The Grain God

Book One

of the

Saga Of The Rah

Susan Shepherd

PREFACE

"When Krakatoa exploded on August 26, 1883, it caused widespread destruction and loss of life on the coasts of Java and Sumatra. Blast waves cracked walls and broke windows up to 160 km away. Tidal waves, reportedly up to 36 meters high, inundated the shores of the Sunda Strait, destroying nearly 300 towns and villages, and overnight more than 35,000 people lost their lives."

J.V. Luce, The Changing Face of the Thera Problem

"Ships navigating the seas in the vicinity of Krakatoa reported that floating pumice in some places had formed a layer about 3 m thick. Other ships, 160 miles off, reported that they were covered with dust three days after the end of the eruption. In fact the dust cloud completely shrouded the area, so that it was dark even 257 miles away from the epicenter. The period of darkness lasted twenty-four hours in places 130 miles distant and fifty-seven hours 50 miles away. The black-out in the immediate vicinity continued for three days and was so total that not even lamp-light could penetrate it. Stunningly beautiful sunsets were observed during the winter months in both America and Europe, thanks to the suspension of fine particles of dust in the atmosphere."

-Christos G. Doumas Thera- Pompeii of the Ancient Aegean, p. 141

"Estimates of the volume of material displaced by the Thera eruption indicated an intensity five or six times as great as that of Krakatoa..."

-Dr. Floyd McCoy, in Ground Truth, Earthwatch Research Report

"After the eruption of Mount Pelee in 1902, "St. Pierre was a cityscape that made Dante's hell look shamefully mild. All the horrors hatching out- the blackened things, the charcoal people, the dead and the still-moving dead – all of these had required just ten thousand cubic yards of vaporized rock dusted less than half an inch deep over eight square miles of the city. Survivors' accounts of the Pelee death cloud provide only the slightest glimpse of how the eastern half of Crete must have suffered in the aftermath of Thera.
Thera blew a thirty-cubic-mile hole in the earth. Thera was fifteen million times worse than Pelee."

-Charles Pellegrino, Unearthing Atlantis (1991) pp 72-73

"On the west coast of Turkey, just north of the island of Rhodes, is a small body of water whose shoreline is like an ever-narrowing funnel. Its open mouth faces west, toward Thera, and anyone living behind that mouth

might just as well have been a flea located in the throat of a cannon. As the shock wave surged east between increasingly confined shorelines, the waters piled higher and higher until at last they became a foaming white mountain eight hundred feet tall. The wave penetrated thirty miles inland, in the general direction of Mount Ararat; and when it receded, it dislodged house-sized boulders, scoured the soil and carved out channeled scablands. Elsewhere, on a strip of Turkish coast only ninety miles north of the funnel, the wave seems to have risen barely twenty feet high. Tsunamis are like that – capricious."
-Charles Pellegrino, Unearthing Atlantis (1991) p. 87

"The death cloud deposited a dense ash layer hundreds of miles east of Thera, but penetrated west only sixty miles, stopping at the island of Melos. To halt the cloud at Melos, the headwinds from the west must have been very strong, and from the meteorologists came word that Westerly squalls were almost exclusively a September through November phenomenon on the Aegean, suggesting that the volcano exploded in autumn."
-Charles Pellegrino, Unearthing Atlantis (1991.

CHAPTER 1

He is tackled, brought down like prey on the Burial Mound Road.

He struggles like a civet in a net, wild, scratching, biting. He is small compared to the man who is pinning him but he is athletic, strong like a small animal is strong. All sinew, speed, panic. The assassin is surprised by the boy's strength, surprised he did not consider it before, add it to his plans. He had seen the boy dance. Fool, he thinks to himself.

The second surprise is the boy's scent. It makes no sense to the assassin at first why, in the rage that always precedes a kill, he is bathed in delightful fragrance. Later he will realize that the priests have bathed the boy in holy oils- hyssop, myrrh, lotus blossom, cherry. But here, in the act of murder, his senses reel with confusion. The scent is sensual, expensive, sacred, and innocent. He fills his lungs with it, how can he not? His exhale is a sigh, a bizarre thing in light of what he is here to do.

Release. Re-pin. His signature. It has yet to fail him. The boy has spun himself onto his back in the release. Now the assassin is crushing the air from his lungs, weakening him quickly. He sits up, grips the boy's hips between his strong thighs and knees, smashes his left forearm down into the boy's chest and slips his gold handled dagger up to rest against a tan silk throat.

"Quiet, little cat." His Minoan still maintains a Hittite accent. But the phrase, in Minoan, forms a hiss all the same. He is a baritone giant compared to this lithe creature, and he is quite aware of how terrifying he can be. His is a deadly face, obsidian-eyed, oddly pale skin for this climate, which makes the black, jeweled eyes even more terrible. A square jaw, thickly muscled neck, and bullish shoulders. The very features that draw the women to him, his hot, black eyes, his strong brow and chin, his massive chest and arms and thighs, are the features that frequently paralyze his prey with fear. But this boy is far from paralyzed until he feels the cold

1

blade against his larynx. Then he freezes, and in a panic, lifts his eyes to those of the assassin.

And Rush, as if knocked from a horse, is stopped cold.

The boy peaks his brows, struggling to gulp the lungful of air allowed him by the man's hesitation. Then he opens his mouth and yowls like a tiger cub plucked from its mother's teat.

Rush blinks down at the boy, clearing his vision in the dust.

He has watched this dancer perform, he has taken his time with this kill. He has studied the boy under torch light in the Great Hall of Knossos. He has measured the symmetry of his dance against all others, has stood in awe of the boy's athleticism and balance and timing. These things are burned into the assassin's brain already. But he has never been close enough to know that, without face paint, the boy is even more beautiful. He has never actually looked into these striated, blue-green eyes. The boy's wheat colored lashes are too long, too thick. His mouth is too perfectly bowed, his teeth too even and milk-white, except for the slightly longer incisors.

It is the face of a cat, some blonde feline treasure from Africa, from Egypt.

Two parts of Rush, one a stranger to him, are in hand-to-hand combat. And Rush the Assassin, the Terror of the Aegean, has lost his edge. He is a dull blade, a prop. He cannot slice home.

And the boy is howling.

Rush slaps his left hand over the pretty Cupid's bow mouth, cupping it away from the teeth so that the boy cannot sink those incisors into it. The blue-green eyes are riveted to his. The boy is struggling for another lung full of air. His chest is heaving against the assassin's forearm.

Rush breaks his second cardinal rule and eases up off the boy's chest, letting him take a natural breath. Even so, the boy renders a whimpering cough and for a moment Rush fears that he has caused some permanent damage. Insane! He should have the boy's head by now.

He utters a Hittite oath, pulls himself to his feet, the dancer in his hands. He throws the thrashing body over his shoulder and trots down the embankment to the spot he had planned to leave the lower portion of the corpse. By the time he has reached it, the boy has torn at and bitten his back, bringing up bloody welts and bite marks that will last for weeks.

Rush tosses him to the ground, eager to remove the nipping and scratching teeth and nails from his now raw back.

"Run and I will break your legs," he says in Greek. "Cut off your head and leave the rest for the wild dogs to eat. I only need your head to prove you dead."

The boy has landed on his rump, and with this news, which he can just decipher, having learned some Greek from the merchant who sold him to

Crete, his startling eyes widen as he shakes his head "no" and drops his gaze down and to the left in the universal slave sign of submission. He does not look up again, not even when the man grabs him up and out of the brambles and takes his chin in his hand.

"Look at me." He shakes the boy by the chin. Blonde curls fluff prettily about the dancer's head and settle back into ringlets.

"Look at me again, damn you," he growls in Greek and jogs the sharp, newly bristling chin again. It would be comical, he would laugh heartily if it were some other assassin and not he, Rush, who was addressing the head he should have severed and should be carrying away in a sack by now.

It's those eyes! Those crazy, blue, gold and green eyes. He must be regarded by those eyes again. He will, by God! Then he will find his wits and cut this cub down like a fawn.

The boy is trembling. His body is so perfectly and leanly muscled that the curling golden hairs running down in a diamond from his solar plexus to his loins are shimmering in the fading Mediterranean light with his tremors. The assassin's eyes follow the movement involuntarily. He is fascinated by so much gold. Golden down. Golden eyes, shot with blue. Golden skin, golden hairs along the apricot-golden arms. The boy is dipped in gold. In sunlight and honey.

He lifts his eyes to the face he is still holding. The boy's striated blue-green irises reflect and scatter the twilight. They are almond, perfectly almond and tip-tilted like a cat's eyes, the honey-gold lashes thick and straight like brush bristles. He wants to touch the lashes. Are they as soft as they appear? Or bristly like the tiny golden hairs along the boy's sharp, symmetrical jaw line? He wants to run his fingers along all these sparkling golden hairs.

He is Hittite by birth, but has never seen a foreigner like this one. He has seen a green-eyed Ethiopian, a light skinned tribe of barbarians from the north, but never this. Nothing so feline, yet human.

The boy's face screws up into a scowl as he attempts in vain to free his chin from the assassin's fingers, which have become vice-like. His golden brows furrow and a little noise escapes him again. Like an animal his noises all seem to come from his clavicle, that secret place where cats purr. The assassin amazes himself one more time by laughing aloud. Is this a fox? Shape-shifted into a human form for the amusement of kings by some bored, comedic god? He runs his broad thumb across the boy's girl-soft mouth.

"Shh-h. I cannot kill you. Be still and live, or bolt and meet my blade." He can see that the boy understands him, although this he has spoken in Minoan. "You know some island tongue." The boy nods carefully. His eyes wander as he relaxes ever so slightly. They drop to the assassin's shoulders, chest. He swallows. Rush notices the tight gold bracelet around his throat for the first time. There is another around his waist. This is how they chain the slaves at night on Crete, even the God-slaves. It serves two purposes, for if a slave becomes too fat, he will cut himself in half with his own gluttony. Rush has slipped a finger under the gold waist cuff, absently wondering how tight the thing is, does it hurt him? But there is enough room even for his thick index finger to slip back and forth between the cold metal and the boy's tawny belly, which is glossy with sweat but as hard as bone.

"For you? Not kill?" the boy offers, struggling with the Minoan. He looks back up into the assassin's face hopefully.

"Mother god," the assassin mutters, pushing the boy out of his own reach suddenly. "I cannot kill you, nor can I take you for myself."

The boy catches his balance and takes a few careful steps backwards.

"I am an assassin for the court of Cyrus, you understand?" Rush says in Greek.

The boy nods.

"I am ordered and paid to cut off your head and bring it to Cyrus, so that Knossos loses his corn, his grain, and so his army. Kill the golden dancer of Knossos. These are my orders."

The boy's eyes are saucers.

"Do I think it will work? Do I think separating a head from a torso will solve Cyrus' problems with Knossos?" Rush absently stuffs his blade back into his belt. "Bring Knossos to his knees? Bring a plague of locusts on his wheat? No I do not. But Cyrus has not paid for my opinion. Only for your head. Because I am the best. A man must enjoy his work to be the best. Until now," he waves his hand at the boy gruffly, "I have always enjoyed what I do."

The boy takes a step back. He is wicked fast and quite capable of out-running this hulking Hittite if given a few yards leeway, and he has been stealing these, inch by inch, as the assassin muses. He is taking deliberate, circular breaths, eyeing a clearing to his right which he knows opens onto a path that will take him quickly back to the Bridge Road and so, back into the city.

The assassin chuckles at him. "If I want you dead you will be dead, little cat. You may outrun me but not my dagger." He gestures to the blade he has returned to his hip. The boy's multi-colored eyes drop to the dagger and remain there. Rush watches as his silken chest rises and falls in that purposeful pant. So he is willing to take his chances with the accuracy of a flying dagger from the hand of a marksman, though a moment before he offered himself to the same murderer in exchange for his life. He is not a little fascinated by the boy's nerve.

"You do this before the dance, yes? You take in air." Rush has lapsed back into Minoan. He thumps his own brutish chest. "You pant, for air, for strength."

The boy flicks his eyes back up to the assassin's face.

"To dance," Rush says again in Greek. He is startled now only by the gentleness in his own baritone voice.

The boy cocks his head at him. "Dance?" he repeats the Greek word. His voice, in strange contrast to his features, is dark, dusky. There is something wrong with his tongue.

Rush nods.

Then the boy does a startling thing. He lowers his body, softly, to the earth, in a full and supremely elegant bow before Rush. At the bottom of this feather-soft motion his arms extend, palms up, his fingertips touching the ground. His golden curls fall to cover one knee. One would salute a king, were one graceful enough, with no greater show of humility. Certainly, no one has ever offered such a salute to an assassin.

It is the boy's final bow, his bow to the King at the end of his performance.

The gesture, with its elegant respect, twists a dagger of unlikely emotion in the assassin's belly. His throat tightens.

The boy lifts his head. He looks up, directly into the assassin's eyes.

The assassin hesitates for only a second. But it is enough time for the dancer to leap, as on springs, to his feet, pivot, and sprint away up the path like a deer.

He is two kilometers from the Villa of Mochlos when he escapes Rush. He runs the distance at top speed and approaches the gate breathless and spent. He is let in by two junior priests who demand to know why he is acting like an idiot, why he is embarrassing the house of Mochlos with disgraceful behavior. A holy dancer must always conduct himself in a manner that is befitting his station and the boy had better understand this and behave accordingly or he will be flogged to within an inch of his life.

The household has been instructed to speak Greek when addressing the boy, for he has only a smattering of Minoan, and Mochlos has learned from experience that it is prudent to keep god-slaves in the dark, though the boy's personal attendants, Aros and Pyrus, ignore the rule. These two priests are Minoan and the boy is unable to express himself sufficiently in that language to describe the attack. In his panic he has developed a stutter and this, coupled with his mangled tongue, makes him sound quite retarded to the priests. His story is brushed aside. A man? What man? Where is he now, did he not follow you? Why were you still running, you silly fool? There is no one chasing you. You have imagined the whole episode. Now go to the shrine of your god and bathe and ask forgiveness for your mischief. You are trying to avoid your obligation to visit the mounds, that is all. You want us to believe that a ghost followed you home from the cemetery, eh? Do you think we will believe you were attacked by a ghost just because we are priests?

The boy is frustrated, but happy to go to the baths, which are deep in the sanctuary of the house. He does as he is told. When he arrives he tells Tuma of the man that attacked him, but Tuma only chuckles and shakes his head. "You will have to run fast on Crete, boy, if you want to avoid what your giant had in store for you. You are going to find that these Minoans lust for beauty and grace in either sex like no other race on earth."

That night the boy is visited by his dead sister. As always, he is in a twilight state when she comes, conscious but completely paralyzed. He awakens to a yellowish light as dawn crests the Aegean, and there, standing to the left of the window and haloed in this light is a girl his age. She is his twin but for her femininity, that is, she wears a short white shift and her blonde hair reaches her waist. She is as whole as any corporeal being except that the center of her face is gone, eyes, nose, mouth hidden by a dark blur.

"Ahalai, my brother," she says in the tongue they once shared. "You must flee."

Trapped, as always when she comes to him, and tormented by his own body, which does not obey him but lies like a corpse on his pallet, the boy attempts to speak, for she is fading.

"Ileah, don't go!" But he cannot make his tongue work before she is gone.

The boy has no doubt that his dead twin has come to him from the land of death with a grave warning, that she has come to save him from his own otherwise certain death. But it is not a priest's knife on the cliffs of Juktas, nor the tidal wave which the bowels of Thera are already preparing, that he imagines will take his life. It is the murderous black eyes of Rush the Assassin he imagines. That horrible giant that attacked him on the path to the burial mounds, whose clutches he escaped by the breadth of a hair. He shudders, imagining again the monster's impossible weight on him, crushing the wind from his lungs. He sees the cold black eyes, center-less, the eyes of a shark, the oddly pale skin. Most of all he remembers the man's lethal strength, pinning him as easily as one might pin a moth by the wings. The boy starts when he hears attendants enter Mochlos' bedchamber. He is covered in a fine sweat when his own attendants, Aros and Pyrus, come somberly into his room through the beaded drape.

"Poor baby," says Aros, unchaining the boy and casting a miserable glance at Pyrus. "You must come with us now. There will be no gymnasium today."

"Those bastard priests have given the master a reason to. . . discipline you." Pyrus mutters close to the boy's ear so that the others in the next room cannot hear him. "Now listen to me. The reed is nothing, only pain. He will not allow you to be permanently scarred with it. But when they put you in the drowning pool take several deep breaths just before they force you down. Do not allow yourself to panic. You must pretend, boy, and I have seen you can pretend. Thrash for them as long as you can but be still before you begin to breathe water. They will not let you drown."

It is all Pyrus has time to say to him before several of Mochlos' junior priests come for Rah and drag him down to the punishment chamber in the bowels of the villa.

CHAPTER 2

Taken as an infant from his home in the north, he was purchased by the trader, Kephas, from Illyrians at an auction on the coast of Mycenae. Having changed hands several times by then, he knew no modern language, but the Illyrians spoke a dialect close enough to Greek to allow him to communicate reasonably well in that language.

He would always speak with difficulty nonetheless, every new language creating ever more frustrating obstacles for the impediment of a cleft tongue. Orphaned as an infant, his mother slain by Gauls, he and his twin sister were taken first by that nomadic tribe of horsemen. As children, they were taught to dance for their food, a pair of freakish blonde angels kept alive for entertainment only, and when his sister died in her seventh year the boy would continue to speak to her ghost in his dreams. Nearly perishing from the same fever, he survived to become an expert horseman before a tribe of Illyrians wiped out his kidnappers and took him themselves for a slave.

The Illyrians, also horsemen, gave him the status of stable keeper when he was only nine summers old and by the time he was thirteen he was training the new colts and winning death defying acrobatic riding games among a people who rode before they walked. Having such difficulty with language perhaps gave the boy a special affinity for animals, and his ability to communicate with and train any beast was uncanny. But when a stray party of Greek soldiers, returning from war in Tarsus, slaughtered his master the boy was again seen as nothing more than a freakish novelty and was brought to auction on the coast of Mycenae. Kephas purchased him there.

Twice aboard ship, for the Captain traded all along the Mediterranean coasts and kept the boy on board for many months, the boy took fits. In fact he was since infancy an epileptic, his seizures coming on only during certain high emotional states, and part if not the entirety of his speech impediment was the result of his biting his own tongue nearly in half during one such episode. He had trouble making certain sounds, the Greek "Ka" mostly, and compensated by training his throat to echo when his tongue could not serve him, thus the guttural, cat-like noises, sensual and even sweet in such a face, that Rush had heard.

The boy would never know the name his parents had given him, or any term of endearment they might have had for him. Nor would he ever know his sister's birth name. Those who stole him from his mother named the twins Ileah and Ahalai but these names were lost in the exchange of hands. In the land of the Minoans he will have no name until he earns the name of the deity he is to represent.

He is just sixteen summers when he is sold to Mochlos, the highest ranking priest in Knossos.

Mochlos is at first startled by, then titillated with, the boy's strange appearance. The boy's eyes are the colors of the sea, deer-soft and almond, and Gods, the lashes! A double row of lashes above and below, one fine and platinum over a denser row of amber bristles, lynx long. He is like this all over his body, white blonde hairs darkening to honey where his maleness is beginning to express itself. Ah, thinks the high priest. He will be a living torch in the Great Hall under the torchlight!

Beauty always stimulates cruelty in Mochlos. It is a link in his mind whose mother he has never traced. The fine, cat-like features of the boy's face are neither wholly male nor female, and had Mochlos been accustomed to the Hebrew concept of angels, he might have thought that one of these had fallen into his grasp. But tickling his innards is a vision of this creature under his lash, mewling with pain and fear.

He licks his lips, and his coterie of slaves shudder silently. They have seen this look on their master's face.

Mochlos has a rich man's zeal for concubines and is in no shortage of these. He is not particularly stimulated by males except as subjects of a good beating, a game of drowning. But this one is going to set his twisted heart spinning. He will never know if he loves or hates this boy, but he is obsessed with him from the first moment he lays eyes on him.

Mochlos is taller than the average Minoan, though not as tall as Kephas, and lean as a whippet. He is not ugly by any means. It is only the sharp, wanting look in his eye that makes him unattractive, a man to step around, a man to leave be. He is too rich and too clever, a loner, one who trusts no one and, like most religious down through the ages, he thinks only that he is too smart to believe completely in what he preaches. In truth the coin is his god, and it has served him well.

If at the end of a series of competitions over the next three moons Mochlos can convince the King to choose his new slave to be the representative of the Grain God, the boy must yet undergo the Dying to the God ceremony, a ritual in which his body appears to expire, and be reborn with the soul of the Rah. This will be an easy illusion to pull off with Mochlos' arsenal of potions and drugs, but the less the boy knows, the better.

In the meantime, to prepare his human body for the God, the boy will be given three concubines to lie with. On Crete sex is as necessary as air, and a Grain Dancer must be fully satisfied to insure that Rah himself is pleased, and generous in return. It is a simple matter. If you want your crops to grow fat, ripe and pregnant, you had better satisfy the sexual fire of the god of fertile valleys. How better than to satisfy his human representative?

The girls are Minia, Siriona and Trinadea. Rah will love them all but his favorite will be Siriona, who is a voluptuous African beauty even at fourteen summers. Until he came to Crete Rah had never lain with a woman, nor a man. He had always been an outcast, a freak, having been a slave from infancy, and from a toddler kept with the hunting dogs, then later with the barbarians' horses. Kephas kept him safe aboard his merchant ship, for damaged goods are of no value. So when Rah is taken to the baths at Mochlos' villa, stripped by the big, jolly servant of the baths, Tuma, bathed in holy oils and given three lovely girls just his age he is like a two year old colt let into a field of fillies.

Tuma is a bull of a man, an architecture of muscle, ebony black and shaved from head to foot. He wears a short linen skirt embroidered in gold, and reed sandals. After the master has examined the boy he is stripped of his barbarian clothing, his deerskin vest and breeches, and he is fitted with the golden collar, belt, bracelets and anklets he will never again be free of. His nipples are pierced with tiny golden rings denoting his heart's enslavement to the god and Tuma takes him to the holy baths. These are outdoor pools built on the rooftop of the villa, equipped with a sophisticated plumbing system which allows them to be maintained and always pristine. Great trees from many lands surrounding the Aegean have been planted in huge stone pots, palm, fruit and flowering. Neophyte priests and concubines lounge in the perfumed waters or lie about under the influence of holy medicines made from the poppy plant. Each pool is dedicated to a god and each has a shrine to the deity at one end where gifts of lilies, roses and grain are laid. Tuma takes the boy to a spacious and unoccupied pool under an enormous shrine to Rah. Then Tuma introduces him to perfumed water and emollients for the first time in his sixteen summers.

The boy is like a puppy in the frothy water, slapping and splashing in it as Tuma pours oil of rose and lavender over his head. He has been on a merchant ship for four months, watching the blue-green Aegean slip by beneath his feet. He is not afraid of water; rather he is like a seal in it. He was let to bathe in the Aegean and taught himself to swim and dive, finding animals of breathtaking colors to swim amongst, to reach out and stroke, for the seas were teaming then, before mankind hunted and poisoned them near to death.

He slides deep into the bathwater, slips from Tuma's grasp, stays down so long that Tuma becomes alarmed and nearly falls in himself while reaching about. He yanks the boy up by the hair, but the water saves the boy from the anger in Tuma's yank. He shines a sunny smile at him. "I can swim, Tuma. I cannot drown unless you hold me down." And Tuma laughs, a big, booming African laugh, slaps his chest and answers, "But I can drown, boy, trying to catch you!"

Once he is bathed properly, the three girls are brought to him, and the boy is allowed the rest of the day to cavort with them in the pool under the shrine of Rah. By sundown he has deflowered all three, all under the supervision of Tuma, who must not allow certain acts to be performed before the boy has died to the God. His only limit in taking his pleasure is that he must not beat or sodomize the girls, which would offend Rah, a kind and generous god bent on creation only.

Tuma, in this case, has an uneventful afternoon. Rah will woo a girl with the same cat and mouse patience that he has learned to woo a filly, or a cur. He can only seduce, never take, and with his unusual beauty in his favor, it will appear to Tuma that the girls were begging for his seed.

First is Siriona. More mature than the other two she approaches the boy haughtily, like a dominant mare, slaps the water under his nose as he stares at her naked breasts in the water, then laughs before she turns and dives under to escape an advance he has not yet made. The boy dives after her, and although he can catch her easily, for he is as powerful a swimmer as he is an acrobat, he merely swims beside her, admiring her, as he would a brilliantly colored fish. Siriona comes to the surface for air and looks about her, unable to find her suitor. When the boy pops out of the water behind and whispers "pretty girl" in her ear, she spooks, then turns to slap him. But he is easily out of her reach, and is soon playing a game of retreat with her until she has backed him into a corner of the pool, and in furious frustration made a move to slap at his chest. The boy laughs, catches her wrist, then plants a kiss on her mouth, ducks back under the water and slips away.

While Siriona looks about for a sign of him swimming, the boy makes his way to the other two girls, who have been giggling together in each other's arms at the other side of the pool, watching his antics with their braver counterpart. Suddenly Trinadea trills a playful yelp as she feels him slip past her, sliding his fingers across her hips and belly. This is enough to bring on Siriona's jealousy, and she makes her way over to her rivals to pull their hair and chase them out of the pool. But the boy intercepts her, splashing water in her face and laughing at her as she turns on him. Again he lets her advance toward him, backing him into a corner until they are under the shadow of the shrine of his likeness. But this time when she raises her hand to strike him he does not attempt to avoid her blow. He stares her down. His eyes now reflecting turquoise in the bath water are serious and vacant. They fix on hers, drop to her mouth, her breasts, return to her face heavy-lidded. She lowers her hand, reaches out, strokes the honey-gold skin of his shoulder, his left pectoral muscle, where the nipple is still plump and angry from the piercing. He remains still, touching her face and breasts only with his gaze. Her anger shatters. She slips herself into his embrace and he kisses her voluptuous mouth, slipping the tip of his tongue along her lips, between her teeth. And Siriona is his. This mare is rideable. In the water he mounts her like an eel, takes his own pleasure, then slips away from her without a thought. When she tries to keep him from the other two girls later he will placate her with kisses and restrain her from hurting the others, until she understands that there is more to gain by being part of his harem than by opposing him. He will have all three, and that is that. When Tuma awakens from an afternoon nap he will find the golden boy under a pile of lovely, if deflowered, dark maidens, all cuddling together in a happy litter.

When the sun begins to set, the boy is taken to a chamber next to Mochlos' own suite of rooms, outside of which stands an armed guard. He is fed. Then he is chained, by the neck, the waist and the ankles to the wall above his sleeping mat. The chains are short and although he has enough room to turn or to sit up he cannot stand. Mochlos sleeps in the next room and the two rooms are connected by a passage through a wall two feet thick, separated only by a beaded drape. There is a single tall window in Rah's room, but no means to it from the outside. The villa is high on an outcropping overlooking the sea, and only an assassin could find a means to enter there.

In the morning his personal attendants, who must ready him for his first practice, march briskly into his room through the only entrance, the beaded drape that separates his chamber from Mochlos'.

"Too pretty for his own good," titters Aros, who is middle aged, balding and fat but moves and speaks like a king's concubine. He unchains the boy and straightens his loincloth, which is twisted and falling from his hips. "Where on earth did you come from, hmm?" He lifts the boys chin and runs a limped finger over his jaw. "Mostly baby's down, but he will need a shave all the same, or we'll all feel the priest's reed." He is referring to Mochlos' penchant for flogging with a stiff beech reed, which stings but rarely cuts.

"You would gladly 'go to the mountain' to be as pretty, Aros," quips Pyrus, who is younger than his helpmate by a generation and as narrow as Aros is fat. Pyrus, once a minor dancer himself, will apply the boy's face paint for the first time today, and every day he dances hereafter. Although only twenty-three summers, he has already earned a reputation as one of the finest face painters in Knossos. His wizardry with paint is rivaled only by Aros' wizardry with cloth and bead and feather. The boy is sent with a steward down to the latrines and baths. When he returns Aros flutters about him with a bolt of jade green cloth, explaining to two seamstresses the skirts and sashes he wants made by the end of the day. Pyrus is fussing with the jars of paint on the vanity.

"Enough, Aros, it's only a training garment, not a costume for the Great Hall." He takes the boy by the shoulder and leads him to the stool in front of the vanity.

"And you? You are painting him for the gymnasium today?" Aros counters.

Pyrus has already begun applying paint to the boy's cheek.

"I need to come up with a new face, don't I? I can't do it without his." The boy turns to the vanity to reach for a pot of yellow goo, which he brings to his nose and sniffs.

"Leave it," Pyrus slaps his hand with the back of his brush. "Be still. Look at me."

The boy obeys, and Pyrus' progress is stopped in mid-stroke.

"What eyes you have." He seems lost a moment in wonder. Aros has come around behind the boy and is peering at Pyrus' work.

"What is this? You're making stripes!"

"Hush, Aros. I have an idea, that's all."

Aros shakes his head and wanders over to a trunk full of last year's costumes. "One day you will go too far, Pyrus. Then you will be painting the faces of the bulls under the palace." He rummages through the trunk, now and then pulling something out that seems to interest him and putting it aside. After some time, Pyrus steps back from his work and puts his fists on his hips, pleased with himself.

"Aros, look here." He turns the boy about on the stool to face Aros.

"Good heaven, what are you doing to his face! You have made him a devil!"

"Not a devil, Aros," Pyrus smoothes the boy's hair back from his forehead. "A cat! Has he not the face of a wild cat?"

The boy, who has been sitting for the painting innocently enough, pulls back his ears, flattening his brow like an angry feline. Aros moves closer to consider this metamorphosis. To him, painting this golden boy into anything but a beautiful girl is lunacy. Yet the green and orange stripes bursting from the boy's nose and eyes and into his hairline are brilliant and alarming, and Aros loves theatrics. But Aros does not notice that the boy has developed a mischievous light in his pale eyes. When the boy makes an eerie hum in his throat, bares his teeth and leaps off the stool at him, Aros' face is inches from his. Aros shrieks and jumps back several feet, his hand on his breast.

Pyrus and the boy burst into laughter, Pyrus so hard that he cannot catch his breath.

"Merciful gods, you little beast," Aros pants, struggling to compose himself. "Yes, I see your point, Pyrus." He fans his own face with his hand. "It is quite. . . . breathtaking."

"You just put your mind to a costume to match, Aros. And we will have the winner, that is, if our cat can dance."

Aros lets his gaze wander over the boy's body. "He looks like he's been dancing all his life."

In the gymnasium the boy is a leopard. The trainers are stunned. Where did a slave learn to move like this? He is more graceful than the girls, more powerful than any male. He is brilliant with the bulls, but even more extraordinary on his own. His leaps are higher, his spins faster, his gymnastics so precise and impassioned that Dimius, the Dance Master, has tears in his eyes when Rah drops into that seductive bow that will so touch the heart of the assassin. They cannot know that the boy and his sister learned to dance as the slaves of barbarians, that they danced for food, even as children. They cannot know that the Illyrians who took the boy were acrobats on horseback and, for amusement, used the animals in games requiring immense skill, balance, and gymnastic ability far exceeding anything that could be performed on a simple minded bull.

CHAPTER 3

A fortnight will pass before the assassin lays eyes on the Grain Dancer again, those two weeks an eternity in a sea of brown-skinned, black-eyed island natives.

A double agent who holds favor with the north King for certain secret treasonous acts against his southern enemy, Rush is welcome in the Palace of Knossos, even holding a high rank in Court in the guise of Ameg the Merchant. When the high priest, Mochlos, presented the boy to the Court for the first time that spring the performance was a scandalous success and his value soon became evident to Cyrus. Knossos, certain that this new dancer possesses such unique beauty and talent as to secure the favor of the Grain God, Rah, and so, a bountiful harvest that year, promises to make Mochlos an even richer priest than he is if he can convince the people of the city that this dancer is a worthy surrogate, by winning the competitions. The prize for his success will be the commission of a fine new villa in the city, near the palace, and twice the size of his current one at the foot of the Bridge Road.

The yearly competitions for the title of The Grain God are a recent development in Knossos. And Mochlos, ever the businessman, has been a prominent proponent of the games. Until four years ago the games were restricted to bull leaping. But that summer Mochlos, High Priest of the Moon Goddess, added a new component to the games. He offered, in addition to bringing bull dancers, to entertain the city with his own private troop of temple dancers, knowing he had the finest in Knossos. The trick worked like a charm. The following year, three other high priests, Ananou, High Priest of the Sun God, Enenoch, High Priest of the Sky God, and Tyrus, High Priest of the Bull God, all brought temple dancers to perform. A competition sprung from the diversity, and Mochlos won the first. His lead dancer was titled Surrogate to Rah, the Grain God, and he continued to perform for the city at all of the most important holy days throughout the summer and fall.

At the autumn equinox, he was sacrificed on Mount Juktas, in a private ceremony that only the priesthood attended. His crime? That he was unable to please Rah sufficiently to continue the growing season, and to stop the coming of winter.

And a tradition was born.

The boy's reward for winning the debut challenge this year is longer practice and more stripes. Mochlos must allow his potential slave god access to the dead, and so the boy is given the freedom to leave the villa alone three days a week and pilgrim to the burial grounds of the ancients high on Mount Ida, about four kilometers from Knossos. This is his only freedom, and it is precious to him. He is sent with offerings to the ancients, to leave with Ting Ya, the Asian slave guardian and tender to the mounds. It is on such a visit that he is attacked by the assassin.

When Rush sees the Grain Dancer again he is performing before the entire city of Knossos in the Great Hall of the King. This dance is expected to be even more scandalous than the first and the entire city, loving a scandal, is in attendance. The boy is in full colors on this night, green and gold and blue silks trail about his hips like dragonfly wings, his face a mask of paint in like hues, his body more defined even than when Rush held him in his hands (it seems a dream now, that this creature was ever in his hands) his dance breathtaking, surreal. No dark skinned native can match his speed, his balance, his time, and even if they could have, how beastly they would be in comparison to this golden mystery, this exotic cat-boy.

The Grain God, Rah is the son of the Sun God and the Moon Goddess. He is the god of harvest, of grain, of all that has made Crete rich. There is a consensus among the most important in the King's Court that he has never been better represented than by this golden, sea-eyed boy. Already the crops of Knossos have doubled, and it is clear that Rah is pleased by the Moon Priest's choice for his representative. Rah is a god of harvest, bounty, pleasure and sexuality, fertility and birth, therefore his slave-god's dance must reflect this. In the three years since the beginning of this tradition, the dances have become more and more erotic as the priests have competed to seduce the Soul of Rah. But in this new dancer there is something more. There is innocence beneath the beauty, and grace beneath the erotica.

The city is in love with Mochlos' new dancer by the end of his performance, and Knossos himself is so engaged by the dance that when the boy bows before him, he does the unthinkable. He stands up, leaving his Queen, to steps down from his dais for a better look at the creature.

The King has never left his throne for any dancer. If the audience is pleased with a performance they throw lilies and saffron flowers at the dancer's feet at the end of the dance, the more flowers, the greater the accolade. But the most the King has ever done is clap once or twice in applause. Tonight, the new performer is nearly covered in flowers as he drops to his bow that, three weeks ago, silenced an assassin and saved his life. The giddy audience laughs as he gracefully frees himself from their tribute and shakes his blonde head, dispersing a head full of petals about him. He has won this leg of the journey to Mount Juktas, according to the crowd. He now must face the King and Queen, as well as the court, which is seated to the King's left and right in order of importance. Rush, in the guise of Ameg the Merchant, is among the court, to the very left of the Queen.

The irony of this turn of events has not escaped Rush. Here he is, occupying a seat of honor in the Great Hall of Knossos, enjoying the gifts of a dancer he should have beheaded weeks ago. When the boy turns to face the King, head bowed, arms down and back, palms forward, collapsing into what appears to be a puddle of green and gold silks in the most submissive of gestures, he sees the same bow that cost him his self-respect as an assassin the day he held this golden ghost in his hands. When he sees the boy fail to raise his eyes to Knossos, even when ordered to do so, he recalls his respectful downcast eyes the day he planned to kill him. But Knossos, having watched those blue-green beauties sparkling prettily in the torchlight for an exquisite hour, will demand that they be raised to his, and this will place the little cat in a dilemma, for if he raises his eyes to the King he is showing disrespect, a thing that could lose him his head all over again. Kings are like that, short-sighted and fickle.

There is a hushed murmur as the King rises from his seat on the dais and steps down, first one step, then another, almost to the floor of the hall, to have a closer look at the boy. Three attendants immediately surround him. A forth has followed him down the steps to keep the train of his robe from touching the ground. Rush is no more than a few meters from the boy, though he is a dozen steps above him. He can see that the boy has begun to shiver with fear. His priest is not at his side to tell him what to do. Mochlos is in fact on the dais with the rest of the court and in no position to interfere here. And this is new ground. Even the Queen has an expression of surprise on her heavy, masculine face. For once her King has made a decision without consulting her.

The boy is breathless and physically spent. He has been poked, prodded, stroked, bathed, clothed, pinned, chained, flogged and nearly drowned since his arrival on Crete. He is not proficient with the language of this country, but like any clever slave who wants to survive he has become proficient with the customs. Here on Crete, one does not raise his eyes to his betters, least of all a King. As always when he is in a state of confusion and fear, he frets that he may take a fit. He does not know that Mochlos is aware of his infirmity, having been forewarned by Kephas, the trader he purchased the boy from. Both men knew it made the boy an even more extraordinary acquisition for a Crete high priest, for seizures here are considered a sign that one of the gods has delighted in playing with the afflicted now and then. The boy only knows that his illness gained him nothing but scorn and ridicule from those who had owned him previously, who considered him retarded, and a freak.

One of the attendants has been called to the King's side and has been given an order. Now that attendant, a tall, older man with shaved head but for a braided tail, moves to the boy's side and leans down to speak into his ear.

"The King wishes that you approach and regard him."

The boy flicks his eye up into the attendant's, and the attendant blinks, a bit startled. He regains his composure, nods for the boy to do as he is told.

Now the boy lifts his eyes to the raised seats behind the King in search for his master. Mochlos allows himself a barely perceptible nod to the boy, and the boy drops his gaze to his feet, takes one deep breath, and steps before the King, lifts his eyes to the sovereign's long enough to be considered obedient, then drops to the ground in an even deeper bow than the last, his golden curls sweeping the dust.

Rush cannot help but be amused. The King's face registers none of the frustration he is surely feeling. This is not what he wanted, but it must suffice. Rush knows the King wants to lift the boy's chin, look into that magically androgynous face and memorize it. It is a fine painting, a piece of living art just days from the fire. It is a moment, like the last day of a rose before the petals fall. Rush knows, as does the King, that the boy will never know his full height, will never grow a full beard, will never be allowed to be anything but this year's Grain Dancer. His youth is what is keeping him alive, and it is momentary and heartbreaking.

When Rush returns to Cyrus prepared to inform him of his failure to kill the dancer, he discovers that Cyrus has had a change of heart. His Queen has convinced him that killing the boy may cause more harm than good. Clearly he is pleasing to Rah. If that is so, perhaps the god will visit even more misfortune upon their city. Cyrus now wishes for this assassin merely to keep track of the boy, to study his movements, to learn all of the secrets behind Knossos' success. Do not kill the boy, but study him. What is he doing that so pleases our Mother, the Moon? Our Father, the Sun? How is it that he has seduced the earth for Knossos while Cyrus' southern fields are burning with drought?

Rush informs Cyrus that the boy is given license to pilgrim to the Burial Mounds on Mount Juktas and that on these days, from sunrise to sunset, he is a target. Although any good citizen of Knossos who harasses or harms or even touches him will have their arms ripped off by bulls, he is yet quite vulnerable to thieves and assassins from rival governments, and Rush is not the only one of these.

"You must protect him, then!" cries the king. "For if I am privy to this, and do nothing, am I not accountable for his fate?"

"I am not a baby sitter," growls the assassin, "but a killer. Pay me to kill, and I am yet in your service."

"You have it," answers Cyrus, "Name your price. But only keep the boy safe from those like yourself, and I will pay you handsomely for each head."

Several days pass before Rush spies the boy leaving Mochlos' villa at the top of the Bridge Road with a cage full of doves. Rush is covered head to toe in white muslin. He wears a loose hood and carries an olive staff with a bone head carved to resemble a beetle. It is the costume of a priest of the dead, and it allows him to move about outside of the city freely in the daylight. A priest of the dead cannot enter the city, however, therefore he must use his Knossos identity, Ameg the Merchant, once he crosses the bridge. But out here in the farm fields, the cemeteries, the wood, he is simply one of the tongueless priests who prepare and bury the deceased, going about his solitary business. Rush is still Rush, however, and beneath his muslin robe he carries an arsenal of weaponry, including a golden handled dagger strapped to his ankle and a rope made of reed grass that is strong enough to hang a man and thin enough to slice his throat to the bone in the process. The staff is also a weapon, a rather nice one, in Rush's hands. The carved head is made of the jawbone of an ox and has a sharpened side that could, if need be, open a man's skull.

Rush hangs back, following the boy at several hundred meters' distance, until he unexpectedly leaves the paved road and begins to hike up through a meadow of goats toward a stone wall on the crest of a hill. This is strange. The doves are a sacrifice to the gods of the dead and are meant to be slaughtered by the Asian woman who tends the Burial Mounds of the Ancients on the south side of Mount Ida four kilometers from the city. One can follow the paved Bridge Road, which hugs the coast, for two kilometers, but the dancer has cut into the countryside and is headed south early. He is disobedient. He will have been told to stay on the Bridge Road until it cuts into the countryside toward the Mounds. For what?

Rush follows, invisibly, and watches the boy set the cage on the top of the wall, which is nearly to his shoulder, then hop the wall effortlessly like the acrobat he is and disappear behind it, snatching the dove cage from the other side. Rush increases his pace so that the boy is not out of his sight for too long. By the time he reaches the wall, his heart is pounding in his chest with anxiety. But as he peeks over the stones beneath a cherry tree he sees that the boy has walked another hundred meters or so and has dropped to his knees. He fiddles with the cage, then sits back on his haunches. Rush sees that he has one of the birds cradled in his hands close to his bare chest. He is, it seems, whispering to the bird as he strokes its breast. He takes his time with this and it is several minutes before he tenderly inverts it and puts it his lap, then takes a second bird from the cage. He performs the same ritual with the second bird, the third, the fourth and fifth. There are five birds lying on their backs on his thighs, immobile, when he takes the sixth out of the cage, pets it, and places it on his left shoulder. It sits there calmly.

Rush is fascinated. No one plays with doves. They are to be eaten, a dainty for kings, or sacrificed to the gods. Beyond this, a slave representing a god can have no contact with base animals. In fact, the boy must touch only pure white and unblemished animals. This is why he is allowed to take the doves to the city of the dead. The boy is a complete mystery to Rush, disturbingly wild yet as tame as a dove himself. He loses himself in fascination and rests his chin on the stone wall to watch what happens next.

It is a clear spring day on Crete, the sky a vibrant sapphire blue, the clouds stacked but ever moving on the Aegean breeze. He has a clear view of the boy, who has lifted the five birds in his lap, one by one, and set them upright on his outstretched arms. They sit like clay pots where he has placed them, on his wrists, forearms and biceps. Now he rises like a spirit from his ankles, with all the grace and balance that has made him a superstar in Knossos. He rises to his toes, lifting his arms up with eerie slowness until his wrists are above the height of his shoulders. He holds that position, then bends knees only until he is half that height. His next movement is so fast, so athletic that Rush cannot follow it. It starts with a leap and a spin in reverse, at the top of which the boy extends one perfectly straight and vertical leg in an arch over his head. The doves fly off in six different directions just as he reaches a height Rush would not have thought possible. It ends with the boy folding in on himself in a graceful bow, as if he were weightless and hitting the ground causes no more percussion than a feather.

Now the boy is still. In a trance? What is this? Why does he not stand up and walk? Has his soul departed with the doves?

Presently Rush sees another figure out of the corner of his eye, stealthily approaching on four legs the bowed head of the boy. He is unaware that he has found his dagger under his cloak and is fingering it. He is unaware that his jaw has tightened and that his heart is beating fast again. He is utterly mesmerized by the scene before him. The creature that advances on the boy is a cur dog. Its fur is a dirty yellow-white and its ruff is bristling like a wolf as it trots up to the dancer with its snout to the ground. At first it seems to Rush that the boy does not hear the cur. But even when it is upon him, sniffing his head and nosing his sides the boy does not react. Presently the cur starts to paw and whimper as if it has found something it wants in the boy's lap but cannot reach it. The boy lifts his head and the dog jumps back, dancing to and fro in excitement, singing like a fox. The boy slips his hand into the folds of his skirt, then extends his hand, opened, to the cur, who gulps down the contents, tail wagging. Now the boy rises to his feet and walks casually over to the cage, which he has left on the ground where his dance began. He drops to his knees, turns over the dove carrier, which is made of hollow reeds. He takes a package out of the floor of the carrier, where there is another compartment. He unfolds the olive leaves that make up the wrapping and sets the contents on the ground. The dog has followed him, but waits patiently, watching. The boy turns to give the dog a stern look, then raises an index finger. The dog sits. The boy makes a motion with the same finger, a little circle. The dog stretches out onto its front paws, then rolls right over onto its back. The boy raises his finger again and the cur rights itself, yelps and leaps to its feet. The boy throws his head back and laughs. It is a lovely thing, the laugh, springing from pure innocence, a jolly, teenage giggle that has its beginnings in the boy's belly. Rush feels some satisfaction that he is probably the only one to witness it since the boy set foot on Crete. The dog sets to the package, which Rush surmises is meat stolen from Mochlos' kitchen. The boy lies back on an elbow and watches the dog. When the dog is finished he licks the boy's face from chin to brow. The boy, still giggling, drops to his back, allowing the dog to cover his face and chest with kisses.

Rush shakes his head, mumbles to himself, "You'll smell like cur breath when you get home, boy." But he is chuckling a bit himself.

Over the next few months Rush will see the boy and dog together every several days, whenever he visits the Burial Ground of the Ancients. They will meet this way in the field, greet one another with meat pilfered from Mochlos' kitchens and with canine kisses, then walk side by side up through the fields and wooded hills to the cemetery. It is utter blasphemy. From the theft of the meat to the release of the doves to cavorting with a dingy cur, the boy is committing reckless crimes against the King, and Rush knows Mochlos well enough to know that although he would do nothing to jeopardize the boy's position as Grain God, he would welcome a reason to whip or choke or drown him for his disobedience. But Rush will never tell, not Mochlos nor anyone in Knossos, nor Cyrus, who pays him for the information. He will guard this secret, that this slave boy who has been stripped of his own identity and forced to stand in for a god, has seduced the harvest not with rituals and sacrifice, but innocence and kindness. Nor will he tell of the Asian slave woman's treason, that she knows of the dog, of the doves, feeds the boy forbidden sweets made of barley, corn sugar, and pine nuts that have been left as sacrifices by the relatives of the ancient ones. No, he will tell no one. He will only tell Cyrus what he wants to hear, that the boy takes a sacrifice of six doves to the keeper of the mounds. That he is released from the House of the Moon, unattended, to do so every several days. That he practices the dance from sunup to sundown on the other six days and eats no meat, no fish, only fruit, grain, and milk and cheeses from a white goat kept behind the kitchen. That Mochlos has given him his three youngest concubines, virgins, to lay with, that the whole household dotes on him, but holds him fast to the religious rules of his place: He must be chained after dark by the golden bracelets and belt he wears, he must raise his eyes to no one above his own status, he must obey the priest in everything. For like begets like, so the slave who represents Rah obeys the priest, assuring that Rah himself must obey the priest and bring the King a bountiful harvest.

CHAPTER 4

The King has twenty horses, white Arabs out of North Africa, and they are kept in a guarded field above the city. The boy has discovered the horses and has crept into the field, unobserved by the guards, on at least two occasions that Rush has observed. He is amazed at the boy's bravado, for to do such a thing is madness. A commoner would be thrown in the labyrinth to be gored by bulls. A slave, especially one who represents a god, would meet with an early disembowelment on the mountain at best. Rush is equally amazed at the boy's stealth, for the King's best men, as many as he has horses, guard the field. But most especially he is awed by the boy's antics with the beasts.

Rush is not unfamiliar with horses, having trained to fight amongst the Macedonians. But he has never witnessed anything like this. The boy does not dominate the animals, he befriends them, as he did the cur dog. He creeps into the field after carefully discovering the location of the guards, who tend to congregate in groups of four and five under the fullest trees along the border, then keeps out of sight of them and slowly approaches the furthest beast. Rush can observe him only by doing the same. And the animals already know the boy and come to him freely, nuzzling him and ignoring him as they do one another. A young colt, still dappled, trots over to him without ceremony when he sees him. He is awarded a treat.

The boy has not yet had the gall to attempt to mount one of the animals, and Rush cannot imagine that this could be in his plans. The horses are untamed to harness and kept for their novelty only. Nevertheless, the boy's antics are worrisome. Will he have to take on an entire squad of soldiers, albeit mediocre ones, to keep the boy from harm? And keep him from harm he must. He has already forfeited the peculiar pleasure of taking his head for his king. He will surely not stand by and watch a bunch of fools cut him down like a calf.

Rush watches the boy befriend the colt, run his hands over his flank, under his belly, down his legs. Presently he slips the colt another treat, then moves away the way he came. When he reaches the wall of stones along the eastern side of the field he takes care to see where the guards are and then slips over the top like a lynx.

Just as he disappears over the wall the guards on the eastern side of the pasture stir from their afternoon game of dice. One of them has seen some movement in the grass in the pasture, perhaps a fox. He begins to advance in Rush's direction.

Although no threat to Rush, who can disappear from view easily enough, or take down a few guards without even rustling the grass, the man's approach has made it impossible for him to follow the boy. He knows well enough where he is headed, having followed him before to the City of the Dead, where an Asian woman tends the spirits and lives on gifts laid at the gate by their patrons. He knows the old woman loves the boy, having been treated to his dance and his flirtations on more than one forbidden occasion, and that she feeds him sweets made of dates and honey and pine nuts, which Mochlos would flay him for eating. So Rush gives up his pursuit and retreats to the north wall, over and down the hill to the Bridge Road and to the city of Knossos. He will pass Mochlos' Villa on the way and pay him a visit as Ameg the Merchant. He will discuss his new shipment of silks and spices which Mochlos, a lover of luxury, style and fashion, will pay extra to get first dibs on. He will inquire after the priest's household. Any new developments with his pick for this year's Grain Dancer? Is it true the boy takes fits (he heard this at court from another merchant, who heard it from Kephas himself) and does Mochlos believe, as the Egyptians do, that this is a sign that the boy is a favorite plaything of the gods?

In fact, Rush hates Mochlos passionately, not especially because he owns the boy, sees him daily, and can do what he wishes with him. He has always hated Mochlos, and believed him a sneak, a cheat and a hypocrite long before he purchased the boy. He would gladly cut the man's genitals off and feed them to his own chickens for half of what he normally gets for an assassination. Perhaps he can convince Cyrus that it is Mochlos, and not the boy, who has brought about Knossos' recent prosperity.

But he will not concern himself with ending Mochlos' life today.

Rush presents himself at the gates of Mochlos' villa as Ameg the Merchant. He is escorted into a courtyard overlooking the sea. Over the wall of the courtyard are the rooftops of smaller homes descending down the shallow cliff to the beach. The place is open to infiltration by a good mercenary like himself. He can easily scale those rooftops. It is common practice on Crete to grow flowering and fruiting vines along the eastern wall of one's home and he will take advantage of this custom. At the base of the villa is a low wall, a narrow lawn, and lo! steps leading to the second floor. Then a kind of parapet skirts the upper level. He can leap to a window from that. All he needs now is the layout of the upper floor, which will contain the master's sleeping quarters. The boy will not be far from that, he is certain. Priests keep their best dancers near them at night, where the security is sharpest and where they have easy access to them.

Rush makes his visit with Mochlos, who is in a private courtyard entertaining several other merchants on the opposite side of the house. This yard, also surrounded by a low wall, overlooks a canal across from which can be seen the city and the palace of Knossos. Two other merchants and Mochlos' three personal advisers are lounging about a stone table, drinking and eating delicacies. The merchants are pacifying the priest with pleasantries about his house, his servants, his exquisite sense of style. When Rush arrives Mochlos loses interest in their patter. They cannot compete with Ameg, whose fleet is one of the largest and furthest reaching in Knossos. Mochlos is intent on learning what Ameg the Merchant has brought from the east in his newest shipment of silks, for he needs something special to dress this year's Grain Dancer in for the upcoming competition.

Rush allows Mochlos some bit of excitement as he describes a gold encrusted, sky blue silk he found in the orient and purchased with Mochlos in mind. This is in fact true. The silks were purchased months before, while the boy was still sailing the Aegean with Kephas, his final destination unknown. The irony of this is not lost on Rush; he will be providing the silks the boy will compete in for a chance to be a human sacrifice at the age of seventeen, when just a fortnight earlier he had the little dancer pinned beneath him in fear for his life. But there is much irony in the life of a double agent. Mochlos agrees to a price on the silk and Rush, after taking part in a few pints of mead, takes his leave. He will let himself out.

Without much difficulty he slips over the wall to the upper parapet as soon as he leaves the private courtyard, then easily moves about on the second level until he finds his bearings. No one guards the high priest's chamber during the day and he enters, moving through the room, around an enormous bed heavy with exotic furs, and silently slips through the bead doorway to the slave chamber. Here there is a small stone pallet against the far wall. Above it are two circles of bronze for chaining a slave. There is a basin in the center of the room into which well water can be pumped, and about the walls are several trunks, some opened and overflowing with brightly colored costumes. There are silks, embroidered and woven linens, feathered head pieces, beaded gloves, fur boots and belts of woven leather. On one wall is a low vanity, and upon it a jumble of face and body paints and brushes. There is a large mirror across from the pallet against the opposite wall. This is made of polished bronze.

He has found the grain dancer's dressing room and sleeping quarters.

Rush fingers the gaudy costumes in the closest trunk, musing. Has he seen the boy dance in any of these things? If he found one he would take it home, a prize.

He picks up an embroidered vest, sniffs the fabric. The perfume of cherry, myrrh, lotus blossom and hyssop bring his head up as if he has been slapped.

The boy's scent. For an instant it is twilight on the Bridge Road and he is pinning the dancer again, about to take his head when he is struck stupid by those feline eyes, struck dumb that a boy smells like a holy concubine, rendered impotent by confusion.

Fool.

Twice a fool. For all of Mochlos' dancers would be bathed in these expensive oils.

He tosses the garment back into the trunk and moves to the bed.

The pallet is plain, harsh, a thin deerskin over a stone slab. He runs his hand over it as if checking for the heat of its last occupant. It must be cold at night, he thinks, when the breeze comes through the open window, and here the boy is chained by the neck, the waist, the ankles, unable even to stand or move about except to sit up on the bed.

He considers robbing Mochlos of one of his furs and leaving it on the boy's pallet. The boy, who seems more beast than boy at times, would find comfort in a fur.

But Mochlos would of course accuse him of taking it and beat him half to death.

Rush purses his lips, annoyed at his own nonsense. What is it to him if Mochlos leaves the boy to shiver on a cold pallet all night while he is drowning in furs in the next room? Did he not himself frighten the dancer half to death only days ago?

It is time to slip away before someone enters Mochlos' room and hears him in here.

Rush moves to the window, peers out, careful not to be seen from below. But there is nothing but rooftops and a gorgeous Mediterranean sky. Why not in daylight then? He hops the ledge, drops six feet to a narrow parapet below. Over that wall and onto a rooftop, and he is soon strolling out of an alley onto a backstreet toward the Bridge Road.

Back in Knossos he visits his own house, which is on the opposite side of the palace and the city. He attends to his household. He visits his stable, where he keeps two barber bred ponies for traversing the mountains between Knossos and Cyrus. And he thinks of the boy, out in the King's pasture in broad daylight, risking his life to play with a colt he will never ride.

That night, in bed with his Minoan wife whom he loves (he has another in Mycenae whom he rarely visits), it is the boy's face he sees as his member enters her. It is the boy's face, covered in blue and green paint, dancing for the King and the court of Knossos, the boy's strange, catlike features, his unearthly sea-green eyes sparkling in the torchlight.

CHAPTER 5

Throughout the competition, the dances were performed at each of the Holy Houses of Knossos. The last dance takes place again in the Great Hall, and everyone of importance is in attendance, in addition to the general public, which has packed the house. Together, by their applause, they will decide who is to be the Grain Dancer of Knossos, the true representative of Rah. The King and his Queen and highest ranking officials sit on a dais on the short side of the hall, entering and exiting behind a mosaic wall two stories high and depicting the city and the Bridge Road to the west. Their private chambers are further back, on the south end of the palace.

Mochlos, being the richest priest in Knossos, is no fool. He has paid a handsome price to have his performers give the very last dance of the evening. He has ordered Dimius to hold his group in the practice area after the normal intermission between troupes has expired. When Dimius hears the crowd growing restless, he is to come out himself, into the center of the arena, bow to the King and Queen, and beg forgiveness for the delay. His lead dancer has sprained a foot only this morning while practicing for the competition and he may not perform at his optimum. Does the King wish to see him dance with the injury, or shall Mochlos' house, with all due respect to the Court, scratch the performance?

Of course this is outrageous. The Court, and the city, have been talking of nothing but the golden god-slave since his debut dance. There could well be a riot if he were not to perform, sprained foot or no. What Mochlos does not yet know is the Queen of Knossos has plans for this boy, should he win the crowd's favor today. She has instructed her King of these plans and has insisted that the boy dance. The King is servant to the Queen in Knossos, a king in name only.

He will have him out in the arena even if he has to be dragged out.

The King's face betrays his impatience with Mochlos and his tricks. He speaks softly to his right hand man, who slams his staff down once on the stones, indicating the King's decision. Then he bellows loud enough for the whole hall to hear, "You will dance, House of the Moon!"

In fact there is nothing wrong with the boy's foot or any other part of him. His welts have faded and his lungs recovered from his punishments the morning after he ran from the assassin. He has been coddled since then by his attendants, his trainer and his concubines and kept safely out of Mochlos' sight. When the priest asks how the boy's practice is progressing he is assured by all of his handlers that Mochlos' lead dancer will be unrivaled at the competition. Having a tin ear and no sense of rhythm himself, Mochlos has no interest in dance, and has left the boy to them.

The dance begins with Dimius narrating the story which the dance will reflect. Then the dancers enter to timpani, lute and string. The air is dark and smoky for the many torches lighting the Great Hall have been burning for hours. It is the perfect setting for the dance.

The boy is naked to his hips and dressed in a skirt made of many lengths of green and yellow silk and sewn together painstakingly by Aros' best seamstresses. Matching bits of silk are woven to his golden bracelets, anklets and collar. His feet are bare. His face is a fantastic explosion of green and yellow stripes, although clever Pyrus has added a startling thick blue line under his eyes that reaches his ears. The blue under his large and ethereally pale eyes is magical, even to an audience watching from a series of elevated stone steps.

For the Grain Dance competition, each of the four Houses of worship must perform a dance telling a story of their god or goddess, and this year Dimius has built the House of the Moon's story around Pyrus' genius with the boy's face. It is the story of a boy created from the forbidden love between the Moon Goddess and a tiger. The boy, half god, half tiger, is so beautiful, with stripes made of moonlight and eyes the color of the sea, that he is hunted down, ravished and stripped of his pelt by the people of Knossos. When the Goddess learns that her son has been defiled thus she calls forth the wrath of her first love, the Aegean, who rises up and drowns the city in a great tidal wave.

The audience is both shocked by the boldness of the story and seduced by the boy's performance of it. They throw saffron flowers and yellow lilies at his feet and roar with delight when the King stands up and steps down from his place on the dais to honor the House of Mochlos with his acceptance of the boy as the new Grain God.

The next day the Dying to the God ceremony must take place. The ceremony will begin in Mochlos' gymnasium and end in the City of the Dead four kilometers from Mochlos' Villa. Eleven of the highest ranking members of Court will attend. The boy must appear to die so that the God Rah can fully possess his body. If he can convince the eleven Watchers that he has indeed taken into himself the soul of Rah, he will be the God's representative on earth throughout the growing season. And in the fall, unless he can hold back the winter, he will be sacrifice on Mount Juktas to the God.

CHAPTER 6

At the Villa of Mochlos the boy is led down to the gymnasium as usual after a morning meal. Today the main arena is empty of dancers. Instead, it is occupied by Mochlos himself and a group of neophyte priests and ten young girls, bare-chested and dressed in white and yellow skirts to the floor. These are the Concubines to the God, chosen from the various households who hold high bureaucratic rank in Knossos. To have one's daughter chosen as a concubine to Rah is a great honor. The girl will become a priestess, a mistress of the God she is chosen to serve, and go to live in the Palace.

The priests are the students of Mochlos, and of the House of Ananou, devoted to the Sun God. All are dressed in white robes and yellow sashes. Mochlos is dressed formally as well. He wears a robe of white and yellow, with sheaves of grain embroidered in gold about the hem, representing Rah, and a bronze hat, a round golden ball with two crescents facing outward on either side, representing the Moon Goddess in all of her phases. In his hand he carries a bronze staff with the same symbol of the Moon Goddess on the head. Old Ananou, head of the House of the Sun, wears a similar robe of yellow and white, but embroidered with a great golden sun. He also wears a bronze hat, his with a fan of bronze rays making a half circle above his head.

Seated on the raised steps along the west wall of the gymnasium, perpendicular to the line of priests in front of the boy, are the eleven dignitaries from the Court of Knossos. These are all hidden in hooded black robes. Today these dignitaries are standing in for the Night Watchers, spirits of the dead. They will view the proceedings and make a decision as to whether the boy has truly died to the God and whether Rah himself has possessed his body.

Among them is Rush.

Since his beating with the reed and the ensuing drowning, the boy is quite terrified of Mochlos and the high priest's appearance in the gymnasium in ceremonial garments sends a sickening misery through his bowels. He falters as he is led before the group but strong hands grip him on either side and continue to move him forward. He is loved by the servants of the House of Mochlos who know him but the men handling him now are the priest's private henchmen. He wishes in vain for his own attendants, Pyrus and Aros, who would have managed to give him some advice or encouragement in Greek, or his trainer Dimius whose instructions at practice have always held a note of affection toward his favorite pupil, or Tuma, whose baritone African boom would soothe him and give him courage now. But none of these are present.

An altar has been set up behind Mochlos and Ananou, who stand together waiting for him. Somewhere behind the priests timpani and reed flute are being played in an eerie, even heartbeat. These will continue, following behind the procession to the Burial Mounds of the Ancients, until the slave boy is pronounced dead by the priests. Then they will cease, signifying the boy's last heartbeat and breath. A thick cloud of smoke rises from pots of incense burning on the altar.

When the boy reaches Mochlos he is forced to his knees without much effort. His knees were already weak at the sight of the man who took such pleasure in beating him, first yanking his head back by the hair after having him chained by his wrists facing a wall, then giving him an angry, open mouthed kiss after applying a reed to his seat and thighs until he thought he would vomit from the pain, then having him dragged to the drowning pool and held under until he passed out.

Now Mochlos is speaking in a droning tenor in high Minoan, the dialect of the priesthood, and the boy cannot make out a word of it, which is a mercy. After what seems like an eternity to the boy, who is on his bare knees on the sand floor, Mochlos turns to the altar and takes from it a bronze plate upon which lies a little mountain of purplish powder and a bronze cup. Mochlos uses a utensil to scoop up a bit of the powder and mixes it ceremoniously in the cup. He makes another proclamation in high Minoan. Then Ananou takes the cup and lifts the boy's chin, offering him the brew.

The boy has only one objective this morning. He is going to avoid another beating. He squeezes his brilliant eyes closed, takes a few panting breaths for strength, and opens his mouth for Ananou, accepting the liquid. He swallows the gritty, drug-laced wine obediently, before his throat spasms closed against its bitterness.

Almost immediately he feels a heat rise in his body, from his belly outward. His heart begins to talk in his chest, a bang, then rapid timpani. He tries to take a step backward and finds himself half in, half out of his own body. He can think clearly, he can see, it seems in slow motion. But he cannot co-ordinate his movements or direct his own limbs. The step backward becomes a step forward. His attempt to balance himself becomes a spastic gyration of his arms. He wants to speak, but words are grunts now, his tongue disobedient. He fears he will bite it near in half as he did when, as a child, he fell into his first fit and mashed the length of the right side so badly it has left him with a lifelong speech impediment. He wills his tongue to be still, but it jumps like a worm in his mouth, threatening to choke him. He commands his body the simplest task, to maintain his balance and continue to stand before the priests, but a tremor runs through his maverick limbs so violently that he falls to the ground, his muscles jerking and spasming, pulling him into painful contortions. His thighs Charlie-horse and his brain screams with pain, but from his mouth comes only an ugly cawing.

He has been an epileptic all of his life, but has never experienced his own palsy. Yet here he is, conscious in a body that now reads his internal commands like gibberish. He has become the polar opposite of himself, no longer a skilled acrobat capable of stunts of balance and grace most only dream about, but a palsied idiot.

Behind the cowl of his black hood, Rush is stillness itself. He is seething with hatred for the priests, who have chosen this particular drug to usher the God into the body of the boy. Twice before he has witnessed the Dying to the God ceremony. The first time a boy was paralyzed, the second, blinded, both recovering from their infirmity upon rising from the Dying Altar as Rah. But this is more abominable, the ultimate sin. They have robbed this amazing creature of his very essence, his physical grace. It stinks of Mochlos who, like a rapist, cannot be content paying for a whore but must attack a nun. Mochlos the sadist, the clever showman. He has concocted this monstrous defilement out of the poisons in his own sadistic mind. He has determined that nothing would so convince the Watchers that the boy is gone from his body as this, this robbery of his athletic beauty. Yes, only Mochlos would consider this angle.

It is almost impossible for Rush to watch the boy, who has fallen on his contorted face in the sand, his arms and legs stiff but spasming as he attempts to operate them, his agile body twisted, his wrists bent back and fingers splayed. He fixes his gaze instead on the man who will pay for this. He watches Mochlos' wily face in the haze of the incense smoke, observing his ugly work with glistening eyes. Rush has seen that look in the eyes of the rich old men who visit the finest brothels to pay to "break in" a girl of nine and ten summers. The priest is enjoying this, he is even excited by it.

He is inside his victim's head, feeling his distress and confusion, his helplessness and shame. He is dizzy with his own power to disgrace grace.

But clever Mochlos has not considered that there is a bigger devil than he watching the ceremony that he has contrived.

Rush, the assassin, watches and waits. When they truss the boy in a linen shroud, strap his spasming body to a leather stretcher and begin the procession to the Burial Ground of the Ancients, he follows with the other Watchers. He will watch for the signs of the God, as he is expected. He will, with the others, make the decision whether or not the boy has indeed been possessed by Rah.

But sometime hence he will give Mochlos a taste of his own poison. He will give him back the gift of his own meanness, with interest. For Rush has seen the world, the high, the low, the great, the evil. He knows that a sadist is merely a masochist who lacks courage.

As he walks solemnly along with the other Watchers, behind the two high priests and the stretcher but in front of the neophyte priesthood, he considers his options. He knows that Mochlos delights in flogging and drowning his dancers. He has on occasion even performed this meting out of punishment in front of guests. It is his right, a luxury bestowed to him because of his priesthood, and he seems to have a penchant for torturing his most gifted boys. But Mochlos is just a slack bellied pansy. He has no real idea of how many ways there are to torture, and not much imagination. He hasn't a soldier's understanding of the limits of the physical body, or a mercenary's knowledge of how to maintain the fine line between his victim's endurance and blood loss, he has no idea how long one can really take if one has the stomach for it. Rush has the stomach for it. He was an elite soldier first and is now a highly paid assassin. His work has not always required the death of his mark. Sometimes he is sent only to extract information, or to blackmail.

The road to the Burial Mounds of the Ancients runs along the coast. It is paved with round stones for half a kilometer, then brick as it curves south into the hills. As the land rises it becomes less a road and more a wide path through grass and brush, and then farmland and wood. The mounds are on the side of Mt. Ida, a nest of man-made caves with faces of squared stones. More recent burials tumble further down the side of the mountain, and there is a commune of priests living among the dead to tend to them properly. After a season, corpses will need to be exhumed and cleaned, the bones then returned to their family grave.

But only Ting Ya, the old Chinese slave, tends to the ancients whose bones are already cleaned by time and considered too sacred to move or to rearrange. Ting Ya lives in a small mud brick building near the stone entrance to the mounds, and when the procession reaches its destination she will become part of the ceremony by opening the gate to them, then walking with the "corpse" of the boy to the Altar of Rah.

The Mediterranean sun is high and hot, the sky an opalescent blue as the procession begins to ascend the mountain. The boy has become quiet. Perhaps he has been overtaken by the drug and become unconscious, or else paralysis has set in and he remains aware. If this is the case his ordeal must be horrific. Rush considers the fact that he could stop this farce right now and slaughter most of these priests without much thought. He is never without his weapons, and under the black robes he wears are two daggers strapped to his ankles and two smaller but deadlier blades in leather holsters that sit under either arm pit, their straps crisscrossing his bull-like chest. He would need only to rid himself of his outer garment. But the boy would still be in the psychic hell of the drug. Beyond that, if he is indeed conscious, his recognition of Rush, in that state, would doubtless be more terrifying to him than anything else that has happened today.

The sun has peaked in the sky and is on its descent when the group reaches the gates of the ancient cemetery. Ting Ya meets them. She is wearing a thin white veil that covers her entire head and face and disappears into the folds of her white robe. She opens the gate, steps aside for the two high priests, then comes beside the pallet and the trussed and shrouded boy. Rush notices that, walking along side the stretcher, she quietly slips one small hand out of her robe and rests it on the boy's right arm. His heart warms to her. Even this small show of friendship must be a comfort to the dancer right now.

The procession comes to a halt in an open area surrounded by burial mounds. Before them, inside a circle of shallow stone steps, is an altar also made of stone. The pallet upon which the boy lies is lifted and placed on the altar, then the pallet bearers step away from it. Torches have been lit in a ring around the congregation, as night is approaching. Ting Ya lights votive candles around the base of the altar and steps away from it. The priests and Watchers arrange themselves on the steps, kneeling around the "corpse" of the boy while Mochlos and Ananou loosen the trusses that strap him to his stretcher. Mochlos passes his hand over the body and Rush sees his offering of seed, dried corn kernels and millet drop from his fingers about the boy's chest and shoulders. Then Mochlos backs away from the body and kneels in front of the priests, his own knees pillowed by the many layers of his embroidered garments.

The priesthood begins to murmur, at first incoherently, then in rhythm. It is a chant, a call for Rah to come and inhabit the body they have prepared for him.

The congregation waits for the boy to stir, chanting as the sun begins to drop in the western sky.

Ting Ya kneels on a step several feet from the boy's head, her hands on her knees, her elbows tucked in like a serving girl. All is still but for the drone of the priests.

Suddenly, high above the chanting voices is heard the flapping of wings. Several of the Watches lift their cowls to see a flight of doves, not ordinary pigeons but large white birds with yellow beaks and big dark eyes, descend to settle about the limbs of the boy on the altar. There are six of them, the holy number of Rah.

The birds light on the shroud one at a time, cooing softly and walking back and forth, pecking at the seed and corn that the priest has surrupticiously dropped in the folds of the boy's shroud. The chanting stops abruptly. Mochlos rises from his knees, stealthy and slow so as not to disturb the doves. Six! This is better than he had planned. He had hoped for one or two wild pigeons, not a perfect six of doves! He must be sure to take full advantage of it.

He raises his arms out to his sides, his robes making wings. He is himself a great white bird.

He whispers to the congregation, "See the purest spirits of the earth come to worship him! It is Rah!"

At the same time, and to the delight of the high priest, the boy begins to stir. Perhaps the birds cooing and pecking, their cold, clawed feet skittering along his arms, have ushered sense back into his limbs. The congregation is awed to fearful silence.

To Rush's utter relief, the boy moans, lifts his shrouded head a few inches, and then giggles when he sees the birds strutting and pecking along his arms. It is that jolly little sound he made when the cur dog licked his face. As if unaware of his audience, he sits up slowly, lifting the birds on his linen draped arms, setting two on his shoulders, where he nuzzles their white breasts.

Rush has to bite his own lip to keep from laughing himself. Surely these are the same doves the boy set free in the field weeks ago.

Rush watches as the boy extends his arms out on either side of him. The doves flap casually to steady themselves but none leave him. He makes a quick upward movement with both arms and the birds obediently take off into the sky. Then he is on his feet on the altar, and the shroud has fallen in loose coils about his body. It is no impediment to one who danced in a cloud of colorful silks in the Great Hall before a king. He hops, without ceremony, off the slab.

The boy looks about at the circle of spectators, priests, black robed Watchers and bare breasted virgins, kneeling around his altar on the stone steps. He spots Ting Ya, kneeling to his right at the head of the altar, and he gives her a respectful nod, dipping only his head, like a dove. He is unsure of what is expected of him. Best to give his master, who stands now in front of the kneeling congregation, his humblest bow.

A murmur runs through the Watchers. One, chosen before the ceremony to bring their collective decision to the priests, now steps up to Mochlos and Ananou and pronounces their verdict.

"Blessed be Rah, son of Moon and Sun. Praise to Rah, for he has accepted the offering and has come to inhabit the body of this Grain Dancer. He has deigned to live among us for a season."

This is a rote proclamation. With it, Mochlos has succeeded in bringing Knossos its third living sacrifice to Rah in as many years. He is a rich man, for the King has already assured him a house beside the palace if the boy is proclaimed the vessel of the God. He turns to face the congregation, hands lifted like a magus in the air to summon the group to their feet. His face is fat with satisfaction.

"You have heard the verdict of the Watchers. We must now celebrate, for Rah has found favor with this human vessel!"

At this the ten virgins, bound now for the palace and a life of esteem and luxury, fill the hills with their joyful ululations. Minstrels who have carried brass drum, reed flute and lyre up the mountain behind the procession now begin to play the Song of the Grain Dance. Roasted lamb, yogurt, bread and retsina, which were brought up the mountain road on wagons and unloaded during the long wait for Rah to awake, are distributed. As the girls form a circular dance around Rah, the neophyte priests form a line to bow before Rah and lay a single lily at his feet. Then they move off to join the festivities.

Rah stands peacefully beside his altar, watching the priests drop to their knees before him. A pile of yellow lilies lies at his feet. His shroud is still draped about his shoulders but is falling in loose loops about his body. His face is innocent until Mochlos, who has been hemmed in by well-wishers and sycophants, takes his place at the end of the diminishing line. When he reaches the grain dancer he whispers instructions to the boy in Greek.

"Dance now, Couple with the virgins. You are Rah. Do not disgrace me."

The boy looks up at him, eyes wide, sees the tiger lurking in his master's face, and drops his gaze, down and to the left.

"Yes, master."

He may be playing the part of Rah now, as he played the role of the tiger-boy, but Mochlos is still Mochlos, and as dangerous as ever. Rah will do exactly what the high priest says.

Ananou has come to offer Mochlos a bronze chalice filled with retsina. Mochlos slips his fingers into a pocket in the lining of one of his sleeves, then passes his hand over the top of the cup. He hands the drink to Rah.

"Don't be afraid," he whispers to the boy in Greek. "This drink is pleasant. It will give Rah stamina."

Rah takes the chalice, closes his eyes and takes a sip, hoping a sip will be enough to pacify the priest. It is not.

"All of it," Mochlos whispers. The boy swallows what he can in one gulp, liquid splashing down his chin and onto his chest.

"Good," whispers Mochlos. "Now you will dance. Dance and couple with the virgins. Rah must sew our fields with wheat and barley."

The priest takes the empty chalice, pretends to drink from it, passes it back to Ananou. The boy bows to his master. He is in full possession of his limbs and when he hops back onto the altar he hushes the crowd. His shroud has fallen from his shoulders leaving him naked but for the short asymmetrical skirt Aros dressed him in that morning.

As the drug takes its effect, the priests, watchers, minstrels and food carriers fade in his vision. The torches seem only capable of lighting the sweat shining on the plump breasts of the girls who continue to circle him in a subdued dance. He feels himself respond to them, his loins almost painful with need. He picks out the prettiest one, not for her face or form but for her grace. He is picking out the mare with the best movement, light-footed, well conformed, flexible and energetic. Oblivious to the circle of bureaucrats drinking and smoking opium in the cemetery he drops his head, takes a few imperceptible deep breaths, and vaults himself up into the air.

Somersaulting in a double flip off the altar, he lands on his feet, a little blonde leopard. He stalks the girl he has chosen, moving to the rhythm of the drums, then captures her in his hands and twirls her lightly. He catches her again and the two become familiar as he matches her movements, creating a dance around her dance. He is backing her around the altar in a circle counter to the circle of the nine remaining girls who continue their chain in the opposite direction.

When he has made a full circle around the altar, Rah leaves his partner, retreating with a series of cartwheels and back-flips, scattering the other girls out of his way. He is following the edge of the top step, and by the time he is back where he started, his locomotion has slowed until his last flip is a walk backwards from a handstand to his feet. For one long moment his back is arched so impossibly high it appears he must snap in two. The crowd of celebrants laughs, claps, cheers.

Then he is standing before the girl again, somehow taller than he was when he stalked her. He takes the fingers of her left hand and she stops, unsure of what she is to do. He steps forward to show her, shoulders up and back, spine arched, toes pointed each step. At first she steps back awkwardly, her movements brittle. Then, understanding, she begins to mirror his ballet in reverse, backing herself up to the altar. She is a kitten dancing backward. He is a panther.

When her haunch hits the slab she leans back with nowhere else to go. And he is on her.

Rush has seen the priest pass his hand over the drink he gave the Grain God. He knows the boy has no real power of reason now and is possessed entirely by the effect of the drug. He himself is possessed by voyeurism and is planted in his tracks. He watches the boy couple with the girl on the altar, as prettily as if this, too, is part of the dance.

The celebration continues until sunrise. At some point, Rush has turned away from the boy's dance with the concubines. By early morning most of the celebrants are scattered about the ancient graves, sleeping in the grass, or else have left the festivities and gone home. Even Rush has allowed himself a few hours of rest, although he has remained cautious of too much retsina. When he rouses himself at dawn he is the first awake.

Still dressed in the black robes of a Watcher, he throws back his hood, no longer concerned that the boy might recognize him. After last night, he must still be sleeping, and will no doubt be unconscious until noon.

Rush moves about the slumbering priesthood silently, making his way to the altar. It is a high point from which he quickly spots the corn silk head of Rah a hundred feet away.

The boy is surrounded by, and covered with, sleeping concubines. As Rush approaches he sees that Rah is lying on his back in a thatch of tall grass between two shallow outer burial mounds. Girls sleep on either side of him, snuggling together or else sprawled out on the grass near him, one or two clutching his leg or arm in their sleep. One girl's dark head rests on his belly, her long black hair replacing his skirt, which is not in evidence. Another maiden lies with her head resting on his ribs as if, in sleep, she listens for his heartbeat. Rush moves closer silently until he is standing above the boy, blocking the rising sunlight that had been playing in his golden hair. In sleep the boy is angelic, his thick lashes creating shadows on his cheekbones, his Cupid's-bow lips parted so that a glint of incisor and the tip of his tongue peek from them. His cheeks are flush, perhaps from the drug, despite his golden tan. This sleeping child is surely not the young man who coupled like a satyr with the girls he now pillows, nor the fierce little cat Rush himself pinned and struggled to hold down several weeks ago. Surely he did not put a dagger against that innocent throat before he was struck useless by the boy's alien beauty.

He shakes his head, frowning but peering at the face of the sleeping Grain God all the same, looking for a clue. A clue to that moment of paralysis, of unexplained impotence in him. He has killed beauties before, more than one mistress or wife of privilege, who cried for mercy and found none in him. He has never faltered in his work. Killing was nothing to him, until now.

The conflict within him irritates, challenges.

"I may put a blade in you yet, cub," he murmurs to himself. "I am what I am."

The boy makes a sudden sound, "Gah!" in his sleep as though in response. His right hand comes up to find the girl's head on his chest. He calms, his fingers stroking her hair gently in his slumber.

"Mother god," Rush mutters, shaking his head again.

He steps carefully away from the pile of sleeping lovers to find his way out of the cemetery before the priesthood awakens.

CHAPTER 7

"Did they stop your limbs, or put you to sleep only?"

Aros is playing with the new Grain God's hair today in front of his vanity. Something different, something more ethereal now that he has been proclaimed a heavenly vessel. How would these curls react if he cut them into a halo about the boy's head? Would they stand up, rays of sunlight? Or lie limp and make the God look like a soaked house cat.

Rah is more interested in the sharpened bone which Aros is whirling about his head than in remembering yesterday. He watches the razored edge of the bone instrument flying back and forth in front of his eyes with distrust. Now and then he snaps hold of Aros' soft wrist, viper-fast, if it comes too close to his face, then frowns at his attendant with disapproval.

"Let go, you'll ruin the cut if you keep doing that, you silly thing. I won't hurt you. Now tell me! What magic did our master put in the drink? What was it like to die, and then to awake a God?"

"It make me sick," Rah shrugs, his Greek still imperfect and always in present tense. His eyes still follow the blade. "Then later, another make me strong."

"No, no, tell me everything. The first drink. How did it make you sick?"

"Oh for god sake, Aros, don't be such a ghoul. Leave him alone, he doesn't want to remember." This is Pyrus, hands on hips, watching his counterpart chop and feather the boy's beautiful hair. His stomach is in a fist for he is sick with worry that Aros will ruin that glorious head of yellow light.

Rah tries again. "It give me fit," he makes himself ridged, neck bent, arms stiff and wrists curled under, in an ugly imitation of himself. "But I am awake this time. Then I cannot move at all and Ileah, my sister, come to be my arms and legs."

Aros looks at Pyrus, eyes wide, over the boy's head. A sister? He mouths.

"The talented are always half mad, Aros, I don't know why you bother."

"Ileah?" Aros tries again, fussing with a few arrogant curls at the boy's nape.

"My twin," says Rah.

"My god, two of these?" Aros tips the razor at the back of Rah's head, glaring at Pyrus.

"He was dreaming, Aros. He had a dream in the drug, that is all."

"No!" Rah shouts at Pyrus, then, frustrated, he captures Aros' wrist one more time, this time refusing to let go. He speaks deliberately, slowly, staring into Aros' face.

"Ileah come and I am free. I run ahead to the mountain. I play in sky with doves."

Pyrus rolls his eyes. "I told you. He had a dream in the drug. You'll get nothing but nonsense from him about this."

"Ileah, Ileah, pretty name," Aros muses, "What is that. Dorian? Gaul?" Aros tips Rah's shoulders back so that he can see the result of his work. "There, Pyrus, look. I have made a halo!"

Pyrus steps in front of the boy, arms crossed over his narrow chest. He fluffs Rah's hair a bit here and there, a grateful smile beginning to play on his lips.

"Thank god you didn't ruin it, Aros. You had me worried."

"And we can stiffen it-"

"No, no none of your spikes. Let it bounce and move. . . here, boy, shake your head."

Rah shakes his entire upper body like a wet dog. His curls fluff about his head, then settle.

An idea lights Pyrus' face.

"I can paint the sun on his face, Aros, this is brilliant!"

"Better than the tiger!"

"Nothing will ever beat the tiger," says Pyrus. "But Dimius will love it. Come, we're late. Get him dressed and down to the gymnasium."

"You dance for the King tonight, eh, Sunlight?" says Aros as he tosses the boy a clean loin cloth skirt to tie himself into. "A private dance, only the King and Queen and the Court, hmm? I hear he's entertaining guests from Egypt. I would be terrified." He shakes his head.

"You are a fuss pot, Aros. Always fretting and seeing the worst outcome. A good dancer, like this one, uses his fear like a drug. A drug to make him focused and perfect. Yes, Rah?"

"Oh, and I suppose you would say that, having leapt the bulls yourself. Well, what do I know, I was a seamstress until I became a dresser."

"What do you say, Rah?" Pyrus looks at the boy.

Rah shrugs at Pyrus, tucking the tie to his skirt under the waistband. When he is finished, he looks up at the face painter.

"Aros afraid for Rah," he says simply. He steps behind Aros, who is fussing with his own reflection in the big bronze mirror, and puts a kiss on his attendant's ear so quickly that Aros flinches, then stares at Rah as if the boy had slapped him.

"Aros, Rah can dance," the boy smiles at him. "King will like," he winks at Aros and plants another quick kiss on his mouth before turning away.

"Yes, Sunlight," Aros looks after him, dazzled. "That's what I'm afraid of."

CHAPTER 8

The summer solstice is a holy day in Knossos. Each year, the chosen Grain God comes to the Palace to perform a Dance to the Sun before the King and Queen. There are usually diplomats from other countries present, and this year they are Egyptians.

Knossos and his Queen are especially interested in impressing the Egyptians, whom he considers his most sophisticated contemporaries and his allies in many ways. The Egyptians share the Minoan love of style and physical grace, and are particularly awed by the athletic displays performed by the Minoan bull dancers. There is rumor in Egypt that Knossos keeps a thousand bulls under the palace, that there is a bull-headed monster living within a labyrinth of tunnels under the Great Hall, and that enemies of the state are thrown to the monster to be eaten, at the King's whim. Knossos does nothing to correct this rumor, in fact, he has made a point of implying its validity. In reality, the basement of the palace is a labyrinth of tunnels, but these are filled with textiles, pottery, military equipment and amphora holding thousands of pounds of grain. There is a sunken bull pen near the Great Hall where two wild bulls are kept and it is true that murderers and thieves have been thrown in with them on occasion. But there is also a leopard pit used for the same purpose. These are hardly monsters, or even unusual deterrents to crime.

Tonight is the Dance to the Sun, and the Grain God will be performing before the court of the King and his Egyptian guests. Rah's face has been painted in a burst of hot colors, yellows and oranges, to represent the sun, his hair fluffed and stiffened into a yellow-gold halo of sunlight. His costume is made of orange and gold silks, flames that flutter from his wrists, neck and ankles. He will dance last, after the bull jumpers, and his dance with tell the story of the Sun God.

On Crete the Sun God starts life as a shepherd boy who loves his

44

flock so much that when the time comes he refuses to take his sheep to market for slaughter. For his punishment, the people of the city pin him to stakes high on a mountain in the noonday heat of the summer, to be burned for seven days. But the Sky takes pity on the boy and calls on the Wind to carry the clouds to the top of the mountain and rain upon him, protecting him from the Aegean heat and giving him water to drink. When the people of the city see that the Sky has favored the boy and kept him from harm they declare him an equal to the Moon, who tamed the Sea for love of mankind. They give him two fine white horses and a golden chariot and dress him in purple robes. But the Sky has fallen in love with the boy and wants him to herself. When he steps onto his chariot amid the cheering crowds, she calls again upon the Wind, who fashions wings for the horses out of clouds and air. Then the horses carry the shepherd boy up into the heavens where he remains united with the Sky forever, a bright yellow star in the day, God of the Sun.

When Rah's dance is finished, his audience shakes the floor of the Great Hall with their stamping feet and applause. Once again they cover him with lilies, and Mochlos spirits him away before the King and Queen can have another look at him. He is in the palace gymnasium with the other dancers when Mochlos and several of his attendants come to collect him.

"Well, boy, it seems you have pleased the King sufficiently to earn a private audience. Now listen carefully. You will do exactly as he wishes, for he has paid me well for your company tonight. It seems his Queen is quite taken by you and believes you the answer to her prayers." He looks about at his men. "And we all know who is the true King of Knossos is."

With that, the men around Mochlos burst out laughing, for Knossos is a city of illusions. It is the Queen's line that matters, and the King is more of a figurehead and president of a merchandising company than a mate for the Queen. The Queen can take any lover she chooses; therefore her fertility is not dependent on one man. This Queen has only male children and she needs a daughter.

On Crete, it is believed that like begets like. The pretty, golden Grain Dancer has no rival for physical grace and androgynous beauty, and the Queen has determined that he can give her what she wants. What has sealed the deal between Mochlos and the King is the fact that all three of Rah's private concubines, Siriona, Trinadea and Minia, are pregnant. And no male has touched them but Rah.

So Rah is taken up to the King's private chambers to meet the Queen. Still in face paint and costume silks, he is walked through a maze of hallways by a handful of guards to a large and elaborately decorated room. His wristlets are clipped together behind him and he is left in the company of two armed men.

Rah looks about the room patiently. He is used to being restrained by his bracelets, his collar, even the circle of gold around his waist, though he has always been obedient and gentle. These walls are painted in fine and colorful murals. There are dancers and bulls, dolphins and birds, amazing flowers and fields of grain traversing every wall. The furnishings are made of olive wood, cedar, of gold and bronze, and there is fabric draped everywhere, even covering the ceiling. There is an enormous bed on a dais in the center of the room and sheer curtains are draped all around it. The bed itself is thick with sheepskin and exotic furs.

Presently Rah hears footsteps, and the rustling of a skirt or gown, approaching from the hall behind him, but his guards do not allow him to turn around. Voices, one male, one nearly as deep, but female, accompany the footfalls. Something about the deep female voice sends a wave of fireflies up Rah's spine. He takes a deep breath, forces himself to breath normally. He does not want to meet the owner of that voice, which echoes an archetype of dominance through his soul and fills him with dread.

"Ah, the dancer. No, Cleos, do not turn him. Let me take my time."

Hands, long-fingered and light, take him by the shoulders, and as many times as he has been touched without invitation on this island he cannot help but flinch at the touch of these hands. Cold, greedy hands. He finds them difficult to endure, but they skim down his back and flanks, rest on his hips. Ownership, they say. This is mine.

"Such skin! A baby's skin. And yet you are as hard as marble. Mochlos keeps them so lean. Now turn him to face me, Cleos. My husband tells me I must be sure, or he will pay for nothing."

Rah is turned to face the voice. He has surmised he is in the presence of the King and Queen and drops his eyes.

"Ohhh," she takes in a breath. "Gods, he is more beautiful at close range. Lift your eyes to me, now, come!" she taps his chin and he reluctantly obeys. She is tall, taller than him. As tall as the King who stands beside her. But she is broader than the King. Broader than any woman Rah has seen on Crete. Her face is masculine, her jaw square, her forehead wide, though she is not unattractive. Her eyes are large and lined, like an Egyptian royal, in black paint. They are as black as the paint that exaggerates them.

When Rah looks into them he feels a hawk's talons in his guts. He steels himself to maintain her gaze, but he cannot. Who could? No slave could.

This only serves to make him more intoxicating to the Queen, who lifts a long-nailed finger to sweep through those brush-thick lashes.

"Tell Mochlos he may have his house if the boy stays with me for three days."

"No, Ninaea, this is a God slave, he must stay in the house of the

High Priest. The people cannot know he is being kept here like a rooster-"

The Queen merely flashes a dark look at the King and he stops in mid-sentence.

"I will have a daughter, Knossos. He has filled three virgin concubines. He is potent." She turns and takes the King by the arm, drawing him aside but still within the hearing of the boy. "No one but Mochlos himself needs to know the boy is here. Dress another dancer in these silks, cover his head and take him out of the palace through the gymnasium. Let the people see him leave with Mochlos' dancers. Then on the third night we will smuggle him back to the priest's villa in a cart, eh?"

The King nods. "I will speak with the priest."

"Be quick, Knossos. Cleos, have his attendants come and take this costume from him."

Rah has no desire to be alone with this greedy, masculine woman, but he is beginning to understand what is expected of him. He has always done what he is told to do, at least while in the company of his master, or the servants of his master here on Crete. But now he is expected to do something that his body recoils from, like eating rotten flesh. This woman is a she-wolf who snarls and snaps, bullies and bites. She is hunger itself, forever gulping, forever unsatisfied. He is less than a flea on her back, and yet she wishes to consume him, too.

The Queen has her men release his bracelets and strip him of his costume, then she sends her servants away. But each time she approaches him her hunger precedes her, foul and deadly, and he finds it impossible to tolerate her touch, much less respond to her.

The first of the three nights Rah is given to the Queen ends in her frustration and a nip from those slightly elongated incisors.

"Little beast! I could have you skinned for that!" She leaves him to tend to her wound, which is no more than a bruise and two tiny pricks on her shoulder. But this does not deter her. Like most of the affluent and powerful, she finds what she cannot have easily all the more valuable. Rah's reluctance simply whets her appetite. She will have his seed! The second night she has the boy drink as much retsina as her men can get down his throat before they brings him to her chamber. But drunk, his lack of interest is even more obvious. Finally, on the third night, she binds him, blindfolds him, and summons a young priestess, one of the girls who danced for him at the Dying of the God ceremony and whose place it is to serve the Grain God. She has the girl seduce him and, when he is at last ready, she straddles him herself like a great open mouth and consumes him.

The boy who stands in for Rah that first night, and is taken from the palace dressed in his costume to fool the people of Knossos, is Tiko. He is a slave from the east, purchased by a Minoan trader on the coast of

Anatolia. He is Rah's age and though slightly less compact, his approximate height and weight. Tiko has the features of the orient, a single upper eyelid, a small, flat nose and low bridge, a high, flat forehead, straight brow and planed face. He possesses a very different beauty than Rah and has been Rah's chief rival since his arrival on Crete.

As with most rivals, there is little love lost between the two boys. Tiko has great precision but lacks Rah's strength, nor does he possess the wildness in Rah's dance, which at times balances on the edge of obscenity. Twice before in the gymnasium the boys had to be torn apart when one whispered a vicious comment while passing the other during practice.

"Will you fuck your audience next, Blonde?"

"Better fuck than put them sleep, China!"

"What is wrong with your tongue, Blonde, you eat the priest's shit?"

"I make you eat shit, China!"

No one in fact, can get a rise out of Rah like Tiko can.

So when it is Tiko who is selected to wear Rah's costume, in order that Rah may lay with the Queen, Tiko is furious. First Rah steals the title of Grain God out from under him, then he pleases the Queen, a thing that could lead to a dancer's release! He vows that he will undermine this scheme and make Rah sorry he ever learned to dance.

Two days later in the gymnasium, Tiko has his chance. Rah has shown up late and missed his first practice with the troupe who will support his character in a new routine, ironically enough, the story of a slave boy who wins a queens favor and so, his freedom. Rah is late only because Pyrus held him in his dressing room that morning to work on the new face he will need for this part. But when Rah arrives at the gymnasium, Tiko will give him no peace.

"What does the priest do with you, Blonde, chaining you up in a closet behind his own bedroom? You're the priest's whore, late to practice servicing Mochlos, and so we all must suffer for it."

Rah manages to ignore this taunt. After his three days with the Queen, he is more subdued than usual, even brooding. Tiko sees that he must try a little harder to achieve his goal.

"So now you are a woman's woman, eh, Blonde? How did the Queen like fucking a girl? I always thought she preferred men. Or does the Queen have a member, as they rumor it, and likes to use it on her favorite maiden?"

Rah has just removed his sandals when this barb is whispered behind him. Tiko has chosen to say it in front of several other dancers who have also been put out by Rah's lateness and who now hoot with laughter. Rah's reaction is too fast even for Tiko. He has leapt to his feet, spun and punched his tormentor in the eye before Tiko has had time to duck. Tiko stumbles back but maintains his balance. He snaps out with a fierce side-kick, an oriental move that Rah is unfamiliar with. The blade of his foot connects with Rah's chest and sends Rah onto his back in the center of the sand arena. He is on his feet like a cat, his face dark with fury. He rushes at Tiko, plows his shoulder into the Asian's midsection and takes him to the ground, where his superior strength gives him the advantage. Tiko did not expect this strong a reaction, but he takes advantage of it. He allows Rah another punch to his head without blocking it. The punch splits his lip.

When the boys are pulled apart, Rah is suffering from nothing more than a sore rib and looks no worse for the wear. Tiko, whose own face is as delicate and beardless as Rah's, looks a fright. His left eye is swollen, the white of it turned bright red, the area around the socket quickly bruising. His lower lip is split open and his nose is crooked.

Disfiguring a holy dancer is a serious offense, even if another dancer is the culprit. The Dance Master, Dimius, cannot look the other way, for he is responsible for what happens in his gymnasium. He has no choice but to report the incident to Mochlos, even knowing what that must mean for Rah.

"Let us be honest with one another, Dimius," says Mochlos to the choreographer and gym instructor that afternoon. He has summoned him to his private courtyard since hearing about the fight, which seemed to amuse more than upset him once he learned that Rah was not hurt. It never occurred to him that there was much fight in Rah, who has always appeared docile when standing before him, although he realizes now that the energy of the boy's dance should have perhaps suggested to him otherwise. Mochlos is a bit perturbed that he has missed this side of Rah, but of course the boy is either dancing or taking a beating while in his presence and so has never been in any position to express the spirit that he showed today.

As for Tiko, Mochlos' interest in the dancer from China is minimal, especially when he discovered that the boy, perhaps because of his early upbringing, is quite stoic, refusing him so much as a whimper, and therefore no fun to beat or drown. Well, his face would heal. And Mochlos had been thinking of selling him to Ananou anyway. Ananou had a taste for Asian exotics. Most of his concubines were from the Far East.

"Tiko is not worth half of what Rah is worth to me. My little Grain God has already made me a fortune and has sealed me the Queen's favor. Tiko can be replaced. If the two fight again, and neither of them seems capable of maintaining a peace, Rah could be injured, or disfigured. I cannot let that happen. We must keep them apart until Tiko's wounds heal, then sell the Asian boy to Ananou."

It always amazes Dimius how tame and calculating Mochlos can be when discussing his dancers, and yet how passionately he beats them whenever he can find cause. Most especially, Rah. The boy has been allowed to dance today, but Mochlos will have his reed on him before the day is out. Dimius has learned not to hold out much hope for mercy from Mochlos. He knows the priest is looking forward to punishing Rah, despite his seemingly mild reaction to the offense.

"Perhaps you could spare the boy the reed, then, Master, if this is to be the case. Rah has never shown any animosity to the other athletes. He is really quite obedient, and I wouldn't want to see his spirit broken by--"

"You speak out of turn, Dimius." Mochlos, who is lying by a low table and has been eating dainties, now lifts his eyes to Dimius, standing before him. His look is slow and sly, and rakes Dimius from calf to head. It is a look that sends a warm panic through Dimius' bowels.

"Yes, Holiness, forgive me."

"Send him to me after his practice. After Tuma has bathed him."

"Of course."

"Don't worry, Dimius," Mochlos cannot resist a taunt. "He will be at practice tomorrow."

CHAPTER 9

The next morning Aros is the first of Rah's two attendants to enter the boy's chamber. Rah is still sleeping when Aros pulls open the drape to rouse the boy. He is lying on his stomach, wrapped up in his chains as a result of tossing about all night trying to avoid lying on his wounds. Aros' first reaction is to slap his hands over his own mouth to prevent himself from screaming.

"What is wrong with you, Ar-" Pyrus stops in his tracks behind Aros when he sees the boy's naked back.

"Holy Mother god, what has he done to you?" he hisses, moving to the bed to unchain Rah. He must keep his voice low, for Mochlos is yet in the next room being attended to by his own servants.

Rah makes no attempt to sit up. He grunts lifting himself off his pallet in a push-up, and from there moves to his hands and knees before stepping gingerly onto the floor.

"For fight with Tiko," he tells them. And between clenched teeth he adds, "I am kill Tiko."

"Tiko is to be sold to Ananon. There will be no more fighting," says Pyrus, ever the

pragmatist. "And if we don't get you down to the gym on time today, our backsides will all match."

"But he needs to be cared for, Pyrus. We must send him to the baths!" Aros whines.

"No!" Rah grabs Aros' chubby arm and pulls him nose to nose. "I go to gym!"

Pyrus pushes Rah away from Aros gently. Then he turns to Aros.

"Dimius will send him to the baths, Aros. Put something on him. Come."

"Oh, you poor baby," Aros whimpers, rubbing his own arm once Rah has released it. "You are in such pain, Sunlight." Aros' eyes are tearing up. "How can we send him down to work like this, Pyrus?"

"By thinking of the safety of your own fat bottom, Aros. Now come."

Rah is at practice that day, as promised, but after failing to execute one of his simpler somersaults and falling on his knees rather than his feet, Dimius takes him aside. His head coach, Akbar, accompanies him with Rah into a little room off the arena where bull leaping equipment is stored.

"Let me see what he has done to you, Rah. It may be you need a few days off to soak in the baths, eh?"

Rah has suffered enough humiliation in the past few days, beginning with his treatment by the Queen and ending with another flogging from Mochlos, whom he now believes is completely insane. He will pass on this offer.

"Pain always with dance," says Rah, stepping away from Akbar when the older man attempts to lift his skirt for Dimius. "I do better, I show you. Let me dance. Prove it."

"Do as your teacher tells you." Akbar takes his elbow and turns him around.

Dimius is sickened by what he sees. Rah is bruised from the small of his back to the bottom of his thighs. The area is covered in welts and cuts that will scar if not tended to.

"Get out of here, now. If his cruelty leaves you with marks it will be my backside opened up next. Go to the baths, show Tuma. You need a poultice, herbs. He will know what to do."

Rah goes to the baths, angrier at Tiko now than he was after his last insult. He wants only to dance, only to practice. Only to be left to do what he does best, to speak not with his mangled tongue but with his body. But instead he must be treated like an invalid, sent like a child back to his mother. To Tuma, who will make all manner of fuss over his bruises and will probably manage somehow to make him laugh at all of this, perhaps even at the Queen's humiliating use of him.

But when he reaches Tuma he is greeted by his three concubines first, for Aros has informed Tuma of Rah's encounter with the priest, and Tuma knows what will heal Rah faster than any poultice.

The girls flutter and fret over Rah, their light hands soothe, their voices minister. They have missed him, for he has been away from them for almost a week. Siriona teases Rah, even dares to pinch his bottom after a poultice of herbs is applied to the cuts and welts, and Rah is laughing before he is taken down to his dinner in the kitchen. Even there he cannot brood, because the kitchen slaves have also learned of his flogging and have secretly prepared him his favorite meal and a special treat of honeyed pine nuts.

CHAPTER 10

After dying to the god, Rah is allowed to come and go with greater freedom. His visits to the mounds, and so to the king's pasture, are more frequent, and for several weeks he has been working with the dapple colt. Thus far he has been unnoticed by the king's guards who take siesta at the height of the day, leaving only one on each fence line to watch for thieves from the countryside.

Rah has coaxed the colt to follow him and even to trot along beside him with treats of sweetened grain he has snatched from Mochlos' kitchen. The young horse has become accustomed to the boy's hands running along his flanks and belly, and will allow itself to be led about with a leather rein stolen from the bull master. Last week he seduced the beast into tolerating a thick woven pad and a small sack of sand, on its back. Soon he will replace the sand with his own weight.

Rush has followed the boy from the Villa today. He has not done so since the Dying to the God ceremony. He has been in Cyrus, and across the sea to Mycenae briefly to see his Mycenaean wife and daughters. His daughters are married to soldiers and both are pregnant. Rush also has twin sons by his Minoan wife, fourteen summers old and identical. They are the image of their father, already taller and bulkier than Rah, who barely reaches Rush's shoulders.

Rush is unaware that the boy has been working to mount the colt. He follows casually, leaving some distance between himself and the boy. He knows where Rah is headed and does not mind if he loses sight of him now and then. When he reaches his hiding place along the stone wall of the king's field he is surprised to find that the boy and the colt are only twenty meters from where he stands. The boy is feeding the animal treats and rubbing its flank and haunch. Presently the boy makes a noose of a long leather rein he had been concealing in his skirt. He deftly constructs a bit-

54

less bridle from the rein, then slips it around the animal's head while he continues to feed it bits of grain. Gradually he steps away from the colt. When the colt turns to him looking for more treats the boy raises his right hand away from his body and makes a sound with his tongue.

"Ttk, Ttk."

The boy's vision is pinned on the colt's left flank. His left shoulder is at a right angle to the colts left shoulder. The colt moves off to the left in a trot circle at the end of the tether, which the boy lets out gradually until the animal is making a twenty meter circle around him.

Rah coos at the colt, and even Rush can understand that the gentle sound is one of praise. When the colt tires and slows or attempts to stop and face the boy, the boy pursues him visually, stepping always toward his haunches, yet never changing his position relative to the colt's. Presently he bends his knees and raises his right hand again, adding another sound to the first. The colt's immediate reaction to his crouched position is to canter away from it, but he must do so at the end of the leather line. Rah praises him and stands up quietly, lowering his hand. Each time the colt slows he repeats the new sound, the crouch, the raised hand. His patience is remarkable to Rush, who can only compare him to his own two, typically impatient teenager boys. Fascinated, he does not immediately notice movement along the opposite wall of the pasture.

When he does, his heart slams in his chest. At first he assumes the guards have awakened from their slumber to find the Grain God playing with the King's horses. But these are not the king's guards. First one, then three dark heads pop over the stone fence on the south side of the pasture, then disappear again. They are visible long enough for Rush to see that they wear no head gear and that at least one of them is bearded. Knossos' soldiers are always clean shaven and normally wear leather headgear. So someone else has been watching the boy, someone Rush has somehow failed to notice until now.

His reaction is that of rage. The need to lop and slash, crack bone and open bowels sings in his veins. But Rush is equally dismayed at his own oversight. How could he have missed this? These common dogs, for surely that is what they are, paid garbage from a neighboring government without the kind of resources it would take to hire an assassin of his own caliber, have been watching the Grain God long enough to know his habit to visit the pasture when the guards are resting. They mean either to kidnap the little God or to kill him.

They mean to do it right under Cyrus' highly paid assassin's nose.

Always his greatest adversary, his fiery temper overtakes him. He considers circling the paddock and dealing with these men while the guards are still dozing, but this would leave the boy open from another quarter. There is no guarantee that the three men are working alone. He must ignore his first impulse. No, he will stay out of sight and see how many are involved in this plot. He will not be made a fool before Cyrus and have the boy stolen out from under his nose and taken to Malia or Gournia. Cyrus has been paying him handsomely to watch the boy and may yet want him for himself, if he has the guts to steal him from Knossos.

Rush waits until the boy has released the colt before he understands that he has made yet another mistake. This boy is turning him into an idiot! For Rah is now retreating to the south wall of the pasture, which is his normal path, right into the hands of the hirelings! If they snatch him as he hops over the wall, they may spirit him away before Rush can intercept them! Now he will have to catch up. He has no doubt that he can, and at this moment would follow them to Egypt, but he may not reach them in time to stop them from slitting the boy's throat if that is their intention.

Rush quickly calculates the guards' positions and activity. Grateful that they are still enjoying their siesta he slips over the wall and across the pasture. Not surprisingly by the time he reaches the southern wall of stone there is no sight of Rah, nor the hirelings. There is also no sign of a struggle, which means they have chosen to follow the boy and put some distance between their attack and the ears of the king's men.

Rush follows the men's tracks, which are obvious and evidence that the thugs are amateurs. They are, as he expected, leading to the second field, higher up Ida, where the boy always meets the cur dog before continuing on to the Cities of the Dead. Rush is soon convinced that the three men he saw at the pasture wall are working alone, for he is not being followed himself. He is not far behind the hirelings and is anticipating that the sound of the boy's strange howl will alert him when the men overtake him. Rush has not forgotten Rah's eerie, strangled scream the day he attacked him himself. If the thugs don't wait until the boy is far enough away from the king's men, they too will hear it and no doubt come running to investigate. Rush is hoping that this is not the case. His blood is up, and he wants these three all to himself. They are wolves now, hunting a lamb, but they are also aliens in a strange country. No one knows them, and if they disappear no one will miss them.

Rush has advanced a kilometer up the path when suddenly an inhuman sound breaks the noonday stillness. It is the sound of an injured animal, a horrid, heartbreaking thing, far worse than the one Rush recalls the boy making the day he nearly took his head himself. There is something wrong. Something he did not count on is going on ahead of him. He breaks into a sprint, heedlessly plowing through brambles to shorten the distance between himself and that sound. Here is the wall around the field where he leaned to watch the boy release the doves only a few weeks earlier. His palms smack the top of the wall and he is over it on a current of adrenaline that lifts his hind quarters and legs perpendicular to his hands, vaulting him clear over the top. He hits the rubble on the other side, stones left by the slaves who made the wall a hundred years ago, and rolls. His knees are ripped open by the impact but he is on his feet, his two crescent blades already released from their sheaths under his arms and securely in his hands.

Trained to kill first and think later, the assassin finds his closest target. It is the bearded man, standing over the limp body of the dingy white cur which has been slashed open at the throat. Still holding the heavy blade with which he stabbed the animal in his right hand, he has turned around in surprise at the thud of the assassin's body hitting the ground behind him.

The haunting wail that has been driving a sickening pain into Rush's brain stops abruptly. Rush realizes now that it was not the dog that was making that inhuman noise. The nightmarish sound was coming from Rah, who, pinned between the two other thugs, was struggling not so much to free himself from them but to get to the dog. Rah's golden face is ashen, his luminous eyes huge as they move from the body of the dog to the blades in his assassin's hands. The wail dies in his throat.

The bearded man hesitates, unsure whether he should attack this intruder or flee. His hesitation is his death. Rush has cleared the distance between them. He strikes with the blade in his left hand, across and in, driving the edge through the man's right forearm just above the wrist. The man screams and drops his knife as Rush pulls him forward on the fulcrum made by his blade and the space between radius and ulna. The assailant falls into Rush, making a weak attempt to head-butt him onto his back. Before he connects, Rush has whipped his second blade across his face from left to right, neatly slicing it in half from ear to ear. He pulls the blade in his left hand free and swings his arm up in a roundhouse that ends when it plunges sideways into the back of the man's neck, separating the base of his skull from the top of his spine.

Rush uses the man's fall forward onto the ground to propel himself at his next target, the man on Rah's right. That man has barely had enough time to release Rah and attempt to use him as a shield, pushing him forward and onto his knees. The third man has also released the boy and is turning to flee. But there is no time. Rush has closed the distance and opened the man on the right from liver to lung, slicing inward and upward with his left blade and shoving his collapsing body out of his way with his foot before the man on Rah's left has had time to pivot on his heels.

Rush drops his blades and tackles this man from behind.

The man is instantly overwhelmed by his weight and he hits the ground with a sickening thud, several of his ribs snapping like twigs under Rush's momentum. His pleas for mercy are abbreviated when Rush pulls him to his feet by his hair and sinks the fingers of his right hand around the sides of his trachea.

"Who sent you," he snarls into the man's face. "Tell me and die quick, or else you will die slow." He releases the man's throat long enough for him to take a breath. When he does not answer immediately Rush pulls him back and over, cracking his pelvis over his knee.

The man manages a gurgling scream.

"Who," Rush brings the man's upper back over his knee.

"Ananou!" the man cries. "Please," he gasps, "I am a poor man. . . trying to feed his family. Please. Let me live!"

"You are already dead," says Rush, as he yanks the man's head back and drives his larger blade, the dagger he has just released from its sheath on his ankle, through the space under the jawbone, into the back of his victim's throat and up into the bottom of his brain.

Rush drops the man's gurgling body and turns to find the boy, but Rah has disappeared. The body of the cur still lies where it fell, bleeding out from the wound in its neck. It has begun to rain lightly and the cur's blood is mingling with that of his killer.

"You tried to protect your friend, eh? And so they cut your throat," he says to the dog, bending to stroke its unconscious head. He kicks the bearded corpse that is lying next to the dog, hoping there is enough life left in the man to feel some more pain. But the body is motionless. He looks back at the other two men, both dead. He will come back to clean up this mess later. But first he wants the boy.

Rush considers his course only a moment. Rah will not run back to the Villa. What comfort waits for him there? He will not return to the colt for the king's men are surely up from their siesta by now. No, he has run up the mountain, past the Cities of the Dead and the village of priests who tend them, on to Ting Ya's little house in the cemetery of the ancients. He has run to Ting Ya, who would have known his relationship with the cur. The boy had been bringing the dog with him on his visits to her and she will share his grief, or at least offer him some understanding and solace. Ting Ya will comfort him.

But not before Rush has had his hands on the boy and has learned what he needs to know.

If being devoured by a hungry she-wolf in the guise of a Queen, then flogged black and blue by a madman who kisses you between lashes, if having one's dog killed before one's eyes, being kidnapped, and then saved only by the one thing more frightening than any of these, were not enough to put Rah's incomplete brain over the edge, then being tackled by his assassin once again, this time only a few hundred meters from Ting Ya's door, is.

He is walking now, walking in a light rain up the dirt track to Ting Ya's door, and weeping for the dog he had given the only love-name he had ever known. Hali. Now and then he must stop in his tracks, fall to his knees and give himself to his sorrow. When the impact of Rush's tackle shoves him forward into the dirt, filling his mouth with grit and smearing his tear dampened face with mud, his last thought is 'a bear!' before he leaves his body behind to his epilepsy.

And Rush finds himself holding the boy together, fighting to keep this wiry little athlete from bashing his own head in on the rocky path or biting off his own tongue.

Rush has seen a man take a fit before. More than one soldier at his side or, later, under his command, seizured after a head injury, or simply discovered his infirmity during battle. He has seen a man bite the end of his own tongue off. But even Rush is surprised by the strength he needs to use to trap the spasming body of the dancer in a hold tight enough to keep him from harming himself, and there is little he can do for his tongue except to shove the boy's chin up against his skull and try to keep his jaw closed.

The attack takes several minutes to sweep through Rah and let him go. When his body stills, Rush turns him over onto his back and eases him down onto the dirt track, waiting for his mind to return. He maintains a grip, straddling him, for the boy is wicked fast and he cannot give him a chance to roll to his feet and run. He would be too fast even for Rush to catch.

Presently the boy's mind returns. He is confused, knows a sadness in his heart but cannot remember the source of it, remembers only the image of his assassin carving up a bearded man, then pouncing in his direction. When he realizes that it is Rush who is on top of him, pinning him again, his reaction is wild. He twists and scratches and yowls, his face a panic.

Rush gives him enough leeway to spin himself over onto his belly. Trap, release, trap, release. He has done it a thousand times to a thousand opponents. He lets Rah weaken himself, spinning onto his back, then his stomach, trying in vain to wrestle himself out from under the big man's crushing mass and gain some ground. When the boy is heaving and exhausted, Rush gives him one last release. But instead of spinning himself onto his back again, Rah surprises him by twisting like a cat and sinking his teeth into the assassin's forearm. It is a nip, a snap and retreat, a warning only. But it stings and draws two small dots of blood. For a moment Rush can only look down at the two crimson drops and blink. Were he fighting a matched adversary he would have smashed his opponent's teeth from his mouth by now. But the boy's bite is more pathetic than fierce. His feline nip fascinates Rush, draws his attention back to the boy's cat-like face. He stares down at Rah, who is still on his belly, no longer golden but covered in grime and panting with fear and anger, and he forgets himself.

He slips his left hand into the boy's curls and palms the back of his skull. He tightens his fingers and pulls the boy's head back and around to him. Covered in dirt, Rah's face is even more feminine, his fair eyes more brilliant in the mask of mud. Rush brings his mouth down onto those cupid bow lips, licks at the gleaming, bared incisors, and pushes his tongue past the pearl teeth, daring them to bite again.

But Rah cannot bite. He cannot breathe. He is smothering under Rush's weight, his head is twisted back over his shoulder and he is gagging on the assassin's tongue. When he feels the man's organ nudge his thigh, a new panic flies through him, but he can do nothing to defend himself. He moans into Rush's mouth in helpless misery.

Rush pushes the boy's skirt up over his haunch with his right hand. His palm connects with the uneven ridges of the welts left by Mochlos' reed.

And he comes to his senses.

He lifts his upper body off the boy. He shoves Rah's face back into the rain damp dirt, and investigates the welts.

"Who-" Something catches in his throat and pinches at his eyes. He swallows and tries again. "Who did this to you, boy?"

Rah squirms, trying to twist his face out of the mud to answer. The assassin makes no attempt to release his grip on the back of his head.

"Huhhg," there is mud pasting Rah's tongue to the roof of his mouth.

"Who?"

"Moch-" Rah manages, choking.

"The priest?" Rush pulls Rah around to face him. "The priest Mochlos?"

"Pffhh," Rah spits, trying to dislodge the mud from his mouth to answer.

Rush narrows his eyes at the boy.

"Y-yes." Rah stutters. He tries in vain to twist his face away from the assassin's.

"And why does Ananou send cheap dogs to kill the Grain God?"

Rah blinks up at the assassin helplessly. His blue-gold eyes are saucers. His eyelashes are caked with mud. He shakes his head.

"You know more than you think, boy," Rush studies him patiently.

Rah shakes his head again. He is trembling with exertion, his mind is knotted. Ananou? He recalls Pyrus' comment that Tiko was to be sold to Ananou. This is all he has to give. His tongue is thick and trips his speech but when he finds the words, he pushes them out in a jumble, eyes squeezed closed with the effort.

"Tiko-" he begins.

"Tiko?"

"Tiko call me girl. I fight with Tiko. Mochlos sell Tiko," he gasps, "to

Ananou."

Rush considers this.

"Who is Tiko?"

"China. China dancer. My second."

"Your second. So if you cannot dance, he is first."

"Yes."

"He taunts you into a fight, and you are beaten for it."

Rah nods.

"Then Mochlos sells Tiko to Ananou."

"Yes."

Rush is sitting on Rah's hips, breathing evenly, his black eyes dull and unblinking. "And with you dead, Ananou then has the next Grain God."

Rah looks away and Rush grabs his chin. "Well? Is he good enough or not?"

"Tiko is good," Rah agrees reluctantly.

Rush frowns and leans back.

"No one can match you, boy. But if you are dead, the next runner up, no matter how far behind, is still the winner."

He gets wearily to his feet, pulling Rah up with him.

"I don't want to hurt you." He pulls Rah close, gives him a shake and looks into his face. "I don't mean to hurt you, you understand?"

Rah eyes him warily.

"Go to Ting Ya now and let her clean you up. They are all dead, those dogs who attacked you. You are safe, for now."

The boy looks at Rush's grip on his arm, then back up at the assassin. Rush knows that the second he releases him he will put as much distance as he can between himself and the man who admitted he was paid to kill him.

"Cyrus does not want your head any more, you understand? I am not paid to take it. Only your secrets. He pays me for these, now."

Rah shakes his head. "I have none."

"You are nothing but," Rush releases his arm and the boy takes several steps backward before he flees up the path to Ting Ya.

CHAPTER 11

Mochlos is dreaming. He is in Egypt, in a great room full of exotically dressed dancing girls. There is music playing and much gaiety about him. Men shouting and playing dice, women shrieking with laughter. He is drinking golden nectar out of a chalice and talking earnestly with the pharaoh's statistician. He is trying to win an argument. He is discussing wealth, his wealth, the pharaoh's wealth, Knossos' wealth. He is trying to convince this fat Egyptian bureaucrat that he is as rich as a pharaoh now, as rich as a king, that he has a dancer made of gold who is inhabited by a god, yes! That through an amazingly clever deal he made with a trader he is now the richest man in the world! The statistician asks him, what did he pay for the gold he made the dancer of? Mochlos answers smugly, "I got it for nothing! Ameg gave me silks, and in the silks I found threads of gold. I took the gold and made the dancer. And now I am the richest man on earth!" The statistician shrugs, "Well," he says, "these things can happen right before a wave, you know. You must eventually give the gold back to the silk merchant, or else we all will drown." Mochlos is about to ask him what he means. A wave, what wave? When suddenly water begins to rise around his feet, blue, green and gold water rising all about him and everyone is panicking, and he is trying to get above the water but his feet are stuck, he cannot move in the water, he is pinned down. He cannot take a breath! The water is crushing the air from his lungs and he cannot breathe!

"Wake, priest. It is time to dance," says the face of Ameg, hovering above his own as he lies in his bed.

"Ameg!" Mochlos hisses with what breath is left in his lungs. But no, this is not Ameg. How could he have thought so? This is a bear of a man wrapped in black. His voice is a baritone growl, unrecognizable. His eyes, the only part of his face exposed, are black shadows in the cloth. Ameg is a gentle silk merchant, a Greek. A refined man, who keeps his nails manicured and his beard trimmed. This animal is Hittite. Yes! He can hear the accent, even in the growl. This is an assassin from the land of Hatti. But Mochlos has cheated so many, he is at a loss as to who could have sent this beast, and so, for the moment, has nothing with which to bargain for his life. He waits for the man to speak. Surely he will not kill him without giving him a chance to bargain.

But the thing that is sitting on him, the thing that has now slapped a hand the size of a bear's paw over his mouth, says nothing. It is the needle sharp tip of the dagger that is resting on the socket under Mochlos' left eye that speaks.

"I have blinded many men." The Hittite accent is thick now, though the voice remains a whisper. "Fast and bloodless, a finger here, in and out with the ball. Deserters. But you, I blind bloody."

Mochlos feels a terror he has never known, paralyze his thoughts. The paralyzing weight of the assassin, denying him air, is easy to endure in comparison. He feels a part of himself step away from this terror in wonder. He is watching himself from another part of his mind.

And then the beast removes his hand from Mochlos' mouth and with it rams the priest's jaw back, shoving his head into his pillows and, holding his face tight, he begins cutting. Mochlos feels the tip of the dagger split his flesh just under the eye. A line, tracing the socket, surgically precise. Tears of blood spilling from the wound run down Mochlos' temple into his ear.

Mochlos finds his brain.

"Anything!" he says through his locked teeth. "I can give you anything! I am a rich man. Don't be a fool. No one can pay you what I can! Only do not take my eyes!"

"You think I am a fool, priest?" The assassin is drawing something on the priest's cheekbone just under the first cut. Even so, the priest feels surprisingly little blood running down his temple and into his ear. The assassin tips the knife in, around, and makes a hole in Mochlos' cheek. A hole!

"My god, man, have you no ears? I can make you rich!" Mochlos spits.

"I am already rich, priest," says the assassin casually. He seems to be finished carving designs into the priests face.

"What in hell do you want then. Tell me what you want!"

The assassin lifts his shrouded head. The picture he makes in the moonlight slicing through Mochlos' window is infernally ugly. The dark fabric tightly wrapped around his skull has turned him into a black mummy, but his shoulders are the shoulders of a bull, not a man. He has no eyes, only the shadowy holes in the fabric. He has no mouth or nose. He is sitting on the priest's soft belly and his thighs are huge, strapped with muscle, their heat against Mochlos' abdomen is sickeningly intimate. The priest can feel the man's organ and his stomach curls with revulsion. He feels a hatred for this monster greater than he has ever known. His heart is a rock in his chest made of his hatred. He clings to this hatred to keep himself from drowning in fear.

"I want to satisfy you, priest." And Mochlos is suddenly off the bed being dragged by the front of his nightgown to the doorway. Good! His guards will attack this man the moment he steps out into the passage.

But when the assassin shoves him through the opening into the hall, Mochlos' foot strikes a pile of clothing and he trips over it. He falls onto his hands, rolls over and realizes that he has just fallen over the body of one of his men.

"Speak above a whisper and I will take your tongue," the Assassin growls from somewhere above him in the dark. Then he lifts the priest onto his feet again and shoves him down the passageway.

"Where are you taking me? How do you know your way around my house?" Mochlos grasps about his mind for some advantage. If the man takes him out the front of the Villa the priest's private guard will cut him down with arrows. If he attempts to take him out the back, over the parapet of his private courtyard, the sleeping priesthood on the first floor will surely hear him on their roof and alert his men.

But the assassin does neither. He pushes the priest forward through a maze of halls and down a staircase. With deepening dread Mochlos realizes that he is taking him to his own private punishment chamber.

The man seems to be able to see in the dark. He moves soundlessly, shoving the priest in front of him, now and then pricking him with the end of his dagger. "How long can a priest hold his breath?" he muses. "Surely longer than he can hold his tongue."

They reach the chamber which is directly under the baths but three stories down. The assassin has found the drowning pool in the dark. It is in the center of the room, no bigger than a cart wheel, a baptismal font. He pushes the priest down onto his knees at its edge and palms his head. He has replaced his dagger in its sheath and now he draws the priest's right arm behind the left, trussing him up in his own limbs. Then he thrusts him head first into the water and holds him there.

Mochlos is so desperate for air that he is about to suck water into his lungs when his head is finally lifted out of the pool.

"Anything!" he gags. "Anything man!"

He is plunged back into the water before he can say more.

The priest's own drowning game has been visited on him for over half an hour before he is at last pulled away from the pool and deposited, in a state of exhaustion, onto the cold stone floor.

When he has begun to catch his breath, water still running from his nose and mouth like a slow bleed, he begins again where he left off.

"Take my finest dancer. Take the Grain God! You can do no better. He is priceless."

The mention of the grain dancer creates an eerie silence above the priest and he wastes no time in taking advantage of what he hopes is the assassin's peaked interest. "Yes, take the dancer, then. Let me bring you to him. See for yourself." He peers up into the darkness in an attempt to catch the man's reaction.

"But that is just why I am here, priest," he hears above him in the dark. For a moment, it seems as if the man has lost his Hittite vowels. Then the accent returns.

"Ananou has sent me to kill the dancer, you see?" He drags Mochlos to his feet and hisses this last into his ear. "You see what you have done? You have sent for me yourself. By selling the Asian to Ananou."

"But why-" The priest understands before he has finished his sentence. He changes gears, hoping to avoid another drowning. "But why do you do Ananou's work, man, when you can work for me? I tell you, there is nothing I will not give you."

The assassin seems to be considering this.

"Perhaps we can do business." He releases Mochlos suddenly and steps away. Mochlos is lost in the dark. When he attempts to grope for the doorway he comes upon the assassin's massive chest and stumbles back. He recovers quickly.

"Let me take you to him," he offers again.

A deep chuckle, oddly familiar, sends a chill up Mochlos' spine.

"Your meanness knows no limits, Holiness. You would bring me to him to slaughter in his sleep. No, priest. I am your nightmare tonight."

He brings Mochlos to his knees with a blow to the belly, then snatches his throat with iron fingers and squeezes.

"You and I will do business, priest. On my terms. You will pay me to visit Ananou, and Ananou will send no more assassins for the Grain Dancer. You will pay me with the contents of your fastest ship. You will pay me half of what is on board each time it comes to harbor. I will know what is on board, priest. I will take the skin off your back and make a flag of your hide for my own vessel if you cheat me out of one jug of oil. I have many such flags, priest. Be careful."

Mochlos is appalled at the price the man demands, but only for a moment. He will have his life, keep his eyes, even take revenge on Ananou, and protect his prize possession. The very beast sent to kill his cash cow will protect it. Half the contents of his fastest ship is a fortune, but he has many ships. He can afford it.

He is about to open his mouth to complement the man's wisdom when another blow, this one to the kidney, knocks him over face down onto the cold stones of the floor. He feels the man's mass hovering above him like a bear playing with a beehive.

"Hold your tongue. I will send a representative to work out the details of our arrangement. He will have the goods transferred to one of his own ships whenever your vessel returns to port."

"Yes, of course, it will be just as you say, I swear it." Mochlos forces the words through a jaw clenched in pain. The assassin is bending over him. He is so close that the priest can feel his breath on the back of his neck through the gauze that wraps the man's face.

"You are mine now, priest. Mine to play with, mine to whip or drown as I desire."

This last sends a sick chill through Mochlos' bowels, not entirely unpleasant, but utterly terrifying.

Then he feels something probe the flesh under his jaw, a thick finger. It traces his mandible to the hinge, pushes in, finds a tendon and jabs at it. "Cut this, and a man can no longer chew. A simple thing, just here and here, and a man becomes a dribbling invalid."

"Oh god, no, man." the priest breathes, a sob of hopelessness escaping before he can catch it.

"Your money can not buy me, priest."

Mochlos chokes on another sob.

"But I will take it from you, because it is so precious to you."

Then he draws away, and is gone. But it is half an hour before Mochlos has the courage to pick himself up and rouse the household.

CHAPTER 12

"I see this man, Rah. I see him watch you at Die to God Ceremony." Ting Ya is washing Rah's hair in a basin in the kitchen portion of her little hut. "He is big important man. Close to King. I see him follow you here some days. It is same man."

"He is wolf, Ting Ya. He is pack of wolf. He come out of ground, he come all direction!"

"No, I tell you. This is big man in city. This is powerful man."

Rah pulls his head out of the basin and shakes himself like a dog. His curls spring up around his head despite its dampness, thanks to Aros' skill with the razor.

Ting Ya hands him a cloth. "You wash now, Rah. You go back to Villa like that, you get whip again. Give me your clothes. I soak."

Rah manages a soft smile that sets the dimples in his cheeks off.

"You bad old China woman. You like Rah no clothes." He grabs her, bends her over an arm, tips her into a deep arc, so that her braid, which is nearly as long as she is tall, brushes the floor. Then he draws her back onto her feet, sweeps her around in a circle, and kisses her full on her mouth.

She pushes him away, slaps at his chest with the back of her hand, clucks her tongue at him. Rah laughs and winks at her, turning away to untie his skirt.

"I like you dress or naked. You like me old or young. No matter. We always be friends. Many lives, we always friends."

Rah shakes his head at her, smiling. "If Ting Ya say."

She looks at him, serious, stern. "I know so."

Rah hands her his muddied skirt and loincloth, the smile fading from his face.

"Ting Ya, my sister-" He cannot think of how to say it. "She come to me. She tell me I must flee that man. Or I die."

67

"Cannot be. You sister is ghost. Ghost lie. She not know this man. I see him watch you. I see his face. He fall in love with Rah. He never hurt Rah."

Rah has never seen her look so serious. Or speak such foolishness.

"One day you must go with this man. He will take you away. When he understand his heart, he will take you off island to his home. I see this in dream. My dream no lie. You must leave island, Rah. Wave is coming."

He frowns at her. "He is one man made of many wolf. You tell Rah, 'Let wolf carry you off! In the north we have bear. You have bear in China? All teeth and claw. Today, I think I am attacked by a bear." He shakes his head. "He so hungry, Ting Ya."

"You listen to Ting Ya," she pokes his chest with a gnarled finger before she shuffles out to wash the skirt in the cistern.

While she is gone, Rah washes off the mud he is covered in. Then he goes out to meet her. She is hanging the skirt on a branch in the sun.

"Hot day. Won't take long to dry." She turns to him and gives him a maternal look. "Come to Ting Ya, boy."

Rah obediently walks up to her, his nakedness no more uncomfortable to him than it might be to a child of two or three summers. He is taller than Ting Ya, who is quite diminutive.

When he reaches her she opens her arms wide to him. He hesitates.

"Come," she says softly. Then he is on his knees, his head cradled against her chest, and she is rocking him. Only the movement of his shoulders gives away his silent weeping.

"Dog still here, Rah. She here with you now. She sit beside you, watch you. Ting Ya sees."

"Hali gone, Ting Ya. Men kill her for fight for Rah," he says between sobs.

"Tonight she come to you, you will see. Tonight she lay beside you, just this one night. Then she must return to Sun Goddess."

"T-hah," he has to laugh at her mistake. "It Moon Goddess, silly China woman," he looks up at her from his knees. "Moon Goddess. Sun God."

"No. My people say Sun Goddess." She ruffles his hair, kisses the top of his head.

"Rah must dance in dress then," he squints up at her mischievously and the sun catches the blue in his eyes and turns them sapphire. His tears are drying.

She looks into his eyes, shakes her head at him, then hugs him tightly.

"You too beautiful, Rah. You not made for this world. Piece of sunlight, fall to ground. Everyone want. No one know how to catch sunlight, put in pocket. You make them-" she spins the tip of a finger against her temple. "But this man, Rah, he can catch sunlight. He catch by letting go."

Rah gets to his feet. He puts his hands to his temples dramatically.

"Ting Ya, you make Rah head hurt." He shakes it. "Please, no more talk about wolf. Tell Rah story about Ting Ya. Little girl Ting Ya in China."

Rush is home in Knossos. He has spent several days here, with his wife and sons. When he leaves he will be gone for a fortnight. He will be Ameg the Merchant, overseeing his shipping business. But for now he is spending his time teaching his growing sons to fight, and to handle an assortment of weaponry from around the world. Hittite javelin and club, Mycenaean spear and mace, Chinese throwing discs, Phoenician swords, Sardinian shields and slings.

His Minoan wife has been quiet these past few days, leaving him to the boys, who need him more even than she. But tonight she goes out to the stable to find him. She approaches him while he is grooming one of his ponies.

When he hears her footsteps he looks over his shoulder and smiles at her. It is a hard thing for such a face to do, a smile few are privy to.

She returns it, then comes to his side, laying a hand gently on his arm.

"A word, Antaris?"

"As many as you need, Josepha."

She looks down a moment, considering how to begin. She is not a handsome woman, but there is the light of intelligence in her dark eyes. She is sturdy, plump, and though a decade younger than he she looks to be his contemporary. But when she lifts her eyes again to his something comes alive in her face and she becomes beautiful.

"You are here with us now," she begins. "You are here. But you are not here, Antaris. I have never complained that you are so little with us. But I have always hoped that you would let me know where you were when you were not with me."

"Ah," he nods, "I see." He turns back to the pony, continues to stroke it with the grooming brush.

"Of course, you owe me nothing."

"Neither owes either anything," he murmurs. It is their code, their connection.

This is the hard part. She has never said anything to him like this before. Even she, who has never feared him, must take her hand away and step back before she presses on.

"Let me help you, Antaris. Please. This is my battlefield. On this battlefield, I am as good as you are on any other."

He jerks his head around at her as if she has just appeared from thin air. He looks into her eyes a long time, straining to see it. And he sees it.

"How can you know, Josepha?"

"Do you know another assassin, my love? Though I could walk by him in the market and think him a simple farmer, a cripple, a cobbler. You know him. Do you know which man carries a dagger, what kind of dagger he carries, how well he can handle it? Though I would walk by him and think him a priest or a beggar? So I know the dagger that is in your heart, even if you refuse to acknowledge it. I have that same gold handled dagger in mine."

He can say nothing for some time.

"I'm sorry, Josepha. I'm sorry for both of these daggers."

"Will you lie to me now?" she counters.

He shakes his head. She is always ahead of him. The one opponent whose moves he could never anticipate.

"Then what is your advice, wife? What do I do?" He frowns, feels a fool. "What did you do?"

"I let what I loved be what he was. I loved what he was. I love what he is."

He lifts his hand to her face, strokes her cheek.

"You are a champion on this battlefield, madam."

"Take it out, do you hear me, man? I want it out of here."

"But Holiness, this pond is part of a complicated and delicate balance that feeds the entire villa fresh running water. To take it out is difficult. It could damage the entire system."

"Then fill it with sand." Mochlos is picking at the poultice over his left eye and cheek. He has not been able to leave it be since Tuma dressed his wounds in the baths this morning. The cuts on his face are small, but hideous. The beast carved the symbol of the bull, Taurus, under his eye. He will wear the scar like a tattoo of tears for the rest of his life. He has been told by his top advisers that the assassin that visited him last night is known all over the Aegean. He has earned the name Rush because of the swiftness of his delivery of death. He generally leaves this mark on his corpses, and Mochlos is quite lucky to be alive.

Mochlos does not feel lucky to be alive today.

An ugly image suddenly dances through his head.

"Never mind the sand. One can drown in sand. Just remove it. I don't care what it costs. Get it out of here."

"Yes, Holiness."

"By tonight."

"Yes, Holiness."

Mochlos has advised the captain of his guard to put five of his best men in front of his bedchamber night and day, but he is not particularly comforted by this new arrangement. The assassin had no difficulty cutting down two men without waking the priest. So how difficult will five be? The more than likely outcome of his plan will be five dead guards. He may as well leave a sign outside the Villa's front gates requesting that the Assassin please wipe his feet before entering the premises.

"And put locks on all three entrances to the baths, good sturdy ones. Double keyed. Leave the keys of one lock with Tuma, the other with the Captain."

"Yes, Holiness. But I am not a locksmith. . ."

"Then get one. Do you have ears in your head, man?"

"I'll arrange it."

"Good, good. And lock this up when you're finished. Keep the key. I don't want it."

In the gymnasium today the dancers crowd around Rah, pressing him for details. Surely he heard something. He sleeps in the next room, separated from the priest by nothing more than a drape of strung beads. But Rah shakes his head, backs away from the assault of questions. He has lost his tongue and he has no desire to learn more about the terror that entered the Villa last night unnoticed by the guards, the beast that roamed the halls of the Villa in the dark and cut down the two men assigned to watch the priest's chamber.

That night he did awaken, but not to noises in the priest's bedroom chamber. He woke to a full moon, beaming like a far away sun in his own narrow window. He woke to the cold wetness of Hali's muzzle in his right palm. He did not open his eyes, afraid to frighten the spirit of the dog home to Ting Ya's Sun Goddess. He woke giggling, feeling the cool moist nose just in the center of his palm where she so often placed it as they walked side by side up Mount Ida. Then he fell back asleep. When he was awakened again in the early morning to a household in turmoil, he felt for the muzzle, but it was gone, and when Aros and Pyrus came running into his dressing room to see if he had been hurt or stolen, he was curled up in a fetal ball, weeping like a chained angel against the stone wall behind his pallet.

"Leave him alone, all of you." It is Akbar, come to break up the group and get the boys' minds on practice. "Next week is the Midsummer Celebration at the palace. You are all so perfect that you do not need to practice today?"

Rah is happy to go back to practice. When he is dancing he is dancing. When he is dancing he can forget the dog. And he can forget the wolf.

But the wolf cannot forget him.

Rush is away for two weeks. He has sent his man to Mochlos' to discuss the arrangements for transfer of half the merchandise of his fleetest ship to a port on the coast of Anatolia, where he will take possession of it.

During his travels back and forth across the Aegean he visits Thera. He has a home here, kept mostly as a place to rest between voyages, store merchandise, arrange shipments. On this visit the mountain is steaming, the sky white above it. There is talk that the gods are at war in the center of the earth and that the steam is the smoke from their many battlefield fires. Rush considers moving his goods off the island in the month to come. Whatever is steaming in the bowels of Thera, it is best to be cautious.

When he returns to Crete he looks for the boy even before he returns to his own house in Knossos. But Rah has been taken again by the Queen, smuggled to her chambers after the Midsummer Festival. Rush discovers this when he visits Mochlos as Ameg the Merchant with a new shipment of silks. Mochlos' face is healing and he sports the Tears of the Bull with some drama, constantly touching the area, unconsciously pointing to it by resting his chin in his palm and leaning his cheek on his index and third finger as he lies beside a low table, eating honeyed walnuts and exotic cheeses and drinking retsina in his private courtyard. Perhaps, thinks Rush, it has become something of a badge of courage for him. I survived Rush the Assassin! Fear me! Rush muses about putting a matching mark on the priest's other cheek.

"And how goes the work on your new house in the city, Mochlos?" he inquires, for Ameg is a gentleman and always curious about the goings on in town while he is away.

"We will see. I've had to give Queen Nanaea the slave god, Rah, for another try at impregnation. Don't ask me how she can imagine the whole city is not aware of her scheme. Do servants not talk? If he manages it this time, I should have my house by spring."

"This time? She has taken him to her bed before?" Rush is glad to be standing, facing away from the priest and looking over the parapet wall when he hears this news, for even he has a difficult time maintaining a casual expression. Had he a swig of retsina in his mouth he might have choked on it. He cannot imagine how this information could have escaped him, if it is indeed common knowledge among the servants in the palace. He pays well for such information.

"I'm afraid so. She seemed pleased enough at the end of three days last month, but apparently his seed did not find purchase, shall we say, within that rock." Mochlos chuckles at this little joke before continuing. "Poor thing was spooked when he came back to me, too, let me tell you, I was almost sorry I let her have him. But she believes he can give her the daughter she wants, you see, because of his" he waves his hand, "well because he appear so-"

"He is beautiful, as beautiful as any woman, Mochlos, don't be modest."

Mochlos looks up at Ameg the Merchant, a smug worm twisting his lip at one corner.

"Well, you have said it. And like begets like."

Rush has to laugh at this bit of Crete superstition, for while his daughters in Mycenae are as strong as oxen, and tall as their husbands, they are certainly female.

"And how long does she get to play with the little Grain God this time?"

"The same, three days."

"And if she is again unsuccessful? What becomes of your house by the west gate of the palace?"

"You know how fickle she is as well as I, Ameg. It could be up in smoke, my new villa. I will beat him senseless if he disappoints her this time."

"Of course," agrees Ameg the Merchant, who is no milksop with his own slaves. "Well, we shall see soon enough, eh, Mochlos? I must be off." He puts down his cup and moves to the archway, which leads down an internal garden path to the street.

On his way out he slips through an adjacent hall to the gymnasium.

Rush moves along under an overhang, where he is in shadow, toward the back of the gym and spends some time watching, and listening to, the dancers. Rah is not here and somehow this seems to tone down the brightness of the great, open yard, and even reduce the impact of the dancers' colorful costumes. There is a new boy taking Rah's place, easy to distinguish because his costume is made of the silks Rush himself selected for the Grain Dancer. Rah's new "second" is dark and slight of build, a mediocre dancer who was no doubt given the position because he excelled as a bull jumper. But Rah's grace, his fluid strength, his brilliant golden presence is missing, and the dance practice is a dull thing to watch without it.

"Are you made of eggs, Praxis? Move like you are made of feathers, not like you are springing over a bull's horns and trying not to get gored!"

"There's no point berating the boy, Akbar, he is a good enough technician, he just doesn't move like Rah," says Dimius to his coach. "Nobody does," he adds with a tinge of longing in his voice.

During a break Rush, as Ameg the Merchant, steps out of the shadows to chat sociably with Dimius.

Dimius knows Ameg as a merchant much in Mochlos' favor, and also as an important member of the King's Court, which is comprised of the most successful businessmen and traders in Knossos.

"I am honored, Ameg," he makes the light bow of a servant among his betters.

"It is always a pleasure to take a moment out of a day filled with details and matters of money to visit the best gymnasium in Knossos," Ameg returns. "I see your Grain Dancer is absent. But where is his second, Tiko?"

Dimius purses his lip. "I'm afraid he has been sold, to Ananou, to the House of the Sun." He looks off at his athletes, muses. "Nonsense in my view. Boys fight all the time. Rah is tough enough and can hold his own. But Mochlos fusses over him, you know, he simply wouldn't have anyone laying a hand on him." He glances back at Ameg carefully. "Anyone but himself, of course."

"Of course."

"So we have to make do, you know, with what we have, while-" Dimius, normally quite discrete, realizes that he is about to disclose a palace secret and so, rephrases his thought. "While Rah is gone."

"Yes. I have heard he has been pressed into service to the Queen," he gives Dimius a knowing look and the imperceptible flick of a wink. "Perhaps in error," he nods at the boy, Praxis, who is across the arena, panting and fatigued, bent in two with his hands on his knees, from the difficult routine he just attempted. It is Rah's routine, and much of the footwork, as well as several leaps, spins, and flips have been edited to fit the new boy's abilities. But it is still too much for Praxis.

Dimius looks down, shaking his head. "In more ways than one. Rah was not himself, when he returned from his last visit to the Queen, not for many days. It will be worse this time."

"Why do you say that, Dimius? If he can not accomplish the task, what is there for her to do but send him home?"

Dimius looks away. He has said too much already. But Ameg is trusted among servants in Knossos. None have ever suffered for giving him too much information. Rather, some have become quite comfortable as a result. He is not entirely surprised when the merchant presses a full coin pouch into his palm. When he looks up into the merchant's face, however, he is startled. For one fleeting moment, it appeared as if Ameg, gentle, polished Ameg, had disappeared, or else had simply grown a new face. Something fierce and utterly cold glitters in his half closed eyes, and then is gone. He is himself again, smooth browed, soft eyed.

Dimius blinks, swallows.

"Rah is. . . . different, Ameg. His is not. . . . whole, you see." He draws a breath, considering what to say. He has never put this in words before.

"He takes fits," Ameg offers quietly.

Dimius has to allow himself a quiet chuckle. "You are well informed, sir."

Ameg makes no response. He waits.

"It is not only the palsy, Ameg. He. . . . he is different in the mind, in other ways. He has difficulty speaking, not just because he is a foreign born slave. He is bright enough to pick up language. But even so, he speaks with difficulty. This," he lifts his hand and motions to the arena floor, "this is his voice."

"He doesn't need to speak to fuck." Ameg's brutality causes Dimius to snap his head around to him. But the merchant's face is unreadable.

"No. No, of course not."

"What is it, Dimius?"

"He is like a boy raised with dogs, Ameg. Or else some other mute beast. He does not think like . . . . he does not see the world as you and I see it."

"Retarded?"

"No, no not at all."

"What then?"

Dimius is squinting up at Ameg in the sunlight. His sharp face is pinched with feeling.

"Purity."

"You are a romantic, Dimius. No wonder you create such genius." But Ameg is looking at him with the light of understanding dawning in his face. He puts a gentle hand on the choreographer's shoulder, leans toward him and speaks this next softly.

"But if what you say is so, then care must be taken not to injure that . . . purity, lest we offend the host god."

Dimius looks up with surprise and hope. "Yes, that's exactly what I am saying, Ameg. That's precisely it."

"Let me see what I can do. I think perhaps I can abbreviate the boy's visit to the palace, and have your Grain Dancer sent back to the House of the Moon before that she-wolf has had another bite of him."

Dimius is looking at Ameg the Merchant as if he has never seen him before. How can this bureaucrat, this dandy, utter such words? And how can he carry out such a promise? But Dimius knows his place. He drops his eyes and makes no answer.

"No, I know you cannot respond to such disrespect of the Queen. But I also know you are a smart man, Dimius. And so I know you will not breathe a word of what I have said to anyone, not even Akbar. Because you like waking up in the morning and know that as wealthy a merchant as I can pay for your head. Nevertheless, let us make a wager. You will have a happy Queen in the palace and an undamaged Rah in the Villa by tomorrow morning."

Dimius can only swallow the saliva that has collected in his throat and glance up at Ameg silently. Ameg is smiling, but it is the smile of a shark. He gives the gym instructor another slap on the shoulder, this one far from light, and strides away.

At the palace there is a stir.

It is early afternoon. It is the second day of Rah's visit, and the first day did not go well. The Queen is sporting another nip mark, this one on her hand, and she is in a sour mood. Told to ply the boy with mead today, the Queens guards have realized, too late, that a boy of sixteen summers hasn't the tolerance to alcohol of a palace guard, which is considerable. They have overdone it, but they are not entirely at fault. The boy was able to entertain them with single hand stands and other amazing feats of balance long after he lost his ability to rise to the challenge of his visit to the Queen. Now they are ushering him back to her chamber through the colonnade behind the great hall. Before he reaches Nanaea, he will be muzzled and blindfolded. But at the moment he is no harm to anyone, needing support to walk between two of the five guards who surround him.

Rush has just come from the Villa of Mochlos, the House of the Moon. He is dressed as Ameg in a fine yellow linen robe. His hair, which he maintains at waist length, having served for many years in the Hittite military, is now pulled into a meticulous plait at the back of his head, the length hidden under a small merchant's cap. He wears heavy gold jewelry about his neck and wrists. As Ameg, he walks with a bit of a lilt, as if on his toes, his thickly braceleted wrists held neatly at his sides. As he approaches the group of guards with the boy he appears an utterly refined, handsome and immensely wealthy dandy.

He reaches the group of guards, whose progress has been slowed by the boy's wriggling, and he offers a salutation, which the men return with a respectful come-to-halt and bow, for Ameg holds high regard in the King's Court.

But when the boy looks up at Ameg he sees only Rush, not a merchant, nor a dandy, nor a statesmen. His drunk for a moment interrupted by shock, he yanks violently against the hands holding him upright and slurs, "Th-the wolf!"

The guard in charge of the group quickly steps between Rush and Rah and offers his apology to the merchant.

"He is drunk on mead, sir, Queens orders. I suppose he's seeing things now. We. . . may have given him a bit too much."

"I should say so, Ramicus. He can barely stand. How do you propose to service the Queen with this?" He waves his hand in the direction of the still squirming Rah, now hidden behind Ramicus.

Ramicus looks at him with some surprise, and Ameg counters with a look of boredom.

"Yes, yes, her scheme is all over the town. I'll wager the only ones who still believe it a secret is Her Majesty and Her Majesty's cunt."

Ramicus draws his head back as if he's been slapped. He drops his eyes and remains silent.

"Let us not play games, shall we? There is no time for it. Now I ask you again, how do you propose to please the Queen with this drunken cat?"

Ramicus gives the guard to his right a quick, angry look, the look one gives a party responsible for one's troubles, then looks down. "We don't expect her pleasure, sir."

"No, and you won't get it. But her expectations must be met, Ramicus, unless you look forward to sleeping with the bulls tonight." Ameg strokes his beard, waiting for the guard's response. When none comes, he slips his hand into a fold of his robe and takes out another pouch, heavy with coins. He presses it into the head guard's palm.

"Now hear me. Give me a quarter of an hour with the Queen, take the little Grain God back to your quarters. Put him to bed." Ameg is speaking just above a whisper, but he has taken the tone of a commander, and Ramicus has snapped to attention. The merchant is taller by a hand than the guard and now peers easily over his shoulder at Rah.

"He looks to be taken with fever if you ask me. He's red as a pomegranate, trembling like a rabbit. Give him plenty of water, make him drink as much as you can without drowning him." He moves Ramicus to the side with a firm hand, takes a step toward Rah, and sniffs.

Rah is staring up at him, shivering, and watching him with big, frightened eyes.

"Fortunate for you, the priests soaking him in holy oils as they do. He still smells like a temple concubine and not a drunken kit."

"But sir, she expects him immediately," says Ramicus suddenly, having found his tongue. "We are already delayed."

Rush has not taken his eyes off Rah.

"In a quarter of an hour, announce yourself at the Queen's chamber door. She will not admit you." He turns to Ramicus. "Tell her guard then that the Grain God has taken ill with fever."

Ramicus looks over at his men. They look to one another, nodding.

"She will not want him near her if he is ill," agrees Ramicus.

"Take care, Ramicus." Something black, like the wing of a crow, passes over the merchant's face and Ramicus takes an unconscious step away from him. "Do not let him come to any harm," Ameg speaks just above a whisper, "while he is in your care."

"No, sir," He stuffs the coin pouch into a pocket in his skirt. "A quarter hour."

Rush steps in front of Rah again just as the men move to take him back down the hall in the same direction from which they have just come. He tips the boy's chin up, leans down to close the distance between his face and the boy's. "I'm a wolf, am I?"

Rah pulls back, still held tight by the men at his sides, and makes a vibrating noise deep in his throat.

Rush chuckles.

"Silly little cat," he murmurs. "Are you growling at me?" Then he turns to addresses the man he has just paid off, still holding the boy's chin.

"It takes a he-wolf to take a she-wolf. Not a rabbit. Leave the bitch to me."

CHAPTER13

Queen Nanaea is pacing like a tigress in her bed chamber. She has been waiting for her guards to bring the god slave Rah back to her for another attempt at his seduction. She strides across her chamber, rubbing the back of her left hand where the boy nipped her the night before. This has become a fiasco, exasperating. In her heart she no longer believes that the unwilling boy can give her what she wants. She knows that she has frightened him too badly. He has curled in on himself. He's a strange thing, that boy. A breathtaking angel when he dances, a feral animal when he is cornered. She has enjoyed playing with him, has even enjoyed his resistance, which is so new to her. But she cannot waste this month on play. Her months are running out. She is not a young woman of twenty any longer. Her oldest son is just Rah's age. She is running out of time.

She is not surprised that she frightens the boy so. She frightens most men and this boy is barely sixteen summers. All of her life she has been something of a challenge to her elders, her handlers. Hers is a long line of dominant, dangerous females, no coddled kittens these. As a girl she jumped the bulls, and as a young woman, she learned to use a blade to defend herself. She was always tall for her age and large boned and she beat more than one brother or cousin in a game of wrestling. On the whole she thinks little of men, considering them less than equals and of little use beyond procreation and overseeing the paltry details of merchandising. She has been surrounded by sycophants and dandies all of her life at the palace and the foreigners who have visited Crete, even the kings, have been little else. She rules the dominant city on Crete because of her husband's business acumen (in trade he is a genius, in the bedroom, a mild mannered bore). She has the world at her feet.

Except for this. She needs an heir. A girl-child, strong and bright and dangerous, like herself, to keep her safe in her later years. To maintain her line in Knossos.

Queen Nanaea's pacing is interrupted by a guard at her door. It is Pallox, her door guard, bringing her Ameg the Merchant's request for her audience.

Ameg. Now there is a curious character. Urbane, refined, smart as a fox. She has propositioned him more than once and even offered him a liaison on strictly business grounds, but has been met with a polite decline each time. He eludes her offers by insisting he could not satisfy such a woman, pretending to be inclined only toward his own sex, which is nonsense, as everyone knows he has a wife in Knossos and at least one more overseas. But Ameg is a powerful man, possibly the most powerful man in Knossos next to the King. And Nanaea has never for a moment believed he was the dandy he pretends to be. On more than one occasion she has seen the mask slip, seen the wolf lurking in his black eyes. One would have to be a fool to think a man could be as successful as he is without a set of fangs behind his smile.

"What is his business?" says Nanaea, as she turns to her guard, irritable that they have not yet produced the boy for her. "Where is the Grain Dancer? What is taking them so long with him? He should be inebriated by now. Tell Ameg it will have to wait-" but her guard has stumbled awkwardly aside and she is facing Ameg himself.

"Have I interrupted something urgent, Nanaea?" Eyes like black stones regard her. Is that contempt she sees in his face? No, not contempt. Nor respect. Something lurking behind the mask today. He has his own urgency, his own agenda.

"Ameg, how kind of you to visit me in my bedchamber, when I have so often invited you to do just so and been declined. What sort of business could possibly be so important as to lure you here into this dangerous territory at last?"

Ameg turns to the guard, Pollax, who is still chagrined at being shoved against a wall by the impudent merchant. But when Pollax looks up into the merchant's face to challenge him with a haughty look, he instead finds himself stepping back as if away from a blow.

"Is there anything else, madam?" he asks the Queen, hoping she is willing to handle this intrusion herself.

Nanaea is looking at Ameg with amused interest. "No Pollax, go back to your post. And admit no one until I tell you may do so."

"Madam," he bows and exits.

Nanaea has stepped toward Ameg, a curious tilt to her head, as if she sniffs the air. She peers at the merchant as she would a slave on a block, up and down. She moves around him in a circle, a bird of prey, considering.

"What is it, Ameg. Have you come on business, or is this a social call?"

Rush has not moved, but is watching her all the same as she circles him, knowing that she is enjoying her little dance of domination. She will dance his dance soon enough. He waits.

She steps in front of him, finds herself curiously excited by the fact that she must tip her head back quite far to look into his face. She has not smiled like this, she realizes, for some time. Her teeth are bared. She is having fun.

"Ameg, must I beg?" She is flirting. To her own amusement, she finds she is flirting. Like a commoner. How refreshing. She has never stood near Ameg without sensing a certain violence in the man, under the immaculate robes, the trimmed and oiled beard, the polished nails. She has often wondered how it is that no one else could sense it. It is like a smell that links one type to its own. Like the musk of a deer. He has fooled the Court. But no, he has never fooled her. There is something of her own nature under those robes.

This is no boy, unwilling and snapping with fear. This is a man. Dangerous, like her. This is an equal.

"You are ready for something, woman, which you will not find elsewhere. I have come to save you from making an even bigger fool of yourself than you have already made."

Nanaea's eyes flash at the insult. Her face darkens, she has lost her smile. And yet, who else would have had the nerve to tell her what she already knows? This thing with the boy, the Grain Dancer, it is the miscalculation of a desperate woman. What Ameg has said can be taken as treason, or as heroism, depending on the cleverness of the listener. And Nanaea is nothing if not sly.

She recovers her poise quickly. There is a vulpine pull to her smile.

"And how do you propose to save your Queen, Ameg."

Ameg the Merchant looks down at the snarling smile of the Queen and pulls back his lips. He lifts his right hand, settles his fingers at the back of the Queen's neck. It is barely perceptible, this touch, yet wildly suggestive to the Queen. She has not been touched, uninvited, for a very long time, if ever.

Nanaea feels a sense of vertigo momentarily as she is drawn toward the dark, wild strength she has always felt behind the facade of Ameg the Merchant. It is like a common throbbing that, when in close enough proximity, must rush into itself, into the other, snapping and snarling and panting. Black eyes fix on black eyes. She leans her neck back against those fingertips. Ameg takes a fist of the Queen's hair in his hand and pulls her head back, drops his mouth to her throat and licks it, nuzzling, biting. Nanaea moans. Drawn toward the strength she feels coming off him like a mist, she slips her hands up to his neck and closes her fingers around it. Her hand is on his throat, her fingers slipping over sinew taught and thick as a tree's trunk.

He lifts his head to brush her mouth with a fleeting kiss, then spins her around with a vicious jerk and clamps his forearm about her waist, lifting her heavy skirting.

Nanaea the Queen sighs with delight.

And lifts her tail.

CHAPTER 14

King Cyrus has lost his appetite. This is not a thing that happens often. In fact, it has not happened since his infancy, when he colicked on his wet-nurse's milk. His mother having died in his childbirth, Cyrus learned early in life to compensate for his lack of maternal love. Food became his mother. And when he became a man, food remained his lover.

So the Grain God, the slave boy whose beauty and dance so pleases the gods that Knossos' fields are fat with fruit and grain, is a fascinating subject for King Cyrus, who spends his day exploring the world of exotic foods which he has shipped to him from all over the world. Today he is lounging at table in his private courtyard with several of his favorite men, gastronomes like himself, tasting a new wine from the Arpa River region. But Cyrus is distracted, even distant. He joins the conversation only for the sake of courtesy.

"What is on your mind, today, Cyrus. I have never seen you so disinterested in a fine wine!" says his best friend, and nephew, Ikarus.

"Fine wine," muses Cyrus. "We have fine wine on Crete, too. Most years. But this year the wine is fine in the north, bitter in the south. No rain, you see. All the rain falls north of the hills. North, over Knossos' fields. All because of the little Grain God."

"Oh come now, Cyrus. You can't really believe that priestly nonsense. He is just a dancer. Gifted? Yes. Holy? No."

"Oh, I believe, Ikarus. I believe that Rah loves the little dancer. I believe that he has favored my enemy because of that lovely child. I also believe that if they take him to their Mount Juktas in the fall and disembowel him like they did the other two, there will be a terror on this island the likes of which we have never seen."

Ikarus has put down his cup, fascinated by his uncle's words.

"You cannot mean this, Cyrus. I know you to be a reverent man, but surely you do not think that the gods will bring down wrath upon all of Crete simply because Knossos' high priest has slain one imported slave in offering?"

"Not the gods, Ikarus. The Moon Goddess herself. His mother. And yes, I believe it with my whole heart and soul." He picks up a bit of cheese, looks at it, puts it in his mouth, nibbling without interest.

"I had a dream last night. I dreamed of a dove. A brilliant white dove from the far north. He came to Crete on a merchant ship. He was purchased by the high priest Mochlos and released over Mount Ida, into Knossos' fields, and the fields became abundant with grain. But then another priest bade his archer shoot the dove in the heart as he flew over the fields, as a sacrifice to the gods. Then the sky darkened and a wave came, tall as a mountain, from the north. A wave of water. It wiped out Knossos and all of the cities to the north. And then another wave, of men in ships, came from the west. Greeks, soldiers, landed on Crete and-."

"Come, Cyrus, you are depressing us all. Put these thoughts aside, and drink with us. Or else let us plot to steal the little slave-god from Knossos! Steal him, and kill him and start war with Knossos," says Lutarus, who is Cyrus' mother's brother. He waves a bit of pita in emphasis before dipping it into a dish of seasoned yogurt.

"And can you and your men defend me from Knossos if I do, uncle?" Cyrus takes a measured look at the man to his left. Only a few summers older than himself, Lutarus is Captain of the Palace Guard and Cyrus' right hand. Lutarus has been overseas to fight, and was a mercenary soldier before he returned to Crete to become his nephew's guardian.

"This island is too peaceful for me. We need a fight. We are becoming women, all of us. We are too soft and we will pay for it. I am ready for Knossos. Steal the boy. I will defend you."

Cyrus looks at his uncle solemnly. "You are a good friend, Lutarus. But you don't believe a word of what I've said. You are a soldier who forever looks for an excuse for war."

"Perhaps so. Nevertheless, I do not need to believe your dream to fight Knossos. I need only men and equipment. Give me enough of these and we can take him."

"A dancer," says Ikarus, watching both men with amusement. "A war for a holy dancer? And a dream? The wine has gone to your heads, both of you. And you, Cyrus, sound as mad as Media. No dancer can make the harvest prosper. This is a high priest's invention, a new way to line priestly pockets with gold."

"This one can, Ikarus," says King Cyrus, who has had to run his government without a proper Queen for several years now. "This is the real thing, I tell you. Perhaps the priest did invent the tradition, but this slave," he puts down his cup, having barely sipped from it, "this slave is nothing like we have ever seen. This is no ordinary temple dancer. Knossos is on fire for him. Their crops flourish, their trade increases. This is Rah, Ikarus. This is the son of the Moon and the Sun."

"Soon you will be spending your days wandering in the cemeteries with your wife, talking to the dead. Then we will have neither King nor Queen to rule Cyrus," quips Ikarus.

"You have no faith, Ikarus, in anything but a good cup of wine and a fine meal. There is more to life than food and drink. There is an accounting for our actions at the end of our days. If a god fell from heaven, would we know it? Would we have enough sense to see it? Or would we go on, eating and drinking and trading and hoarding and thinking only of today. What if he were Rah, Ikarus? What if this boy really did 'die to the god' and take on the soul of Rah? What then?"

"Well, according to Knossos priesthood, then he must be sacrificed on Mount Juktas." "Sacrificed to whom? To himself? He is here." Cyrus pounds the table suddenly. "He is here, and if they kill him, we will all suffer for it. Our world will be lost forever."

The two other men are looking at Cyrus as if he has grown another head. Cyrus, their jolly epicurean friend and king, talking like a fanatic priest!

"You sound as if you have been listening to Media's nonsense, my friend," says Lutarus.

"Media may spend her days in the cemeteries talking to the dead, but she is not mad, Lutarus, she is lucid, a seer. And she has told me the meaning of the dream."

Ikarus has had enough.

"Am I not at table with the same man who sent a killer to collect the head of this very slave boy, two moons ago?"

"That was before I had the dream. That was before I knew. Now I know. And now that I know, I have no excuse. I must find a way to stop this from happening." A light of hope pass over his heavy face. "That is it, Ikarus. You have given me the answer! I will pay that same man to protect him!"

"And how is an assassin to protect a slave from such a thing, Cyrus? Short of killing every high priest in Knossos?" wonders Lutarus.

"You know the man. You found him for me," Cyrus murmurs.

Lutarus takes a deep breath, blows it out slowly. "You play with fire, Cyrus. I found him for you for an assassination. I found you the best, an elite killer. I risked my own neck doing it, I can tell you. My contacts on the mainland are trustworthy, but this is no baby sitter. I would not ask that one to be a body guard for a dancer. You are liable to have your own head handed to you in a sack for the insult."

Cyrus considers this. Then he claps his hands and a servant, waiting at the entrance to the courtyard, approaches and bows.

"Get me the messenger."

The servant bows again and exits.

"You know where to find him?" Ikarus asks in surprise.

"No. But he knows where to find me. When I wish to see him, I send a messenger to Knossos, with a gesture of goodwill to the palace, a gift from abroad. Then he knows I am in need of his assistance." He looks at Lutarus. "When his spies in Knossos tell him of my gift, he will be here within a day or two of its receipt."

"You play with fire, Cyrus," Lutarus warns again. "He is not one to trifle with."

"I am not trifling, Lutarus. I am trying to save Crete."

CHAPTER 15

The morning after Rush's visit to the Queen, Rah is returned to the Villa of Mochlos. He is packed in a cart pulled by donkeys, hidden amongst offerings to the priesthood from the King. When he arrives he is taken immediately in to Mochlos' private courtyard to give his account of what happened. Why has he been sent back two days early? Is the Queen dissatisfied? Is the deal off?

Rah knows nothing of his master's bargain with the Queen. He is badly hung over and sick. His head aches and he wants only to hide his eyes from the brilliant Mediterranean noon that beats down in the courtyard garden. He is pale and drawn. He remembers little and his head is spinning with a dark image he cannot escape, an image of two wolves pacing him through a murky wood, one male, one female, hungry beasts that circle and sniff, muzzles down, hungry and wanting. He shivers, moaning, as the priest's men shove him in front of Mochlos. He wants only to be brought upstairs to his pallet and allowed to sleep.

But here is Mochlos' wine sweetened breath on his face, Mochlos' leaning over him, his leering mouth demanding answers. Mochlos the tiger, his thin lips drawn back over his long teeth. Rah turns his face away from the priest's involuntarily. He puts his eyes down, and to the left.

"Tell me exactly. From the beginning. Every detail."

Rah feels his stomach twist. He tries hard to remember, but sees only the palace guard surrounding him, laughing, handing him cup after cup of retsina, urging him to drink, to drink and to dance for them.

"They make me drink wine," he squints up at Mochlos hopefully. Is this enough?

"Yes, yes. I see you have been drowned in wine. But did you couple with the Queen? Is she satisfied with you?" The priest wrings his hands. "Why would she send you back after only one night?" he hisses, turning as if speaking to himself.

"The wolf!" Rah suddenly blurts, eyes big as a rabbit's.

"The wolf. What wolf?" Mochlos peers at him, then shakes his head, twisting his mouth in disgust. "Simpleton. A wolf. I should have sent a spy with you. You wouldn't know if you coupled with a bull in this condition." He waves his hand at a servant. "Send him off to the baths. Perhaps Tuma can sober him up and get something out of him. A wolf. Idiot."

So Rah is sent to Tuma, who takes him roughly from the guard and, with bluff and bluster, promises that he will extract some information for the master. When they are safely out of earshot he laughs softly to himself and gives Rah's corn silk head a gentle tousle.

"You are not made for wine, boy. I will give you a drink that will make you sleep and when you wake, you will be fit to dance. You will see. Tuma has a magic root to fix your belly." He gives Rah's sore stomach a little pat.

Sick and confused, Rah is happy to be babied by Tuma today. The gentle African giant gathers some toweling and feather pillows from the priest's supply room and makes a bed of them in a dark recess near the Pool of Rah. He gives the boy a drink made of a powdered root and lets him sleep. He sends Siriona, who is his own sister's child, down to the kitchens for a simple vegetable broth, and when the boy awakens he awakens to his three concubines, who feed him the broth and fuss over him until he begs Tuma to let him go down to the gym.

"They will be glad to see you," Tuma agrees. "The new boy, he has broken his neck, poor thing. Trying to jump and spin like Rah, this way, that way, upside down and inside out." He pats Rah's head. "No one can jump like Rah. There is no one. You go, boy."

Dimius and Akbar are as glad as they are shocked to see Rah this afternoon.

"You think you are ready for practice, Rah?" asks Akbar. "You don't want the remainder of the day to rest up? Start fresh in the morning?"

Rah shakes his head. Then looks at Dimius carefully. "How does he fall, teacher?"

Dimius sighs, looks at Akbar.

"Trying to be you," answers Akbar.

"But which jump?"

Akbar opens his mouth but Dimius lifts a hand to silence him.

"No. I won't have him focused on it." He looks at Rah. "Just do flat work today. Tomorrow, the jumps."

Akbar gives Rah a searching look. "You are-" he taps his own temple, "you are alright today? You can dance?"

Rah blinks at him, frowns. Something lurking in his head, something dark, low to the ground, breathing behind the brush. One, then two shapes. No, it was a dream. He dreamed of wolves, that is all.

"Rah is good," he says.

Dimius peers at him, considering how to ask the question on everyone's mind. He is not one to pry into what is none of his business, but the Grain Dancer is his business, is he not?

"Will they. . . she. . . send for you again?"

Rah looks away, knits his brows, strains to see what he does not want to see. "No, teacher. I bite her."

"You bite-?" Dimius widens his eyes. "You bit the Queen?"

Rah drops his gaze to his feet, remembering. He makes a little vibration in his throat.

"She sent you home, after you bit her?" Akbar blurts out, stunned.

"No," Rah keeps his head down. "After he . . . . after the w-w-. ."

"The what?"

"Never mind, Akbar," Dimius interrupts. He is recalling Ameg's words. Whatever happened, the merchant was certainly involved. And given his warning to Dimius yesterday that his involvement must not be mentioned to anyone, this is all better left unsaid. "Go and join the others, Rah."

After he leaves, Akbar looks at Dimius with astonishment. "He bit the Queen? And he is alive to tell?"

"Well, no one is supposed to know of his visits, are they? She can't very well skin him if he isn't there. And then send Mochlos back a corpse? Even if it were common knowledge, he is the Grain God, and even the Queen would have to answer to the priesthood for harming him before the equinox. She took a gamble. Apparently she lost."

Akbar shakes his head. "Ninaea doesn't lose," he says. Then, grinning he adds, "Maybe she liked it, eh?"

CHAPTER 16

The House of the Sun God, the Villa of Ananou, is on the dark side of town. Half the size of Mochlos' Villa, Ananou's house is built on a sun bleached outcropping on the east end of Knossos, past the poorer neighborhoods where houses are low and single roomed and dirt floored, on the road to Gournia. But the Villa itself, which sits behind an eight foot wall of brick and marble, is full of light, open and spacious. Decorated in the tradition of the sun worshipers who inhabited Crete before the coming of the people of the moon, in the dawn of island civilization, it belies its builder's masculine leanings. Much gold gilds the interior and many bronze renderings of beautiful youths with broad shoulders and nipped waists, bringing saffron offerings to the Sun God, festoon the walls and courtyards. The House of the Sun is a stronghold of masculine dominion in a land where politics designate a feminine supreme being, and a female ruler.

Ananou is an old priest who hates and fears the matriarchal society he lives in. His chief enemy is Mochlos, head of the House of the Moon. But the truth of his hatred for Mochlos, and his hatred of the feminine deity, he holds in his heart. On the exterior, he is a devoted high priest who understands his place as head of a lesser church. But deep in his soul he knows that the Sun rules the Moon and her children, and that man ultimately rules woman. So when Mochlos offered him Tiko, he accepted with much pretense of gratitude but with a heart filled with secret hatred. He had seen Tiko dance, thought him exquisite, and coveted him from the start. But upon acquisition of the boy, his frustrated heart whispered to him that Tiko should be Grain Dancer, that if it wasn't for the blonde, who should have been disqualified for the very simple reason that he is imperfect, flawed by a mangled tongue and a speech impediment, he would be. What god wants to be represented by an imperfect, indeed blemished, slave? Tiko, on the other hand, is without flaw, possessing an Asian beauty as stunning, if only this island had the eyes to see, as the blonde, in his own right. And now Tiko is his.

So Tiko has fast become his prize possession, and he is treated as such. The fact that Tiko hates him passionately and makes no attempt to hide it only serves to make the Asian dancer more adorable to Ananou. Such spirit. Such heart! And such precision. He must be Grain Dancer. He must take the blonde's place. And why not? Now that he is Ananou's. So Ananou makes a sloppy attempt to have the blonde slaughtered on his way to the Burial Mounds, although it is high treason to do so. He is an old man. He will restore some power and respect to the House of the Sun before he dies. It is now or never.

But the attempt fails. Either the three thugs he hired took the down payment and ran, or else they met with a bad end themselves. Ananou never saw them again, and the blonde dancer is still driving this city crazy. Well, he will just have to try again, this time taking care to find a more reputable killer. And so he sends out word, into the darker streets on the east end of the city, word that he is in need of such a man or men.

It is twilight, and Ananou is praying in his western courtyard to the setting sun when such a man appears.

His prayers have been long and he is yet focused on them. He has been praying to the Sun God for help with this endeavor. When he rises from his knees he is still bent over his folded hands in an attitude of devotion. It is not until he lifts his eyes in the dim light to find his way to the arch leading back to his chamber that he notices a huge shadow leaning against the archway.

At first Ananou's old heart jumps in fright. The darkness has come to life, and the black archway has stepped forward with the head of a man and the torso of a bull. As the shadow incorporates in the moonlit dark Ananou realizes what he is looking at. It is a man dressed in black from head to foot, a black sackcloth hood wrapped tightly around his head. His physical aspect, his size, his silence, his dominant, wide legged stance, is frightening enough, but his energy is like a thunderclap. It hits Ananou in the chest and the old priest steps back involuntarily.

An assassin! The Sun God has answered his prayer.

He waits for the man to announce his purpose. But the man says nothing.

Finally Ananou breaks the silence.

"You have come," says the priest to the eerie figure as it takes another soundless step forward into the courtyard.

"Yes," says the man in Greek. "Death has found you."

A chill of wavering apprehension skitters through Ananou's testicles.

"I am in the market for an assassin. I will pay you handsomely," says Ananou.

The figure makes no move to answer. It stands looming in the moonlight, motionless, and Ananou, who is beginning to lose his confidence, feels pressed to continue.

"I want the head of the Grain God," he offers.

Silence. With the mention of the dancer the air about the man seems to have gained weight. It presses down all around Ananou like a blanket.

"You are here because you have heard that I need an assassin. Name your price for the head of the new Rah," says the priest.

Suddenly the figure is advancing. One step. Two. Faster and faster, as if without legs, like a ghost from a grave and he has covered the distance between himself and the priest and the priest has stepped back and stumbled and hit the courtyard wall with his back and is already cringing, waiting for the knife that is surely coming.

"Who sent you then, if you are not here to kill for me?" he blurts, cowering now as the shadow looms over him, breathing like a bull.

"You have sent for me, old man." The baritone voice is hell-deep, a growl, the accent foreign. "You sent for me when you sent cheap dogs to kill the boy, Rah. Your dogs are dead, old man. I am the wolf who killed them."

Ananou is pulled out of his cower and lifted up against the wall by the throat. His feet struggle and stretch for purchase on the ground so that he can take a breath to speak.

"Who are you?" he squeaks.

"You know who I am," says the beast through the sackcloth hood. The hand that has been squeezing the old man's throat is now shoving his head against the wall tightly by the jaw. A glint in the moonlight at Ananou's left eye belies the dagger in his other.

"My god, will you kill me for failing to find you first? I will pay you twice what I gave them!"

The tip of the blade alights on the folds of skin above Ananou's left cheekbone.

"Twice a dog's pay is nothing to Rush the Assassin." The man is carving into the priest's cheek with the tip of the dagger.

With the mention of the terrifying legend, Ananou stiffens, understanding finally what his religious fervor has bought him.

"How much? Name it! Name it, man!" the old priest whimpers.

The black sackcloth head lifts, intent on its work on the priest's cheek. Then the dagger is withdrawn and Ananou's neck is wrenched as the assassin shoves the priest's face back over his shoulder, into the wall behind him. Ananou feels the man's breath through the cloth, tickling his ear as he growls his price. "Tiko."

The word sends a lurch of nausea through the priest. "What? Tiko? No--"

He is pulled forward and slammed back into the wall, his head cracking against the stones.

"A boy for a boy."

"No. No I-" Ananou is defeated. This he cannot pay. Not Tiko. His shoulders shake as he breaks down with a sob. "It is for Tiko that I want the Dancer's head, man. So that he can become the Grain God. What good is the blonde to me dead if Tiko is dead, too?"

The assassin draws back, releasing the priest, who slides down the wall in a crumpled pile of robes, sobbing.

"A boy for a boy. That is my price, old man. I will give you Rah's head, and you will give me Tiko's."

The priest can only shake his head, whimpering. His sniveling is ended abruptly when the assassin backhands him in the face, bloodying his nose and mouth.

"You insult me with dogs, then call me for hire and change your mind."

"Please, I am a foolish old man. I meant you no insult."

"You play in deep waters, priest. My waters. Now I will teach you to swim. Come. Lead me to Tiko."

Ananou's face pales. He looks up at the assassin.

"What will you do to him?"

But the assassin has answered him for the last time. He lifts him onto his feet by the front of his robe and throws him toward the archway.

Tiko awakens to torchlight.

He squints, raises his hand to shade his eyes, sees two shapes looming over his pallet, one the old priest, Ananou, the other a giant wrapped head to toe in black. His chamber is off a short hall, in the anterior of the villa, not far from the priest's rooms. It is windowless and dark but for the torch in Ananou's hand. Tiko's heart thumps in his chest as if he has been struck by a master's side kick. He cannot believe what he is seeing. He pulls himself up onto his knees on the bed. He is chained only by the ankles to the wall behind his pallet, but the chains will not allow him to move further or to step onto the floor.

"The assassin!" he gasps in awe.

Ananou's face is a study in misery. The hulk in black says nothing.

"Take these chains off of me, old fool!" Tiko spits at Ananou. "Let me die with honor as my father died and his father. I will kneel before a master!"

Ananou moves to do as the boy has demanded, then stops to look up at the assassin for permission. The assassin has not taken his eyes off Tiko.

"May I not release him?" Ananou begs.

Rush makes no answer, but steps up to the boy's pallet, takes both of his ankle chains in his hand and yanks them out of the wall with a single heave. It is a sickening feat of brute strength that should have sent the boy into a corner. But the boy is still. Rush throws the loose bolts in Tiko's lap, showering him with bits of brick and dust. Tiko flinches as the bolts land in his lap but his eyes are fixed on Rush with something closer to adoration than fear.

"Well, did you not ask to die on your knees?"

The boy scrambles to the floor, kneels, lowers his head as if in prayer.

"No!" Ananou has thrown himself in between Rush and the boy. He has fallen on his knees as well and is grabbing at the assassin's legs with his free hand. "No! Kill me if you must punish me for my sin against Rah. I deserve it. I see this now. But do not harm this boy. I beg you, let him live. Let him live!"

Tiko has not moved. But he lifts his head, his eyes hot with hatred, searing into the priest's.

"I will die at the hand of a master, you old prick. You cannot take this from me." And then to Rush, bowing his head again, "Do it, sir."

Rush pushes the priest off him with his foot, and the priest falls onto his back, still holding the torch upright. Rush has drawn his gold handled blade and now uses the tip to lift Tiko's face by the chin.

"You have the heart of a warrior, boy. How did you come to be a slave?"

Tiko looks up at the assassin's wrapped face. Only the shadowed eye holes give it humanity.

"My father died in battle, sir. My father was a warrior, as was his. My line goes back a thousand years. All men of war. I am not afraid to die. I am honored to die at the hand of a master assassin."

"And so you shall."

But Ananou, weeping, has taken hold of his forearm. "I tell you I do not want the head of the Grain God, at any price. May he live forever in paradise! May he live in glory and riches beyond imagining! I will pray for him daily! I will fill his church with my offerings! Only do not kill this boy!"

"And what will you give me to spare him, Ananou?"

"Anything! Name it! My own head!"

Rush has to chuckle at that.

"Until now you have made no enemies, and so your head is of no value to me. No one wants it." He is silent a moment, as if considering. "But I will take this boy."

"The boy? But why? For what? What will you do to him?" says Ananou suspiciously, his own desires coloring his picture of the assassin's.

"I will go with you!" says Tiko to Rush. "I will polish your weapons. I will wash your clothes! I will do anything you ask! I will-" he bows his head again, this last clearly hardest for him to acquiesce. "I will be whatever your need."

Rush ignores this. He turns to the priest.

"Have him at the gates of the Villa, ready for my man, in two days. He will come at dusk." Then to Tiko. "You know some Chinese hand to hand?"

"My father taught me everything he knew. He was a master of the martial arts."

"These secrets, will you share them, or will you make me break your legs and throw you into the middle of the Aegean?"

Tiko has boldly risen to his feet. He is staring directly into the shadows that house the assassin's eyes.

"You are taking me to teach the ancient fighting art of my ancestors to soldiers? Until now I have been treated like an old man's whore. You give me a chance to be a warrior. You come to take my life and instead you give me back my life. I will not disgrace my ancestors by dishonoring such a trust. I will make your men masters of hand-to-hand combat. I will teach them everything I know."

The assassin has sheathed his blade. He is thinking of his daughters, both big with child, in Mycenae. He is thinking of his sons-in-law, both soldiers. And his own twin sons, here in Knossos, who will grow to be soldiers also. He will give the Asian boy to them as a gift, and perhaps the tricks the boy can show them will spare their lives in battle one day.

But he is also thinking of Rah who, with his chief competitor off Crete, will never be threatened by a jealous priest who owns the second best dancer on the island.

Uninvited, the image of the dancer visits him. Rah, sprawled in the mud beneath him, Rah, covered in mud and more beautiful than ever, more exotic, still smelling like a temple offering, struggling like a wild cat, snapping at his forearm and drawing blood. And just as uninvited, the taste of the boy's mouth, puppy sweet, returns to his tongue. And then the feel of his flogged haunch, the smooth skin raised in uneven welts, hitting him in the heart like a thunderbolt from a protective god, saving him from thoughtlessly taking the boy by force himself.

For a moment the only sound is the breath easing back and forth against the cloth that covers the assassin's face. Then he grabs the torch, which has gone to embers, from Ananou. He moves silently back to the doorway, taking the only light in the room with him. And he leaves the boy and the priest alone in the dark.

CHAPTER 17

In Knossos, Josepha is in her garden tending the chickens. Her house is a two story dwelling built around a square courtyard. It is one of the most palatial homes in Knossos, located in the center of town just east of the Palace. Her sons are at practice in the gym, which is on the first floor of the west wing. They are taking instruction from a wrestling coach imported from Hatti. But Josepha is enjoying the cool of the day in the shade behind the kitchen. She throws grain out to the chickens in a circular motion and muses about love, about what it means to truly love, and about the challenge that her husband is now facing. She smiles, in awe and wonder, that the One God, the God of her people, should deign to give her own love, Antaris, the same challenge that He once gave her. For it is a challenge that ultimately brought her the contentment that she knows today. It is the thing that made her a woman content to listen to the soft avian murmur of her chickens scratching under her skirts, though her husband's heart is captured by another, and was before that only in love with war. She is far from the place of her birth, far from her parents and siblings, living in the land of her people's enemies. She is a thousand kilometers away across the sea from the land of Goshen, living in the land of the Philistines.

Josepha is known in Knossos as one of the more reclusive ladies of privilege. She comes to the required events at the palace and has seen several of the new Grain God's performances. She comes to the necessary feasts. She dresses appropriately for the wife of a wealthy dandy. But at home, Josepha wears a simple muslin sheath dress of homespun fabric. She wears her hair in a braid down her back and simple, peasant sandals. Josepha has no need for fabric and jewels, nor for the recognition and honors given nobility in this society. She was content long before her husband brought her here, and she remains content.

So today Josepha is singing to her chickens, returning the gift of their calming avian purr with her own lovely soprano hum. She is thinking of her husband Antaris, and of the miracle that is the Grain Dancer.

She knows Antaris better than anyone, yet she has never pretended to understand his heart. Nor to own it. It has always been the errant nature of his heart that has maintained her love for him. She lives satisfied in invisible chains, chains stronger than any chains that bind the slaves on Crete. Even stronger than the golden chains that keep the Grain Dancer earthbound, or her people bound to Pharaoh. But this new slavery is freely given. She alone owns the key to her chains, not even Antaris has access to them. And so she is content.

For before Josepha came to Crete she was a Hebrew slave in Egypt. Antaris, already a soldier of fortune, assassinated her Egyptian master, a royal. He found her pleasing, purchased her freedom and brought her to the place her people called Caphtor. He needed a wife in Caphtor, and she, being foreign born, was a perfect choice, for he had many identities in many cities. Here she became the wife of Ameg the Merchant, was given a home, and her sons. All that was required of her in return was her acceptance of the arrangement, and this she gave without question. Antaris had killed her master and purchased her freedom. She would not, in return, become his master and take his.

And now, sixteen summers later, she would live to see Antaris take up invisible chains as strong as those that bound her to him.

And so Josepha muses in her garden amongst her chickens about the little golden dancer who stole her husband's heart, stole it without wanting it, stole it without knowing it. And she must laugh to herself at her God's choice for Antaris. She has seen the boy dance in the great hall, a little blonde leopard with the balance and grace and strength of a cat and wildness matched only by Antaris' own heart. She smiles at her husband's predicament. For such a man to be tamed by such a creature!

"I will help you, Antaris," she says to the chickens. "In this, you will need my help."

While Josepha feeds her chickens behind her kitchen in Knossos, the Grain Dancer is playing with the dappled colt in a guarded field above the city. The colt has accepted his weight on its back and is learning to move off his leg. He has fashioned a bit-less bridle from leather straps pilfered from the gym, with two long reins that he can use seated or standing on the animal's croup. He has not tried this last yet, but is considering an attempt today.

Today, and every second day, Ramicus and his men are guarding the westtern flank of the pasture from dawn to dusk, when a special night guard takes up the post. Two of Ramicus' men are outright drunkards, and two are hardly more than boys, lads who came to the palace looking for work and finding drudgery in the stable more tolerable than life on the eastern edges of the city. They were hired to bring the horses up to the pasture in the spring, and kept on as alternate day guards.

Rah is working the colt near the western wall today, not far from the shade tree where Ramicus and his men are snoozing. So fixed is his concentration on the animal that he has lost track of the time, and the men are rousing from their afternoon siesta. One of the stable boys has risen first and has spotted Rah on the colt's back, but he is so struck by the sight, having never seen a blonde in his lifetime, that he has said nothing. He is looking over the top of the stone wall, mouth open, when Ramicus stirs, tips his hat back from his eyes, and mutters, "What the hell is wrong with you, Ophos?"

"A boy with yellow hair, he is standing on one of the horses!"

Ramicus' first thought is of the only boy with yellow hair he himself has ever seen. By this peculiar description, he knows Ophos has seen Rah. That the Grain God would be capable of standing on an unbroke horse he has some doubt, although he has seen him walk on his hands with so much alcohol in him he could not have told you where he was. But here? In the King's field of priceless Arabians? Ophos is playing a trick to get him to jump to his feet for no reason. Then he will be the butt of his men's jokes for a week. He keeps his wits and gets to his feet casually.

"Perhaps you prefer cleaning the Queen's latrines, boy, to napping in the afternoon all summer under this tree."

But by now the other boy, brother to Ophos, has leapt to his feet to peer over the wall.

"It's true! What's he doing with that colt?"

Now Ramicus is fully awake, his whole body flushed with adrenaline. He jumps up and shoves the two boys out of his way, and he sees Rah standing on the colt's hip while the colt trots in a twenty meter circle at the west edge of the pasture.

"Crap," says Ramicus, who has seven of his own sons and no end of patience for their mischief. "That, men, is the Grain Dancer of Knossos, keeper of the spirit of Rah, priceless possession of Mochlos of the House of the Moon."

The two older men have now risen as well and are looking over the wall at the boy on the colt. They recognize the little blonde acrobat they plied with wine for the Queen. One of them, the one who did the most plying, looks at Ramicus, then at his partner, and bursts out laughing.

"Better at mounting horses than Queens, eh, Ramicus?"

The others howl.

Ramicus only frowns. "We are in a pickle jar, men."

"How so, sir? What's the harm? They say that he can dance like the

Sea itself. Let us see what he can do on a colt," says one man.

"Breaks up the day, eh?" says the other.

"What's the harm?" answers Ramicus. "I'll tell you the harm. He could get hurt. Kicked. Fall and break his neck. If he gets hurt, we'll have to bring him back to the priest, and what will we tell him? That he was riding the King's horses under our noses and we just watched him do it to entertain ourselves out here, break up the monotony of our day?"

Ramicus strokes his beard, thinking.

"We must not disturb him now, or else he could fall. We must catch him before he leaves the pasture, then we will see what is what."

So Ramicus sends the two older men to the southwestern wall, where Rah is most likely to exit to return to the Villa. He sends the two boys to the northwestern wall in case the Grain Dancer is on his way up Mt. Ida to visit the dead. He himself remains on the western wall to cover all three options.

With his men gone he has nothing left to do but wait and watch Rah work the colt. The boy has been taking little hops while standing on its back. The colt is still trotting in a small circle. Ramicus is more than a little impressed that the colt seems undisturbed by the change in weight as the boy increases the height of his jumps. "You've been on him before," he murmurs to himself. "You've been doing this all summer, haven't you, you little monkey, right under our noses." He shakes his head, thinking of Ameg's warning the night he saved all of their heads by taking the boy's place with the Queen. "Let no harm come to him while he is in your care," he repeats aloud to himself. "Well, this is my post. I am responsible for the field and the horses. And whatever or whoever is in it." He thinks of the heavy coin purse Ameg pressed into his hand the day he rescued Rah, and Ramicus, from the Queen, and wonders casually what Ameg's interest in the boy could be. A financial one, for sure. But the connection escapes Ramicus, a simple soldier who never had a head for business. "He will want to know, in any case, and will no doubt pay for the information."

Suddenly the boy takes a somersault off the back of the colt, landing adeptly on his feet with a little bend in his knees. The colt has spooked but quickly recovers and trots up to the boy. Rah removes the bridle, wraps the reins around it, offers the animal something from his hand. Then he deposits the bridle behind a pile of stones at the northwestern corner of the wall. The colt has followed him, and is nudging his back with its muzzle, no doubt asking for more treats. Rah turns and rubs the length of its head roughly, then moves off toward the north wall behind which the boys are waiting, the colt, uninvited, continuing to follow him, nudging and phlegming his back with its lips.

Ramicus leaves his post to meet them, not sure that two dimwitted stable boys can catch, or for that matter hold onto an athlete of Rah's caliber. But first he whistles for the two other men. They peek over the southern wall and he gestures to them to follow him, then heads for the northwestern corner of the pasture.

He turns the corner and is in time to see his two boys grappling with Rah. He is about a hundred meters away, and as he trots to the melee, notices with some annoyance that the boys are about to lose a two-on-one wrestling match with an opponent smaller and younger than either of them. Each time one of the youths appears to have pinned Rah he twists and spins and is on top. The other boy then attempts a clumsy tackle, only to have his legs swept out from under him or to be thrown by a double kick to the chest, or simply by the momentum of Rah's whirling energy.

Ramicus breaks into a run, closes the distance between himself and the three wrestlers, and reaches down to get a good handful of Rah's pale curls while he is under Ophos. At home he has a houseful of sons, and they fight often. Experience has taught him how to end such conflicts quickly.

"Get off him, you numb skulls."

He walks Rah to the pasture wall, still holding him by a good chunk of curls at the back of his head. The boys follow, berating one another for their ineptitude.

Rah has quieted, like a cat held by the scruff. He allows himself to be tossed against the wall and pinned by the shoulders. He keeps his eyes down. But these are not his betters and he is angry. He has had enough of being tackled by surprise on this island. His jaw is tight with the need to snap at something. He looks down at his own feet, chest heaving. Only a very good ear would pick up the hum rumbling in his throat.

"Rah, look at me," says Ramicus. When the boy fails to do so he shakes him lightly by the shoulders. "Rah, it is alright. No one means you harm. Look at me, you know me, boy."

Now Rah looks up into Ramicus' face, peers at him, frowns. Does he know this man? He looks to either side. The two stable boys are watching him over Ramicus' shoulders with fascination. He does not recognize either one.

"Look at his eyes!" says Ophos. "He's not human!"

"He is a ghost!" says the other.

"He is a foreigner, that is all. A boy, same as you," says Ramicus patiently.

Movement to Rah's right takes his attention. The two other men are walking casually up to the group. Ramicus ignores them. But Rah recognizes these two men, recognizes them and feels a nausea overcome him. He squints, grits his teeth. His head is beginning to hurt.

Ramicus sees the recognition cross his face. He puts up a hand to the two men, who stop in their tracks a few meters away.

"You remember now. We guarded you at the palace. They," he tosses his head at the two older men, "gave you too much wine."

Ramicus is speaking Minoan, a language Rah is still struggling with. But he knows the word for wine. Rah gives the two men a wary look.

"No more wine," he says to Ramicus in Minoan.

Ramicus laughs for the first time and releases Rah's shoulders. "No, no more wine. Just talk." He nods to his men to come closer, just in case the boy decides to try to slip away again.

"No one gave you permission to go near the King's horses, Rah," he begins.

"No," Rah lifts his head at the mention of the horses. His expression lightens. "I go myself."

Ramicus considers this. "Rah, you cannot do this. You break the law."

Rah shakes his head. "No. I teach horse good. I jump with horse."

Ramicus takes a deep breath, blows it out slowly. "You cannot do this," he repeats. "You break the law. You could be punished if the King, or even your own priest, finds out, Rah. You don't want to be punished do you?"

"But you do not tell King. You do not tell Mochlos," Rah says simply. The light of excitement in his face, he looks about at the other men for support.

The four guards standing behind Ramicus look at one another. There is an energy coming off the boy like heat. They rarely get to see the bull jumpers or the holy dancers at the palace although it is part of their duty as palace guards to keep the crowds controlled before and after the performances. This strange golden boy is the best of them, and he is offering them a summer-long performance, on horseback.

"You could be hurt, Rah, and then I am to blame," says Ramicus with a father's patience.

Rah looks at him as if he is an idiot. "Horse cannot hurt me."

Ramicus frowns, looks over his shoulder at his older man, Thymus, the one who poured the most retsina down Rah's throat.

"Like talking to a beet," says Thymus, grinning at his captain's predicament.

"A very valuable beet," sighs Ramicus. "We either take him in hand to the priest, right now, and tell him what the boy has been doing, or we keep our mouths shut and let him work the colt." He scratches the back of his neck, thinking.

"Alright, Rah. You show us tomorrow. But only the colt you've been handling. And only down here on the western end of the pasture. If the men guarding the other three quarters see you, I cannot guarantee they will keep quiet."

Sunlight spilling over Ramicus' shoulder strikes Rah's irises, snapping them suddenly closed and turning his eyes to pure gold. Ramicus steps away. He does not believe the superstitious priesthood, that Rah is the corporeal host of the true Rah, God of Grain. But the golden dancer is eerie just the same. He gestures for the boy to be on his way and for his men to return to their post on the western flank of the pasture. As he follows them he recalls Ameg's words one more time.

"Someone should set a guard on him," he says, more to himself than to the others. "He shouldn't be out here alone."

"Then the grain would wither!" says Ophos helpfully, turning about and walking backward as he addresses his captain. "Rah must be free during the daylight and chained at night. That is the law!"

"Horse crap," grumbles Ramicus. But he is not convinced. He wishes to himself that he had never laid eyes on the Grain Dancer. He wishes the boy had never come to Crete.

CHAPTER 18

Aros is picking up laundry in Rah's chamber. The boy drops things where he stands, seeming to have no concept of order or cleanliness beyond his own person. Aros is dawdling, as

he always does when he is around the boy or any of the things he has been in proximity to. He fusses with costumes strewn about the room and stuffed without thought into trunks. He fiddles with the order of the pots of make-up on the vanity (these are really none of his business but Pyrus has come to expect him to rearrange and dust them off periodically). He stands at the window, playing with a feather collar that smells faintly of cherries, sighing. Aros is miserable. He can no longer keep his dread inside. He can think only of Rah's fate come the autumn equinox these days, and pictures of the boy strapped to an altar on Mount Juktas gagged and tied, torment him day and night. Rah, beautiful Rah, bound to a slab of rock, the muscles in his arms and legs cramping from being trussed behind him for hours on his way up the mountain, all because of a priest's sadistic imagination.

"We have to do something," he says to the yellow and green feathers he clutches in his hands, feathers that hugged Rah's neck the night he played the tiger and still smell faintly of him. He stuffs his nose into the feathers, breathes deep. Cherries. An undertone of lotus and myrrh. But the boy favors cherries and has coerced Tuma to use this oil in his baths more heavily than the sacred ones. Aros is surprised when the feathers come away from his face moist. He blinks away a film of tears.

"Oh, I cannot bear this. The others, they were bad enough. But this one. No." His doughy face becomes fierce suddenly, his soft brown eyes hot. "No. This we have to stop. I would rather," he sobs into the feathers, "go to the mountain myself, my angel!"

A narrow arm slips around his ample waist. Pyrus has entered the room and come behind him, Pyrus, unexpectedly offering him comfort.

"Don't say it, Pyrus," says Aros. "I don't want to hear it."

"Say what, Aros?"

"That we must bear it. That it is our backsides that will suffer if we attempt to interfere, or tell the boy the truth."

"We don't know the truth, Aros."

Aros snaps around. "What is that supposed to mean? That if winter never comes, the boy will live? Does anyone really believe that Mochlos can stop the winter with a slave dancer? Oh, this is all such madness. The world has gone mad. And you with it."

"I only mean to say that he is but the third. Only two slave-gods precede him to the mountain. Neither of them were particularly special, and neither did much for the crops. Look what has happened to Knossos since Rah came here. The city prospers, other cities have no rain, their crops fail. Gournia is battered by sea storms. Pheistos is plagued by mud. Isn't it possible that Mochlos could have a change of heart? Keep Rah on for another spring?"

Aros looks up from the feather boa, his face for a moment hopeful. He purses his full lips together. "I suppose it is possible. But what if they do it again, Pyrus? Snatch the boy from his bed one morning right under our noses, and take him up the mountain like a goat to slaughter? What if they do it to Rah? To our Sunlight? How can you stand by and watch?" Aros begins weeping again, strokes the feather collar in his hands as if it were a housecat. "How can any of us stand it?"

"I don't know that I can, Aros. But there is nothing to be done about it," Pyrus sighs. "Let us think of today, and let tomorrow alone. There is yet time. Much can happen in three cycles of the moon."

"I try, Pyrus," Aros sniffs. "But every time I look at him I see him on that mountain again. I see those eyes of his, so full of pain and fear. And surprise! And the priest standing over him--"

He stops at the sound of quick, light footsteps padding though Mochlos' chamber, at Rah slapping at the curtain of beads to enter the room. The boy is breathless with excitement.

"Dimius say I must have wings! You make wings for Rah, Aros! Big, big!" He stretches out his arms to show how big he needs them. "Can you make wings for Rah, Aros?" In his enthusiasm he has dropped to one knee before Aros, dramatically grabbing his attendant's hands, feather boa and all, in his. He looks up at Aros with peaked eyebrows, pleading.

Aros looks down into his upturned face and lets out a shrieking sob. He falls to his knees and throws his arms around Rah, burying his face in the boy's shoulder.

Rah flinches as Aros' bare chest slaps his, but he tolerates his attendant's embrace, even lifting an arm to return it. He looks up at Pyrus in confusion.

"Why wings make him cry?"

Pyrus is for once stumped. He lifts his hands and shrugs.

"Why wings make you cry, Aros?" Rah pushes Aros gently away from him, holding him by his shoulders. Aros face is a disaster. He is weeping quietly.

"My poor Sunlight," sobs Aros, reaching up to stroke Rah's curls.

"Come, come, Aros," Pyrus has slipped a hand under Aros' arm to bring him to his feet. "It's not the wings, Rah. He's," he frowns as he comes up with a viable lie. "He's had a fight with his lover. That's all."

Rah give Pyrus a quizzical look. Then he looks at Aros and bursts out laughing. "Aros has lover?" He yips with delight, spills himself over his knees, clutching his abdomen, howling with mirth. His peals of laughter get higher and higher until he is struggling for breath and squeaking.

Aros looks down at him with a hurt expression. But he has stopped crying.

"Well, I don't see the humor-" he whines.

But Rah's laugh is infectious and Pyrus has joined him.

"No, it's not very funny," Pyrus says, making a gallant attempt to soothe Aros, but Aros' pique only starts up his laughter again. He turns away, shoulders shaking with mirth.

"What, I can't have a lover?" Aros is looking from one to the other.

Rah has gotten to his feet, still giggling. And then, to Aros' utter bewilderment, he steps right up to him, his giggling dimming to a single chuckle. His eyes are soft, their twinkle of mischief dissipating. He cocks his head at his dresser, and when he speaks, he is so close that Aros can feel his breath on his cheek. His hooded voice is only for Aros, a dark vibration coming from deep in his throat.

"No lover, Aros." He says, dead serious. "Just Rah." He puts an innocent kiss on Aros' mouth. It is butter soft and silken.

"Now make wings," he gives Aros a smile bright with dimples, winks at his dresser, and walks casually out of the room.

It is evening when Rah returns to his chamber to be chained to his bed. Aros is not present, although it is normally his duty to clip Rah's golden anklets, necklace and belt to the thin gold chains hanging from the rings above his pallet.

"Aros not here. Make wings?" Rah asks pleasantly as he reclines on his pallet, making his ankles available for Pyrus to secure. But Pyrus ignores his question. He seems distracted, only half there himself. He fiddles with the fixtures with frustration and distaste.

"Aros is better at this," he mutters. "Quicker fingers. God I hate this nonsense. 'Chained by the golden threads of his father through the dark of the night, that his mother the Moon' blah blah. Hog turds."

Rah is looking at him as if he has never seen him before.

"Oh, I'm sorry, Sunlight." Pyrus has looked up from his work, finished securing the chains. "I'm sorry." He gives the boy a pained look, then ruffles his hair without much energy. Rah continues to look at him strangely. His face is paling.

"Something wrong," he says, his muscles tensing. His irises are pinpoints.

Pyrus has seen this look before. On at least one occasion, it preceded a fit.

"No, no. Everything is fine. Rah? Don't do that. You scare Pyrus."

Rah is unconvinced. He has flattened his forehead, his ears back.

"Where is Aros? Why no Aros? Why everyone is so-" Rah squints at Pyrus, looking for the word in Minoan. "Scare."

Pyrus takes a deep breath. The boy picks up energy around him like a cat. There is no use trying to hide one's fears from him. Hidden, they are even more disturbing to him. But Pyrus straightens up and folds his arms over his chest, determining to tell the boy as little as possible for his own good.

"I just don't like to chain you tonight, Sunlight. I've got a bad feeling. There, I've said it."

Rah is looking at him with distrust. "You do not tell Rah everything."

Pyrus frowns. "We are none of us our own masters, Rah. Not you, not me." He lifts his hands in frustration. "What do you want from me, eh? What can I do? I paint faces. Lucky to be good at that, or else I'd be living on the east end, selling myself by now, I suppose. What do you think happens to an aging bull jumper, eh?" He has never been this mean spirited with the boy but he is at his wit's end. And he has no answers.

Rah's angry glare stops his rant.

Pyrus shakes his head and turns to leave. "You just don't understand what you do to people, baby."

But Rah has snatched his attendant's wrist and pulled him back. He narrows his eyes at Pyrus. "No chains," and offers his ankles to the attendant to unbind. "You take off."

"You know I can't do that, Rah." Pyrus manages to twist free before Rah can take another limb. He backs away, shaking his head. "You know I can't."

"No chains!" Rah shouts at him, his tongue thickening. But Pyrus has backed through the beaded curtain and is running down the hall to find Aros.

A half moon is spilling through the narrow window in Rah's chamber several hours later when Mochlos brushes the beaded curtain aside, careful not to make a sound, and enters the room. He needs no torch. The moonlight has illuminated a slice of the room and is playing with Rah's pale curls. In it, they appear silver, as if the Moon Goddess has taken a delight in painting her son's hair in the colors of her own country.

Mochlos has had no appetite for beating or drowning his dancers since the assassin visited him some weeks earlier. But he has not lost his keenness for the boy's physical beauty. For days he has been plagued in his own bed by his proximity in the next room and by the ease in which he might take advantage of it, had he the sexual prowess to do so. Having never possessed sexual strength or stamina in his body, the priest has long leaned toward his sadistic streak to satisfy his lust for male beauty. Unlike his female concubines, who must tolerate his swift weakness, beautiful males required some force. The pool and the whip had provided Mochlos with a sense of dominance he would otherwise not have, but now, stripped of these, he must rely on the golden chains that tie his victim to his bed.

So Mochlos approaches Rah with some trepidation. He sees the boy is curled up against the wall, his back to the priest's doorway, and he carefully moves around the basin in the middle of the room and eases himself down onto the boy's pallet, attempting not to wake him. He sits at the edge and touches a wisp of curl at the boy's ear. He lifts his hand to touch the boy's golden shoulder, then thinks better of it. He casts his eyes down the length of the dancer's body, which is exquisite. Golden-tan, well-muscled and lean as a leopard, perfectly proportioned broadening shoulders and nipped waist. Mochlos skates his fingers along the ridge of Rah's ribs, his hip and down his exposed thigh.

Rah is awakened not by his touch but by his own shivering response to it.

The priest's fingers are like the scales of a snake slithering along his body, sensuous and revolting at once. Rah takes in a hissing breath through his teeth, turns his head just enough to see Mochlos leaning over his shoulder as he sits beside him on the pallet, and involuntarily spins himself over and flattens his back against the wall behind his bed.

"Gah," he says.

Now Mochlos is treated to the very vision of the boy that has tormented him in his own bed of furs these past few nights. Rah is glaring at him under silvery gold brows, the moonlight creating long brush-like shadows off the tips of his lashes. His eyes are a transparent sea green in the light, the irises dominant. He is breathing his slow, circular dancer's pant, and his chest is rising and falling evenly, calling the priest's hungry eyes to the little golden rings piercing his nipples. The boy's torso is long and utterly naked of excess, as if the thinnest layer of silk, and not human skin at all, were lain over the long-trained muscles. Like six perfectly matched horses in harness, his abdominals bunch and pull with each breath. Mochlos is too enchanted by this vision to hear the hum, the deadly little warning hum, vibrating in Rah's chest.

He must touch. He must have. He must enjoy. Is this not his?

Relying on the strength of the chains that bind the boy, and on his well-known fear of the lash, Mochlos reaches with long, flat fingers to stroke him.

The boy pulls himself even flatter against the wall. Undeterred, the priest bends to nibble and lick at the rings on his chest and Rah makes a little noise of distaste, "Tugh," wincing and turning his head away.

At which Mochlos lifts his head to him. Eye to eye for once, and seated on the pallet together, the boy and his master exchange glares.

"You don't like me very much, do you, handsome?" chuckles the priest. He is sure now, by the boy's tolerance thus far, that he has calculated correctly. He will tolerate this invasion. He will grit his teeth but bear his master's lust to spare himself a beating.

Rah narrows his eyes at the priest, defiantly failing to lower them as he should. The little muscles along his jaw are bunching rhythmically. The hum in his throat is barely perceptible, hardly a noise at all.

"No, you don't like me. But I don't mind that, I'm quite used to it. In fact, I rather like it." Mochlos reaches for the boy again, this time skating his fingers along the length of that fine abdomen and over the golden belt that binds him by the waist to the wall. His fingers find the upper edge of Rah's loincloth. He slips them under the fabric and they feel for the golden brush at the boy's groin.

Rah has pulled his lips back in a silent snarl, but the priest has dropped his eyes to peer, in the weak light, at the golden fleece covering the boy's loins.

He is instantly flat on his face against the rough leather mattress, a panther's strength pinning him there by the throat. Then a tussle above his head and his neck is released almost at the same instant that he feels himself lifted by a hand the size of a bear's paw and thrown clear across the room, back though the curtain and into his own chamber.

It is Rush the Assassin, silently observing the priest from the shadow to the right of the narrow chamber window, who catches the glitter of the boy's pearly incisors in the moonlight and moves before they strike. In an instant the boy has snatched the priest's throat with both free hands and thrown him down on the pallet, then leapt on his back. He is about to drive his teeth into the back of the priest's skull when Rush intercepts him, pushes him off Mochlos with some difficulty, and tosses the priest across the room toward his own door.

In the priest's chamber, Aros is feeling his way along a wall to the opulent bed in the center of the far end of the room. He has not brought a torch, only the butcher's knife he pilfered from the kitchens after dinner. This he stuffed into the hidden pouch he sewed into the back of his skirt that evening while Pyrus was putting Rah into his chains for the night. Now he has removed the weapon and holds it gingerly, in both hands, by the handle, unsure of how best to wield it when he plunges it into the priest's heart.

He had no trouble entering the room, as Mochlos has given up on guarding his door these last few nights. Rumor in the kitchen has it that, as he has had no further nocturnal visits from the assassin, the priest has decided that the killer was satisfied with the goods his man came for last week and that he is in no immediate danger. Either this, or the priest has accepted the obvious fact that there are not enough guards in the Villa to protect him, and that as he will ultimately face the beast alone, there is no point allowing the man to kill them by the handful every time he visits.

The fact that Mochlos has dismissed his guards for a more sinister reason has, as yet, escaped the tender hearted Aros.

But when he reaches the edge of the bed and finds no priest lying in it, a cold claw of horror grabs at his heart, and he instinctively looks up toward the doorway to Rah's room.

There is no sound coming from the room. Suspicious. Rah would be making noise, perhaps not human noise, but noise, if the priest were on him. But there is nothing, not so much as a whimper.

Aros moves around the edge of the bed toward the beaded curtain doorway. He has already determined that he will find the priest in Rah's bed, and pictures himself raising the knife and with all of his might plunging it deep into his back.

But when he touches the curtain, barely tinkling the beads, he is greeted with the force of a catapult slamming into his solar plexus and throwing him back half way across the priest's room and onto the fur strewn bed. He attempts in vain to take a breath and for one terrifying moment, thinks he never will again. Then his lungs respond to his brain and he fills them, just in time to have the air pressed out of them as the flying body of Mochlos falls on top of him.

The priest rolls off him and alongside him on his own bed. There is enough moonlight coming from his own window for him to see Aros, knife still clutched in his left hand, sprawled on his back in the furs.

"I-" Aros stutters," I heard a noise in the hall."

A look of astonishment passes over Mochlos face. This fop came with a kitchen knife to protect him? It seems he has misjudged more than one member of his household this night.

"The assassin!" he hisses at the dresser, nodding to the curtained doorway.

At that moment a heartbreaking mewl, something between a whimper and a growl, rises in pitch behind the beaded curtain.

"Rah!" Forgetting the priest, Aros pushes his chubby bulk off the fur laden bed, the butcher knife still in his hand, and runs toward the noise.

CHAPTER 19

The thing he encounters is a hulking shadow, a mummy wrapped in black muslin. It is standing in the moonlight, its back to Aros, a surreal vision, an over-sized demon, a wingless gargoyle. It is watching Rah tighten himself against the wall at the end of his chains and yowling like a cat in a hot cauldron.

Aros cannot bring himself to approach the horror in the middle of the room. But he is determined to get to Rah. He inches along the wall in the direction of the boy's pallet, his knife in both hands, turned at the assassin.

But Rush has forgotten, for a moment, the priest he has just picked up and thrown across the room with one hand, tossing him like so much grain through the bead curtain and back into his own chamber. He has forgotten, for the moment, why he has come to the villa at all, forgotten as well the man whom, moments earlier, he heard rustling the curtain and elbow-smashed in the solar plexus.

He is watching Rah, who has turned completely wild.

In the moonlight slicing through the chamber window the boy has become a leopard in chains. There is no human recognition on his face, no human sound emanating from his throat. He is a feral animal tethered to a wall. He is crouched on his pallet, his back to Rush, his chest, his palms pressed against the stone. He is scanning the ceiling with wild eyes, as if looking for higher ground, some crack or hole he can hide in, some means of escape from the one who is here to protect him. His savior is his worst nightmare, a monstrous black presence standing at his back, part man, part bull, all wolf.

Rush has been to see Cyrus and has agreed, to the king's great relief, to stop the impending slaughter of the Grain God on Mount Juktas at the autumn equinox. Tonight he came to the House of the Moon Goddess to convince the high priest Mochlos that the boy's death on Juktas, should he as high priest fail to create a reason to spare him, will precede his own by mere hours. Rush came through the boy's window to avoid another encounter with the guards he expected at the priest's door. Tonight he had no need to silence these, as he would not be taking the priest past them. He needed only to visit the man in his bed. Rush did not expect a difficult nor a lengthy meeting. For the priest, it would be simple. Agree, or find your tongue and eyeballs on your bureau in the morning.

But he did not anticipate that he himself would create a problem by hesitating in Rah's room after slipping through the window. He did not consider that he might be mesmerized by the sight of the boy in chains, drooling from parted lips as he slept on his mean leather mattress. And when the beads rustled behind him as he stood there, Rush the Assassin, once again made stupid by his fascination with a simple slave boy, had time only to disappear in shadow.

Aros has made his way half way around the room when the assassin takes notice of him and of the unwieldy butcher's knife held out from his belly like an angry phallus.

Behind the gauze of his mask, Rush blinks, not believing what he is seeing. Then he must bite his own cheek to keep from laughing out loud.

"And you are?" he murmurs with thick, Hittite vowels.

"I-" Aros falters, looks at Rah, who has turned toward his voice, "I am Aros, a dresser," he says. He nods to Rah. "His."

Rush looks from the attendant back to Rah, who seems to be settling down at the approach of his attendant. The rustle of the curtain behind him turns the assassin's wrapped head in that direction. The priest has re-entered the room and is standing timidly against the wall beside the beaded doorway.

"I suppose there is no use rousing the guards so that you might cut them down like so many sheaves of wheat," he says peevishly.

Rush barely acknowledges his presence.

"What is wrong with him?" he whispers at Aros as he turns back to the boy.

"I- I don't know. I've never seen-"

Rah is still straining against his chains, but has stopped mewling. He is looking from Rush to the priest, with love for neither.

Rush shakes his head. "No. I mean to say, what is he?" he whispers.

Aros moves toward the pallet protectively. "He's just a boy," he says. "Just a boy."

But Rush is still shaking his head. "That is not 'just a boy. '" Then he moves to the doorway, takes the priest by the arm and shoves him back through the beads into his own chamber.

He looks at Aros once more before he follows the priest out of the room.

"Put that back where you found it, dresser," he is nodding at the knife. "Before you cut yourself."

CHAPTER 20

Rah awakens to a triangle of sunlight on the wall behind his bed. He is not alone. The soft corpulence of his dresser is pressing him into the wall, and Aros' gentle snore is tickling his ear. Rah looks down the length of his own body to find his attendant's arm draped over him. In his sleep, Aros has tucked him against himself like a favorite doll.

Rah turns to speak over his shoulder. "Aros? Why you are here? Wolf gone."

Aros snorts and blinks awake to see that he has fallen asleep with the boy in his arms. The assassin never came back through Rah's chamber, and must have gone out down the hall. Had he killed the priest?

He lifts himself off the pallet, putting a finger to his lips. Rah nods.

Aros walks gingerly across the room, looks back at the boy one more time, and carefully opens the beaded drape.

The priest is snoring rhythmically in his bed.

"Where this comes from, Aros?" says Rah, lifting a thick fur rug off his legs.

The two look at one another, eyes widening.

"It's the priest's!" says Aros, his own eyes big as a pigeon's eggs.

Rah gives him a look of perplexed innocence. He shakes his head softly.

"No, Aros. Mochlos does not give Rah this fur. Rah-" he mimes his attack on the priest on the bed, grabbing air and pinning an invisible Mochlos to the bed by his throat.

"Rah, say it in Greek. I don't-" Aros starts. "Oh. You attack him." He has drifted into Rah's chronic present tense.

Rah nods. Affirmative.

"Then who-?" Aros and Rah exchange another wide eyed look of realization.

"No the wolf, Aros?" says Rah.

Aros recalls the assassin's frozen form when he first saw him in Rah's room. The man was staring down at Rah as if hypnotized by the boy in chains, panicking at the end of his tethers, clawing the wall for some avenue of escape. His was not the attitude of a killer. Something was clearly wrong with the man, and Aros suspected it was Rah. Advised by his own tender feelings for his charge, Aros is putting together a picture in his mind. The assassin came through Rah's window, found the priest on the boy, tossed him across the room through the doorway, followed him, and yet spared his life. Aros and Rah had remained awake for some time after the man left the room, waiting for a sound from behind the curtain or a revisit. None came, and they eventually nodded off together on the pallet. The assassin then returned and deposited one of Mochlos' finest fur coverlets over them as they slept.

"My god, he came to protect you, Rah. Rush the Assassin came here last night to save you," he turns and points to the priests room, "from him!" He looks at Rah with awe. "The assassin! Saved you!"

"What this means, Aros?" Rah is looking down at the mottled gray fur, probably wolf, and swallows. "This is wolf." He does not look happy. "He is wolf," he murmurs to himself as he paws at the skin.

"It means," Aros blinks away a film of tears, "It means you won't die on the mountain, Rah. He saved you from the priest once, he'll do it again."

Aros is interrupted by the sound of Mochlos' attendants entering the next room, then Pyrus pushing through the beads.

"Aros, what the hell-?"

"Don't, Pyrus, It's been a long night," Aros gives him a warning look and a nod of his head toward Rah.

"Why is there a knife in your bed, Rah?" Pyrus picks up the weapon, "and a fur?"

Aros grabs his arm, pulling him away from Rah, who has thrown the coverlet off the end of the pallet and is kicking at it with his bare feet. "You brought the keys? Give me." He snatches them quickly from Pyrus' hand and goes to release Rah. "Go on. Go to the baths. I'll have your practice things ready when you get back."

Rah hops up from his pallet as if it is on fire and, still eyeing the skin, backs away and pushes through the priest's curtain doorway. There is a moment of silence on the other side of the curtain, then the sound of Rah's bare feet slapping the stones in the hallway as he sprints down to the baths. A murmur is heard from the priest's chamber, and Mochlos pushes through the beads into the room. He gives Aros a sheepish look.

"Yes, I am still in one piece, no thanks to you and your expertise with a kitchen knife." He looks about the room, eyes settling on the fur, and exhales a breath.

Aros immediately moves to waylay his suspicions. "It was here when we awoke, Holiness."

"Well, I didn't think you came and stole it from under our noses while I was entertaining the Prince of Tartarus, Aros." Mochlos looks at him humorlessly and pulls back one side of his mouth in a frown. "He took it last night. Wants the boy to sleep with it."

Pyrus, standing behind the priest, is looking at Aros as if their master has grown a second head.

When no one answers him Mochlos continues, gesturing to the fur. "Why the hell is it on the floor half way across the room? If that infernal beast comes back here and finds it anywhere but on that bed I'll be made into a flag and flown all over the Aegean at the helm of the devil's death ship!"

Aros is at a loss. "He. . . he hates it, sir. He kicked it off."

"Well, kiss the Moon and call me a jackass, he's got to sleep with it, damn it!" Mochlos has put his hands up to grab at the sides of his shaved head. "What have I done to deserve this?" he says to himself, rubbing his pate. Suddenly his eyes lighten with a crafty thought and he turns to Pyrus. "You, you paint his faces, yes?"

Pyrus nods carefully.

"Well then. What has Dimius dreamed up for the Midsummer Celebration, eh? Anything we could add a wolf to?"

Pyrus blinks. "A wolf?"

"Yes, damn it!" Mochlos appears to be edging toward hysteria again. "A bloodthirsty wolf! Find a way to put one in the dance, you see?"

"No sir. I mean, yes, sir. But. . ."

"He is to be costumed as a dove, Holiness," says Aros helpfully. "I am making him the wings today. Perhaps," Aros is feeling more alert than he has ever felt in his life, as if he can see though walls. "Perhaps we can add a wolf, a great hungry wolf, who falls in love with the dove."

"Awful," mutters Pyrus, who is completely at a loss as to what is transpiring in the priest's mind, but has long since had enough of Aros and his themes of love.

"Yes! That's it, Aros! Take the fur down to Dimius. Tell him he must add a wolf to the dance. Make them practice in it. When the boy sees the fur dancing, he will sleep with it."

It is Aros' turn to blink in disbelief. Forgetting his place, he whispers, "My god, that is genius, Holiness." He looks over at Pyrus as if his friend were in on the scheme. "It's true. If he sees the fur dancing, he will no longer fear it. It will become his friend."

CHAPTER 21

Half way up Mount Ida, in the City of the Dead, Rush the Assassin is dispatching with four bodies, two men and two women. He has long held arrangements with the Priesthood of the City of the Dead. He is a generous benefactor. He is also an unholy terror. Every priest who lives and works in silence in the City of the Dead knows that Rush the Assassin will beat them to death with their own bones and bake them in their own furnace if information ever reaches Knossos of his use of their facilities. Every priest knows because one fool priest, a new man, took exception to his practices early on and became an example for them all. He was dismembered, alive, and cooked. His fellow priests then obediently cleaned his bones and buried them.

Now every priest in the City of the Dead is Rush the Assassin's grateful servant. Grateful not to be amongst the bodies it is the priesthood's duty to clean and bury daily. So when Rush the Assassin, clothed in the white hooded robes of a Priest of the City of the Dead, brings four well-dressed corpses, on the backs of two barb ponies to their furnaces, several silent priests immediately make themselves available to him. They assist him in removing the dead from within the rugs Rush has rolled them, cooking and cleaning them, and hiding their bones among the families of Knossos.

After leaving Mochlos to shudder with images of the skin from his back flying on a pirate ship, Rush turned to filter through the household like a ghost and leave the way he had the first night. But something was so filling his head with rage and his heart with pain, a feeling he would one day identify with love, that he stood still at the end of the priest's bed for some minutes.

"I have told you I will declare him sacrosanct, beyond reproach. A chalice of the true Rah. He will not be sacrificed on the mountain. My god, man, why do you stand at my bed like that, why do you continue to haunt me? I have done everything you have asked, have I not?"

But Rush was not seeing or hearing a priest cowering in his opulent, fur-pillowed bed. His mind was in the next chamber, watching an angel and a cat and a boy, all sharing the same skin, straining at the ends of golden chains in a panic to escape the very one who would decapitate anyone who laid a hand on him to harm him.

In this embroiled state, Rush was still rearing over Mochlos like a great bear. He could feel the teeth in his mouth aching to tear out a throat. This he had done on more than one occasion while in the service of the army. The Hittites were fond of close contact, hand to hand. And everything is a weapon to a warrior.

Rush looked down at the plush furs covering the priest's bed and felt his throat close. The boy lay on a hard, friendless pallet with nothing but a deerskin mattress between him and the wood frame. Rush pulled back his lips to speak, unable to unclench his jaw.

"Why do you leave him on that hard bed while you sleep in here like a king?" he growled between his teeth. For once Mochlos had no answer, and Rush waited for none. The moonlight through one window was providing minimal light but night fighting and much night killing had trained his brain to see what he needed to see in half a moon's light. He reached down, one hand sweeping the bed, and he found what he was looking for. Wolf.

"This stays with him." He picked the coverlet up and shoved it at the priest, momentarily smothering him with it. He took it with him back into the rear chamber, found the boy and his attendant sleeping, and tossed it over their legs. Then he left by the priest's window.

Rush returned to his house in Knossos that night, but only to tack up two ponies. While Josepha and his two boys slept peacefully on the second floor he closed the gate quietly and left for Malia, where he had business he had been putting off.

The following night he arrived in Malia, a peasant from Gournia looking to sell goatskin sandals in a richer town. He left his ponies tethered on a hill above the city and spent the day spying, searching for his prey, in this disguise. By nightfall he knew where his victims slept. In Malia, as on most of Crete, the houses had no windows on the first floor for fear of burglars. But this did not discourage or hamper Rush. On Crete it was a common custom to plant flowering and fruiting vines along the eastern walls of one's house, typically against the kitchen wall, above which were the masters' chambers. This gave a good assassin just enough purchase on an otherwise challenging surface. Rush was in his victim's bedrooms in seconds and all but one died before they awoke. That lady was the last. She roused when she heard her husband stop snoring, as if she had been waiting for his last breath for some time. Rush treated her to the frustration and anger that had been lying wait in his veins for a suitable vessel. She and her husband had kidnapped, tortured and sold the virgin daughter of the man who had hired Rush. Apparently they had been enjoying quite a successful business for some time, kidnapping and selling Minoan girls this way to foreign markets.

Rush gave the lady a taste of her own poison before she died.

Then he gathered up the bodies, one by one carrying them over his shoulder up the hill behind the city to his ponies. He wrapped them in rugs, managed a few hours sleep, and rose early to deposit them with the Priesthood of the City of the Dead.

After ridding himself of his burdens Rush releases the ponies to graze and moves down the mountain. He will come back for the animals later, and the priests will be sure they have been grained and watered and groomed when he does. He knows many ways down the mountain, many ways back to the Bridge Road, but he is helpless not to take the path that Rah will take today if he visits Ting Ya. An hour's walk down the path he sees the boy coming toward him and his muscles twitch, his mouth involuntarily filling with saliva, as it did when, during his years in the army, he spied a small herd of antelope after having been fighting without supplies for days. He came this way for this very reason, on the chance to pass the boy, to have proximity to him without frightening him. He is still dressed in the robes of the priesthood, his cowl pulled loosely over his head. He pins it with one hand at the throat as he closes the distance between himself and the boy, who walks alone, head down, kicking stones with sandaled feet.

He immediately picks up the boy's distress. This is not Rah, the boy who, in the past, he has watched walking along this very path, eyes up, scanning to the very tops of the trees for life in the leaves, his face open and pleasant, those maddening dimples bracketing his pearly incisors, his blonde mop of curls brushing his gold silk shoulders. He made a sound then, for he was singing softly, mumbling a little melody, a foreign lullaby Rush thought he recognized. The babyish tune, carried on the boy's dusky voice, seemed to hum through the soft summer air and alight on Rush's belly like fingers reaching to tickled his loins. But today the boy is not humming a lullaby. He is whining irritably. The noise goes up and down, patternless. It is the noise a housecat makes when it is caught in a corner. His own noisy murmur makes it impossible for him to hear Rush's ever silent approach, and when he at last looks up to see Rush, only a few meters in front of him, he takes a little spring backward, squints at the hood of

Rush's disguise, and gives the 'priest' a wide berth.

Rush nods, as would a priest, in the boy's direction, and the boy manages to return the salutation as he takes a few backward steps. Then he turns away, toward Ting Ya's house, and sprints up the path.

There is a pain in the assassin's breast, as if a small fist, perhaps a child's, with the strength of a javelin, has struck him in the sternum. He takes a deep breath, unaware that he has pulled the cowl off his head. He is suddenly hot. He forces himself to continue moving down the mountain toward Knossos, although his hunter's heart pants to turn and chase the boy.

In town he makes a quick visit to the palace, where he hears word that the Queen is pregnant. There is much excitement and gaiety in the halls and as Rush walks back to the north wing to congratulate Nanaea, two of her stewards rush past him, heads together, twittering about her instructions for creating a nursery out of the maid's room adjacent to the Queen's suite. At the palace he also learns of the Midsummer Celebration. Word is, the House of the Moon has changed their program, and Dimius has cooked up a rather provocative tale. Of course, the Grain God will play the lead, and there is talk that he is to be costumed as a bird.

At the Queen's door, waiting for the guard to gain him permission to enter, Rush is picturing the boy in wings, white silk perhaps, and finds himself grinding his teeth. He barely has time to refashion his countenance to that of the popular and gentle Ameg before Pallox returns to invite him in.

"Ameg, what a pleasant surprise!" Nanaea tosses over her shoulder as she hands two harried maids several bolts of brightly colored fabric that had been strewn across her bed. She chases them out, their arms full, and closes the door on them.

"A second visit to my chamber! And this one unnecessary, considering the results of the first!"

Nanaea is in rare form. She is beaming and when her dark eyes alight on Ameg they are burning bright, like two black fires.

"I am happy for you, Nanaea," says Ameg with genuine feeling. "I pray that the child is all that you hoped for."

"Oh, yes, Ameg. She will be. My soothsayers tell me so, and they dare not be wrong."

"I wouldn't put my hopes in soothsayers, Nanaea," he cautions.

"No, you wouldn't. That's because you are a man, Ameg, despite what you pretend to be. And men do not set store in soothsayers."

"Nanaea, the child in your belly is mine. That is the simple truth. And so I must protect it." He turns to look out her window up the hill behind the palace. His shoulder is to her, his head slightly raised. Something is catching in his throat, burning behind his eyes. Where is the boy now? Up on the mountain, taking forbidden treats from Ting Ya? Or is he stumbling up the path, weeping for a cur dog? Or playing with the dappled colt in the kings fields? He is barely sixteen summers. Young enough to be my son. Even if the priest does not slaughter him, he dies. How much time did any of them have, anyway?

"Ameg, what is it?" For once serious, no haughty edges to her words, Nanaea has moved to stand beside him and look up into his face.

He turns to her, puts a hand on her bare shoulder. "Nanaea, I am no soothsayer. But you must believe me now. Thera is dying. The mountain has been steaming for weeks, and her cloud sails half way across the sea to Crete. You are no longer safe here. None of us is safe here."

The Queen is peering into the merchant's face. She studies his eyes and sees that he believes what he is saying. She knows he is a smart enough sailor to understand the moods of the sea, but does he really believe that an eruption on Thera, so many leagues away, could harm Crete? And what is she to do if it does? Move a city? To where?

"Ameg," she says, because she is not one to waste time on argument. "How long?"

"Weeks, months. No more."

She is silent.

"What are you suggesting, Ameg. That I flee, leave my people to fend for themselves, in order to protect your child?"

"Do you think I am giving you a choice?" he answers, the affectations of Ameg fleeing from his face before the man beneath them.

She is too surprised to answer.

"Why do you tell me this, then? If I have no say in the matter?"

"Because you are a Queen, Nanaea, but you are also a survivor, just as I am. With enough time to think it over, you will agree to flee, and let me take you to a safe place to have the child."

"Give it to me then. Leave me," she says, dismissing him like a servant.

He turns to go, thinks better of it. "I am sorry, Nanaea." When she gives him no answer he adds, "I have already moved my assets off Thera."

She is standing by her bed, where only a few moments ago she was happily sifting through fabric for a nursery she will never complete. When she looks up at him, there is no anger in her face, only sadness. "Thank you, Ameg. I will do the same."

That night Rush dreams of the boy walking toward him up the path to the ancient burial mounds and Ting Ya. In the dream the boy is wearing wings, silvery-white. And when he looks up to see Rush approaching he opens them like arms and smiles. In the dream Rush feels something break open, like a cool volcano, in his chest and energy flows out of him. It is something he has needed to be rid of, something that had been trapped in his chest but that now flows easily and with clarity and certainty toward the boy. He walks, then begins to run, down the shallow incline toward him. His face feels strange, pulled in new directions, and a curious foolishness makes him bring his hands to his cheeks to feel the broad smile.

But as he feels for the smile he comes instead upon a snout, long and bristled. His fingers feel for the lips and he cuts the end of his index finger on a row of shark like teeth. He cries out, "No!" but sees that the boy is no longer ahead of him on the path but has sprung into the air, his costume wings have become real and they flap, like those of a falcon at the end of a tether, lifting him high above Rush's head, into the trees.

"Then I will chase you down and eat you," Rush thinks, with dream world logic, and he too springs into the tree from powerful, primeval haunches. He catches the boy's thigh in his muzzle and hears the boy scream, a high pitched whimpering scream, like a woman's pleasure.

And awakens. His wife is whimpering like a kitten beneath him. His teeth are on her throat, he is inside her.

"My darling," she murmurs, clutching his sides.

Rush removes his teeth, kisses Josepha roughly, finding the back of her throat with his tongue, imagining the boy's sweet mouth the day he tackled him in the mud. She arches and moans, accepting him deeper.

He sleeps no more that night, but lies awake reliving the dream. In the early dawn he awakens Josepha, who is cuddled against his side, to ask her if she has ever feared him.

"I have only feared that I should one day never see you again, Antaris, and never know what found you, out there in the dark where you live, and took you from me."

He shakes his head, brow twisted with confusion, gets up to leave the house.

"Antaris, what will you do?" she whispers, sensing his pain.

"I will take him. And I will break him."

"Not this one, Antaris. This one will break you."

His eyes flash at her.

"I am not you, Josepha."

"No. You will never be me, Antaris. But you will be broken all the same."

CHAPTER 22

On the night of the Midsummer Celebration Rah is carried out of the Villa with the other dancers in his troupe in the back of a cart drawn by two strong oxen. The bulls that will be used for the bull jumping are provided by the palace and will be kept in temporary pens in the Great Hall when the jumpers arrive. In Rah's lap, jostled along in the back of the ox wagon, is a cage of white doves that Rah has been allowed to play with for several weeks. This he did behind the kitchens in the company of the dove keeper, who took a fancy to him from the day he arrived at the House of the Moon. Old Galateo had been handling the birds out in the aviary alongside the kitchens that day and when Rah arrived in the servant's dining hall to take his first meal he spied the old man through the open air windows, petting and cooing to the birds. Leaving his supper to go cold, he cautiously padded outside to watch more closely, fascinated to see a man handle and stroke a live bird. It was a thing he had never seen. Galateo, in turn, had never seen anything so achingly gorgeous as Rah. When he lifted his head from his work with the pigeon and noticed the strange blonde boy standing quietly in the dining hall doorway, head cocked like a curious puppy, eyes wide and blue-green as the sea, he smiled, motioned for him to come near and gently handed him the bird. From that day on, Rah found time to visit Galateo before dinner to handle the birds. It was only a matter of time before he was dancing with them.

The birds with him now will be used in the dance, and jumps similar to the one he performed alone in the field where he met the cur, a jump thus far seen only by Rush, will be part of it.

This dance is called The Tears of the Moon Goddess. Dimius has created a story about a boy who could tame doves which, to Minoans, are considered to be the earthbound tears of the Goddess. In the story, the boy's ability to seduce and tame the birds so enchants the Moon that one day, watching him with the birds, she weeps so hard that a flock of doves descends upon him. Vowing to make him a heavenly creature she tears off the clouds that fly alongside her and gives them to him as wings. The next portion of the dance is a display of Rah's ability to dance in a difficult costume while the birds remain perched on his arms and shoulders. But Rah and Galateo have trained the birds to remain motionless when he is moving slowly, and to explode in all directions into the air when he jumps. They then alight on him again when he comes back to a bow.

Aros has fashioned Rah's wings from sheets of silk, white and silver-gray. They are not great domes of stiff feathers rising from behind his back. They are no more than strips of fringed fabric sewn to his gold collar and then attached with string to his biceps and wrists. The fabric moves like a cape, fluttering in feathered pieces that drape to the floor when he is still, but lifts and soars above his shoulders and trails behind him like smoke when the air and energy of his kicks and jumps fill them, thus creating the illusion of wings.

When Mochlos insisted that the wolf skin be used in the dance, Dimius, like any good choreographer, found a way to make the addition improve the story. And thanks to the nature of his lead dancer, the addition gave the story the edge of scandalous erotica it had until then been missing. He had two dancers carry the skin over their heads, the one in front wearing a large and terrifying wolf head mask with huge teeth and bristling hackles. When the wolf sees a boy with wings he thinks, how good this dove boy will taste! He hunts him, but the moon is ever exposing him to the boy, allowing him to run before he can be snared by those evil jaws. But one day, during the new moon when the Goddess is doomed to walk on the other side of the world, the boy fails to see the wolf coming in time and is trapped in his jaws.

During this part of the dance the two wolf dancers tear Rah's wings from his back and the dancer in charge of the head brings the jaws of the huge mask down on Rah's torso. But Rah is not content to merely lie like a pinned dove under the wolf. Even on his back, he is still dancing, and the scene becomes a scandal. As the wolf devours him, Rah uses his entire body, all sinew and strength and grace, to writhe and buck in a seductive dance under the horrid jaws. The audience is rapt.

The stage lighting for the Tears of the Moon Goddess is bright during the scenes when the moon is full, more subdued as she goes to the new. While Rah is writhing under the wolf three other dancers, entirely dressed in black, stand behind the wolf with torches so that the audience can see the action. This lights the hair of Rah's head, and the now sun-bleached platinum hairs on his arms and belly and legs. His entire body is a living torch.

At the end of the dance the crowd is so wild that Ramicus and his men, as well as every other palace guard and available steward, are called into the Great Hall to keep them from storming the floor. When the torchlight comes up (stewards must run about the hall relighting torches that were doused as the "moon" went to new) and the audience has quieted, Rah is sent back out to bow to the King and Queen and their court.

Rush, and Josepha, are amongst them, seated to the very right of the Queen.

Rah steps out into the empty arena from the dancer's entry point at the far left of the hall. Aros has quickly reattached his wings (a second set was made for this purpose, as the first were thoroughly trashed in the last scene). As if on cue a gentle breeze blows through the hall behind Rah, lifting his "wings" about his shoulders and sides. His face is painted white and haloed by short white feathers pasted to his hairline and jaw. His aquamarine eyes are ethereal, eerie and translucent in the ghost white face Pyrus has painted.

Rah arrives before the court and halts appropriately ten meters out from the King's seat. He is glossy with sweat, his chest appears made of glass. His eyes remain lowered until he reaches his destination. Then he lifts them, only for the barest instant, to alight on the King's, then the Queen's, before casting them down to the floor. As if in slow motion, he flutters to the ground in his signature bow, arms drawn back like wings, palms up, his forehead touching his knee, his curls sweeping the dust.

Josepha can hear her husband's teeth grinding. She puts a light, dry hand on his knee, as if to caution him to remain in his seat.

But she does not anticipate what Rah does next.

The boy has turned his head, in position, to the right while still at the bottom of his bow. The King and Queen are still privy only to the top of his golden head. But Rush, and so Josepha, catches the very corner of his face tilting at him. One blue-green eye, shaded by a brush of lynx-long lashes, is fixed on his. One silvery brow is flattened hard against those lashes, the lid is at half-mast. It is a look of absolute hatred.

Before he stands, the boy spits in the dirt in Rush's direction. Then he lifts himself softly to his feet, makes one more, smaller bow to the court, and spirits backward out of the arena.

Josepha has to squeeze her husband's leg to bring him back from wherever his mind has gone. The expression on his face is black. He is no longer Ameg, although he sits among the court. He is Rush, dandy robes or no. And he is full of death. It is like a smell on him, and for a moment she feels true fear for the boy. Then she sees that he is regaining his poise and she settles back in her seat and removes her hand.

She has seen what the boy has done, but to her, a mother of two teenage boys herself, the look was no more than a defiant scowl. An "I will not!" or "Leave me alone!" Apparently to her husband, it is a challenge. And he is too seasoned with much war and murder to take a challenge from a slip of a boy without exacting a high price, even if that boy has his heart.

"He is only a boy, Antaris," she whispers as the crowd erupts with applause once more.

"So I am forever being told, wife," he answers, clapping with the others and smiling through his teeth.

"He wants to see the priest about Rah, about the purchase of Rah, Pyrus! He is taking our Rah!"

"Calm down, Aros, Mochlos has no desire to sell him. No matter what the merchant offers him. Besides, Ameg is a merchant. He has no time for dancers. Worst comes to worst, he will take ownership of half the boy and pay for his keep here, where he can continue to dance with the troupe."

Pyrus, in fact, is nearly correct. Ameg has come to speak with the high priest about an arrangement that the priest himself devised. He has no use of the dancer during the winter months, and his presence on Crete, while the fields are barren, would be a difficult thing to explain. Therefore, he needs a wealthy partner, one with assets elsewhere, in Mycenae perhaps or even in the land of the Hatti. This boy would do well performing anywhere in the Mediterranean with such Nordic beauty. Perhaps Egypt.

Naturally, the first person to come to Mochlos' mind is Ameg, a man with money, stores and homes all over the Aegean, and a man most people believe has a penchant for his own sex. So Mochlos has summoned the merchant to discuss a deal that will both save him from the wrath of Rush the Assassin, and that would further pad both of their already swollen pockets.

"I have reason to keep this Grain God on for another summer, you see. Dispatching with this one on the mountain at the equinox serves me no purpose, does it? Who will replace him in the spring? Some mediocre local talent. And what will the city think if I suddenly cannot produce a representative of the God of this one's caliber? They will decide that the House of the Moon has lost favor with Rah and look elsewhere for him. Something like this comes along once in a lifetime at best and I am no fool. I shall squeeze as much juice out of this golden pear as I can. But what do I do with him in the winter months? He cannot stay here. How can Rah co-exist with winter? No, I need someone to take half his ownership, take him off Crete for the winter months, use him, he is a money maker, and he is twice the dancer he was when he came to me, working with Dimius and Akbar all summer. What do you say, Ameg? You have seen him dance. I have seen you at every performance. Do what you want with him all winter long, just bring him back to me in the spring in one piece."

The two have been chatting in private at table in the priest's courtyard. Only the servants, coming in and out at intervals to fill their cups with retsina (for Mochlos) and mead (for the merchant) and bringing them dainties to eat, have interrupted them. Ameg appears disinterested and has said nothing, allowing the priest to ramble, to try too hard. Too late, Mochlos realizes this. He determines to say nothing more until the merchant has given him some sign of interest.

"I have seen him dance," is all Ameg offers.

"And? You think Crete is the only place in the world that loves beauty, or the only Knossos the only court wealthy enough to pay a fortune for such entertainment?"

Ameg has pursed his lips, as if considering this. But he looks troubled. There is something keeping him from committing to the deal. Mochlos strains to find it. Perhaps it is time for him to appear indignant.

"What? You think I am trying to cheat you, that the boy has developed an illness and will be of no use to you by the time you take possession of him?"

"I hadn't thought of that, Holiness," the merchant's eye flickers over the priest's face as if amused. "Although that is a point. I will want to take a good look at him first. No, I am thinking he must be something of a hellion when he is not dancing. I am not a man who likes conflict, if you understand me. I'm not interested in trying to tame a wildcat for six months out of the year."

At this Mochlos smiles, relieved. "Merely show him a lash and he will be as meek as a lamb, I assure you. Oh I know, I know, it is all over town that he bit the Queen." Mochlos cannot help a chuckle at this image. "Hell, I would have bitten her myself." Then his face becomes serious. "I won't lie to you Ameg, he has a strangeness. Dimius thinks he may have been kenneled with dogs as a child, somewhere along his travel down the Amber Road, I suppose. Idiot barbarians, don't know gold from brass. But even so, he is quite obedient." He looks Ameg up and down as if to make a point. "He will respect you, Ameg, I'll see to it."

Ameg's black eyes seem to have suddenly turned to glass under his gentle brow. Mochlos feels a peculiar chill touch his spine. Then the soft-eyed merchant returns and nods. "It could be a very lucrative deal, my friend. But I don't want damaged goods. I will gain my own assurances that I can handle him. You will give him to me until the quarter moon. I will take him into my own home. I will see for myself whether I want to keep him for the winter. If I can handle him, I will return him to you until the equinox. Then I will take him from you in secret, and return him to you in the spring just as you say. That will make an easy explanation for you. At the equinox, 'Rah has returned to the heavens, he has ascended to his mother. ' And in the spring, 'Rah has returned to fertilize the fields and usher in the harvest. ' We will discuss what is a fair share of my winter profits after I have agreed to the deal." He rises. "Now let me see the boy."

Rah is in at baths, playing with his concubines, when word comes that Ameg the merchant wishes to examine him. The servants tending the priest during the discussion have already alerted Pyrus and Aros of the meeting, and Aros in turn has told Dimius, who sends word to Tuma. It is Tuma's unfortunate job to explain what is happening to Rah, who, if he hears it from anyone but a friend, is likely to earn himself a beating.

Rah is cavorting with Trinadea in the pool when Tuma gestures for him to come to the edge, under the statue of the god.

"Come here boy, quickly. I must speak to you before the priest's men arrive."

Rah gives the water a slap under Trinadea's unsuspecting nose and she squeals and dives under to tickle him in the same place the priest's fingers crept, nearly earning him a mouth full of loose teeth in his head. When she finds what she is looking for, Rah giggles, pushes her hand away and swims off under water. His soaked head pops up at the far end, under the statue of the god and Tuma's great shadow. He cocks his head to look up at the bath master from directly beneath him, water pearling on his eyelashes. He is in a playful mood and grabs one of the African's ankles, attempting to jerk it out from under him. This earns a gale of laughter from the girls, as it always does, for Tuma, it is well known, is terrified of drowning.

"Ah! Bad boy!" Tuma pulls his ankle free and squats at the edge of the pool. "Now come close, I do not want those hens to hear." His skirt is within range of Rah's reach and Rah tips his head to peek under it, and is rewarded with another peal of giggles from the girls, who are watching intently from the other side of the pool. He turns to them, still bobbing in the water, and spreads his arms wide.

"So big!" he tells them, laughing his strangled laugh as they put their hands over their mouths giggling, but half believing him. Tuma's elegant black fingers take him by a shoulder and shake him. "Rah must behave now! Priest's men come to take you to the merchant, Ameg, to be examined! Ameg wants to buy you, boy, and take you with him for the winter!"

Rah blinks up at him as if he has not heard correctly. "Take me, Tuma? Where take me?" The name Ameg means nothing to him, for he has never made the connection between Rush and the name of the merchant. He has come to realize that the man that tackled him on the path to the Bridge Road, and the man who took him down like a deer on his way to Ting Ya, and the man who slaughtered the three who killed Hali, are all the same. He has come to understand that the wolf in dandies clothing who appeared the night he was plied with retsina at the palace, and the man who sits on the right of the Queen in the Great Hall during his performances, are the same man. And he alone, because he senses with a dog's senses, knows that the black clad monster who visits the priest in the night is the same wolf. But the name 'Ameg' he does not know.

"Hurry now, out of the water. Dress. Towel yourself dry, boy, put on a skirt. They are coming."

But there is only time for Rah to slip out of the water naked and to shake himself, spraying Tuma with droplets, before the priest and the merchant, accompanied by two of Mochlos' guards, approach.

Innocent as a doe, the boy, hearing the stomp of the guards and the priest's reedy cajoling, stops in mid-shake and stands waiting for them. It is Tuma who has the presence of mind to consider his decency and tuck a towel around his hips.

Mochlos is, even now, trying to convince Ameg that he would be better served if he let the boy learn of this transaction from his own staff, thus giving him some time to adapt to the idea.

"He does startle easily. Dancers tend to be overly emotional. All of them are. I suppose that's what makes them so expressive, eh? Temperamental lot. This one more so, a bit slow in the head, but not difficult to handle, no, not at all. Just show him the reed, he'll heel alright."

But Ameg is paying him no attention. He walks through the baths as if he owns the Villa, spots the boy at the far end, and struts in his direction without further discussion.

When Rah recognizes him his entire body stiffens. His eyes widen, then narrow. By the time the merchant is a few meters from him he has recovered enough sense to drop that glare, down and to the left, but his jaw is still clenched. His hands are at his sides, but balled into fists. The boy's golden brows are flattened and his ears are back, his face a picture of feline fury. Tuma, standing behind him, has picked up his distress and has placed a hand on the back of his neck to keep him still, or from taking off like a jackrabbit.

"You know this man?" he whispers to the boy. Then clever and empathic Tuma adds, "Perhaps he is your giant, eh? Not too many Minoans this tall."

Mochlos has finally given up his attempt to dissuade the merchant from seeing the boy immediately. He stands behind Ameg, vainly attempting to take Rah's attention and so manage him. But Rah is aware only of Rush, of the wolf who has stalked him relentlessly since he arrived on Crete, first threatening to slice his throat open, then to take him as one would a girl, and now to claim ownership of him.

Rush has walked directly to Rah, to tower over him, arms crossed over the rich fabric of his robe. He looks down at Rah in silence, allowing the weight of the presence of Ameg the Merchant to engulf him.

This is his revenge for that spiteful little spit on the floor of the Great Hall. And it is sweet.

Rah cannot stand long in the presence of the wolf, nor of the richest man in Knossos, before his body begins to tremble. He is making noises in his throat over which he has no control, though he is trying so hard to be silent that he has squeezed his eyes shut with the effort.

The merchant moves haughtily around the boy, as if considering his worth, and Tuma moves back to allow him room. Rush's eyes skate up and down Rah's flanks looking for any sign of a flogging since his first visit to the priest. There is none. He reaches as if to lift the boy's towel from behind and Mochlos interrupts him, suddenly reminded of Rah's reaction to his own curiosity the night the assassin tossed him like a coin back into his own chamber.

"He is intact, of course. Well, he could hardly represent the God of Fertility-"

Rush lifts his eyes and the priest is silenced.

"Of course," says the merchant. "I was there, you recall, at the Dying to the God ceremony, Holiness." He releases the edge of the towel, amused that he has succeeded in further goading Rah, whose cat-like buzzing has thickened. He too recalls the boy's reaction to the priest's advances and knows that Mochlos' brain is in knots, worried that the dancer will react to the merchant the same way. He is enjoying playing with the priest almost as much as he is enjoying his revenge on the boy.

"Ameg has been gracious enough to agree to take ownership of you for the winter months, Rah," says Mochlos. "This will- " he considers how to put it, "allow you to dance for us next spring, you see? Ameg has agreed to take you now, for a few days, to his own household. You must be obedient, you understand? Do as you're told and," this he emphasizes, "try to behave like a human being."

While Mochlos is chattering, Rush has circled the boy and is in front of him again.

"That means no teeth," he says softly, unable to resist tapping Rah's cheek with his finger. Go ahead, he wants to say, snap at me. But Rah only tightens his jaw. Rush smiles with triumph. I've got you, little cat, he thinks. You're mine now.

He is having more fun playing Ameg, the dandy, than he has in some time.

"Very well, Holiness, let us give it a try. He seems docile enough. Have your men bring him to my house after dusk, when the city is sleeping. No point having a riot of admirers at my door, or thieves breaking in the middle of the night to snatch him. Let us keep this arrangement to ourselves," he says, looking around the bath at the priests and servants milling about, "as best we can."

But he cannot resist taking the boy by the jaw, forcing him to meet his gaze, before he leaves him. Those eyes. Those strange, alien eyes. Right now they are reflecting the blue pool water, as if they are colorless glass that pick up the hues that surround them.

Rah seems to have become resigned to his fate. He looks back at the merchant dully.

Finally Rush regains his thoughts.

"I can only take him for a few days, so I will leave you his attendants for now. But if I agree to take him for the winter, I will need more than a talented but brokenhearted dancer. I will need to take his troupe with me to Mycenae. His costumes, his dresser, his face painter, his teachers."

"Well, of course." Mochlos is nonchalant, but secretly delighted that he will be relieved of feeding a score of men through the winter months.

When the merchant and the priest have left, Rah remains where he stands. He is still clenching his fists and his teeth, and even the ministrations of his concubines cannot relieve him of his misery.

In the evening he is taken, on foot, to the house of Ameg by several of Mochlos' men. The streets of the city are dark, lit only by lamplight in second story windows, and their progress is unnoticed. Rah's fair hair is hidden under the hood of a cloak, and the group of men appear to be no more than a contingent of palace guards escorting a woman of some importance to the house of a member of the court. When they arrive at the merchant's compound, two burly black dogs rush at the gate, snarling and barking loudly. They are not the gentle hounds that Rah is familiar with, the lean and obsequious deer hounds he was kenneled with as a child. Nor do they bear any resemblance to the fox-like cur he befriended when he first arrived on Crete. They are like some hellish marriage of wolf and bear, and when they jump onto the iron rails of the gate, lips pulled back to reveal fangs the size of Rah's thumbs, their paws reach over his head.

Rah's knees buckle. When he recovers he spins and leaps backward, very nearly managing to clear the two men standing guard behind him. But the lead man holds a chain that has been clipped to his belt and collar. He jerks it roughly, catching Rah in the throat and taking his breath, and the boy falls back against him. Then he is pulled to his feet and held fast.

Presently the merchant himself appears in the doorway of the house. His frame is back-lit by lamplight and his silhouette fills the doorway. He is alone, and when he whistles through his teeth the dogs instantly rush to his side, tails wagging, muzzles down. They remain beside him as he approaches the gate.

Rah makes a miserable sound as he watches the merchant unlock the gate, but the dogs remain obediently at the man's side, their open, dripping muzzles now panting and smiling as if receiving guests. Rah can focus on nothing else. He is shoved through the gate, the chain handed over to the merchant.

"He is all yours, sir," says the head man. But Ameg refuses the lead.

"That isn't necessary. He's not an animal." He gestures for the man to unsnap the chains from Rah's collar and belt, then lets the men out of the gate and locks it. Rah has remained standing, immobile, head down and shivering. Rush turns from the gate. He takes a moment to look the boy over. The hood of the ladies cloak he is wearing is off his head.

Rush clicks his tongue at the dogs and they abruptly sit, looking up at him attentively. He puts his hand on Rah's shoulder. "Leave it," he says to the dogs. They wag their tails. One drops to lie on its belly, a further show of submission.

Rush makes a quick move with his hand, gesturing to the back of the compound.

"Go," and the dogs obediently trot off in that direction.

Rah lifts his head to watch them go, still trembling.

"They won't hurt you," Rush says softly to him. Then, as a precaution he adds, "Just don't try to go over the wall."

Rush moves toward the door of the house, deliberately turning his back to the boy. Rah hesitates only an instant. His choice is to remain out here, in the dark and alone with the pack, or to go inside with the alpha. He follows Rush's retreating protection into the house and down a dimly lit hall.

At the back of the main house Rah follows Rush through a narrower hallway, past the kitchen, and up a set of stairs. At the top Rush taps a brass bell with a wooden stick. A servant, lean and stooped but nearly as tall as Rush, opens a door and bows. "The room is ready, sir." He moves aside and allows Rush to pass. Rah looks at the servant, hoping for some little nod or wink of camaraderie. But the man's head remains bowed. Rah steps past him into the room.

There is a lamp lit in a corner, and a window opened to the west. A small bed, raised and heavy with clean linen and a sheepskin coverlet, stands against one wall, a dresser and mirror against another.

"Ham will show you the latrine and the bath below," Rush nods toward the floor. He sees the boy eyeing the open window and frowns. "Remember what I told you about the wall, Rah. I can control the dogs when I am amongst them, but I cannot promise you that they will not make a toy of you if they catch you out there alone." He gives the boy a stern look. In reality, the dogs are trained to guard everything within the compound, including people, and will merely keep the boy from scaling the wall should he wander outside. But it is best to let the boy think the worst.

When Rush leaves, Rah is taken to the latrines and then returned to the room and left to himself. He has made no attempt to communicate with Ham, and the servant, in turn, has offered him no conversation. For a long time he stands at the open window, unconsciously enjoying the freedom of not being chained to a bed at night. His sensitive ears have picked up the rustle and blow of stabled horses and he cranes his neck attempting to catch sight of the animals, but the back end of the servant's wing prevents him from seeing where the sound has come from.

When Rush returns several hours later to check on him, he is asleep on the sheepskin, which he has pulled off the bed and thrown in a ball under the window. Moonlight is stroking his curls with silver fingers and a light sea breeze is lifting and scattering them, like loose feathers, about his cheeks.

CHAPTER 23

He is awakened at the break of dawn when something lands hard on his back and pins him. In an instant he is pure panic. He spins, too easily for what he is expecting, pushing a slender leg off his trapped arms and shoving a lithe body into the window ledge before realizing that Tiko is laughing so hard he cannot take a breath. His laugh trills upward like a bird's song.

"Blonde!" he wheezes, holding his stomach. "You thought I was the master! Come to take you like a little slave girl! Hah, hah!" He is still laughing when Rah shoves him hard in the chest, double fisted, slamming him against the wall under the window a second time. But Tiko's mirth is undaunted.

Rah blinks in the sunlight streaming through the window over Tiko's shoulder. Not believing his eyes, he shoves at Tiko again, assuring himself that the Asian is not a dream.

"Tiko, how you are here? You go to Ananou-" He is half annoyed, mostly grateful to have his old rival here with him in the wolf's den.

"Ananou! Screw that old whore! Rush, Master Assassin, Terror of the Aegean, takes him by his old balls and squeezes! 'I will take this boy to teach my sons to fight like Chinese warriors! Best fighting men on earth! This boy is priceless!' And so now I teach his sons, and will go across the sea to teach his sons-in-law. Rush, he has two armies, one for hire in Mycenae, another in Hatti. I teach them all to fight like real men!"

He springs to his feet, punching the air. Even Rah is surprised when he manages to fit a flying crescent kick into the tiny room. He brushes the opposite wall with a sweep of toes, his enemy the shadow made by Rah's head in the sunlight.

Rah is still on the sheepskin. He rubs his eyes, gets up, unwilling to give Tiko further attention. He turns and leans out the window, cranes to see the back of the compound in the morning light.

"I hear horse last night, Tiko. Wolf has horse?"

Tiko, who has been hopping on his toes like a boxer and punching the air, relaxes and walks to the window. The boys are the same height, both beautiful, yet a study in opposites. Tiko's straight black hair is braided tightly in a single tail behind his head to mimic his new master. It shines like a crow's wing. His single-lidded eyes are exotically tilted, black pearls. Rah's head is a mass of smoke-soft platinum curls. His eyes are green in the soft morning light.

"How can you call the master 'wolf'?" Tiko shakes his head. "You are so stupid, Blonde. What a thick head." Tiko raps his knuckles against Rah's temple. "I always knew you were an idiot."

Rah frowns at him, batting away his hand. "Shut up, Tiko! You walk right into wolf mouth. You stupid!"

"Ah, hah!" Tiko pokes his arm. "You are jealous! I will teach the master's sons to fight! What will you do, eh? Cheer up, Blonde. Not so bad, to be Rush the Assassin's concubine!"

Rah can take no more goading, least of all this kind. He pivots, shoves Tiko half way across the room and leaps on him.

They have been wrestling for several minutes when Ham comes in. Tiko, who is at the moment on top, quickly hops off Rah and backs away. Rah, who is still on his back, looks up at Ham from the floor, then at Tiko.

"The Master will have you go down to the kitchen and take a meal, Rah."

He steps out and closes the door softly behind him. Rah is still blinking in confusion.

"Why you stop?" he says to Tiko.

"Because I am not a stupid Blonde. The master knows I can kill you with my bare hands! So he says, 'do not fight with Rah. Rah is no match for you.'" Tiko shrugs. "A good warrior obeys his commander."

Rah frowns at him. "Big talk, Tiko." He makes crocodile jaws with his hands, opening and closing them. "Big mouth."

"After you eat, I meet you in the gym," says Tiko, ignoring the jibe.

"You come." Rah offers, suddenly meek. He does not know what to expect when he leaves what he now feels is the safety of his room. The thought of the wolf pacing about as he tries to swallow a meal makes his stomach turn over.

"I am already up an hour while you sleep, lazy Blonde. I have eaten. But I will show you the kitchens." Tiko pretends to offer him a hand which Rah foolishly reaches for, a dancer's habit. Tiko slaps away his hand and pats his shoulder, rolling him back onto his rump.

"You are so slow, Blonde," he teases as Rah bounces to his feet to follow him.

When Tiko and Rah enter the kitchen it is empty but for a stout cook, a cook's helper, and a large ginger cat who is helping itself to a plate of scraps on the floor. It is a large sunny room facing south with a row of ovens under large open windows on the far wall. At the west end is an archway leading into a room much like the dining hall in Mochlos' villa with parallel tables and benches filling the room perpendicular to the doorway. Another archway, on the east end of the room, appears to be decorated more expressively and meant for the master and his family.

But all Rah can see is the stable at the very back of the compound, behind a garden, a neat yard and a small area for livestock. The horses he heard from his room are finally visible to him from the windows over the ovens. They are barb ponies, dun colored, husky pack animals, like the ones he trained in Gaul, and later, Illyria.

Used to moving about at the priest's villa as he likes, he drifts toward the door leading out to the yard. The cook, who is preparing a morning mash that will be fried into cakes, looks up from his work and shouts, "No, no, you cannot go out into the ladies garden, boy!" But when Rah turns his attention to the man, the cook stalls, straightens up, his hands dripping mash over the mixing bowl, and stares, open mouthed.

"This is the Grain Dancer, Janus. Don't look so surprised. They all look like this in the far north." Tiko is shaking his head with disgust at the cook's reaction to Rah. "Eat and come up to the gym, Blonde, so I can make an example of you for the master's sons."

Rah looks back at him and nods, although he has no idea where to find the gym. A gymnasium? In the wolf's house? The cook, and now his helper, stand transfixed by Rah's appearance, their work momentarily forgotten.

Rah looks from one to another, as ever innocent of his effect on people. "Why cannot go?" He says carefully, word by word, in Minoan.

To the cook, who is born and bred Minoan, Rah's accent is a singsong northern lilt. It is hard enough to decipher the Minoan in it. But the boy also speaks as if his own tongue is in his way, and the man can barely make out the question. He leaves his bowl and walks up to Rah, pointing with a mash-caked finger out the window. "Do you not see the lady of the house in the garden?"

"That is lady of house? Not dress like lady. She dress for servant."

The cook is staring at Rah's mouth.

"What is wrong with your tongue, boy?"

Painfully used to this question, Rah gives him a bored blink and shrugs. "I bite it off. Fit." He then pushes his way out the kitchen door into the garden before the cook can think to grab him.

Josepha has sensed the boy's golden presence through the kitchen windows. Like a ball of light entering a dark room, he is impossible to miss. She is at the dovecote by the west wall, leaving grain for the birds. She waits for his approach, light feet padding the moss (he has forgotten his sandals) to stop two meters from her. A soft, tickling flower of energy reaches her. My God he is lovely, is the first thing she thinks to herself, although she has not yet raised her head to regard him. She is holding a dove in her hands, turning it over to check the ring on its foot for ownership. When she looks up, she will not allow herself to stare. She will be ready for Rah.

"This one is not mine," she says. "But loves my garden." She lets a moment pass. Then, "Someone is missing him." She looks up to allow her eyes to alight, like doves, on the boy's.

He is standing as still as a deer, his head cocked, his eyes gold-green in the morning garden, fastened on the bird in her hand. Now she can take him in. Softly, she turns the bird back over, makes a single gentle stroke of her fingers down its feathers, and opens her hand. The dove merely descends to the ground to peck. Rah's pretty eyes follow it. You are a pastry, she thinks, and Crete is a land of hungry children.

Rah is making a cooing sound from deep in his throat, his lips barely parted. He watches the bird. The dove wanders toward him, pecking the ground.

He giggles. Looks up at her. The flash of his blue-green eyes, now invaded by sunlight, cause her to take in a sharp breath, despite her precaution.

But Rah is incognizant of it. He smiles at her, dimples exploding on his cheeks. He drops lightly into a squat, stretching out one arm to the bird. He makes a different dove-sound, rolling and changing the coo ever so slightly as he watches the bird. The animal hops on his wrist, pecks his forearm, hops down to peck between his legs.

Rah looks up at Josepha from his haunches, squinting in the bright morning sunlight. He shakes his head. "This the priest bird. This Galateo bird. This bird does not come home for days, then," he snaps his fingers, "he is back."

She smiles down at him, surprised at the husky darkness of his voice. It is an unsuspected voice coming from such a bright face.

"And does the priest miss his bird?" she asks him softly.

Rah makes a little pout. "Priest does not miss bird." He looks back at the dove, pecking in circles between his knees and cooing contentedly. "Galateo miss bird."

She smiles. "It would be hard not to miss such a beautiful bird."

Rah rises effortlessly from his squat, the bird forgotten.

"Cook say you are lady of house!" He steps toward her casually, without deference. The scent of cherry blossom and myrrh, her favorites, advances with him.

"I am Josepha," she says, offering him a small hand. Everyone must want to touch you, she is thinking. I want to touch you.

He takes her hand.

In a clearing in her mind, she sees a vision, hears men shouting, smells battle fire. A dirty and foul smelling man, his face a thicket of matted hair. He wears a horned, bowl-shaped helmet. He storms into a thatched hut with a fighting blade in his hand. He is growling like a bear. A woman screams. She is young, barely twenty, lithe and delicate, golden haired. Beautiful. The boy's mother. The man shoves past her into the small dirt-floored room, overturning a table upon the edge of which a bassinet is set. There are two pale heads in the basket! One topples out on top of the other. The man picks one infant up. A boy. Holding it by its ankles he lifts it into a spin, smacking its skull against the edge of the overturned wood table. The woman screams again in anguish. She throws herself at the convulsing body of the child. The man throws his blade down and grabs the girl by her thick blonde braid, which is so long it nearly sweeps the floor.

The vision dissipates.

Rah has made a light bow, her hand still in his. The bow is greater than necessary for the station he believes she holds, far too casual for the station she in fact does.

"And you are Rah," she smiles back at him. "Good morning, Rah."

"Good morning, Josepha," he says slowly, mimicking her accent.

"That's very good, Rah. What other languages do you speak?" She takes his forearm and begins to lead him toward the chickens.

"I speak Greek," he says proudly, "Illyrian, Gaul, little Minoan." Then, suddenly freezing in his tracks, "Where are dogs, Josepha?"

His fear is palpable. She can feel the muscles in his forearm harden to stone.

"It's alright, Rah. The master takes them up into the wood to hunt for hare and grouse in the morning whenever he is home. They will be gone for a few hours yet."

He searches her face for truth, decides to believe her, relaxes.

"He won't let them hurt you, Rah. Come, help me gather some eggs for breakfast. We have a fat white hen. She is a good layer. We will find two fat white eggs under her for Rah," she cannot help but pat his arm as they walk together to the chicken pen.

"Rah can only eat egg from white hen, milk from white goat," he agrees, apparently pleased that she understands his limits. "No meat," he continues. "Only white fish."

In the coop, she does indeed find two white eggs under a large white hen. "These are for you, then," she hands them to him. "Now come in and we shall have the cook boil them for you."

But when she turns to return to the house Rah stands his ground.

"Wolf has horse," he says, lifting his chin to the stable at the back of the compound.

"Wol- ? Oh! yes, Rah, the. . . wolf. . . . has two horses. Ponies. But," she reaches to take his arm again and thinks better of it. "Perhaps you should call him the master while you are here. The. . . wolf. . . is also the master." She must tighten her cheeks to keep her smile to herself. Oh yes, he is quite the wolf. Was he hired to kill you when Knossos' fields began to flourish? Cyrus, no doubt? But he couldn't, could he. She sees an image of her husband holding a blade to this golden throat. No, he couldn't slice through that. Not likely. He must have felt that he was drowning in those eyes of yours. What a surprise for him to fail at what he does so well. And that is your hold on him, isn't it, Rah? That is his fascination for you.

To Rah she says, "You want to see the horses."

He nods.

"Well, you had better not go near them without the master's permission. He allows no one in the stable without him. Not even Philip and Quintus. I think. . . it is best that way." She does not voice her suspicion that there may be more of her husband's work in the stable at times than the two pack horses.

When she enters the kitchen, with Rah close behind her, the cook and his helper turn from their work and bow.

"Madam," says the cook nervously. "He walked right through the kitchen into the garden. I tried to stop him but," he lifts his spatula at Rah, "you see how he is."

Rah is blinking at the cook. By the time Josepha has turned to him he has dropped to his knees, his curls scattered over the tiled floor. He makes no attempt to rise.

She bends to touch his shoulder lightly. How silken his skin is. Her fingers brush across his back to rest on the top of his head. She sees the bassinet crashing off the table again, sees the man take the babe by his chubby little legs and swing him in an arch over his helmet.

"My God," she whispers aloud, "how did you survive?"

Rah has not moved.

"It's alright, Rah. You've done nothing wrong. We are friends now, so it is no matter whether I am a lady or not, is it? We are already friends." When he looks up at her she is smiling at him. She taps his head. "You remember this. Friends." She looks over at Janus with a less-than-pleased lift to her brow. "If that is alright with the cook."

"Madam," says Janus, bowing lowly, his spatula still raised in his right hand.

Josepha extends a hand to Rah, which he takes as he rises to his feet. She puts the hand he has given her to her breast.

Horses. Pounding hoofs. My God, so fast! She is standing on the backs of two roan mares, a treble of mares race alongside. She is performing for the barb horsemen. The five mares are flank to flank, moving together without tack. She controls them by a double set of reins attached to bit-less bridles on the two center mares. They turn together in harmony. They jump a stand of brush in harmony. A felled tree. She cannot fall. She and the horses are one. She is their heart.

"You will continue to call me Josepha."

"Josepha," says Rah shyly.

"Boil these eggs for Rah, Janus. Here," she takes the cook's spatula, a plate from a stack at the end of the counter, scoops two cakes off the stone in the oven. Ladles a generous spoon of honey over the cakes. She hands the plate to Rah, motioning for him to go and sit down in the servant's dining area. He flinches from the offering. He has never been served by a lady. But when she presses it at him again he bows low and then takes it.

"Now go eat," she says, "and then I will tell you how to find the gym."

When Rah arrives there, Tiko is demonstrating blocking and punching techniques that the twin sons of Rush the Assassin have never seen. Philip is convinced that punching without a roundhouse swing is useless. Quintus, the more studious and docile twin, is eagerly soaking up everything that Tiko demonstrates, determined to use these moves on his sometimes arrogant and bossy brother.

"No! Like this! Like this!" Tiko's voice is as quick and sharp as his movements. Rah cannot believe that he is speaking to the sons of the assassin in such a manner. But more disturbing than Tiko's training tactics are the boys themselves. They are images of their father, softened backward in time to puberty. And they are identical to one another.

Rah stands at the archway of the gymnasium. He is bathed in buttery morning light pouring over his shoulders from the clerestory windows above. He is paralyzed by the image of the assassin's identical twins, whole and healthy and together as all twins should be.

He has never hated the assassin more than at this moment.

He blinks reddened eyes, swallows under the invisible chain that is tightening around his throat, and begins to step backward away from the scene. He will have nothing to do with this. Better to be eaten by the dogs when they return than to tolerate another moment of the hot pain that has exploded in his heart.

He is unaware that he is backing into Rush, flanked by the two very dogs he expected to meet at the wall.

What he feels first is the silken cloth of Ameg's robe against his bare back, for Rush had little heart for grouse and hare this morning, knowing that a fine dove roosted in his very house today. He came back from hunting early, watched the boy and his wife in the garden from his own bedroom chamber above the kitchen, and dressed as Ameg knowing that he must meet a ship from Thera at the harbor that afternoon.

Rah feels two large hands settle on his biceps. It is not the Queens greed, nor a guard's callousness that he feels in them, but the things they say to him are less welcome than either of these. They rest on his arms gently, huge, protective, absolute, denying him an exit.

Then the assassin speaks over his head.

"Where are you going, little cat?" The burly voice is amused. Rah attempts to take a step forward out of that grip, is unsuccessful. His body hardens. The dog to his left strokes a wet nose across his thigh possessively.

By now the twins, always alert to their father's presence, have spotted the movement in the archway. Their attention is completely diverted from Tiko, who stands where he has been demonstrating a proper inside punch. The boys are walking over to their father, who seems to have brought them yet another amusement from his travels.

"What is he, Papa?" says Philip.

"Is he ours?" asks Quintus.

Rush gives Rah a little push forward toward them. Rah stumbles, steps back into Rush, at this point the lesser of evils.

"These are Philip and Quintus, Rah. My sons." As if it were necessary to identify his two likenesses. Rah drops his eyes, down and to the left. He has, at least, ceremony to fall back on.

Rush tugs a lock of curls at the nape of his neck playfully forcing his head back up. "No, you will treat them as you do my wife," he bends to put this last softly against the boy's ear, "with whom it seems you are quite comfortable."

Rah reluctantly looks up at the boys, who are taller than he though far yet from their father's height.

Philip is grinning ear to ear. Quintus looks startled, then spellbound.

"Look at his eyes!" says Quintus.

"So who do you think he is?" Rush asks them.

"It's the dancer! The Grain Dancer!"

"The Grain God!" they say in unison.

"Why have you brought him here, Papa? Is he ours now?"

"He is a visitor." Rush pats Rah's shoulder. "And he can wrestle like no one I have ever seen. Like Tiko, he is here to show you something new." Then he pats Rah's cheek. "But no teeth."

Philip has already grabbed Rah's arm. His brother takes the other and they both begin a thorough interrogation as they half-lead, half-drag him between them toward Tiko.

"Where did you come from?"

"They say you were born of a woman and a tiger! Is it true?"

"They say you can jump like a panther! Will you show us how?"

"Can you really bend backward and touch the ground with your fingers?"

Rush reluctantly turns to go. He takes a step out into the hall, thinks better of it, peeks back around the archway wall. He is not concerned for his sons. Philip already has Rah in a rough embrace as he leads him toward the center of the gym floor. He will dominate but he will not break his new toy. Quintus, the sensitive one, is probably already half in love with the superstar he has heard much about but never seen, a boy with the eyes of a cat and the compact body of an acrobat.

It is proud and ambitious Tiko that Rush is concerned about. Can he keep his jealousy under control?

"Tiko!"

"Sensei!" Tiko makes a full half turn toward Rush and snaps to attention, making his idea of a proper military bow.

"He is a dancer, not a warrior. You are responsible. I leave him with you in one piece, I expect to find him in the same condition."

"Hei!"

Rush must turn away before Tiko sees him shake his head and smile.

Several hours later he returns from his business at the docks and goes up to check on the boys. He peeks in just as Tiko is executing a series of flying spins and kicks in the center of the arena. The display is all show for it is far above the abilities of the two students he has only just begun to work with. It takes Rush only a moment to see why the Asian is wasting his son's time with such nonsense. At Philip and Quintus' urging, Rah gets up from his seat on the sand floor and walks to the center of the arena. He stops, head down, takes a few panting breaths, and proceeds to perform the very same routine, with higher jumps, more extended kicks, and a lighter landing. He has turned Tiko's series of sharp and aggressive martial art moves into a dance, powerful, sinuous, elegant. When he has finished, he walks over to punch Tiko in the arm.

"More strength, mean lightness, Tiko," he says in Greek. "Rah in air longer, but move slower." He is not bragging, his face is soft, conciliatory.

Tiko frowns, shaking his head. Philip and Quintus are hooting and clapping. They jump to their feet when they see their father, pointing at Rah.

"Did you see that, Papa?" says Philip.

"Wasn't it beautiful?" adds Quintus.

"Hah, maybe pretty, but not deadly," says Tiko.

"Tiko is right," says Rush from the archway, his arms crossed. "But wrong to show my sons these things. You teach my sons to raise their legs like that on a battlefield, Tiko, and I will have no grandsons," he moves toward the Asian, his brow hard.

"Yes, Sensei!"

"Leave the spinning kicks for dance. Not battle. No wonder Rah makes it prettier." He strokes a glance down Rah's body. "That is his job."

Rah's face has turned to marble at the approach of the assassin. He tucks his chin.

His eyes still on Rah, Rush asks Tiko, "Have you taught my sons anything that can save their balls today? Or do I feed you for nothing?"

Tiko nods at Philip. "Show the master what you have learned, please."

Philip executes a few simple punches and blocks, then a turn and inside jab meant to crush an opponent's windpipe. Quintus follows.

"Good, you eat tonight," Rush winks at Tiko, the corner of his mouth turning in an abbreviated smile. "Go clean up now," he tells his sons. "Show Rah the bath, Tiko," and Tiko makes an abrupt bow and grabs Rah's arm.

On his way out, when he thinks the master is not watching, Tiko gives his rival another poke.

CHAPTER 24

Media is walking in the Hall of the Kings. She has only a torch to light her way, and the ghost of her mother, a gray shade moving like an agitated smear in the dark ahead of her, to guide her.

Media is the Queen of Cyrus, and the Queen of Cyrus is mad. But Media can hear the voices of the dead in her dreams, mad or no. Media goes down to visit the bones of the kings under the palace on each new moon. She carries only a torch and a scrying bowl, and returns with the future.

Tonight her mother's specter is more agitated than usual. She moves from left to right along the corridor, as if bouncing from one side of the narrow passageway to the other, twenty or so paces ahead of Media. She chatters, like a leaf scraping stone, in Media's head. There are no words in her chattering. She was insane during the last decade of her life, the only decade Media remembers. She is equally insane in death. But she leads Media on each night of the new moon through the hall of the kings, to the sepulcher of Heritas. And she speaks, through the scrying bowl, to her daughter.

Media could not have found the tiny room herself. The hall of the kings is a maze beneath the arena of the great hall of Cyrus and few have visited it since the last flood. Few now even know of its existence, for kings are buried now beside their queens, in the hills above the city, in these days of feminine monarchy. Few remember now that the kings were blamed for the flood, two hundred years ago, the kings and their bloodthirsty wars. And so now all of Crete worships a mother god, and the god of war is forgotten. And Queens rule all of the cities.

One night in a dream Media's mother showed her the entrance, which, when she found it, appeared no more than a forgotten cellar behind the pottery mill. Media's mother told her that the secret of the kings was buried there with them; that the kings brought on the flood not by war, but by greed. When Media entered the forgotten tombs she found them filled with bronze and gold and silver, proving to Media that Cyrus had no reason for envy. But when she set the scrying bowl on the sepulcher of Heritas, the first King of Cyrus, there formed in it a watery vision of a bountiful harvest in the fields of Knossos, even then, rival to Cyrus. And in the water vision Media saw the last true King of Cyrus hire an assassin to kill Knossos. Then the sea became wild, because the sea loved Knossos, and it rose up, and swept over the cities in the north, destroying all but Knossos. And earthquakes plagued the island, making it impossible to rebuild the cities, until Heritas died. Then the people of Cyrus condemned the King and turned to the feminine deity, to the moon, who governed and soothed the sea. They elected priests to the moon goddess, and determined that there would be no more kings, only queens, in Cyrus.

Gradually people forgot the truth. They allowed the queens to marry and to call their husbands kings. But these new kings had no power, except to execute the will of their queen. As the cities of the north began to rebuild, they too adopted a matriarchal kingdom, and a supreme mother god.

Now Media has learned that a new flood, far more terrible than the first, is coming. This flood would come with fire and ash and darkness, and wipe out all of Crete, unless the Grain God of Knossos, son of the Moon, was protected.

Her husband has assured her that he will be.

But she is not convinced.

Now Media's mother leads her daughter down the hall of the kings one last time, to show her a final vision. Media reaches the sepulcher of Heritas and places her scrying bowl on the tomb. Her mother's shadow shrinks against a far wall in the little room, a gray mist, waiting. Media speaks her incantation, and looks into the bowl. But there is only the reflection of her torchlight.

Until her mother's specter screams.

Media looks up, and sees a halo of yellow light forming against a corner of the little room. In it is a golden haired boy, trussed and convulsing, lying in a pool of blood against a blood spattered wall. Media peers through the yellow halo at the vision. Where? When?

On the wall above the boy's pale head is a mark. A family seal. It is a goat in a pentagram. It is the family sign of her husband's uncle, Lutarus.

In the evening after a bath, and a meal with the servants in the western dining room, Rah returns to the servant's quarters. The sheepskin he slept on the night before is back on the bed. Another, one twice that size, one now lies on the floor under the window. Rah moves about the room in a circle, to the window, the bed, the door, the dresser. Back to the window. He is pacing like a thing in a cage.

Despite the dogs, the open window beckons. He would prefer his chains tonight.

The vision of the assassin's identical sons, whole and together, clogs his mind. A longing so powerful that it threatens to steal him from his own body has settled in his breast. He feels around in his mind for his own twin, but she has withdrawn. He cannot find her. Without realizing it, he has sunk to his knees on to sheepskin under the window. He has wrapped his arms, tightly, around his own abdomen, as if attempting to keep something inside. His fingers dig into his sides. He folds over his knees and drops his forehead to the floor. A single embryo. And silently, with only the dog-like sounds he cannot keep from making in his throat, he weeps.

Ham has come to the door with a fresh loincloth skirt for tomorrow when he sees the boy drop to his knees clutching his abdomen. He backs away quietly and pads quickly down the west wing stairs to find Josepha. If the boy is ill, she will want to know.

He finds her in her sitting room in the east wing. She is weaving in lamp light, but turns from her work the moment he enters the room.

"What is it, Ham?" She jumps to her feet. Quintus is sitting cross-legged on a richly colored rug in the center of the room, playing a flute. And Philip is whittling a piece of wood into a shape with a small, sharp knife his father brought him from Anatolia. Her family is whole. But her heart is breaking, cracking in half like an egg.

"It is the boy, Madam, he appears to be ill. He . . . rocks on his knees at the window as if poisoned." It is the best Ham can do. He has seen poisonings. Yes, it is just that way with the boy.

"I will go to him," she says, dropping her weaving bow to the floor.

She finds Rah where Ham had left him, kneeling on the sheepskin under the window, his arms still clutching his abdomen, his head to the floor. He is whimpering like a lost puppy. He does not seem to be aware of her when she comes to kneel beside him on the sheepskin.

Her heart wants to speak, her hands, to take hold, to comfort. But she steels herself. She sits back on her heels and waits, and slowly, the whimpering subsides. He picks up his head slightly, aware that someone has entered his space, but does not turn it. But he remains in his fetal ball.

She lowers her torso over her thighs, tightening her shift into a cocoon around her. She cannot match his flexibility, and her own physique becomes her obstacle. But as best as she can she forces her body to conform to his. She clutches her abdomen and bends to rest her forehead on her knees. She turns her head to him in that position and waits.

He turns his head towards her. His eyes are gold shot emeralds set under his too-pale brows. A look of confusion passes over his face. He blinks. A crystal tear falls from a lash onto the sheepskin.

Sweet child, I know, she wants to say. I know what it is to be an orphan, to lose one's parents, one's siblings, one's people. To be lost in a sea of strangers, in the land of one's enemies. I know.

But she does not speak. She remains, though her body is beginning to scream for adjustment, in position, mimicking his embryonic ball.

Twins.

Presently he lifts his upper body, sits back on his heels, tips his head at her.

"Josepha?" He stretches out one long fingered hand, strokes the flat of his thumb under her eye. His touch is electric. His thumb comes away wet. "Why you are crying?"

She returns his gesture, sweeps a thumb under one of his brilliant eyes, allows the backs of her fingers to rest on his cheek a moment. "I am lonely, Rah," she says.

"How you are lonely? You have home." He sweeps one elegant arm across and behind him, toward the interior of her house. Every move he makes is dance. "People."

She makes the same gesture, sweeping her own short, plump arm behind her. "But I have also lost a home." I have lost all that is behind me, she is saying. All that you cannot see. "And a people."

"Oh! Wolf take you, Josepha? Away from home?"

"Come here, Rah." She opens her arms to him, and after a brief hesitation, he allows himself to be embraced. She slides her knees across the sheepskin so that she is alongside him. She pulls him in, presses his head to her shoulder. You're only a child, she thinks.

"Who do you cry for, Rah? You had a twin, yes? A sister?"

He coughs, takes a hard little breath as if his throat has closed. "I think I have sister. I am child when she die." He lifts his head. His face is inches from hers now. Her maternal feelings are strong for him, but the proximity of the embrace, the scent of holy oils heated by his silk skin, are making her head light. And his eyes are not a child's eyes. Not by far. There is heat in them as well. She begins to untangle herself.

"I see her in dream sometime," he says in his dusky, strangled voice.

She has begun to lean away from him, and seeing her do so he sits back on his haunches as well. The loss of his proximity is palpable, as if he has somehow rent a hole in her chest and is pulling energy out from it. Her head is spinning. She begins to bring herself to her feet, but he is on his, taking her arm before she can do so, helping her up as if rising to one's feet was a piece of art one must perform with grace. When he lets her hand go her head spins so violently that she must take a step forward to avoid falling.

"Well, that's pretty."

Rush is leaning against the edge of the door, arms crossed over his chest, watching the scene. When his wife looks at him, one corner of his mouth turns up in a sardonic smile.

She looks back at Rah, whose elastic body has become rigid. The child-soft face has been replaced by a look of wary hostility.

She walks toward her husband. When she is under his chin, at the doorway, she looks up at him and whispers, "You are a bull in a pottery, Antaris."

He looks down at her, eyebrows raised. "I may be a bull, dear wife, but that is no clay pot."

"Perhaps not, but he is fragile. It will not serve you to shatter him." She gives him a pleading look before she makes her way through the door.

"I don't mean to shatter him, Josepha," he calls after her, then turns to regard Rah, who continues to watch him with suspicion. "Just break him." He pushes himself off the doorway and moves toward Rah.

The boy has begun to pace again, back and forth at the window. His movements are rapid and confused. He does not look at Rush, but at the floor, the ceiling. But there is little time for him to continue this display. Rush crosses the room in three strides and steps in front of him. Rah backs away, head down. He turns in the other direction. Rush moves in front of him, blocking him again. There is no room left for Rah to move. He turns his head this way, that. Rush looms over him, sets his bullish chest in front of the boy's turned face. His arms are still crossed in an aggressive posture. He is staring at the boy with fixed eyes, deliberately intimidating, and although the boy does not look up into them he appears to be painfully aware of that black, intense stare. Rah takes a step backward but there is not a full step to take. His back slaps the stone wall. A wavering murmur rises from his throat, the warning of a feral cat. He flicks his startling eyes up to Rush, brow flat. They are full of fear and hate.

Rush backhands him across the cheek, a sweep up and over, catching his jaw and spinning him around into the wall. The blow is light, but enough to take the wind out of the boy, who is stunned to silence. Rush takes a handful of his curls and tilts the boy's face back. Rah has cut his lip open on his own incisor and a pearl of scarlet sits in the corner of his open mouth. He is breathing short, hard breaths and his body is rigid, as if waiting for the next blow.

Instead, Rush holds him by the scruff, shakes him lightly, and releases him. The boy settles his cheek against the cool stone wall, eyes down, waiting. His long, thick lashes shade his eyes. He waits, unaware that Rush has become mesmerized, once again, by his feline features.

Without thinking, Rush runs his thumb along the edge of his jaw. The boy has not had his morning shave, normally Aros' favorite job of the day, and pale bristles have developed along his chin and cheek since last night. His lips are parted and one long, pearly incisor is exposed. The moist, pink tip of his tongue presses against it. Perspiration has blossomed between his shoulders, making his back appear as if it has been dipped in honey.

Rush puts the palm of one hand against the boy's back and presses him deliberately against the wall. Stay where I put you. He drops his head, letting his beard skim that gleaming shoulder and Rah responds with a sickened moan. Rush nips at the back of his neck, aggressive, bullying. Don't you move. Don't you breathe. When he gets no resistance he sets his teeth against the boy's ear, breathes heavily in to it, lifts his head to bare his teeth against the boy's skull, growls.

Rah has squeezed his eyes closed but is otherwise motionless. He swallows, shivers against the wall.

Rush pushes him harder into it, licks the blood off his open mouth, enjoying the feel of those cool, angry teeth. Still no resistance. He spins the boy back around to face him.

Rah keeps his face turned as far as he possibly can from Rush's mouth.

"Look at me. Look at me with some respect, little cat."

But this Rah cannot do. He begins to tremble but he cannot lift his eyes again.

"You give my dogs more respect than me, boy. But I am their master for good reason."

In an instant he has taken Rah's throat in his jaws. As quick as a wolf, he has snatched the boy's windpipe. He sets his teeth into the sides of the column, pinching just enough to make it difficult for the boy to take a breath, not enough to break the skin or strangle. The taste of myrrh and lotus blossom is on his tongue as he squeezes, releases. He has torn more than one throat from a man his own size this way. But he means no harm to Rah. He will speak the boy's language, and he will not cover the same ground twice.

After a moment, the boy's body lets go. The tension drains from his limbs. Even the muscles in his neck release. He makes a small submissive whimper. Rush removes his teeth from his throat.

"You will not disrespect me, you understand?"

Rah makes a little nod. His eyes remain down.

"Look at me."

Rah swallows, shuts his eyes, flicks them quickly up, then drops them.

"Don't make me ask you again."

Rah clenches his jaw, but looks up at the assassin. His eyes are wary, but tame. His jaw is shaking with the effort to keep his face tilted up and his eyes on the master's.

"Better." He is rewarded by a stroke from the same hand that struck him, as the assassin brushes the backs of his fingers down his abdomen, then takes a fist full of his curls again and pulls his head back to gaze into those strange sea-colored eyes. They are dull now, but not dead.

"A little fire is good," he gives Rah a shake of the scruff for good measure. "Too much, and I will take it out of you. You understand?"

Rah is staring blandly at him now. "Ja," he says. Yes. And then, "Isha nahhan." It is Hittite. Respect the master.

Rush opens his eyes at the boy, then narrows them.

"Ja." He agrees, nodding his head as he allows his eyes one final walk over the boy's beautiful, feline face before reluctantly releasing his curls.

"Enough for tonight, eh? Plenty of time." He steps away from Rah, gives him one more sharp, even suspicious, look over his shoulder, then leaves him to the evening.

On his way past the kitchen he meets his wife.

"Where are you headed, my dear?" he lifts one arm, corralling her in it and changing her direction. Now she walks back the way she came, to the east wing.

She looks up at him sheepishly. "You know, Antaris."

"Come to see what's left of him? Patch up the pieces?"

"Antaris, he is so --" she begins in earnest.

"So what, Josepha? Innocent? Fragile? Have you not been paying attention? Do you not see what he has done to this city? He is a wind from the north, and I fear that wind, Josepha."

"You are in love with him, Antaris."

"What is there more to fear?"

She smiles up at him. "For you? Nothing." And then she adds, "Have you ever known fear, Antaris?"

"Battle is all fear. There is no battle without it." He is talking to himself. "And you, wife? Did you think you were immune to him?"

"He is just a boy," she protests.

"Don't lie to yourself, Josepha, it does not become you."

"Well of course he is beautiful," she begins.

"Answer me this, in such delicious proximity to his 'beauty' as I witnessed you enjoying earlier this evening, did you feel him 'just a boy' Josepha? Is that what you felt?"

She says nothing.

"The cat has got your tongue, my sweet wife."

She sighs. "I'm afraid the cat has got both our tongues, Antaris."

This cannot help but make him smile. He is recalling that feline face, tipped up, the plane of one cheek against the cool stone wall, a drop of crimson blood at the corner of that apricot mouth. Forever soaked in holy oils and smelling like a temple concubine. Yes, that cat has got my tongue, he thinks. But what of the cat's tongue? I will see what has become of the cat's tongue.

"That is not just a boy." He repeats, but he is smiling now. "Now come to bed with me, wife, and be his hero tonight."

She looks up at him, confused.

"That is if you wish to spare him any further abuse from me. That is your best avenue."

Rah has remained where Rush left him, pressed against the wall at the window of his little chamber. His body is glistening with sweat, though it is a cool evening and a breeze lightens the air. A cat, the ginger he saw in the kitchen that morning, walks along the edge of the first story tiles. Its motion has caught Rah's notice. The boy turns, pushes himself slightly from the wall, edges toward the window. He watches the cat move along the very edge of the roof, crouched as if stalking some beetle or moth that is scuttling ahead of him, out of eyesight. Rah kicks off his sandals, slips one foot onto the sill, which is waist height. Another. He crouches in the window on his heels, his arms around his shins, watching.

The cat trots to the end of the roof top, then disappears down a gutter that is part of the rain-water collection system. Rah hops gently, soundless, onto the roof tiles. Hugging the outside wall of the second story, he checks to see if there are lamps lit in any of the windows nearby. The servants' rooms appear to be dark, deserted. He slips toward the edge of the first story roof, hoping that the coming dark will cover him.

At the south edge of the roof, over the kitchen, he sees that the cat is on the ground now, trotting off toward the chicken coop. There is no sign of the dogs in the yard. Rah finds a pebble in a crevice in the tiles and tosses it down onto the mud-brick patio. The sound is loud enough to alert guard dogs, not significant enough to cause alarm in the household. He waits. There is no response from within nor without. He eases down the south face of the house into the garden, using a trellis built against the house for flowering vines. He waits at the bottom, utterly still. The yard is silent.

He moves forward to the stables.

And is paralyzed by a barely perceptible growl behind him.

An hour later, Rush cannot sleep. It is an instinct. Something is amiss. He has not heard the dogs for some time.

"Isha nahhan," he says aloud to the ceiling.

"What?" mumbles Josepha, stretching her hand out for him. But his side of the bed is already empty. He is on his feet, tying on a loincloth skirt.

"It's what he said to me. I asked him if he understood me. He said, 'Isha nahhan. ' That is 'respect the master' in Hittite. I wonder what it means, that is all." He is installing his daggers in their sheaths at his ankle and sides as he speaks.

"What did you want him to understand?" she murmurs, still half asleep.

"That he should respect me. I told him it was alright for him to give me a little trouble, but too much disrespect and I would take it out of him."

He is strapping on his sandals. "He said it in Hittite," he says again.

She has risen to one elbow. She rakes her moss brown hair back from her face, scratching the back of her head.

"That is strange," she says.

"Why strange?"

"Because I asked him today what languages he speaks. He said Illyrian, Gaul, a little Minoan. He did not mention that he spoke or even understood Hittite."

Rush stops dressing to look down at her.

"When has he heard you speak Hittite?" she tilts her head to peer into his face, eyes half closed with thought.

"Never. But," he nods suddenly, lifts a finger. "Ah, I should have known you would figure it out, Josepha."

"What is it?"

"The assassin. A Hittite accent."

"Ah."

"Still, I do not understand why he would use the assassin's tongue to answer me."

She has pursed her lips, not sure if it is better he did not know.

"You know. You understand that baby mind of his, Josepha."

She takes a deep breath, expels it.

"He will respect the assassin, Antaris. He will fear and respect the assassin." She looks up at him again, this time with pity. "But that is all."

Rush's face is lit by moonlight reflecting off a bank of clouds, passing the master chamber window. His eyes have turned to stones.

"He is only-" she begins.

"Then it is time for him to grow up."

Rush leaves by the ground floor door at the south end of the east wing. He whistles for the dogs, but there is no response. Something is amiss alright.

His blood is beating in his throat. He is in a black mood, and hopes for burglars. There is plenty of space left yet for bodies under the manure pile where he has built a cold cellar for just such nuisances.

He moves about the outside of the house, below his sons' rooms, to the front portico, around the western wing, back toward the kitchen. His house is secure but the dogs, where are the dogs? He moves toward the stable.

As he approaches the two canines come trotting out of the building, tails down, tongues lolling. No burglars. Unless they dispatched them after they found them in the barn, which is unlikely. They would have caught them coming over the wall and ripped them to shreds. That which is invited into the compound is protected, and held for the master. That which enters the compound without the master is torn to bits. Rush himself taught them this. The command he used to teach them the latter must be spoken in Greek, and is the word 'toy'.

He ignores the dogs, moves quietly to peek into a small window in one of the stalls. But it is too dark inside to see anything but the rump of one of the ponies. He moves to the opposite side of the building, looks in a larger window, this one lit from behind by moonlight.

The snorting of horses. The munching of hay. And a little singsong lullaby, Hittite, he is sure, being hummed by a boy with half a tongue and the voice of a man twice his size and age.

The blood in Rush's throat turns to a claw and tightens. Now it is his heart that is thumping so loudly it hurts his own ears. His eyes are stinging, as in battle fire.

He turns around, leans on the outer wall of the building, not sure if he wants to kill or rape or lie down his life for this blonde demon who has come to Crete like the vapors escaping from Thera. Beautiful. And disastrous.

And he disobeyed me!

And now he has put a fine blade in my heart as I stand here like a girl with tears in my eyes listening to that broken lullaby. My lullaby.

He lets his mind have its way for a moment. In it, he has entered the stable, grabbed hold of the boy, beaten him half senseless, then loved him as he has never loved his wives. If I could devour you I would. But then you would be gone. It is the same with all force. I can break you. How long does it take to break an unwilling boy? Once? Twice by force at most? But then what would I have? Not Rah. Not Rah.

He is turning me into a woman.

Cut his throat.

Get it over with. How long do you think you can stand this?

Forever, if it will keep him safe. If it will keep him Rah.

He will destroy us all.

Rush turns back to look into the barn window. The boy has sung himself to sleep. He is in a corner of one of the ponies' stalls, tucked between the front wall and a half bale of hay. He is curled up in a sitting position, his head resting on his arms, which are stretched out over his knees. The pony gently flems his hay-colored hair with its lips before returning to the real thing.

One of the dogs is making an invisible nest next to him. It circles, then drops to lie against his legs. Protecting him. Mother god, are you protecting him from me? When he rounds the building to the doorway, the second dog is standing at attention there.

"Very well. Watch." The dog smiles its mouthful of daggers at its master as if to say, good, we agree. It drops to its haunches, then stretches out its paws to lie down at attention.

Rush takes a deep breath and walks back toward the house.

Something is amiss, alright.

CHAPTER 25

Lutarus is sharpening his sword.

It took him two weeks to make a decision. But when the finest assassin in the Mediterranean world agreed to babysit the Grain God so that Cyrus' dream of destruction would not come true, he was forced to make up his mind.

It was time for war. So he would have to kill the boy himself.

So far as Lutarus was concerned, war was long overdue. The matriarchal rule on Crete had effectively destroyed a man's role in this society and the island had become nothing more than an effete storehouse, a money changing port. One hundred years of emasculated kings and unchecked queenships, one hundred years of worship to a feminine god, had turned the island of the Sun King into a spineless business district, a society of priests and fops and dandies who could not stand up to the armies of Mycenae waiting to rape her.

That would be enough to have convinced him. But then there was also the plight of the sun priest, Ananou, the last representative of a once male-oriented society, who had solicited for an assassin, come face to face with Rush, and lost his favorite dancer as a result. The next night Lutarus came to him, unaware that Rush had been there the previous evening. He came to answer the call for an assassin, hearing of the priest's desire to kill the Grain God and knowing that Rush had sworn to protect him. When he discovered that Rush had taken Ananou's dancer as a punishment for his trespass against his charge, he offered himself to Ananou as an avenue of revenge, promising he would not only kill the boy, but Rush as well. All he needed was enough money to pay an army.

Lutarus was a man of war, not an assassin. He took the assignment only as a means to instigate his war, and he truly believed that the fate of Crete, and his nephew's kingdom, depended upon that war. He was convinced that Knossos would not stand for the theft and murder of the phenomena that had brought such wealth to his city in only a season, and he was gambling that he could win a war with Knossos because he himself had access to an army for hire in Mycenae. His contacts with the Greeks remained strong long after he returned to Crete from his own mercenary exploits. Lutarus believed that if Knossos fell, all of Crete would follow. Then he and his nephew would be assured a position of government in a new, Mycenaean state.

It all came down to bringing about a war on the island, using the Grain God as bait and then calling in Mycenaean troops to finish the job. And now he had Ananou, who believed that the boy was responsible for the loss of his dancer, to foot the bill.

Had Lutarus paid heed to dreams, he may have seen himself in Cyrus' dream of a priest who sent an archer to kill a holy dove, bringing on the destruction of Crete. But dreams meant nothing to him. Even advised of the disastrous results of his scheme by the very man he wished to protect, Lutarus failed to see that he, himself was the archer in the king's dream, and that it was Ananou, not Mochlos, who would dispatch him.

As to his promise to kill Rush, well, one rarely has the luxury of going to war against an easy opponent. If he managed to kill the boy and start a war before Rush caught up with him, his paid troops would land in days to overtake the island, protect him and set him up as governor. If not, he would at least die a manly death.

So he studied the boy's patterns by sending spies into Knossos to discover them. He knew the Grain God had free access to the burial mounds of the ancients on Mount Ida and that he visited the old grave keeper there several times a week. It would be during one of these visits that Lutarus would take him, bring him back to Cyrus, and make a public spectacle of his death. Knossos, of course, would believe that Cyrus put him up to it, and would launch an attack.

Rush could not watch the boy day and night. But just in case, Lutarus has brought five of his best men with him. They have been living out of doors for three days, camped near the old grave keeper's hut and waiting for the boy to arrive.

Rah is awakened by a rooster a half hour before dawn. He is still in the corner of one of the stalls but the pony he shared it with, who can enter and exit the barn into a small paddock as it pleases, is gone. Rah eventually laid down in his sleep. He is on his side now, his face toward the wall. The dog that was guarding him lies against him, warming his back. Still foggy with sleep, Rah reaches one hand behind him and down the dog's spine before he realizes it is the assassin's monstrous hound and not Hali who leans against him. But the dog merely throws its massive head back over its shoulder and exposes a mouthful of shark long teeth, then licks the boy's face with its long, hot tongue. Rah falls back onto his shoulder giggling, and the dog hops to its feet and continues to slobber on his face and chest, forcing Rah to pull himself up into a ball to protect himself from the hound's rough affections. The second animal stands at the door of the mud brick barn, on its feet, watchful and panting.

Rah stands up, careful not to move too quickly, his posture one of deference to the dogs. He moves quietly out of the barn and through the yard to the house. He walks to the dovecote, spends a moment talking to the birds, and then wanders toward the west wall. But as he nears it he notices that the dogs have begun to circle him, whining anxiously. Certain they are only an instant from barking and awakening their master, Rah casually strolls back toward the house. He reluctantly returns to the trellis, which he scales like a monkey. He slips over the rooftop and back into his window, settles down on the sheepskin, and waits for Tiko to take him down to the latrine and the kitchen as he did the previous morning.

When Tiko arrives, Rah jumps up immediately, happy at least to see a familiar face.

"So, Blonde, you please the master last night like a good concubine?" Tiko teases, for whatever happened overnight, his rival does not look any worse for the wear. He puts an arm over Rah's shoulder and fakes a punch to his stomach. "Today you show off. Show the master's son's how you wrestle. I am not so good at wrestling. Stupid sport. Who wrestles on the battlefield? You get that close, you use your weapons, or your fists and feet. But the master wants them to learn something from you."

"What is wrestle, Tiko," says Rah innocently, following him out the door and down the stairs.

Tiko looks at him with awe. "No one taught you to wrestle, Blonde?"

Rah shakes his head.

"Pretty good for no training." He looks Rah over, signs. "Fighting without fists, eh? When you try to pin your opponent before he pins you, that is wrestling."

In the gym, Quintus and Philip are practicing what they have learned from Tiko yesterday. When the Asian enters, they snap to attention as he has taught them. He bows, and they relax. Rah, unfamiliar with these formalities, stands passively behind Tiko waiting to be called upon. But Tiko has a surprise for him. He pushes him out into the arena in front of him and his two students tackle him in unison.

Rah is instantly sent into a panic. It is as if the two halves of the assassin, the bully and the possessive lover, have split into two and attacked him. The boys outweigh him on their own, and together take him down easily. But his acrobatic strength and ability to twist and squirm out of their grasp, coupled with a cat's panicked speed, soon puts him on his feet again.

Tiko, laughing, orders the boys to cease their attack.

"Why you do that, Tiko? How I can fight both of them, both big!" Rah is looking at Tiko as if he has lost his mind.

"He goes crazy!" says Philip. "You can't pin him!"

"Where did you learn that, Rah?" says Quintus, his eyes wide with adoration.

Tiko is still laughing. "You think a dancer is weak? We are both dancers," he puts an arm around Rah. "We are strong! You think it is easy to jump a bull? No one has stronger legs than a dancer." He slaps his rival on the back, his face losing its humor as he catches Rah's eye. "Or stronger heart than a slave, eh, Rah?"

It is the first time Rah has ever heard him admit to their commonality. Tiko reaches up and ruffles his hair, then pushes him toward Quintus. "Now one at a time."

That evening Mochlos' men return to escort a 'lady' in a hooded gown back to the House of the Moon Goddess. Rush must bring the boy out to the gate to them. It has been raining and his house is somber. Quintus is complaining of a stomachache and has gone to bed. Philip is moping about in the yard, kicking any chicken stupid enough to get in his way. Even Josepha seems saddened that Rah must return to the Priest, however briefly, although Rush has assured her he will be theirs permanently in two weeks time.

"But until then he is safer here, Antaris. Anything could happen to him in two weeks. The priest lets him wander up to the cemeteries alone. It is only a matter of time before someone takes it into their head to kidnap him. Ransom him. Maybe even kill him. You yourself were called to do just that."

"I have no time to babysit the Grain God, Josepha, and if I am not here to keep an eye on him who is to say he will not take it into his head to slip away on his own? You see how he is. Let the priest's men watch him while I use this time to move Ameg's stores and ships to Cyprus, and you and the boys to Anatolia. In two weeks I will return for him and for his troupe. Nothing will happen to him in two weeks time."

Rush finds Rah in his room, with Tiko for company, that evening. He is amazed to find the Asian and the Grain God together during the last hour of Rah's stay and he takes a moment to listen outside the door before entering the room to take Rah down to the priest's men waiting at the gate. He cannot hear a conversation, only the murmuring of two teenage boys sharing secrets, much as he might hear if he stood outside his own sons' door in the evening. When he looks in on them he finds them sitting casually together on either end of the sheepskin bed. Tiko is seated upright and cross-legged and Rah is slouched against the wall and leaning on one elbow, his long legs extended. Rah is playing with something in his hands and giggling his strange, dark giggle. Something Tiko has just said. It is the first time Rush has ever seen him smile at this range and the beauty of it, the soft, golden energy in his face, his dimples pleating his cheeks, nearly knocks the assassin over.

He is unexpected, and Rah is still smiling when he lifts his blue-green eyes to see who stands in the doorway. At the sight of Rush he drops them, his smile disappears, and he and Tiko rise to bow to their master.

"Time for Rah to go, Tiko," says Rush, still dazzled by the memory of that smile. Tiko makes to exit, but manages to give Rah a quick, light punch in the arm before he goes.

"Good fortune, Blonde," he says softly to Rah, and Rah nods.

"You also, China."

When Tiko is gone Rah remains as he stands, head down, waiting for Rush to order him to follow. He is still fiddling with something which is hidden in his right hand.

Rush has lost his desire to take the boy down to the gate. He wants to see that smile again. How have I never seen it? Am I such a monster? My sons smile at me, they smile at me all the time. Tiko can barely keep from grinning ear to ear in my presence. What have I done to you, little cat? I've turned the world over to protect you, and still you fear me.

"I have to give you back to the priest for now, Rah," he begins, wishing that he had somehow learned to make the boy comfortable enough in his presence to come closer without having to be corralled. "But in two weeks you, and your dance troupe, come with me for the winter."

Rah nods, head still down.

"What is in your hand, boy?" Rush has lifted his, and Rah looks up, obediently walks to him, deposits the item in his open palm.

It is a wooden dove. Philip's work.

Rush has to swallow the knot that is tightening at his windpipe. "My son gave you this?"

Rah flicks his eyes up at his master.

"Yes, sir," he says softly, not lowering his eyes as he should. "And Quintus, this." He lifts his chin. Tied to the golden collar at his throat is a dove's tail feather.

"They are quite taken with you," Rush murmurs.

There is a noise behind him. Ham has come with the green ladies cloak Rah arrived in. Rush turns, takes it from him, nods for him to go. Ham retreats.

That knot in his throat is threatening to choke him. Rah has dropped his eyes, probably when Ham entered. Rush opens the cloak, puts it over the boy's shoulders, ties the neck closed. He has turned me into a woman, he says again to himself as he settles the hood over Rah's head. A servant.

A slave's servant. But he feels no anger, except at himself. Josepha's words are haunting his mind. Two weeks is a long time.

He is about to tell the boy to come with him, turn his back on him and take him down to the gate, when Rah lifts his eyes again.

"And Josepha, this," he says to Rush, his face curiously open. He has pushed back the left side of the hood, and a lock of curls, to expose his ear. It has been freshly pierced. There is a single white pearl against the lobe.

Rush blinks at it, lifts his fingers to it. Touches it. Rah flinches lightly and makes a child's embarrassed giggle. "Still hurt," he explains.

"My wife did that?" Rush says, his brow knotted against the thing that is threatening to tear itself free of his chest.

"She make," says Rah, innocently pantomiming a jeweler's work with his fingers, as if his master did not know his own wife's hobby.

"Yes, I bring her the gems, Rah," says Rush, "and she fashions them into trinkets." He swallows. "So," he cannot believe his own ears as he hears himself say this last, "the pearl," he releases Rah's ear and pulls the hood back over his head roughly, "is from me."

At the gate, the dogs, who have followed Rush from the house, raise their hackles when the lead man takes Rah and clips chains to his collar and belt. And when he yanks the boy roughly out onto the street, it is only their master's firm voice that keeps the dogs from attacking him.

"He is half mine now," Rush calls after the men, no longer bothering to play Ameg. "If you bruise that half that is mine, you will be wearing your own balls for earrings by the end of the week."

There is no further roughness from the priest's guards as they walk the boy down the rain- dampened street toward the villa.

CHAPTER 26

"Let us take the grave keeper's hut, sir. We are wet and miserable. We have been out here for four days. Let the men at least be out of the rain."

"He needs to be in the hut when we take him, Turios, I have told you this. He is a god damned dancer, an acrobat. If he sees something is strange at the house he will run like water. We will never catch him."

"A grave then, let us hole up in one of the mounds. Let me find one we can use as a post."

Lutarus has been standing in the rain, taking the guard, allowing his men to shelter themselves along the north wall of the burial ground where the cliffs of Mt. Ida form a shallow refuge from the weather. These are the best men he could find in Cyrus, but they are dainty fools, afraid to get wet for fear of fever, afraid of a day without rations for fear of a cramp. He cannot wait to be joined by real soldiers from Mycenae to fight his war with Knossos. But for now, he must coddle these pansies to get the job done.

"Very well, Turios. Take Aktor over the wall and find an open mound here on the north end of the cemetery. Look about on the ground. See that there is no disturbance to the vegetation. If you can find something agreeable to me we will use it as a post. But I will still need a man to watch the gate and another to watch the old woman."

"Sir."

Standing in the rain, Lutarus considers the information he has received from his spies in Knossos. The Grain God was absent from the House of the Moon for three days. Just his luck. He and his men out here on this barren mountain top waiting in vain while the dancer is holed up at some other location, unable to take his constitutional up the mountain to be snatched. As a result, one of his five men has already deserted him. If Lutarus were a man who believed in omens, or in gods for that matter, he might have considered these combined misfortunes signs from above. But as it stands, he only believes himself to be unlucky and ill informed by a couple of paid-for spies who are in reality no more than two glorified stable boys working for the palace guard for the summer. These two neither knew where the Grain God was being kept during his absence from Mochlos' villa, nor when he would return. They were hardly more informed than his own men, sitting like wet fowl behind a dreary cemetery on a mountaintop four kilometers from Knossos. In fact the boys, Ophos and his brother Eknos, are the same two boys who have been watching Rah train the dapple colt in the king's field all summer, and their information is only a few minutes fresher than what Lutarus and his men could learn for themselves, another kilometer up the mountain. But the boys, eager for extra pay, have embellished their virtues as spies, and led Lutarus to believe that they work at the priest's house and know Rah's schedule as well as his own attendants.

Lutarus pulls his soldier's leather, a simple rectangular piece of deer skin used to wrap pack, to line bedding, and protect one from the weather, over his head and shoulders and submits to the prospect that fortune does not seem to be smiling on his plans thus far. But all that will change once he has the Grain God in his hands. Then he will take the boy back to Cyrus, cut him down in public in the name of the king, and instigate war with Knossos.

When Rah is returned to the House of the Moon he is immediately brought before the priest, who is eager to learn whether or not Ameg has decided to take him, and his troupe, for the winter. Still in the green ladies cloak, which is rain dampened and clinging to him, he is shoved at the priest by one of the guards who walked him home.

"Well, my little goose, did Ameg enjoy your company these last two nights? Or did you put your teeth in someone's head and screw up my lucrative deal with the richest man on Crete?"

The guard has pulled the hood of the cloak off Rah's head as the priest is talking, unintentionally drawing back Rah's damp curls as he does so, and the first thing Mochlos, with ever an eye for value, sees is the single stunning pearl in the boy's left ear.

Rah looks up at his old master with disrespectful familiarity. He has lost his fear of the priest in these last weeks and is irritated at the question, which suggests that Mochlos had no qualms about lending his dancer to the wolf as one would lend a concubine.

He need not answer the question posed him in any event. Mochlos' eyes are riveted on the pearl, an incredulous look passing over his crafty face.

"My god, boy, what the hell did you do to earn this?" His fingers stretch to touch the stone. Rah winces, not in pain, but at the man's touch, and turns his head away.

"I teach his sons to wrestle," says Rah defiantly. But his disrespectful attitude is lost on Mochlos, who is too satisfied by the obvious outcome of his gamble to pay it any heed.

"Well, you are just a bundle of surprises, aren't you, handsome? And here I thought you'd have taken one of his fingers off and ruined me. Good boy," Mochlos is rubbing his hands together cheerfully. "Good boy. You see, it's worth being a bit . . . friendlier . . . to the right people, isn't it? No need to be so snappish. You make a man like that happy, boy, you can have anything you want. Anything."

Rah is shaking one leg under the cloak, tapping his heel with angry energy.

"What are you fidgeting about? Can't you take a compliment from me at all?"

Rah flicks his eyes back at the priest. There are golden daggers in them. "Only want to dance. Want to stay here and dance. Not go with wolf. Not go away." But here he stops himself. He has not said so much to the priest since his arrival on Crete in the spring.

"Well, well. You have developed a bit of pluck now Ameg has taken a liking to you, haven't you? Well he's taking you with him and that is that. Don't screw it up. Hasn't anyone told you you'd have been sacrificed on the mountain if he hadn't stepped in? He and that . . . that black thing from the netherworld that visits my nightmares."

At this, Rah turns his full attention back to the priest, and stares at him with dazed eyes. When the guard pulls him away and turns him over to his dresser, to be put away for the night, Rah barely acknowledges his friend.

Aros lets him be, filling their walk up to his chamber with cheerful banter about the goings on in the priest's household during the three days of his absence. Galateo has six new birds. One of the bull jumpers has broken his arm. Dimius is working on a new dance and may use one of the female bull jumpers as Rah's partner. She is really quite amazing, a slave from Gaul, strong as a boy. Rah shows no interest in the gossip.

Pyrus has joined them on his way back from a late dinner, but Rah ignores him as well, scuffling along in the wet cape with his head down and an eerie whine in his throat.

Aros has filled Rah's little room with lilies in his absence and the scent of the flowers is overpowering when they arrive. He has smuggled a bowl of the boy's favorite treat, honeyed walnuts, up from the kitchen and put it on the floor by his bed. He has even added a few pillows to his mattress, which he pilfered from the priesthood's quarters. But the boy is intractable and takes no notice. He walks glumly to his pallet, dropping the wet cape on the floor in typical Rah fashion, and throws himself down on the deerskin mattress. When Aros attempts to secure his chains he sits up, crosses his legs under himself and tucks his hands under his arms. It is impossible for the dresser to untangle those strong limbs to chain them.

"What is it, Sunlight? What are you angry at me for?" Aros must pretend to pout. He has been miserable since Rah left and is delighted to be in his company again, whatever his mood.

But Rah only turns his head into the wall and makes a little "uff" of disgust.

"Sunlight-" Aros moves to touch Rah's head but Rah slaps his hand away faster than Aros can follow it, then tucks his fingers back under his own armpits, folding his torso in half so that his gold belt is equally inaccessible.

"What are you mad at us for?" Pyrus pipes in over Aros' shoulder.

Finally Rah looks at his attendants, first Pyrus, then Aros. "You know," he begins, struggling to put into Minoan what the priest has just revealed to him. "You both know priest mean to-" he gives up, and attempts a rather amazing pantomime of a priest cutting the heart out of a human sacrifice.

"Oh, baby, everyone knew," says Aros, immediately understanding Rah's gesture.

"We all knew from the moment you came to us. Two boys before you were sacrificed, Rah," says Pyrus. "But they were common, native bull jumpers. Not like you. We were hoping that it would never come to that."

Aros is tearing up. "I did. But I wasn't going to let him do it, Rah. That's why I came to your room the night the assassin saved you. I wasn't saving you from the assassin, Rah. I didn't know he was here. I came to kill-"

Rah gives him a wary sidelong glance. He is still folded over himself in a knot only an acrobat could sustain. His pretty eyes are hot under the half-mast lids. He is trying to look fierce. He is succeeding in looking like a kitten with its tail caught in a door.

"Rah, I would do anything for you, don't you know that?" Aros has moved to sit beside Rah on the pallet. He looks up a Pyrus helplessly. "One way or another, I would never have let it happen. Never. Not even if it meant my own life." He slips an arm around Rah's waist. When Rah fails to push him away, he gives him a little squeeze. "I'm always your friend, Rah."

Rah straightens up a bit, still hugging himself, and looks at Aros suspiciously.

"You come to kill priest?" he asks his dresser in a whisper. "Night wolf come, you come to kill priest for Rah, Aros?"

Aros, blinking at tears but smiling now, nods proudly.

He is rewarded with a soft, golden smile from Rah. Then the boy's pale brows bunch again in annoyance.

"I like to kill priest," he says. "Hate priest." He looks up at Pyrus. "This why he buy me?" he says to Pyrus quietly. "To-" he starts his pantomime of the grizzly death on the mountain again.

"The assassin saved you, Rah. We all heard about it while you were gone," says Pyrus.

"He told the priest that night that he'd be dead before you were cold on the day he killed you," adds Aros gleefully. "And now Ameg wants to take us all to Anatolia for the winter. All of us. Pyrus and I as well."

As Rah begins to unfold his limbs, Pyrus, who has the keys to his chains tonight, makes an attempt to secure them. Rah folds up and shoots him a dangerous glare.

"No. No more chains. I sleep without chains now." He has flattened his brow at Pyrus, and fixes him with the same hateful stare he gave Rush the night he danced with the wolf.

"Oh, not this again," says Pyrus, lifting his hands as if to surrender.

Rah is on his feet. He has snatched the keys out of Pyrus' hands. He stands nose to nose with him, fists clenched.

"No more chains," he repeats, challenging.

"Rah if I have to call a guard in here, so help me I will," says Pyrus, but he makes no move to do so.

"Oh what's the difference," says Aros. "Don't you see? Ameg didn't chain him. He's had two nights of freedom. You don't know what it's like to be chained up like that every night, Pyrus," Aros looks up suddenly into his friend's face. "Oh, sorry."

"I know what it's like, Aros. I was a dancer."

At this, Rah's sullen look fades. He looks from Aros to Pyrus. Back to Aros.

"You too, Aros?" he says.

"This is Crete, baby. Slaves are chained at night. Until I became a dresser, I was a seamstress. Worked in the palace factory. We were all chained."

Rah takes a heavy breath, nods. He puts his open palm out to Pyrus with the key in it, which Pyrus takes cautiously.

"Then I also," he offers Pyrus his wrists.

When he is settled on his pallet, Pyrus and Aros seem reluctant to leave. Pyrus moves to the dresser to fuss with some pots of makeup. Aros arranges a vase of lilies, then comes back to Rah, picks up the bowl of honeyed walnuts and offers it to him, popping one cluster in his own mouth as he does so. Settling himself next to Rah on the pallet, he munches the treat thoughtfully and asks, "So, what is he like?"

Rah looks at the dresser with big, wary eyes. "He is wolf."

"Ah," Aros chuckles, "another wolf. All big men are wolves to you, you silly thing."

"No. Tuma not wolf. Tuma big, strong, but soft, inside like woman." He taps his chest with a fist, "big heart. This man he is hard, like bear, so fast! All teeth, he take and push and-" he grabs Aros by the neck and whips him down on the pallet under him so fast that Aros shrieks, though Aros outweighs him by half.

"You are mine!" Rah barks in Aros' face. "You obey me! Or I bite! " Quick as a snake he has nipped the dresser's throat. Then, satisfied that he has made his point, he lets Aros go, leans back, and stretches out his legs on the pallet to the length of his chains.

Aros pushes himself back into a sitting position on the bed next to Rah.

"Doesn't sound like a very nice man," he mumbles, grabbing another cluster of honeyed walnuts.

"Is he really married?" asks Pyrus. "He has twin sons, they say, his very likenesses. Is his house full of gold and jewels?"

"He has gym," says Rah, finally noticing the bowl of candied walnuts and taking one. "And horse. Two." He chews, musing. "And white chicken. Doves. Wife make this." He pushes back some curls to show off his earring.

Pyrus walks over to look at the pearl and whistles, impressed.

"His wife gave you that?" Pyrus looks at Aros, who rolls his eyes and shrugs.

Rah nods, munching. "Nice lady." With his permanently crimped tongue and a mouth full of walnuts he is almost impossible to understand.

"Did Ameg know his wife gave you this pearl, Rah?" asks Pyrus, winking at Aros while Rah reaches for another treat.

"I show him. He say, 'This pearl I bring her. She make. This pearl I give you." He flicks his eyes up at Pyrus, leans back on his elbow, licking honey off his thumb.

Pyrus is chuckling. "You are a brat, Rah. I don't believe for a minute you don't know what you do to people. Not for a minute." But he reaches down to ruffle the boy's hair all the same. "Poor Ameg," he laughs.

"You both come with me?" Rah has turned to Aros. "He take you too?"

"Yes, Rah. We're all going."

Pyrus bends, hands on his hips, to speak into Rah's face. "So you needn't fear the wolf. When he comes to 'bite' you, Aros will smack him on his muzzle and tell him 'Leave my Sunlight alone, you horny wolf!'"

Rah kicks at Pyrus, who jumps nimbly out of the way in time. "Maybe he come bite you, Pyrus," he warns.

"What are we going to do with you, now the priest is afraid to beat you, Rah?" Pyrus shakes his head. "Maybe keep you in chains day and night, eh?"

"You know why he doesn't use the reed on his dancers anymore?" says Aros. "Or the drowning pool? The assassin gave him some of his own medicine, that's what. Took him down to the pool and drowned him for half an hour." Aros is looking from Rah to Pyrus, who apparently hadn't heard this bit of gossip. "One of the stewards in the priesthood's quarters told Agatka in the kitchens. She heard two of the junior priests talking about it. Mochlos told them the assassin took him down to his own punishment chamber in the dark, drowned him for half an hour, beat him. Now he can't even stand to go in the room. He's locked it up. No one's been beaten since."

Rah has pulled something out of the pocket of his skirt and is fiddling with it, ignoring Aros. Aros' attention is immediately drawn to Rah, who has never shown an interest in any object, so ensconced is he in his world of motion.

"What have you got there, Sunlight?"

"This from wolf son. This he-" he pantomimes Philip carving the bird, using the bird as his prop.

"Mother Moon," breathes Pyrus. "There three days and everyone is giving you presents. And the feather on your collar, Rah? I suppose that is another?"

"Yes. Quintus." Rah has forgotten the feather until now and feels for it with his fingers.

"Well, let us take them for you for safe keeping. You won't have them a day if not," offers Aros. He puts his hand out and Rah obediently hands him the wooden dove. Aros unties the feather and takes it as well.

There is rustling in the priest's chamber and the two attendants quickly stash the rest of the walnut clusters under the vanity and move to the beaded curtain doorway.

"Good sleep, angel," says Aros, taking one last look at his charge before he retires to the servant's quarters.

"You want the fur, Rah?" asks Pyrus before he leaves. The skin has fallen off the side of the pallet and out of Rah's reach.

Rah looks at it, tries to reach it, is trapped by his chains. "Priest not come since wolf is here." he whispers to his attendants, pointing to the skin. "Good wolf. I take."

Pyrus goes to pick up the fur and hand it to Rah, who smashes it into a pillow and flops down on it.

"Good wolf," agrees Pyrus.

But the good wolf is in a foul temper the following morning. He has arranged to have the entirety of his compound moved to his house on the coast of Anatolia and hired men from that locale are in the process of loading the household onto carts and readying to take it to the harbor, where Ameg's personal ship waits to sail. He has been batting men on the backs of their heads for not moving fast enough, kicking one so hard in the buttocks that he fell on his face and broke a box of pottery underneath him, but in fact Rush has no desire to leave Crete at all, least of all without the boy and his troupe. After two hours of doing more harm than good, he agrees with Josepha to leave her in charge of the remainder of the moving and meet his family at the dock at noon.

"Go, Antaris, see that the priest keeps him at the villa for us until we take him. He is safest there."

So Rush leaves his compound for the last time, taking his two dogs for company, as no one else can handle them, and his house is to be closed up. He sets out for the House of the Moon as Ameg one last time, dressed in a fine linen robe and expensive Greek sandals, his fingers covered in jewels, his long nails manicured as if for a meeting of statesmen. In fact, his nails are honed for war, in proper Hittite tradition. For everything is a weapon to a warrior.

Rush approaches the gate of the House of the Moon, but as he does so has a change of heart. Something is irritating him, something he has recalled of the boy's movements. Ever plagued by perfect recall of every meeting, every observation he has had of Rah since his first encounter, his memory is stimulated by a row of wildflowers growing along the stone wall of the villa compound. They are white lilies, dappled with flecks of brown. The colt. The King's Arabian colt. His mind visits the day he watched the boy lunge the colt on the south west corner of the King's field. Only moments later he was attacked by the three would-be assassins from Ananou on his way up the mountain to the burial mounds and Ting Ya. His mind jumps to the day he met Rah on that same path, himself disguised as a Priest of the Dead. How easily he could have snatched the boy that day, had he the intention to do so. Trying to keep Rah from harm was like trying to save Crete from Thera. One had to set one's priorities or one would go mad.

The boy himself made it impossible to cover all the possibilities. He was only half tame, like the cur dog he had loved.

"You never really obey anyone, do you, little cat? You just happen to be doing what we want most of the time. Child's mind, dog's mind. Off in some, smaller world. " He recalls the sound of the boy's dark voice humming that Hittite lullaby in his own barn. The boy would rather sleep under the hooves of a horse than on a luxurious sheepskin bed in a rich man's house, and would happily risk his life to train and ride an unbroken and uncut colt, right under the noses of the King's guard. And then there was Ting Ya. What hold did she have on him? Mother he never had? Or was it just the treats? He himself like the horses and the cur dog he was so adept at training, responding to a handful of candied walnuts, a reed whip, a set of strong teeth in his throat, faster than he would to any command.

He will want to visit Ting Ya, thinks Rush. He will want to visit the colt while I am gone. And nothing will stop him. If I order the priest to keep him in, he'll just seduce a house servant into letting him out for a few hours. His dresser would walk through Tartarus for him. Who else is under his spell? He'll find a way to get out. Two weeks is a long time.

Rush has no time to take the walk to the King's pasture this morning. But he has time to visit the Palace, so he heads in that direction, his burly wolf-hounds at his heels. When he reaches the guard he is instructed, respectfully, to tether the dogs outside.

"They come with me," he informs the two men standing at the archway of the palace.

"Beg pardon, sir, but such beasts are not allowed in the palace," says one of the guards, a man of half Rush's girth. His fellow gatekeeper appears his twin.

Rush scowls at him, pulls back one side of his mouth. "Are you here for decoration only?" He looks from one to the other.

The man clears his throat, realizing he is in a difficult spot. Everyone knows that Ameg is the father of the Queen's pregnancy. Everyone knows he can a buy and sell Knossos. And everyone knows that lately he has not been himself at all, that the dandy, Ameg, seems to have grown a set of balls to rival the bulls in the sink pit.

"My deepest apologies sir, but these animals will frighten the staff half to death. You will clear the palace."

"These dogs go where I go, and only attack on a single word from me, a word, if spoken by me even in error, that will raise their hackles and put whomever I address inches from a bloody death," says Ameg cheerfully.

The man has begun to tremble. His partner, on the other side of the archway, seems in danger of losing his bladder.

"Yes sir," is all the first guard can manage.

"Would you like to hear it?" asks Rush.

"No, sir!" blurts the guard, eyes big as grain cakes. The two dogs stand at attention on either side of Rush, ears pricked, tongues lolling, as if awaiting the command.

"Very well then. Perhaps, if I cannot enter with a civil and respectful audience from the front guard, I will put my question to you, man. Who guards the King's horses, specifically, the western quarter?"

"That is Ramicus and four men, sir. Two stable boys and two older men who have been with him for years. That is, four in seven days. On alternate days two men from the King's private guard take the post."

"And why two on some days and five on others?" asks Rush without much interest in the answer.

"Quality of the guards sir. Ramicus' bunch are really only two stewards from the grain vaults and two boys from the west end, shall I say, a bit less than up to the task of soldiering, though I'll vouch for Ramicus myself. As good a man as they come, sir. The King's private guard are trained Greeks, sir. Paid for."

Rush has his own opinion of the general worthlessness of the 'guards' at the palace. He is more surprised that the King is using two of his small staff of paid-for personal guards to watch the field half the time than he is that he has entrusted slackers to work the other half. Except for the boy, no one has paid much mind to the King's horses. It would be a difficult task to steal them and transport them to another queenship on Crete as they are all but wild. So the guards are more for show than need.

Rush considers the man he is speaking to. He is young, nervous, probably only just put on the position of entry guard. A freed slave? A poor man from the east end with a family to feed? He can be bought in either case.

"Well, here it is then. I am to be out to sea for the next two weeks and I need information in the meantime. You tell Ramicus that Ameg the Merchant wants to know all there is to know about the little Grain God's comings and goings in and around the King's pasture. Everything. Anything suspicious. Anything unusual. That is what I will pay for. He is to be my eyes and ears. And you, to keep your mouth shut in the mean time, will take this," at which he presses an ever present coin purse into the man's hand, "and do so. Any questions?"

"If you are to be at sea, sir, how will Ramicus bring you the information?"

"He will give it to the boy's dresser, a man named Aros, at the High Priest Mochlos' villa. He will smuggle any important news through the kitchen staff. I have dealt with the kitchen staff at the House of the Moon before. Pass the information on to Agatka, and so to Aros."

"As you say, sir."

"And remind all involved that my information is mine alone. If I hear that anyone but me has come to know what I have paid for, I will find the tongue that slipped and cut it out."

"Yes, sir!"

At this assurance, Ameg the Merchant leaves the island of Crete with his household on his own private ship bound for Anatolia. He will return with a second ship, readied to move any remaining cargo, including the boy and his dance troupe, in two weeks' time.

CHAPTER 27

In a field above Knossos a blonde boy in a dirty loincloth skirt is standing on the back of a dapple colt as the animal moves in a double loop around the west end of a pasture. Four men, two dimwitted stable boys and two whose minds are slowed by years of too much drink, watch from the stone fence line. A fifth stands in the center of the north loop of the animal's travel, wondering how he managed to fall so far from his superior's wishes, and making his best attempt to keep the boy from breaking his neck.

In the center of the double loop, where the colt's path bisects itself, is a makeshift jump, a pile of felled tree trunks and brush, measuring about a meter in height at the center. So far, the boy has only fallen once, landing on his feet somehow, then tumbling in a controlled tuck and rolling some distance from the colt's pounding hooves before coming to inertia. That is when Ramicus decides to enter the field and spot him. He leaps over the wall, his sudden strength reminding him of his youth, and runs to the boy to drop to his knees at his side. The tumble has sent Rah's weakened brain spinning, a thing that all jumps do, unbeknownst to his audience, but falls especially. As his mind finds its balance, spinning late of his body to the point of inertia somewhere within his skull, he pushes himself up from the ground like a swimmer coming out of the water and looks at Ramicus as if he has never seen him before.

"Rah! Are you hurt?" Ramicus shouts in his face.

But Rah only chuckles, leaning on his hands to catch his breath. "I fall always, no problem," he tells Ramicus. "I am behind him, need to be more-" he leans his body forward. Ramicus has come to understand the boy's language, which is like a sign language of the body, everything expressed in gesture, with some kind of internal grace that fairly sings when the dancer moves. He is telling Ramicus that he did not lean forward enough when the colt went over the fence. It never looks like he is leaning at all, this tiny discretion is his alone, a thing his injured brain has left him with, like an idiot savant. He is telling Ramicus that he was an inch or two behind the horse's center of balance, and so, was 'left behind' the motion of their jump together. Given this advantage gravity, ever in love with the acrobat, took him greedily from the horse and brought him to the ground.

"I don't know how much more of this I can take, Rah," says Ramicus grimly. It is not just the security of his post he is speaking of. It is the affection he has come to feel for the boy. He can imagine feeling no greater horror if it were one of his own sons falling eight feet from a leaping horse.

Rah manages a smile. It is almost wicked, most of all because it is both ruthlessly innocent and mischievous at once. He leans toward Ramicus, whom he has come to believe is his friend, and in his husky, broken voice he says, "You can take more, Ramicus." Then he gets to his feet, brushes himself off as best he can and clucks to the colt. The long reins have been dragging and the animal has halted not far from the jump. It stands waiting as Rah approaches, then allows itself to be captured, patted, re-mounted.

Now Rah has taken the jump on the colt several times without mishap and Ramicus is about to order him, for what little good it will do, to dismount and be done for the day. But when he looks over at his men, he sees that one is missing. One of the stable boys is not watching from the wall.

Assuming the youth has taken a trip into the brush to relieve himself, he returns his attention to Rah, who has the colt in a canter. He takes one last jump over the makeshift obstacle, circles at the far end of the eight, slows the animal to a trot, and somersaults off his back as if the horse were not in motion at all, twisting in the air and coming to earth with a gentle dismount.

As Rah rewards the horse with a generous rub and a treat, Ramicus returns to the wall. Eknos is still not back, and none of the other men seem to have noticed his absence, so intent are they on Rah's performance.

"Have any of you idiots noticed that Eknos is missing?"

"Said he had to take a dump, sir," offers Thymus, one of the two older men in his charge. Ramicus shakes his head, at first only annoyed. No one is to leave their post without first asking his permission. Then he recalls the message he received last night from the palace gate. Ameg the Merchant was paying him to be his eyes and ears out here. Anything unusual, anything at all, was to be reported to him. He has to chuckle to himself. How unusual was it for a half-witted stable boy to fail to ask permission to go into the brush to relieve himself? Not very. Nevertheless, Ramicus is an old soldier. He was given an order. He will obey it.

When ten minutes later the boy has not returned, he begins to have misgivings about his failure to act immediately. Ameg would not have given such an order without good reason. He had suspicions. Ramicus looks out over the stone wall into the pasture. Rah is spending a little extra time here today, apparently trying to seduce one of the mares with something he has hidden in the pockets of his skirt. Ah, yes. I knew it would come to this. He is not content to ride the back of one animal. He is going to start working with a second. How many did he say he could jump at once on the Steppes of Gaul? Five? He is too simple minded to lie. My god, what have I gotten myself into?

But he is glad that the boy is still in the field. Something is amiss.

"Thymus, go get Rah away from that mare. Kleitos, go find Eknos and bring him back here. Ophos, you stay right here with me, boy, you and I are going to have a little talk."

"How do you expect me to find a boy taking a crap on a mountain, sir?" says Kleitos, still a bit hung over from last night. Ramicus heard the stewards guarding the grain vaults brought in some girls from the east end in to the palace cellars last night. Apparently Kleitos, who had worked the vaults until he was assigned to guard the King's horses under Ramicus, had joined his old cronies for the party.

"Take the cemetery road. The path you see Rah take up the mountain. When you find him, tell him his brother was helping Rah and was kicked by the colt, maybe dead. Get him back here, Kleitos. Do it now and do it right or you can explain to Ameg yourself when he returns why Rah is missing."

"Rah missing, sir? But he's right-"

At that all three men look over the pasture wall to see that Thymus is having some difficulty with Rah, who is backing away from him toward the north wall of the pasture. They have looked up just in time to see Thymus take a leap, attempting to tackle the boy, and Rah jumping twice as far backward, then scaling the wall like a lynx and disappearing.

"Thymus!" shouts Ramicus. "What the hell have you done?"

Rah has jumped the wall and darted up the path to Ting Ya. He had let the colt go, stowed the tack under a rock, and walked off toward a group of grazing mares when he noticed that the man called Thymus, the man who had given him too much retsina at the palace, was stomping toward him from his post at the west wall. Rah had decided weeks ago that his next step must be to gain the trust of the colt's mother. He knew she was the dapple's mother because the colt had told him so. Each time Rah released him after training, he nickered to her. He did not approach the other horses until the mare lifted her head and responded. Then he trotted up to the group, running his nose along the ground in submission until she wandered over to him and herded him about for a few minutes. Finally, convinced that he still accepted her as his superior, she would drop her head to graze and he would do the same.

She was a young horse herself, and the dapple colt had probably been her first foal. Their bond was still strong. Rah wanted her because he knew that that bond would make a double jump, one in which he stood on both horses, possible.

But when Thymus came stomping toward him from the stone paddock wall he instantly startled. That man had been melded in his brain with the sickness brought on by too much wine and with the distasteful memory of the Queen's touch. He did not like Thymus, did not like the way his breath smelled of stale wine day and night, did not like his slow speech and broad movements. Had he any memory of the barbarian who had entered his mother's thatched hut on the Nordic peninsula and taken him up by the ankles and smashed his infant head into the side of a wooden table, he might have made the connection between Thymus' foul, sweet smelling breath and the barbarian's. He might have made the leap between that slow motion ride through the air, the impact that forever distorted his brain, and that man's drunken movements. But he did not. He only had instinct. And his instinct told him to run.

Rah's agile muscles twitched as Thymus approached. When the man called out callously to him to get his blonde butt over to Ramicus, he could only assume that his attempt to advance on the mare had gotten him into trouble with the captain. He began to back away from Thymus, who immediately leapt at him in an attempt to bring him down. That was enough to send Rah over the north wall and up the path toward Ting Ya's house, unaware that what he ran to far outweighed in danger that he fled from.

Eknos has sprinted up the path toward the cemetery of the ancients ahead of Rah by twenty minutes. He knows Lutarus' men are hiding out in one of the oldest mounds in the far end of the burial ground, just over the upper wall. He has been told to let them know when Rah is approaching and has been promised a month's pay for his trouble. Eknos has no malice in him toward Rah. He is motivated by the prospect of earning extra money to show his father that he is not as worthless as he is constantly being told he is. It has never occurred to him to question Lutarus' desire to know Rah's movements. He will pass on the information, in secret, as he was told, and will innocently expect to watch Rah performing on the colt the next day he is assigned to guard the King's field.

When Eknos reaches the exterior of the far wall of the burial mound he finds Aktor snoozing in the shade amongst a patch of wildflowers and the buzzing of bees. He shakes the big man by the shoulder and yells in his face, "He is coming now! Up the path! Tell your captain I have come!" Aktor takes a moment to understand that the boy is referring to the Grain God of Knossos. After blinking stupidly at the youth a moment he dutifully scales the wall and rushes down the side of the nearest mound to the moss covered door. It is half open for air, but he bangs on it to make his point, making a sound like a small clap of thunder that echoes off the surrounding mounds.

"What the hell is it, man? Is he coming?" hisses Lutarus from the dark interior.

"The boy says he's on his way, sir," answers Aktor.

"Well, get down to the gate! Turios, take those two and surround the house. Don't let her see you! When he is inside, I will enter behind him. Then you three watch that he doesn't flee from a window, and if he does, Aktor, you grab him at the gate!"

The men stumble out of the dank burial chamber and do as they are instructed. Eknos, having fulfilled his end of the bargain, watches them move off in various directions, attempting to be invisible. When they are out of view, he realizes it has been some time since he told Ramicus' men that he was going into the brush to evacuate his bowels. He returns to the south wall of the cemetery, scales it, and begins sprinting back to the King's pasture.

He is intercepted by Kleitos.

"What in hell are you doing up here?" Kleitos pants, out of shape and breath. "Captain wants you down at the pasture. Ophos' been kicked by the colt helping Rah. Maybe dead."

Eknos' eyes go round with fright. He bolts past Kleitos, who is done running at any rate, and heads back to his post, passing Rah on the way without a thought for anything now but his brother.

Rah is disturbed to see Eknos coming down the path from Ting Ya's house at a run. When he next comes upon Kleitos, another unsavory character in his experience, he nevertheless stops before him, blocking his way back to the pasture. Careful to remain well out of the man's reach, he looks at him with spooked eyes and says, "Something wrong now."

Kleitos is glad to have a shot at bringing the Grain God back to Ramicus, who apparently promised Ameg the Merchant he would keep an eye on him. What that arrangement is, he figures, is none of his business. Except that if it involves pay, and dealings with Ameg, as every servant at the palace knows, always does, he wants to be in on it.

"Come here, boy, Captain wants to talk to you, is all. Now don't run from me like a damned maiden, will you?"

He has stumbled upon perhaps the only verbal means of coaxing Rah into returning to the field, for the dancer is by now painfully tired of being wanted like a maiden here on Crete.

Rah narrows his eyes at Kleitos. "Why he runs like that?"

Kleitos blows out a puff of air. "I just told him Captain wants him, is all. Been gone too long." He lifts one arm as if to corral Rah and turn him back down the path toward the horse's field. "Come now, don't cause me any more trouble today."

"No, I go see Ting Ya. Something wrong," answers Rah, and he begins to edge his way around Kleitos by moving into the brush and leaving the path.

"Damn it, boy, this has got nothing to do with Ting Ya!" But Rah has already skirted him and bolted up the path to the burial mounds.

Back at the pasture wall Ramicus has learned from Ophos that the boys made a deal with a man to alert him when Rah is on his way to the burial mounds. It is Ramicus' expertise as a father, and the correct mixture of patience and bribery, that brings forth the information from the lad. When Eknos returns, breathless and relieved to see his brother standing, he is given a handsome slap across the back of the head, then ordered with the others to take up their weapons and follow Ramicus back up the path to the burial mounds to rescue Rah. They will pick up Kleitos on the way.

Rah arrives at the gate of the burial mounds of the ancients, his ears pricked for danger. There is movement in the brush beside the gate, and as he passes through the archway he deliberately gives that side of the entrance a wide berth.

"Ting Ya!" he calls out toward the house, but refuses to enter it. Something is heavy in the air. He feels eyes on him. His senses are burning and alert.

Ting Ya calls to him from the house. "Jin yu! You wait there." It is her love word for him, and in her language, means 'gold in abundance. ' But it is also a warning. So many times she has said to him, "Jin yu, you are a treasure many lust after. Must be careful!"

Now Rah is all ears and eyes. When Ting Ya opens the door and steps out of the house she gives her head a little shake. "Bad day, Jin yu. Remember what I say."

It is all he needs to hear. His heart is pounding now, full of fear for her but also for himself. He does not wish to leave Ting Ya alone with the danger. But he is electric with panic. He begins to move away from her, toward the western edge of the cemetery where the wall is broken and he can scale it quick and leave enemies behind.

But as he backs away in that direction, Lutarus steps away from the brush behind Ting Ya's door. He grabs Ting Ya by the braid, pulls her body into his and puts a knife at her throat in full view of Rah, who screams

"Ting Ya!" again, helplessly. She does not seem surprised or frightened by Lutarus. Her eyes are quiet as she looks toward Rah. "Jin yu," she says again, her voice soft with tears, "remember what I say."

Rah is paralyzed. His mind is already in flight but his body refuses to leave Ting Ya. Three more men step out of the shadow behind the house, then another approaches from the gate, all dressed as Lutarus is dressed, in the uniform of the palace guard of Cyrus.

"It's you we want, Rah of Knossos. Give yourself over and the China woman lives," says Lutarus. The man is nearly as tall as Rush, broad and powerfully built. Ting Ya is a diminutive jewel against his uniform. Rah loses his posture of flight. His spinning mind comes to rest somewhere in his injured brain. He steps forward, the panic flowing out of his body like the silken wings of his dove costume coming to rest against his back, or the rain soaked ladies cape, slick against his legs. He cannot leave Ting Ya, he is trapped by his heart. He bows his head, his arms against his sides, palms forward. He has made an upright bow of surrender and submission.

The air is still. So still one can hear the buzzing of bees in the flowers growing along the outer wall of Ting Ya's house.

"Turios, take him," says Lutarus. But his voice is not the commanding tenor he wishes to project. It sounds weak in the summer air, as if trapped in the stillness Rah has created with his posture.

Turios has not moved. He is standing erect, blinking stupidly at Rah. The other three men have come around the back of the house and stand dumbly beside him.

"What the hell is he," says Turios finally.

"Jin yu," says Ting Ya one last time. She is addressing the boy, but also answering the man's question. Gold in abundance. Flee.

Rah lifts his head. He catches her eye. She is smiling at him her soft, ancient Asian smile. She makes a fist, bumps her chest with it, extends her hand to him, fingers opening. Many lifetimes, always friends.

But still Rah cannot move, cannot obey her. He lowers his head, returning to a submissive erect bow.

"Take him, damn it!" barks Lutarus, finding his voice.

Turios moves at last, striding up to Rah and grabbing his arm. He meets no resistance, but steps behind the boy and quickly trusses his wrists together with a rough rope. He shoves Rah ahead of him toward Lutarus.

Lutarus has pushed Ting Ya aside. The woman is useless to him now, dead or alive.

The men gather around their prize. Rah's chin remains tucked against his throat, his eyes to the ground. Lutarus' first impulse is to capture Rah's jaw and lift his face. When he does so he is struck in the chest as if with a golden club. All of the men are staring with equal astonishment at the boy's face.

Rah returns their stares with his fiercest scowl.

"Well, he's a pretty little thing," comments Turios finally.

This brings Lutarus to his senses. He releases Rah's jaw and shoves him at Aktor. "Take him. Turios, tie the woman up and leave her in the house. Let us get down off this damned mountain and back to Cyrus to finish what we came here to accomplish."

Five minutes later Ramicus and his men arrive at the gate. By then the cemetery is empty but for Ting Ya, and the souls of the ancient and Sun worshiping dead.

CHAPTER 28

By nightfall Lutarus and his men are back in Cyrus. They have not returned with their prize to the city itself, but have set up camp in the cemetery above, where the families of Cyrus have buried their kin since the last flood. They are holed up in Lutarus' own family grave. This is a stone walled crypt built into the side of a hill, with room inside for the men to bed down for the night against the tombs. There is no ceremony of bone cleansing in Cyrus and so no priests living in the cemetery. There is no keeper of the dead in Cyrus at all. The graveyard is empty of life, but for a pair of owls and a small colony of bats living in one of the older family crypts, the door of which was smashed in by thieves years ago and left to decay.

Rah is made to sit in a far corner of the crypt on the damp stone floor. His wrists remain tied behind him. His ankles are also bound and another rope ties the bonds at his wrists and feet to his collar. He is miserable and in pain, for the ropes are tight and cutting into his flesh. His lean, dancer's body has no excess, and his seat is already raw from sitting on the rough stones. Lutarus has left Turios and Aktor in charge of him while he and the two other men return to the city to prepare Cyrus for the public display of his killing. His plan is to proclaim the coming assassination in the street outside the palace. He will do this alone. The other two men are to remain hidden. If Lutarus is taken into custody these men are to return to the cemetery and slaughter the boy on his orders. But if he is able to stir the people in his favor and given leave to return for the boy, he will do so, and at an appointed time the following morning he will bring him down to the city and take his head off in front of the palace. Then he will send the boy's blonde head back to Knossos in a pigskin bag.

That should be enough to bring Knossos to arms.

After he and the two other men have left for Cyrus, Aktor and Turios leave Rah in the tomb and settle down outside the entrance in the sun for a game of dice. They remain within earshot of the boy as they have been told. They have two orders, keep him tied in the tomb and keep him alive, for as Lutarus has explained to them, bringing Cyrus a dead Grain God will be far less effective than bloodying a live one in public. But it is not long before an eerie yowl is heard coming from the crypt. It is a low vibration breaking the late day stillness, but it is unmistakable.

"Sounds like some animal trapped in there," says Turios, looking up from the game suddenly. "I'd better go have a look. Wouldn't want the little scamp to get bit." He lifts his considerable bulk off the grass and leaves Aktor to throw by himself a bit or just relax against the outer wall of the tomb.

Inside it is dark except for the light coming from the now opened tomb door.

Turios becomes alarmed when he realizes that the cat-like yowling is coming from the corner where the Grain God was left, trussed too tightly to be able to move from whatever is making that noise.

"You alright, lad?" says Turios, slouching toward the corner. In the dim light he can just make out Rah's form. There is no answer, but the whining has ceased abruptly. Turios moves without much concern for himself toward he boy. Anything making that noise will surely be more afraid of him than he of it. When he reaches Rah, he crouches in front of him. Even in this light that pale mass of curls is evident and easy to find. There is nothing in the corner but the boy.

"Was that you making that racket?" says Turios to the shadow under the hair. No answer. But then, from the same shadow, comes the warning hum of an angry cat.

"What the-?" Turios turns back toward the doorway. "That's him making that noise!" he shouts toward Aktor. "Maybe went to take a leak," he mumbles to himself when he gets no response. Rah is still making a feral warble.

"Well, no need you sitting in the dark over here by yourself. Nasty place, eh? Damp, dark. No place for the living. Come on, let's get you in the light over there where it's dry." With that he looms over Rah, feeling for the knot in the rope at Rah's wrists, and releases it. He does the same with the boy's ankles, then lifts him roughly by one arm and pushes him toward a rectangle of sunlight at the bottom of the stone staircase that lead up to the sunlight.

"Well go on, set your little butt down here and I'll tie you up again."

But Rah makes no move to do as he is told. Instead he walks right into the wall at the bottom of the stairs, presses himself against it, his back to Turios, his eyes lifting toward the light at the top. He makes a miserable whimper.

"Poor little thing, you're in quite a mess, aren't you," muses Turios. "What in hell are you? Half cat? Do you speak, boy?" He turns Rah around to face him.

"Hurt," says Rah, in the voice of a man Turios' size, flicking his eyes down to show Turios the bruises and cuts on his forearms from the rough rope. Then he crosses them high over his chest, hiding his hands under his armpits and shrinking against the wall away from the guard, who is peering at him with unchecked curiosity. Rah tucks his chin in an effort to dampen it, but Turios immediately takes hold of his jaw and turns his face back toward the light.

"Where do you come from, boy?" he says, staring at Rah's eyes like a jeweler looking through a glass.

"North," says Rah. "Far north," he adds, when the man makes no move to release his jaw.

"And there's something wrong with your tongue, too, you can't talk right. Did they cut a piece off?" He has squeezed his fingers into Rah's cheeks, forcing him to open his mouth. "Stick it out, never seen one," says Turios. "Why did they do that to you?"

"Turios, what the hell are you doing down there? You owe me money," says Aktor from above. And Turios, suddenly reminded of his responsibility, drops Rah's face at last and snatches his wrists in one hand, binding them together.

"Here then, I'll tie them in front, how's that?" He is quick with a rope. The instant Rah's wrists are secure he pushes him down into the corner and ties his bound wrists to his ankles.

"Now you quit that howling. Take a nap," says Turios. He seems to be looking about for something. Not far from where Rah has been deposited is a pile of gear the men threw down the steps when they arrived at the tomb. He rifles through it, finds a soldier's leather, shoves it under Rah's seat. Then he stomps back up the stone stairs and out of the tomb.

An hour later his heavy footsteps awaken Rah, who has indeed dozed off in a seated position in the corner.

"Come down to give you a bite to eat. You have to pee or something?"

Rah looks up at him glumly, shakes his head 'no'. To his surprise, Turios plops down right beside him in the corner. He has a round of pita in one hand, a water gourd in the other. He tears a chunk off the bread, shoves it toward Rah's mouth.

"Come on, open up," says Turios pleasantly.

The man is dirty and smells of days outdoors without a bath or change of clothes. Rah feels his stomach flip at the thought of taking food from his hand. But when he turns away from the offering Turios puts down the water gourd, leans over him and begins pushing the chunk of bread at him doggedly. It occurs to Rah that if he does not take the food voluntarily he is going to be forced and probably choked by this buffoon, who clearly has no intention of releasing his wrists and allowing him to feed himself. Eyeing Turios warily he pulls back his lips, nips a bit of the bread from the chunk in Turios' finger and, fighting a powerful the urge to spit it back at the man, manages a few disinterested chews.

"There. Good boy. You thirsty? You must be. Here, I've brought you some water," says Turios, turning to find the water gourd. This too he presses at Rah, who is ready for him this time. Even so, water splashes down his chin onto his chest as the man tips the skin too forcefully into his mouth.

"So who exactly do you belong to, eh? The King? The Priesthood?" Turios asks after a time. Rah has managed to take another bite of bread without vomiting up the first, and is chewing it determinedly.

With an effort, he swallows the morsel. "To wolf," he says, shooting Turios his blackest look.

"Wolf? Who is wolf?" Turios chuckles. "Wolf." He shakes his head, bemused.

"Wolf is assassin," says Rah.

This peaks Turio's interest. "Assassin? What assassin? Why would an assassin own the Grain God of Knossos?"

Rah looks at him as if he is an idiot. "He try to kill me. Cannot. When I dance I spit at him. He is mad. He buy me to punish."

It is Turios' turn to give Rah a quizzical look. "Sorry I asked." He offers him the rest of the pita but this time Rah turns his face to the wall. Turios gives him a long look over. His breathing is louder than before and Rah automatically bunches himself as tightly as he can into the corner, as if expecting a blow, or worse.

But the big man only shoves himself off the stone floor and gives Rah's head a pat before he stomps back up the stairs to sleep under the stars. At the top he calls back softly, "Well, good night, then." Then he closes the tomb door and leaves Rah to his first horrible night in the tomb.

As night falls the House of the Moon is filled with the wailing of a trilogy of temple maidens. The concubines to Rah, all three months pregnant by him, have stripped naked and covered themselves with filth. Even their eyes and hair are stringy with dung. Now they walk in circles around the columns in the villa's public courtyard, striking themselves bloody with reed whips and howling with grief. They are doing what it is only their duty to do, following proper protocol for this event. But the girls are sincere in their misery, and their voices cut through the night like the screech of mating owls. They will not relent until Rah is returned to them, or until they themselves are put out of their misery.

It is not only Rah's three concubines who are mad with grief. All the house is in chaos. The dance instructors, Dimius and Akbar, the bath master, Tuma, the pigeon keeper, Galateo, the dressers and face painters, most especially Rah's own, all of Rah's dance troupe as well as the kitchen staff are stricken with horror that their beautiful Grain Dancer has been kidnapped and may already be dead.

Mochlos, pacing like a caged rat back and forth in his private courtyard and wringing his hands, has refused any interruption from his staff other than that of good news. He is determined to find Rah alive before Ameg returns to collect him. Always a man to rely on wit first, he believes he only needs to figure this out. Over and over he has repeated to himself that Rah is worth more alive than dead. How could it be otherwise? He refuses to despair. When Ameg returns the little Grain God will be back here at the villa where he belongs, being coddled by an entire houseful of grateful staff.

Right now Mochlos is awaiting the arrival of the Asian gatekeeper, the woman whom Ramicus brought back with him when he returned to the city to tell the priest what had happened. She is being held by his guard now, and he has decided that his first step must be to interrogate her. The two idiot stable boys could only tell him that the kidnapper wore some kind of uniform and was a big, powerfully built man with piercing eyes. It was not a uniform they recognized.

Mochlos has thoroughly interrogated Ramicus and sworn him to secrecy, though Ramicus has no intention of honoring the later. As soon as he leaves the House of the Moon he will send his men out into the city to leave word for Ameg that the Grain God has been taken.

But Ameg is at sea, cruising slowly against southern winds toward Anatolia, where he plans to oversee the move of his Minoan household into a fortress twice the size of the Palace of Knossos. The fortress is Rush the Assassin's safest nest. It is surrounded by a trained mercenary army and boasts the finest Hittite charioteers in the Mediterranean world.

Mochlos has learned from Ramicus that after he and his men discovered Ting Ya and released her they searched the burial ground for clues as to where the Grain Dancer may have been taken. They found evidence of an encampment on the outer wall of the south end of the cemetery, but nothing more. It appeared to Ramicus that four or five men camped out behind the wall for several days, obviously waiting for Eknos to alert them when the dancer was approaching. They were able to stow their gear and disappear in a matter of about a quarter hour, as long as it took for Ramicus to get to the mounds. Mochlos is relieved to discover that the men took the boy alive and had done no harm to him in Ting Ya's presence. It is a good sign, in his estimation, that Ting Ya has been spared as well. Ting Ya was able to give Ramicus the names Turios and Aktor, the only names she heard spoken by the man who was clearly in charge of the kidnapping. Eknos was of the least use, although he had had the most dealings with the man. He did not know his name or even which city he came from. He only knew he had paid the boys to spy on Rah and to give him a sign when he knew the Grain God was on his way to the mounds.

"The Asian woman, Holiness."

A guard has led the diminutive Ting Ya into the priest's private courtyard. She is dressed in her ceremonial gown, the veil pulled back. Odd, since she would have had to have been surprised by the kidnappers. Why would she be dressed this way on a common day?

Ting Ya offers the priest her Asian bow, then maintains lowered eyes.

"Let us dispense with ceremony, Ting Ya," says Mochlos quickly, waving the guard away. "I know you and you know me, and today we have a common enemy."

"Yes, sir, common enemy, common friend."

"And who is our friend, Ting Ya?" asks the priest with ever an ear for the possibility of an unexpected solution.

"This is great man from city, sir. Rich man, one who will take boy with him far from wave."

Mochlos stares at the little woman blankly. There is only one man she can be referring to, but what is this about a wave? Involuntarily, Mochlos recalls his dream the night the assassin first visited him. Water flooding the floors of an Egyptian palace where he was bantering with a statistician about the vastness of his wealth as a result of a golden thread he found in the silks he bought from Ameg. And then the statistician saying something about a wave. These things happen before a wave, he had said. "You must eventually give the gold back to the silk merchant or else we all will drown." Yes, those were his very words. And then water, blue, green and gold, like the boy's eyes, sucking him down, pulling at him, climbing up to his chest. And then the sense of smothering, the pressure on his lungs so great that he could not take a breath. And waking to the assassin sitting on his belly with a knife to his throat.

"You speak of Ameg, the merchant," he says, shaking a long index finger at her. "But why do you call him my friend? The man will be very unhappy with me indeed if he finds that the Grain God has been kidnapped out from under my very nose. I shudder to think what his money can buy me for losing him."

Now Ting Ya lifts her head, boldly looking the priest directly in the eyes. "Ah, this man, Ameg, this is only man can save Rah now. Only man. No time to waste. You must contact this man. How much angrier will he be if you fail to give him time to save Rah? He want Rah. He will kill you many time, many ways, if Rah is dead before he return."

Mochlos' eyes widen at this thought, which has as yet escaped him. Ting Ya is right. If he keeps this secret from Ameg, and fails to find the boy alive before he returns, he will be in even greater peril of making an enemy of the merchant than if he found a means to let him know what has happened, thus giving him an opportunity to use his vast wealth to bring about the boy's safe return.

"You are a clever woman, Ting Ya. But Ameg is at sea, already eight or so hours out. I have no means of reaching him, as his ship is the fastest in the harbor."

"Then you cannot catch him with ship. Cannot fight water with water. Must fight water with air."

"With-" But suddenly Mochlos' understands. He slaps his own head with his open palms. "With air! My god, the doves! Guard! Bring me the dove keeper! Bring me Galateo at once!"

In the lamp lit servant's dining room of the House of the Moon, several of Rah's closest allies are keeping a vigil. No one in the villa has had the stomach for a meal, and at any rate, the kitchen has been closed for the evening. All have been ordered to fast tonight and pray for the safe return of the Grain God.

Those who keep the vigil in the dining room have their theories as to who stole Rah and why. Dimius believes it is Ananou, but his theory is challenged by Akbar, who reminds him that the men had foreign uniforms (this he learned from the guard at the gate who let Ramicus and his men into the compound). Akbar thinks these men are from Gournia or Malia, that they were sent to kill the Grain God of Knossos because the people there believe he has caused the sea storms and quakes on the eastern end of the island. Pyrus has kept silent most of the evening, but at length offers that it is possible that Rah was taken by Cyrus, and meant to be kept alive in hopes that possession of the true Rah will bring much needed rain and end the drought that has all but destroyed southern crops on Crete this year.

"There's no point being overly optimistic, I suppose," says Pyrus. "But you'd have to be an idiot, or mad, to believe that Rah is worth more dead than alive."

"Ameg himself would pay a fortune for him," adds Aros tearfully. "You can't fool me when it comes to matters of the heart. That man is completely captivated by Rah. Didn't any of you see him at the Midsummer Celebration? He looked like he wanted to kill our 'wolf' and take his place right there on the arena floor. It was no surprise to me when he came for Rah the next day."

"Ah, that boy could dance with the sea," smiles Galateo from the end of the table. The old man has been sitting quietly, listening to the talk, petting a dove he holds close to his chest in both hands. The dove was found in the House of the Moon aviary this morning after missing for over a week.

"Let us not speak of him as if he were already dead." It is Tuma's baritone boom. Tuma has been standing by the doorway like a bronze statue, his arms crossed over his powerful, hairless chest, listening silently to the table. "Our boy has tricks," he continues, giving the Galateo a wink.

"Indeed he does," says Galateo. "This dove seems to have followed him home from Ameg's house. Rah and I found it in our own coop this morning before he left for the burial mounds. Rah told me it had a mate at Ameg's house. I said to him, "Rah, how did you come to play with the doves of the merchants wife?' For everyone knows the lady keeps the doves. He says, 'Josepha let me. '"

"That's the wife," agrees Agatka. "That's the merchant's wife, Josepha."

"Imagine, he's at the House of Ameg a few days and the lady of the house is letting him play with her own birds," chuckles Galateo.

"The merchant has moved his household to Anatolia," offers Agatka. "Ramicus told me this before he went to speak with the priest."

"So the lady's doves are on board ship. This one lost its mate this morning when the house was locked up and abandoned. So it came back here." says Galateo, considering.

"She gave Rah a pearl earring worth a king's ransom," offers Aros. "He told us she made it for him. Pyrus asked him, 'Does Ameg know she gave you this pearl, Rah?' He says to Pyrus, 'Wolf say, This pearl I bring her. She make. This pearl I give you. ' That's what he calls Ameg. 'Wolf. '"

"Our boy has tricks," Tuma says again, nodding.

"It's true," agrees Agatka. "Who among us didn't find ways to spoil him rotten? I was always making him his favorite treat, those little-"

"Honeyed walnut clusters," finishes Aros. "And I was always finding ways to sneak them into his room at night. There are still some hidden under the vanity from last night." Aros begins to tear up again. "I was so happy to have him back, even though he was mad at me."

"What for?" Puts in Dimius.

"I think the priest finally let him know he was headed for the mountain," says Aros.

"And that Ameg, and the assassin, saved him from it," adds Pyrus.

"Have none of you ever considered-" begins Dimius, then thinks better of it.

There is a sudden stillness in the room. It is Tuma who breaks the silence with an almost inaudible chuckle. All eyes turn to him.

"They are the same," he says.

Aros is looking at him with a queer expression. He drops his eyes, smoothes out the napkin he has been twisting in his fingers all evening, bites his plump lips. Finally he looks up and around the table. Pyrus is giving him a warning look.

"What is it, Pyrus?" asks Dimius.

Pyrus gives him a frown. "Oh come on, we all knew. But who among us had the balls to tell the priest? Or anyone for that matter," he breathes.

"I would if it could save Rah," blurts Aros suddenly.

Another moment of silence is broken by the soft voice of the dove master.

"Perhaps it can."

At that moment Galateo is summoned to speak with the priest. All eyes are on him as he passes the dove to Agatka, and gets slowly to his feet. As he leaves the table he puts a hand on her shoulder.

"Hang on to him, woman, there is hope in that dove."

Mochlos is pacing again when Galateo arrives. Ting Ya has been standing quietly in the courtyard, her hands folded in front of her, her head bowed as if in prayer. When Galateo approaches she looks up to catch his eye, although the two have never met.

"This man we need. This man can fight water with air."

Mochlos strides up to Galateo without ceremony. "I need to reach Ameg at sea. Can a dove do it?"

"Can a dove catch a ship? Yes. It's done all the time, Holiness. That is how the Greeks communicate with their vessels. But the dove must have a motivator. A reason to fly to the ship."

"Damn!" spits the priest.

"If you speak of Ameg's ship, Holiness, I have a dove with just such a motivation. I have a dove with a mate aboard that ship."

"My god man, I could kiss you. How is this possible?"

"Why only this morning Rah told me that he had seen a dove which had been missing from our coop at the House of Ameg. No sooner did he tell me this, than that very dove came to alight upon our coop. As you know, Holiness, all of our birds are marked with a twist of wire strung with the colors of the House of the Moon, yellow and white."

"Yes, yes. But how did Rah know this bird had a mate at Ameg's house? And that the bird would be aboard ship? And how will this bird know to find his mate if it is stowed in the hold as most household animals are?"

"Well, Holiness, Rah saw the dove approach his hen. There is quite a bit of ceremony involved when doves, who mate for life, greet each other after a separation. As to the latter, the lady of the house told Rah that her husband had had a dovecote built on the foredeck. She wanted her birds to enjoy the sun and air, you see. Pigeons often sicken in the hold."

"And you think this bird will fly out to sea to find her?"

"I believe it came home because the house of Ameg has been

deserted. The coop closed, the birds brought with the household out to sea. If I withhold food, it may look for her, and for the rest of the flight. Birds are strange creatures, Holiness, doves stranger. We can only wonder how they navigate the seas, but they do, as if they had maps in their bellies. It is not a certainty that this dove will fly to the ship, but it is a possibility."

Mochlos, a man never to shrug off a possibility, then calls Aros and Pyrus, Rah's two personal attendants, to the courtyard.

"You two know the boy as well or better than anyone. I need some trinket, something that can be tied to a dove's foot, something that Ameg may have seen him with."

At that Aros looks at Pyrus, a wide, teary smile breaking apart the misery on his full face. Pyrus returns the smile with an upturned corner of his lips and a wink.

"Holiness, he came home last night with gifts from Ameg's house. A pearl earring-"

"Yes, of course, the earring. You needn't remind me. A token of affection from the merchant himself, worth a small fortune. Losing that alone will cost me my balls. And I have lost it and the boy."

"But there is more, sir," offers Aros, his big eyes twinkling. "Ameg's sons, the twins, each gave him a gift."

"Well for the love of the god, man, don't keep me in suspense," Mochlos throws his hands in the air. "Anything light enough to be tied to a dove's foot? A dove with a mate aboard Ameg's ship! A god damned lovesick dove who may just head into southerly winds to find his mate in a dovecote on deck, especially made for the lady so that her doves could enjoy the light and air above decks?"

"A feather, holiness," says Pyrus. "A tail feather tied with a red ribbon, and a small carving of a dove, made of wood as light as air itself."

"All you need do is drill a hole through the wood with a needle, and tie it to the leg," adds Aros, turning to Pyrus and shrugging at the simplicity of the plan. "Tie the feather to the other."

"We must wait until morning." It is Galateo. "It will not fly at night. I will shut up the other birds tonight, separate this dove, and withhold grain. Then in the morning we can release it, and pray."

Mochlos gives Galateo a sharp nod. Then he turns to the two attendants. "You two have these items?"

"I took them from him for safe keeping last night," says Aros. "He drops things where he stands, you know. He would have lost them in an hour."

"Give them to the dove keeper. Have one of my jewelers fix them to the dove's legs securely. If he loses one in flight, there is still the other. Ameg is clever enough to figure out the message. We need only pray that the dove finds the ship."

"They have only been out a day, sir. If we release the dove at dawn he may well find the ship by dusk. Doves are powerful fliers."

"Air dominate water," says Ting Ya, who has been listening to the men in silence. "Must return Jin yu to the wolf, then leave island. Earth create air. Air dominate water, and bring wave."

"Oh, to hell with the wave, Ting Ya. I've got to find this boy alive or I won't be around to drown in a wave."

On the morning of Rah's second day of captivity by Lutarus' men, Turios opens the tomb door to find the Grain God moaning and shivering at the bottom of the stairs.

"Bad night, lad?" He grabs the boy by the rope binding his wrists to his ankles, unties it, and attempts to drag him to his feet. But Rah's hands and feet are numb from lack of blood. He is unable to stand and crumples like a ragdoll to the floor. Turios is forced to throw him over his shoulder and carry him up the stone steps into the daylight.

"I don't know what we're waiting here for," growls Aktor as Turios steps out of the tomb and tosses Rah to the ground. "Captain would have been back last night if he hadn't been arrested. The other two must have taken off, left us to rot up here." Aktor has apparently just returned from a water source with two filled gourds and a larger leather water carrier. Seeing the boy's condition he offers one to Turios. "Here, give him some of this."

Turios takes the gourd and offers it to Rah, who is not yet in control of his numbed hands. Rah reaches for the gourd but is unable to close his fingers around it. It falls through them, its contents spilling out onto the ground.

Aktor's immediate response is to bend his apish bulk over Rah and slap him across the face.

"You spastic idiot! I walked half a mile for that!"

Aktor's blow has thrown Rah onto his back. He looks up dizzily at Aktor, who is still bending over him. The man's eyes are hot with violence, beneath which an unsettling curiosity has developed.

"You are a pretty little thing, aren't you? I wouldn't mind having a go at you," he says, reaching to untie the skirt of his uniform.

Turios grabs Aktor's arm. "Hey, we're supposed to watch him, not kill him. Anyway, he's sick or something. He's burning up."

Aktor pulls his arm out of Turio's grasp. He reties his skirt, but looks at Turios with a leering grin. "Make you a deal. If the Captain isn't here by tomorrow morning, I get to do whatever I want with him."

"Deal," agrees Turios, not one to back down from a bet. "Captain will be back. Maybe stayed the night at the palace. He is the King's uncle, after all."

But Lutarus did not sleep at the palace last night. His bid for war was quashed when he arrived before the gates with his proclamation.

"I have the Grain God of Knossos! People of Cyrus, we all know he is the cause of our failing crops! Join with me and my men! Take up arms against Knossos! Let us slaughter the god publicly here before the palace and take the fertile north country! I have powerful Greek allies and I can guarantee our success!"

But Lutarus is not the man he thinks he is. Neither the leader of armies nor the powerful orator he would have to be to launch a revolt such as this one. The palace guards report immediately to Cyrus that their captain, his uncle, claims to have kidnapped the Grain God of Knossos and is in the street outside of the palace attempting to incite a riot and worse, war with Knossos using Greek allies.

"Why, the Greeks will take everything. Has my uncle gone mad, now, as well?" Cyrus shakes his head, not particularly concerned. "Take him off the street as quickly and quietly as you can. Surround him and tell him he has my audience. Then bring him before me and we will see what the truth is."

Lutarus is hopeful when his nephew the King grants him a formal audience for this occasion. It means that the court will be present and he can make his bid for war before them. He strides into the palace with the guard, men he considers to be loyal to him first, and presents himself before Cyrus who has by now gathered the court in the Great Hall.

But the first words out of Cyrus' mouth are not encouraging.

"Do you not recall that I have paid the 'Terror of the Aegean' to protect the Grain God of Knossos, Uncle? Did you not find this man for me yourself? Did you not say one must not trifle with such a man? Do you think I will have the boy I paid him to protect slaughtered publicly so that you can have your war with Knossos? I have no desire to explain to the assassin one night in my bed while he is carving my eyeballs out of my head, why my uncle slaughtered the Grain God I hired him to protect, so that he could incite war with Knossos. You are a dead man, uncle, and I do not wish to follow you into the grave."

Lutarus is allowed to stay in the palace guard quarters, under the arrest of his own men. He has refused to give Cyrus the location of the Grain God, and has sworn to him that the boy will be killed if he is not allowed to return for him. But Lutarus' plans are crumbling. The two men he took with him back into the city have, unbeknownst to him, given themselves up to the guard since his arrest, hoping that they might avoid execution if they give the King the location of the kidnapped boy. In the morning, Cyrus will send a contingent of men to the burial ground to arrest Turios and Aktor and to rescue the Grain God.

CHAPTER 29

On his second night in the tomb, not long after Turios closes the door on him, Rah escapes.

His body has begun to scream with the pain of being bound, wrists to ankles, on a cold stone floor. His back is burning, his thighs cramping. His neck, always delicate as a result of that ride through the air and the blow to his head against the table as an infant, is torturing him. The pain chases his soul about in his body, and when he can stand it no longer, his soul flees. The bonds he is trussed in cannot keep him from bashing his head against the floor of the stone tomb that surrounds him as he leaves his body behind to his epilepsy. After the fit, he sleeps. And in his sleep, he is visited by his twin, Ileah.

Rah opens his eyes to blurred yellow light. He is in that twilight place he always visits between an epileptic seizure and full consciousness. At the far end of the tomb a childlike but obviously feminine figure evolves out of the haze. It is his twin, Ileah, at the age she died of fever. She is tucked into the corner, on her feet but turned partially away from him. She hides her face behind long platinum blonde curls that cascade down her back. She wears a dirty white shift, sleeveless, too big for her tiny form. She is shivering, her face turned away and pressed against the wall. She is weeping, a child's terrible, lonely weeping. She is as opaque as Rah.

In his fevered brain Rah forms the words to speak to her but he cannot operate his vocal chords. His body will no longer tolerate him as master. He is in the grip of a paralysis, like the drug induced paralysis he suffered as a result of the potion Mochlos made him drink the day he was proclaimed the Grain God. He can only lie where he is on the cold tomb floor, feeling the floor, feeling his sister's tiny whimpering along the nerves of his spine, unable to reach her or speak to her.

Then a voice booms from above, as if emanating from the very core of the hill into which the tomb is built. Like an explosion it shatters the image of Ileah into fragments. It is neither male nor female, this voice, and although cataclysmic and deafening, it is also beautiful.

"Ahalai, you must flee," it says. It is not a suggestion. It is a command. Ileah is gone but something else, something colossal and transcendent, descends upon him from above. Music, chords beyond the limits of any chords he has ever heard, a symphony of sounds unknown to his world, heralds its descent. Looming over him, somehow unhampered by the close, tight walls of the tomb, mighty wings flap with the power of horses, thundering against the tomb walls on either side of him. Within his paralyzed body his soul curls up in terror. He is an embryo.

"Come," says the voice. And suddenly Rah is plucked out of his body. He shoots up, like a dolphin exploding out of the sea, into crystal white light. It is a gorgeous feeling, this freedom after such bondage. He is wrapped in a warm and physical sense of love, as in a mother's arms. He is elevated, up, up, through the hill above the tomb and into the stacked clouds above the southern skies of Crete. He is soaring, high above the mountains on warm currents of air, flying north, toward the House of the Moon, toward the sea.

Josepha is on deck with her birds, looking south toward Crete in the early evening of Rah's second day of captivity.

There is still enough light to see the horizon and for a time she believes she is merely watching a lone gull, an unusual sight this far from the coast, which disappeared yesterday evening. Curious, she watches the bird. It is flying too high for a gull or cormorant, and appears to be heading straight for the ship. As it continues to approach it becomes clear that its flight pattern is that of a dove. Amazed, Josepha takes some grain from the pocket of her shift and waits. The bird continues its direct flight and is soon clear enough to recognize. It is indeed a dove, pure white, and as it makes its descent she realizes, with some alarm, that there is an object tied to one of its feet.

In the morning Turios opens the tomb door to find Rah at the bottom of the stairs moaning and shivering. He has moved several feet from his original corner and is no longer sitting on the soldier's leather. Blood is caked in the curls at the back of his head for he has smacked his skull on the stone floor during his seizure. He has also bitten his lower lip and it is swollen and bloody.

When Turios comes down the stairs and leans over him Rah's eyes open and roll in his head. Afraid they may have killed the boy with neglect in one night Turios picks him up, still bound, and carries him up into the light.

"Something wrong with him," he tells Aktor, depositing him on the grass near the opening of the tomb. "Get me some water."

Turios takes Rah's face in his hands and shakes it, further insulting his concussed brain.

"Wake up, boy," he demands, slapping the boy's pallid cheeks. When Aktor comes with a gourd of water Turios splashes some in Rah's face and the boy pulls his head back and opens his eyes. He quickly squeezes them shut again against the daylight and moans.

"Head hurt." He manages to force the words past his parched, thickened tongue. "Eyes." He tries to pull his hands up to his eyes to cover them but they are still tied to his ankles.

Turios tries to untie the rope at Rah's wrists but it has tightened with his struggling over night and is impossible to loosen. He pulls a short handled dagger from his belt and cuts through the knot, then cuts the bonds at Rah's ankles as well. The boy's wrists and ankles are raw and bleeding.

"Come on, boy, get on your feet," says Turios, lifting Rah up like a doll and attempting to plant his feet under him. But the boy cannot stand. His balance and strength gone, he melts to his knees. Before he can fall on his face, Turios slips an arm under his legs, one under his torso, and lays him back down on the grass. Rah rolls into a ball, shivering and moaning.

"What the hell is wrong with him. He looks like he's dying," comments Aktor.

"Burning up. Fever," says Turios.

"Awful lot of jewelry for a slave, eh?" considers Aktor, bending over Rah and slipping thick, simian fingers under his golden belt, which has become quite loose. "What say we cut all this gold off of him and split it between us? Captain must have been arrested. Someone would have come back by now."

"Captain said stay here, watch the boy," says Turios, looking down at Rah with a perplexed expression.

"We're on our own, Turios. Captain's been arrested. Those other two never came back to tell us. May as well make the best of it." He begins looking around for something with which to strip Rah of his golden collar, belt, and anklets.

"They're too thick to cut," says Turios.

Aktor comes up short, turns to the other man. "Well, he's near dead anyway. Fever or something. May as well put him out of his misery. Then we can chop him up and take the gold without cutting it."

As the two men stand over him considering this, Rah moans and turns his head away from the sunlight streaming down over their shoulders. His curls flop away from his ears and the pearl earring catches the morning and gleams.

Aktor whistles, dropping to his knees to investigate the gem. "Will you look at that." He fiddles with Rah's ear, then comes to his feet with the pearl earring in his hand.

"Half of that's mine," says Turios.

"Well, we'd better pack up and get out of here," says Aktor. "If the captain's been arrested, it's only a matter of time they'll come up here looking for the boy. We'll be arrested next."

"What do we do with him?" asks Turios, looking down at Rah with something like compassion passing over his simple-minded face.

"Leave him. Put him back in the tomb so it looks like we deserted him before he got sick. Long as they find him alive, we aren't murderers. Come on, grab the gear. We can live for a year in Malia on this."

Turios lifts Rah without much effort and carries him back down the steps to the floor of the Lutarus family tomb. He sets him back on the soldier's leather in the corner and stands up. The boy is in a delirium but seems less restless now that he is out of the morning light. Turios kneels one last time and pats the boy's head.

"Sorry, lad," is all he can think to say before he trudges up the stairs with the gear and shuts out the daylight.

An hour later a contingent of men and two horses arrive at the burial ground. The Lieutenant and leader of this expedition is half Lutarus' age and possesses twice his ambition. Before leaving the palace he has carefully examined all of the men available to him for the rescue. In addition to taking the ten best men he can find, he has chosen five others who excel as trackers, as well as his personal friend, Horus, a man who has previously demonstrated his intelligence and loyalty to him. He has also spoken with a palace physician to be sure he takes appropriate supplies along on an extra pack animal. Whatever the Grain God's condition is when they find him, provided he is still alive, the Lieutenant does not intend to lose him to whatever injuries may have been inflicted on him during his captivity.

The two men who were arrested following their confessions last night are bound and brought along. When the soldiers arrive at the stone wall at the bottom of the burial grounds these two are shoved ahead, lances prodding their backs.

"Find the tomb and be quick," says the Lieutenant. He has already made it clear to his prisoners that he is a man to be obeyed promptly and that anyone who slows his progress will pay a high price. That morning, before leaving the palace, he cut an ear off each man, then had the palace surgeon cauterize the wounds so that the men could make the trek up the hill to the cemetery without passing out from loss of blood.

"I take these from you for your treason against the King and Queen of Cyrus," he explains while the men howled in pain. "For listening to the

Captain of the Palace Guard instead of his sovereign. These ears have failed you. I trust those remaining on your heads will listen only to the will of your King. He speaks through me when I tell you that you will lose the other two if I have not found the Grain God of Knossos, alive, by noon."

The two men, trussed like fowl, now stumble forward through the gate of the burial ground toward Lutarus' family tomb. The Lieutenant, a handsome figure on horseback, trots behind them, his lance unsheathed and lying against his right thigh, ready to be swung skillfully and sharply through the air should either man attempt to escape. He is fond of decapitating from the back of a horse, and only recently returned from Mycenae where he spent several months practicing this skill on Greek prisoners of war. But his enjoyment of this sport is thwarted today as the two men head straight for the Tomb of Lutarus and drop to their knees in front of the door.

"He was to be kept here until the captain returned," says one, "or until we came back without him."

The Lieutenant does not need to order his men to open the tomb. Three of them have done so, kicking the prisoners aside and storming down the steps into the darkness before the Lieutenant has had time to dismount and hand his reins to a fourth.

"He's here, sir!" says one from inside the burial chamber.

"He's alive!" says another.

The first appears at the doorway with the unconscious boy in his arms. The Lieutenant strides up to him, peering with suspicion at the limp body. He places three fingers against Rah's throat, checking for a pulse.

"Just barely," he murmurs, then places the palm of one hand on Rah's forehead. "He's burning up with fever." He strokes the boy's damp curls back, then turns Rah's face gently to one side. "He had an earring. Look here." His eyes travel down the length of Rah's body. "But they left all this gold. So they left quickly, and stupidly." He turns to address a tall man standing directly behind him. "Horus, take the five trackers and find them, they cannot be far." The man he has addressed nods, beckons the trackers, and gestures for them to spread out to look for signs of the kidnappers' route of departure.

"Don't waste time in here, Horus," says the Lieutenant, turning back to Rah. "Start at the gate. Men stupid enough to do this would not have the sense to go over the wall."

The Lieutenant opens his arms to the man holding the unconscious Grain God. "Give him to me." He takes the boy, who seems to weigh nothing, and nods toward the second horse. The animal is burdened with several large leather sacks and a roll of linen. "Bring me the water and the linens. We need to bring down this fever before we move him."

Now the Lieutenant drops to one knee with Rah in his arms. "Spread the linen under him," he orders. "Then we will soak it and wrap him in it to cool him."

As his men obey his orders the Lieutenant takes a closer look at Rah's face. The boy's eyes are closed, and his face is drawn and pale. His lower lip is puffed and bleeding as if he has been punched in the mouth. The curls at the back of his head are caked with blood as well. Even so, his extraordinary features are obvious.

"He is exquisite," murmurs the Lieutenant, sitting back on his heels. He lowers the boy's body onto the linen, which has been soaked with cool water. He wraps the wet cloth around the boy's limp form, then takes another cloth, which has been dampened for him, and uses it to wash the blood and sweat from Rah's face. Then he turns Rah's head to one side to examine the wound at the back of his scalp

"Give me a gourd of water." He washes the blood out of Rah's matted hair and finds a deep cut which he rinses patiently. A man standing behind him, leaning over his ministrations, offers him a small pot.

"What is it?" But the Lieutenant has already removed the cover and dipped a finger into the coarse bluish mixture.

"Surgeon said it would heal up an open wound faster than without," says the man.

The Lieutenant applies a generous dab of the concoction onto the wound. Then, satisfied that he has done all he can for now, he gently sets Rah's head back on the cooled linen sheet.

"Someone is missing this boy," says the Lieutenant, taking a deep, purposeful breath.

"They say he can jump like a leopard, sir, that he can make the moon weep to watch him dance," says the other man.

"Someone wants him back," the Lieutenant responds. "Someone powerful." He shakes his head, getting to his feet. "God help Cyrus if we don't deliver him alive."

When Rah's body has begun to lose its feverish heat, the Lieutenant orders his men to wrap him in a dry linen sheet. He mounts his horse, then has Rah handed up to him. He settles the boy in his arms and picks up his reins. Then he and his men begin the trek down the hill to the city.

Half way down the hill the horse, although a seasoned and docile animal, spooks at a movement in the brush. A fox has been disturbed by the men's tramping feet. The Lieutenant instinctively snatches Rah against his chest, maintaining his balance by clutching the horse with long, well trained thighs. When the animal settles, he looks down at the boy in his arms. He is greeted by a pair of gold flecked, blue-green eyes gazing up at him beneath cat-long lashes. The Lieutenant sits up in his saddle and blinks foolishly at his burden. For a moment, he is utterly captivated. His men have stopped their progress and are standing about, waiting for his command.

"Gah," says Rah, trying to focus on the face above him. Then he begins to struggle in his cocoon of linen. Although he is barely conscious, he is a horseman on a horse and in the wrong position, and his body, like a gyroscope, is twisting to put him on his seat.

"Be still, boy, you are rescued," says the Lieutenant, still dazed by those eyes. The face, angelic in sleep, has twenty times the impact when they are opened.

Rah moans, his eyes rolling back, and passes out again in the Lieutenant's arms. But it takes another moment before the man is able to recall his own priorities and nod for his men to continue forward to the palace.

On the morning of Rah's rescue, a small boat, launched from Ameg's private ship the night before and meant for an emergency exit on high seas, lands in the harbor of Knossos. From it, Rush the Assassin, once again sporting the fine garments of Ameg the Merchant, steps onto the pier, then catches a sack tossed to him by the man who will wait for him here until his return. Two burly wolf-dogs, black as death, hop onto the pier at his sides, their tongues lolling with thirst. Ameg's private vessel has orders to deposit his household on the coast of Anatolia, then turn around and make the trip back to Crete, this time with the help of southern winds, to take Ameg and the remainder of his valuables home to the Land of Hatti.

The assassin is in a fine temper this morning. Last night his wife, screaming his true name above decks, sent his body into a state of war before he even knew the cause. He has not eaten or slept since. When he reached Josepha on the foredeck and saw her standing in her simple white shift like a ghost against the darkening sky, a dove in her hands, his first thought was that she had merely overreacted to the injury of one of her pets. This launched a fury in his balls she would never understand. His muscles were already charged with strength, he was ready for a bloody fight, hoping to slaughter her attacker. Some fool he had hired in his haste to take his family off the doomed island thought he would have a taste of Ameg the Merchant's gentle little wife. Well, he would instead watch his own limbs being hacked off and thrown overboard to the sharks. Then the rest of him would be tied to the stern and eaten like chum while he was still alive, head above water. But when Josepha looked up at him with horror in her eyes and lifted the dove to show him the tiny carving hanging by a red ribbon from its foot, his mind truly went blank with rage.

The message was obvious. Someone had taken Rah.

It was to the priest's credit that he did not attempt to hide this event. He would be rewarded for that bravery in good time. But first, Rush the Assassin would be going hunting.

Upon reaching the harbor at Knossos Rush stows his sack in his own private storehouse, now all but empty, gives the dogs fresh water and locks them in the building. Then he trudges up the beach to the Bridge Road and Mochlos' villa.

Upon his arrival the gate seems to open itself. Two young priests have spent the night taking shifts awaiting his possible arrival and upon seeing him, a huge man dressed in fine yellow robes making his way up the Bridge Road from the harbor, the two pull the double gates back and fall to their knees until he has passed through. A bell lodged in a small guard tower atop the house begins to clang, awakening any who are still asleep inside the villa. Mochlos is not among them. He is down at the front door of the house before Ameg reaches the stoop.

"They took him alive, five men, when he arrived at the burial mounds yesterday afternoon. They were wearing uniforms. One idiot stable boy and Ting Ya saw the uniforms but the boy is useless, can't even remember the colors. He and his brother were being paid to alert the kidnappers as soon as they knew for certain Rah was on his way to the cemetery. They were assigned to Ramicus to watch the King's horses, and apparently knew his habits."

Mochlos has not stopped talking since Ameg reached the door. Now he pauses, shuddering under his own elegant robe, waiting for the man's response.

"Have you kept these boys for me?" is all Ameg says, not bothering to address the priest with his eyes. He is looking over his head, scanning the house. "And Ting Ya?"

Mochlos turns to the two young priests who have been following at a distance. "Bring me the stable boys and Ting Ya!" he screams at them, near hysterics. Then to Ameg, "Is there anyone else you wish to question?"

"They did not kill Ting Ya," says Ameg, who seems to be talking to himself. "That means they have a plan. Something long range. They wanted us to find them, to know who did this." Now he looks down at Mochlos, stroking his beard, his speech slowing. "Clever priest, put that fine mind of yours to work for me. Tell me, who would want such a thing?"

The priest stars up at the merchant, his eyes open wide in recognition and horror. The voice coming out of Ameg's mouth has been changing as he speaks, the refined Greek of the dandy merchant growing darker as the man talks, easing first into a baritone growl, and then into the Hittite hiss of the assassin.

He had thought that Ameg could buy him a nasty death by the assassin, but such a thought allowed the wily priest the belief that he would have time to flee. He now realizes that there is less than an arm's length between himself and his worst nightmare.

"It was you," he whispers. But he is interrupted as his own men return, shoving the two stable boys, Ophos and Eknos, in front of him.

"Which one alerted the men?" Rush addresses Mochlos. He is speaking Minoan now with a heavy Hittite accent.

"This one, Eknos," says the priest, pointing to the older boy.

Rush turns his attention to the youth. "You will tell me every detail of what you know, with perfect recall, about the theft of Rah." He nods in the direction of the younger boy. "Or I will cut out your brother's heart right here, in front of you, and eat it."

He had been standing with his arms crossed. Now he puts them to his sides. Two crescent shaped blades, embedded into curved handles, gleam from their nests within his palms.

"He'll do it, boy!" Mochlos takes a few involuntary steps away from Rush.

The boy has fallen to his knees, weeping. "I've told the priest everything. A man came out of the wood one day while I went to take a piss. He asked me if I knew anything about the Grain God, about his habits, if he was ever alone. He told me he'd give me a month's pay for information that would help him catch Rah. I told him I worked here, in the House of the Moon and could tell him anything he wanted to know. We'd been watching Rah playing with the King's horses all summer, you see."

"Good god," Mochlos breathes, certain that this bit of information will cost him his head. But Rush merely nods at the boy. "I'm getting hungry, boy. This is nothing," he grunts.

The boy looks up at him with terrified eyes. "I told them, he had a uniform on. A skirt embroidered in blue, and a hat, like a bucket, with silver trim."

"He didn't tell us this!" says Mochlos, wagging a finger at the boy. "He couldn't recall the colors!"

"No, I remember! He had a-" the boy opens his hands to demonstrate, "a short sword, about this long. He carried it in a belt at his waist."

"That is what Ting Ya told us. This is nothing we don't already know."

"It is the palace guard of Cyrus," murmurs Rush without taking his eyes off the boy. "But you will tell me something Ting Ya could not know, boy, or else I will show this sloppy priest what he has yet to discover, how to take a heart clean and beating."

"He called him 'Captain'!" shouts the younger brother suddenly. "You said he called him Captain!"

"Called who, you imbecile?" cries Mochlos, grabbing the boy and shaking him.

"The one who sent him!" says the other, looking up at Rush hopefully.

He is still on his knees but no longer weeping. "It's true. He said, 'The Captain will give you a month's pay. ' That's what he said!"

"He's making it up," moans Mochlos.

"No," says Rush, nodding at the boy at his feet. "It is Lutarus. It is the Captain of the Palace Guard of Cyrus." He breathes out a sigh. "I know the man."

"The Captain of the Palace Guard? Why would he want Knossos to know he kidnapped Rah?" asks Mochlos, struggling to answer the question the assassin originally assigned him.

But it is the assassin who answers it for himself.

"For war," he spits between clenched teeth. "And so he shall have it."

Rush next interrogates Ting Ya. This he demands to do in private, and so the priest leads the assassin and the diminutive Chinese grave keeper into his own private courtyard and orders a servant to bring them refreshment. Rush no longer feels a need for haste for he knows that Lutarus' scheme cannot succeed without the King's consent, and Rush knows King Cyrus well. The man has paid him a fortune to protect the Grain God and will have nothing to do with anything that could jeopardize him. Nor can Lutarus succeed without the consent of the people of Cyrus, and how will he earn that, when the Queen is as mad as a hare and believes that if any harm comes to the boy Cyrus itself will be destroyed? No. It is the hair-brained scheme of a small man desperate to prove he is a big one. Rah, if he has survived his kidnapping, will be in the hands of the kingdom of Cyrus before Rush can cross the mountains to find him. And once in the hands of Cyrus, if his effect on Knossos is any indication, it will take more than an assassin to extract him. He will have to come willingly. And for this, Rush will need some information from Ting Ya.

"I am stricken by envy of you, lady," says Rush, settling himself at last in some comfort on a bed of pillows at a low table in the center of the garden. He has gestured for Ting Ya to join him, and she does in her own fashion, sitting upright and resting back on her heels. Rush has addressed her as he would a lady of the court, but she has not responded to this honor with anything less than humility. She keeps her eyes to the ground, her head bent in a gentle bow.

"He loves you." he muses, playing with one of his daggers. "I wonder, how does one obtain that love?"

Ting Ya raises her eyes and offers the assassin a soft, patient smile. "I call your boy Jin yu," she says, as if she has not heard him. "Jin yu mean 'gold in abundance'. What need does such a treasure have for more gold? This energy from Sun Goddess, this light that come to us, it come to illuminate, not take. Jin yu want nothing for himself. Only to shine. This why he dance. He give his beauty to the world. You chase Jin yu, he will always run from you. You must extend finger," and here she lifts her hand

and does just that, extending an index finger as if offering it to a dove for a perch. "Perhaps he come to you when he is ready."

"If I lived like that, Ting Ya, I would have starved to death on the plains of Troy years ago. I do not wait for anything to come to me. I am a soldier. I advance."

"Jin yu will teach you how," she says, nodding her head at him confidently.

"Tell me something I will need to know to catch him, Ting Ya. I have no time to wait for Rah to come to me. Thera is angry. She empties steam into the skies of the Aegean, steam that stretches south and west like fingers. Only a fool would fail to see that this island is not far enough away to survive her explosion. The volcano will not wait for Rah to perch on my finger, Ting Ya. I must get him off this island, him and everything he loves, before she erupts."

Ting Ya nods. "But my answer is the same, sir. Only one answer. Cannot change for you. If you chase Rah, he will always run." She hesitates, then adds, "Darkness cannot catch the sun, night forever chasing day. Never catch."

He lifts himself up from his prone position. "Well put. But if he drives me to it, lady, this darkness will put out that light."

She puts her hands flat on her knees, lifts her eyes to his, this time boldly. "Then you must learn to live in darkness."

At the palace of Cyrus, the Grain God is met at the gates and taken from the Lieutenant by the King's own valets. He is carried on a pallet to the King's suite where the King's personal physicians, the palace surgeon, and the King himself, wait for his arrival.

Immediately upon being relieved of the boy's body, the Lieutenant jumps down from his mount, hands his horse to one of his men, and strides after the valets. His job is technically completed and, were he a simple soldier, he would return to his assigned post, perhaps never to be recognized for his accomplishment. But the Lieutenant, though just twenty two summers, is not a simple soldier. He will make sure the King knows who rescued this treasure and he will be assured that the King provides him with continued access to the boy. He will introduce Rah not as an unconscious and pathetic victim, but as the matchless prize that the Lieutenant believes he is. Above this, he has no intention of leaving the boy in anyone's care without gaining full access to him himself. If he left him at the gate as any simple soldier would, he would probably never even know where the boy was to be kept.

The Lieutenant pursues the valets, his long legs quickly catching them in the palace hall. When, now striding importantly in front of them, he reaches the king's chambers, he puts up a hand to signal for the men carrying the pallet to halt behind him. Thereby denying the King a view of the boy before first forcing him to address him as the boy's rescuer, he makes a graceful bow to one knee in the doorway.

"You are the man who found him?" says Cyrus, getting up from his couch like a commoner to address the Lieutenant.

"Yes, sir. He was found in the Lutarus tomb as we suspected. He was burning up with fever. We brought the fever down before we moved him." Now the Lieutenant moves aside and motions for the two valets to bring the stretcher into the room, just under a rectangle of light cascading from the clerestory windows above. The physicians and the surgeon have approached as well, and now stand about behind Cyrus, looking down with curiosity at the pallet.

But the Lieutenant has considered this introduction ahead of time. As he passed the valets in the hall he pulled the linen still shrouding Rah over his head so that the King, and his doctors, see only a body shaped bundle of cloth until he uncovers the boy himself.

Now he gently lifts the shroud away from Rah's face and says, "This is the Grain God of Knossos."

The reaction of Cyrus, and the group of physicians who flank him, is nothing less than the Lieutenant expects. There is a gasp from the King, an exclamation from the surgeon, and the physicians are blinking stupidly and muttering words of admiration among themselves. The golden luster of the boy's hair has been restored, to some degree, by the Lieutenant's ministrations in the field. His swollen lower lip, now clean of blood, only makes him more appealingly victimized. His halo of platinum and gold curls is a perfect frame for his remarkable feline face.

"Beautiful child," murmurs the King.

"He is exquisite," says the Lieutenant a second time.

"Put him in the Queen's nurses' room," says the King, now addressing the Lieutenant as if he were his personal man. "I want him guarded day and night." He looks up to the Lieutenant now. "What is your name, man?"

"I am Nikolaos, sir. And if you want this boy guarded properly, may I suggest that I and my men, having found and saved him, feel a very personal responsibility for his continued safety and will devote our very lives to the task."

"Yes," says Cyrus, looking piercingly into the Lieutenant's gray eyes, "I imagine you will. Very good. And where are the men who were keeping him in the tomb?"

"I have sent five of your best huntsmen, as well as my personal friend, to catch them." The Lieutenant allows himself a subtle, but smug, nod. "You will have them, sir. I guarantee it."

Again the King gives the Lieutenant a penetrating glance. "I seem to have found the Grain God, and a new captain of my Guard, on the same morning. I like you, Nikolaos. You have authority from me to do whatever you believe is necessary to keep this boy safe. Until we decide what is to become of my uncle, you will continue to be addressed as Lieutenant. But you will act as Captain hence forth. Do you understand?"

"I am your loyal servant, sir." The Lieutenant makes a light bow, turns to the two valets and in a commander's voice says, "Bring him into the Queen's nurses' room," and follows the valets out.

Rah is properly bathed and placed on a fine feather bed piled with silk pillows. He stirs from his dream world once more before the Lieutenant leaves him to arrange a schedule of guards for his new charge. While Rah is awake the Lieutenant, sitting next to him on the bed, offers him fresh water. Dehydrated from fever, Rah swallows all he is given, then falls back on the mattress and quickly passes into a comfortable slumber. It will be four days before his concussed brain will allow him to lift himself without help off his new bed and begin creating chaos in the city of Cyrus.

The Lieutenant assigns three men in shifts round the clock to the door of Rah's chamber. Then he turns out a steward who had been living in the adjacent room, sending him down to the servant's quarters, and takes that space for himself. "I am given authority to do whatever I feel is necessary to guard the Grain God," he tells the indignant man. "I would not complain to the King if I were you. You are liable to be sleeping in the stables tonight." When he is satisfied that he has done all he can for now to assure the boy's safety, he visits the wing of the Palace Guard. Lutarus is still under house arrest there and has been stripped of his uniform but is otherwise being treated casually.

"I am the head of this regiment now by the decree of the King. I have full authority to do whatever is necessary to safeguard the Grain God, whom I retrieved from the Lutarus family tomb this morning. The boy was near death. This man has proclaimed his desire to kill the True Rah to incite a war we can neither win nor do we wish to fight with Knossos. I want him in shackles twenty four hours a day. If he escapes, whomever is responsible for that escape will be executed by me personally. And as you know, I am fond of beheading."

On the morning of Rah's second day in Cyrus the sun fails to appear. The sky is curtained in darkness and a wave of rain clouds grumbles and growls over the city. By mid-morning, the leaden sky releases its burden and the parched earth opens its mouth to the gift of rain.

The people of Cyrus run in to the streets, their hands lifted to the rain like thirsty flowers. The women take their scarves from their necks and spin, dancing on sandal-stripped feet, and ululations lift outside the palace to the window of the chamber where Rah is still recovering from the latest assault on his brain. The King of Cyrus, looking out onto the spontaneous celebrations in the street, turns to his nephew, Ikarus, and says, "Do you believe me now, nephew? He is the true Rah. And he has come to save my people."

"He is a pretty boy with a lovely head of yellow curls and a concussed brain, uncle. And it happened to rain today. We were long overdue."

Cyrus shakes his head. "You are a cynic, Ikarus. What, I wonder, would ever convince you that there is more to life than fine wine and a good meal?"

"Perhaps I will believe your boy is a god when he turns this rain into wine," winks Ikarus, and putting a hand on the King's shoulder he adds, "I have one firm belief, Cyrus. I believe we must enjoy every moment we can in this life, because there is no other. I am a devout hedonist. And so let me give you my advice. Enjoy your little god, Cyrus. Enjoy him to the fullest. The rain would have come either way. But the boy is a tasty treat fit for a King, and he is lying on your plate."

The rain continues, held over the vineyards of Cyrus by a southern breeze. Rush has donned the clothing of a traveling sandal merchant once again, this time without the help of his two pack horses. With most of his weapons under a simple, unbleached robe, he hoists his sack over his powerful shoulders and takes his wolf dogs with him across the mountains to the city of his highest paying client, King Cyrus, who knows him only as the black mummy who visits him when he least expects it and takes his money to do what no one else can.

When he reaches the peak of Mount Juktas, Rush rests at the site of the two previously sacrificed Rahs. It is a simple clearing cut into the eastern side of the mountain with an altar made of a stone slab. He stops to consider the weather he is heading into, and to run his fingers over the top of the stone, feeling for the fear and agony of the two boys who were laid here, trussed and gagged, waiting for Mochlos' knife to open their veins. Someone's sons. For nothing. Who were they? Local bull jumpers, mediocre when set against the barometer of this year's Grain God. Rush allows himself to imagine, for one clear instant, his Rah lying on this slab awaiting the knife. But he cannot take the scene to its conclusion.

"I would take that blade from that hand and cut off that hand. I would make him eat his own balls with the other," thinks the assassin, meaning every word, and seeing that scene clearly. "Then I would kill the rest, all who watched and waited to see the spectacle of your death. And I would take you for myself." And now his mind goes there. Taking Rah. It always ends up there. But every time it does, the boy is howling as he did the day he tackled him on the Burial Mound Road. He is howling like a wildcat caught in a trap, struggling, his amazing, compact acrobat's strength against an adversary easily twice his weight, struggling to exhaustion. And when he is finally exhausted, still fighting with his very refusal to submit to pleasure. "Because I would make it pleasurable little cat. I would take you very, very slowly. Plenty of time." These thoughts drive him mad, but also drive him off the sacrificial altar, down the south side of the mountain, toward Cyrus and toward Rah. The one Rah. The true Rah. His Rah.

When he reaches the cemetery of the families of Cyrus, he stops to rest again. It is evening. He is a day behind Rah, who reached the palace of Cyrus only a few hours earlier. He has not slept in nearly two days and decides to camp here with his dogs for the night. He chooses the very back of the cemetery, near the Tomb of Lutarus, for his camp site.

In the morning Rush is not especially surprised to find evidence of a recent encampment and a sloppy exit all around him. He is quickly informed by the dogs that something very interesting spent a considerable amount of time in the tomb, and when he follows them down the stone stairs he finds the soldier's leather, left in a crumpled pile by the Lieutenant's men in their haste to remove the Grain God from his nightmarish prison. The tomb is too dark even for Rush to see that the leather is soaked in blood from the gash at the back of Rah's head. But when he brings it up the steps into the light he roars like a mother bear who has just lost her cub to a pack of jackals. He smells the leather, even tastes it, rubs the blood on his face like war paint. This is you, this is your essence. This is your life. They kept you down here in this damp hole with the dead. You were injured. But not killed. They either took you with them, still alive, or they were interrupted and you were taken by another. By the looks of it, they left in a hurry, leaving evidence of themselves. There was no battle. Probably knew their plans had failed and then fled to avoid arrest. But you were not killed, not here.

He offers the leather to the dogs to sniff. "Find it," he says. And the dogs circle anxiously a minute before trotting toward the cemetery entranceway, turning and whining at him to hurry. He folds the leather up carefully and puts it at the bottom of his sack as he follows them down the hill toward Cyrus.

CHAPTER 30

Rah is dreaming. For two days and three nights he has been swimming in and out of his dream world. Sometimes he is a dove, flying above the ship of Ameg, alighting on deck at Josepha's feet to peck the grain she scatters for him. Sometimes he is an orphaned slave child running through blue and yellow wildflowers, hand in hand with his sister, the two laughing with joy at the round of bread, the wedge of goat cheese and the gourd of milk the old soothsayer gave them for dancing behind her wolf-skin tent that morning. They will not go hungry today. Sometimes he is a scrawny boy standing on the croup of a dun mare, controlling her only with a bit-less bridle and a set of long reins, flanked by a trio of identical animals, flying at a soft canter over hand-built jumps to impress the barbarian horsemen of Gaul. And sometimes he is a slave-god, dancing in silks, his face painted in brilliant greens and yellows, and he is performing for the King in the Great Hall of the Palace of Knossos.

Right now, though, he is being eaten alive.

It started in Mochlos' punishment chamber. He was stripped of his skirt and clipped to a wall by his golden collar and belt. The crazy priest had provided an elegant silk pillow for him to kneel on and once his collar and belt had been fastened, making it impossible for him to wriggle away, had pulled his head back by his scruff and kissed him long and wet enough to drown him. Now the priest is taking the reed to him, but there is no pain. The reed is warm and insistent and strokes him here and there, on his shoulders, his sides, his hips, his thighs. He tries to push himself off the wall but it is impossible, the chains are too short. Another kiss, this one brutish and choking, nearly suffocates him. Then the mouth releases his and strong teeth take the side of his neck, give a little shake, pressing hard and painfully but not breaking his skin. The mouth returns to his, nipping open his lips and an intrusive tongue slips up and under them and licks at his incisors before it finds his own retracting tongue and strokes it like a mother wolf licking its cub. The priest's mouth was insistent but smaller, dry and miserly. This kiss is generous, a flood of wet strength and ferocious emotion. And there is fur about the mouth. Bristles rake his own tender skin. This is not the priest. This is a wolf. His dream eyes open to see a huge black snout, like the snout of the wolf head that was used in the Tears of the Moon dance, opening on his. He feels a sharp-clawed paw take hold of his hip and flip him over onto his back and he is somehow no longer chained to a wall but lying on a soft bed and all the hardness is above him, nudging, licking, nipping at him as if it would take its time, take forever to devour him. The teeth return to snap at his ears, his neck, the tongue laps at his chest, his pierced nipples. The hungry muzzle opens on his ribs, sucking and licking as if it would take the meat off the bones.

He wants to wake up. He struggles against the currents of his sleep. He must wake. He does not want this wolf to eat him while he is helpless and unconscious. But the dream is too thick. He is embedded in it and cannot rise up out of it.

"You have lost your earring, little cat," a baritone voice murmurs as the wolf laps at his left ear. "I will have to find it for you, or Josepha will be very angry with me."

The words jolt him to a surface. There is something huge, big and black and wrapped in muslin on his chest, but he cannot find his arms to push it off. He is still half in, half out of the dream world, in that twilight place he always goes between a fit and full consciousness.

"Wake up, little cat, you can do it. Wake up or I'll take the best bite of you first, eh? Down here in all of this golden fleece. And then set to the rest."

Teeth nip across his belly, pulling at the triangle of hairs that point like a gold arrow to his loins. A huge, hot, sharp-nailed paw slips under his waist and lifts his lower body up, pressing his belly into the tongue of the wolf. He is angry suddenly. Furious. And in his fury he comes full awake. He finds his hands, he grabs at a great, black head hovering over his belly. He digs his fingers in, pulls at it, taking away a strip of muslin.

And the wolf looks up from his meal. In the light of the single oil lamp that has been left lit in Rah's chamber, one eye is revealed through the torn fabric of the assassin's mask and it is hot and heavy lidded. The muslin around his mouth has been opened to allow him to nibble at Rah, and his mouth is an unexpected gash.

"Ah, there you are." The fiend sits up on the edge of the bed, putting a single finger across Rah's lips. "Now be very quiet or I will have to suffocate you with this pillow. You must tell me, in a whisper, exactly what happened to you."

"Wha-?" It is the first word Rah has attempted to speak in four days and his tongue is stuck to the roof of his mouth and cannot finish the sound. He lifts his head, but drops it immediately back down on his pillows. His neck cannot support it, and his brain is spinning in his skull. Pain like a blow from the back of an ax throbs in his ears. A sudden wave of emotion, grief, loss, hurt, sadness, washes over him. He is trapped in the body of an infant. An infant with an injured brain. His nose clogs, he snuffles back snot, tears run down his temples into his curls. He swallows for saliva to wet his tongue and finally manages to whimper, "Head hurt, so bad."

"Yes. You've been injured."

"Why you are bite me, Wolf?"

The assassin must close his eyes, lower his head and smile before he answers. "Because you taste good, little cat," he says. He gives Rah a moment to take in his presence, to return to the world.

"Now tell me what you remember."

Rah's eyes drift past the assassin's black-wrapped shoulder and go out of focus.

"I remember bad man, he is holding Ting Ya. He has knife-" at this he begins to snuffle again, tears leaking out of the corners of his almond eyes, "here." He puts his fingers to his collar. "He say, 'Rah of Knossos, you come. Then we do not hurt this woman." He looks at the assassin's one exposed eye and swallows, sniffling. "I can run fast, away, easy over wall. But I cannot leave Ting Ya. I stay. Let them take me." He is beginning to pant, to take in too much air, He makes a little choking sob.

"Easy, little cat."

Rah blinks, struggling to control his breathing. He looks up at Rush hopefully. "I think they do not hurt Ting Ya."

"Ting Ya is at the House of the Moon, being treated like a queen on my orders." The assassin sits up. "They took you to the cemetery, up the hill here in Cyrus. Kept you in a tomb. Five men took you. I know the identity of one. I want the others."

"They wear-" Rah points to the wall behind Rush. "Like him." He is pointing to the Lieutenant, whom he knows sleeps in the next chamber. "Like them." He points to the guards he believes are still standing in front of his door.

"Yes, the Palace Guard. Did you hear names, Rah?"

Now Rah opens his eyes wide, remembering. "Aktor! He is like-" he brings his arms up, although he is still prone, flexing his pectorals and biceps. They jump prettily, a reminder of his body in motion that distracts Rush momentarily. "He is like big monkey. The other -" Rah bunches his brows, suddenly angry. "He tie me, like chicken. Put me in grave. He is tall, strong like bear." He looks up into Rush's single exposed eye, an expression of surprise passing over his face. "Turios!" he says proudly. "I remember!"

"Turios and Aktor. Which one took your earring, Rah. The monkey or the bear?"

"Monkey," spits Rah. "He want to-" but here he remembers who he is talking to and his cheeks flush. He looks down and away.

"Yes, I can imagine. But no one got a chance, did they, Rah? The King's men came. They left you there in the tomb, bleeding and delirious. Lutarus, the ringleader, came down here to incite the city. The other two have been arrested. These two who held you in the tomb, they are still at large."

"How you know all this?" Rah peaks his brows at the assassin.

"I have been awake while you sleep, Rah. I have been about, learning what I can from the street. Now tell me, who is this man," he nods his head to the wall behind him, "who wears a palace guard uniform and takes the chamber beside yours, eh? Taking an awfully personal interest in you, Rah. Don't you think?

"He find me. He is on horse. I ride with him here to palace."

"Ah. And you liked that, didn't you." Rush's voice is getting lower, reminding Rah of the wolf. "A horseman."

"He sleep there," Rah nods at the wall behind Rush again. "So he can watch Rah."

"Keeping an eye on you himself, eh?"

Rah nods.

"Will you tell them the wolf has come for you, Rah?" muses Rush, looking down at the boy curiously.

Rah nods again.

"I thought so." The assassin lifts himself off the bed and noiselessly crosses the room to the door.

"Guards there," whispers Rah, innocently pointing to the doorway.

"Sleeping," says the assassin, his single exposed eye winking at Rah as he opens the door.

In the morning the palace is in chaos. There are three dead guards in front of Rah's chamber. The Lieutenant is tied to his bed and sporting the Tears of the Bull under his right eye. And Lutarus has been stolen from the Palace Guard barracks, right under the noses of over a hundred men.

It is not hard to guess who is responsible for the attack on the guards and the Lieutenant. And there is only one man on Crete who could have managed the kidnapping of Lutarus. The wound under the Lieutenant's right eye is a well known mark all over the Aegean, and the expertise of the killing of the three guards alone is a dead giveaway. One of the men, apparently the only one standing and awake at the time of the attack, was garroted from behind while the other two were probably stabbed simultaneously, both blades entering the thorax from above and plunging with perfect precision into their hearts while they dozed against the outer wall of Rah's chamber. Added to these facts is Rah's boast that morning to the King himself that his 'wolf' has come for him and wanted the men who had hurt him. When questioned further, he explains that his 'wolf' is an assassin, has two pleasant ponies, two identical sons, and two dogs he may have stolen straight from hell. Also that his wife is a "nice lady" who had given him a pearl earring that the man who walked like a monkey had taken from him. His recently pierced and now naked left ear confirms this last.

The Lieutenant, ungagged and unbound once the bodies of the guards are discovered, makes straight for Rah's chamber, followed by the King himself, who had awoken across the hall early, leaving his bedchamber for his private latrine down the hall, only to trip over one of the bodies. His shouts brought the palace physician, who occupies a room nearby, and his two personal stewards running down the hall. The queen, who occupies a completely separate wing of the palace, has not yet been informed of the attack, and will learn of it from her own servants before she hears it from her King.

"Rah, you're awake!" says the Lieutenant, trying to regain his normally serene bearing after a night he will never forget.

"Wolf wake me," says Rah, sitting up for the first time in four days. "Head feel better now," he rubs his ears dramatically.

"Wolf? He was in here with you, Rah? Did he hurt you?" The Lieutenant has come straight to Rah's bedside, oblivious to the fact that he has just stepped in front of the King. The King, who appears calmer than anyone, stands in his nightclothes at the doorway patiently taking in the scene. Yesterday the boy was in a coma. Now he is not only awake and quite alert, but rather cheerful. The man he entrusted with the job of keeping the boy safe, and whom he has considerable faith in, was no match for whoever went through three guards like a hot knife through heavy cream. There is no doubt in the King's mind that this is the work of Rush the Assassin, and that they are all lucky to have survived the night themselves.

"He is bite me," says Rah in his oddly husky, singsong voice. He pinches himself here and there to show just where the wolf nipped him. "He is try to-" now he must struggle to pantomime Rush's kisses down his abdomen toward the golden down at his groin. He looks down at himself, frowns, gives up. "I think he will bite me here and I am mad! Wake up. Grab head." This he does a good job of expressing in pantomime with the invisible assassin's head. "He say, you tell me everything. I want these men that took you. I must find ear-" he pulls his left ear, "ring, or Josepha is mad."

At this the Lieutenant looks back at the King who shrugs, puzzled.

"He bite you too," says Rah, pointing to the Lieutenant's face. "Hard." Then he shrugs. "He does not bite me so hard." He lifts his arms away from his sides again, unconsciously treating his audience to a better view of his exquisite physique while he looks about for wounds on his own person.

"You're not bitten, Rah," says the Lieutenant, misinterpreting Rah's manner of speech.

"No, he's quite . . . unharmed, I'd say. But you-" says the King, his attention brought back to the Lieutenant's face by Rah's search for wounds, "are quite the spectacle, Lieutenant. Perhaps you'd better have a physician clean you up, put a poultice on that."

"Sir, the man killed three of my best men, stole a criminal out from under a hundred men assigned personally by me to guard him with their lives or have their heads cut off. I think my wound is a small matter given the circumstances. There is too much else at stake here. I must recover our criminal and bring the monster that attacked the palace last night to justice."

"You are young, Lieutenant, but surely you were not born yesterday," says the King, stepping casually up to the tall, young Lieutenant. "You have as much chance at bringing that man to justice as you do at laying a clutch of eggs for our breakfast." The King motions for one of the physicians to come forward and look at the Lieutenant's face, which is a dreadful sight. Blood from the hole Rush carved on his cheekbone has run into his hairline and dried, giving him a wild and theatrical look. He is light skinned and gray eyed and he looks hysterical with the bruised and swollen area under one eye still weeping from the wound. "It needs a poultice." The King nods to the physician, who takes the Lieutenant by the arm and attempts to lead him away.

"And as for that 'criminal', Lieutenant," adds the King as the Lieutenant reluctantly allows himself to be lead to the door, "He happens to be my uncle. If you should find him alive, which I very much doubt, you will treat him like the royalty he is, even if he did commit treason against me. Now," he says, turning to the boy on the bed, who is looking up at him fearlessly as if he were no more than a steward. "Tell me, Rah of Knossos, what interest does Rush the Assassin have in you, beyond protecting you on my orders?"

"No," says Rah, shaking his head of tousled curls emphatically and pointing at the King. "You are Cyrus. You pay him to kill me. I remember! But he cannot. He want for himself. He chase and chase," says Rah, frowning and shrugging his shoulders in wonder. "And one day I spit at him and he is mad! So he come to priest and he buy me." He makes a firm nod. For once he has been able to make his point without the interruptions of his own pantomimes. "I am his. You steal from wolf, wolf will bite you." He points at the retreating Lieutenant. "Hard."

"Yes, that is for certain, Rah of Knossos. This wolf bites hard."

At the tomb of Lutarus, Rush and his prize are getting reacquainted. They were never well acquainted to begin with, Lutarus having hired Rush by word of mouth in the streets on the east end of Knossos. They had one meeting, brief and to the point. Cyrus would pay handsomely for the head of the Golden Grain God. Lutarus brought Rush an advance payment and neither he, nor Cyrus, ever asked for it back. Instead, Cyrus allowed Rush to apply it to his new assignment, that of stealing Rah's secrets, and finally, of keeping him from harm.

Now Lutarus, who is still in the shackles ordered by the Lieutenant, which made Rush's theft considerably easier than it might have been, is lying on his face outside the tomb of his family. He has been kicked and shoved and whacked in the back of the head innumerable times on his way to his own grave. He has made no plea for his life. He knows the man who has kidnapped him, although he never saw him in his black assassin's wrap. His deal with the killer was made on a moonlit night outside the walls of the City of the Dead, half way up Mount Ida in Knossos, and the man was dressed as a priest of the dead in a white and hooded robe. But the size, strength and talents of this man, who has snatched him from the palace guard of Cyrus like a fox snatches a chick from a hen house, makes his identity a simple matter. And the familiar, hell-deep Hittite growl is the final clue.

"What business is this of yours, Rush the Assassin?" says Lutarus from the ground, although he knows full well the answer. He has been asking this question, between blows, all the way up the hill to his family grave. "The boy is owned by a priest of Knossos, and none of your concern."

"I am paid to protect him by your nephew, the King, and well you know it," answers the black behemoth. He is removing Lutarus' shackles as he speaks. Where and how the man obtained the keys (they were in fact under the Lieutenant's pillow, not a very imaginative place to put them, in Rush's view) is beyond Lutarus, but he is happy to be free of his bonds. "Get up, Captain Lutarus, that I may give you your war."

At this, the ex-captain of the Palace Guard feels his heart leap with excitement if not joy. No sooner is he on his feet, than he has instinctively caught the dagger that has been tossed to him by the hilt. Now he is a man in arms, a soldier again. He forgets the blows that a few minutes ago promised to drive him into unconsciousness. He is being given his opportunity to face the enemy. He will fight well, though he does not expect to win.

But his enemy has thrown him his own dagger, and seems to have kept none for himself. The assassin stands like a thing risen from the very graves he now haunts, a huge bull-chested beast wrapped head to foot in black sackcloth, his feet planted in a dominant wide-legged stance, his arms folded in front of himself.

"Arm yourself, man," says Lutarus stupidly.

"I am armed, Lutarus. You are a soldier. Do you not recognize a weapon when you see one? I am my weapon."

"I am Captain of the Guard of Cyrus! I will not plunge a knife into a man who will not at least address me in an attitude of war!" cries Lutarus, growing unsettled by the man's lack of fear.

"You are nothing, regardless the title or the weapon you hold. I am greater than you, though I am without both," says Rush. "You hold in your hand the golden handled dagger of Rush the Assassin. It has executed two kings, a dozen generals, and hundreds of soldiers of your caliber. Now see, Lutarus, if it is the weapon, or the man, that makes a soldier."

"You arrogant bastard," spits Lutarus. "You are a fool, and you fool no one. You want that boy for yourself. Yes. I saw him. I know your thoughts. He has your balls. A pretty little dancer owns the balls of the great Rush the Assassin. Ananou spoke the truth! To hell with your boasts. Here is your blade!"

With this he charges at Rush, forward, then quickly to the right, attempting to cleverly avoid the big man's frontal defense and plant his own famous blade into his left side. But somehow the blade is gone, flying like a silver and gold bat through the moonlit night above his head, and Lutarus is spinning around, his knife arm snapped in two just above the wrist, and he is being shoved toward the door of his family tomb, with his other arm twisted in an impossible angle behind him, the shoulder having come out of the socket to accommodate the new position.

Ahead of him the wooden door of the tomb flies inward as the man throws the latch and kicks it open, and Lutarus is tossed, as if already dead, down the stone steps into the snarling darkness below.

"There is your war, Lutarus," says Rush the Assassin from above. And then, in Greek, he utters one word more.

"Toy."

CHAPTER 31

"Rah cannot eat this," says Rah, slapping the silver tray up and over and spilling its contents down the robe of the steward who has just attempted to place the boy's breakfast in his lap. Rah tips his head curiously at the mess running down the man's chest and giggles. His pretty eyes are viridian this morning, and seem to have absorbed the color of the sea a mile away. In another month Cyrus will be carbonized in the catastrophe that is Thera, and four thousand years from the day Rah, sitting cross-legged on a lush bed of silks in the palace guest room, chuckles in his too-deep voice at the reaction of the steward he has just painted with egg yolk and cereal, it will exist only as a layer of undiscovered flotsam under several meters of fertile earth on a local farm. But today Cyrus is Rah's kingdom. Thanks to the wolf, he is no longer a slave. He has become a prince, and well he knows it.

"Rah, you must eat. You have taken nothing but a little water in four days," says the Lieutenant, who is wearing a poultice of blue clay on his right cheek. It is rather flattering, though strangely theatrical, under his gray eye.

"Yes, Rah must eat. Grow strong. Dance! You have horse. I will ride horse!" During his body's inactivity it seems his extraordinary energy has converted itself, for the time being, into speedy thought. He jumps from one command, one observation to the next almost too fast to follow.

"Yes, yes, if you like. But you must eat first. You can barely walk three steps, Rah. How do you intend to get up and sit with me on a horse in this condition?" says the exasperated but utterly smitten Lieutenant.

Rah rolls his eyes, folding his arms over his chest. "Rah cannot eat this." He lifts a hand flamboyantly at the mess he has made of the steward.

He is obviously lost some muscle during his ordeal. Even so, the Lieutenant is constantly struck by the grace of his smallest movements. My god, what is he like when he is fit and dancing?

"Rah can only eat egg from white chicken, milk from white goat, no meat, only white fish," he says, shaking his head at the Lieutenant's ignorance. "This all Rah can eat." And then he adds, shrugging at his own forgetfulness, "and grain, fruit, nut, all what come from Rah." He lifts one hand toward the sunlight that is streaming in the window, changing his eyes to turquoise gold as he squints at the Lieutenant.

The rain that has soaked the fields of Cyrus for three days during Rah's unconsciousness has passed south to the sea over night. Now that the morning light has found him, Rah sparkles like a torch, the sun dancing in the pale curls on his head and on the golden hairs along his arms and legs and belly, distracting the normally single-minded Lieutenant for what seems the thousandth time in three days.

"All of the King's chickens are white, Rah, and so these have come from a white chicken. And you say yourself you can eat the grain cakes. Why do you do this?" The Lieutenant nods at the splattered steward. Another is making a valiant effort to wipe the mess from his chest and skirt, and from the floor.

Rah cocks his head at the Lieutenant and smiles mischievously, dimples popping. He shrugs again.

"Alright, Rah," says the Lieutenant, gathering his thoughts, "we will bring you eggs from a white chicken, milk from a white goat, grain cakes and honey. You will eat, grow strong, and I promise I will find a way to carry you on horseback again, agreed?" He is picturing Rah wrapped in linen, weighing nothing in his arms as he negotiates the rocky path from the cemetery of Cyrus to the city. He is picturing the first time those strange eyes opened at him in that feline face, taking his breath away. He is not picturing the boy balancing on the animal's croup, controlling it with nothing more than a bit-less bridle and a long rein, as it flies in a hand gallop over a meter high obstacle. Nor could he imagine in his wildest imaginings the boy's dismount, a backward leap up and over, with a twist, and a flawless flat-footed landing.

"Agree," says Rah smiling. He carefully pronounces the new word, copying the Lieutenant's Minoan perfectly except for a loss of sharpness due to the crimp in his tongue.

When the stewards return with a new tray, identical to the first, Rah, still seated in a cross-legged fashion on his bed, obediently sets into it. He wears nothing but a loincloth skirt, his golden belt, bracelets and anklets. The Lieutenant watches him from a bench by the window, fascinated by every move he makes. He is even beautiful when he eats, thinks the Lieutenant, although he chews and swallows with difficulty, gulps like an animal that is afraid its meal will be stolen, and tries to speak with his mouth full like a commoner. And now he is running the palace, throwing plates of food at the staff, insisting on delicacies, and demanding concubines when he can barely yet walk to the door. He speaks to the King himself as if he were a servant and to me as if I were imbecile.

The Lieutenant has been frowning as he sits with his back to the wall by the window, watching Rah stuff an entire egg into his mouth. The boy is painfully thin from having eaten nothing for nearly a week, but he has the appetite of a starving cur.

"You watch like fox," says Rah, eyeing the Lieutenant with some contempt under the sweep of those ridiculously long, golden lashes. He picks up a honey-soaked grain cake and crams it into his mouth, ignoring the utensils on his tray.

"I am sorry, Rah. You eat so fast I am afraid you might choke yourself," responds the Lieutenant.

"No. You watch Rah like fox," says Rah, wiping crumbs from the corners of his lips as he speaks through a mouth full of cake. "You make wolf angry. Wolf does not like you."

The Lieutenant sighs, a bit angrily. "Yes, I know just how little the 'wolf' likes me. I have a memento of his dislike right here on my face."

"Like priest," says Rah, pointing at the Lieutenant's swollen and poulticed cheek with one hand as he licks honey off the fingers of the other.

"He did this to the priest he bought you from?" says the Lieutenant, his interest piqued.

"Mmm," nods Rah, his mouth full again. "He does not like priest either," he finishes, swallowing. "I think maybe because priest beat me, maybe," he says, shoving the bronze tray to the floor with a clatter. "Now you take me to horse!"

The Lieutenant gets to his feet, shaking his head at the new mess. "No. Now you rest, Rah, rest and get stronger-" But his words are interrupted. In a temper, Rah has sprung off the bed at him like a lynx, making a strange warble in his throat. But his assaulted brain cannot keep up with his body's inherent speed. He takes a wobbly step backward and falls to the mattress on his rump.

"Rah!" the Lieutenant rushes to catch him but the boy is already sitting up, holding his head dramatically with both hands.

"Head spin!" says Rah, chuckling.

"You are not well enough for horses, Rah. Now just settle down and rest a bit. Give it time."

"Girl, then! Three! Rah must have three concubine!" demands Rah, looking at the Lieutenant through the hands that still clutch his head. "You know nothing! Stupid fox!"

"Oh for-" the Lieutenant closes his eyes in exasperation. "Fine. I will get you three girls. But they will do nothing but coddle you, I assure you, or I will take off their heads and you can sleep with them."

Half an hour later, while Rah leans out his window, watching soldiers practice hand-to-hand in an arena conveniently located behind the King's wing, three young girls, wearing nothing but elaborate necklaces and ankle length skirts, are ushered into his room.

Having spotted hoof prints in the arena, Rah is sure that horsemen must practice there as well, perhaps even the Lieutenant and his mount. When he turns from the window and sees the girls, though, all thoughts of horsemanship fly from his head.

They are lighter skinned than his own concubines at the House of the Moon and wear their hair in elaborate loops that stand up from their heads like hats. One is tall and lean, one, of medium height, is plump as a pony with big dark eyes. And one is as tiny as a doll yet quite voluptuous. She stands in front of the other two and seems the boldest of the three. Rah takes a quick step back from the window and loses his balance. His back slaps the wall and the girls laugh, the tall one in back bringing both of her hands up to cover her mouth, the plump one taking a sharp breath. The doll in front, though, has stepped forward quickly as if to offer him her hand. She is light footed and moves with practiced grace, extending her arms to him as if before an audience. It is all the movement Rah needs from her to sense that she is a dancer. He stares, mouth open, his eyes bright with an animal's interest.

"He is like the King's lion!" says the tall one.

"Yes exactly!" says the second girl. "But his eyes-!"

The little dancer says nothing, but stares right into those eyes as she closes the distance between herself and Rah with quick, light steps.

"You dance," says Rah, pulling his eyes away from her lovely breasts to address her eyes.

"Yes," she answers, and surprises him further by dropping into a dancer's bow before him.

Rah's smiles in delight and attempts to return the bow. He makes it to his knee, and loses his balance again, falling on his right hand and haunch.

"Head spin," he says as the girls skate across the floor on bare feet to surround him, fussing and cooing.

"Poor thing," says the tall girl, who has stepped behind him. "You are hurt!" She puts a steadying arm around his shoulder and touches the wound on the back of his head with tentative fingers.

"Come," says the dancer, apparently in charge of the other two. "We must put him back in bed." She takes his hands and pulls him to his feet. The three girls herd him over to the bed and quickly lay him flat out.

The dancer has dropped onto the mattress next to him, her breasts bouncing enticingly. Rah tries to lift himself up onto an elbow to reach her but she quickly pushes him back down.

"You are good dancer?" he asks, looking her over.

"I am in the King's own company." she answers proudly.

"What is this King's company?" asks Rah, attempting to lift himself back onto his elbows.

"Here in Cyrus, the King has his own dancers. We are the best in the city." The dancer pushes him back down for the second time.

"Do you dance?" asks the plump girl, sitting down beside her sister on the bed.

Rah makes one more attempt to lift himself up, but the dancer holds him down by his shoulders.

"No. You lay down. If you fall-" she makes a quick motion across her own throat with her index finger. "I lose my head."

"I am best dancer in Knossos," says Rah to the plump girl over the dancer's shoulder. "Win competition. So now I am Rah."

"Rah the Sun God?" asks the tall one. "Is that why your hair is gold?" She stretches out her hand and touches a curl at his forehead. "Like silk," she nods at the other two.

"Are you really a god?" asks the plump girl.

"Did you make it rain?" asks the tall one.

"Rah is not Sun God. Rah is Grain God. Maybe I make rain. I do not know," says Rah. Although he has given up trying to rise, his fingers have crept toward the dancers breasts as he talks and now he is stroking one absently. The dancer seems not to notice.

"We had no rain for months!" says the tall girl. "All the crops were dying. Now you come, and it rains for three days! Everyone thinks you brought the rain."

"Maybe. I don't know. You sit here!" he orders the dancer, patting his stomach.

"You are too weak," says the dancer.

"How you know? Don't have to stand." He tries to lift her by the hips onto his belly but she moves away, giggling. Now the other two begin giggling as well, and the tall girl takes his hands and pulls them over his head while the dancer tickles his sides.

He lets them abuse him this way a moment, then pulls himself free and slips an arm around the dancer's waist. He makes one cat-quick twist and pulls her over, on top and then under himself. There is not much the others can do to stop him now.

He is inside her when, a few minutes later, the Lieutenant comes striding in to check on him.

"Oh, for the love of god." But Rah pays him no mind. The two unoccupied girls, who have been playing with Rah's curls and stroking his back and thighs while he rides the dancer, must slap their hands over their mouths to suppress their laughter at the Lieutenant's expression. The man looks more like a cuckold than a commander. Although apparently appalled by Rah's antics, he seems mesmerized by the scene before him, unable to take his eyes off the boy's pulsing rump. At length he gathers his dignity and walks out of the room without further comment.

When he hears the door slam shut Rah bursts out laughing, falling over on his side beside the fourth concubine he will impregnate on Crete before hot gas and ash from the volcano that is Thera incinerates her.

CHAPTER 32

Rush is loping up a wooded hill in the rain drenched and steaming morning air. He is breathing evenly, running tirelessly, his dogs unseen but pacing him on either side hidden in the brush. Now and then one comes upon a hare or grouse and flushes it, causing a leafy explosion ahead of the assassin. But there is little else to distract him, and as he covers the distance between himself and the trackers who pursue Aktor and Turios his mind wanders, to the messenger dove, to his wife's horrified scream, "Antaris, they've taken him!" and to the scene he discovered the following morning in the Lutarus tomb. The blood drenched soldier's leather, the length of blood-crusted rope outside, still bearing evidence by the method in which the knots were cut, of the way they trussed him, wrists to ankles, and left him in that miserable dank death hole to wither. He recalls hearing in the streets of Cyrus how the soldiers had found him burning up with fever, delirious and near death, the back of his blonde head blackened with his own blood.

Rush likes to revisit these things. He is looking for clues, yes, but more than that, he is a man who believes in symmetry.

Loping just behind his dogs, whom he can hear but not see as they follow the scent of the trackers, he allows himself to picture Rah in the hands of the two bullies, the monkey and the bear. How they would have shoved him about like a common scamp, paying no notice if they bruised that silken-gold skin, how they would have ignored his feral noises, those strange warbles and growls that come from wherever it is that cats purr, and how untouched they would have been by those paralyzing feline features, those sea-colored, tip-tilted eyes.

Mine, thinks Rush. You took what is mine. You touched what is mine. What I saved from myself, for myself. What I could not diminish by taking. Then the wild animal that snarls in the pit that is his soul threatens to tear open his belly once and for all and leap out into the world on all fours. It roars, and sends all of its ferocious strength and fury through his veins. It lifts its snout and sniffs the air. Where is my enemy? I am coming for you.

At the House of the Moon the concubines of Rah continue their vigil in the public courtyard. They have not eaten for six days. There has been no word from Ameg and, while the hopeful at the House of the Moon take this to be a good sign, the grief stricken girls have come to believe that their God is dead.

The merchant, whose true identity is no longer a secret at the House of the Moon, has left instructions for the entire household to pack and ready for sea. It is now his intention to take the complete compound with him to Anatolia, including Mochlos and his priesthood, the temple concubines, the kitchen and service staff, and all of the bull jumpers and dancers. Word of Thera's impending doom has spread through the city as seamen returning recently from her bring their reports of the ever-increasing steam rising from her volcano. Those who have the ability to flee, with access to ships and security on other shores, are preparing to do so. Those who cannot will remain on the island and hope for the best.

Pyrus and Aros have been the most optimistic of the staff and have been able to maintain lightheartedness among the others. Tuma, too, who has seen Rah in action and believes he could seduce a scorpion if need be, continues to speak of the Grain God in the present tense. Mochlos, having won what he believes to be his most important business deal to date, that of joining up with Ameg and maintaining his priesthood in Anatolia, as well as his shipping business, is full of future plans. The deal is simple. The assassin gets half of all of his profits and the priest gets off Crete before the volcano decides whether to drown him in a wave or incinerate his lungs with hot vapor and toast the rest to carbon.

When Ameg's ship returns the household of Mochlos, along with anything and anyone else left on Crete that Rush chooses to take, will be loaded. If he is not back with the boy they are to leave without him. He will follow on the boat he took back to Crete when he learned of Rah's kidnapping from the messenger dove. His man remains on that boat, taking his meals at the House of the Moon.

"Rah must bathe in holy oil only. This is wrong smell. This water is for pigs!"

Rah has insisted on a bath after his afternoon with the three concubines. Told to give him whatever he wants, within reason, the King's personal stewards have taken him to the palace bath, where he continues to wreak havoc with the staff. He has already nipped the bath master who tried to put him in the pool used by the palace priesthood.

"This is holy water, you little beast!" screams the bath master. "It is oiled with Rosemary, Bergamot, Spikenard! The finest money can buy! Imported from Canaan!" He rubs his forearm irritably. There is no puncture, but his pride is mightily bruised. "No bath on Crete has better holy oils than the palace of Cyrus, you obnoxious little animal!"

"He's been like this since he awoke from his injury, Naiba. No one can control him, not even the King," says the steward. "He threw his breakfast tray at me this morning. And he is driving the new Captain of the Guard to distraction!"

Rah is even now frowning a flat-browed warning at the bath master, a rumble rising in his throat. The tall African is still clutching him in one hand, his long fingers easily circling Rah's wasted bicep. He looks down at the boy and gives him a shake.

"I should hold him under a minute or two, that would take this out of him," he says.

"Perhaps it is the results of the coma," says the second steward, looking at Rah sympathetically. "I have heard this can happen with an injury to the head. A change in personality."

"Yes, or perhaps he has always been an obnoxious little beast," responds Naiba.

"Who can make rain," frowns the first steward.

"I wouldn't be too rash, Naiba," says the second, "that new Captain of the Guard likes to take off heads. You bruise this grape, yours may be one of them."

"I have been bath master of the palace of Cyrus for seventeen summers. I will not have my head taken off because of this," says Naiba, giving Rah one more shake for good measure. Then he leans toward Rah, a menacing grimace on his own face. "Don't you bite me, you little beast."

"What oils did they use in your bath in Knossos, boy?" asks the sympathetic steward.

Rah turns to the steward, his frown turning to a blank stare.

"Hah! Yes, do tell us, Rain God, what did they put in your bath at home, eh?" jibes Naiba, knowing full well that no bath master would ever divulge such trade secrets.

Rah blinks up at the man, then flattens his brow at him again. "Tuma know! Rah does not know! You stupid-" but before he can finish this Naiba has raised his free hand high, intent on a slap that will send the boy spinning into the 'wrong' bath water.

"You will lose that hand," says the Lieutenant, who is striding toward them from the courtyard entrance. The sound of his short Grecian sword, slipping out of its sheath, finishes his sentence.

Naiba instantly lowers his hand. But his face is set.

"He insults me, sir, and the palace bath. He calls my finest bath water fit for pigs only, and demands special oils which he cannot even name."

"He bit the bath master, sir," offers the steward who wore Rah's breakfast this morning. "I saw it myself. He growls and spits like a wildcat. He is not human."

"No. He is a slave-god. And must be treated as such," says the Lieutenant, sheathing his blade. Then, with a conciliatory softness, he addresses the bath master. "Naiba, I have never seen you raise a hand to anyone. Would you strike an injured kitten?"

"That is not a kitten, sir. That is a wildcat. May the gods help us all if he is allowed to grow up."

But the Lieutenant's eyes have wandered from the bath master. He is looking down at Rah, who is making burring noises in his throat as he fidgets and pouts and tries to squirm from Naiba's grasp.

"Sir?"

"Cherry blossom," says the Lieutenant, remembering his ride back to the palace with Rah in his arms. "Cherry blossom, and myrrh I think. That is what he was bathed in. I'll stake my new commission on it."

"That is a simple thing, and far less costly then the oils in this bath," says Naiba, still stinging from the boy's insult.

"Make a bath up with cherry blossom and myrrh, Naiba, and he will get into it," says the Lieutenant, looking at Rah with a self satisfied smile. But Rah has lost interests in bathing.

"Where are dancers? You have dancers. Bulls. I will go to gym." He tugs one more time against Naiba's grasp, this time coming free. He flashes a hot pout at Naiba before turning to look about in an attempt to find his bearings.

"You are far too weak to go to the gym, Rah," sighs the Lieutenant.

"No. I go. Watch only," says Rah, turning his attention to the Lieutenant finally, this time with a softer expression. "Take Rah, please," he adds. He looks up too quickly into Nikolaos' eyes, then takes a small step sideways to steady himself.

"He will drive you crazy before he is through," muses Naiba. He makes a short bow and turns toward the palace bath apothecary to get to work on the oils for the new bath.

"I can show him, sir," says the more sympathetic of the two stewards, after Naiba has gone. He is plump and rather fish-faced. He steps behind the boy as if to take charge of him.

Rah turns his head to observe the steward over his shoulder. One tip-tilted blue-green eye flicks down the man's body, unconsciously sweeping him with golden lashes. "What your name is? You are like Aros," he says.

"He is Fillius," says the other steward, seeing that his counterpart has lost his tongue. "And he has no business offering to take you to the gym."

And turning to Fillius he says, his mouth pursed as if he has bitten something sour, "The Lieutenant has just told you that the boy is not strong enough, Fillius."

"No," says the Lieutenant, "go ahead. If he promises only to watch, perhaps it will keep him out of trouble a few hours."

The steward, Fillius, takes Rah by the elbow and leads him away. Rah is oddly compliant in the hands of the effeminate steward, and wobbles along beside him out of the marble-tiled bath house, taking several fast steps and then losing his balance in one direction or another.

"He will fall and crack his skull," says the remaining steward. "He listens to no one. He is an utter imbecile."

But the Lieutenant is watching Rah with a dreamy look on his chiseled features. "He is utterly adorable, Bacus, are you blind?"

"Oh he is as cute as a kitten, nonetheless, he has been a boil on my bottom since he opened his eyes," says Bacus, frowning. "Fillius seems quite struck by him."

At this the Lieutenant puts a comforting hand on the steward's shoulder. "I will relieve Fillius myself of the duty of watching him once I have finished my rounds this morning, Bacus."

In the gym, Rah's entrance causes a stir almost instantly. The practice comes to a hushed halt as soon as the dance master's attention is diverted from his dancers to the golden boy who appears alone under the archway situated across the arena and behind them. His troupe is practicing a simple circular ceremonial dance in preparation for the burial of Lutarus, the remains of whom were found earlier that morning. It is a dull and lifeless thing, despite the help of a group of musicians accompanying the practice with percussion and lur.

Rah, despite his handicap, has managed to keep up with Fillius on the walk down to the gym and he is even several paces ahead of him when he reaches the gymnasium archway. He has only a moment to observe the dance practice before all eyes turn around to see what the dance master, who has been sitting on a stone bench coaching, has been distracted by.

At first Rah is alone under the archway, framed by the white marble arch and back lit by sunlight. Then Fillius appears beside him as if to demonstrate the extraordinary humor of the gods of creation. There could hardly be a more incongruent couple, one doughy and dark, with a kind, fish-face, standing stoop-shouldered and as docile as a doe, the other slight and fair, and breathtakingly pretty, but with a certain haughtiness in his posture, and a cat-like curiosity in his tip-tilted eyes.

As the dance slows to a baffled halt Rah instinctively looks for the master. He finds him sitting on the bench, looks the man over, then steps tenuously forward onto the sand floor and offers him the bow that stole the assassin's heart.

The dancers stand blinking in awed silence as Fillius, seeing that the boy has wobbled ever so slightly at the bottom of the bow, takes his elbow and helps him to his feet. The tenderness with which he does so, itself dance-like, only serves to enhance the boy's ethereal beauty.

Swallowing the thing that has risen in his breast, the dance master hops down from his bench. He offers a few hard claps of approval and walks through his troupe as if they were so many goats, making a bee line for Rah.

"You are Rah of Knossos," he says, his voice as soft and carefully nonthreatening as if he were approaching a bird that might suddenly lift its wings and disappear over his head. He is still several feet away when Rah's exotic eyes stop him in his tracks.

"What eyes you have," murmurs the dance master.

Paying this typical reaction to himself no mind, Rah informs the instructor, "Rah will dance for you," and waits to be challenged.

But the man only looks him up and down and asks, "Are you able?"

At this Rah narrows his eyes at the man and says, "You see if Rah is able." Then he walks off toward the dancers, who have moved into a cluster in the center of the floor.

"He is not well enough," says Fillius to the dance master as he hurries after Rah. "The Lieutenant will have my head!" he adds over his shoulder.

But when he has nearly caught up to Rah he is shouldered aside by the dancers themselves, who have surrounded Rah. He has walked right into the knot of performers, his movements becoming longer and stealthier as he approaches them, his inherent tempo palpable, his shoulders and arms lifting back and away with the same grace that made his bow remarkable. He cocks his head this way and that at the group of dancers, sweeping his lashes over the girls' bodies, challenging the males. His face has become a theater, a stage set for emotion, and for the dance of expression.

Fillius steps back.

And Rah continues his haughty prowl through the group, stepping up to challenge the males, ears back, a mischievous smile curling the sides of his mouth, seductive and proud. Like a contagion it leads them into their own backward glides away from him, allowing the girls to draw nearer, their limbs defining their rapture as they circle, sway, and roll like waves against his invisible rhythm.

And soft-footed and dangerous-eyed, Rah the cat continues his prowl through the dancers. He is hunting for his partner, as soon becomes evident when he finds her in a maiden who has been matching him move for move, in forward and in reverse, her heels barely touching the ground, her motion elongated and slow. She dances behind her brothers, around her sisters, flirting and slipping away, understanding his language and answering with the feminine counterpart.

And the dance master watches, blinking with disbelief, as the troupe he has trained all summer becomes cohesive and instinctive and balanced and beautiful at last, and without a single direction from him. It shapes itself around the symmetry of Rah's seduction. Without a leap, a twist, a powerful jump or a mind boggling series of leopard-quick somersaults, Rah has created, with only a kitten-weak prowl, an exquisite first act, one far exceeding in impact any that the dance master has dreamed up since the day he first stepped foot in the King's arena.

But even this simple walk is taxing the boy's bruised brain and as he nears his maiden his steps begin to falter. Even then, it is only with unparalleled grace that he takes his dance to the ground, reaching for the girl as he drops to his knees like a dying god. And the girl responds, matching his faltering steps, coming to her knees before him, and stretching out her body to reach for his.

"Enough, Rah!" says the dance master, as Fillius attempts to push himself through the group to help Rah to his feet.

But he has misunderstood.

For Rah, as he creates his death on the arena floor, has communicated a single suggestion to his partner. "Lift me," he winks, and she passes the challenge to the others who surround him, still poised as if watching the Sun God fall from the clouds. And three of the larger males, matching each other move for move, and in rhythm to the timpani that is supporting them, pick Rah's limp body easily up from the sand and begin to raise it. Then three more boys move in to support the first and three more and then the girls come fluttering forward on tip toes to surround the boys and support with gesture only the ascent of the dying god. And Rah is lifted high above their heads on twenty strong hands, utterly lifeless and draped like a silk sheet supported by a breeze.

The dance master, taking a deep breath and closing his eyes a moment, claps his hands. The dancers set Rah on his feet and, laughing and clapping, spread themselves out behind him as if at the end of a performance, as if he were already their lead dancer. They form a loose line behind him, clapping and smiling.

"Now I watch," says Rah, standing with some difficulty where the boys set him down. He makes no argument when Fillius comes to his side to offer a supporting arm and then helps him across the arena to the dance master's bench.

But when the dancers return to their ceremonial circle dance there is something new in their performance. Something months of being told how to dance, with too much instruction and too little freedom, had diminished and that has been reborn in them, something untamed, natural, urgent, something that cannot be taught. And the dance master finally comes to understand what he has never quite understood about dance when, as he sits beside Rah on the bench and observes it quietly, he hears its master purring beside him.

CHAPTER 33

Turios and Aktor are arguing over the pearl.

They have been arguing over the pearl, and the boy, since they left him to die in the tomb of Lutarus. The pair reached Malia on the third day, crossing the mountains on foot, spending what coin they had with them for a room at a brothel in the poor section of town. A hundred kilometers away to the north Thera steams. Five kilometers to the east a piece of the coastline of Crete has tumbled into the sea, battered for weeks by sea storms, and finally compromised once and for all by a minor quake.

But Turios and Aktor know nothing of these omens. Nor will they ever connect their abuse of the Grain God with the monster that is growing out of the earth and sea on Thera. They are only concerned with the pearl. How to sell it, how to split the spoils. Whether to split them at all.

For Aktor, it is a simple matter. He will convince Turios to approach a local merchant with connections in Egypt or Cyprus, sell the pearl, then kill him and take the money. Then he will travel west to Knossos and pay for passage to Greece where he will set himself up in business. Perhaps whores. A small brothel on the road to Mycenae where sailors and soldiers will make him a rich man.

For Turios, a simpler soul, it is a more difficult thing. Although Aktor has given him the pearl to carry (just in case they are arrested before they have time to sell it) he has never felt completely comfortable with it. The thing seems to have taken on the personality of the boy. Now and then he takes it from his own ear (Aktor punched a hole in the lobe and cauterized it with a hot nail for just this purpose) and holds it in his palm. It is a tiny thing in his thick, flat hand, yet enormous in its power over him. Sometimes, in the glossy skin of the thing, he seems to see a vision of the boy, not trussed up and lying on the floor of a dank, dark tomb, but as he was that day they captured him on Mount Ida, shining, even brilliant in the noonday sun. Cat-like quickness in his fine limbs, and those strange sea-green eyes, darting and alert and fearful. And then, after Lutarus' threat to kill the Asian woman, the practiced bow of submission. A shimmering stillness. Water in a parched place.

And Turios thinks of the value of the pearl and becomes confused. They took the pearl and left the boy. But what is the pearl? What can the pearl buy? Something is wrong with the exchange. Here he has in his hand what has no meaning to him except in a memory it holds of the price he paid for it. Why did they leave the boy? They may be hunted down and arrested, forfeiting their lives for their prize, in either case. Why not keep the boy and leave the pearl? Perhaps if they had left the pearl, it could have paid for the boy.

Like the plump breast of a dove, the pearl shimmers, silvery, golden, white, in the palm of his hand. Like the boy he once held in his hands, brilliant and small, and yet more valuable than anything he had ever touched.

Turios keeps the pearl in his ear, and listens to it. It tells him to return for the boy. It tells him he is weak and a fool, and should kill Aktor and return the pearl to that ear, hiding under golden curls, which is the only ear worthy to wear it. He keeps his thoughts secret, wondering if the voice of the pearl will be more convincing in the end than the voice of his companion, who talks and talks of their shared profit, their future as whore masters. And so the two thieves, once soldiers but now criminals for a commander's folly, search the city of Malia looking for a merchant who might be interested in a stolen pearl. They come upon their own kind in the seedy neighborhoods at the edge of town behind the work houses and they hear of a man who steals girls from neighboring towns and sells them over the sea. They do not know that the man is brother to one of the four whom Rush the Assassin dispatched one day in a fit of frustration and rage brought on by a hunger for the very creature whose pearl earring they are planning to sell to him. Nor can they know that the man is the one slave trader in the group that Rush was hired to kill who was fortunate enough not to be in Malia that day, but elsewhere furthering the family business.

Now as they sit in their tiny room on beds that stink of themselves and of the whores they used the night before, they argue. They argue about the pearl one final time.

"You take it to the man, Turios, and tell him it's none of his business where it came from. Does he want it or not? No trade. Payment in coin. That's all there is to it. I'll meet you a mile up the road to Knossos at dusk."

Of course, Aktor has no intention of leaving the pearl or the money it fetches in Turios' hands. He will keep him in his sights until sunset, then follow him up the road a mile and use the element of surprise, and the waning light, to take advantage of the bigger man and ambush him.

"Why not stay here another day or two before we sell the thing," answers Turios. "We have enough to keep us a week. Maybe it will fetch more in Mycenae, eh? And no one knows us there. Someone here from Knossos may have seen the boy with the pearl in his ear, a sailor, a merchant. Could tie us to the kidnapping. May be a bounty on us."

But still the pearl whispers to him. Of course, of course, he who owned the boy owns me also. A rich man. A powerful man. And he is coming for me. And for the boy. Go back. Rescue the boy before it is too late. Pay for your life with me.

"Damn you, Turios, I tell you we have to get rid of that thing! Tonight! No later! Here. Drink some of this for courage. Then do as I tell you. Or else give me that damned earring and I'll do it myself."

But Turios cannot hand over the pearl to Aktor. Any more than he could have stood and watched the man take his pleasure from the boy. He sees Aktor as being dirtier, somehow, than himself. Lower. You can't touch it. It's mine now. Mine. He takes the bottle of wine and pours half of it down his throat. Then he picks himself up from the sodden mattress and makes for the door.

"Don't you get any ideas about leaving me here and taking off with the money, Turios," says Aktor.

"I'll meet you a mile up the Knossos road," says Turios, already sure that he will never part with the pearl, that he will meet with the whore master, just in case Aktor is watching him, but he will only make arrangements, arrangements that will never come to pass. Then he will overpower Aktor in the dark, deserted road leading south and west out of town, back into the hills, before it turns north again to Knossos. And he will leave the man's body to rot in the woods and travel south again, over the mountains and back to Cyrus and the boy.

In the evening of the second day Rush catches up to the trackers. Signals from the dogs let him know that they are just ahead, bedding down for the night in the woods just off the road to Malia.

These are not his enemies, nor are they friends. There are six of them, five local men, good enough hunters but worthless soldiers, as Rush has come to know simply by their weak advance, taking twice what it would take one of his own men to cover the same uphill climb, their sloppy movements forward, leaving their own obvious trail, and their scattered and haphazard encampments. The leader, the one he has been told is named Horus, is a soldier, but not a commander. He has maintained the focus of the trackers and continued to advance, too slowly for Rush, toward his goal. Rush watches the group for only a few moments as they bed down in a copse in the wood for the night. They do so in a routine manner, telling

Rush what he suspected, that it will not be difficult to find them on the way back to Cyrus, when he already has what they are looking for, and deposits with them what he has no further need of, except as a warning and as a bit of conceit for his own art.

Rush gives the tracking party a wide berth and continues up the path. He no longer needs them, in fact, they would only slow him down. They have given his dogs a scent, for their own path co-mingled with that of the two thieves and it was easy enough to know whose debris was whose and give the dogs new instructions. Follow the smell of the "monkey" and the "bear," so rank that even he could at times discern it. Rush and his war dogs continue toward Malia, where the men are headed, he can surmise, to sell the pearl to a merchant with contacts overseas.

Rush knows of one such merchant. The man missed his date with the assassin once but will not be so lucky a second time, not if he happens to be in town. With access to his own ships, the man could well have dodged the wrath of Thera, had the monkey and the bear not brought the wolf back to his doorstep. But he is as good as dead now, and no trouble to Rush. In fact, he will come in handy.

Rush continues toward Malia, the dogs now tracking the scent of the monkey and the bear. They will not rest until they reach the dark edge of town, the rambling and dirty warren of streets and hovels furthest inland, behind the city workhouses. Then Rush will tie the dogs in the woods and enter the city, moving easily about in the darkest corners, shunned for his size and his silence and for the smell of death that comes off him when he is hunting, always recognized by those who consider themselves dangerous and low until they pass him, feeling the fingers of his rank energy caress the air around them. He will pass easily and freely the cutthroats and thieves, the slave traders and the whores, and they will back away, heads down, hoping that he continues on. He will go where the children of men like himself are made to service the sexual desires of the lowest form of life, those who rape the innocent. He will take a room with a bed for the night, but never sleep in it. He will pay for girls, but never touch them. He will pay for information, and he will sniff out the monkey and the bear. And retrieve the pearl.

"Where did you get it? You can't expect me to buy a thing without knowing if it's stolen. That'll decrease its worth. What if someone should recognize it? Then it would be my head, wouldn't it."

He is a fat, greasy man who wears his hair cut like a bowl, an unusual thing for a Minoan. He stinks of burnt weeds, the kind that make men see things and hear things and feel things they cannot otherwise feel. And he stinks of whores, girls and boys alike. Turios dislikes the man instantly and knows he will never own the pearl. It is distasteful for him even to remove it from his own ear and give it to him to examine.

"None of your concern where it came from. It is what it is, and no less, no matter whose it was. It's mine now. Never mind then, I can sell it myself overseas, I'm headed there anyhow," says Turios, grabbing it out of the man's hand as he's ogling it through a glass.

"Don't be so hasty, man, don't you know how to haggle? I'll give you four hundred coin for it."

The man is reaching at Turios like a child whose sweet has been taken. But Turios has already replaced the pearl in his own ear.

"I said never mind," says Turios gruffly. "Too good for the likes of you anyhow." He shoves the man out of his way and lumbers out of the dark hole that is his den, past filthy men coupling with girls young enough to be their granddaughters, then out through a broken door into the light, onto the street. Half way back to his room in a brothel up the street, he is met by a man who looks to be in the wrong neck of town. He is big and broad as a bear himself but a well fed and well fought bear. He wears his hair in a long braid and his beard is trimmed, though he smells of earth and sweat, like a soldier who has been in the field for a week. And something else, something Turios is instantly repelled by.

So fixed is his attention on the pearl whispering in his ear that he does not notice the man until he is clearly blocking his path several meters in front of him. He attempts to move out of his way, drifting further into the street to do so. But as he is about to pass him he is suddenly being flung by one arm, like so much dough, sideways in front of the man into a narrow alleyway. He stumbles, attempting to remain on his feet, and is just as suddenly caught in the throat and slammed against the outer wall of a building. And he finds himself pinned like a woman against the cool rough stone. The man is impossibly strong. His fingers are clawed, the nails knife-sharp, sinking into the flesh of his biceps. He feels his own blood run down his arms and pool at the crook of his elbows. The man is so close he cannot see his face. And then he feels teeth sinking into the ear, the ear with the pearl. A tug, and hot pain runs down his neck and up into his scalp. A crunching sound accompanies the pain, and then the left side of his head is throbbing. The lobe of his ear is gone, he feels a coolness where it once was. The ear, and the pearl, is in the man's mouth.

Then the man is no longer pinning him and he moves to defend himself, lifting his fists. But he is smashed in the face as with the jawbone of an ass and his head strikes the stone wall behind him, the blow putting him to the ground. Another, from the opposite direction, puts his face in the dirt.

He is spitting out teeth.

"Where is Aktor," a bass voice demands in the hole that was his ear. "Tell me, Turios, if you want to die with your balls attached."

The further shock of his own name in the beast's mouth sends Turios' small mind reeling. But when the clawed hand slams into his groin and captures him, he finds within him the sanity to answer, "He --- will meet me in an hour, --- on the road to Knossos."

Two more fierce blows slam his head into the stone wall he sits against. He is blinded by them, and does not see the crescent blades glitter happily in the lamplight above his head before they descend, slicing left and right across his neck, just under the jaw on either side, then once more, down and across from behind, expertly severing his skull from the spine to relieve his body of the burden of his head.

Inside the brothel the whore master is counting money in a small back room. He has heard of the volcano on Thera and is making plans to take his best stock east to one of the many Minoan colonies along the shores of Canaan. He will do well there, and only stayed on Crete as long as he did because his brother's wife, a Minoan by birth, had family here she would not leave. Now his brother is dead, and there is no reason to stay longer than it will take for him to put together enough coin to set himself up in business across the sea.

The whore master is interrupted by a child half Rah's age, who has enough sense to knock before she enters, having lost the thumb of her left hand as a result of forgetting to do so one too many times. She is scrawny and crawling with lice, but there is still the vestige of the beautiful child she was when the whore master's thugs brought her to him, having stolen her from her family in Pheistos. Her features are perfect and symmetrical, huge dark eyes, exotic and feral, high cheekbones and a delicate jaw.

She steps into the room and holds the dirty drape open, a sin that could cost her another thumb, had the whore master time to punish her for it.

But there is no time. A shape has filled the doorway.

He is huge in the way a lean, well fought bull is huge, hard muscles strapping his arms, neck, and calves. His chest, though hidden under the garb of a simple street merchant who has come from another town to sell wares here in Malia, is likewise the chest of a hard fought bull. A linen robe, tied at the waist, hangs to his knees, and his feet are strapped in a soldier's sandals. His hair is caught up behind his head in a long braid, and his beard trimmed like a nobleman.

The whore master lifts himself up from his seat at the small table where he has been counting and stacking his coins. Fear strokes his balls with its muzzle. It has entered his whore house with the man, as if the man brought it with him, as if he kept it on a leash at his side and now releases it to come and sniff and snuffle the whore master's privates.

"Who are you? What do you want?" he says, his voice a nasal wheeze. He is backing away from his table, toward the knife he keeps on the window ledge behind him. His eyes are fixed on the brute in the doorway. They flick about his shoulders as if to see behind him, but the intruder is so large that this is impossible. Where are the two thugs he pays to keep things like this from happening to him when he is counting his money?

"Go," says the man in the doorway. But he is not talking to the whore master. He is addressing the child, who had been standing against the drape to keep it open for him and has stepped toward him. She stops, looking up at him. Her face is without fear, only wonder.

"Ameg," she whispers up at him, and her lips quaver as if trying to remember how to smile.

The whoremaster's eyes dart from the man to the child. "What the hell is going on? Who are you? Get out of my house!" He reaches for the blade, finds it, his confidence building now he is armed. He holds the stubby bronze weapon like a man who once knew how to use it.

But the man in the door is ignoring him. He has turned his head to the child. Good. I will rush him and stab him in the belly, thinks the whoremaster.

The man looks down at the child, one hand gently tips the girl's chin. He scans her face.

"I am Marta," she says. "My father sent you! I know he did!"

But the whoremaster has lunged across the room from his corner, his blade thrust ahead like a lance. He sees his goal and lusts for it. Yes! I will give you something to take away with you! You dare to challenge me for what is mine! The tip scratches the intruder's robe. He feels it tug lightly across the fabric before his head explodes with light and fire.

He is on the floor, looking up, seeing nothing, only light.

The man, he can feel it, steps over his body to the table. "Take this, Marta, and wait for me outside on the street."

The whoremaster hears the child scamper close. He hears his coins tinkling together as if being poured into a pocket or a sack, then the light scuttle of the girl's bare feet retreating out the door.

"I am blind, you monster! You have blinded me!"

The whore master can feel the man's enormity near him and suddenly wishes he had said nothing, pretended unconsciousness. He senses the man kneel and overshadow him. He hears his garment rustling, as if the man reaches for something hidden underneath.

"You could never see." The hell deep voice is suddenly thick with long Hittite vowels. A broad, hot palm slaps over the whoremaster's forehead, pressing his skull into the dirt floor. A pinch under his right eye turns into a burning pain, like a heated nail. The man is carving something into his face.

"Rush!" cries the whoremaster.

"The same," says Rush, finishing his work without much interest, then slamming the entirety of his weight down, on one knee, into the whore master's chest and collapsing seven ribs and a lung before he turns his attention to the lower half of the man's body and removes his most offensive organ.

This he crams into the whoremaster's open and screaming mouth.

When Rush steps back through the drape into the dingy den, it is empty but for the whores, its patrons having fled in terror at the gurgling screams coming from the whore master's private back room. Their coupling interrupted, the women stand or lie about staring at the man who emerges from it, a man so tall that he must stoop to move through the den, with a thick black braid of hair cutting his powerfully muscled back in half, and the eyes of an executioner. He scans the room looking over the women. He seems to be considering them, as if now his job is done he would take his pleasure here. He takes only an instant to choose.

"You come," he tells a tall girl who has been standing by the exit as if about to slip out of the place. Her eyes are alert, unlike the others. They dart about the room at her sisters. Why me? Then they return to Rush, staring at him like a hare stares at the fox it cannot escape. She says nothing, but steps away from the door and drops her eyes. He nods. He has chosen the right one.

"I will need a wife," he says, taking her arm and shoving her ahead of him out into the street.

Outside he sees that a man has approached Marta, who holds the sack of coin behind her as if she will swing it at his head if he comes closer.

"You want my daughter?" says Rush. He lifts his eyebrows at the man, a small weasel with mean eyes.

A look of disbelief crosses the man's face as he steps away from the girl. He backs away. "No trouble, I want no trouble," then he darts across the street and walks toward the workhouses, looking over his shoulder only once to see that he has avoided it.

Marta has run up to Rush as if he were in fact her father. She hands him the sack. "Here, I kept it safe for you. Will you take me home now, Ameg?"

Rush looks down at the child, a perturbed discomfort on his face. The girl he has taken for his 'wife' stands obediently beside him, watching the exchange but saying nothing.

"You carry that one for me, Marta. I have another." He looks at the whore. "Go down that alley. Pick up the sack there and bring it to me." He tips his beard at the alley where he left Turios.

The whore nods and retreats toward the alley.

"How long have you been here, Marta. And where is your home?" he says to the child.

"Two months, I think." She looks down at the stump that was her thumb, as if to help her to remember. "Yes, about that. I come from Pheistos. That is my home. My father has a vineyard there."

"Ah," says Rush, recalling a transaction with a vintner in Pheistos as Ameg the merchant. "You saw me there, did you? Speaking to your father?"

"Yes!" she smiles. "You have ships! To sell our wine over the sea! He has paid you to come for me!"

Movement from the alley catches Rush's eye. The whore has returned, dutifully, with the sack. She totters, her face pale, holding the leather pouch away from herself as she approaches. When she reaches Rush she attempts to hand it to him, but he makes no move to relieve her of her burden.

"Now you see, woman, I give you a choice. You will travel to Cyrus, to be my dutiful wife for a time, this our child," he nods at Marta, "or I will marry you to the man you met in the alley, and the two of you will kiss forever in that sack. What is your answer?"

The whore looks as if she will vomit. She manages to raise her eyes to his only long enough to respond, "You, sir," before she drops the sack and falls against the front of the brothel, retching.

"She is sick from weed," says Marta casually. "Or maybe she is with child." She slips her hand into Rush's. "Can we go now?"

"Get up, woman. Your name is Cara now. Take up your ex-husband and lead us to a bath house. You are running with lice, as is your daughter here. You will both bathe, then we will purchase decent clothing for you and a wagon to take you to Cyrus. I will meet you there in two days. You will use the money to take a room at a fine inn. You will wait for me. Do not think you will escape me and steal what is mine. Your ex-husband thought as much." He nods once more at the leather sack she has picked up and holds gingerly and at a distance. "You had better look like a lady when I see you again, Cara. And this child had better be the happy daughter of a rich merchant."

"Yes, sir," says Cara, the whore who has become the third wife of Ameg the merchant. "I swear it, sir. I will do exactly as you say."

Aktor has been sitting on a rotten stump a mile up the Knossos road, waiting for Turios as the late afternoon fades toward evening. The north sky, which he faces, has turned from a bird's egg blue to a pirate's blood red flag before his eyes. Tomorrow he will sail for the first time in his life. A red sky at night means safe travel for sailors, or so his captain always told him. Lutarus had crossed the sea many times, so he had told his men, and often entertained them with tales of his passages. Aktor looks up over the treetops toward the sea to the north and the blood red horizon fills him with a sense of pleasure. He feels lucky. Tonight he will dispatch his friend Turios, here in the twilight wood on the road to Knossos. He will ambush him, kill him quick, take the money he carries from his sale of the pearl, and pull his body into the wood for the wild dogs to eat. Aktor does not believe in an afterlife. Either way, he will have no time to tarry over his friend's corpse.

He has given himself a good hour to prepare and to wait, and is only a little surprised to see the large, bearlike shoulders of his friend slowly advancing toward him up the steep hill. Quickly he removes himself from view. The man advancing on him wears a simple, short belted tunic and sandals. He appears to be looking about him, oblivious of the danger ahead in the form of his soldier-brother and friend, Aktor. He has Turios' dark hair and beard. In the waning light it appears to Aktor as if his friend has been to a barber and purchased himself a fresh tunic after selling the pearl. Good, thinks Aktor, he is carrying the money. I have persuaded him to sell that damned pearl. The thing was talking to him, I swear it. Full of demons. I'll be glad to be free of anything to do with that boy. Ever since I first lay eyes upon him, all hell has broken from the gate. Be glad to be rid of it, and of Crete.

In the long minutes it takes for his prey to lumber up the steep hill through the wood toward him, Aktor loses the remainder of the daylight. By the time the man is parallel to his hiding place, only a sliver of moonlight and the torchlight from the city below illuminate his form.

And as he leaps out from behind a copse to drive his dagger into his friend's back he has an odd moment of confusion. For the back he springs at is too broad, even for Turios, the outline of the belted tunic too well-shaped, the waist a hard, clean line, the buttocks tucked and athletic. What has happened to Turios in the span of an hour, thinks the monkey.

Then the truth turns to slash its own dagger across his brow, left to right, and he is blinded with the blood pouring into his eyes. He instinctively reaches for them, is spun by an arm and flung to the ground on his face. He feels the man's knee slam down on his mid-back with enormous speed and force, as if launched from a catapult. His back cracks and numbness floods his legs like ice water. A hand like a bear claw palms the back of his head and yanks his face out of the dirt. Aktor waits for a knife to slice his throat with the same swiftness. But it is not there.

"Who are you?" he has time to choke out the words as the thing that attacked him, the thing he believed was the friend he meant to kill, tears at the back of his tunic. Now he can feel the man yank the loincloth beneath it down, exposing his buttocks to the warm Cretan air.

"I am the one you stole from," a voice snarls at his ear, deep as the river to Tartarus. "You would have what is mine, eh? Now I will have what is yours, Aktor, now I will have you," and splicing fire explodes through his tenderest parts as the man drives his diamond sharp, foot long dagger into his rectum.

CHAPTER 34

At the Palace of Knossos, Queen Nanaea is preparing her departure. All of the city is well aware of the volcano that is steaming on Thera. The wealthiest merchants in town keep storehouses and ships on the island, just a hundred kilometers north, and during the past few weeks they have been transporting their wealth elsewhere, abandoning what will become, in two months' time, the greatest catastrophic natural event in written history. Nanaea herself has plans to transport her household and her immediate staff to a Minoan settlement on the coast of Canaan and many of the top officials of the town will do the same. But just as many have refused to leave Crete, and have decided to stay, believing that an explosion 100 kilometers away cannot affect them to any great extent.

Nanaea has learned from Ramicus, delivering the message from the House of the Moon, that the Grain God has been stolen, and that Ameg has returned to Crete on nothing but a skiff, intent on rescuing him and taking him to Anatolia with him. As a gesture of good will toward the father of her pregnancy, and unaware that he has made plans for his own ship to return for him, she has prepared a vessel to replace the skiff. It is a ship second in size only to the one upon which she will flee Crete herself, and it has ample room for a gift of twenty Arabian horses. Ramicus has been instructed by the Queen to round up the animals and bring them down to the harbor, then to care for them until Ameg returns. The ship has been equipped with a crew and sufficient food and water for his passage to Anatolia.

Ramicus and his men, including the two stable boys, have dutifully and painstakingly caught the twenty horses and brought them to the Queen's storehouses at the harbor, which will serve as stables until Ameg returns. In the meantime the House of Mochlos, which awaits the return of Ameg's private ship to transport them to his sanctuary in Anatolia, continues its vigil for the return of Rah. Most of Mochlos' own ships are out to sea, and those that remain in the harbor are cargo vessels and not fit for the transport of an entire villa. The three concubines have disappeared, and it is suspected that they have made a pilgrimage to Mount Ida, to the Burial Ground of the Ancients, where the god Rah first entered the slave boy. No one questions their absence, as it is customary for the concubines of a slain slave-god to take their own lives with poison or bloodletting at the site of his birth.

Ting Ya remains at the House of the Moon, her things having been gathered by the priest's men and brought back to the villa for her. She is, perhaps, the most optimistic of those awaiting Rah's return, and continues to speak of Ameg's rescue of the boy and his transport overseas as if it is a thing already accomplished.

In Cyrus, Thera is considered no threat for although she is only the breadth of Crete further away than from Knossos, Cyrus is buffered from her by the mountains. The people are confident that no wave resulting from her explosion could reach the city. Nor has Cyrus been plagued by the quakes and sea storms that cities to the east and west have suffered. Its only plague was drought and, now that the Grain God is theirs, the surviving crops are green again. In fact, the Minoan's genius for irrigation has prolonged the life of much of their agriculture and the drought, followed now by late summer rain, promises to sweeten the grapes and make this year's wines exceptional.

So Cyrus, unlike Knossos, is focused on celebration and thanksgiving for the Grain God. The locals are quick to forget that it was the captain of their palace guard who very nearly killed the boy, and cheer instead his rescue by the new captain, Nikolaos. The streets are abuzz with hope for a prosperous future for Cyrus, and if the volcano does indeed send a wave crashing over the northern coastline of Crete, such a calamity could make Cyrus the strongest and wealthiest city on the island.

It is unanimously believed that the little dancer from the north is indeed the incarnation of the Grain God, Rah, and he has become a celebrity and a superstar overnight.

The story of the boy becoming the incarnation of the god by winning a dance competition has filtered down from the palace concubines and dancers to the stewards, the kitchen staff, the guards, even the palace plumbers, and on to the street. Now the people of Cyrus are demanding a demonstration, a dance! For if an unconscious slave-god can bring rain from drought, what can a dancing Grain God do? And so the King has ordered his dance master to create a story-dance for the people, an unusual thing in Cyrus, where dance is limited to ceremonial circles or lines. This new dance is to be performed in the great hall of Cyrus for all to attend.

Rah himself will tell the story in dance, with the accompaniment of the King's own troupe. It will be the story of Rah himself, his capture in the barbarian lands far to the north, his sale to the priest of Knossos, his winning of the competitions among the Houses of the Gods, and his assumption of the soul of Rah at the Burial Ground of the Ancients.

On the morning Rush is circling the trackers and descending swiftly down upon Malia, Rah awakens in his chamber howling.

It is the sound of an animal, a lost kit, or cub, a high, singsong warble, heartbreaking and driving. Nikolaos is the first to rush into the room, his short Grecian sword at the ready. Behind him tumble the two stewards and the King, who is this morning accompanied by his wife, Media, both in bedclothes.

Immediately upon gaining an audience, Rah stills. He is sitting up in the middle of his opulent feather mattress in a full lotus, his fine, flexible limbs relaxed into the position as if it were as natural as bending to tie one's sandals. He blinks his blue-green eyes at Nikolaos as if just awaking, takes a huff of air, and looks at the others in confusion.

"Why you are here?" he asks finally, when the audience makes no move to address him.

"You were screaming, Rah, like someone was killing you. What the devil is the matter? Did you have a dream?" says Nikolaos, relaxing and sheathing his sword, then crossing the room to stand over Rah.

"Moon, she is angry now. Give Rah bad dream. Rah must sleep in chain. Gold. This how priest do to make Moon happy. Rah hate chain-" he pantomimes a struggle with invisible chains as he sleeps, "but must have. Rah must sleep in chain. Here," he takes hold of his own collar, "and here," his belt, "and here," his anklets. He slumps into a dejected whole-body pout.

"Chains?" says the King, stepping up beside Nikolaos. He looks back at his wife, who is following him across the floor. "Why would he want to be chained?"

"No want," says Rah miserably, looking up under the curtain of his lashes. "Must have. This why Rah sick. No chain. Too long no chain. Rope no good. Must be gold. So to please Rah."

"He tells his story," says Media, coming to stand beside the King, then plopping down on the bed next to Rah and stroking his curls. Since she first lay eyes on the boy two days earlier, as she was heading out toward the pottery shed past the gymnasium and he came tottering through the archway with Fillius, she has been following him around, cooing and petting him with the abandon of a concubine. She has shown no sign whatsoever of her dark illness, has made no further trips to the Hall of the Kings, and has brightened her appearance considerably. Gone is the hag's black sack cloth. She is a queen again and wears colorful silks and fine jewelry. She has even been to the bath master to soak in rare oils and to the hairdresser, and last night, for the first time in three years, she slept with her King.

"They chained you at night in Knossos, Rah?" asks the ever practical Nikolaos. "Is that why you believe you must be chained here?"

"This is not Knossos, Rah," adds the King, who has never chained a slave.

"Sweet little kitten," says the Queen. "You will have chains if you wish. Get the locksmith, Cyrus, and have it done, just as he tells you. Gold." She considers Rah for a moment, purses her lips. "Thin links, like necklaces, you see? So as not to mar him."

Rah gives the Queen a furtive glance. He has tolerated her affections well these last days, although he seems disturbed by them. Something is wrong with this Queen. She is a pleasant enough creature, not hard and manly like the Queen of Knossos but gentle and feminine, fine boned and soft. But there is an energy in her like a door sealed shut, or like a mare that cannot foal. As she runs her fingers down his back absently he flinches lightly, bites his lip. He looks up at Nikolaos as if for help.

"Too thin, I break. Bad. Must be strong enough."

"Just as you say, kitten," says the Queen, putting a light kiss on his shoulder. Then she rises from the bed. "Now have some breakfast, hmm? Get him just what he likes, Bacus," she says to the steward.

"Of course, madam," says Bacus, bowing low and exiting, with a sour expression, to do as he is told.

When the King and Queen have retired back to the King's chamber Rah hops off his mattress and steps past Nikolaos as if he is invisible to peer out the window.

"Are you feeling better, Rah?" asks the new Captain of the Guard, stepping behind him as if to look over his head to see what his men are doing in the practice arena this morning. Fillius has remained in the room as well, for it has become his habit, much to the consternation of Bacus, to take Rah down to the latrines and the bath before attending to his own daily duties.

"Rah is feel better," says Rah, only half aware of the Captain's intention to draw him into a conversation. He seems to have lost the edgy energy with which he has plagued the staff since he arose from his delirium.

Over the boy's gold and platinum curls the Captain can see that several men have hauled a chariot out of the stable block, behind which another leads a rather high spirited chestnut colt.

"Hah," Rah tips his chin at the men. "They will lose that one. He is too strong today." He turns to the Captain, a bit unbalanced to see he has drawn so near to him that he must look directly up into the man's face. Nikolaos is looking down at him with no such discomfort.

Rah furrows his brows at the man, takes a step back and bumps the window ledge in an attempt to create a more comfortable distance.

"Rah is show Fox, Rah is good today. Then go-" he points out the window. He folds his arms over his pierced nipples and cocks his head at the Captain, waiting for an argument.

"And how will you show me that, Rah?" asks Nikolaos softly, enjoying the moment. The boy was bathed in a cherry blossom and myrrh oiled bath yesterday and the scent has put Nikolaos back on his horse, Rah in his arms, on his return to the palace from the cemetery.

Rah gives Nikolaos a withering look. Then he dips out from under the Captain's chin and executes a double back flip to a hand stand before falling on his rump.

Nikolaos stands blinking at what he has just seen, while Fillius rushes to Rah to help him to his feet.

"I do again, not so good," says Rah. But Nikolaos has caught him by the arm. He looks down at the boy with something between awe and anger. Rah returns the look with one of dismissal. He yanks his arm out of the Captain's grasp.

"You promise," he says.

"I promised-?" But Nikolaos cannot remember what he has promised Rah in these last three days. He frowns, searching his memory.

Now Rah is smiling a smile of conquest. "Yes!" He points at the Captain, even stabs him in the chest once with an arrogant finger. "You say, Rah, when you are better, I take you to horse! Yes!" He looks at Fillius for support. Fillius in turn looks at the Captain and lifts his hands, shrugging.

"I suppose you did, sir," he says, having no intention to do anything that might make Rah angry with him and thereby forfeiting his morning walk to the latrines with the boy.

The scream of a horse followed by a crashing sound and the shouts of men draw Rah and the Captain back to the window. Rah points at the disaster and yips like a happy cur. "I tell you! This one too strong today!"

The horse has bolted, apparently just as the men were attempting to harness him to the chariot. Now he is running at a full gallop around the arena, chased by his harness tack which follows him close behind, furthering his hysteria. The chariot has overturned and one wheel is even now rolling across the arena as if determined to remain with the horse. One man is down and another attends to him. Three more are making a weak attempt to corral the animal.

"They scare him," says Rah. "More hard to catch now. I go." He puts two hands on the window sill and makes a neat little spring to bring his feet up beside them.

"Dear gods," mutters the Captain, hooking one strong arm around the boy's waist and pulling him back into the room. "Alright, Rah. I'll take you." Then through the window he bellows to the men, "Let him be! Let him run it out! Clear the arena and shut the gates!"

The men look up to the window, see their captain, and obediently back away from the hysterical horse to clear the wreck of the chariot.

It is a simple matter to gain access to the practice arena from the King's wing. The Captain leads, with Rah happily bouncing beside him, now and again hopping into the air and spinning down the hall in a cartwheel or a flip. The Captain has given up his attempts to curtail his exuberance, which is infectious at any rate. He shakes his head and watches the boy's antics, amazed. So this is Rah in motion. If I ever see him in stillness again my heart will break into a thousand shards.

Down one long hall, a stone stair, another long hall, and they are out an archway almost directly under Rah's chamber window. Fillius has followed at a lumbering trot behind them, unable to keep up with either. One stride of the Captain's long legs requires two of his, and Rah is like a sprite, bouncing and flitting with more ethereal and magnetic energy than Fillius has ever known in his entire cautious and patient life.

But once he has stepped through the archway into the high light of the arena Rah's spinning motion suddenly quiets. He is several paces in front of the Captain when he steps out of doors, and his focus is instantly pinned on the horse, which is, as it happens, closer to him than to the men returning to the arena from the stable block, where they have deposited the wrecked chariot. Rah, his eyes fixed on the horse, lifts one hand to the men, the elegance in the gesture enough to halt them in their tracks. Nikolaos, coming to a halt in the archway, nods to the men and tips his head at Rah. Careful, he is saying, stay where you are. His first concern is that if they spook the animal any further it could easily trample the boy as he attempts to approach it.

"Let me catch him for you, Rah," tries the Captain, reaching to take Rah's shoulder. But the boy has had enough coddling from Captain Nikolaos. He shoots him a dismissive look. "Stupid fox," he speaks slowly, deliberately, his crimped tongue fighting with every word. "You think you know everything. But you know nothing. You watch and watch Rah, but never see. Never open hand, never let go. Put bird in cage, never let fly. How you can know bird?"

So struck by this observation, coming from a boy who can barely make himself understood under the best of circumstances, is Captain Nikolaos, that he can only stare at Rah in disbelief. There is a pain he has never felt before in his chest, as if the claws of a kitten have closed on his heart.

Now Rah turns from him and walks deliberately into the arena. He is to the right of the horse, who, at the approach of the boy, has come to a lathered halt fifty meters away but continues to worry at his trailing tack.

Rah begins to make a noise, soft and soothing, as he walks not toward the animal but parallel to it, across the arena, keeping his left shoulder to the beast. His head is down, as if he is searching the ground for something. Nikolaos notices that the horse, still blowing, has lifted its head at him, as if to tear off again on another wild loop around the arena. But now Rah has begun to move away from him, even turning his back on him, and as he does so, he continues to search the ground, finally coming to a soft halt himself and dropping to his haunches to pick at a few weeds that have managed to sprout in the sandy earth.

The colt, for it is no more than three summers, is watching, its head alert, its sides still heaving lightly from its gallop around the ring. The three men in charge of it have begun to move toward Rah, but Captain Nikolaos has raised his hand, ordering them to back off. They do as they are told. Meanwhile the colt has begun to move, very slowly, one tentative step at a time, toward Rah, who pays it no mind but continues to pick in the dirt, collecting whatever vegetation he can find in the well-kept arena. As he does so he continues making his light, whistling purr, so soft it is barely audible.

The colt is twenty meters away when Rah lifts his head with unutterable slowness and meets the animal's eye. He does so only for an instant, then returns to his grazing. He creeps along the ground on his haunches, picking tiny weeds, purring like a winded horse.

The colt continues to wander toward him, now with its head down, as if it, too, would search for grass in the barren arena. But finding none, it meanders toward the boy, muzzle down until it is at his shoulder, finally snuffling at the hand that holds the bits of grass and weed.

The whole episode has taken a quarter of an hour. But now something is happening between the horse and the boy that Nikolaos and the men at the opposite end of the arena cannot see or hear. As moments pass, the bizarre picture of the horse, spooked and lathered only moments earlier, and now pushing at the boy's shoulder as if to say, "Give me! Open that hand!" seems perfectly normal. Then Rah does indeed open his hand to the animal, who finds a few threads of grass and takes them. And Rah strokes the animal's head, gradually takes the reins that hang from its headstall and quietly rolls their length up into a neat circle.

Off the ground, the reins are no longer a predator chasing him, and the colt allows Rah to stand up. He does so slowly, not facing off the animal but shoulder to shoulder. He leads the horse, not toward Captain Nikolaos, but toward the chariot men. From Nikolaos' point of view, it appears as if he is dressing them down. And the strange thing is, they appear to be taking the telling quite well. One shuffles his feet, as if bashful and embarrassed. Another turns smartly toward the stable door. He will return with a bucket momentarily. The third man takes the cavesson Rah has removed from the horse. Then he takes the headstall and reins Rah offers him before the Captain realizes what is happening.

The colt is now free of tack and virtually impossible to catch.

Snatching the bucket of grain from the man who has gone for it, Rah marches right back into the center of the arena. The colt throws his head in the air, as if giving the chariot men his own dressing down, and follows Rah. He nudges Rah's back, makes a few attempts to nose dive into the grain bucket over Rah's shoulder, but gets a reprimand in the form of a tap on the muzzle and dodges away. It has all become a happy game to the colt, who was brought out cold to do a job he had no aptitude for in the first place.

Now Nikolaos sees that Rah has detached one of the long chariot reins from the headstall and kept it for himself. He unrolls five or six feet of it and begins to whip it lightly at his own feet, encouraging the colt to move away from him and the bucket. But the colt wants the grain and is unwilling to move too far from it. He begins to circle Rah, playfully dodging in and out for the grain as Rah swishes his makeshift whip on the ground in front of him to keep him out in a circle.

Soon the colt is lungeing himself around Rah in a quiet trot to the right.

Nikolaos can only look on in wonder.

He and the chariot men watch from opposite sides of the arena as Rah continues to free lunge the colt. After a time the boy curls up the rein he has been using as a whip and takes a handful of grain from the bucket. The colt trots in to take the grain from his hand and as he does so Rah runs his hands over the animal's neck, shoulder and flank, carefully stepping around him to his right side. When the colt has finished the grain in his hand Rah lifts the whip, this time forcing the colt to move off to the left.

Soon the animal is free lungeing in a quiet trot in the opposite direction.

Rah curls up the whip and offers him another handful of grain. Good, thinks Nikolaos. Now he will bring the horse in and demand his own breakfast.

Rah has returned to the chariot men, with the horse passively following him. He has an exchange with the men, and even from this end of the arena Nikolaos can see those dimples explode as one man hands him back the headstall and the remaining rein. Then, to Nikolaos' complete amazement Rah gives the man a theatrical bow before turning to the colt and gently replacing the headstall. He walks the animal out a few paces, stroking its neck, shoulder, belly and flank and running his hand along its back from wither to croup. The horse is unfazed. Satisfied, he puts a hand in its mane and takes a few hops, as if to mount. The colt remains unconcerned. It nuzzles at his skirt pocket, apparently having discovered that Rah has a stash of grain in one. Rah strokes the animal's head, offers it a bit of the grain, and slips onto its back so lightly that even Nikolaos can feel his weightlessness. The colt makes one awkward step to the right, then quiets as Rah continues to stroke both sides of its neck simultaneously, rub the length of its mane, scratch either side of its withers. He moves the animal forward a few steps, then lifts himself effortlessly up into a handstand, balancing on its wither. The colt seems oblivious to his change of position. Rah returns to his seat, then takes another weightless hop and he is standing on the animal's back, the long harness reins gathered in one hand.

In this manner, Rah begins walking, then trotting, the animal in a circle.

It is not until he feels a hand on his shoulder that Captain Nikolaos realizes that the King and his Queen have been watching Rah along with him under the archway.

"Quite a creature," says the King, who has dressed for the day. His Queen stands beside him, one arm wrapped around her husband's ample waist. The top of her head reaches only to his shoulder, although her new hairdo competes for height with his clean shaven head. Neither competes with Nikolaos' elegant height.

"He is the true Rah," muses Media the Queen.

Rah has somehow returned to a handstand on the colt's wither, the reins now loose in his hands and hang in loops against the animals shoulders.

"He will break his neck," says Nikolaos, helpless.

"Don't be such a hen, Captain," says the King. "I think this is not the first time he has performed such feats on horseback. He looks quite competent, no?"

Bending at the hip like a switch blade, Rah has returned to sit the horse. Now he draws in the rein and brings the colt to a square halt. The colt drops its head submissively, and Rah hops to the ground, light as a leaf, and offers the animal the remainder of the grain in his pocket. When the chariot men begin to cheer and clap, the colt pays them no mind. Intent on Rah's pockets, he follows the boy back across the arena toward them.

And when Rah makes an abrupt halt a few meters from them the colt does the same, as if allowing him his moment in the spotlight. It patiently waits for him to complete a stage bow.

Rah hands off the reins to the men, then turns to run his hand over the colt one more time before returning to Nikolaos.

He is glistening with sweat and panting lightly when he reaches the trio under the archway. When he sees the King and Queen he offers them another bow and Nikolaos finds himself dumb with confusion. It is the first time that the boy has recognized their station appropriately.

Media has released her husband to step toward Rah. She puts an arm around his glistening shoulder, kisses his cheek, and squeezes him against herself.

"You are a confection," she says, "A sweet."

"You are the true Rah," murmurs the King, looking at his transformed wife and then the boy.

You are going to drive me straight out of my mind, thinks Captain Nikolaos. And here I stand hoping you will allow me to continue to babysit for you, when I have a guard to command. What in hell is wrong with me?

But when Rah lifts his morning-lit, blue-gold eyes to the Captain and gives him a lopsided smile, Nikolaos forgets his frustrations. He smiles back broadly, docile as the colt.

"Would you like some breakfast now, Rah?" he is struggling to keep his eyes up. The boy's panting abdomen, bunching and relaxing with each breath, is a fine team of glistening horses.

"Yes, hungry," responds Rah between breaths. "Where Fillius?" He looks behind the Captain down the empty hall.

"Gone to get it for you, I suspect," says Nikolaos.

"Bath first, then breakfast," says Rah, making another short bow to the King and Queen and then walking off in the direction of the baths. Nikolaos immediately moves to follow him.

"Come now, Captain," smiles the King. "If he can manage what we just witnessed, I

expect he can find his way to the latrine alone." He takes his wife by the hand and leaves the young Captain to his day.

CHAPTER 35

Early the next morning the third wife of Ameg and her new daughter, Marta, are being jostled together in a cart drawn by two ass over a rocky road into the mountains and toward Cyrus. Cara wears a good linen dress, appropriate for a traveling lady, with a scarf pulled over her head to protect her from the sun. In fact, she is a light skinned girl, originally from Pheistos herself, where there is a small enclave of immigrants from Thrace. Her family came to Crete with a shipping vessel when she was only Marta's age, settling on the southern coast of the island to prosper as saffron farmers. The girl who is now Cara was engaged to marry the son of a local vintner, unrelated to Marta, before she was kidnapped by the whoremaster's thugs and taken to Malia. She had only been at the brothel two weeks herself when Rush the Assassin changed the whoremaster's plans, curtailing her sale to a higher class brothel, where her virginity and her voice would make her a fine prize. For Cara was quite well know in Pheistos for her singing, and she had hoped she might earn a decent enough living on it to avoid marriage altogether before her father made arrangements with the vintner's son.

Cara is not singing now. In fact, she has barely used her voice at all since the assassin left her in charge of their 'daughter', relieving her of the sack with the head of her 'first husband' before he disappeared. She sits in the wagon as it bounces along the rocky path up the mountain, Marta nodding sleepily against her side, and contemplates her fate. She did not love the man she was intended for, a man more than half again her age and in possession of less than half her wit and no looks at all. And while she is relieved that she has avoided her impending sale as a high priced sex slave at a foreign brothel, where she was almost certain to have been purchased by someone even less appealing than her husband-to-be, she is in something of a state of shock as to with whom she has ended up. Although not by law, she is suddenly married by fear to a vicious killer, a butcher who cuts men's heads off and leaves their headless bodies in alleys behind whorehouses, taking their heads, she supposes, as souvenirs.

Since first laying eyes on the monster she has felt nothing but dread of him, although to be fair their introduction was partially to blame for this. She had been coming down the stairs that led from the women's rooms above to the vestibule at the front of the brothel, when she saw him enter and immediately take down the whoremaster's two security thugs. She watched from above, drawing back against a wall, as the beast slammed them both to the ground with his massive fists before either could draw a blade, then slash their throats with as little reluctance as she might slap at a louse. He tossed their bodies in a heap behind the door, then strode into the brothel, the smell of death so high on him that she could sense it from her perch at the top of the stair.

She had intended to run back upstairs and hide as best she could, except for Marta, who she knew was down in the brothel serving drink and drug. She had not known the girl in Pheistos, but felt a certain loyalty to her given their common origin. And so she came down the stair and into the brothel, looking for the girl but not finding her. It was not until the child ran happily past her and out the door with the sack of coin that she realized the man had not come to hurt a child, but to do business with the whoremaster of the house. In the next instant the awful, gurgling screams coming from behind the draped doorway at the back of the den froze her in her tracks. And then the man appeared in the doorway himself, and looked right at her.

"I will need a wife," he said, in a huge voice, like an angry bear. Why me? was all she could think. By what star am I cursed thus?

And the man hated her, there was no doubt in her mind. He believed her a common whore, and clearly had no use for the vocation. Here she is, the virgin daughter of a reasonably wealthy saffron farmer. . . .

Of course she is not really a virgin. Who is, these days? No, a handsome soldier-for-hire, traveling through town on his way to the battlefield had taken her virginity (she would never call it innocence, believing she never possessed much of that) two summers earlier and then left for war, or so he said. May the crows eat the eyeballs out of his corpse on the battlefield.

So here she sits in an ass-drawn cart, dressed like a traveling lady, on her way to a city she has never been to, to be the wife of a man she is utterly terrified of. Here she is, rescued from being sold as a virgin by a man who believes her to be a whore, and she is neither. Here she sits in a cart with a child she would have had to have given birth to when she herself was sixteen summers. She knows as much about children as she does about acting like a 'lady.' And that is next to nothing.

Now the child has stirred. She looks up at Cara, smiles, pats her hands. These are folded in Cara's lap in her feeble attempt to develop a habit she believes lady-like enough to keep her head on her shoulders until she can figure out some way of convincing her new 'husband' to 'divorce' her amicably.

"Don't worry, Cara, Ameg is a good man. Very rich, too! He will make you a fine husband!"

She looks into Marta's huge eyes and frowns. No point talking down to the girl. Marta has seen more in the past few months than most girls of her station see in a lifetime.

"This is all pretend, Marta. You see? He needs us as a disguise. He stole the money from the master and he has stolen us and we are to pretend to be his wife and daughter so he can avoid a well deserved execution."

"Ameg is rich!" laughs Marta. "He does not need to steal from a brothel!"

Cara rolls her eyes and gives up. She has not had the stomach to ask Marta what she saw transpire in the back room of the whorehouse, but the man she calls Ameg had not yet set upon the master when the little girl came running though the den with the sack of coin. The whoremaster's horrific screams came later. And then the giant appeared in the draped doorway, stooping to pass through, never able to stretch to his actual height of heaven-knows-what until he was out in the street.

"I am a dead goose," murmurs Cara, frowning.

"Silly," Marta smiles up at her, patting her hand again. "He likes you, Cara! Did he not give you a sack of gold to hold for him?"

But this is where Cara can and will part with the truth to spare the girl her own sickening knowledge of what the man is capable of. "Yes, Marta. He did indeed."

"And he is so handsome, Cara!" beams Marta. "I wish he would marry me!"

At this Cara must swallow the bile in her throat. How different perceptions can be. How could a child think a beast like that handsome? All she herself could see was lethal strength, unbound cruelty, and coal black eyes that flashed and snarled like the devil's own.

"Be quiet, Marta, I must think. I must think," Cara pushes her scarf off her head and runs her fingers through her long, loose hair, unconsciously enjoying the feeling of it, now that it is clean. The bath he insisted she have was wonderful, she had to admit that. She had forgotten how it felt to be free of lice and to bathe in perfumed water. "Maybe just take one thing at a time, solve one problem at a time, hmm?" she nods to herself. "I do just as he says, to the letter. Like a soldier with orders. I can do that. Get to know him better. Figure him out. Maybe he likes to be sung to, why not? They say wild beasts enjoy the human harmonies." She looks down at Marta, who seems to have nodded off again. She scratches her scalp, a habit developed from a fortnight of lice. "Well, at least the part about the happy daughter is done." She gives the child a little squeeze and begins to hum a tune. Better exercise this throat, she thinks. If he likes what comes out of it, perhaps he'll leave it in one piece.

On the morning of Cara and Marta's journey toward Cyrus over the mountain road in a hired cart, the camp of Horus is in a state of panic and confusion.

Horus is sleeping in his palace guard uniform, the insignia of his station embroidered on the breast. He is Second Lieutenant of the Guard. A good enough commission, though perhaps less than he expected at his age. Horus is dreaming of his first wife, who died in a fire when he was but twenty-four summers. He often dreams of Sonia, a foreign born slave girl he fell dead in love with at first sight and never changed his course to buy and free her until it was accomplished. Then he lost her a year later when a cook overturned a pot of hot oil, burning down the camp kitchen. Sonia had taken a job as cook's helper just to be near her new husband while he was fighting for hire overseas. Her hair caught fire, that beautiful river of yellow-gold hair he married her for. She went up like a torch. But now he feels her hair on his cheek as he so often did when she made love to him, her riding his hips and moaning and purring like a she-cat in heat. Her hair wisps across his nose, his eye, tugging at his lashes, brushes his forehead. He chuckles in his sleep. He knows he is asleep, knows, after all these years of longing that he is only dreaming of her, but his heart is glad just the same. He lifts a hand to stroke the side of her head, brush back the hair.

And the god of ugly-jokes-on-the-brokenhearted opens Horus' eyes.

At first he thinks he must still be dreaming, or else has gone mad with longing for his beloved Sonia. The thing waving above his head does indeed have hair loose and long enough to tickle his face. But the hair is dirty, matted and brown, the face bloodless and grimacing in a horrific exaggeration of surprise. The head is twice the size of Sonia's and has no shoulders, only an awful stump that is the drying vessels and muscles and bone that had been its neck.

Horus' mind swims in a delirium of confusion, then basic instinct takes over and his body fights to remember how to take a breath. This done, he lets out a bellowing scream and awakens the rest of the camp.

From across the copse comes an echoing screech, higher and then higher like a man at the onset of madness. Horus rolls out from under the head of Aktor and stumbles to his feet. What is happening? He sees that one of the trackers, a slender boy of twenty summers, is crab-walking out from under a second head. He is still yodeling wildly. The head swings calmly above him, back and forth like a pendulum, several feet above his bedroll. It too has an expression of surprise, as if its owner were shocked that the boy should have such an unreasonable reaction to it.

"It's them!" says one of the other trackers, a braver man who has come forward to stop the head's swinging and take a closer look. "See here!" He takes a strip of cloth that has been stuffed into the head's mouth, pulls it out, unfolds it. "The insignia of the Guard!"

Now another man has approached the head. "Someone has torn off one of the ears," he says.

Horus pushes past the two trackers and takes hold of the head himself. The man with the piece of cloth opens it to show him the golden embroidery that matches his own.

"Look under the eye," says Horus, "A fresh mark. It is the mark of the bull." He looks about at the men that have gathered around him. The boy has stopped screaming, but has yet to come to his feet and join the others. "This is the work of the assassin." He looks about past the men, into the wood, as if Rush might still be lurking there.

The men are looking at one another nervously.

"He has given us a message to take to the King," says Horus. He seems to be addressing the wood. "And so we shall," he says in a loud voice. "On my word we shall."

Rush the Assassin is taking the Knossos Road on foot, back to the House of the Moon. He is no longer burdened with the heads of the two thieves, and he has fed and freed his dogs, which now trot along, parallel to him, in the brush on either side of the road. They will remain invisible to anyone but him unless they are called to his aid.

Rush has a single errand in Knossos. He is on his way to pay a visit to Ananou, the master of the House of the Sun. His name was uttered only once by Lutarus before he was made a toy and a meal for Rush's two wolf dogs in his family tomb, but that was enough for Rush to put together the connection between the two men. Lutarus would have needed money for his bid for war. By promising the priest, who would have blamed Rah for his loss of Tiko, that he would kill the boy, he would have had the priest on his side to finance that war.

As he lopes along the Knossos Road in the bright, late morning Cretan sun, Rush has time to think of Lutarus, who captured Rah, left him in the hands of two simple minded buffoons, and returned to Cyrus to pursue his own personal dream of manhood. He left Rah to two dogs, for Turios and Aktor were nothing more, maintained his focus on his goals, despite meeting the boy, maintained his decision to kill him.

This, perhaps more than anything else Lutarus had done, cost him his life. For in this, he bested Rush.

Lutarus' jibe that Rush had lost his balls to the boy has been gnawing on Rush for days. That he has been made impotent as a killer by a boy of sixteen summers is a thing he has never stopped struggling with. It was the thing that tore at him as he watched the boy sleeping in the stall while he was yet with him at his own home in Knossos. In truth, each time he is near the boy, he struggles within himself, for in the mind of the assassin his failure to kill the boy is his only flaw as a man. His authority as an executioner was lost to him the day he could not finish that job, and there will always be resentment in him toward Rah for that.

He cannot deny to himself that Lutarus spoke the truth.

Lutarus' mention of Ananou is yet another set of teeth in Rush's side. From it he learned that Ananou still wished to kill Rah, even after his visit from Rush. Why? Because Rush had taken Tiko from him. Until then, Ananou wanted Rah dead so that Tiko might be Grain God. But now, it is revenge. Revenge against Rush himself. An eye for an eye. A boy for a boy.

Alright then, Lutarus. I will prove to us both that had you had your way with the people of Cyrus and had come to the moment when you were standing before them, knife at the ready, to take Rah's life, you would have found it as impossible as I did. I will show you by giving Ananou the same opportunity. Ananou, the man who has wanted Rah dead since he first laid eyes on him. I will set him in my sandals. He will trade places with me, and spend some time wrestling with this wolf in my breast. Or to put it another way, I will give him my dagger, as I gave it to you, Lutarus. And we will see in whose heart that dagger ends.

Rush continues his steady pace toward Knossos until dusk, his hell hounds shadowing him in the woods on either side of the road. When he reaches the city he deposits the dogs back in the storehouse on the harbor. He stops at the House of the Moon to bathe, to dress as Ameg the Merchant, and to take a meal. Then he leaves for the House of the Sun to make his proposal to Ananou.

When Rush arrives at the gate of the House of the Sun he is dressed in gold silks. His beard is perfumed, his Hittite braid wound up under a merchant's cap. He wears expensive sandals and a sash embroidered with pearls. The pearl he ripped off Turios' head has been removed from its nest in the man's disembodied ear and cleaned by Mochlos' jeweler. Rush wears it in his own ear for safekeeping.

He is immediately let in by the guards, led into an opulent room full of pieces of statuary and wall art depicting perfect male bodies, and a few moments later is greeted by a pretty Asian youth who offers him a tray of refreshments.

"The High Priest Ananou will be with you shortly, sir. He has asked me to tell you that it is his honor to have you in his house."

"I am equally honored to be entertained under his roof," answers Ameg with the rote response.

He is not left to himself long.

"Ameg, to what do I owe the pleasure of a visit?" Ananou has apparently just come from his sanctuary of prayer. He is dressed formally, in the same white and yellow gown he wore during Rah's Dying of the God Ceremony, with a great sun embroidered on the back, the rays of which encircle him, reaching around the front of the garment as if embracing him. His bronze hat is missing, however, and his shaven head gleams in the sunny room and seems to reflect the many bronze and gold statues surrounding him. He comes forward to give Rush a formal embrace, then extends his hand to offer him his choice of pillowed settees on the floor. When Rush returns to the one he had been lounging on, Ananou settles himself on a smaller arrangement to his left.

"Ananou, I come to you today to bring you much joy, I suspect, for I have something that was once yours and that I have been told you value above all else."

At this Ananou's old eyes open with the excitement of a much younger man, and Rush the wolf imagines he can hear the old man's heart jump against the cage of his ribs. Ah, he thinks, already I see I have you.

"What is it you speak of, Ameg? What have I lost that is of such great value to me?" Ananou's attempt to hide his joy is a weak one. Although he still leans back on his couch of pillows, his body has become rigid. Rush can see a bead of sweat collecting on his brow. Enjoying the moment, Rush leans forward conspiratorially.

" Why, Ananou, do you not remember the dancer, Tiko?" It is all he has to say to crush the remainder of the priest's facade of complacency.

Ananou's old eyes narrow at Ameg momentarily. Then he regains his poise and forces a smile. "I do indeed, Ameg. But what is that to you? The boy was stolen from me by the assassin, Rush. He is gone forever."

Now Rush leans in closer. "No Ananou. He is not. For I have purchased him myself. He is mine." Rush takes his time with this next, watching the old man's face, feeling his innards with instinctive fingers as they shudder with hope and want. "And for a price, he can be yours."

Ananou is as still as a hare that knows it is too close to flee the fox, and so awaits its death.

"Have you no offer?" asks the patient Ameg.

"I do. I will give you what you ask," answers the priest, too enrapt by the thought of once again owning Tiko to barter.

Rush lifts his brows. "That is a steep price, my friend. For I took my life in my hands to deal with the assassin and obtain the boy."

"If I have what you want, it is yours," says the determined Ananou.

Now Rush allows himself the corner of a smile

"I have a proposition to make," he says, his obsidian eyes glinting with mischief.

"Speak, man," says Ananou.

"I know a second thing that you desire, almost as much as the first."

Now Ananou narrows his eyes at Rush, himself at a loss. A second thing? What could he desire beyond the return of Tiko?

"Can you not tell me what it is, Ananou? What you were willing to set Knossos at war for? What you paid the Captain of the Palace Guard of Cyrus a fortune to accomplish, but will never see accomplished, because the Captain is dead, Ananou. I heard it only yesterday from a merchant just in town from Cyrus. Lutarus is dead, his plan foiled, and your money gone. Do you not still wish to have the head of the Grain God, Ananou? For what good is Tiko to the House of the Sun if the blonde still lives?"

"Tiko is worth two blonde mutes," says Ananou haughtily. But Rush can see the greed rise and yawn in his eyes. There is the House of the Sun to think of. He waits.

"What is your proposition, Ameg?"

"Will you leave Crete, Ananou?" asks Rush suddenly, ignoring the question for the moment. "The House of the Moon is even now packing and making ready to wait out the wrath of Thera on more distant shores."

Only partly distracted by the change of subject, Ananou scoffs. "What can a mountain one hundred kilometers north do to Crete? We have survived flood, earthquake. Can the lava reach us? No, the House of the Sun will not leave Crete. We are built high and on a good stone foundation. Fire cannot harm us and flood cannot reach us. We stay."

"Then here is my proposal. Come with me to Cyrus, where the blonde has become the star he was in Knossos overnight. Come with me and I will give you your very heart's desire, my friend. You may have Tiko, if you can kill the blonde yourself."

"If I could do that, I would have done it already," scoffs Ananou. "I am an old man."

"I will make it possible. You need only drive in the blade."

"Leave my house? Travel over the mountains? Where will I stay, Ameg, have you a house in Cyrus?"

"That is easy enough to accomplish. What is more important is that I own the Grain God in Cyrus. You need not ask how this is possible. You will see plainly enough that it is so."

"Why would you give me Tiko and let me kill the blonde also? What is in this arrangement for you, Ameg?"

"What is in any arrangement for a businessman? Money, my friend. You will pay me what you paid Lutarus to kill the boy, only you will have the privilege of killing him yourself, and will have Tiko back as well. You cannot do better than that."

"And how do you propose that we kill a superstar without notice, without detection? Without begin beheaded ourselves for the crime? This is nonsense. You joke with me."

"No. We merely blame it on the assassin. We mark the boy with his sign, with the Tears of the Bull. I have seen it enough times to know how to execute it."

"Ameg, I am not a fool. You do not need my money."

At this Rush takes a moment to stare blankly at the priest. For a moment it seems his eyes have turned hard, like polished black stones. He takes a heavy breath.

"If I tell you the truth, Ananou, you will not believe me."

Intrigued, the priest tips forward on his pillows. "I knew it! There is more to this. Tell me, Ameg. I sense that you, too, have a desire to see the Grain God dead, though you say that you own him. Why, I do not pretend to guess. But if this is so, why not do it yourself?"

Again, Rush is silent. Finally he answers. "Because I cannot," he murmurs, and looks down at his hands as if it is they who have betrayed him.

Ananou cannot hide his curiosity. It is like a craving for a drug, which, having been partially satisfied, now demands more.

"But why, Ameg? He is worth a fortune. And why can you not take his life yourself, or else hire the assassin to do the job?"

"He is my weakness, Ananou," says Rush, looking directly at the priest to find his ugly brother in the man's eyes. "And I cannot tolerate my weaknesses."

"This much I understand," nods the old priest.

Now Ameg smiles. "And why should I hire the assassin, whom I would have to pay a fortune, when I can take the same fortune from you with the same result."

"Hah," says the priest. "You have answered me honestly, Ameg. I will consider your proposition."

"Do not consider it for too long, Ananou," says Rush, rising to his feet. "I am leaving for Cyrus this morning. If you are not there in three days, the deal is off." He smiles wryly. "Tiko is a pretty little thing, is he not? I could do worse, keeping him for myself. Perhaps I could learn your taste for Asian exotics."

That is enough to bring Ananou to his feet in a huff. "Do not damage the boy before I have taken him from you, Ameg. I am not interested in spoilt goods."

"I will keep that in mind," says Rush giving the priest a light bow and turning to find his way out.

"Ameg." The priest has taken his arm. "I will give your proposition the greatest consideration."

Rush cannot help a self-satisfied chuckle. "You may ask for Ameg the Merchant at the Palace of Cyrus."

"You are staying at the palace?" asks Ananou, incredulous.

"I am the King's honored guest," responds the assassin. "Quite convenient, as the little Grain God has been kept at the palace since his rescue from Lutarus' men by his own guard." As he utters this last it seems his face has hardened, and a dark energy, like the shadow of a bird of prey, hovers over Ananou. For an instant the priest has a recollection of horror, a flash of the dark form of the assassin in his doorway, his rapid and soundless approach across the courtyard, the thump of his own body hitting the wall as the beast's energy slammed him into it.

"How can we blame this on the assassin, Ameg. Will he not discover the lie and come for us?"

"I wonder you didn't consider that when you made your deal with Lutarus, Ananou? No, if he were to come for you, he would have done so by now. Surely he holds no more interest in the Grain God and has left Crete himself. He is too clever a man to remain long on a doomed island."

"Yes, I am sure you are right in that, Ameg. If he were going to come for me he would have done so by now. He is swift in his delivery of retribution, is he not?"

"He is indeed," responds Rush, making another light bow to the priest before he leaves him.

CHAPTER 36

Cara has arrived in Cyrus.

During the rocky climb by ass-drawn cart up through the mountains and down again toward the southern coastline of the island, Cara has had time to part with her earlier self. Now Cara is Cara and no one else. The woman she was, the daughter of the saffron farmer, the girl from Thrace, the betrothed of the stoop-shouldered clod who was the vintner's son, is gone. As is the whore who spent two weeks in Malia scratching at lice and washing the house clothing behind the whorehouse in an irrigated basin that was once a rich man's bath. For the whorehouse was once a rich man's home, before the town of Malia, battered by the wave a hundred years earlier, sank into the disrepair of its current state and became a factory town. She has been reborn, given a new identity. And she is not entirely unhappy with her fate.

In fact, it rather suits her. For Cara has always believed she would be a woman of many faces.

As the cart driver helps her down from the cart bed along with her small bag of newly acquired clothes she looks about her, absorbing her surroundings like a chameleon absorbing color. The inn is on the main road entering the city from the east, and she can see the upper levels and rooftops of the palace over the skyline. The top of the palace is like a mountain to Cara, or like a great, broad-backed camel with several sand colored humps of differing heights. Some of the roofs gleam as if painted in gold. Large things have always frightened her, a childhood fear. Her head swims a bit as she takes in the enormity of the city and of the palace. Stop it! Look, the child dances ahead of you into the inn like a deer, laughing and spinning. Are you a rabbit? Where is your courage?

You are a lady now. You are not afraid of palaces and cities and men that tower over you like trees and lop heads like the barbarians.

It is a fine inn. The man who kidnapped her had asked the cart driver to take her to the finest one in Cyrus. From the back of the cart she saw him press a pouch of coin in his hand, take hold of the hand, squeeze the hand until the cart driver looked as if he would faint. He whispered something to the driver then that she did not hear. Nevertheless, she has been treated quite well by the driver, who offered to stop here that she might relieve herself, there that she might consider the lovely view at the very top of the mountains. She herself thought she might faint, then, having a fear of heights she often believed was the parent of her fear of big things. Now he has deposited her at the doorstep of a fine inn, one that is surely used to entertain rich merchants and dignitaries who enter the city from the east. Well, he will have been paid well for his obedience, even if there were no coin purse involved. Even if it were his own head he had earned by being obedient to the man Marta calls Ameg.

Now Marta runs back for Cara's hand and begins pulling her toward the archway into the open air entrance to the inn. It is busy here. There are more servant men and women coming and going on errands, or people of higher rank, wearing expensive clothing and intent faces, entering and exiting the inn and the surrounding buildings than she has ever seen in one place in her life. And we are yet a mile or so from the palace! If it is this crowded here, how much more so is the center of this city? I will pass out. Her hand on her breast, she pulls in a thin breath of air and closes her eyes. She imagines herself in her father's saffron fields, picking the delicate red lace from the faces of the flowers in the golden summer sunshine, and she can breathe again. Marta tugs her hand, gives her a sharp look.

"Are you pregnant, 'Tia? You look as you did when Ameg gave you the bag of money. Don't you vomit now, here in front of this fine inn!"

Marta has continued to call Cara by this abbreviation of her given name since they left Malia. It was the name the whoremaster used to address her.

"I am your mother, now, Marta. You must call me Mama, or some such endearment, or Ameg will be displeased with me." She swallows the bile rising in her throat. Oh, god, what does a rich child, one of breeding, one with education and tutors, call its mother? "And no, I am not pregnant. Will you please stop asking me if I am? You know as well as I that the master was saving me to sell as a virgin."

But Marta only laughs. "You will sleep with Ameg soon, 'Tia, and you will be with child then, and I will have a little brother!"

Cara can only roll her eyes at the child. Then she grabs her shoulders and squats in front of her, her expression firm.

"Now no more of this, Marta. Now, let me hear you say, 'Mama, can I go and play with the other children?' Say it."

"Mama-" but this only sends Marta into peals of laughter. "You are too young to be my mama, 'Tia!"

Mother Moon save me, thinks Cara. "Yes, Marta, I am too young to be your mother, who was old when she had you. But I am not too young to be the mother of a child your age. Ameg wishes for us to pretend I am your mother. And he your father. You must call me Mama, and him Papa. Surely you know how to pretend, Marta. Pretend, as if you were an actress in a play, or a dancer in a story dance, you see?"

Marta's eyes grow wide at this. "Yes! Like in a story dance! We saw one once when I was but six summers, in Pheistos, at the first full moon of spring! Oh, it was so beautiful! Someday I will dance in a story dance! I will be the best dancer ever!"

Ah, now we get somewhere, thinks Cara. "So, shall we go in and find our lodging, daughter?"

"Yes, Mama!" says Marta, offering her new mother a smart little ladylike bow. "Yes, please."

Breathing a sigh of relief, Cara rises to her feet and turns her 'daughter' toward the doorway. A man in a green linen tunic has come to meet them.

"Can I be of service, madam?" he bows to Cara. She mimics him with the identical bow. "Yes, sir. I am the wife of Ameg the Merchant, and this is our daughter. I am to wait here for my husband, who is completing some business in Malia."

"Ah, Ameg, yes! He stays with us frequently. Such a pleasure to have you with us, madam. He always takes two rooms on the upper floor when he visits. As it happens, they are available. Come, let me take your bag and show you to the baths so that you may make yourself comfortable after your long journey. Your rooms will be ready by the time you have finished. Then I will send up a good dinner of roast chicken. And something sweet to cleanse the palate."

Two baths in as many days, thinks Cara. And a good meal, too? And a clean bed, one I may occupy all by myself, with neither louse nor drunken whore to disturb me? And when my new 'husband' the homicidal maniac arrives, then what? I cannot dazzle him with my talents in bed for I have none, having been taught nothing but how to wash stains out of drawers at the whorehouse. Nor can I feign virgin innocence. Think, woman, think. What does he want? Give him exactly what he wants. A lady. Obedience. An obedient lady.

Once again, I am neither.

Goddess help me.

That very night, Cara and her new husband meet again for the second time.

She has requested, as she assumes any lady might, a small pallet for the child in the less attractive of the two rooms she has taken. The larger bed in this room will be her own, and the more impressive room she leaves for Ameg. But the child keeps her up to all hours chattering about her new life as the daughter of the rich merchant, who will certainly be able to purchase her a place in a good dance company in the city as soon as she is old enough, perhaps next year? When Cara finally convinces her that her 'father' will be angry if she is not a good girl and gets to sleep (and lets her 'mother' sleep as well so that she looks less like a tired whore and more like a young lady, if not a virgin, in the morning), she can only do so by putting a door between her ear and the child's imagination. And so, she is curled up atop a delicious feather mattress in the finer room, wearing only a sleeping shift, when Rush discovers her.

Weary from two days of travel, mostly on foot, with little sleep, the assassin has arrived at the inn in the wee hours. He has taken his sack of gear from the wharf storehouse in Knossos but has left the dogs behind, with instructions given to his man on how to feed and water them without becoming their food and drink, himself. He has visited the Priesthood of the Dead on his way across the mountain to Cyrus, taken some food there, and changed his identity. Now, entering the room he intends to sleep in at the inn at Cyrus, he is dressed only in a white robe, which he removes the instant he closes the door behind him.

But he is ever Rush, and so, silent in his coming. He has descended onto the bed before she is awakened by her own body rolling into his when his impressive weight hits the mattress.

It is to her credit that she does not let go the scream that begins with enough intake of air to sing an aria.

"Why are you and your lice in my bed, woman?"

But she cannot speak to answer him. He has clapped an enormous palm over her face and all that is left to express herself with are her eyes, which she can only blink at him with owlish intensity.

"M-mmph-" she makes as much sound as she can from behind the bear paw, promising him in her mind that she will be off the bed in a flash if only he will remove that paw, which is in itself enough to keep her from doing so by pinning her head to the mattress.

"Scream and I will be a widower before you hit the floor," he hisses with disgust before releasing her face. Then she scrambles off the bed. But she is not foolish enough to rise to her feet. Oh, no, I do not dare to look down on this man. I stay here on the floor, on my knees, here, see? I am obedient. But he is not looking at her. In the moonlight she sees him frowning, turning his own hand over in the dim light to check for lice where he has touched her.

"They are gone, sir," she whispers. How has she found the courage to speak? "The bath oils killed them. I do not itch now." She is edging, on her knees, toward the door that separates this chamber from the smaller, where her own bed calls her. Foolish woman, it says. Why are you not in here sleeping on me where you would have been safe?

But the answer is lying on the bed she has just been discharged from. For she cannot take her eyes off the naked Ameg.

"Mm," he is still frowning, unconvinced that he has not been tainted by her somehow. "A whore without lice is nevertheless poisoned. What other diseases you have to offer, I am not in the market for. Now get out. I am tired."

But she is not moving. She is caught, like a hare in a net, by the sight of him raising himself up on one elbow to address her from the bed.

For Ameg undressed is simply impossible for her to fear, his body so beautiful to her eye that her head is spinning a little, as if she is standing on a high place looking down. And her eyes have run the length of it, like a butcher eyeing a good cut of beef, before she can stop herself. Then she gulps down the saliva that has filled her throat and squints with discomfort at her own mistake, anticipating his angry reaction to her eye's unbelievable arrogance.

Instead his face softens with a moment of confusion. Then, an edge of irony in his voice, he mutters, "You have never seen a naked man?"

Not as many as you think, and never one like you, she thinks, then blesses heaven that the words have miraculously remained in her head and are not lingering now in the air like clods of dirt. Get on your feet, you idiot. Bow. Yes. Bow, and get out, do as he tells you. Obedience!

Instead she hears herself say, "I have." My god, now you make a conversation!

He takes a heavy and exhausted sigh. Black eyes blink coolly at her. He is waiting for her to finish whatever it is she wants to say.

"I am not diseased, sir."

Are you out of your mind? Are you offering him your services, then? Look at him. He would rent you in two. Probably strangle you afterwards. And besides that, you know nothing. What that soldier taught you about lovemaking you could have learned from a monkey.

His brows have knit again. Poor thing, he really is tired. Hard work, cutting people's heads off I would guess. Then a look of recognition crosses his face.

"Ah. I understand. You would seduce the rich thief, eh? Join forces?" He shakes his head. "Woman, you try me. I have but a few hours to sleep. Get out or I will throw you out a window."

"Sir," she manages a kind of bow from her knees, then gets to her feet and scurries out, though her mind is still in bed with him, rolling into all of that heaviness, that long, roped muscle that fairly sings of his strength, into all of that masculine beauty. Again and again she rolls into him on her own bed, in her dreams, until she rises in the morning and peeks into the next room to find he is gone.

King Cyrus is not nearly so happy to see Rush when he is visited by him in his bed at the palace a few hours later.

"Hello, Cyrus," says Rush, now wrapped head to foot in black linen, the wingless gargoyle of Cyrus' nightmares, and Cyrus is for once thankful that his wife declined to sleep with him last night but took to her own bed, having imbibed a bit too much local wine at dinner.

"Hello, Rush," says the King, his lips half an inch from the long edge of the assassin's dagger.

The man is sitting on his belly, as if riding a horse. He says nothing, and so the King, feeling pressed to make conversation, continues. "Have you been to see the boy? I think you will be pleased. He is well cared for and happy. Eating like a little horse, dancing with my own troupe and making something quite lovely of them. Even playing with the chariot horses. He does just as he pleases, does he not? Quite a handful."

"It is the boy I come to discuss," says the assassin. "I trust you will keep your voice low, so that we might speak like gentlemen."

"Oh, you have my utmost assurance of that, sir. You'll be lucky if you can hear me yourself." Released from his own bed when the assassin withdraws, he sits up, sets his feet on the ground, places his hands on either side of him.

"You paid me to kill him, and I did not. To steal his secrets, and I have yet to uncover them. Protect him, and yet he was injured near to death. And so I owe you, Cyrus, for services never rendered."

"Oh, my good man, think nothing of it. Nothing! Thank Rah himself you did not follow through with killing the boy on my orders."

"No," says Rush, leaning now against a wall near the window. Cyrus has not had the heart to set a guard at his door since the assassin's interest in the boy became evident. Why waste a good man's life? But by the way the assassin now and again scans the King's private courtyard below through the second floor window Cyrus believes he is correct in his assumption that the man came through the window tonight and intends to exit the same way.

"A deal is a deal, Cyrus," says the assassin.

Now the King forgets his fears long enough to sigh and put his open hands in his lap. "Rush," he says, like a parent talking to a child. He looks from his open hands to the shadowy hell standing in the moonlight by the aperture. "For the love of heaven, you gave me back my Queen. You owe me nothing, I, you, everything."

"Your Queen?" The black mummy's head tilts, and for a moment the picture is almost endearing. He is but a confused, misguided monster. Then the head tips to scan the courtyard again and the illusion fades. "How did I give you your Queen, Cyrus? Has the boy driven her out of madness and back to sanity?" The hell-deep voice has a derisive edge.

"In a word, yes, Rush. One morning she passed him in the hall. That is all. She has been following him around ever since, petting him and cooing at him and giving him everything he wants at the moment, which is considerable, and everything she can anticipate he may want tomorrow. She is a changed woman. As clean and fresh and kind as the day I first took her."

"Then it is Rah who gave you back your Queen. Not I. No, Cyrus. You cannot change my mind. I owe you. If only for the fact that if it were not for you, I may never have discovered my own weakness."

But this, Cyrus will not address. One does not ask such a creature about his weaknesses.

"Tell me what will ease your guilt over this perceived debt, Rush. If it is in my power to make it right in your mind, I will."

Now the mummy folds his long, powerful arms over his chest and lifts himself to his full height, and the gargoyle has returned. A shudder of dread runs through Cyrus' veins at the apparition.

Dear gods, get him out of my house, he thinks. But to Rush he says nothing.

"I have sold the boy to the merchant, Ameg. You will ask me why. Let us just say that he is kin, of a kind, and that I trust him. He will take the boy to his home in Anatolia, where he has a compound the size of a small city, and an army for hire. I believe the boy will be safe there, and your city safe from him."

"You think him not safe here?" Cyrus' dread is deepening.

"No."

In the silence that follows the two men peer at one another across the room, the gargoyle at the window through a mask of black linen, the king, from his bed, in a thin nightdress.

"You speak of Thera," says the King.

"Yes," says Rush.

The King finds a weak laugh in his throat. "My wife thinks the boy can save us."

"And I think the boy and the volcano are the same disaster. Married, somehow, like moon and tide."

At this Cyrus picks up his head with a look of surprise. He waits for Rush to explain, but his quick mind needs no help. Of course, he thinks. They co-occur. Though why Rush sees the boy as a disaster and not a redeemer is beyond him.

"You cannot blame the volcano on a dancer, Rush. You are a man too grounded in the physical world to believe that such a connection exists."

"I witnessed the ceremony that made the boy a god." And it would take a god to weaken me, he thinks, but does not say. "I see what has happened to Knossos, to the cities to the east and west, even to Cyrus since that day. And I have seen Thera, once a port for the wealthiest merchants of Crete, become a ghost town at the same point in time." Rush grunts and peers out the window at the courtyard once more. "That is not a boy, Cyrus."

"But here his presence has had the opposite effect, Rush. The crops sweeten with rain. The people rejoice. My Queen is lucid. Even my palace dance troupe is transformed from a stiff and soulless thing to a... a melody of talents."

"Yes. And in a day, a week, a month at best, your city will be reduced to a landscape from Tartarus. I have seen it, Cyrus, what a volcano can do, how far reaching its effects. I have seen it from the coast of Sardinia. Across the sea the poisons fly on the wind to burn and choke the shores of distant lands. It may be that the fire and the wave do not reach Cyrus, but the air will be poisoned all the same."

Cyrus is silent a moment. Then he sighs heavily.

"You are a depressing man, Rush."

"I am trying to save you, Cyrus, and your city. By taking the boy. By sending him with Ameg to Anatolia."

"That is your favor to me then?" He shakes his head. "My city will riot, Rush. They believe that the boy is their savior."

"I care not what they believe."

"And Ameg? You would send this.... this cursed boy.... with him to his home?"

"I believe that I can control him."

At this Cyrus peers at the assassin in the gloom. Ah, there it is. You are as stricken by him as we all are. You want him for yourself. This Ameg is just a merchant, a cover, who will pretend for you in daylight that he owns the boy now, and will transport him for you to your personal sanctuary.

"The people of Cyrus will not let a merchant, no matter how rich, walk away with their Grain God. How do you propose to get him out of the city? If I may be so bold as to ask."

"The boy will do that himself, Cyrus. Is he not even now demanding certain treatment, designed by the priest who invented him? Will he not eat only certain foods, does he not demand concubines? Has he insisted he sleep in chains yet, Cyrus? Golden chains? Or has he neglected this detail?"

"This is all true, Rush. What does it mean?"

"He believes he is Rah, and Rah requires these conditions. There is another. He must visit the Burial Ground of the Ancients, in Knossos, the very place where he was captured by Lutarus. He must visit and bring gifts to the ancient dead. If any of these conditions are not met, he believes he will die, that the god will leave him. Whomever he was before the ceremony, is dead, Cyrus. At least in his child's mind. Whoever he was is no more. There is only Rah. And if Rah leaves him, there is nothing."

"And from one of these visits, he will simply never return, is that it? But he likes it here, Rush. He will not go willingly."

"As I said, Cyrus, I believe I can control him."

Rush is approaching Cyrus in the dark, now, as he speaks. A shudder of fear moves through the King when he sees that he is to be tied, blinded and gagged before the assassin leaves.

"It would be easier for me, Cyrus, to leave your head on a post in the courtyard there, and take the boy with me now. Easier and far quicker. Remember my kindness, Cyrus, when Ameg comes to visit the palace."

This is kindness? thinks the King. Nevertheless he is grateful when the devil, having gagged, tied and blindfolded him, leaves him thus to wait for his stewards to find him in the morning.

CHAPTER 37

"Rah talk with body," explains Rah, picking himself up from the gymnasium floor, where he has just completed a dazzling series of leaps, spins and flips, and thus ending his practice of the last of his solo dances in the Story Dance of the Grain God. He is speaking to his dance troupe, the Dancers of Rah, formerly known as the dancers of the Palace of King Cyrus. His audience stands in rapt attention around the gymnasium floor, awed at his performance. They have never seen anything like Rah. Never knew such jumps were even possible, nor such passion expressible in dance. In Cyrus, bull leaping was outlawed years ago when a youth broke his neck and remained alive in that condition for fourteen days. Since then, dance has been reduced to mundane ceremonial circles and lines. But since Rah's arrival in the gymnasium less than a week earlier, dance has come alive again and become the living art it once was. The King's dull troupe has been transformed by Rah's energy, and daily the gymnasium is electric with anticipation of their upcoming production depicting the story of the incarnation of Rah.

Rah takes a soft bow before the dance master, who is seated on his stone bench watching his world turned upside down by the whirlwind that is Rah dancing. Although he lost the reins of this chariot the day Rah tottered into the gym and performed his resurrected god, the dance master remains, in name, the driver of his troupe. No matter. It has been impossible not to fall in love with the boy. Watching him dance is in itself like falling in love, or like hanging onto the sides of the bucket while the horse charges on, out of control and yet quite beautiful as it enjoys its passion for freedom, in full tack but no longer in communication with his charioteer. One loses all sense of time and distance, can think only of what may come next. Will we strike a rock? Will we lose a wheel? How long can this continue?

Rah has given the dance master the respect of a superior, although both understand that he has nothing to teach this performer. Whatever taught this boy to dance has left no stone unturned.

"We need paint now!" says Rah, panting, glistening, his muscles pumped from exertion. He has gained all of his muscle back and more in less than a fortnight and he is no longer the tottering kitten. He is a young lion, his small stature a clever camouflage for his sinewy strength.

The dance master can only look about at his other dancers with a curious expression. "Paint, Rah? What does a dancer need with paint?"

Rah glides toward the master as if he slides on polished marble and not a sand floor. His face is wide with disbelief. "You dance no paint?" he raises his arms, opens them wide. Every gesture is theatrical now. "How you can dance, no paint face? Must paint face to show who is who! How can Rah be tiger first act, sun god next act, dove, next act, no paint? Costume only? Bahh!" He cuffs the master's shoulder. "Must have face paint!"

But the master is used to Rah's antics by now. He merely laughs, shakes his head, pushes Rah's hand away in a wide swing. "Bahh yourself, Rah. No one paints faces in theatre in Cyrus. I know what you are saying. I have seen this in Pheistos theatre. But we have no skilled painters here. Here we dance in costume only."

"Must have paint!" says Rah, and now it is a plea, and so he drops to both knees, lifts his hands, wrists together as if tied by Turios' rope. He is begging for his life, as he will beg the wolf for mercy in the last act of his story dance. This he made up himself, for he has elaborated on his life on Crete without discretion. "Better this way," he has told the dance master repeatedly, when the man insisted that his death at the end would be unsatisfying. "This make people keep Rah here," and he taps his halo of blonde curls, beneath which his battered brain spins. Then he continues to explain, as if talking to a simpleton who has never had a creative thought in his life, "Wolf kill Rah at end, people cannot forget, no forget Rah." And he smiles, a smile that fairly puts the poor dance master on his back. It is pure golden noonday sunlight appearing in clouded skies, and fairly crackles with electric beauty. He presses a fist against his breast, "So Rah in people heart, always."

But today the dance master can only look at him in wonder. Does this boy ever stop dancing? And if he did, could anyone survive it?

"This is a simple matter," comes the voice of the Queen behind the dance master. She has been watching the practice, as she has done every day since the idea evolved. Today she sits with her husband's nephew, Ikarus, on a golden bench brought in for her for this very purpose. The two have become an inseparable pair in the days following Rah's awakening and her own return to sanity. They share a fascination for the boy's talent, but also a love of pleasure that even the King falls short of.

"My ladies can paint his face. Come, my sweet kitten, we will paint your face for you, anything you like. They will be delighted to have such a face to set a brush to." She rises and steps toward Rah, who gets to his feet, a look of surprise bunching his golden brows.

Hah, thinks the dance master. That will teach you. Now you will spend your afternoon in the Queen's clutches with a bunch of hens fussing over you, instead of here in the gymnasium where your heart is.

"It's alright, Rah," offers Ikarus, seeing the boy's distress. "They really can paint faces. They are imported from Greece, you see, and worked for a dance troupe there at one time."

Rah can only drop his eyes and bow to the Queen, with an obligatory, "Madam," then allow Media and Ikarus to take him by either arm and draw him out of the gym and down the hall toward the Queen's own wing of the palace.

In her salon he is made to sit on a stool in front of a vanity twice the size of the one in his own chamber at the House of the Moon. A polished bronze mirror hangs behind it. Media calls for her ladies and explains that the Grain God must have a face to match his various costumes. One for the tiger dance, one for the charioteer, one for the sun dance, one for the dove. The women are instantly electrified by the challenge. They have had little to do with face paint since the Queen imported them only a year before her descent into madness. In the last week they have taken turns working on her own daily make up, and now they are to paint the Grain God! And look at him! They have all seen him from a distance but none of them at such close range. How could you ruin that face? Look at the planes of his cheek, those cheekbones, those eyes! It is an actor needing only a costume, a theatre needing only a troupe!

As the women prepare their potions at the vanity and take turns tipping his chin up to better study their canvas in the daylight, Rah settles onto the stool, resigned to spending the rest of his day in their company. At first his attention is drawn only to the clutter of jars and brushes on the vanity, which he paws at and tips over indiscriminately, until he finds the shades of green and yellow he is looking for. These he presents to his audience of three as if they were filled with emeralds and citrine and not mixtures of vegetable matter and quarry dust in an egg yolk base.

"This!" he says eagerly, "and this! Here-" he makes a brush of the fingers of his left hand and sweeps them back from his cheeks to his hairline, painting invisible tiger stripes. "And this-" he has found a blue green that matches the natural explosion of color in his eyes, "like this-" he takes the tip of one pinky and draws another invisible line under his lashes and up to the top of his ear.

"This how Pyrus do," he says, then sighs, suddenly saddened by the absence of his friend, a thing he has not noticed since his kidnapping. But presently he begins to take notice of the women who flit and fuss about him, picking up the spilled paint jars, scolding him gently and slapping his hands. They are not maidens, older by half, perhaps, than he, but they are trim and well made, and smell of clean linen and flowers. And they are pretty enough to wait on a queen. He studies each one's face as she takes her turn to paint him, he fixes her with his stare, only squinting and blinking his brilliant eyes when she gets too close to them with her brush, and then unintentionally sweeping her fingers with his lashes. His chin is chucked over and over for he persistently tucks it to peek down the front of their dresses. Each one, in turn, is at some point mesmerized by her subject and finds herself staring into his face until one of the other ladies slaps her hand and says, "Come now, my turn! You can't paint him all yourself!"

The Queen and Ikarus have left Rah with the face painters and gone down to the palace courtyard to entertain businessmen with the King and take some refreshment. By the time they return, Rah's face is a maze of yellow and green stripes, bursting outward from his eyes, which have been outlined with a deeper blue-green line that streaks back and up into his hairline. Rah himself is delighted with the results, and is standing on his stool in front of the mirror, snarling and arching, to see his tiger come to life, when the Queen arrives. The women are laughing and clapping. "Wonderful! Look! How the lines beneath his eyes make him fierce! How the stripes from his brow to his hairline give him the forehead of a tiger!"

Seeing her enter, Rah turns on his perch, a circus tiger on a stool, and looks at the Queen. His fierceness fades and is replaced by a long, docile stare, his face tipped to avoid the sunlight streaming through the window, so that he regards her under the feral brush of his golden brows.

The picture is enough to strike Media still.

She stands like a bronze likeness of herself, one hand on her throat, captivated, as Rah blinks at her in the bright afternoon light.

"You will tell your uncle nothing, Ikarus," she says finally.

And Ikarus laughs like a man who has not heard a joke in a hundred years and now hears the clowns coming down the hall.

"Only if I can watch, Media."

"Do as you like, nephew," says the Queen, stepping toward the tiger.

Rah is still looking down at her with docile innocence when she reaches up for his hand and takes him off the stool to lead him, with her ladies in tow, into her own bedchamber.

"Where is fox, Ikarus?" yawns Rah some hours later. He is on his belly, his face turned away from the pile of happy females occupying the better portion of the Queen's bed. His face paint is all but gone, except for the stripes around his eyes and the exotic blue-green line that now drifts into his hairline like smoke. The rest of his face is a pea green smudge, and his lips are bruised and blushed from kisses.

Ikarus, true to his threat, did indeed witness his seduction and molestation by the four older women, all possessing husbands and, with the exception of the Queen herself, lovers, and all quite skilled at the art of satisfying a male and maintaining his interest long after he thinks he has lost it. Now an arm slips around Rah's waist and pulls him away from the edge of the bed, where he has wriggled after a much needed nap.

"Well that was quite something," is Ikarus' only response. He is lounging on a settee under a mirror on the wall opposite the open windows. "And I thought I had seen it all."

Rah is resisting the arm that has encircled his narrow waist and is now making some effort to remain at the edge of the bed by digging his fingers into the mattress. The disembodied arm has found a companion, bedecked with the Queen's bracelets, which comes from the other direction and slips around his chest.

"Come, kitten," murmurs the voice of the Queen behind his halo of curls.

Rah giggles. "She is like lioness!" he whispers at Ikarus. One of the Queen's ladies has popped a disheveled head up behind the Queen. "Where is he?" she pouts. "My turn."

"Where is fox, Ikarus?" Rah asks the King's nephew again as the Queen tips him over onto his back and he loses his grip on the edge of the mattress.

"Some business about heads, Rah. His men came back with two heads. Don't concern yourself."

"He is not like this, he is be mad at Rah now," says Rah, shaking his head dolefully as he is overwhelmed by the Queen's kisses.

"No," chuckles Ikarus to himself, "He will not like this a bit." And then, considering, he adds, "That man needs a mentor. Perhaps I shall take him under my wing."

But in the Palace Guard barracks under the great hall the Fox is in a serious mood. The man who marked his face has sent him the heads of the two traitors, Turios and Aktor, both sporting the identical mark, the Tears of the Bull, the mark of the assassin.

Nikolaos has questioned his man, Horus, for an hour. Did they see nothing? Did they never suspect that they were being followed, overtaken in fact? What other signs could they gather from the treatment of the heads? How could a man tie a head above your sleeping sack and you not hear a sound, not wake, though you may thank your own personal gods that you did not! But Horus can tell him nothing more than he has. That he awoke to the hair of the thing moving across his face, that it was bloodless and swinging gently. That the young tracker boy did the same. No other signs of an intrusion into their camp were evident. Not a twig could be found broken. Although, adds Horus uneasily, we did feel as if we were being watched as we took the things down and packed them to return to the city.

Nikolaos dutifully interrupts the King's business lunch to report the incident. To his credit, he does not bring the heads with him.

"This is not a thing to discuss over lunch, Captain," is all the King has to say. "I am entertaining guests, as you see."

"Yes, sir, but this is a matter of grave importance. I believe that this... message... was meant to be delivered to you, and that it is a threat. He marked the heads, sir, as he has marked me, the person you left in charge of Rah, sir. It seems obvious that he is telling us that anyone who believes they can take Rah from him will meet the same fate. I believe you are in great danger, sir, and so it is my duty to tell you, even if I must interrupt your lunch to do it."

Cyrus sets down his wine cup, takes a deep breath, seems lost in thought a moment. When he raises his eyes to Captain Nikolaos, his weariness is evident in them.

"Captain, you cannot protect me from Rush the Assassin. An army of Captain Nikolaos' could not protect me from Rush. The man is responsible for the death of two kings and a dozen generals. That we know of. If he wants to kill me, I am already dead. And if he wanted to kill you, Captain, you would not be sporting that tattoo so handsomely in a living head."

"I believe he was warning you by marking me, sir," says the ever serious Captain Nikolaos.

"Warning me of what? Warning me that I am not to consider the boy is mine, no matter how he has blessed my city with his presence here? Warning me that he will leave my head on a stake in the middle of my own courtyard for all to see if I try to keep what he considers his? I know this man, Nikolaos, his very existence is a warning. He need not repeat himself. No, he marked you because you show a personal interest in the boy. He is warning you, Nikolaos. Though why he spared you at all is yet to be explained."

At this Nikolaos blinks and jerks his head back as if he has been slapped. The thought that the assassin has somehow observed his interior, seen into his thoughts, thoughts that even he has not fully admitted to, is a further insult. And a bit embarrassing.

"Why would he think I have a personal interest in Rah, sir?" says Nikolaos, off balance.

"Captain," continues the King, seeing the man's reaction. "It was you who rescued the boy."

"On your orders, sir."

"And then took a room next to his."

"To personally guard him, sir. To keep him from further harm. As I promised you I would."

The King, seeing where this is going, makes a little frown and looks at his guests, offering them a conciliatory shrug, all the while knowing that they could have hoped for no better entertainment this afternoon.

"I take it the bodies were not found?"

"No, sir."

"Well, give the heads a proper burial, Nikolaos, for the sake of their families. They were decent soldiers, once. And let us speak no more of this incident."

Nikolaos makes a reluctant military bow, and leaves the King to his guests. But he has not let go of the episode. He is still stewing in the juice of his own pique when, after failing to find Rah in the gymnasium, he runs directly into Ikarus, who has left the Grain God in the capable hands of the Queen and her ladies to find some good wine and perhaps some female company for himself.

"Ah, Captain! Just the man I was hoping to catch!" says Ikarus, realizing at once that the Captain is heading for the Queen's wing.

The captain offers the King's nephew a stiff bow. "Sir." He is only half aware of the man, however, and continues to look down the hall in either direction as Ikarus takes his arm and turns him around.

"I was hoping we could have a little talk about Rah," says Ikarus, knowing full well that this is one subject Captain Nikolaos never loses interest in.

"Rah, sir? Is there a problem?" Nikolaos has halted and turned to look down at Ikarus, who barely reaches his shoulder.

Taking the man a bit more firmly by the arm, Ikarus leans into him conspiratorially.

"Captain, it is a matter of much importance." He looks over his shoulder as if to be sure no one is listening, although the men are quite alone. "Can we not find a good wine in the cellars to discuss it over?"

"Sir, I am on duty-"

"Yes, yes, Captain, as always, but Rah is your main concern, is he not?"

"He is, and I have been distracted this morning over the matter of the heads of the traitors and have in fact been lax in my guard –"

"Come now, Captain," Ikarus fights the urge to make a cynical expression. "No one would ever accuse you of that. Besides, the boy is in good hands. He is with the Queen herself, having his face painted by her ladies, you see? He has insisted on face paint for his various roles in the Story Dance of Rah." Ikarus gives the Captain a moment to digest this. "It will take the rest of the afternoon, I have no doubt. You know how women are about face paint."

The Captain gives Ikarus an odd look, then peers over his head down the hall toward the Queen's chambers. "Very well, Sir, if it concerns the boy. But I cannot tarry long."

An hour later, over a bowl of Egyptian mead, the two men are becoming better acquainted. The Captain, as it happens, is inexperienced with alcohol, having always had his mind too finely tuned toward his goals as an officer, and now as the primary guardian of Rah. He has moved from his typical, saturnine demeanor to a more vulnerable and, so, pleasant one. He has questioned Ikarus thoroughly regarding the 'matter of much importance' which is that Ikarus believes that the Queen has fallen in love with Rah. Ikarus had not even considered what the 'matter of much importance' would be until he had the Captain in tow on his way to the cellars. But it has become clear that his choice of a ploy to get the Captain away from Rah and the Queen is a good one. As Ikarus sees it, Nikolaos, being all soldier and no soul, and a baby at twenty-two summers at that, would certainly consider it his duty to bring the information about the Queen's afternoon dalliance directly to the King without considering what good it would produce and how much unnecessary bad. It is not so much that the Queen, this or any other, does not have carte blanche when it comes to taking a lover, it is the fact that the lover is a sixteen-year-old boy, quite a blow to a man thrice that age! At any rate, the conversation quickly turns from one of concern over the welfare of the King and Queen to Ikarus' seeming confusion as to how a boy of sixteen summers is so successful at seducing the female sex at all.

"I tell you, man, I have been studying this subject my entire life. I should be a world- class whoremaster by now! Instead my best efforts seem to earn me friendships, which is all well and good. I like women! I would be a friend to all! But gods! I have needs! They are so hard to read, aren't they? So hard to please. You are nice to them, give them gifts, treat them like you would your own mother and they go off with some dim-witted soldier (no offense, Captain) or some brute who doesn't wash himself but once a week!"

"He is beautiful. Ikarus. Women… men and women alike, love a thing of beauty," says the mead-softened Nikolaos.

"Oh, it's not just the look of him, though granted, there is plenty to look at. And of course he is, well, gracefully made-"

"He is grace itself," interrupts the Captain, now on his fourth cup of refreshment on an empty stomach, for Horus and the trackers were at the gates this morning with the heads as he was but rising and he has had no time to take a meal. "Grace itself," he repeats, his grey eyes misting.

"Well, here now, you are no slouch when it comes to grace, Captain, and here is my point. Here you are, young, handsome, a soldier, everything a woman who would reject me would take to her bed the same evening. You should be an absolute scoundrel, Captain, and have women waking you at all hours of the night to offer themselves to you."

"Oh, no, Sir!" says Captain Nikolaos. "I do not encourage such behavior! I will take a wife when I have made something of myself. Until then, I will apply myself to my duties! I have seen too many men do otherwise and amount to nothing. My father one," he adds, his lips turning down a moment like a pouting child.

Ah, here it is, thinks Ikarus. It always has to do with a bastard of a father with this type.

And so the conversation continues, far beyond the hour at which Nikolaos attempted to get up from the table and return to his responsibilities. On past mealtime, on until dark, when finally the two men, having imbibed enough mead to make Thymus proud, stumble off in each other's arms toward their respective chambers.

CHAPTER 38

"You will take a suite of rooms here at the palace then, of course," says Cyrus, after the Captain of the Guard has been persuaded to leave the matter of the heads alone and the King to his guests, they being Ameg the Merchant from Malia, his wife Cara, and a high priest from Knossos who arrived this morning with several servants. The priest was a surprise. The merchant was not, although the bloom on his young wife is an unexpected delight. More often than not, businessmen bring their first wives with them when visiting Cyrus, which is known for its fine garment district. The older women simply love the shopping, and having the means to enjoy it, will spend much of their days doing so, and staying out of their husband's way. But Cyrus can see why Ameg has chosen to bring this wife on his visit. I wouldn't let her out of my sight either, chuckles Cyrus to himself, not for so much as a day.

"We will gratefully lodge here, if it is convenient," says Rush with rote civility. He is still smarting from the interruption and audacity of Nikolaos. I should have taken his head, thinks the assassin, and left it on the King's pillow.

"And you also, Holiness. I would not think of allowing you to lodge elsewhere," says the King to the High Priest of the Sun, Ananou. The old man shrugs humbly, nods and murmurs, "I would be obliged, Sir, for your kindness."

"Well then, my stewards will show you to your rooms," says the King, assuming all has been settled.

"There is the matter of the boy," says Rush, and his wife jumps a little at the tone in his voice. The note of civility is lost, the merchant's tenor has dropped dangerously and the baritone of the assassin has appeared to her trained ear for an instant. But Cyrus has missed it.

"The boy? Why, yes, I understand your authority over the boy, sir, now it is established he is your property. But he is quite safe, his chamber is just across the hall from my own, and the Captain of the Guard himself has taken one beside it."

"Yes," growls Rush, too irritated to play the dandy. "I am aware of it. But now he will be moved to my quarters."

You have spent time in the military, thinks the King. And are used to giving orders as well. Is that where you became a 'kin' to Rush?

"Just as you say, sir," he offers the merchant a weak smile.

"And the priest as well."

Now this is over the top, thinks the King. But when he looks at the priest, he sees that the man is nodding in agreement, as if the merchant has made a wise decision on his behalf. I'm letting this one go, thinks Cyrus. They can sleep in the same bed, for all I care. I see why you get along with a man like Rush.

"As you wish," says the King, rising to end what has become an uncomfortable dialogue. "My stewards will take you now." And with the customary bows and pleasantries, the party divides to go their own ways.

Once left to themselves in their own suite of rooms, Rush advises his 'wife' that she and the child are to take separate chambers at the end of the short wing, which, as it happens, is above the stables. Marta has been left in the hands of the palace Mistress of Children and will spend much of her time segregated from her 'parents' while at the palace, but she will be sleeping in the family suite. Rush has advised the King's stewards, Bacus and Fillius, that Rah will take the room beside his own and the priest the room across the hall. No, the Captain will not take a room in his suite. His services will not be necessary. On second thought, yes, put him on the other side of Rah. And to himself he thinks, then I will not have to bother to take out a few more clay pigeons to finish him, as I should have done last week. But I needed him until now. The conceited ass is in love with the boy and watches him like a hawk watches a field mouse. One alert fop in uniform is a better guard than none.

But it is already late, and so Rush will leave Rah's change of rooms for the following day.

It is dusk when Rah returns to his own chamber, having been spirited out of the Queen's rooms by her staff and deposited in the hands of Bacus and Fillius, who are just back from taking orders from Rush.

"I don't believe he owns the boy for a minute!" squeals Fillius as soon as he has the ear of one of the Queen's stewards, for Bacus will not entertain his dangerous talk. "How do you like it, he walking in here and claiming ownership just like that? And the King believes him? On what grounds, may I ask? Well I'll tell you what, if he does not own Rah, the boy will make it plain enough tomorrow when he meets him! Then what will the

King do?"

Of course, this information quickly travels through the servant's quarters and down to the street. And when Fillius is given leave to take Rah down to the baths, as instructed by the Queen's servants, he questions Rah himself.

"You know this Ameg, Rah? This man who says he owns you?"

But Rah only looks at Fillius with tired irritation. "I tell you this already," he frowns. He is sitting in a raised wash basin the size of the priest's drowning pool. His face is a froth of bubbles as Naiba scrubs vigorously at the remains of the paint.

"This paint will not come off in one bath, boy," says the bath master, who is delighted to hear that someone has come to claim ownership of Rah, someone who seems to think he can control him.

Rah looks up at the bath master, who is leaning over him from behind, and shrugs. His eyes are a soft, gold-smoked turquoise now, a marriage of the blue bath water and his apple green face, and even the still-smarting Naiba must push the boy's jaw to one side and scrub the opposite cheek hard, or else become like every other lovesick fool at the palace and be ruled by them.

"What do you mean, Rah?" asks Fillius, who is standing in front of the bath, determined to have his answer. "I understood that the assassin owned you."

Rah is pulling at the bath master's wrist. "You hurt!" and begins to struggle.

"Oh leave his face for a moment, will you, Naiba! Let him answer me!" says the frustrated Fillius.

At last Naiba releases Rah's jaw. "Answer him, before I strangle you, little beast," he gives the back of Rah's head a shove.

"Ameg. This same man. He own Rah now," says Rah. He shrugs again. "He buy Rah from priest."

At this Fillius finally relents. "Well, there it is. But I'd like him to try to take you out of this city. He will be torn limb from limb!" Fillius' eyes are tearing up. "He won't take you from us, will he, Rah? He'll stay here with you in Cyrus, at least for a while?"

Rah has stood up in the bath font and is shaking his body like a wet cur as Naiba ties a towel around his loins. The bath master has learned to be quick about this, or Rah will slip away from him without one and go wherever he pleases naked as a newborn babe.

"He will take me," answers Rah, utterly oblivious to the stricken look on Fillius' face as he speaks. "Over water. Take Rah across big sea to his home. Ting ya say this. I can do nothing. I tell her, this man, he is one man made of many wolves. Rah do not want to go with him." He lifts his hands, helpless, then slaps them on the side of the basin and makes a little cat leap out of the water and onto the tile floor two steps down.

"Leaps like a wild animal. Cannot step out of a bath with dignity like a man," mutters Naiba.

"But he chase Rah, like wolf," Rah continues, ignoring Naiba. He throws a wet arm over Fillius' shoulders, leans into him conspiratorially. He smells of his usual cherry blossom and myrrh, but there is an undertone of almonds as well, from the oils in the soap Naiba used to scrub his now chartreuse face. Only the stubborn blue-green line under his lower lashes remains intact. "He is love with Rah. Ting ya say this also." Rah shakes his head. "Ting ya say he is not hurt Rah. I think he is hurt Rah. So strong this man! Love? Love Rah like wolf love meat!" He looks into Fillius' face earnestly. Then the thought is gone, a sunny smile replacing the sober attitude. "We go to kitchen now."

But the distracted Fillius remembers the honeyed walnut clusters the kitchen maids have pressed on him at dinner to give to Rah at bedtime. He pulls the package from his loose skirt pocket. "They won't let me leave the kitchen without them," he sniffles. "At least let me take them up to your bed and put them on a plate-"

But Rah has snatched the package out of Fillius' hands, laughing at the man's slow and uncoordinated attempts to recover it. He holds it out in front of him for Fillius to chase, dancing to and fro in front of him out of the bath house and down the hall.

"Too slow, Fillius!" laughs Rah, finally losing interest in the steward all together and sprinting to the stone staircase at the end of the lower hall and on up to his own chamber above.

When he reaches it, he finds the Fox slouched uncharacteristically on the end of his bed, his back resting against the wall behind, his long legs extended. Rah stops on his toes at the doorway.

"Fox, why you are here?" His eyes drift over the man's long body warily. "Rah must sleep now," he says. His normal haughtiness when addressing the Captain is absent.

Nikolaos is staring at him with drunken intensity. He pats the bed beside himself.

"So sleep, little Rah. I shall watch Fillius put you to bed… in golden chains…. Rah, in chains. Rah the dancer. Rah, the Grain God…." He hiccups. "Mmmh, Rah the cat-boy." He suppresses a burp. "Rah the horse-tamer." He is struggling in his inherently graceful body, to rise. "I shall sit…" and he walks uncertainly across the floor to plop into the chair by the window. "Here."

Rah takes a deep breath and gives him a look of disgust. He waits until he hears Fillius' footsteps coming down the hall toward his chamber, then moves to the bed. Having lost interest in his bed-time snack he drops the package of honeyed walnuts on the floor as he does so.

Nikolaos points at the package. "You dropped your…. treats, Rah." He gets up for them but by now Fillius has entered the room. Fillius looks at Nikolaos, blinks in confusion, looks at Rah with some concern.

"Sir?" is all Fillius can manage.

"F-fillius?" responds the Captain, sitting back down with a smack. "F-f-illius. Fillies. Fellatio, what a f-funny name. Hah!" Now he has begun to chuckle to himself, a startling and even frightening thing to the other two, who have never seen the man smile, let alone laugh. Rah looks at Fillius with a worried expression.

"Maybe no chains tonight, Rah?" suggests Fillius softly.

"Oh, yes." Now the Captain is on his feet again. He seems to have recovered his ability to balance himself on them. "Oh, yes, Rah needs his chains, don't you, Rah?" He peers at Rah menacingly. "Rah must have golden chains! Or the moon, his mother, will be mad! And we will all die!"

Rah is backing up toward the opposite wall now, eyes bright with fear.

But the Captain only takes Fillius by the arm and shoves him toward Rah. "Go on, chain him." He steps back and once again falls into the chair by the window.

"Come, Rah," says Fillius, gesturing toward the bed miserably. Rah has not taken his eyes off the Captain, but obediently walks forward and sits lightly on the bed, allowing Fillius to snap the newly installed chains to his neck and waist rings.

"I'll leave your feet, Rah," whispers Fillius in Rah's ear as he does so, thinking it the best he can do and keep his head.

When he is finished he gives Rah a little pat on the shoulder. "Alright then," he looks over at the Captain, who is staring at Rah with a maudlin expression. "Good night, Rah." He waits a moment, hoping the Captain will rise to follow him out with the lamp.

"Leave it," says Nikolaos, "There." He points to a short table on the opposite wall. "I shall keep Rah company for a while."

Fillius swallows, looks one more time at Rah, who has remained sitting up in bed, his body tense as a coiled snake. "Yes, sir." He puts the lamp on the table, leaving the door half open behind him as he exits.

Now Nikolaos sits up in his chair, still staring at Rah like a fox watching a hen. Finally he speaks. "It makes you vulnerable," he says, lifting his chin at the chains. "Like the day I found you."

Rah stares back at him, challenging, but he has begun to tremble. When the Captain lifts himself out of his chair and moves toward him, he flinches. The Captain seems to take no notice, and sits down beside him as if to chat with a good friend. He reaches to touch the collar under Rah's chin, and Rah draws back, pressing himself into the wall, straining at the limit of the chains. He flattens his brow and makes a little warble in his throat.

The Captain's eyes flick up at his. He slips one long index finger under the collar and his eyes drop to trace the curve, as if distracted by it. "How cat-like you are," he murmurs.

Rah is losing the last measure of his composure. He makes a quick twisting movement and manages to dislodge his collar from Nikolaos' grasp. "Wolf is kill you," he whispers, but his mouth is dry and his tongue is thick and the words are barely audible.

At this the Captain loses interest in the collar and looks again at Rah, a dangerous light in his sharp, grey eyes. "I don't need threats of your 'wolf' to keep me off you, Rah," he says softly.

Rah's warble has become a low rumble. His lips are slightly parted, exposing his incisors. But the Captain only smiles. "Will you bite me, Rah?" he snatches the boy's jaw, turns it to one side, to the other. He studies Rah's pale green face. "Rah must have face paint! Rah must have chains!" He narrows his eyes, noticing the darker line under Rah's left eye. Holding Rah's jaw with one hand he traces it with a finger from the other. His finger follows it into the hairline, where it finds a stray curl. He lifts it, blows on it as if it were a milkweed pod. Rah recoils from his wine sweet breath. Suddenly he releases Rah's jaw and sits back on the bed. "Why do you hate me, hmm? Didn't I rescue you? Don't you remember?" He gives an ironic chuckle. "I remember. I remember finding you." He shakes his head, blinking, as if struck. "Sometimes I wish I'd never found you." He sighs, leans his head back against the wall. "But mostly I am … so very grateful that I did." He stares up at the ceiling, lost a moment in his own musing. Then he blinks, comes back to present, looks over at Rah, who has quieted but continues to watch him guardedly.

"I only hope I'm there," says the Captain of the Palace Guard, as he puts his hands on his knees, pushing himself up off the mattress wearily. "I only hope," he says as he looks down at Rah, all of his father's rage harnessed again in the light tack that keeps him ever on his course. He looks down at Rah, and his face is soft with what he can no longer hide, even from himself. "That I'm there when that wolf comes to take what he thinks he deserves of you, Rah. For who will protect you then, beautiful Rah? When your guardian becomes your assailant? Your defender, your foe? Who will defend Rah from him." He bends to ruff Rah's curls. "Rah the slave. Rah the temple dancer. Rah the Grain God."

"I hope I'm there for you then, Rah," says the Captain, as he stumbles out of Rah's chamber to fall into his own bed next door.

CHAPTER 39

There is an owl perched on Cara's window ledge. It is a small, oval-faced bird with large, haunting golden eyes, a heart shaped breast and a smooth, earless head. Cara has been watching it for some fifteen minutes or so, wondering at its meaning. She is a strong believer in omens, especially those brought by birds. And this one, perching on her chamber window ledge with a cold, full moon over its mouse-brown shoulder, is an all-time champion omen.

Cara had crawled into her bed and fallen asleep with the ease of a child as usual last night, after bowing a 'good evening, sir' to Ameg at his chamber door. It looked for a moment as if he might be considering her 'services' for the evening, might be mulling over the possibility of putting aside her status as a diseased harlot. His hungry eyes, for that is what she saw when she looked into them, a ferocious black hunger, flicked down her body to her ankles, back up to pause at her breast, the plump curves of which were displayed prettily by her Greek-inspired dress, then narrowed as they returned to delve her own. But ah, she was mistaken. He was only letting her know he understood her harlot's brain better than she did, that there would be no joining of forces between them. Don't think you will outsmart me with your sex, woman.

One thing she was beginning to understand about Ameg was that he craved most what he could not have. More to the point, to pique his interest, he required a chase. He was a consummate predator. The world was full of men like this, and the fact that this was a common ailment of men in general was why her parents were able to arrange a marriage with the son of one of the richest men in Pheistos. It was because she was one of a mere handful of women who didn't want him. For Cara had the peculiar habit of loving beautiful things above all else and riches meant little to her. Cara loved beautiful sounds, beautiful words, beautiful music.

Beautiful men (thus the loss of her virginity to the handsome if inept soldier). But Ameg, Ameg was a title-holder. And a title-holding, world class predator.

And so, after a medley of dreams she could not remember, she had awakened when it was still dark and the moon was high, to find the omen of the owl perched upon her chamber window, blinking and staring at her as if she were the world's biggest fool. She had awakened to her own inner voice scolding her. What are you doing in this room alone? You were kidnapped from a whorehouse, for the love of the goddess. And how did you manage to get yourself kidnapped twice. Twice. First by a vicious, money-hungry troll, then by a crazed, murdering thief.

He is a very beautiful nightmare, responds the other side of the argument that always develops in her head in times such as these. You're a very sick woman, responds the other.

I should have been born a man, thinks Cara, as she rises from her bed, causing the omen to start at her effrontery and then flap away into the night, back to the cemetery of the families of Cyrus, to the empty tomb beside that of Lutarus, where it makes its home.

There is a dresser by her bed. From it she takes a comb she had purchased in Malia at the bath house, that and the necessary toiletries of a lady. She strokes the comb through her hair, peers into the mirror in the dark, runs her tongue across her teeth. Takes a sprig of parsley from the vase atop the dresser and bites the top off. Chews, moves to the window and spits the rest out.

He'll kill you, says her rational mind. He'll cut you down like a dog.

No he won't, says the clever challenger. He is a man. What have you learned about men in the last two weeks?

You deserve what you get.

Down the hall, silent as any creature with perfect hearing and perfect pitch can be, Cara pads on naked feet. She is drawn like a snake to heat. His chamber door seems to glow with it as she approaches. I will crawl in beside him. That is all.

The door has been left opened a hair and, as she pushes it in, she sees that the full moon has illuminated his room almost as if it were dawn. She peers in. He is not in the bed. He is standing at the window, in the moonlight. He is completely naked but for the weapons holstered at his sides and the daggers strapped to his ankles, and the sight of him sets her heat banging, half in fear, half in desire.

"Cara."

"Yes, sir," is all she can manage.

"Why do you not fear me, woman?" He has not turned to address her. He stares out into the night, his hands leaning on the window ledge.

He has given her an opportunity to look him over as if he were a bronze casting of a man, without the challenge of meeting his eyes. This is what they are supposed to look like, is all she can think. This is what they are supposed to be like, comes the second half of the conversation forever taking place in her head.

"I…of course I respect you, sir." Ah, very good.

He is caught off guard with that one. He drops his head, chuckling. God you are beautiful, thinks the huntress that has a twin in every woman's heart. Now who is the predator, says the evil commentator in her head.

He turns to look at her in the doorway, shakes his head. "Thank the gods women do not wage war. Or there would not be a man left standing." But he is smiling. Smiling! I did not think that face could smile!

Now a look of puzzlement has replaced the smile. He peers back out into the night.

"I am not diseased, sir," she hears herself whisper, taking a tentative step toward him. He looks at her, the puzzlement still pulsing between his brows.

"Go to bed, Cara. I care not if you are diseased."

Why does he make me angry? Oh but he does! You bastard! You are all bastards! No, that is not what I feel at all. I just want him to… I just want him. Try again, then. Take him down, you bitch-in-heat. Or will you wait for another woman to do it?

"He took me from Pheistos only a fortnight before you…. before you killed him, sir." Go ahead, before he throws you out. Finish it. Give him something to sleep with if not with you. "I was to be sold as a virgin. So you see, I am not spoiled. I am clean." My eyes, my eyes, they roam like wild dogs. I am looking at him as if I was the man and he the woman. Put your eyes to the floor, you fool.

"You want to lie with me, woman?" He is incredulous. "Your breed has a strong stomach."

"I am only the daughter of a saffron farmer, sir. That is my breed."

Now he gives his head another little shake, wagging the braid that trails down his back to his hip. "I speak of your sex," he says. He turns back to the window.

Now I bid him another embarrassed good-night and back out the door. But instead she is moving toward him, walking right up to him, and he towers over her. She could easily rest her head against his breast. She would have to stand on her toes to touch his chin with the top of her head. But she feels no fear. Unless this thrill I feel is fear.

He is looking at her with a confounded expression but he is no longer protesting her presence. When she reaches him, she puts a hand on his arm, looks up into his face. Still no protest. Then she puts a kiss on his chest, just there where his heart beats. She lays her lips against the swell of muscle there, unable to move, unable to release the kiss. She can feel the pulse. My god how powerful you are! You are all blood!

His organ has lifted against the fabric of her nightdress. It nudges, an unruly appendage, the most fascinating of the gods' creations, so far as she is concerned. Hard as stone and soft as warm silk. Nothing is as ugly nor as beautiful. Nothing as weak, nor as strong. Nothing made of so many opposites.

I am empty until you fill me.

And so she is filled for a time. And then sent to her own bed. Emptier than she has ever been in her life.

Across the hall, Ananou is preparing himself.

The challenge ahead of him is monumental. He must drive the dagger that Ameg has given him into the Grain God. As High Priest of the House of the Sun, Ananou has never had to perform a human sacrifice, that honor having always been bestowed upon the High Priest of the House of the Moon. For this Ananou was always secretly grateful. Mochlos had a taste for such things. He did not, most especially because the sacrifices had thus far been boys in their puberty, subjects which Ananou had a particular weakness for. It was bad enough he had to be present during the killing, representing the House of the Sun, and on these occasions he always made sure he was quite drugged himself during the procedure so that the boy's screams for mercy were not vibrating in the hollows of his own bones, but seemed only echos in a far off distance, perhaps across the sea.

He had been present for the Grain God's incarnation, and he knew as well as any how beautiful the boy was. His preference for Tiko was not based on outer beauty, although Tiko had plenty of that, nor on Tiko's worth as a dancer. In truth, he knew as well as anyone that the blonde was beyond compare when it came to athletic power and grace. He was not a fool. No, his partiality for Tiko was based on the Asian's unwavering arrogance, his haughty pluck, his outright gall in his attempt to challenge the blonde in the first place. And later, once he owned the boy, his love for Tiko was born out of the boy's resolute hatred for Ananou himself.

All Rah had to offer was grace and beauty and obedience. But no one had ever challenged, belittled and abused the High Priest of the House of the Sun like Tiko had.

And so the High Priest, Ananou, sits at the edge of his bed in the moonlight, fingering the silver dagger Ameg the Merchant has lent him for the specific purpose of ending the reign of the Grain God. He has to shake his head and laugh at the irony of the thing. A silver dagger? Wielded by the Priest of the Sun? To be plunged into the heart of the one heralded as the true Rah, the single offspring of the union of the Sun and the Moon? Could anything be more religiously offensive? If he succeeded there ought, by rights, to be no light in the sky over Crete until somehow some reparation had been made, or else the boy was reincarnated. And how could that happen? With Mochlos even now dismantling his household to move it, in its entirety, to Ameg's compound in Anatolia?

Well, he was an old man now and, religious consequences be damned, he would do this thing, somehow, and he would have his Tiko back.

Ananou runs his thumb carefully along the sharp edge of the dagger, considering. Ameg had already created a situation in which he could easily slaughter the boy in his bed. He was in the chamber just across the hall, and although the man he had allowed to act as the boy's guard, a man highly respected for both his efficiency and his devotion to Rah, was to be sleeping in the room next door, there would be no guard posted in the hall. Ameg was a clever fellow, there was no doubt of that. Clearly, he allowed the Captain of the Palace Guard to take a room in his suite in order to make it appear that he was doing everything possible to protect the Grain God. The boy would be considered perfectly safe, and yet the assassin had already tied the same man to his own bed and then proceded to slaughter the three guards posted outside the boy's room and visit him personally. If he could get to the boy once with Captain Nikolaos sleeping next door, he could certainly do it twice. It would be obvious to everyone who killed Rah. Not the old priest sleeping soundly across the hall, but the very same assassin.

Motive? Who would spend time questioning the motives of an assassin? It was usually money, was it not? Someone paying him to kill?

So there it was. Everything all sewn up. Except the actual deed itself, of course. The plunging in of the knife. Into that breast. That would be the true challenge of his fortitude.

Ananou hears a thump and a moan across the hall and smiles an old man's smile. Yes, I remember that. Ameg is enjoying his new wife and well he should. Will you be plunging into her as I plunge this blade into the blonde tomorrow, my friend?

Slowly he replaces the dagger in its nest of priestly clothing in a cedar case brought into his room by one of his servants. Then he draws himself back onto his bed, pulls the fine bed linens over his tired limbs like a shroud, and passes into sleep.

As Ananou prepares himself for the task of executing his first human sacrifice, one not performed for his gods but in spite of them, Fillius is returning to the servant's quarters from his visit to the palace kitchens.

Fillius found what he was looking for, a long, easily concealable poultry knife, one that could be drawn and thrust into the back of a man engaged in sexual congress with an unwilling Grain God, without difficulty. But he hesitated before picking it up and slipping it under the pile of fresh clothing he was carrying back from the laundry to the servants' quarters.

He had never killed so much as a rabbit, and now he was about to take the life of a man, not just any man either, but the Captain of the Palace Guard.

Fillius does not expect Nikolaos to be in Rah's bed by the time he arrives with the pile of laundry and the knife. It is already nearing dawn and what is done is done. No doubt the man had long since returned to his own room to sleep off his drunk. Fillius would hide the knife in his own mattress and take it with him tomorrow night, concealed in his skirt, when he puts Rah to bed in his new room next to Ameg's in the guest suite. There were two unoccupied rooms left in the suite, on either side of the room the priest would be sleeping in. He would hide in one of these and keep an eye on the boy's door. Nikolaos would have to use the hall to enter Rah's new room if he had intentions of abusing the boy again. Well, he would never get the chance. Fillius would see to it. Whatever the cost.

Fillius makes a detour to the servant's quarters to slip the poultry knife out of the laundry he is carrying and into his mattress. Bacus is yet sleeping in the adjacent bed, and Fillius takes a moment to watch his friend snore, open mouthed, against his pillows. "You wouldn't do that if you'd sleep on your back like a normal person," he murmurs affectionately to his friend. Then he picks up his burden and marches toward the King's wing and Rah.

He is a bit surprised to find Rah also lying on his belly and snoring lightly into his favorite feather pillow, with a peaceful expression on his lynx-like face. The boy does not look any worse for the wear, assuming there was some wear. In fact, he is, in the breaking dawn light, the picture of untainted innocence.

"F-f-t-t-t, Rah," whispers Fillius, in an attempt to rouse him without waking Nikolaos in the next room. But Rah does not stir. So Fillius touches his shoulder lightly, feeling somehow like a thief as he does so.

Rah makes a little "m-m-m-f" and, still on his belly, turns his head toward the wall. He is naked but for his golden belt and collar and Fillius purses his lips, looking about for the towel Naiba tucked around him after his bath last night. He finds it in the bedding. This tells me nothing, he thinks, forcing himself to touch Rah's shoulder again. The skin is butter soft, the muscle beneath, unyielding as cast bronze. This time the boy grunts and rolls over on his side, blinking in the soft first light of morning.

"Fillius," he offers the steward a lopsided smile, sits up and lifts his arms to make a long, satisfying stretch over his head, then draws his elbows behind, arching and yawning. Then he shakes himself as if to awaken his still sleeping brain. Having completed this customary routine, he lifts his chin for Fillius to unsnap his collar. Fillius obliges.

"Captain was drunk last night," offers the steward, moving to release Rah's golden belt. His face is very close to Rah's as he bends to unclip the chain but he is making a point of avoiding the boy's eyes.

Rah says nothing, but the steward can feel his eyes on him, the blink of his long lashes creating puffs of air that pat his cheek.

Frustrated, Fillius stands up, his hands on his hips. He gives Rah a determined look. "I will not move from this spot until you tell me what he did to you, Rah. That is all there is to it. We will stand here all day, I swear it."

Rah frowns at him. "Rah is good, Fillius," he says, and gives him a dismissing look. When he sees that the steward will not relent, he looks down. "Fox does not hurt Rah." He waits for the steward to step away from him so he can make his usual hop off his bed, but the steward only frowns at him, unconvinced. Then the Captain's tall shadow, leaning across the floor behind Fillius, catches his attention.

"No, I will not be sleeping through the morning, as you will both have hoped," grumbles Nikolaos. He walks to his usual post at the window, looks out over the practice arena, folds his arms over his chest and takes a deep breath. "Rah, I want to apologize to you for my behavior last night." The Captain gives Fillius an irritable glance, "and to you, too, Fillius." He looks back at Rah. "I'm afraid I allowed the King's nephew, Ikarus, to seduce me into a drinking game, and I will admit I am not as accustomed to wine as most soldiers are."

Fillius has stepped aside, allowing Rah to get to his feet. But Rah remains seated and cross-legged, oblivious of his nakedness. Fillius tosses the towel into his lap, turns, finds the package of treats still lying on the floor where Rah dropped them last night, and picks them up.

Rah is watching Nikolaos with cautious curiosity. He says nothing, then blinks at the man with nonchalant disinterest and hops off the bed, dropping the towel and reaching for a loincloth skirt from the pile Fillius has left on the floor.

"Go to gym now," he says, his back to Nikolaos.

Nikolaos leans on the edge of the open air window, arms still crossed over his chest.

"No breakfast, Rah?"

Rah turns to regard him evenly as he ties his skirt around his hips.

Nikolaos waits a moment for an answer, then gives up.

"Rah, you will be moved to the guest quarters today, to a room in this… Ameg's suite. Man says he is your master." He makes a little "hmph" of irritated disbelief. "And I suppose he owns the moon as well," he adds, glowering.

At this Rah pulls himself erect. He gives Nikolaos his own version of a scowl. "Yes," he says with some triumph. "This Ameg, he own me now."

A look of surprise opens Nikolaos' face. Then he regains his composure. "Really. Well, then you won't mind staying in the room directly beside his, for that is his wish." The look of trepidation and alarm that flashes across Rah's face makes Nikolaos instantly sorry he was so cruel in his delivery of this information. "I will be next door, Rah, right next door, just as I am here," he adds softly. But it is too late. Rah's face has closed like a lily at dusk. Gods, I am a fool, thinks Nikolaos. Why am I trying to frighten him? He is already as shy of me as a mouse is a weasel.

"Rah go to gym now," Rah says in his dusky, thick-tongued voice. "Please." He has dropped his eyes, and waits for the Captain's permission.

You never waited for permission before, thinks Captain Nikolaos, feeling an odd new pain in his heart. Where is that willful spirit of yours, Rah, have I broken it so easily? Am I no better than Lutarus' men, blundering about like cows in a pottery?

"You don't need to ask, Rah," he says wretchedly to Rah, waving at the boy to go, and Rah is gone in a flicker, taking off on bare feet down the hall toward the gym.

The Captain gives Fillius a miserable look. "Well, I've managed to make myself even less likable, as if that were possible, to our little Grain God." He pushes himself off the window ledge.

"Sir," begins Fillius, seeing an opening. But no, he cannot bring himself to discuss last night with the Captain. I will keep my head today, thinks Fillius.

Nikolaos is about to stalk past the steward on his long, horseman's legs when he suddenly stops at his shoulder. He looks down at the man with irritable gloom. He leans over the servant, narrows his grey eyes and speaks deliberately, in a near whisper.

"He is nowhere safer than he is with me, Fillius. You remember that." He is about to leave when he turns back and adds, "No matter what my condition."

"Yes, sir," responds Fillius, wondering how he will smuggle the poultry knife out of his mattress and back to the kitchens in daylight.

Down in the gym Rah is greeted by the sight of his dance master arguing with forced civility with an eight-year-old child.

"But I can dance! I can! You must let me dance with the King's troupe, or else my father will have your head, Dance Master!"

"Little girl, this is a production of grave significance! I cannot interrupt our progress with the tantrums of a spoilt child! Why have you brought her here to me, Mistress, what are you thinking?"

The dance master is clearly beside himself, impatient with the interruption and highly insulted by the Mistress of Children's belief that he should have to baby sit a rich man's child when he has the Story of the Grain God to produce. He stamps his foot, looks up at the mistress, fists balled. She shrugs her ample shoulders, her wide, African smile belying the wisdom that has come with her many years of rearing privileged children.

She can weather this child's moods, just as she can weather his.

Then, like a ball of unruly light, Rah comes to a skidding halt under the sundrenched archway and, stunned to see a child in the gym, stands still as a startled fox except to gently settle on his heels. As usual, all eyes turn to enjoy his golden entrance. He is the sun peeking over the ruby shoulders of the poppy fields of Cyrus, and the disturbed murmurings in the gym hush to silence.

"Oh!" says Marta. "Oh, he is beautiful!" She puts a hand to her mouth. "It is the Grain God!" she says, answering her own question before she has had time to ask it.

"Little girl," says Rah. He looks over her head at the dance master and points at the child. "This good! Now we have Iliah." His evening with the Captain is forgotten.

But Marta is already running up to him. "Oh, Rah! Will you let me dance with you?" she beams up at him. "Will you teach me how? I will learn fast!" She takes his hand and pulls him back where she stood to dress down the dance master. "Rah will teach me! Hah!" She sticks her tongue out at the offended teacher.

"No!" Rah has spun her around to face him with a whip of his wrist. He has knelt to his haunches to meet her height, his opposite hand guiding her torso so that the spin looks polished and elegant. Marta laughs with delight. She throws her arms around his neck and kisses him soundly on his mouth. But Rah takes her shoulders and pushes her firmly back, even gives them a little shake.

"No. This teacher. Even Rah must treat with respect. So you-" he takes her face in his hands, "must also respect."

Marta is looking into his eyes with open fascination. "Your eyes are so green, Rah! And your face is green, too! Can I have a green face?"

Rah picks up a lock of her dark hair. "No. But we make you-" he drops the tail of hair and runs his fingers over his own scalp, "like Rah. We can do this?" He looks up at the dance master, who is blinking in disbelief.

"There are ways to take the color out of her hair..." he answers apprehensively.

"Good," Rah gives his head a firm nod. "What is name, little girl?" Marta has wrapped her arms around his neck again and he must untangle himself from them in order to stand up.

"I am Marta. I am Ameg's daughter!" she says proudly.

At this Rah's eyes widen. "Ameg?" He looks up at the dance master with surprise. "This Ameg daughter."

The dance master stares back, undaunted. "I don't care if she is the Princess of Egypt. She will not come in here, into my gymnasium, and ruin our production." He looks over at the Mistress of Children. "Do something!"

But the mistress only shrugs again, smiling at his distress. "What harm can she do? She is only a child," she says brightly.

"Marta," says Rah, looking down into the child's eager face. "Can you play ghost?"

Marta has not let go of Rah's hand. She looks up at him with delight, tugging on it as she hops up and down in excitement. "Oh, yes, Rah!" And then, with some trepidation, "If you will teach me."

"I can teach, no problem," says Rah. Now he turns her hand over. Where the thumb should be there is only as stump. He looks long and hard at the stump, then into her face, eyes wide. "No thumb!" He says.

"No," says Marta, suddenly sad. "The whoremaster took it. Because I didn't shut the curtain in time."

Rah blinks at her as if he has been slapped. "Took thumb?" he says. "Why take thumb? Stupid master. How you can shut curtain better with no thumb?"

Marta is tearing up. "I can't dance without a thumb, can I Rah?" she sniffles. "I have to be beautiful to dance, like all of you." That gets a murmur of compassion from the knot of other dancers watching their interplay.

Rah frowns, shaking his head. "Cannot jump with no thumb," he looks at her gravely. "Need thumb to-" but this he cannot explain in words, and so he makes a quick leap backwards onto his hands, walks on them a few meters, then bends backward onto his toes with his characteristically breathtaking flexibility before sending himself into a long and complicated line of somersaults, cartwheels and backflips to the very back of the gym. He comes to a halt under a row of morning-bright clearstory windows.

Marta is no longer sniffling. She is watching Rah with round eyes. "Oh!" is all she can manage. The dancers, who have formed a line behind her to better view Rah's antics, smile and wink at one another.

Rah begins his walk back across the arena on soft, cat's feet. The other dancers are already nodding and pointing at him, for his walk has changed into something they remember. No longer a boy, he has elongated his stride, softened his movements, created a rhythm, transformed. By the time he reaches Marta his walk has become the regal prowl of a jungle cat. His chest is up, his back arched, head is tilted at her seductively. His green eyes sparkle with mischief. He circles her, stalking, his shoulders back, his feet stealthy. He spirals closer and closer. She turns round and round on her heels to follow his movement. He lifts his arm, drops his chin, his eyes hot and fierce under the ruff of blonde brows. Now his fingers extend like claws reaching for her, while his torso pulls back as if fighting his own longing for her. Marta has forgotten her tears. She is giggling. She lifts her hand, the thumbless hand, offers it. Instantly he has closed the distance between them and launched her into a delicate inside spin on her toes. She giggles, spinning into him, his arm supporting her by her tiny waist. He guides her to lean back, fully trusting that he has her. He bends her backward and backward as he slips one knee beneath her arched back. Her hair skims the ground. He leans over her, his face a portrait of the immortal longing of love. He is the Grain God.

After a moment of stillness, Rah's passionate face decomposes. He smiles, dimples popping, and winks at his heroine.

Marta is giggling hysterically. Rah is holding her like a bouquet of lilies over his thigh, one arm supporing her, the other drawn back away from his body, elongating the picture.

"Don't need thumb to dance, Marta," he says in his dusky, thick-tongued voice to the little girl in his arms, before releasing her and setting her on back on her feet. The row of dancers claps. Even the dance master smiles in spite of himself.

"He could make a cow dance," mutters the dance master, shaking his head, as his dance troupe engulfs Rah and draws him back out into the arena to begin this mornings' practice of the Dance of the Dove Boy.

Rush is awakened by hammering in the room next door. He is on his feet, blades drawn, and across the floor to the opposite corner of the room, the corner behind the door, when the voice of Bacus meets his ear though the open window.

"They can chain him to a rock out in the practice arena all night for all I care. He's been nothing but a nuisance since his rescue. Fillius thinks of nothing else. I haven't seen him in days, except to take instruction from the merchant about moving him into this room."

Rush relaxes, slips his palm-sized crescent-shaped weapons back into the holsters under his arms, pulls on his merchant's fine yellow silk robe. He walks on Ameg's high-arched feet into Rah's new chamber to greet Bacus and two workmen who are busy fixing bolts into the wall behind the bed for Rah's golden chains. Bacus steps back from the work, gives Ameg a low bow. "Sir," he says, "I hope we haven't disturbed your sleep."

Rush looks the man over, says nothing. He walks to the wall where the bolts are being embedded, pretends to examine them. *So you are Fillius' lover, and Fillius is mad for Rah, and so you are immune to Rah. Is that the secret of immunity then? Must Rah become my rival in a game of love?*

"This is to your satisfaction, sir?" asks Bacus nervously. For even as Ameg, Rush's silence is disturbing.

"The boy asked for the chains, not I, Bacus," says Rush. "He was taught by the priest that the chains are necessary to his station, you see."

"You would not chain him then, sir?" Bacus ventures. He is beginning to like this Ameg, the mere size of whom is enough to set his heart racing.

Rush gives the servant another sweeping glance. It is the glance of one male who finds interest in another. It is Ameg's best disguise, better than the dandy's rings and robes, better than the tenor pitch of his voice. Better than the toes-first walk. It will convince the servants of the household that he is interested in his own sex, a gentleman of the world with refined tastes. It is the best of sheep's clothing within which this wolf hides.

Bacus drops his gaze. Did he just see a light of attention in Ameg's eyes? His head swims a bit. You deserve it, Fillius, he thinks.

A movement at the doorway draws his attention. Ah, it is the merchant's young wife. How like a fresh peach she is. A fruit tree in bloom. And kind in her demeanor, although she seems a bit tense around her husband.

"I heard a noise," she fastens Rush with a besotted gaze. "I'm sorry," she steps back as if to exit, but clearly she cannot. She looks at him like Fillius looks at Rah, thinks Bacus.

Rush makes no effort to answer her. He gives her a casual glance, takes a handful of the golden chain that has been snapped to the bolts in the wall, gives them a feeble yank. "I have never understood the chains," he murmurs, as if to himself.

"Who is in chains?" asks Cara, and then looks around the room as if someone else has said it.

"The Grain God of Knossos," answers Rush, flicking his eyes at the woman and then holding her gaze there, "The reason we are here." And Bacus watches, amazed, as the truth of the man's affection for the boy strikes his wife for the first time. It seems to leap at her from the intensity of his stare, snarling, warning her off the subject. Suddenly the air in the room is cool, although the morning is hot and steaming outside the window. It is as if she has been struck, and the woman steps back, even wobbles. But she will not relent, she stares back into her husband's face. Her pain strikes back at him weakly. The merchant walks toward her, and she steps aside as he walks past her and out of the doorway. Nothing has happened. Everything has happened. Why am I witness to this, thinks Bacus. It is the boy. It is the boy again. Look, look how her heart breaks. It is the boy.

The woman has her hand to her breast, as if she has lost her breath.

"Are you alright, madam?" Bacus walks forward, takes her arm. She looks at him, offers a false smile.

"Oh, yes," she looks into Bacus eyes, locks them in a painful grip. He sees himself mirrored within them. He puts his hand around her shoulder.

"Poor dear," he says.

"He saved my life," she murmurs, blinking at Bacus.

"How so, dear?" says Bacus, his servant's taste for gossip awakening despite himself.

But she has begun crying, bringing her hands to her mouth to weep into them. "I'm so confused," she squeaks, "I'm sorry. I shouldn't be telling you this. He'll kill me, I know he will. He's a monster."

Bacus waves the workmen out. They have been standing about, finished with their chore, watching like emptyheaded fools. When they are gone, he sets her down on the bed.

"It is quite natural, dear, to confide in a stranger, when you have been though a trial and have nowhere to turn, and here you are, in a strange city, far from home no doubt." He pauses, rubbing her shoulder. She is sniffling, but taking care to make no sound. Afraid of the husband, no doubt, thinks Bacus. That man fools no one. He is nothing to be trifled with.

"He is so…vital," she looks at Bacus, and here each finds their twin in the others' eyes. She sees the glitter of agreement in his face and she begins to giggle. To giggle and sniffle. "Isn't he, Bacus?"

Bacus bites his cheek until the tears come. No use. He begins to giggle too.

"Say it," she says. "Say it."

"I will keep my head today, madam," says Bacus. He lifts his eyebrows, scolding. But he is smiling too.

"What do I do?" she whispers at him, as if he knew.

Bacus peers at her, an earlier idea intensifying in his head. "It is the boy, you know. This Grain God. This Rah. Have you seen him yet?"

"They spoke of him yesterday, the King and … and Ameg." And though it is morning, the sun sets a moment in her face as she utters her husband's name.

"Well, he is down in the gym, as always. Dancing. Always dancing. Or cavorting with the palace concubines, or taking over the guards' practice arena, playing with the chariot horses. It is ridiculous the way he is allowed to do whatever he pleases." Bacus shakes his head, looks down in his lap, spreads his fingers as if to see that his nails are properly filed. He picks at one. "My Fillius is absolutely smitten. As is the Captain of the Palace Guard." He looks back into her face. She seems wholly captivated by what he is saying.

"And you?" she watches him for his answer, though it is clear from her tone that she knows it.

Those eyes! thinks Bacus. Who can escape that scrutiny? How like an owl she is, thinking and thinking and staring into the world with those great, dark eyes.

He purses his lips. He gives her knee a quick pat, stands up. "I will show you. I will let you see for yourself."

"Oh, but I must put on a more appropriate costume. This is just a sleeping dress," she looks down at herself, discouraged. "What was I thinking, coming in here like this? Chasing after his voice? It was his voice, you know. Not the hammering. That voice, my god, what a voice he has. I've never heard such a voice, have you? Oh, I am awful!" She lifts her hands in despair, looks at Bacus helplessly.

But the servant is speechless.

Now she looks down at her dress, picks up a handful of the linen, looks back up at him. "I have so very little with me, you see. He gave me so little time. And what does a lady where? I had no idea what to choose, although he was very generous…"

"No matter, dear, Bacus will find you the perfect dress in which to appear in the gymnasium to watch the Grain God practice. Why, the Queen has no idea what is in her wardrobe, she only recently came out of mourning. Give me a few minutes. I will be back with a breakfast tray and something suitable for the wife of a wealthy merchant." He moves to the door.

"Bacus," says Cara suddenly, but as he turns back to look over his shoulder at her, she stops in mid-breath, closes her mouth, bites her lip.

They eventually remember I am a servant, thinks Bacus.

"She was mad as a hare for years, you know," he says, continuing his train of thought as if she had not interrupted it. "We all suspected it was because the King could not give her a child." He looks down at his feet. "Well, servants will talk. Who knows the truth? Perhaps her mother's sickness, handed down." He shakes his head. "But one day the Grain God appeared. Rescued from a kidnapping, near death. It took three days for him to awaken from his delirium. And when he did, the most amazing thing happened. It began to rain! A city in drought, rescued from disaster. The crops turned green again, after months of dearth. And the people were overjoyed. They danced in the streets outside the palace. They cried out in thanksgiving for the mercy of the gods. They-" He looks back at her, she is staring at him, dissecting his story like a bird of prey pulling at the mouse in its claws. "They fell in love with Rah. Just like that. And then the Queen saw him. And just like that, she was cured of her madness. Made whole. Returned to her King's bed. And she has been following that little minx around spoiling him rotten ever since."

Cara continues to stare, a look of dismay now passing like the shadow of a cloud across her features. "But is he a god, Bacus? They say he was made by the High Priest of the Moon in Knossos. They say he is the true Rah. In Pheistos, Rah is a minor diety. Sexual in nature. Something of a nuisance even. The god of infatuations."

"He is that indeed," spits Bacus. "Everyone here is infatuated with him." He lifts his head. "Everyone but me, and perhaps Naiba, the bath master."

"Why the bath master, Bacus? Does he have a lover who has fallen for the boy as well?" She slaps her hand over her mouth as soon as she has uttered the words, then giggles.

But Bacus is unfazed. "The little cat bit him the first day he tried to put him in a bath! Said he was using the wrong oils! Imagine! Bath master Naiba is a genius! And Cyrus has the best baths on Crete!"

An hour later, Cara is led down to the gymnasium by Bacus who bows ceremonially and leaves her at the archway with a quick tip of his head toward the center of the arena. "Well, there he is," he whispers, his scowls of disapproval for her alone. But Cara's attention has already been drawn away from him by a whirling white light too high above the arena floor to be human, and she has lost interest in Bacus.

"My gods," she murmurs to herself, watching that light descend like a feather, a dove's white feather, to the gymnasium floor. It spins downward, as if only dancing with gravity, as if only paying it tribute, and lands and becomes a boy with sun gold curls and the high-boned, heart-shaped face of a lynx. "My gods," she says again, so dazed by her first vision of the Grain God that she fails to notice her husband has come up behind her to tower over her shoulders.

"You can go in and sit, Cara, they have provided seats for the Queen and her guests, there." He takes her by her arm and tips his beard at the seats behind the dance master's little pillar. Beside him the priest, Ananou, dressed formally, comes to an abrupt halt. He leans with exaggerated importance on his priestly staff, the top of which is bedecked with a sun cast in bronze.

But Cara cannot move. She cannot take her eyes off Rah, not even for Ameg. She tips forward on her toes, resisting his hand.

"Please, may I watch from here a moment longer?" she whispers. "I don't want to disturb him."

The Grain God is rising to his feet and a female dancer, a little doll of a creature who only reaches his height as a result of an elaborate hairdo, flits out onto the arena to take his extended hand. Rah has lifted his opposing shoulder and turned to the archway, facing Cara, but his attention is fixed on the doll. She mirrors his turn. He reaches for her, making an impossible extension of his body, his face sly, pale brows feathered. The doll recreates his moves in reverse. Rah's face is a picture of longing, of hot, feral desire. Gods, what does it feel like to have him look at you that way, thinks Cara and then looks up at her husband foolishly as if she has said it aloud. But Ameg is watching the play, watching with the intensity that a pack of wolves watches a deer.

Rah has taken his little dancer by her waist and launched into a series of turns and extensions, spins and throws. The doll keeps up, her carefully made-up face exaggerating her obvious enjoyment of her partner's prowess, his ability to create her dance, to make her more than she was. This is what he does, thinks Cara, this is why they desire him. He is Rah, the Pheistos Rah. This is what love does; it makes us more than what we are. She looks back and up over her shoulder at Ameg, whose dark eyes burn as he watches the little Grain God perform with his concubine.

"He is magick," she whispers up at him. "He is not human. Not really."

And for the first time since their meeting, Ameg looks back at her with something more than pity.

"You see it too?" he says, not fearing her hungry eyes on his for the moment.

"I see it as easily as I stand here and hear your voice," she says, and thinks, the most commanding voice I have ever heard.

He narrows his eyes at her briefly, before looking back at the boy and his concubine. They have separated, and Rah has stopped the practice. He seems oblivious of the fact that his master, the wolf, is at his door. He cannot see me when he is dancing, thinks Rush.

"Must have three, Dance Master!" says Rah. He has stopped and turned, letting his little doll go on an outstretched arm. But the loss of his energy has taken her grace. She fumbles, spilling to the ground like chaff falling from the wheat on the threshing floor.

"This dancer, she is Siriona. Rah must have Minia and Trinadea also. Must have three." He is glossy with sweat, his abdomen, that miniature team of horses, trots a bright little pant. His hair is a halo of pearlescent curls, bleached even paler gold by a summer of Cretan sunlight.

"Choose them, Rah," laughs the dance master from his pillar. "I deny you nothing." He waves an arm at his remaining dancers, and the girls come forward to be chosen.

"Ta-hah," says Rah, seeing their eagerness. "Maybe we must take all, then. Maybe girls fight, if Rah does not choose. No good." He shakes his head. His back, his skirted rump, is to Rush and Cara. He lifts his hands in a gesture of indecision, head tipped to one side, and seven girls scamper onto the arena floor, giggling and shoving one another out of their way playfully.

"No fight!" says Rah, but he has been surrounded, he is being mauled by girls, and now the dance master must take some control of his troupe.

"Enough!" he shouts, clapping twice. "Step here into a line and let him choose. Or I will ban you from the practice!"

The girls immediately obey, forming a row to Rah's left. The little doll, determined to maintain her position as Siriona, steps behind Rah, her gesture saying to the others, 'I am the first chosen. '

Rah, still panting, turns to the doll, takes her face in his hands, gives her a brushing kiss. "You are Siriona. First concubine of Rah." The doll smiles triumphantly.

Rah turns back to the line of maidens. He is already dancing. He moves toward the girl closest to him, takes both of her hands, spins her, releases her and has the next in an embrace then the next and the next until each girl has been appraised. "This how we do. Like night Rah is made. You, and you, be Minia, Trinadea. Then next act, you are all temple concubine, like night Rah is made. All of you, maiden of Rah."

"Yes! Yes!" the girls clap.

"Now we need priest," he turns to the male dancers, his face angry. "Need two priest." He moves to the boys, stalks through them, having to look up at most. He takes two by their forearms and pulls them before the dance master. "These are priests. They make Rah. I show you. Need bench now." He has taken the dance master's pillar out from under him, waving for the two tall boys to help him carry it into the center of the arena.

"Oh for gods' sakes," says the dance master, who must now stand, or else sit with the Queen and her company in the benches that have been set up behind his pillar.

"He will perform the Dying to the God Ceremony now," whispers Rush to Cara, "and I have no Mochlos to abuse when I see him enter into the terrible spasms of the priest's drug, as he will of course mimic in dance until I want to put him out of his misery myself." He nods at the two 'priests'. "Only a couple of silly, besotted dancers." Cara looks up at him to ask him his meaning when she is suddenly attacked from beneath by Marta, who has come running across the arena floor to join her parents. She wraps her arms around Cara's thighs, clearly overcome with delight.

"Oh, isn't he beautiful?" she smiles at Cara, then releases her and wraps her arms about Rush in the same manner. "Oh, thank you, Ameg, for taking me here. I have met my husband! I will marry Rah, one day!"

This sends a jolt of heat through Rush's nether regions like a donkey's kick.

"No one marries a slave-god, Marta," answers Cara simply, putting her hand on the child's head and patting her roughly to silence her. "Don't be impertinent."

"Then I will be his concubine," announces Marta smartly, beaming.

"You will go home to your father and be glad of it," growls Rush, in no mood to play Ameg, or father, now. The interruption of the child has disturbed him. I should have left her in the whorehouse, he thinks. He looks over her head, his ears perked for the sound he ever longs for, a sound she has violated, that thick-tongued too-deep resonance, that lilting northern accent. He finds Rah looking straight at him, still as a startled deer.

Rah drops his eyes to the ground. The room has hushed. His attitude of submission has startled his audience. Then he takes a step toward Rush, a single step, although it is a distance of fifty meters between them. He stops, takes another dramatic moment to stand as still as a picture, before dropping into the elegant bow that stole the assassin's heart in the first place.

He is dancing, thinks Rush. He is still dancing. You arrogant little bastard. You have always known what that bow did to me. You have owned my balls ever since.

Still he cannot take his eyes off the vision of Rah at the bottom of that bow. How is it that you are so light and yet so strong, thinks Rush. You float, soundless, upward, downward, it matters not. You are like a bird, hollow boned, or like a cat, whose muscles are so toned that you appear to lift nothing in lifting your own weight. But I have lifted you, little cat, and you are weightless. You are no illusion. Rush grinds his teeth and glares at his possession as Rah maintains the bow, his palms up, his arms stretched elegantly behind him, inverted fingertips touching the ground, his platinum-gold mane falling to cover one knee.

"Papa grinds his teeth," says Marta warily, looking up at Cara with concern. "Is he mad because Rah is so beautiful?"

Cara squeezes the child's shoulder. "S-h-h, Marta. This is not a game." She regards Rush with trepidation.

From the seats behind the dance master comes the sound of a single pair of hands clapping. It is the Captain of the Guard, Nicholoas, a tall, stylish character in uniform, who has stepped forward to address what has become a crowd.

"He proves what we all wonder, sir, that you are indeed his master." His voice belies how bitterly he makes this observation.

Rush takes his eyes off Rah with difficulty to find the source of this acknowledgement. When he sees it is the Captain, his black eyes narrow with distaste.

Rah has lifted himself to his feet. He stands docilely facing Rush, eyes down, waiting permission to continue his practice. Rush shifts his attention back to the boy, his eyes sliding in their settings like marbles. You little rascal, he thinks. You are enjoying this. Safe from me in a crowd, eh? But tonight you sleep in chains in the room beside my own. He nods with casual disinterest at the Captain.

"Dance, little cat," he says, his deep voice carrying easily across the arena, although he speaks softly.

Rah takes a few elastic steps backward, makes a shorter bow, and turns back to his 'priests', motioning them to help him carry the pillar further out into the arena.

"This how they make Rah," he says deliberately, speaking to the group of dancers, to the dance master, to the Queen and her company seated behind him. Taking the two 'priests' by the arms again, he walks them to the end of the arena nearest Rush.

"This House of Moon," he says to his audience. "Need more to watch," he points to the remaining male dancers who have not yet been prescribed a job, and orders them to stand in a group to observe the ceremony. Then he begins his reenactment of his incarnation, first miming his taking of the poisonous drink from the priest, then refining the ugly spasms of his drug- induced fit, making beauty out of horror, for Rah is in control of his limbs now, his pantomime of his spasming body is timed, rhythmic, and somehow fascinatingly sexual even in its ugliness. Next comes his paralysis. He needs no stretcher now, but orders four of the male dancers to take him up as if on a pallet. He makes a board of his body, is carried this way across the arena, up the invisible hills, to the maidens standing by the pillar on 'Mount Ida' waiting for him.

Suddenly Rah leaps from his invisible pallet. "Need Ting Ya!" He looks about, finds Marta, and, this time ignoring Rush, he gestures for her. "Come, come! Marta is Ting Ya, now."

"Good, small," he tells her when she reaches him. He looks at the dance master. "Need dark hair here," he says.

"Yes, yes, we'll make her a yellow wig for the other part, the 'sister'." The dance master turns to the Queens ladies. "Is it possible?"

Behind him the ladies twitter amongst themselves. Then one says, "Yes. A flaxen horse tail is all we need. Captain?"

Nikolaos opens his eyes at the affront, then remembers himself, and bows to the Queen, who has lifted an eyebrow at him.

"Of course, there is more than one flaxen chestnut in the stable." He purses his lips. "I will find what you need, ladies. You have my promise." The Queen nods at him approvingly, even offering him a sweet smile.

Rah has set his 'TingYa' on her knees beside the pillar and lined his maidens up behind her. He has forgotten the second drink, thinks Rush. But no, now he brings his two priests to stand beside the pillar. He confers with them softly, takes a light hop onto the pillar, which is not as long as the altar on Mount Ida, but just long enough to support him from head to calves.

"Need dove," says Rah. "You have dove keeper? Rah must have time to train dove."

"How much time, Rah?" says the dance master, finally losing his patience. "We've only two weeks before the fall equinox. Your dance is to be performed then, in addition to the normal celebration. You know this!" He looks at the Queen, exasperated.

"How long will it take you to train your dove, kitten?" asks the Queen, addressing Rah.

With a bit too easy familiarity, Rah looks at Media, then down, a shy smile producing a single dimple. "I think… two, three week," he says.

"Oh, for heavens' sake, Rah, you don't know anything about doves, it would take months to train a bird to work with you," says the dance master.

Rah looks at him ingenuously. "No, I can train," he says. He looks at the Queen for support, but she can give him none. She shrugs at him.

"If he says he can train a dove in two weeks, he can train a dove in two weeks," says the Captain with irritation in his typically well-mannered voice.

This draws Rush's attention. He peers at the Captain thoughtfully. "He can," he says in a murmur meant only for Cara, but heard by Ananou, who stands leaning on his staff to his right.

"He can," agrees Ananou, nodding, and then adds, "He recreates his birth with accuracy, does he not, Ameg?"

But Rush is silent. His first glimpse of Rah after more than a week was that of his descent from one of his inhuman leaps back down to the arena floor, a descent so weightless that for an instant it seemed his limbs must be made of light. Now, casting Ananou a furtive glance, he thinks, I am like a wolf that will chew off its own leg to be free. But I will put that dagger you hide in your garment case in your eye tonight, Ananou, and then carve the bull's tear beneath.

"Well, we know he can train a horse, Captain," says the Queen, "But a bird is quite another matter. Can you dance with an invisible bird, Rah? Can you make us all believe?" asks the Queen with a mother's patient smile.

"Yes!" says Rah, excited by the challenge, and nods with certainty. "Rah make you see dove-" he extends his arms, lifts them out on either side and makes a wave from one wrist, though his shoulders, across his back, to the opposite to wrist. He looks down one arm, smiling at a row of invisible doves, looks down the other. The air in the arena has stilled, the soft light pouring through the clearstory windows hazes, his audience as silent as ghosts, as he lowers himself, arms still extended carefully to support his birds, and across the arena Rush can see them fluttering to maintain their balance as Rah drops to a crouch, and now he is the boy in the field with the white cur dog and Rush feels the sting of knives behind his eyes as he watches Rah recreate his dance with the doves on the afternoon he spied him from behind the stone fence in the robes of a Priest of the Dead. His throat closes. The boy has leapt into the air to perform that slow-motion reverse crescent kick that scattered the birds that day, birds who would return to him on the night he was to be reborn, and made a god.

Rah descends to the arena floor. His birds are gone. But there is no Hali to wake him. He remains in his bow at the bottom of the descent.

The first hands clapping are those of the Captain, and Rush's eyes snap with ferocity as he watches the man step forward, clapping, leading the entire arena in a resounding applause.

The dance master is weeping openly.

Cara has drawn her hands to her mouth, and whispers, her face wet with tears, "I saw them. I saw them. He makes us see."

Ananou, standing to the right of Rush, has lowered his head over his staff. His face is hidden.

The Queen has risen from her seat. She is clapping as she moves forward toward Rah. And Media is not weeping, but smiling the radiant smile of a woman who has just been handed her first born babe.

She walks forward, steps in front of the dance master, lifts her hands to Rah, who takes a quick, nervously glance at Rush before rising and stepping toward her obediently.

"You can indeed make us believe, Rah. But that is enough for this morning. Our Captain has informed us you have had nothing to eat, so now you will obey your Queen and go to the dining hall with your dancers and have a meal." She lifts her eyes to Ameg, across the arena, and with a courteous smile she adds, "And perhaps your master, and his family, would accompany us to the palace courtyard for some lunch."

CHAPTER 40

"I am Siriona, I am the first concubine of Rah."
"I am Minea, I am the second concubine of Rah."
"I am Trinadea, I am the third concubine of Rah."
The girls are gathered this afternoon around the altar where the god incarnated. They make an incongruous picture. The sun is high overhead, and although it is autumn on Crete, normally a rainy and dank time of year, the day is clear and dry, and great, dove-wing-white cumulous clouds are stacked overhead in a cerulean blue sky. Since their pilgrimage up the mountain to the birthplace of Rah the girls have been staying in Ting Ya's little house at the Burial Ground of the Ancients to continue their vigil. If the god is to return, he must return here. If he will not return, there will be a sign at the place of their pilgrimage. But nothing has disturbed the stillness here near the summit of Mount Ida, nothing but the call of gulls far down the mountain along the emptying shorelines of Knossos and the eerie screech of the graveyard owls at night. Nothing, until their shared dream last night.

The girls are dressed in the customary rags of mourning, the same garments they left the House of the Moon in ten days ago. Their hair, their faces, their bodies are filthy. But their hearts are refined by fasting, their minds cleansed by solitude. They are teenage girls, the oldest, Siriona, only eighteen summers, the youngest, Trinadea, is but fifteen. But they are ready for their ordeal. Last night they dreamed of the dove, all three sharing the same dream, a single dove, descending onto the altar of Rah, turning into a golden boy with blue-green eyes and the face of a cat. A boy that could dance like the tide dances with the moon on a summer night, like clouds dance with the wind in the fall, like the grain dances with the breezes, feeding the people, filling the hungry, turning the world gold and green in the spring.

303

The girls are ready for their ordeal. The sign they waited for has come. A single dream. A shared dream of a descending dove who became a boy who could dance like the grain in the spring, Rah.

Siriona is the first to take the drink. It is a poison kept safe from the priests at the House of the Moon. It is a secret well kept by generations of temple concubines. It is a death drink, made to walk the mourning maiden through the door of the soul without pain. It will reunite them with their god, who has returned to the sky to dance on silver wings with the sun.

The drink is bitter and Siriona, even now after so many days of fasting, spits out the first mouthful. She steadies herself. She must show the others the proper decorum. She will not have her love dishonored by her own childishness, which even now, on this last day of her eighteen years of life, plagues her. She takes a second sip, puts her hand to her mouth, drops her head, closes her eyes, forces herself to swallow. A tear trickles along her nose, runs into her mouth as if to help sweeten the bitterness she still tastes there. When she has recovered her poise, she passes the drink to Minea.

Minea looks at her sister with wide eyes. Her chin is trembling. She is terrified. I must show her no fear, thinks Siriona.

Siriona smiles, always the courageous one. "We will be with him in half an hour," she says, encouraging Minea, always the most timid of the three, to take the drink.

Minea stares at her sister as she takes the cup, a simple drinking vessel made of olive wood and found in Ting Ya's house. She lifts it to her mouth, her cheeks damp with her tears. "Does it hurt, Siri?" she whispers, her lips quavering.

"No, little sister, there is no pain," says Siriona, already feeling the drug's euphoric effects. "Don't be afraid, now. I do not go to him without you." She looks at Trinadea. "I share him with you forever."

Minea takes a quick gulp of the liquid, swallows before she can taste the fullness of its bitterness, hands the vessel to Trinadea, whose fingers are stretched and waiting for the cup.

Trinadea finishes the liquid in two swallows, coughs, regains her composure, looks at Siriona for approval. Siriona smiles at her and nods. Now, and always, we are one.

"I am first concubine of Rah," says Siriona, concluding the ceremony.

"I am second concubine of Rah," says Minea.

"I am third concubine of Rah," says Trinadea.

"Into the greatness we rise," says Siriona. "Through the door of death. To join with our god."

"To be with our god," says Minea.

"To be with the Grain God," says Trinadea. "To be with Rah," say the three pregnant and dying teenage wives of Rah in unison.

"How can we leave without him, Pyrus?" weeps Aros as he moves about Rah's old chamber packing the last of the cases of the boy's costumes for the ox-cart that will take them down to the wharf to board Ameg's vessel. The ship returned last night and rocks softly on the water beside the Queens vessel, which is already loaded with the King's horses, now Ameg's, by Ramicus and his men, and ready to sail. Except for these two vessels, the harbor is empty, and makes a desolate and haunted picture from the second story window of the now unoccupied room next to the priest's.

"He will find him, Aros." It is Pyrus, turning from the window to answer this question for what seems to be the thousandth time. "That man would walk into Tartarus and cut the balls off the Prince of Darkness to have Rah." He sighs, shakes his head. "I wonder sometimes if the boy would be better left unfound. Who is to say any of us need to leave Crete because a mountain smokes one hundred kilometers to the north? And what fate awaits him in the hands of Ameg? How is it that you can still trust that man with Rah, when you know now who he is?"

Aros is smiling though his tears now. "I have always knows who he is, Pyrus." He pushes himself to his feet, moves to the window to watch the train of servants and carts moving down the Bridge Road toward the harbor with the contents of the House of the Moon. "There is a look in a man's eye when his heart is in chains…" he trails off.

"He had no face, Aros. You are being theatrical again. You never saw the assassin's face."

Aros turns to look at his friend. He has stopped weeping and his eyes are open and guileless. "No Pyrus. I saw it. The night he saved Rah from the priest. I saw it." He looks back at the harbor, considering. "Rah has captured him, Pyrus. Rah has captured the assassin's soul. He cannot live without him, even if he thinks he can."

"You think with your heart, Aros," says Pyrus, turning from the window and picking up the last case for his friend. "And so you think everyone else lives by the same tender feelings as you. That man has no master. Least of all Rah. Come now. What is done is done. And cannot be undone. We must be on our way or we will be left behind, too."

"Sometimes I think I would be better off also, Pyrus," says Aros, "left behind." He is beginning to weep again. "For wherever our Sunlight is, there is my heart also."

"The assassin will find him, Aros, if he has not done so already. He will find him, and he will bring him to his home in Anatolia. And we will be there waiting. And you will dress your Sunlight in silken wings and make a halo of his yellow curls again." He puts an arm around his friend and gives his soft shoulder a pat. "And I will paint his face a thousand colors, to match his eyes."

Ananou is eating in the servant's dining area. This is not an unusual thing, for despite the honor a high priest of another city is typically given should he travel to any other on Crete, and despite his riches, he is and always must be regarded as a servant, a servant of the people, a servant of the god. So Ananou does not take his lunch with the King and Queen and her company and with Rush and his wife. He takes his repast with the servants.

He reclines at a low table in the dining hall which rests on an elevated stone floor furthest from the kitchen and is maintained for such honored visitors.

But Rah is also an honored visitor, a slave-god, and host of the true Rah. So Ananou will eat with Rah today at the table he has come to know as his. And among the others seated at the table, in addition to the priest's own three servants who accompanied him to Cyrus, are the dance master, Rah's three concubines, and as many of the dancers as can fit around the large olive rectangle, or lounge about it on the raised floor on their own pillows.

Rah has been watching Ananou like a cat watches a bird since the old man took the head of the table, normally his place, seconds before he reached it. It was easy for the old man to arrive before Rah who, ever hampered after a practice by his dancers, was stalled in the arena by them as they crowded about him, hoping that his talent might somehow be shared by proximity.

He arrives in the dining hall just in time to see the old man gather himself to sit in the place that had until then been his. It is the first time he has seen the man since the old priest stood beside Mochlos during the Dying to the God Ceremony, in the House of the Moon's gymnasium, to assist in Rah's creation.

Now Rah lies back, pretending his leisure, at the opposite side of the table, picking with his fingers through what is set before him, pretending to take food to his mouth, and watching the old man under a screen of thick, pale-gold lashes. And his ears are tipped to hear, down the length of the table, what the old man is saying. For Rah remembers.

He remembers the Assassin tackling him like a bear on the path from the King's pasture to Ting Ya's house. He remembers returning to consciousness after a fit, to find himself in the grip of the beast, a beast with the strength of five men, a beast that could have torn him limb from limb but instead only played with him, allowing him to believe he could break free, over and over, until exhausted, he lost himself to his instincts and snapped at the limb closest to his teeth, breaking the skin with a nip on the man's muscle-roped forearm.

He remembers how the man drew back then, took him by the hair at his scalp, twisted his head over his shoulder, and how, choking in mud and fear and anger he was made to look up into the face of the thing that had him, the thing he had believed was a bear, and discovered was worse than a bear.

For in that heated battle, in that proximity of flesh and fight and sweat, the only thing more frightening than war with such a thing was to be the object of the thing's passion. And the hunger in the man's face, in those jeweled black eyes, was the hunger of a pack of wolves, or of a fire descending on a field of dry barley.

And Rah remembers how, caught like a hare in a net, he could only submit as the man brought his mouth down over his own, stopping his breath, choking him with teeth and tongue, finding the back of his throat to lift and stroke and suckle his own shy and mangled tongue which shrank away like a worm. He remembers choking on that muddy and unwanted hunger as the brute held him down, crushing the air from his lungs. He remembers the nudge of the man's phallus against his bare thigh and the dizzying panic that slammed him like a horse's kick, threatening to send him into another fit when the assassin pushed away the loincloth covering his wounds. And when suddenly, miraculously, the monster was instead repulsed by the very stripes by which Mochlos had punished him, he remembers how the man released him, and sat on him, shoving his bruised mouth back into the mud and demanding in that hell-deep voice, "Why does Ananou send cheap dogs to kill the Grain Dancer?"

Rah takes a bit of food, brings it to his mouth, moves his jaw as if to chew. But he cannot eat, cannot chew, for his jaw is clenched tight with rage. Ananou. At his table. At his place at table.

Cyrus sent the assassin to kill him. But it was Ananou who sent him the assassin's desire.

Rah watches Ananou as the old man's eyes flicker and light on his own, subtly at first, then more lingering. Rah draws back his brow, an imperceptible warble building in his chest. He gives Ananou his fiercest scowl.

From across the table, Ananou blinks. Have his eyes deceived him? But no. There it is again. The blonde is glaring at him, those lynx-green eyes of his furious. He hates me! thinks the priest. And no sooner does he think it, than a ripple of pleasure sings though his bones, igniting an old, half-remembered fire in his loins. He hates me. But why? Does he know I have paid twice now for his death, once by incompetent fools who found their own in Rush's blades, and once by Lutarus and his men, who no doubt met the same fate? Ananou stares at the Grain God with renewed interest and, as he does so, his boldness earns him an even fiercer scowl from the enigmatic dancer. Delighted in the exchange, he smiles at Rah, provoking him deliberately. What will he do? What is he capable of?

wonders Ananou. He does not have to wait long.

"Sweet Rah, why do you pout so? And you have had no breakfast. Eat for your Siriona!" says the doll who sits beside him, stroking his curls back and bending to kiss his cheek as she does so.

"And for your Minea," laughs the girl who has been sitting cross-legged behind him as he lounges on his right side, his long legs extended, his temple resting on his right hand. She leans over his side, tickles his belly, a move that usually results in her wrist being snatched and her body being pulled over him into a playful game of wrestling, which, if she is not careful even here in the dining hall, will end in copulation. But today Rah only murmurs something under her range of hearing and pushes her hand away. Then he is on his feet, quick as a housecat, staring down the length of the dining table at the priest from Knossos.

"Ananou," he says, his eyes fixed on the old man in the white and yellow robes of the House of the Sun. "Rah does not eat with this priest. No one who love Rah eat with this priest." And he has picked up his side of the table and shoved it into Ananou before he can be stopped. Two of the female dancers scream. But the rest of the table only stares in shock. Rah's anger is insufficient to move the massive olivewood table more than a hand's breadth, but the force of his rage is palpable. A slave does not act in anger, not even a slave-god. The table is hushed, not in fear of Rah, but in fear for Rah. The entire dining hall has quieted, and some, closer to the kitchens in the back of the room, have stood up to see what has happened. There is a murmur of concern and dread when the servants and slaves that have been laughing and eating together whisper to each other what those in front have witnessed. A kitchen maid, standing at the end of a table with a pot of cold soup, drops the container and slaps her hand to her mouth to cover a shriek of alarm.

All wait for the reaction of the priest, who should, by rights, now call the slave master, or else the Palace Guard, to take the offender away to be aptly punished.

But Ananou can only stare up at Rah from his reclining place at the other end of the table. His three servants look from Ananou to Rah and back to Ananou, then, more subtly, at one another. They drop their eyes and fold their hands in their laps, waiting.

Rah stands, his mercurial eyes burning gold-green, like cool fires, his breast panting out a fierce little rhythm, as if challenging the old man to react. All three of his concubines have stood up to surround him, unable to disconnect themselves from him even now. Each has a hand on his person, the doll on his bicep, the taller girl at his waist. The plump one has grabbed his hand. In the golden noonday light that fills the dining hall, Rah and his maidens appear to gleam, like fallen angels, and in Ananou's eyes Rah has risen to the status of a young god, perhaps the Sun God himself who stands in all of his youthful beauty on the horizon at daybreak supported by his three spiritual wives: Sky, Wind, and Cloud.

Ananou cannot speak. He looks up, his face moving from age to radiance, amazement to bafflement. He reaches for the hand of the servant to his left. The servant jumps to his feet to help Ananou to his and another, at his right, hands him his staff. Now Rah and Ananou face one another across the olivewood rectangle.

"Do you not see it," whispers Ananou to the servant of the House of the Sun at his right. "How is it I have been so blind and yet I see? A blind old man with a fool's brain. Look at him! He is the very Sun God. The very Sun God himself at daybreak."

And before the entire hall of servants and slaves, the old man bows his head, lowering himself slowly back down to his knees, supported by his staff and the two servants to either side of him. He bows to Rah, penitent, submissive, as Rah blinks in puzzlement and distrust at the old codger, a rumble of resentment still humming in his throat.

By now news of the disturbance has reached the Palace Guard, for a member of their own had been sent down to the wine cellars for more mead and happened to pass the kitchen windows whilst taking a shortcut through the chicken yard behind in time to hear the shriek of the kitchen maid who dropped the soup. Nikolaos is taking his own lunch with his men, and is seated at a small table with Horus and two others when the man comes to report the altercation. Already harboring enough hatred and jealousy for Ameg to put a sword through him with the slightest provocation, his mind now leaps to an image of the burly merchant flogging Rah, a thing Nikolaos can barely standing to imagine. He is on his feet before the man has finished his report.

Dashing down the hall to the servant's dining area, Horus and the two others at his heels, he shouts, "This will go no further, is that understood? Else you lose your tongues for it."

But when Nikolaos reaches the dining area he finds Ananou on his knees, paying homage to the very same slave who had injured him. Caught in a moment of uncertainty, Nikolaos looks to Rah. He is just in time to see Rah spit on the dirt floor, then give Ananou one last look of loathing before he releases himself from his concubine cage and strides past Nikolaos, and out of the dining hall. And the Captain of the Palace Guard has had to step back to avoid a collision, thus creating by his very presence Rah's second capital offense in a matter of minutes.

Nikolaos looks around the table, the anger and frustration that have been building in his gut for days now openly coupling, like wild dogs, in his piercing grey eyes. He makes a fearsome figure, nearly as tall as Ameg, the assassin's mark staring like another eye from his left cheek. The V created by his broad shoulders and lean hip is the silhouette of a bird of prey perched on a falconer's wrist. He looks down the table at the dancers but can find none so brave as to meet his eye. He looks to Ananou, who with the help of his servants, is rising slowly to his feet. He finds he has no patience for the priest, who came with Ameg to the palace and now has done something to alarm Rah and place him in mortal danger. He narrows his eyes at the man. He must think of some way of keeping the priest from bringing the incident to the merchant's attention.

"As the Captain of the Palace Guard, I must ask you to explain what has happened here, sir," he says, "so that I can deal with the slave in a manner appropriate to our country." There, he has told the old fool that our ways are not necessarily his ways. The Queen will not allow Rah to be flogged, surely. No matter if she did, Nikolaos will find a way to avoid it. He will take it into his own hands and that is that.

"He is the true Rah, Captain. By my head. I have been misguided. I did not believe. I have come," says Ananou, his eyes filling with tears, "to believe. I am remiss. An old fool. An old fool."

Nikolaos can only stare at the man in disbelief, for what priest believes his own dogma? But he will not be taken in. This one is up to something. This old boy fools no one.

"What are you saying sir? Did the boy offend you, or not? It is my place to discipline the slaves of the palace. And as long as he is under this roof, he is under my authority, no matter who may say they own him."

But Ananou is an old man rekindled. He waves the Captain off and moves to shuffle past him to find Ameg and rescind their pact. "Leave it go, young man. I seek no more to harm the Grain God. I am his penitent disciple."

Nikolaos can only blink in befuddlement as the priest wobbles past him without a further glance. He stares, dumbfounded, as the golden sun emblazoned on the priest's robe retreats down the hall toward the Queen's courtyard. After only a moment's hesitation, he realizes where the old man is headed and strides past him, intent upon reaching the Queen first to whisper the incident in her ear before the priest has had a chance to demand justice from Ameg.

"Kitten, do not pout so, you ruin your pretty face," says Queen Media to Rah as she sits beside him on the bed that is no longer his, across the hall from the King. Rah has returned to this room with his concubines trailing after, but has taken no solace from them this afternoon. He cannot be persuaded to relinquish the space, which gives him a view of the practice arena and so, instant warning of any equestrian goings on, which he is always quick to intrude upon. He lies now on his belly on his old feather mattress, his favorite pillow over his head, his palms compressing it against his ears.

"Kitten?" Queen Media brushes her fingers across his shoulders, then sets to rubbing his back between the blades, a trick she has learned will bring a line of soft grunts and whimpers from her lover that remind her exactly of a favorite housecat she once carried about the palace as a girl.

Nikolaos did indeed find her ear long before she learned of the incident from her servants. The priest never mentioned it at all, but only asked to see Ameg in private when he had finished his luncheon with the Queen. An hour later there had still been no mention of the episode from either Ameg or the priest, and no request for a proper punitive reaction to the Grain God's insolence. When Media returned to the gym with her guests to watch the afternoon's practice, however, Rah was not present, and she had come looking for him here, where she expected he would be hiding in the familiar safety of his old room.

"No one is going to hurt you, kitten. The priest has dismissed the incident, or else had some change of heart regarding you. He tells the Captain he is your penitent disciple. What have you to fear? Come, come down to dance for us, the practice is nothing without Rah."

Her gentle hands have not elicited the sounds of contentment she'd hoped for, and she looks up at Captain Nikolaos helplessly. "He is like a small child sometimes, is he not?"

"Not scare," says Rah then, twisting over onto his back and tossing his pillow at the Queen. She catches it, pats it smooth against her lap, her patience for Rah endless. He pulls himself up into a cross-legged sit next to her, looks at her under his lashes, contrite. "Rah is not mad at Queen, Rah mad at priest." He leans over his own half-lotus to put a quick kiss on her mouth, then wraps his arms around his chest to hug himself like a sulking child.

"We know, kitten. But why? What has the priest done to Rah?" She strokes a lock of blond curls back from his eyes.

Rah hugs himself tighter, begins to rock lightly on his cross-legged base. "Don't like priest. This priest, he send men to kill Rah. They kill Hali. Then wolf come, kill men, all three, hah! Hah!" He has sprung off the bed onto his feet suddenly, and, slashing with invisible daggers, makes an elaborate pantomime of Rush butchering the three hirelings. He slices down the first assailant, spins to run his blades through the second, shoves his body aside with a kick, tackles the third. When he has finished with him he looks up at Nikolaos from the floor, miserable.

"Rah run away. But wolf chase. Wolf catch. Wolf-" but he has no words for the rest. Not for the bear-like tackle that sent him into a fit, not for his waking to the wolf's ravenous hunger. "He is like you!" Rah pushes his chin toward the Captain. He steps back, away from Nikolaos, a wounded expression on his pale green face. "Want to take Rah like woman.

But Rah cannot-" He is staring blue-green daggers at Nikolaos. "Rah is Grain God!" He says the words deliberately, slapping his chest after delivering each. "Stupid wolf! Stupid fox! Rah is not for wolf. Not for fox. You take Rah, no more Rah. God leave. No more Rah. No more-" Tears are welling up in his tip-tilted eyes. "No more-" He looks from Nikolaos to the Queen and back again, then takes another step backward before dashing out the door and down the hall. His concubines look at each other with alarm, then follow.

The captain and the Queen can only stare at one another, mystified.

"It's something to do with how they made him," says Nikolaos finally. "And this priest, he was involved somehow in a plot to kill Rah."

"But the 'wolf', Captain. He said the wolf saved him. This is how he refers to the assassin. To Rush. He said the assassin saved him from the priest's men. And then wanted him for himself." She is looking at Nikolaos with a woman's knowing eyes. "He said you are like the wolf in that respect, Captain."

"I have never made any attempt on Rah, madam, on my life I have not. I would sooner cut my own throat. "

"I did not say you did, Captain Nikolaos. But he reads your heart."

"What my heart will do I cannot legislate,' says Nikolaos, bringing himself up to the fullness of his height and crossing his arms over his chest. "But I will protect Rah with my life, as I have sworn to you that I would. He will come to no harm while I am with him."

Queen Media rises to her feet. She is diminutive in comparison to Captain Nikolaos, but her queenly comportment is nevertheless imposing.

"Nikolaos," she says, looking earnestly up into his face. "I fear this Ameg. I fear he will take Rah away from us."

"He may well, Madam," says the Captain, and in the Queen's eye he sees his own despairing heart.

"Nikolaos," says Queen Media, "I believe you are a good man. A righteous man. But will you do anything for your Queen, for your country?"

"I am at your service, as always, Madam."

The two exchange a knowing look. There is nothing more to say. Nikolaos bows. As he rises, the Queen takes his hand. She squeezes it, looks again into his eyes with earnest. "I know you are, Captain."

When Rush is finished with the formalities of lunch with the Queen, he returns to his own set of rooms to find Ananou. He has seen enough of Rah's practice today to know that the palace of Cyrus is besotted with the boy, that the Queen has taken him to her bed, and that the Captain of the Guard is not the fop he thought he was, though as obsessed with Rah as he is himself. When he reaches the room across the hall from the one that awaits Rah next to his own, he makes no attempt to be genial in his entry, but lays one fist against the door with irritable carelessness and slams it open against the wall, putting a long crack in the olivewood from floor to ceiling. He finds Ananou on his knees before a small, traveling altar at the foot of his bed.

Ananou fairly jumps up from his kneeler, somehow finding the strength in his old limbs to move out of the way of the swinging door in time to avoid a blow to his ankles.

"Sir!" He can think of nothing more, for Ameg's normally genial and gentle face is momentarily unrecognizable. Then the merchant's features soften as he looks about the room for Ananou's servants. But the priest is alone.

"Forgive me, Ananou, I stumbled in the hall and fell into the door just now." Rush pats the front of his gown, where a roll of muslin strapped to his waist beneath gives him the appearance of a rich man's paunch. "Too much good food and too little physical work makes a man graceless."

"Nonsense, Ameg, you are a model of physical poise," responds Ananou automatically. He brings himself to his feet, finds his staff. "Shall we speak here, or in the courtyard where there is less chance of servants eavesdropping."

Ameg brings a hand to his cheek to scratch his beard. "In the courtyard then, Ananou. If it pertains to the boy."

"It does."

The two find their way down to a small garden off the guest wing. It is designed for visitors to take their leisure in the hot summer afternoons, and several pillowed couches sit under the statues of the various gods that decorate the patio. Exotic flowers and trees provide ample shade, and a fountain in the center adds the music of running water.

The priest settles himself under a bronze of the sea goddess. He chuckles, nodding at the figure as Ameg joins him on the lounging bench with a well-practiced thump to prove the merchant's corpulence.

"A thousand years from now they will think she carries snakes and call her the Snake Goddess," comments the priest dryly. "I have always thought it an ugly depiction. Does the Sea not slap her tail against the shoreline in the waves? Why does she stand like a cook in that bell-shaped skirt."

"The eels perhaps for cooking," chuckles Rush, realizing with some distaste that he and the old priest have this in common. Both believe in a world ruled by a masculine divinity. Ananou in the Sun God. Rush in himself.

Now the old priest's face turns somber. He looks down at his robes, gathers a handful of exquisitely embroidered linen in either palm, looks from one to the other. "I am a hypocrite and a fool, Ameg," he says. "Three times I have sought to kill the Grain God of Knossos. Though I dress in the robes of the High Priest of the Sun God, pretend to stand against a tide of feminine rule to protect him, to maintain his church here on Crete. Though I saw…" and here he stops, choking on tears, "Though I saw him born, even assisted in his birth. Though I saw him incarnate, like a ray of light in the dark, dancing on the crest of Mount Ida." He stops, wipes his eyes with a sleeve, sets his gnarled hands down firmly on his knees and squeezes them. "I cannot do it, Ameg. I cannot kill the Grain God. Not for anything. Not for Tiko, not for all of my wealth, not to save my own life I cannot." He pauses, gathering his composure. Rush says nothing, only watches the old man with a cold expression.

Finally, Ananou turns to look at him. There is the look of absolute certainty in his face. He has found his heart, thinks Rush. After all these years of worship, he has found his heart.

"This boy," says Ananou, "this boy has somehow truly become a vessel of the God."

Rush is silent for a moment. "What has made you change your mind, Ananou, if I may ask? Until today you have been single-minded in your desire to kill Rah."

Ananou gives Rush a sharp glance. "If I tell you this, you may well punish him, Ameg, for his insolence. I could not bear to be the cause of that."

"I give you my word, I will not discipline the boy on your account," mutters Rush, losing patience. "Only tell me what has changed your mind, or I will hold you to our bargain."

Ananou looks at Rush, hesitates. "He read my soul, Ameg. He knew. Somehow he knew. He stood at table, accused me. Spit at me. He knew I had betrayed him. And there, in the noonday sun, his anger blazed at me, Ameg, I wonder I was not burned by it. I tell you he was radiant, Ameg, blinding. Like the morning star."

Ah, thinks Rush. He spit at you. He stood in a bit of sunlight and spit at you, pouting like a cat with its tail underfoot, no doubt. Yes, that would do it. That would set your old bones on fire.

"I do not expect you to return the money I gave you, Ameg," says the priest.

"Nor will I," says Rush. "But Ananou, under these circumstances, you cannot expect me to give you Tiko, either."

The high priest blinks at him with surprise, then shakes his head as if at his own folly. "Tiko," he murmurs. "How many pretty Asian dancers would it take to purchase the Sunrise?" He shakes his head again. "No, Ameg, I do not expect you to return Tiko. And I am quite sure that if I saw Tiko again, he would have diminished in my sight, and could bring me nothing but disappointment. I merely wish to inform you that I cannot relieve you of your 'weakness' as you call it. I cannot drive a dagger into that breast. I would sooner drive one into my own."

Fancy words, thinks Rush. You are no use to me, Ananou, and will not see another sunrise, unless you see it in Rah's face once more before morning.

"Do not pity me, Ameg," says the priest suddenly.

"Pity you, Ananou? You make your own choice, and we are, in the end, both men of business."

"But you believe I have lost, do you not? I have lost nothing. I have found my way."

Rush lifts an eyebrow, then takes the old man's arm and helps him to his feet. "I am glad I could assist you in this," he murmurs kindly in Ameg's soft tenor. But he hears the brute within himself snarl. You old bastard, your "way" is worth less to me than one hair on the head of the cur dog Rah loved. I will carve your eyes out of your head and make you eat them tonight before you die.

In the evening, after he has missed his third meal of the day, as well as an entire afternoon of dance practice, Rah has still not returned to his room across the hall from the King's. It is Bacus and Fillius' job to secure Rah for the night in the room next to Ameg's, and after taking their own late supper in the dining hall they have learned from the kitchen staff of Rah's confrontation with the priest at lunch. None of the servants in the dining hall have seen him since, and a palace guard who happens through informs them that the Captain has already sent a few men looking for him. Thus far, Rah does not appear to be in the palace at all.

"Have you tried the stables?" asks Fillius, as aware as anyone of Rah's uncanny bond with the horses. "He often goes there when he is upset by something. I myself have found him curled up in a stall more than once."

"We've been through the stable with a fine tooth comb," says the guard. "Stable master says he hadn't seen him. I can't imagine he could have left the palace in broad daylight," he muses. "He'd draw a crowd in no time and be torn to bits by a mob of admirers."

"Has anyone seen his concubines?" Bacus offers. "They never let him out of their sight. If you can find them, you can find Rah."

"The dish washer told me they were here alone at supper," Fillius answers. "Has anyone told Ameg he's missing?"

"Hah," says Bacus with a fearful look. "I'll leave that to someone else. Come, Fillius, let us try the Queen's wing again, perhaps he is hiding under Media's skirts."

But when the pair reach the Queen's suite of rooms they learn that no one there has seen Rah all day.

"The Queen spoke with him after lunch," offers one of her maidens. "Apparently he had some words for the Captain and fled them both. The

Queen has not seen him since and has taken to her bed."

After one more search through the palace, Bacus and Fillius are ready to send a man up to the roof when they run into Ikarus, who is on his way up from the wine cellar with an amphora of imported wine.

"Have you seen Rah, sir? The palace is astir looking for him. No one has seen him since shortly after noon."

"That is because he has been with me, my good men. Learning to taste wines properly. Not much of a head for it. I think you will find him in the cellar still, sleeping it off."

Rah did run down to the stable after his words with Nikolaos and the Queen, but he did not come through the way he normally did, that is, from the archway beneath the King's wing and across the practice arena. For several days Rah had been slipping away on his own via the palace roof. It began when, like that evening that seemed so long ago now at Ameg's compound, he spied a cat crossing the palace rooftops from his chamber window, and, careful to avoid the eyes of a few palace guards practicing swordplay in the arena below, he simply slipped out to follow. The cat brought him to the Queen's wing and in through a storage closet in the servant's area. When he exited the closet into the Queen's hall, no one thought much of it, for Rah was frequently seen leaving the Queen's wing. The next day, after dinner when the light was in his favor and the practice arena was empty, he exited his window as he had the day before, but moved in the opposite direction, toward the palace stable, which was actually a separate building, and leapt across a short alleyway to the stable roof. This was no problem for Rah, who then followed the low roof to the back of the stable and jumped onto a pile of hay to the ground. Several of the palace horses, Nikolaos' sorrel for one, were left outdoors at night to enjoy the evening air, and were already chewing on their late day ration of hay. This told Rah that no one would be out back again this evening to feed them, and that he was safe to remain among them until it was time to return to the palace to be found by Fillius and Bacus and put to bed.

So on the afternoon of his disappearance Rah was not to be found in the palace because he was not in the palace at all, but behind the stable block and out of doors. There he talked to the animals in a private language he shared only with his sister as a child and later with the horses he trained and cared for during the years before Kephas discovered him.

It was here, singing a Hittite lullaby he had learned in Illyria while feeding Nikolaos' sorrel gelding the honey-soaked oat cookies he had pilfered from the kitchen, that Ikarus found him.

It was Ikarus' habit, being a man devoted to pleasure, to wander down to the stable after dinner with a flask of good wine to share with the stable master, after which he, too, occasionally stepped out of doors behind the stable to pleasure the palace horses with treats from the kitchen. Ikarus had two reasons for being in the palace paddock that evening. For one, being a devout hedonist, he simply loved to be in the company of fine animals, whether two or four legged. For another, as all true devotees of pleasure know, happiness is a drink best drunk amongst friends.

But when he steps out of the rear doors of the stable into the evening air just before dusk, he is happily surprised to find Rah sitting on the ground beside the Captain's sorrel, which is munching its evening ration of hay. At first glance the boy appears no more than an extra portion of hay himself, being flaxen-haired and tawny as a field of late grain, but as Ikarus approaches the fence, the organic curve of the boy's shoulder appears to him in the twilight and the King's nephew realizes with more than a little delight that the gods have decreed that he should enjoy the company not only of several four-legged beauties this evening, but of a two-legged one.

"Ahah! I have found the hiding place of the little Grain God! Now I have something with which to barter your friendship tonight, for I will tell your concubines and you will lose your last inch of freedom if you do not share your company with me!" laughs Ikarus, slipping through the fence rails, a flask in one hand, to settle himself on the ground in the dirt next to Rah. "What brings you out here this evening, hm? Have you had your fill of the mares within the palace, and now seek to mount these?" He takes a swig from the flask and offers it to Rah.

But his humor is lost on the Grain God, who merely pushes Ikarus' hand away and folds his arms over his chest. "Don't want wine. Ikarus drink too much wine. Will make sick."

"On the contrary, Rah, it makes me well. I am sick without it. Why are you so set against a bit of wine, eh? You take all of your other pleasures easily enough. Did you have a drunken father?" Ikarus has set the flask between his legs and leans into Rah with some concern. "Did he beat you?"

Rah flicks his eyes at Ikarus and all of the day's hurt is in them. "No beat. No father. In Knossos they make me drink to be with Queen, but Queen, she is like a man, big. Strong. Hungry. Take, take," he grabs at Ikarus' arm for effect. "Rah cannot be with this Queen. Her men, they make Rah drink. Too much. Do not remember… This Queen of Knossos, she is like wolf," he says bitterly, then seems to lose his interest in the subject. "Like wolf," he trails off, scratching at the sorrel's forelock when the horse moves to nuzzle his leg briefly before returning to his hay.

"You are very sad, today, Rah. It hurts my heart to see you so. Let me teach you how to enjoy wine, eh? This is a terrible thing, that you should reject the entire world of drink for one bad experience."

"No," Rah pushes the offered flask away again, "make sick." But Ikarus has had harder nuts than this to crack. He sets the flask between his legs again, considering.

"I will make a deal with you, Rah of Knossos. You drink a bit of this fine last-year's wine with me, and I will talk the Queen into giving you your own horse."

This grabs Rah's full attention. He looks at Ikarus with the intensity of an orphaned child offered his first meal in a week. "How you can do that, Ikarus? Slave cannot own horse. Slave can own nothing." But the concentration of his gaze tells the hedonistic Ikarus that the boy believes he can indeed bring about such a miracle.

"Which horse would you take, Rah, if you could have any one, hm?" Ikarus takes a sip from the flask, offers it one more time to Rah, who this time accepts it, and without hesitation lifts it to his lips. He takes several gulps before Ikarus must pull it from his hands and set it down between them.

"Easy, lad, this is too good a wine to drink like punch." He points to the horses, who, having finished most of their hay, have moved off toward the back of the paddock where there is some vegetation to forage.

"Not this ones," says Rah, scanning the animals. "This mare here, you see?" He points to a dun mare in the rear of the group. "She is sore in back, here," he plants the palm of his free hand against his own mid-back. His other has settled on the flask absentmindedly. "Good mare, strong. But not for soft ride." He flicks his eyes at Ikarus, who nods with seeming interest, but is in fact lost in the lightness that has softened Rah's face.

"I see," he says. "And that?" He points to a black.

"Black hard to ride. Bad spirit. Too strong here," Rah knocks his own temple with his knuckles. "Want to be wild, always. No." Rah picks up the flask and takes another long swallow. "No this horse." He chuckles to himself. "Rah fight all the time with this horse then, like man and wife."

Ikarus smiles. "I see. Bad relationship. The one that needs to be on the bottom always wanting to be on top."

"Yes! Yes! Hah!" Rah shoves Ikarus' shoulder playfully. Then grows somber, looks down in the dirt, finds a stalk of hay the sorrel has left and puts it to his lips to chew. His eyes wander past the backs of the animals at the far end of the paddock and up into the hills.

For a moment Ikarus is lost watching the boy transform. One moment he is a sweet and uncomplicated child, almost a simpleton in his determined state of now, next, a misplaced soul, stolen from his homeland, from his mother's arms, perhaps, to be made a god for a hungry people by a greedy priest. Ikarus watches Rah chew the stalk of hay, and for a moment he is made stupid by the simple motion of the boy's jaw as he chews, the muscles moving like seals under the sea-plain of his cheek. Presently Ikarus' silence catches Rah's attention. The boy flashes him a quizzical look, then a shy smile. He points north and east over the mountain.

"Rah has horse in Knossos," he says in a conspiratorial whisper. He has licked the entire reed into his mouth and chewed it into a ball to push about with his tongue.

Ikarus finds himself momentarily at a loss for words. He is busy committing the boy's face to memory, thinking to himself that he must burn into his mind this image of quite possibly the most extraordinary creature he will ever look upon. He takes a swig of the wine. "A horse in Knossos, Rah?" he points to the hills, attempting to entice Rah's mind to return there. "How is that so?"

Rah gives him a perplexed look, as if straining for words. The wine has confused you, thinks Ikarus. I am a devil and a whore for beauty. Purely selfish. Look what I have done to you, just for the sake of a few hours of pleasure.

"Did you ride a horse in Knossos, Rah? Did someone let you ride their animals?" he tries in a moment of guilty sympathy.

"King horse!" blurts Rah, prodding Ikarus' chest with a blunt finger. "Yes-" he frowns, grunts, his tongue grown thick with alcohol. "My horse-" he thumps his chest, "he love Rah. Rah talk, he listen." He taps his head with an index finger. "We speak, no words. But here."

"What was your horse like, Rah? What made it so different from these?" asks Ikarus.

Rah's eyes have drifted up toward the hills to the north again. He squints into the sun setting over the mountains.

"He is like Rah," he says finally. "Both are dancer. Both can dance, yes. This horse, he has-" he makes a frown, unable to find the word. "Like, Rah," he says at last. "Good body," he makes a fist and raps his own chest. "Body know where it is. Always. In air. On ground. Not matter." He extends one hand, splays his fingers, wobbles it in front of himself, tips his body to reflect the motion of his hand. "Always know where body is. Can do anything with body."

"Balance, Rah. You speak of balance," says Ikarus softly. "You have perfect balance, you and your horse in Knossos."

"Yes!" Rah smiles. "Ba-lance," he repeats to himself quietly.

"And a good deal of talent," adds Ikarus, taking another sip of wine.

After a moment of silence, Ikarus begins to lift himself to his feet. "Well," he says. "Now you have had a drink with me, and so I shall honor my part of the bargain. Tomorrow I will speak to the Queen, and perhaps we can figure out how a slave can own a horse. But we cannot go to Knossos and steal your horse from the King. You will have to pick one of these." He takes Rah's arm and attempts to help him to his feet. The boy's body seems to levitate effortlessly, guided by his hand, despite his drunkenness. But Rah is giggling, an infectious giggle that starts in his throat and ends by tickling Ikarus' ear until his own throat vibrates with it. "What is it, Rah?" says Ikarus, smiling.

"Pick from this?" Rah points at the animals at the back of the paddock. "No horse here for Rah. Like old woman!" This thought sends him into a fit of laughter. "Rah does not mount old woman!"

Even Ikarus can see the humor in this. He puts an arm around the boy's shoulder and chuckles, leading him out of the paddock gate and along the wall of the stable.

"No, I suppose that would be pointless." And at that they both break out in peals of drunken laughter, Rah holding the flask to his stomach as he doubles over.

When he reaches the alley Rah had leapt from above, Ikarus leads the boy to an exterior door to the wine cellar beneath the kitchens.

"Where you are take Rah, Ikarus? Rah is tire, want bed," Rah asks, suddenly suspicious of the yawning black hole and the long stairs down.

"It is just the wine cellar, Rah. Don't be afraid," says Ikarus, as he motions the boy to follow him down. At the bottom of the stone steps is a narrow hall, lit only by tiny ground level windows along the exterior side.

Rah looks about, rubbing his arms and shivering.

"Cold here, like tomb." His chuckles have faded. But he continues to follow Ikarus to the end of the hall, which branches off to the right.

"How you can see down there? No light. Too dark for Rah." He looks at Ikarus solemnly, stopping with a slap of his bare feet against the stone floor. "I go back now." He takes a backward step, a frightened look on his face.

"Look here, they keep this fire going to warm the ovens above. And torches here, you see? It is just down this way. Come."

Reluctantly Rah follows his host down another short hall which branches off in several directions. They turn right into a large, dark storage room filled with barrels and amphora from floor to ceiling. Behind it is another doorway that seems to be lit by natural light.

Ikarus moves about the space proficiently, holding his torch up to scan the markings on several jugs at the far end of the room. He finds what he is looking for and holds it up for Rah to see.

"Ah! This is the last one! We must try it. It is made from a white grape, you see? Very unusual. Imported from Egypt."

"What this room, Ikarus?" asks Rah, instinctively drawn toward the doorway emitting natural light.

"Ah, come I show you. We are actually near the outer wall. This room has a window that allows light from the hall we entered by. There. This window is parallel to the exterior window. Very clever. Just don't take a wrong turn on the way out, or you'll have a devil of a time finding your way. Very complex storage system down here. I generally never go beyond the wine cellar myself." He pops the skin off the top of the amphora he has pilfered, takes the flask Rah has been carrying, fills it.

"Let us relax in here. The palace wine master has set it up quite cozily. A good idea if your lover is a cook and works in the kitchen above, as his is!"

He leads Rah into the back room, which has a single couch and a table. The floor is strewn with opulent pillows and there is a lamp for Ikarus to light, and so, set down his torch. The wall opposite the window has been painted in bright colors, the artist depicting a graphically sexual scene with bare-breasted concubines pleasuring their perfect-bodied lovers in a variety of creative positions. Ikarus has offered the flask to Rah as the boy stares at the mural, wide-eyed. Rah takes the flask, takes a sip, then a few gulps. "Sweet, like fruit," he comments, still staring with charming innocence at the wall, tilting his head this way and that. "How you can do that? No one can do like that. Even Rah cannot. Hah!" He makes an attempt at imitating the contortions of a particularly creative concubine, gives up. "This is stupid wall." He takes a few backward steps, trips, falls onto a pile of pillows, laughing.

"Apparently someone would like to believe it possible, though, eh?" Laughs Ikarus. He takes the flask from Rah, who has somehow managed to keep from dropping it, and sets it down as he settles himself on a pillow under the painted wall. "There, now you can memorize these positions while we talk."

Rah looks up at the wall over Ikarus' head and makes a derisive sound by blowing through his lips. He continues to scan the wall, nevertheless, with a child's simple wonder.

Ikarus watches him quietly, puts the flask to his lips, and sets it down. "Where on earth did you come from, Rah of Knossos?" he says finally.

Rah's eyelids flutter as he drops his gaze to Ikarus. He gives the man a puzzled look.

"I mean originally. Where were you born?" Ikarus tries again.

Rah reaches for the flask. "I am so small, Ikarus. When they take me. And sister." He takes a gulp of the wine, wipes his mouth with the back of his forearm. "I think I am come from far north." He squints up at the window attempting to illuminate the room with weak, natural light from across the hall.

"Poor boy. Did you not know your parents?" asks Ikarus.

Rah shakes his head. "No parents. Always slave." He is playing with the mouth of the flask, running a finger around the rim. "I am keep with dogs sometime." He looks at Ikarus. "You know? Little child." He shows how little with his hand, a measure against his own body. His hand cuts himself at the navel, where there is no more than a ripple of lean flesh available to cover the muscular cage of his abdomen. "Little child should not be keep with dogs."

"My gods. Is that so?" Ikarus stretches to take the flask, leaning over his own abundant midriff to do so. He grunts with the effort and Rah flicks his eyes at him and chuckles. "Ikarus eat too much. Food not only thing that make man happy." He leans back against the wall behind him, resting his elbows on his knees so that his open legs make a table for them. He is staring at Ikarus with drunken ease. For a moment it appears to Ikarus that his eyes are made of light, gathered from some internal place, for they seem to glitter despite the dimness of their surroundings. In the poorly lit room they are pale green, matching almost exactly the washed out paint that has stubbornly adhered to his face. Ikarus blinks, suddenly overcome by emotion. This beauty, penned up with dogs? Fed what, scraps? What is wrong with people that they cannot see? I would have spoilt him rotten. Made a little prince of him. He scoffs at his own thought. Yes, and made him fat with conceit. Unrecognizable. How awful. Rah, you are perfected by your suffering. Which is why I am so imperfect. I cannot tolerate the slightest discomfort.

"What makes you happy, Rah? That is, besides dancing, and riding women and horses?"

But Rah has lost interest in conversation. He has closed his eyes for a moment and now nods his head and, as his muscles release, his arms skate down the inside of his thighs to rest together as if in prayer at his groin. Ikarus can only stare at him for several minutes, watching the subtle rise and fall of his chest, listening to his soft cat-like snore. Presently he lifts his weight from his pillows and steps carefully over to crouch beside the boy. The scent of vanilla on his skin, residue from the oils Naiba used to attempt to dissolve his face paint reminds him of a favorite dessert of sweetened and vanilla scented goat cheese, and he squats beside Rah to enjoy it. "What a confection you are, Rah," he whispers, but the boy is engulfed in the anesthesia of alcohol-induced sleep. He does not stir.

Slowly, Ikarus bends to put a soft kiss in the curls at the boy's temple, then pushes himself to his feet, leaving the flask between Rah's legs, the torch in a sconce, and slips out quietly the way he came with only his memory to guide him.

CHAPTER 41

"How could he leave him in the wine cellar?" whispers Fillius to Bacus as he watches the King's nephew move away down the hall toward his own chamber. "The sun has set. What if he wakes and finds himself in the dark? He could get lost down there. He will not think to take a torch and at any rate, cannot read the markings on the walls! He could be lost for days!"

"He will be sleeping off his drunk, Fillius. We will find him before he wakes. Come. Let us make haste."

But they are accosted by Nikolaos before they reach the stairs by the kitchens that lead to the ovens below and the wine cellar.

"What is the meaning of this? You still haven't found Rah? How long did you intend to wait before you informed me he was still missing?" barks the Captain at the two stewards.

"Ikarus has just informed us that he left him in the wine cellar, sir," Bacus is quick to respond. "We are just on our way down now-"

"Ikarus? That idiot," mutters Nikolaos, shoving both the stewards out of his way and storming down the stairs to the cellar.

When he reaches the storage room where Ikarus pilfered the wine he breathes a sigh of relief, for torchlight illuminates the doorway to the wine master's love nest at the back. "Rah!" bellows the Captain in a booming voice, shaking the closely packed amphorae and creating a tinkling ring in the room about him. But he gets no response.

As Captain Nikolaos strides through the wine cellar toward the dim doorway at the end of the room an ugly thought creates itself in his mind. Ikarus took the boy down here to the wine master's love nest? For what purpose? There is only one. A vision of the King's nephew's head rolling off the bloody edge of his favorite sword is the next to appear in his mind. By the time he has entered the little room behind the wine cellar, Captain

Nikolaos is ready for battle.

He finds Rah where Ikarus left him, his back against one wall, knees up, hands folded between them as if in prayer. His head is tipped to one side, eyes closed. He is snoring softly, the rustling burr of a small animal at rest. To Nikolaos, he is the picture of adorable vulnerability.

Nikolaos takes a deep breath, struggling to gain control of his temper. There is a flask between the boy's feet. So Ikarus plied him with wine. For what purpose, comes the question again to his suspicious mind? For several moments he can do nothing more than watch the boy sleep. "Bastard," mutters Nikolaos under his breath, moving toward Rah to crouch over him, intending to pick him up as he is and carry him up to bed.

But the shadow of the man leaning over him in the dim cellar jars Rah from his sleep, recreating the memory of Turios in the tomb of Lutarus. He awakens with a jolt of panic, struggles away from Nikolaos, who is attempting to lift him, and bolts out of the room. In what seems less than a few seconds Nikolaos has gone from finding Rah to losing him in a labyrinth of dark hallways and storage rooms that span the length and breadth of the palace.

"Damn!" Nikolaos makes a hopeful attempt to find Rah in the wine cellar, then steps out into the hallway beyond, which branches off in several directions, most of the hallways leading further into the storage complex beneath the great hall. "Rah!" he shouts, using every fiber of his powerful lungs to fill the hallways to the length of the underground maze. Then he holds his breath, listening like a fox outside of a chicken coop, ears lifted. The faint patting of bare feet echoes in the silent darkness that stretches down the hall in front of his torch. "Damn," he mutters to himself, and turns to rush back up to the Guards barracks to organize a search for the now lost boy.

Rush is in his own suite of rooms, having just returned from the private bath at the end of the guest wing and is readying for bed when a knock on his door interrupts him. He quickly ties his 'paunch' about his middle and wraps himself in a ridiculously over-embellished robe, sewn with seed pearls and tiny shells, and offers the intruder to come in with a modulated voice.

"Sir," says the breathless guard at his door. "The boy has gone lost in the labyrinth. The Captain has ordered a search."

Rush looks the guard over with feigned disinterest. "I see. And has the Captain joined the party?"

"He leads it, sir. He wishes to assure you that the boy will be found. However, although all of the halls beneath the palace are marked, the boy fled without a torch and could be lost for days if he is left on his own to find his way out."

"He is a slave and cannot read Minoan or any other language, in any light," comments Rush. "But you say he fled? Fled from what?"

"From the Captain, sir. Who went down to find him before he woke. You see, the King's nephew, Ikarus, seems to have taken him down to the wine cellar to get him drunk, for whatever reason." The guard looks down with a shrug. "The King's nephew is a funny man, sir. He takes pleasure in the drink and likes company when he does so."

Is that so, thinks Rush, who can imagine only one reason to bring a beautiful, if seemingly dim-witted boy down to the wine cellars and get him drunk. He recalls Ikarus, seated at the left of the Queen at lunch, and again at dinner, a soft-spoken little man with a pleasant smile and a flaccid body. Just the type, thinks Rush. We must meet in private, Ikarus, before I leave Cyrus to wither in the acid breath of Thera.

"Well," he gives a tired sigh, a fat man who longs only for his bed, "I suppose I should join the search. After all, he may be inclined to respond to my voice." He gestures for the guard to lead the way.

Several minutes later he is standing in the cellar hall by the kitchen furnaces at the bottom of the cellar stairs.

"Explain the markings to me, man, for I believe I will wander about on my own down here to separate my voice from the others for the boy to hear."

"They are quite simple, sir. It is a number system. The lower the number, the closer you are to the exit. There are four other entrances to the cellar but each uses a different system. The north exit is used only for incoming deliveries and uses letters. Again, simple. The closer the letter to the beginning of the alphabet the closer you are to the entrance. The other three exits are locked and available only to the Guard and will be of no use to you. Now a symbol.... here, tells you the nature of the storage. Here is the wine cellar. The small red amphora. You see?"

But Rush has already entered the wine cellar and strode toward the back in the dark, using his keen night vision, his uncanny sense of direction and his sense of smell to lead him to the last room Rah inhabited, which glows dully with a bit of moonlight that has found its way into the dark. He takes the torch left by Ikarus, sweeps it about the room, scans the sexual scene on the wall, locates the placement of the last two people to lounge here. Here is Ikarus, under the wall. The acrid smell of the chronic drinker. And across the little room, in a heap of pillows under the square of moonlight, cherry blossom and myrrh. His stomach lurches with desire. His teeth clamp down against themselves, against the saliva building in his throat. Little cat. You fled here, yes? Look how the pillows are strewn. Kicked, this one even torn, here, by your sharp little claws. I have felt those claws in my back, carrying you off the Burial Mound Road on my way to a more private spot to sever your head. And then to find myself paralyzed by those eyes of yours. Can they see in the dark, little cat? I fear not. You fled. And you fled fast and far, for you are fearfully fast. And found yourself alone, away from your attacker, but in some new horror. Alone entombed in these stone halls. Stone walls, like the ones in Lutarus' tomb. And if I do not find you soon, little cat, I will lose your mind again, lose it to the darkness you believe yourself to be enclosed by.

Rush turns to see the guard, who has just caught up with him, standing in the little doorway, a look of bewilderment on his face. He is regarding Rush with a marriage of respect and suspicion.

"How did you find your way across the wine cellar, sir, without a torch? And not a single collision with all of those-"

"I have spent some time in the military, boy. Night fighting hones the senses, and some things never leave you," answers Rush. But even in the dim torch light his eyes have begun to glow, as if collecting light like a feral thing. "Now go, make yourself useful. Join the search and leave me. As you see, I can find my way."

"Yes, sir," responds the guard, whose soldier's ears have picked up the commanding tone that has darkened the dandy's voice. He turns and is quickly swallowed by the dark.

When Rush can no longer hear his footsteps, he drops to his knees and picks up one of the pillows Rah had been napping on. He puts the pillow to his face and breaths in deep, memorizing the scent. There is more here than cherry blossom and myrrh. There are the human smells of the boy's perspiration, the delicate scent of wine on the breath of an inexperienced youth, not sour like that of Ikarus, whose whole body has become pickled in the stuff from years of overindulgence. Your mouth would taste sweet just now, Rah. Sweet as the grape that made this wine.

Rush turns to tamp out most of the fire of his torch on the pornographic wall until it is little more than an orange glow. Then he follows his senses back out through the wine cellar, and stops one more time to imagine where a startled, drunken cat would flee before he chooses his direction.

CHAPTER 42

Rah has lost his way.

It is not so much the dark that surrounds him, or the dank mingling of smells, or even the stone walls that seem to loom toward him, to close in around him, to capture him at the end of every hall until he finds another aperture through which to flee. It is the sound of his own fear, the rapid patter of his feet against the rock floor, the sound of his own breathing, coming faster and faster until he is panting like a terrified animal, the deep grunting of his own lungs against the heavy air down here, air as thick as mud, mud that threatens to choke him like an assassin's kiss.

Rah has lost his way, and in the kaleidoscope of his mind he is no longer in the basement of the Palace of Cyrus, running from the hunger in the fox' grey eyes, he is in the tomb of Lutarus, in the nightmare dream world created for him there by the very man who would be torn and eaten raw by the hell dogs of Rush the Assassin only days after his rescue.

Rah has lost his way, and in the dark labyrinth beneath the Great Hall of the Palace he runs into wall after wall, fleeing no longer from Nikolaos now but from his own nightmare, fleeing deeper and deeper into the labyrinth, and finally, downhill through a narrowing tunnel to an even lower level beneath the cellars, to the little known Catacomb of the Kings.

And bruised and bleeding from his many collisions in the dark, he crumples finally into a shivering crouch at the end of a narrow and winding passageway, at the end of which is a tiny, cave-like tomb. He gropes about for a time, whimpering and mewling, his fingers desperate to find the solace of another opening, another egress through which to flee.

And when his body cannot find its way out of what is in fact the tomb of Heritas, the place where Media first envisioned him, then his compromised brain finds its own escape, and liberates his mind with his own special madness.

Nikolaos has dispatched a contingent of twenty guards down into the cellars to find the Grain God. He has himself been down in the labyrinth for near an hour when he hears the mewling of a wounded animal in the stones that surround him. But try as he might he cannot find access to the sound. It is as if the creature is trapped within the very walls, or else buried in the flooring. Nikolaos is unaware of the existence of the Hall of the Kings, for it is the Queen's secret, passed down from generation to generation until the last, for Media's mother was mad and failed to tell her daughter until after her own death.

Nikolaos spends another twenty minutes desperately trying to find a way to the sound that is beginning to drive him to distraction. Several guards come piling up in the narrow hall where he himself is now wedged and crouching, scanning the stone blocks for some opening large enough for Rah to have slipped through. They have heard his bark, "Rah! Rah!" and believed him to have found the boy. But Nikolaos can only look up at the leader of the group in the torchlight and snarl, "Can't you hear that, you imbecile? He is trapped in some crevice here. Listen!"

After a few seconds of silence, the eerie, feral warble returns. All four men are still, listening to the agony that seems to slip through the damp walls and curl around them in a fog of sound. Nikolaos stands up as best he can in the cramped space, a space never intended for a man of such regal height, and looks at his men with a light of near madness in his pale eyes.

"If he is not found in half an hour I will take an eye from every man I sent to find him. Is that understood?"

"Yes, Captain!" comes the echoing chorus from the four men, who quickly shuffle back down the hall and fan out in odd directions at their leader's command.

"Rah!" barks Captain Nikolaos with every particle of air in his powerful lungs. But the name only bounces back and forth down the stone corridor, like the ghost of Media's mother, and scatters somewhere ahead of him in the unrelenting gloom.

Rush has followed the scent of myrrh and cherry blossom down a series of straight passageways toward the north end of the palace. He is as aware of the direction he is traveling as surely as he is aware that his time here in Cyrus is running out, that Thera has not given up her steam only to grow cold and extinct without first setting the Aegean air on fire with her rage. As he moves in his perfected silence down the corridor, sensing the ever increasing heaviness and chill, he considers his plan. He will kill Ananou, of that there is no doubt. Though he may in the end have only done the old priest a service, sparing him the horror of a death by volcano, yet he must take his life. This is personal. This is not something you leave to a volcano. This is blood he will bathe in, like a wolf masking its scent in the offal of its kill. Then he will take the boy, the woman and the child, and return to Knossos to board the ship that will by now be harbored there waiting for him. He will take the boy to his compound in Anatolia. He will reestablish his church, the House of the Moon, setting up Mochlos there to redefine his godhood. For Rush has come to understand that the boy believes himself to be the deity, and that his mind, damaged early on in his slavery by some accident of fate that Rush may never learn, can no longer be separated from that belief. If the god is defiled or in some way damaged by impropriety, then the god will disincarnate, and the boy will lose his mind.

Rush continues in straight lines, imagining himself to be a frightened and intoxicated boy, blinded by darkness, guided only by what his dog-like instincts tell him, that he must take the shortest route away from whatever spooked him, therefore straight lines are likely, that when that straight line ends with a wall, he must chose a direction, and that direction will be one that his instincts tell him will lead him to light. Rah may have already been half-drunk when he descended the exterior steps with Ikarus into the cellar, but he would have the impulse to move west, always west, for he came in a western doorway. And so Rush continues in straight lines, and when he meets a dead end, he turns west, always west. He is rewarded by the continued, if weakening, scent of myrrh and cherry blossom, and the faint, delicate odor of wine on the breath of an inexperienced pup.

Captain Nikolaos has found a doorway.

He did so by using his intellect. After the three guards fled him he stood up in the cramped and airless corridor and steadied his mind. Now and again his thoughts were interrupted by the heartbreaking sound of an injured animal, a keening whimper that seemed to pass through the stones separating him from its maker, and vibrate through his body. Then he would shake his head and clamp his hands over his ears, gritting his teeth against his own desire to tear at the walls with his nails. I will find you, Rah. I will find you again. You are safe. As long as I live you are safe.

Finally, after several minutes of agony, Captain Nikolaos realized that he was feeling the vibration of the sounds because they were indeed coming up from beneath him. He was feeling the sound in his feet.

"My god, there is another layer of passages!" and then, with horror, "Catacombs!"

The thought that the boy has somehow found the entryway to an even lower stratum of passages, a layer of chambers beneath the storage cellar, an area that could only be of use as a place of rest for the long dead, and that he is even now reliving the very horror of the entombment that Nikolaos had rescued him from in the first place, is almost more than Captain Nikolaos can bear. "What cruelty is this?" he shouts into the shadows.

"That such a light should twice be lost in such darkness? Are you lesser gods so filled with jealousy? Well, I will pull him out of hell as many times as you put him in it!"

Nikolaos pulls his sword, lifts his torch, and returns in the direction that he came. For there can be only one answer to this puzzle. A third layer of walls must hold up the second and the first, else they all crumble. A dead end here, then, is a dead end beneath. He is in a vault directly beneath my feet. If I return the way I came, I will find a passage that falls away downward, to the lower level. Then I must retrace my steps as if I am still here on the storage floor, back toward that dead end, and I will find him in the chamber beneath.

Rush has followed his senses to the archway of the catacombs beneath the palace. From here he can hear the sound he had been listening for since he rid himself of the guard. The keening yodel of a lost and very drunken kit, misery beyond measure in every note, strikes his ear like a cool breeze on a hot day. The dark he faces, the death he smells, is nothing to Rush, who is darkness and death incarnate. His face pulls at itself until he is grinning from ear to ear like a satisfied hound. Still he makes no effort to give away his position, but moves silent as the ghosts who inhabit these halls, toward that heartrending mewl.

"Not even here can you hide from me, little cat," says the assassin, as he ducks though the archway into the Hall of the Kings.

Rah has left the tomb behind him. Though his body continues to cry for comfort, his mind is now free.

In the pitiless darkness that seems to breathe against his ear, prodding him with curious and insistent fingers, he hears a sound and lifts his eyes. He does not understand that the sound he hears is his own whimper, echoing down the length of the stone walls that entomb him. Within the whimper he hears the voice of his sister at last, come to rescue him from his isolation once again.

Rah's body crouches in darkness. His arms are wrapped tightly about it, as if to hold back and stop the panicked mania of his racing heart. But his dream body is braver. It stands up. It looks about and sees that there is light in the chamber now. A light that seems to pulse from the end of the hall and steadily increases as it approaches him has illuminated the small stone tomb, and in the light he sees his sister, Iliah the little girl. Her scrawny body is covered only by the ragged dress they one day found in a heap of stinking garbage tossed to the pigs and meant for a child twice her age, Iliah, standing beneath the dome of the sepulcher within which Rah has run, and facing him. Her face is dirty, smeared with grime and tears. Her hair is long and matted, though beneath the filth the fine blonde strands are pale as corn silk. And eyes, they are his eyes, his eyes at last looking back at him from a human face and not a mirror.

"My brother, Ahalai. You must flee," says the little girl, and her mouth is moving. But the voice is the boom of a thunderclap, it shakes the room, it sends his dream body to its knees in fear. Now the room has begun to glow, brighter and brighter. The glow hurts his dream eyes. He must squint to see Iliah, who has begun to burn, like a torch, or like an ember exploding into flame, as if from the inside out.

"Don't leave me, Iliah!" screams Rah in his dream world, where his tongue is whole and strong, and he speaks in a language he has never spoken but has always understood, the language of his people.

But the dream girl has vanished. Only the thundering voice, which seems to emanate now from the stones above his head, responds.

"Come."

CHAPTER 43

Rush is half way down the passageway to the tomb of Heritas when Captain Nikolaos catches up to him.

"Sir!" barks Nikolaos, momentarily stunned that the dandy merchant, seeming to appear out of the thickened catacomb atmosphere, should have somehow found his way through these tunnels to the sound of the boy one level beneath, when he was only informed of his missing after the search had been going on for an hour.

Rush has heard a man advancing from behind him but only turns now to see him approach. He gives the Captain a quick inspection, sees the drawn sword, recognizes the desire of pursuit on another predator's face, and considers his options.

"You had better not approach Rah thus, Captain. He is deluded with panic and drink and could be dangerous," he says.

"Dangerous?" spits Nikolaos. "He is in unbearable distress, sir. He revisits the tomb I rescued him from. Let me pass!"

Nikolaos shoves himself past Rush, who allows him to do so with lifted eyebrows, and at last enters the tomb to find Rah huddled against the far wall, hugging himself and yowling in panic and grief.

"Rah! You are safe! I am here!" says Nikolaos, sheathing his sword and kneeling to comfort the boy. Rush has followed Nikolaos into the tiny chamber and now lifts his dampened torch to watch the scene. In the time it takes Rush to relieve the Captain of his torch Rah has spun himself about and snapped at the man's face, sinking his incisors into his chin before retreating with a warning snarl.

"Damn!" Nikolaos reaches for the wound, pushing the boy back into the wall with his free hand. He looks up at Rush with some amazement.

"You are bleeding, Captain," says Rush with satisfaction. "As I said, he is deluded with panic and drink and can be dangerous." He moves past

Nikolaos, who has stood up and backed away from the boy, and hands the Captain the torches as he does so. Then he gives Nikolaos his back and looks down at the whimpering blonde bundle with the ghost of a grin pulling on his lupine face.

"'Poor little cat has lost his way. But the devil will find him anyway,'" he murmurs, quoting the popular Minoan rhyme.

Nikolaos regards his back suspiciously.

"How do you intend to get him out of here, sir?" he says with some disdain.

Rush looks over his shoulder at the Captain, his lids at half mast. In the torchlight his eyes glint wickedly, slivers of polished black stone. He makes no effort to answer, but returns his attention to the boy huddled at his feet, deliberately obstructing Nikolaos' view with his shoulders. He reaches under his robe and quickly tears two lengths of linen from the roll at his waist, snatching them between his teeth before he attempts to lean over Rah.

In an instant he has seized Rah by a mass of curls at the back of his head. Rah has had time only to yelp once in surprise before Rush has gagged him with one of the strips of linen and put him to the ground on his face. Then, with one knee planted in his mid-back and crushing the wind out of his lungs, Rush ties Rah's arms together at the elbows behind him.

"This is inhuman!" blurts Nikolaos, stepping toward Rush to intercede. But Rush is already on his feet, dragging Rah up with him and shoving him toward the dark hole of the tunnel exit.

"How can you treat him that way? He is mad with fright already!" barks Nikolaos in Rush's ear as he follows him back up the tunnel toward the storage cellar.

"And how is it that you know your way through the King's labyrinth, and can have found your way down here into catacomb unknown even to the Palace Guard? Who are you, sir?" With this, Nikolaos has taken Rush by the shoulder and makes a noble attempt to spin him around to face him. He has done this many times, to many men, and being powerfully built himself, has never met an obstacle. It is a commanding move, one that sets the lesser man in his place right quick. But the shoulder he reaches for, which should be soft and fleshy with overindulgence, is instead like warmed marble under the prissy, pearl-embroidered robe that the dandy wears, and as unyielding as the stone walls of the corridor. Nikolaos steps back with an intake of breath, startled.

When Rush turns around to face him, it is of his own accord. He does so slowly, taking Rah by the elbows so as not to lose him again.

"Who do you think that I am, Nikolaos?" says Rush, allowing his Hittite vowels to yawn and stretch like lions getting up from a nap. And as his words wander heavily toward the Captain they seem to descend back down the corridor to the Hall of the Kings, down to the depths of the dead, deepening and darkening until, by the time he hears his own name, Nikolaos realizes he is facing the very man who carved the Tears on his cheek less than a fortnight ago.

"Dear gods!" Nikolaos chokes. "You are the assassin!"

"I am. And you are either the living and heroic Captain of the Palace Guard, Nikolaos, who has rescued the Grain God a second time in half a moon, or a dead fool, depending on the choices you make in the next moments, for I will take that poor excuse of a weapon you are so fond of and put it in the hole that is left when I cut out your heart. Then I will kick your arrogant buttocks back into the catacombs to rot, unless you can convince me you are of some value to me."

"I do not fear you, sir," says Nikolaos, standing back cautiously, his weapon drawn but lowered.

"That is your first mistake," says Rush. "You are making your grave with your tongue, Nicholoas. Can you do no better?" Rush has casually turned to lift Rah onto his shoulder and now makes a quick adjustment, his powerful muscles popping the boy's hips into the air briefly as he balances him there.

Nikolaos' eyes cannot help but wander from the assassin's face to the skirted rump of the Grain God, which now faces him. He swallows, teeth grit. His eye slides back to meet the assassin's.

"You will kill him," he says, fairly spitting his words.

At this Rush looks at Nikolaos with some concern for the first time. He peers at the Captain in the dark, rakes him with his eyes.

"And you think you will stop me?"

"I will stop you. For you cannot stop yourself, though you may wish to. You are a killer. That is all. That is your mission. What do you want with him?" Nikolaos tips his sword at the burden Rush carries, "Who has paid you to kill him? No one. You want him for yourself." Emboldened, Nikolaos takes a step toward the assassin until the two are eye to eye. "Why does Darkness pursue Light, Rush, except to extinguish it?"

"Perhaps Death is hungry," says Rush with vicious humor, "and wants a snack."

"You will kill him," repeats Nikolaos, his lips retracting with hatred. "You will kill him for that is what you do. Devour, destroy. You are a self-employed, self-interested pox, a blight, a cancer. You are hunger itself. Never satisfied. You think this boy will satisfy you? You are in hell with your hungers, Rush. Stay there. Leave the light to the living."

"Quite a soliloquy, for a man who likes to lop off heads for battle practice."

Nikolaos must open his eyes with surprise at this. "How do you know me, sir?"

"I make a point of knowing my enemies, Nikolaos of Thrace," says Rush, before turning to give the man and his sword his back once more and starting up the tunnel toward the storage level.

Nikolaos finds himself struck with confusion at the assassin's actions once more. But he quickly recovers and rushes after the retreating image of Rah's pale head flopping against the man's broad back. "You need me, Rush," he persists, quickly closing the distance between himself and the assassin.

Rush does not respond, but continues to trudge up the incline, until he has found the archway to the storage vaults.

"Ah, now south and west again," murmurs the assassin in Ameg's lilting tenor.

Frustrated, Nikolaos stops, then slams his sword into the stones, causing the tunnel to echo with its ring. "Why do you let me live, then?" he screams. "Don't you know I will have you arrested as soon as we reach the palace?"

At this, Rush turns his head over his free shoulder to give Nikolaos a contemptuous look, then eases Rah's body down from the other and sets him on the stone floor. The boy appears to be unconscious, and both men stare at him a moment before returning their attention to one another.

Now Rush turns to face Nikolaos and takes a single step toward him, forcing the Captain to retreat down the passageway himself.

"Then I will kill every last guard in Cyrus, and still I will take the boy. For nothing will stop me from removing him from this doomed island before the throat of the volcano that is Thera vomits forth her bile. And anyone left here will die in her poisons. I have seen it, Captain, when you were yet a babe suckling your mother's teat, I saw such a thing. Your island is doomed. Your city is doomed. Knossos is fleeing, even now, those who can. And my own ship awaits me in the harbor there. I have come to save the boy, Nikolaos, though you say I come to kill him. You are right to say I am death, I do not deny it. But I could not kill the Grain Dancer of Knossos, though Cyrus paid me to do it. And now the boy will perish nonetheless, except I rescue him myself. So death has come to be a savior. Dark to rescue light." Rush nods at the slumbering boy. "The one assigned to kill him, captured like a maiden in the golden threads of that pale head of his." He is fairly snarling now, the quiet rage in his voice is seeping into the walls and sucking up the air. Nikolaos is finding it hard to breath. He takes another step down the corridor, back toward the catacombs.

"You, rescue Rah?" he counters. "An assassin, sent to kill him? Do you really delude yourself thus? You let him be captured by Lutarus, tortured, abandoned in a tomb. I rescued him. You brought the priest, Ananou, with you here. For what? He admits he has plotted to kill Rah.

The boy tells us so himself. Did you not bring him here to satisfy his desire for the Grain God's head? Do you not do everything for your own gain, Rush? To pad you're already bursting purse? To satisfy your unbound greed and lust?"

From the stone floor Rah moans as if in agreement. Then he turns from his crumpled seat against the wall and falls on his hands, retching bile into the gag that is tied around his face like a tourniquet.

Nikolaos has cleared the distance between himself and the boy and, under Rush's shadow, drops to his knees and quickly cuts the cloth away, allowing Rah to vomit onto the floor.

He looks up at Rush with contempt. "You will kill him," he hisses at the dark mass above him. He cuts the linen strip that binds Rah's arms behind him and picks up the unconscious boy, holding him like a groom lifting his bride over a threshold.

Rush has set his torch down while Nikolaos is engaged with the boy. Now he stands erect, filling the only exit of escape from the catacombs with his mass. He opens his robe, and in one swift move removes the crescent blades holstered at his sides. His powerful chest glistens like wet bronze. Slivers of silver glint in his palms in the failing torchlight.

Nikolaos takes in the totality of the thing he faces. The man is like a bear rearing on two legs, its claws extended. He is a thing fit only for war, never meant for society, an impossible foe. Nikolaos looks down at the boy in his arms. He is unconscious again, blissfully unaware of the battle that is taking place above his head, his blonde mop of curls lolling over Nikolaos' arm.

Nikolaos stands his ground. He peers through the gloom at Rush with sharp, intelligent eyes.

"Take me with you," he says.

The assassin lifts his head, then pulls his lips back into something that is half a snarl, half a grin. A moment passes as the men regard one another, their torches dimming.

"Take me with you," Nikolaos says again. "I will lay my life down for him, you see that I will. Let us join forces."

Rush shakes his head slowly. "You are not what I expected, Captain. You are far more foolhardy and annoying. I fear you are a thing that, if not cut down now, before you gain experience and strength, will chase and snap at my heels forever." His eyes drop to skim the body of the sleeping Grain God. His face seems to soften as he does so, his massive chest expelling a dull grunt.

"Why did you bring the priest?" continues Nikolaos, accusing.

Rush lifts his eyes back to the Captain's. After a moment he slips the twin blades back into the holsters strapped at his sides.

"You know I speak the truth, Rush," Nikolaos continues, encouraged.

"You will ravage him. You will rape him. You will consume him. You will take and take and look for more. You will crush the spirit that is Rah from his bones. You will chase his very innocence from his soul. And then the thing you love will no longer be the thing you loved, but only a shell, a broken pottery shard, a wickless lamp."

Rush makes a little chuckle. "'Then you must learn to live in darkness,'" he repeats to himself, recalling Ting Ya's warning.

"You need me, Rush. You cannot keep him safe without me. You are his greatest danger. You will kill him. You know it."

"You weary me, Captain. But you are brave to the point of comedy. And when your ears are dry, you may make a decent commander. Very well. You already wear my mark. I will take you with me. But know this. I will cut you down like so much straw, be it here in the labyrinth or above," he nods toward the ceiling, "where you believe yourself to be safe amongst those rabbits you call guards, if you attempt my arrest." He steps forward, and this time Nikolaos retreats involuntarily. "I will fill your palace with blood, Captain," he says, leaning into the man's face until their breath mingles. "And then I will drown you in it."

"You have my word. Give me yours then. That you will take me with you when the time comes."

"You trust the honor of an assassin?" laughs Rush, whipping Rah from Nikolaos' grasp so swiftly that the Captain can only stand with arms extended as if still holding him while the assassin tosses the boy over his shoulder again.

"I have had this cat's claws in my back on one earlier occasion," he says, turning his back on Nikolaos. "If he wakes unbound before we reach his bed, and I must defend myself, let the outcome be on your head."

"He is passed out with exhaustion and drink and will not wake 'til morning," answers Captain Nikolaos with less confidence than before. Then he picks up the torches Rush has left behind and follows the man and his prize back through the labyrinth of storage rooms to the surface.

CHAPTER 44

At her window in the little room she has been assigned, at the end of the guest suite hall, Cara is singing a soft lullaby to an owl. The bird has visited for the second time in two nights, and she is convinced of its significance as an omen.

Last night the significance seemed obvious. Do not be a fool, Cara. A man like this comes past once in a woman's life, like a comet that illuminates the night with such sudden supremacy that one expects it to take up residence, a new heavenly body come to escort the moon across the friendless heavens. But as quickly as it appears, it is gone, following its own lonely trek through space to some destination far beyond her range, and leaving the goddess to wander in even greater darkness because she once enjoyed his momentary brilliance.

And so she made her decision and went to him. And like a fool she threw herself at him to be used like a whore. How ironic, that I should become a whore only after I am rescued from the whorehouse, she thinks. And all because of you, little bird.

But no, that was not the truth. She would have gone to him just as she had whether or not she had awakened to the reproving eyes of the owl. She would have gone with just as much determination if a great black buzzard had been sitting on her casement ledge and, speaking with a human tongue, had told her in no uncertain terms to flee the monster who lay beautiful and naked in the room down the hall, his blades forever strapped to his sides, even while he slept. Even while he copulated.

Then this morning she learned that Ameg could not be won because a boy, the one they called the Grain God, had won him first. She wanted to kill Ameg then, to take his own weapons from him and slice that magnificent chest open and cut that merciless and worthless muscle, his heart, into strips, leaving it on the window sill like so many mice for the owl to feast upon. Until she saw the thing that owned it. Laid eyes upon the boy. Rah.

And she understood. She understood everything. Why she was taken in the first place, why she was rescued. Why she was here in Cyrus. And why Ameg was in love with the Grain God. For the boy was like love itself, light as air, bright as morning, free like a wild animal is free, to the point of madness. Otherworldly grace, fleeting as the deathbed heartbeat of a loved one, beautiful unto sadness. But most of all fleeting. Fleeting. Like childhood, forever gone, forever longed for. Once ours. Our first love is ourselves. The child we were. He is that child.

And so she sings to the owl, sings an old lullaby she learned in Thrace a thousand summers away, and thinks of the boy, and of how love is like the boy, a piece of the sun's fire, the most powerful of all emotions, yet the most fleeting and weak. She sings her lullaby, until the sound of a commotion coming down the hall abbreviates her song.

Then she stops, listens, hears nothing but the sound of shuffling feet, a door open and closed. Too many feet. She is an expert in the world of sounds. Two strong men. And silence.

Cara continues her lullaby, moving to the window as the owl flaps off, and lifting her lovely voice to the moon to soothe the goddess in her abandoned night sky. And her voice carries in the soft late-summer air, and reaches the sleeping ear of the Grain God.

Rah does indeed awake as his rescuers reach the interior stairs leading up to the kitchens. Perhaps the softer, lighter air, wafting in from the open first floor windows has roused him, or perhaps it is the embrace of the moonlight as the Goddess sees her son returned to her from the crypts beneath the palace. But upon his second step up the stairway, Rush is reminded why he gagged and bound the boy in the first place. He grits his jaw and grunts against the pain as Rah's teeth sink into the bunched muscle of his mid-back. With a single curse he drops him from his shoulder, then puts him against the stairwell wall with a shake. Before the boy can claw his arms he turns him around, pins his wrists together and fastens them with another strip of cloth from his 'paunch'. Taking hold of this, he turns to Nikolaos with a deadly look.

Nikolaos can only shrug. "Now it is you who are bleeding, sir," he says, fighting a grin. "I fear he has torn your dress."

Rush nods. "I owe you the same, Nikolaos," he says, which takes the Captain's cheer.

"Would you have preferred he choke in his own vomit?" Nikolaos counters, then nods to the stairs above. "Let us put him to bed. At least his inverted ride on your back has assured us he is done and will not drown himself in his sleep when he reaches it."

Rush turns to Rah, who is watching this exchange with drunken eyes. Still holding him by his trussed wrists, Rush takes the boy's chin, leaning at him. "You bite me again, little cat and I will ruin your pretty dimples, you understand?" He gives the boy's jaw a shake, and with a softer tone he adds, "Then I will eat you."

Rah's eyes widen. He nods fervently, though Rush still has his jaw. "No bite," he says through his teeth, "Isha nahhan."

Rush nods. "Isha nahhan." He lifts the boy unceremoniously back onto his shoulder and starts back up the stairs.

When they reach the chamber prepared for the boy, Rush drops him onto the bed and unfastens his wrists. Then he turns to Nikolaos.

"Your services are no longer required, Captain," he says with one sharp brow lifted.

Nikolaos looks at Rah, who is examining the chains hanging from the freshly mortared bolts in the wall.

"Oh, but they are," he says. "And I intend to stay close to both you and the boy for as long as it takes to extract him from you."

"That you will never do, Nikolaos," answers Rush with a frustrated glower. But he moves to the door. "I must see to this wound, at any rate," he says, "as you should yours." Then he leaves the Captain with the boy.

Alone with Rah, Nikolaos takes a moment to observe the boy. Rah is awake and alert to his relief, but overly fascinated with the gold chains, which he is attempting without success to fasten to his own collar and belt.

"You need the key for that, Rah. And I've no intention of chaining you to a wall tonight. You are liable to strangle yourself or some other such nonsense. Now go on, lie down. Let me see that you are sleeping and I will leave you."

Rah turns now to the voice that is addressing him. His eyes are wide and innocent, the effects of the wine still there, but less evident.

"Sing," he says. He taps his ear. "No you hear? Sing." He points to the window, through which a soft Aegean breeze, pregnant with the smells of summer's end, wafts in. It lifts the curls at the boy's temple.

But Nikolaos hears nothing. Only the light tread of the assassin returning to his own room next door, having apparently cleansed his wound in the bath font at the end of the hall.

"She sing-" says Rah, getting up to walk to the window. He'll be out of it in a heartbeat, thinks Nikolaos, catching Rah by one arm.

"No," he says, even now unable to be harsh. "Bed, Rah."

Rah looks up at him, his strange eyes near black as his cat-like irises attempt to gather the dim moonlight. For once they are without suspicion or anger as he regards the Captain.

"Rah know this-" he says, making a cradle of his arms and rocking an invisible babe. "You say how?" he asks with earnest.

"Lullaby, Rah? Do you hear a lullaby? Perhaps a serving maid in a room below is trying to put her child to sleep tonight, as I am you. I do not hear it."

"Lull-a-by," repeats Rah, nodding his head for emphasis on each syllable. He looks up at the Captain for approval.

But Nikolaos can only stand, looking at him foolishly, fighting a heat that tastes somehow like grief gathering in his throat. "Were you always a slave, Rah?" he asks softly, releasing the boy's arm.

Rah nods vigorously. "Always," he says. Then, looking to the window, "Always, but" points to the window, "this lulla-by I know."

This puts a fist in Nikolaos' chests like a blow from an unsuspected enemy. He swallows the heat that has closed his throat. "To bed, then," he says, turning Rah by the shoulder and pointing to his bed. "Let her sing you to sleep." This time Rah obeys, jumping onto the plush feather mattress and curling himself into a ball against the wall. When he is still, Nikolaos leaves him, leaving the door open a few inches, and his own, next door, wide.

Having heard that his Sun God, incarnation of the Morning itself, has been lost in the labyrinth beneath the palace, Ananou has been in his room praying at his makeshift altar at the end of his bed. Upon hearing the men return with the boy, for it is obvious from their conversation that they have him, he now waits, his ear to the door, for stillness.

When all is hush, he carefully opens the door, and without his staff, hobbles across the hall to Rah's room.

Rah has rolled away from the wall and stretched himself out on his stomach. His face is pressed against the mattress, his mouth open, his tongue resting between his teeth. He is snoring lightly. There is sufficient moonlight to illuminate his pale green cheeks and to turn his lashes silver. The stubborn blue line of face paint still runs along his lower lids to his temples, emphasizing his feline features. Ananou's eye is captured by the picture of his sleeping god. Here is the morning before daybreak, he thinks. He allows his gaze to travel along the perfect architecture of Rah's elegant back to his nipped waist, and to the pretty dip and dimples just at the turn of his buttocks.

Ananou moves closer to the sleeping boy, forgets himself, leans, like a younger man, to steal a closer look at the superb perfection of his deity at rest.

And loses his balance.

And in his slow motion descent toward that sleeping morning that is Rah at rest, which seems to last a lifetime, he feels the sudden the dizzyingly intimate caress of a strong male arm come round his body, the full mastery of a dominant lover's desire encircling his breast, and the sweet breath of a young man in his ear.

"You old bastard," snarls Nikolaos through bared teeth as he drives his short Grecian sword into the priest's back, slicing his spleen, his liver and his heart in twain as he thrusts the blade up with all of the force of his father's frustrated rage.

The old man grunts, his last expression one of satisfaction, and crumples to the floor at Nikolaos' feet.

Nikolaos replaces his blade in its sheath and looks to Rah, who has fairly somersaulted off the bed and stands beside it, staring at the body of the priest on the floor. He looks from the body to Nikolaos to the body, blinking with confusion.

"It's all right, Rah. He's dead. Good and dead. He'll never get another chance to harm you," says Nikolaos, kicking the corpse for good measure.

From the doorway comes the heavy chuckle of the assassin, followed by two soft claps.

"Well, well, that blade is good for something after all," says Rush. "Skewering an old goat."

"Once again, I was here to rescue Rah when you were not, sir," says Nikolaos, giving Rush a bitter look and moving to pick up the corpse.

"And what do you intend to do with that, Captain? Put it back to bed? Even in Cyrus, murdering a priest is a high crime," hisses the assassin as he enters the room and shuts the door quietly behind him.

"He was intent on harming Rah, and you well know it," answers Nikolaos, looking about the body for some place of purchase that is unbloodied.

"Perhaps, but there will still be a trial. One you may well lose, Nikolaos." Rush shoulders past him and takes the corpse by the head, careful to keep it face down. "This is a job for an assassin," he winks at Nikolaos as he pulls the body, head first, to the window, then rips one of the sleeping gown sleeves from an arm and wraps it about the man's face.

"I think it too late for him to cry for help," says Nikolaos, with bland sarcasm.

"They bleed from the mouth, pup, when they've been butchered within as you, in your incompetence, have done." He picks up the corpse and heaves it out of the open window.

"What the hell are you doing with him!" spits Nikolaos in a whisper and rushes to the window to see where the corpse has landed, with a dull thud, on the parapet.

"Cleaning up your mess, Captain," says Rush. "When I am through with him, it will be obvious that the assassin has struck again here in Cyrus, and your bloated head will remain where it is."

"Why?" spits Nikolaos, grabbing Rush by the arm without much effect as the assassin leans out the window, clearly intent upon following the corpse. "Now is your chance to be rid of me, and yet you save me instead?"

"Perhaps I save you for myself, Captain," winks Rush, with a devilish smile.

"If I was a dishonorable man, I would blame it on you! Have you arrested upon your return."

"We have already discussed the consequences of such action," says Rush, disappearing out of the window and landing, somehow soundlessly, below. He is already invisible to Nikolaos, who searches the lower wall for his enemy without success. When he turns from the aperture he sees that Rah has come to stand beside him and is also scanning the dark for the assassin. After a moment he looks up at Nikolaos.

"This priest, he send men to kill Rah," he says. He is looking at Nikolaos peacefully, his face open and trusting. "Fox kill priest. Fox kill priest for Rah." He gives Nikolaos a lopsided grin.

"Yes, Rah, and I will kill a dozen more to protect you," says Nikolaos, a bit stunned and made timid now that the gold in Rah's eyes has opened to him. He stares into the approving gaze of the Grain God, and finds himself made helpless by it.

"Hah!" says Rah, clapping the Captain's arm and breaking the spell. "Like wolf, he kill for Rah," he shakes his head, frowns. "Now wolf take Rah across water. Ting Ya tell Rah this. This night, down there, down," he points to the floor emphatically, "bad place. Voice come to Rah. Come to lift Rah. Rah fly to House of Moon. See everyone go! Go across sea. Two ship stay. My horse on ship, too! This wolf, he own my horse now! Rah go with him, across sea," he nods, determined. "Rah go," he says, turning from Nikolaos and the window to find his bed in the dark. "Maybe wolf not bite Rah. Now Rah sleep. No more priest. No more wolf tonight."

Puzzled, the captain squints after Rah, frowning. And his own stomach grumbles, as if indicting him, as he makes his way in the dark back to his own room.

In the morning, the palace is in an uproar. The body of the visiting priest from Knossos is found hanging, inverted, from the arm of the Sea Goddess in the small guest courtyard. The mark of the assassin has been carved on his left cheek, and his head has been cut nearly off, and remains attached to his corpse only by the spinal column. The pool beneath the statue of the goddess is blood red, for the corpse has had the night to drain into it. The man is naked, and his member has been severed and returned to him in the most unlikely of his orifices. It seems the assassin had a statement to make about this particular priest and perhaps about his practices. At any rate, it is quite clear who claimed the life of the honored guest, and no further questions are asked. The King especially is determined to make light of the incident. The priest, after all, was a visitor from a rival city, a city that is even now dismantling its government and fleeing the island. It is unlikely that anyone left there cares about old Ananou, the High Priest of the Sun.

As for the three servants who accompanied him to Cyrus, they are sent back to Knossos with the corpse in an ass-drawn cart after the sun has gone down and it is appropriate to move the body of a priest.

Queen Media has called Nikolaos to her chamber to discuss the issue of Ameg further, for the man has made no effort to explain why the assassin, whom her husband has informed her is his 'kin' and sold the boy to him, might have a continued interest in Rah to the extent that he seems to be determined to continue to kill on his behalf.

"Who is this man, Nikolaos? He claims to own the boy, when it is clear that the assassin has the greater interest in him. I fear him. And I cannot bear the thought of losing Rah."

"He believes that the island is lost, Madam, that we are doomed fools to remain here when the royalty in the cities to the north are fleeing." Nikolaos gives the Queen a pained look, walks to her chamber window and looks out toward the mountains. "He is a merchant and a sailor, at one time a military man." He speaks carefully, pacing his words. He drops his gaze, looks down at his fingers splayed against the window ledge, long and grasping. "I believe him."

Media looks at his back, broad and honest, from her perch on the end of her bed where one of her ladies buffs her nails while another arranges her hair. Nikolaos' handsome profile is outlined by midday sunlight, carving a curious memory in her mind forever.

"But the mountains," she murmurs, waving her attendants away. They look at each other worriedly and scurry out of the room

Nikolaos turns, faces her. I will save Rah, thinks the Captain, but it is to you, my Queen, that I owe my first allegiance. I must also save you. I am an honorable man.

"The mountains may save us from a wave, my Queen, but not from the poisonous breath of a volcano the size and strength of Thera. Cyrus is no more."

"But where could we go, Nikolaos? Are we to flee our city and leave the people behind to perish?"

"What good will it do the people of the City of Cyrus for you to stay and die with them? Better the line of the Queen should remain intact. Better you should flee, and when the island becomes habitable again, return to reestablish your reign."

"A queen belongs with her people, Captain," says Media, standing up and walking to the window to stand beside Nikolaos and gaze at the mountains, whose strength she no longer believes in.

"And with the bones of her mothers." She looks up at the Captain. "You must go. If he takes Rah from us, then you must go and protect the boy." She gives him a weak smile. "That is an order, Captain."

"Madam, my first allegiance is with you," says Nikolaos nobly, if not with sincerity.

Media laughs at that. "Nonsense, Nikolaos, you have been devoted to Rah since you first lay eyes upon him. There is no point pretending. I am not one to trust pretty words. It is your heart I trust, Captain, for I know it is bound to the boy. You will keep him safe or die trying. And you are a clever man. I think you will figure out how not to die trying."

Ameg is missing for most of the morning. When he returns he finds his 'wife' in her chamber at the end of the guest wing hall, and advises her to be ready to meet the cart hired to transport the servants of the House of the Sun back to Knossos. She will take their 'daughter', and await him on the ship that stands ready in the harbor for his return.

"But you promised Marta you would return her to her father, Ameg," says Cara, and immediately regrets her hasty words. The only response she receives is a raised eyebrow from Rush, and then the expanse of his broad back as he turns to leave her.

"Of course, I will have her ready," she adds quickly. This earns her another look, one more disturbing even than his dismissal of her.

"Woman, you are yet to be sold. I am no redeemer. You are a commodity, as is the child. When we reach Anatolia, for that is where we are headed, you will be auctioned off for a soldier's wife, the child a servant to the priest of the House of the Moon. Do not delude yourself. I do nothing unless there is profit involved. You and the girl are more use to me alive in Anatolia than you would be if you were to remain here on Crete to cook in the ash of the volcano."

With that he turns his back on her a second time and lays his hand on the door. Stunned, she is silenced a moment and makes no answer. But she is a creature of sound, she cannot keep her voice at rest. The words are out and damning before she can harness her throat to control them.

"Would that you felt for me what you feel for the boy, Rah."

When he turns to her again he is not the Ameg she has become accustomed to here at the palace of Cyrus. He is the man who stepped out of the brothel and ordered her to fetch a man's head in a sack. She backs up involuntarily until she is fairly sitting on the window ledge of her little room, just as the owl did. Would I were as wise as you, little bird, she thinks, and could keep this voice of mine still. "I meant only," she begins, but he is already across the room, breathing in her face, and she is leaning precariously and helplessly out the window to avoid his words.

"That is the last thing you should wish, woman," he says, then takes her face in his hand roughly. "Do not want me."

She can only stare into those viciously hungry obsidian eyes of his and swallow. And then he has released her and he is gone and she is sitting on the ledge staring at the open door like a pigeon.

"I can want nothing else," she murmurs to herself, smoothing her dress and taking a breath. "Now that I have discovered you."

CHAPTER 45

At sundown the body of Ananou, along with his three attendants, Cara and Marta, leave the palace to cross the mountains and return to Knossos. The mood at the palace is somber, and in respect for the dead priest, there has been no dance practice. Rah has spent the day in the arena playing with the chariot horses. A chariot is a new invention for Rah, who, until he came to Cyrus, had never seen a horse used to pull a cart. But in the past few weeks he has transferred his skill with the long rein to the chariot, and is soon delighting the horsemen of the Guard with his uncanny abilities and his obvious potential as a charioteer.

But in the late afternoon Rah's games of horsemanship are interrupted by a shuddering of the earth beneath the palace. The horse he has been handling spooks suddenly and he is tossed from the bucket of the chariot. He has never experienced a quake, and panics like any cat might. His instinct is to hide, and despite his experience in the labyrinth his first impulse is to scramble to a low place. When the rumbling subsides, Rah is missing, and once again, Ameg is informed and a party of guards is dispatched to search the palace.

But this time it is not difficult to find him, and Rush comes upon him first, without the interruption and interference of Nikolaos.

Rah has found his way to the little room behind the wine cellar which, despite the tremor, has remained remarkably undamaged. Still fearful and confused when the trembling world steadies, he remains where he is, unsure of the way out and no longer trusting his instincts to take him to the surface. When Rush appears in the doorway it is near dusk, but the master's massive silhouette is unmistakable.

Rush finds Rah standing in front of the painted wall in the last rectangle of dying light coming through the aperture parallel to the outer windows. In it he is pure organic gold, standing out in living beauty against the bright blue and green background of the wall.

Rush stands quietly a moment, fearing he will spook the boy and even now, though he fills the doorway, may lose him again in the labyrinth.

"Time to travel, little cat," he says in his softest voice. "Cyrus is dying, as is Crete herself. It is the end of the reign of the Minoan Queens. Thera will flatten them and when she is done, and her poisoned breath will be blown out to sea, I will return and with no opposition will possess her, just as I now possess you."

Rah is listening to his master with lowered eyes. He has made no move to retreat further away nor to approach and obediently follow him out of the basement.

Rush shakes his head slowly, incredulous. "Still wild you are," he murmurs, then lets his eyes drift over the boy's head at the pornographic wall behind him. He allows them wander a moment, taking in the scene.

Rah watches his master's face as he peruses the mural behind him. When the assassin's eyes return to him, there is heat in them. Rah looks over his shoulder at the painting, then steps away from the wall as if to dissociate himself from it. Unable to meet his master's intense stare, he grits his teeth against the warbling growl rising in his throat, which he is helpless to curtail.

Rush smiles, a sharks smile, and steps toward the boy.

"A convenient hiding place for me to find you, little cat," he says, quickly closing the distance between them and putting Rah against a wall. The boy flinches in his grip, but keeps his eyes down, down and to the left, and seems to choke on the burring in his own throat.

"I won't hurt you, Rah," whispers Rush against the boy's ear. But his grip is fierce.

"You will kill him," says Nikolaos from the doorway.

Rush turns his head only, lids at half mast. "I should have killed you in the catacombs, Nikolaos," he grumbles.

"You can kill me any time you like. But you will lose the thing you most desire if you do."

"And what is that, Captain?" muses Rush as he strokes Rah's belly with the backs of his fingers absently. "How I love that trembling, pup," he murmurs in Rah's curls as if only mildly diverted by the interruption.

"His innocence. His purity. His godhood," says Nikolaos, slipping his sword back into its sheath.

Rush lets go a bothered sigh, long and deep. He turns back to Rah, chucks his chin, so that the boy's eyes flick up at his briefly.

"Is that it, then?" says Rush, less kindly. "Am I to be tortured by you until I take you, break you to my liking, and then frustrated by my own satisfaction? Tell me, little cat, is that our destiny?"

But Rah can only clench his jaw against the noises in his throat that earned him a blow once from the assassin, against the teeth that wish again to snap. He squeezes his eyes shut, his core shuddering under the assassin's fingers.

"You will make your own destiny," says Nikolaos. "Do not blame him for what he is, nor for what you are." He has crossed the room to come to stand beside Rush, who narrows his eyes at him but makes no effort to release Rah.

"You tell me nothing I do not know," says Rush, as if bored with the intrusion. He is stroking Rah's belly again with the backs of his fingers, like a gentleman strokes his housecat. His fingertips come upon the gold belt permanently welded around Rah's waist and he slips them under, recalling his first encounter with the boy. He takes the collar in the same fashion, then rests his hand on Rah's shoulder and brings his mouth down on the side of his neck, setting his teeth against it, licking the scent of myrrh and cherry blossom into his mouth.

He grunts a satisfied grunt.

Nikolaos has put his own hand on Rush's shoulder. It is not an aggressive move, but a comforting one. In it is sympathy, even compassion.

Rush lifts his head, slides his eye back to regard Nikolaos.

"You want him as much as I do, Nikolaos. How do you live with it?"

"By reminding myself that his is an ethereal beauty, born of purity. That without that purity he is no longer Rah. Then I have nothing."

The two men regard one another silently. They are at close quarters, for once, without war in their eyes.

"Let us take him safely out of Cyrus, to your ship in the harbor at Knossos, out of reach of the volcano," says Nikolaos.

"On foot is safest now," responds Rush tiredly, at last releasing his grip on Rah's arm. "The quakes will come faster. It will seem the earth is in labor, but the child to be born is a monster made of fire and ash and darkness."

"How long, Rush? How long do we have?" swallows Nikolaos, for once allowing his face to soften with the fears of a twenty two year old.

Now it is the assassin's turn to rest a strong hand on the captain's shoulder. He presses his fingers into Nikolaos' flesh until the man's arm begins to numb.

"One never has enough time, Captain. There is never enough time for a soldier to avoid the lethal blow, and yet he does. Time stands still then, seconds are hours. There is never enough time for the commander of a battalion to move his men's hearts to embrace the fever of war, to push them beyond the limits of endurance and attack his enemy's flank, and yet he will. This is no different. This dragon will not defeat me, but I will ride its breath of fire, I will use its force for my own purpose. This is a horse of great speed, but only one man can ride it, and that man can have no fear. Do not show me fear again, Nikolaos, else I will leave you here to cook in Thera's breath and fertilize the fields I will plant when I return to take Crete."

"Sir," says Nikolaos, pulling himself to attention and snapping Rush a short, military bow.

"I will not travel with extra baggage, Captain. See that you leave yours behind, or else stay behind yourself."

"I have the permission of the Queen to accompany you, to see to the boy's safety. I will have provisions for travel readied in half an hour and await you with the boy in the Palace Guard barracks."

"You will not. You will meet me at the Tomb of Lutarus when the moon makes her appearance in her heaven. I will take the boy myself."

With that, Rush takes Rah's face in his hand and gives him a shake. "You try to run from me, little cat, and I will break your legs and carry you, you understand?"

"No run," says Rah. "No bite."

"No run, no bite. See that your little monkey mind does not forget it," says Rush, stroking a broad thumb across the boy's lips and again recollecting his first encounter with this creature. I would be in my homeland by now, he thinks, awaiting the boom that will surely be heard and felt even to the eastern coastline of Anatolia, but for you.

Not long after, Cara, Marta and the three servants of the House of the Sun settle themselves in a small ass-drawn cart to begin their journey to Knossos. They will take the main road, which cuts through the hills and around Mount Ida before it descends to the shoreline on the north side of the island. They are unaware that squalls are even now overturning shipping vessels only a few miles from the harbor, and that massive rainstorms have darkened the heavens over the Aegean and are headed to Crete, storms that will create mudslides in the mountains and use the very route they take, to gather earth and rock and to crash down the southern slopes of Ida, filling the tombs in the cemetery where only a few short weeks earlier Rah lay bound and sick during his ordeal in the hands of Lutarus' men. The muddy waters will lift the bodies and bones of the dead from their resting places and carry them in the flood tide down the hill to their families in Cyrus and will deposit them in the city in time for them to be reburied in the rubble from a second quake.

In Knossos, the House of the Moon has been waiting in the harbor aboard Ameg's personal ship, which returned for him a day earlier. But having seen the storm clouds approaching from the northwest, the captain makes the decision to tie the skiff that carried Rush back to the island to the Queen's ship and leave without him, believing he is giving both the House of the Moon and Ameg the best chance of outrunning the weather. The Queen's ship remains in the harbor. It is sleek and fast. The horses are loaded and bedded down in the hold, and only Ameg's hell dogs remain on shore, kept in the merchant's storehouse at the dock. The man who has been caring for them is unwilling to risk his throat to move them to the vessel, and at any rate, could not control them once they were aboard. He leaves with the House of the Moon, leaving Ramicus and his men to deal with the dogs and to stay behind for Ameg.

When the moon is at her apex, Nikolaos, carrying a sack of provisions for a hike he expects to take the better part of two days, enters the cemetery of Cyrus through the south gate. The sky is clear and oddly still. A strange golden sheen illuminates the clouds that streak the southern horizon, above which the moon, which is at the full, seems to watch the earth with blameless serenity. There is no sound, not even the rustle of leaves. No owl punctuates the stillness with its shriek. A cold fingertip traces Nikolaos' spine and puts the hair up at the back of his neck. For a moment, he believes he has been tricked by the assassin. What a fool I am to have believed him, he thinks. He has taken the boy and deserted me. Now I must head straight to the harbor of Knossos to intercept him.

But presently a whistle breaks the silence of the graves.

Across a clearing he sees a silhouette emerge from behind a tomb. Then another. At first it appears that Rah has taken a liking to his master and chooses willingly to keep within a few feet of him. But as the assassin steps forward into the moonlight, Nikolaos sees the glimmer of a golden line connecting Rush to Rah.

It is the first time Nikolaos has seen Rush in the black muslin wrap of his primary profession since the man carved the Tears of the Bull in his cheek a fortnight earlier and at first he is sickened by the apparition. In the full moon's light he can see it is not what it appears, not a single strip of muslin wrapped round and round, but a cleverly sewn and tightly fitted costume composed of a tunic, a legging and a hood, all made of many strips of cloth sewn together at the horizontal. This is the man I choose to follow? he thinks to himself. This is the man I would take orders from, accept as my superior? This is the man who will save Rah, and myself, from the cataclysm that is to come? He moves forward into the clearing, but keeps a distance of several yards from the beast.

The assassin's low, rumbling chuckle breaks the spell, but adds to his ugliness.

"Why dress thus, sir," says Nikolaos, his hand on the hilt of his sword.

"Doom begets doom, Captain," is all the answer he will get before the man turns, picks up his own sack, and makes toward the north eastern wall of the cemetery with Rah in tow.

"That golden chain will do nothing to secure the boy to you should there be an emergency," cautions Nikolaos, following.

"That is the point of it, Captain," says Rush, turning to address Nikolaos directly.

"Is it not the same jewelry they used to chain him at night?" frowns Nikolaos.

"The very same. And so we are bound together, my little cat and I, by the threads of his father, through this perilous night that is the first night of labor for Thera."

When he reaches the wall he tugs playfully on the chain to catch Rah's attention. Then he nods at the obstacle. "You must keep up with me, little cat, or I will drag you by your belly." With that he is up and over the six foot obstacle like a panther. But Rah has beaten him to the opposite side, and Nikolaos can hear his feather-light landing just ahead of the heavy thud of the assassin's. He quickly scales the wall himself and catches up with the pair as they follow the same path Rush took with his hell dogs when he descended Mount Ida toward Cyrus in search of Rah.

"You are quite in your element, sir," pants Nikolaos after several hours of exertion, for Rush has maintained the pace of an advancing army up the side of the mountain. "Can we not take a short rest? It is midnight or better. I am sure that the boy must be fatigued."

As if to make a fool of him, Rah has turned round to cock his head at the yipping of a vixen somewhere to the east. His face is alert and serene and he is breathing as if at rest. It is as if he, too, is in his element, even tethered as he is to the muslin-wrapped and heavily armed assassin.

"He has the stamina of a wildcat, Captain. It is you who are fatigued. Too much easy living as a palace guard, eh?" quips Rush, but he slows his pace by half.

Another hour up the slopes of Ida brings the threesome to the altar where the first two Grain Gods were sacrificed. There is a cave nearby, one used by the priests to prepare the victim. As if sensing its purpose, Rah has slowed to a halt when he sees the altar. Rush turns to see the boy lift his eyes to him worriedly and then take a step back.

Nikolaos has come up behind Rah.

"What is this place?" he asks the assassin with an apprehensive crease between his brows.

"You can feel it, can you not?" says Rush in something near a whisper. "It is a place of human sacrifice. It is where the priest Mochlos took the lives of the two earlier Grain Gods and where he intended to complete the life cycle of this one."

Nikolaos' eyes have opened at this, for he understands the man's meaning well enough. He looks to Rah, but the boy only gazes innocently at his master, forgetting, for once, the slave's creed to refrain from the appearance of a challenge with raised eyes.

"The place is evil. Why do we stop here? I can fairly hear the ghosts of those two innocents crying for mercy still. Let us move on," says Nikolaos. But Rush has already strode toward the cave and now enters it, giving Rah's golden leash a little tug when he hesitates at the entrance. "The mouth faces south and down the mountain. We are safe here for the night, though a storm is coming. We will take a few hours rest, then make our way down the other side to the harbor in the morning."

Rush has found a smooth place near the entry to lay down a soldier's leather big enough for both he and Rah to sleep on. He tugs the chain once more and Rah steps toward him obediently.

"It will grow cold, little cat, and you will be glad of my warmth tonight," he says gently. Nikolaos has laid down his own leather on the opposite side of the opening. Now he steps out of the aperture to find kindling for a fire.

"I will set snares," he calls to the assassin when he has made a fire outside the cave. "We will have grouse for breakfast."

"He will eat provisions and be glad of it," mumbles Rush from the mouth of the cave but Nikolaos is already gone. "The grouse have more sense than that arrogant puppy, and will stay bedded down until the storm has passed," he adds to himself, but Rah is watching him with big, scared eyes.

"What is it, little cat?" grumbles the assassin, looking more like a mummified gargoyle than ever with his weapons strapped across his chest and at his ankles glinting in the firelight. He has settled himself on the soldier's leather, using his sack as a pillow, and now pats the space he has left for Rah beside him, gesturing for the boy to lay down.

"Wolf no bite," chuckles Rush, mimicking Rah. "Not tonight, anyway." But Rah is whining now with agitation. He sniffs the air, looks about him as if for some higher purchase. He tightens the golden leash, retreating toward the back of the cave.

"You feel it too, don't you. The storm. Or is it the next quake you sense? Well, we are as safe as we can be right here. Now mind me and come and get some rest before I resort to knocking you out, eh?" He tugs the chain once more, and Rah reluctantly complies. He sits gingerly on a corner of the leather against the wall of the cave, pulls in his legs and wraps his arms around his knees.

After a moment Rush realizes he intends to sleep this way, as he did the night he found him in his barn, nodding against a bale of hay beside the pony at his compound in Knossos. He frowns, then nods smugly. It will grow cold, he thinks. You will be huddled against me for warmth. But he pulls a sheepskin from his sack and tosses it at Rah, who is quick to catch it and pull it over his shoulders before resuming his upright nap.

Rush is awake when Nikolaos returns half an hour later and settles himself on the opposite side of the cave opening.

"Waste of time, setting snares," he tells the Captain. "There will be a storm coming. Can you not hear it in the silence?"

"It is unduly quiet," agrees Nikolaos softly. Like Rah, he is sitting up, his back against the opposite wall, with a soldier's wool pulled over his shoulders.

"You will get a better rest on your side, Captain," Rush hisses after a moment. In the dying firelight he is almost invisible now.

"Perhaps, but I am accustomed to sleeping in this position when I am in the field," answers the Captain. He adjusts his wool, shivering as a cool breeze enters the cave and causes it to billow off his shoulders. "In case of attack," he adds, pompously.

This Rush makes no response to, but only turns onto his side, so that he faces the cave entrance, and punches the sack he is using for a pillow, intent on making a high enough bolster to compensate for his broad shoulder and avoid a crick in his neck in the morning.

Sometime during the night a whimpering in his ear jolts him awake. It has grown considerably colder and a breeze is stirring the embers of Nikolaos' now cold fire just outside of the aperture of the cave, but his back is warm and he soon realizes that Rah has lain down beside him and is now cuddled against his spine. The boy is shivering and whining in his sleep, and pressed so tightly into him that at first Rush cannot safely turn toward him without waking him.

The assassin lifts his head and sees that Nikolaos is asleep in an upright position against the far wall of the cave. His wool is tight around his shoulders, his head nodded. Rush slowly wriggles onto his left side, careful not to wake Rah. The boy instantly snuggles against his chest and makes a few satisfied little grunts.

Rush lifts his right arm, holding it out and away from the boy, his brow wrinkling under his muslin mask with a confusion of feelings. Rah's pale head of curls brushes his chin as the boy nuzzles closer against him for warmth. He has turned his face into Rush's arm, using it as a pillow. One of his incisors pricks the muslin and pinches the assassin's bicep.

Rush swallows a thickness in his throat and carefully brings his free arm down, then gently draws Rah closer, offering him all of the heat of his core.

In the morning he awakens to find the boy still burrowed against his chest, lips parted and tongue resting against his incisors, snoring evenly. The front of the assassin's tunic is wet with drool.

Nikolaos has gone out, apparently intent on finding grouse in his snares. Rush struggles with a desire to get up and relieve himself, but cannot bring himself to wake the boy. After what seems an eternity, the captain's silhouette darkens the entry of the cave.

"Nothing," he says, standing at Rush's feet, hands on his sword belt. "Well, that is charming," he adds, frowning.

Rush gently extracts himself from Rah, who has somehow twisted his fingers into the muslin under the assassin's arm. He reaches for the sheepskin and pulls it over the boy's shoulder, then gets to his feet, unclipping the chain that joins them from his own waist. He pulls his hood off and tosses it aside. Without it he is half man, half beast. Like the Minotaur in reverse, thinks Nikolaos.

"Watch him. If he startles and takes off I will have the devil of a time finding him in the storm that is nearly upon us."

A half hour later, Rush returns. He holds a dead hare by its hind legs.

"How the hell did you catch that?"

"Make a fire in the mouth of the cave and we will have a good meal. It may well be our last until we board ship."

Dried fruit from their provisions, and the hare, comprise breakfast for the two men, while Rah can be convinced only to gnaw on a few nuts and dried apricots. As the last of the hare is consumed, the rain begins. At first there is only darkness. Then a great thunder clap booms above them and just as suddenly come sheets of rain, pouring as if from buckets down the cave entrance and making a curtain through which little can be seen. With fearful speed the storm is upon them and rivulets of water quickly form streams that course down the mountain, washing away all trace of their fire and taking branches and smaller rocks with it. As the morning progresses, rivers of washing water begin to break away the earth, creating mudslides. But the cave remains dry, for it faces south and the floor slopes upward from the mouth.

In Cyrus, the dead have begun to return home.

Rushing water has carved a gash in the earth above the cemetery where the bones of Lutarus now rest with those of his ancestors. Mud, rock and fallen branches join the water running down the side of the mountain and find the cart road where only a few hours earlier, Cara, Marta and the priests from Knossos passed on their way around the mountain toward Knossos. By the time the water reaches the north wall of the cemetery it is an avalanche of mud, rock and debris, and it takes down the wall on its way to Cyrus, collecting the dead, and racing toward the palace.

The cart has made it half way around the mountain before the storm hits. Taking a well -traveled road carved into the side of the hills, it too now uses the path of the flood. There is nowhere to hide, and the travelers can only continue forward, hoping for the best. It seems as if they are blessed when they round a corner and come upon a steep trench alongside the road. Surely the water racing down the mountain slopes will follow the trench and allow them to pass along the higher roadway.

Cara sits huddled beside Marta in the cart, drenched and panicked. The child clings to her side crying. The priests, the caped shoulders of their robes pulled over their head, look at one another with dread. The body of Ananou lies in a cypress coffin at their feet. The priest's sun-embroidered robe, which had been laid over the top of the coffin ceremoniously, is soaked through and now clings to the top of the narrow box in bitter irony.

The asses continue to stumble up the road, heading into the weather, their heads low, their gait mincing.

It seems as if the gods are smiling on them when the rain slows momentarily.

And then the second quake hits Cyrus.

The asses bolt uphill, off the track, spilling the contents of their cart, but for the driver. Cara and Marta tumble off the side, still holding one another. They land on the embankment, momentarily stunned but unhurt. The scream of a priest raises Cara's head from the muddy ground. The coffin has landed on his leg and the man's foot sticks from the other side, turned in an impossible angle. The ground is shaking as if some great animal wakes from slumber beneath it and would push itself to the surface. Cara and Marta are sliding down the embankment toward the road, which is running like a river from the flash flood. Marta slips from Cara's grasp in the mud and screams. Cara snatches her right arm, but when the ground shakes again, the girl's thumbless hand offers her no grip and slips through her fingers.

"'Tia! Help me!" Marta cries, addressing Cara by the whoremaster's ugly abbreviation of the name she was born with.

Cara makes an attempt to reach for the girl, but another shift of the earth throws her in the opposite direction. Marta is in the road when the earth opens like a jaw, not along the trench running the length of the road, where the eye insists it must. It must! No. It opens beneath Marta and the three priests, the one still pinned under the coffin by his mangled leg.

And they are gone.

Now it is pouring in sheets and buckets and Cara has all she can do to claw her way several more yards up the embankment against the rain running down the hill. As if satisfied by its meal, the earth has quieted and shifts gently like a man at table whose belly is filled. Cara's hair has long since fallen out of its bun and streaks across her eyes in wet tendrils, hampering her vision. The cart? Where is the cart? There are still the asses and the cart! When the tremors end, she pulls herself to her feet and picks up her damp skirts, which are binding her legs together. She draws them in front of her sex in a roll and looks about for shelter. She finds it in a shallow cave in the side of the hill not far from where she stands.

The asses have pulled the empty cart up the embankment to the cave and stand now, their heads to the back wall, as if tethered there. There is no sign of the driver.

Cara blinks with disbelief at what she sees. The cart has been demolished. The animals' vertical bolt up the stony embankment has not spared the wheels. One is nowhere to be seen, the other cracked in half at the rim and useless. The cart itself is overturned, causing the two asses to be pulled together against the single pole that tied them to the cart. They are helplessly tangled in their tack. But Cara's own personal trunk of clothing is still where she left it, fastened beneath the driver's seat. It is the only thing that remains in the wagon.

Carefully she moves toward the animals, murmuring a soothing lie. "There, now, you are safe. It is over. And you know your way, don't you? You've crossed these hills a thousand times and the road is well marked."

Determined to look forward up the incline and not behind her at the fissure that was once the road, and where even now Marta may be buried alive and suffocating in mud, Cara begins to untangle the closest ass from its harness, being sure to check first that its headstall is still intact, and then keeping a secure grip on its reins. When she has extracted it from the wreck she leads it around the cart to the other side and begins the same process with the second animal. There is no point in attempting to leave one behind or to let it loose, for the two are surely inseparable.

Having gathered the two asses, Cara uses one of the harness cavessons to bind her case to the back of the smaller animal. Then she leads the two beasts away from the wreckage along the embankment until, rounding a corner, she is out of sight of the scene of the wreck. Here the embankment flattens to a gentle decline toward the road.

The rain has lightened to a drizzle and there is even a ray of sun peeking out from behind a bank of clouds to the north. There is no breeze, not even a puff of air. The stillness is disturbing and Cara begins chattering brightly to the animals to fill it. Much is lost. But she still has her voice.

"Here we are. Back on the road to Knossos. You see? All is well. We are safe."

Once on the roadway, Cara mounts the larger ass and begins her lonely journey along the mountain road toward Knossos, leaving the smaller animal to follow on its own.

She will not think of the wreck. She will not think of Marta's little thumbless hand slipping through her grip. She will not hear, over and over with her inner ear, the child screaming her slave name, "Tia!" and begging to be saved.

She has means of reaching Knossos, though she no longer has Marta.

She will do as she was told and continue to the harbor to join Ameg and become the wife of a soldier in Anatolia.

Along a more direct route over the mountain, Rush, Nikolaos and Rah remain in the cave at the altar of sacrifice, awaiting the end of the storm. The second quake has had little effect on their surroundings for they are far higher than the cart road that Cara follows, which skims the outlying hills and valleys of Ida. Rah seems to have withdrawn into a more primitive world since the first quake, and now makes no effort to speak at all, but only whines or warbles when the thunder claps or the earth vibrates beneath the cave. Much to Nikolaos' chagrin, Rush has bound his feet for safe keeping, in case he should spook suddenly, bolt from the cave and be lost in the storm, or swept away by the muddy water that courses down the mountain side along the path they have been travelling.

Rush makes use of this enforced rest by spending most of the afternoon sleeping, with Rah yet tied to him by the golden chain.

"Can we not free his ankles while we rest? Can you not see you drive his mind back into the tomb where I found him, bound thus, like a fowl waiting for the fire?"

"You worry so much about his mind, Captain, that you would lose his body over it. Let us get the body safely off Crete, and the mind will follow."

In the early evening the rain begins to lighten and by sundown a fog rolls in and blankets the mountain, making safe travel over the peak equally impossible. Rush goes out a second time, and to Nikolaos' utter disbelief, returns with another hare.

"And how might we eat that, sir, with no dry wood to build a fire?" asks the Captain peevishly.

"You might have saved us some wood last night, Nikolaos, knowing a storm was coming," answers Rush, skinning and gutting the hare expertly with one of the palm-handled crescent blades he keeps ever holstered at his sides.

"I had no expectations that we would be pinned here a second night," answers the Captain.

"The first rule of war, Captain Nikolaos. Prepare for the unexpected." Rush has cut a clean piece of the hare's flesh from its thigh and is chewing it raw as he speaks, watching Nikolaos with a wolf's keen stare.

"You will be sick on that," says Nikolaos, offering Rah a round of unleavened bread and a handful of dried currants from his own provisions.

"On the contrary, Captain," says Rush, watching Nikolaos squint at him with distaste as he sinks his teeth into the hare's haunch, not bothering to cut the flesh from the carcass this time. "He is fresh," he gives the Captain a dark smile, "And I am hardy."

An hour later Rush goes out again. When he returns he takes the sheepskin from Rah, who releases it reluctantly, and stuffs it into his sack. He folds the soldier's leather and does the same with it, then pulls the hood of his assassin's costume back over his head and clips the end of Rah's golden lead back to his own waist. Rah has not taken his eyes off the sack since his sheepskin disappeared into it, but he keeps his distance from the assassin, maintaining a pressure on the leash. Rush watches him a moment as Nikolaos, realizing they are about to leave their shelter and continue their climb in darkness, quickly repacks his own supplies.

"He's gone strange," he says, noticing Rush's keen attention is fixed on Rah, who seems determined to ignore him, giving the assassin his shoulder but keeping an eye on the rucksack.

"It is the storm. And the quake," says Rush, still watching Rah and tugging lightly on the chain. "It is Thera's loud footsteps approaching. He and the volcano are linked, Captain. As she blossomed, so was he fertile and bright. Now, as she prepares to die, so does he deteriorate."

"That is ridiculous and maudlin," snaps Nikolaos.

The assassin's head turns in his direction eerily, as if the head and shoulders of the man are detached and independent of one another. He says nothing. A finger of panic, sudden and unexpected, runs up Nikolaos' spine. He is reminded once more of the thing that pinned him to his bed and carved the Tears of the Bull into his cheek only a fortnight ago. The fog has lifted, and moonlight from the mouth of the cave illuminates the assassin's silhouette. His strength and mass are palpable, and though he stands some distance from Nikolaos his presence is overwhelming, dizzying, as if he takes all the air in the cave into his own huge lungs and leaves none for Nikolaos to breathe. Completed now with the tight, black-bandage hood, one eye exposed where Rah tore a piece free, he is like a great black bull, breathing invisible fire, capable of turning and charging at any moment.

I must watch my words, Nikolaos thinks to himself. This man is mad. I must keep his trust. I must not challenge him at random.

"What now, sir?" he offers, conciliatorily.

"The fog has followed the rain out to sea. Now we take advantage of the moonlight and the calm to make progress. We can reach the colony of priests on the north face of the mountain by evening tomorrow. It is only another few hours from there to the harbor."

"What is this colony of priests, Rush?" asks Nikolaos sometime later, following the assassin blind now, for the man takes a course all his own over the mountain, and it is unmarked and desolate.

"These are the Priests of the Dead, Captain. They live to clean and bury the bones of the families of Knossos. Knossos rewards them with gifts of food and cloth for their habits, livestock, even some… luxuries."

"Wine and drug, you mean," scoffs Nikolaos. "A colony of drunks and drug fiends. Why rest there? It is the last place I would consider safe."

"Oh, it is safe, Captain," says the assassin, and Nikolaos can hear the smile on his lips. "These men have more than a nodding acquaintance with Rush the Assassin."

"I see," says Nikolaos quietly, letting the subject go at that.

After several more hours of progress Rush moves off his straight, if unmarked, course and tugs Rah into a dense stand of trees. In it is a clearing and a lean-to made of stripped saplings and covered in evergreen brush. It is invisible but from the front, and tucked into a drop, so that if one were to approach it from behind or from either side unknowingly, they would almost certainly crash right through the roof and land on the sleeping occupant. Behind it is a small cooking pit. A stream can be heard burbling nearby.

It is obvious to Nikolaos that Rush is at home here. The assassin calmly attaches Rah's leash to a bolt that has been fixed in a tree near the lean-to, then rummages around in his rucksack to find a water gourd inside, drops the sack at the mouth of the shelter and walks off toward the sound of the stream, leaving the Captain alone once again with the boy.

Nikolaos approaches Rah, who is standing where he has been fixed to the tree. The boy seems lost in his own world now, his head cocked as he listens to the sounds of the night wood. His eyes sparkle vacantly in the moonlight under a snowfall of silvery-blond lashes. He takes no notice of the Captain until he stands by his side, then looks up into his face as if he has never seen him before. He regards Nikolaos with sweet innocence.

"I won't let him hurt you, Rah," says the Captain softly. It is the first and only thing he can think to say, the only thing that has been on his mind since he met this Ameg, this Rush. And I won't die trying, he thinks to himself. If I have to keep this hellish pace up unto the gates of Tartarus, I will. But I will not let him take what is most precious to me. He will not destroy you. He will not put out this light that is in you.

Rah is blinking up at him calmly. He has said nothing since the first quake hit Cyrus and the absence of that dusky sound, that spirited if mangled speech that is Rah's and only Rah's, is depressing. It seems only animal noises remain available to him, noises that emanate from somewhere deep in his throat, down along that lovely sun-bronzed column, just under the perfect hollow made there at the center, where a V of muscles jump along the sides of his neck. You should wear an Egyptian emerald there, thinks Nikolaos, right there in that hollow, to set off those amazing eyes. Then he flinches at his own peculiar thought. What is happening to me? What in hell has happened to me since I first lay eyes on you? What sort of creature are you? You are not just a slave boy.

Presently Rush returns with a gourd filled with clear, sweet stream water. He hands it to Rah, and the boy takes it greedily, guzzling it and nearly emptying it. Rush watches him drink, his expression hidden behind his hood but for the single exposed eye, within which glints a fixed fascination with Rah's thirst. It travels with a bit of spilt water down the boy's neck, down to that very hollow that Nikolaos himself admired only a moment before. But the hunger in the man's eye unleashes the anger that is ever below the surface of the Captain's cool demeanor. He feels his lip tighten as if in a snarl, and must look away.

"I suppose you will be taking the shelter for yourself," he says with practiced nonchalance. "Perhaps I should bed down here, near the boy, as a precaution."

"Suit yourself, Captain," says Rush, taking the sheepskin from his rucksack and holding it out to Rah, who instantly gives it his complete focus. He makes a grab for it but is thwarted by his tether. Taunting him further, Rush holds it above his own head, making the boy come close and jump for it.

"Why must you tease him, you can see he is not himself?" protests Nikolaos as he lays out his own leather on the other side of the tree. Rah is whining, reaching for the skin Rush continues to suspend over his head.

"I see that he is more himself than ever," says the assassin, lowering the hide then and ruffling Rah's curls as he snatches his prize. He watches as Rah settles himself at the base of the tree, punching the skin into a ball and throwing himself onto it. Then he turns to make his own bed inside the lean-to. Once he is settled, he is invisible even from the front of the shelter.

For a time, there is peace.

In the wake of the second quake the King and Queen of Cyrus have had second thoughts.

There is little left of their city, and looters and thieves ransack the palace. The King, his Queen, his nephew and his favorites have abandoned their people, and all but their most precious items, in hopes that the criminal element that has taken over will be distracted by the ease with which they can burgle the monarchy and leave them their lives. The city is, at any rate, little more than a crater surrounded by a field of demolished mud-brick or stone buildings. The palace was split in twain, the Great Hall opening like a mouth to receive the mud and rock and bodies flooding down the hills from behind the broken cemetery walls.

The King, his family, and a small group of servants, including Fillius and Bacus, along with all that remains of the Palace Guard, many of whom were killed in the barracks when the floor of the Great Hall fell in and many who have deserted in the wake of the disaster, have taken two unbroken wagons and four oxen and fled to the coast to board a shipping vessel and depart for a Minoan settlement in Canaan.

Bands of looters, assuming that the quake was island-wide and convinced it is a sign of the end of the world, have fanned out from Cyrus in all directions, intent on plundering other cities that have also been damaged or destroyed in the quake. They do not know that Cyrus is alone in its grief, that the other cities of Crete were largely unharmed by the fickle monster that lives beneath the Island of Thera and spreads its tentacles along fault-lines deep beneath the sea.

Cara has continued her weary ride on ass-back over the mountain road, relying wholly on the instinct and memory of the lead animal to take her to Knossos. She is dirty, damp, and exhausted, but refuses to let herself dismount and find some place to rest for fear of losing the animals. To keep herself company, she sings. She sings a lullaby she heard in Thrace what seems a thousand years ago, when she was yet a child of Marta's age herself. She sings to the asses. And she sings to the spirit of the little thumbless girl who follows her now, calling, "Tia, save me!" from the breeze at the very tops of the trees.

In the still, damp morning air the sound of sandaled feet approaching from the southwest carries upward on a breeze, awakening the assassin. Smiling behind his close fitting hood, Rush rolls softly over onto his back and crosses his arms over his chest, grasping the palm handles of his crescent blades under either arm. A murmur of masculine voices, snatches of Greek, dim to a hush as the footsteps near. They have approached as he expected, from the south, and head directly toward the camp, noticing what is meant to be noticed first, the cook-pit, then the blonde head of the sleeping Grain God chained to a tree on a golden tether that glints in the moonlight.

"Look at that!" says one in a raspy whisper.

"Sshhh! There is the Captain!" says another, so close now that Rush can see the man's sandaled feet step down the drop to the right of his invisible nest.

A second pair of sandals rounds the lean-to on the left, accompanied by the sound of a sword pulled from its sheath.

That is the sound that awakens the Captain.

"Intruders!" he barks, awaking Rah in time to send the boy up the tree to the length of his tether.

But there is already the edge of a sword pressed against his throat. A third man, coming round from the far left, has circled the tree and surprised him from behind. The sound of several more men, running up the rise toward the encampment from the south is the last thing Rush hears before a foot comes through the roof of his den and lands on his chest.

The shriek of the unfortunate owner of the foot distracts the man who has put his sword to Nikolaos' throat. That diversion is all the Captain needs to draw his own sword and thrust it into his attacker's thigh, opening the femoral artery. But the sight of Rah's thick golden collar, belt and anklets glinting in the tree above has made the remaining renegade guards of Cyrus brave with greed. There are yet enough of them standing to overtake the Captain. Two more step toward him as the scream of the man he has just lanced is eclipsed by the yodel of agony coming from the lean-to. The ill-fated man who stepped through Rush's ceiling has lost his foot at the ankle, and now that very foot has come to rest at their feet, causing one to screech with horror at the thing and forget his advance on the Captain, who makes use of this second distraction by driving his sword through that man's belly.

The second man is on the ground before Nikolaos can pull his weapon from the first. It takes him an instant to realize that Rush has rolled from his nest with his blades tucked against his sides, and sliced the man's Achilles tendons.

Rush is on his feet by the time a yelp from Rah turns the Captain's head to see two more familiar faces, men who were a day ago under his command. They have yanked the boy down from the tree by his golden chain, and one now stands boldly with the boy pulled against him, a dagger to his throat. The man is huge, as tall as Rush and broader. He speaks with confidence.

"We care not if he lives or dies, Captain. We only want the gold he wears. Give us no more trouble and we will take him alive, or else follow us and I will cut his throat."

"I had thought you a brave and honest man, Sarturus," says the Captain, subdued.

"I am still brave, Captain," says the giant, pulling Rah backward with him as he is joined by his two remaining cohorts. He gives Rush a quick assessing look, as if assuring himself of this.

"You are indeed," says Rush in a sinister whisper, advancing on him without hesitation, blades drawn.

"Stay back!" cries Sarturus defiantly pressing the dagger against Rah's throat but not daring to cut him.

"Do not challenge him!" cries Nikolaos in the same instant. Knowing this man to be impulsive, he speaks to Rush, but Sarturus lifts his eyes to his Captain with a moment of uncertainty, believing his commander yet to be issuing him an order. Then he looks back at Rush, pulls Rah closer and sets his mind to his task.

Now Rush is circling him, a black wolf with head and shoulders low, his single exposed eye gleaming with calculated pleasure. Sarturus' companions have stepped away from the standoff and watch at a safe distance, unwilling to face Rush's blades. Nikolaos has positioned himself behind the tree, in the only clear direction Sarturus has if he intends to escape with Rah. Sarturus is pivoting in place, between the lean-to and the tree. Determined to maintain the face-off with Rush, his blade is still pressed against Rah's throat.

"Or what?" snarls Rush, circling. "Let us talk, little Palace Guard. Let us talk of what will happen next, once you have cut him. Once I see his blood. Once he is so much as nicked by that butter knife of yours. Once he is bleeding, what will I do with you?"

The man continues to press Rah into his bulk as he trips on Rah's chain over and over in his attempt to keep Rush in front of him. Rah has begun to whine and struggle, making it difficult for him to keep the blade to his throat without drawing blood. He lowers it slightly, resting it against the boy's golden collar.

"You are too fat to dance thus," says Rush, and closes the distance between himself and the giant so quickly that the man stumbles back, lifting Rah up like a shield to protect his own breast as the crescent blade in the assassin's left palm slices through the air inches before his eyes. But he has miscalculated. The second crescent is embedded in his left side, splitting his abdomen just below the ribs and loosing the contents of his belly, which pour down his leg like blood pudding. He screams and releases Rah to bring his hands to his wound in a futile attempt to keep his intestines from spilling from the hole. He is effective only in allowing the assassin access to his right side to complete his disembowelment.

Sarturus looks down at his entrails, which are popping out of his open abdomen in shining loops, or like a monstrous, fast blooming rose, and screams in horror.

The last two renegade guards have turned and fled up the mountain, bumping into Nikolaos and then charging through the thick underbrush to escape. Nikolaos is momentarily stunned at the speed in which the confrontation changed direction. He stands dumbfounded, and is struck into a spin when the powerful thrust of the assassin's shoulder crashes into him as he charges up the incline after the guards.

As if awakened from his stupor by that blow, Nikolaos looks to Rah. Unbelievably, the golden chain, with little more strength than a heavy necklace, has remained intact through the struggle. Rah is still tethered by it to the tree, and stands panting but otherwise unhurt, his eyes fixed on the path the assassin has taken up the mountain.

Sarturus lies moaning in the dirt, holding his intestines against the V shaped flap of belly fat which hangs now from his groin.

The man whose foot lies not far from Rah's tree has bled out, and has crumpled in a fetal position at the face of the lean-to.

The man with the severed heels appears to be dead, but is probably only unconscious from pain. Nikolaos sets to the ugly task of clearing the bodies from the assassin's camp before Rush returns.

In an act of kindness not typical of him, he cuts Sarturus' throat before he hauls him off into the wood. He does the same for the man with the severed heels. Then he goes to the stream to fill his water skins, and offers Rah a drink when he returns. The boy accepts the gift gratefully, but his ears are pricked for his master, and he keeps his eyes on the path Rush took into the trees until the assassin returns.

An hour later the dark shape of the assassin emerges from the wood to the east. His mask is off and tucked in his belt. A grouse hangs by the feet from his left hand. He walks directly to Rah, who jumps up from his nest under the tree and steps toward him eagerly. Rush ruffles his curls with his right hand, then lifts his chin to examine his neck.

"What did you do with them, Captain," he says evenly to Nikolaos as he turns Rah's chin from side to side, checking for a wound.

"I dragged them into the wood, that they might not draw predators to the camp," says Nikolaos cautiously.

"They were not dead, Captain," says Rush. "I was not finished with them." He has released Rah and now steps away from the boy and toward Nikolaos, who has jumped to his feet and stands at attention in an attitude of deference.

"I … cut their throats," he answers guardedly. "Did you catch the others?" he adds, hoping to change the subject.

"I did," says Rush, his mouth curling in a malevolent smile. "Would you like to know what I did to them, Captain? To your renegade guards?"

"You needn't bother," answers Nikolaos, flinching involuntarily.

"I did what you should have done to the other two. I hung them from the feet by their belts." He lifts the grouse and shakes it in front of Nikolaos' face, "thus, in the trees, and cut their bellies open for the birds to pick. They will die slow, as deserters must."

Nikolaos holds his gaze nervously, knowing full well that the assassin has not yet finished reprimanding him.

"Do you know what a Hittite commander does to a junior officer who fails to discipline his men appropriately, Captain?" says Rush, leaning ever so slightly at the Captain and forcing him to step back.

"I know what the Greeks do," answers Nikolaos.

"It is the same. And so next time you think you will spare a man my justice I will mete out the punishment meant for him on you. Understood, pup?"

"Understood, sir."

"Now cook this bird for us for breakfast."

"Sir," answers Nikolaos, taking the grouse gingerly and moving off to find some dry kindling for a fire.

Rush uses the time it takes the bird to cook to strip and wash in the stream, turning the little rivulet red for a time with the blood that has soaked his assassin's camouflage.

CHAPTER 46

Not long after Rush has opened Sarturus' bowels on the southern flank of Ida, and yet before a glowing red sun has breached the mountains, Kleitos and Thymus, drunk and exhausted from a night of tossing in the hold of the Queen's ship through the storm and fighting to keep calm twenty terrified horses, stumble off the ramp and onto the dock to feed the assassin's hell dogs.

They have made this pilgrimage every day for a week and have managed thus far to avoid catastrophe. Each morning before dawn they have together taken a pail of scraps from the evening meal and another of water to the storehouse on the dock where the hounds are kept. Then one man positions himself behind the massive wood door, hands on the heavy oak plank that serves as a bolt, and the second, with both pails ready, waits at the opening, heaving with dread as he leans against the flank of the building.

"Ready!" cries the lucky man who drew the long straw at supper, the man who has the door between himself and the two beasts.

"Ready!" cries the unhappy other, usually Kleitos, for Thymus has always been lucky at games of the draw.

Then the door man pulls the bolt and takes the brunt of the impact as Ameg's snarling hell hounds hurl their fury against it.

And the man with the pails drops his offerings just inside the door.

"CLOSE!" cries the pail man, usually Kleitos, throwing himself back to allow the door man to slam the thing shut while the dogs are distracted by the food, and grateful that he still has arms and a face.

"Fucking hell," breathes the pail man then, usually Kleitos, and wipes the sweat from his eyes miserably. "Your turn tomorrow, Thymus, you cheating bastard. I don't give a fuck for straws."

"We draw for it, you agreed," answers Thymus, less than confidently.

And then, with a chuckle, and slapping his drinking mate hard on the shoulder, "maybe tomorrow we throw a bitch in there first, eh?"

"I swear to the gods, Thymus, I'm through. I can't take no more of this," Kleitos will grumble then, marching behind his mate back up the dock to the ship. "I swear to the gods."

But this morning, once again, Kleitos, having failed to draw the longer straw, is pail man. And once again, he and Thymus march gloomily down the dock to the storehouse to feed the dogs.

"Fucking hell," moans Kleitos. "Feel like I been kicked in the head by a horse this morning, Thymus. You drop the pails today. I haven't the speed."

"We drew for it, Kleitos, fair and square. It's your turn to drop the pails," answers Thymus tiredly.

"It's always my turn," grumbles Kleitos, swinging the pails resentfully and taking an inordinate amount of time to make any progress toward the storehouse.

But when they round the Queen's granary and the view is open up to the Bridge Road and on into the city, what they see shocks them sober and awake.

On the streets of Knossos there is anarchy. The government is dismantled and the palace all but abandoned. The storm has smashed most of the remaining boats in the harbor against the bulkhead and rendered them useless, and social order has capsized as well. Looters run through the streets, breaking into the finer homes near the harbor and carrying out bronze statuary, cartloads of clothing and foodstuffs, even livestock. The din of the looters, whose mass voice could be mistaken for a celebration, is overshadowed by the shouts and screams of the more affluent who have remained on the island to defend their possessions.

Kleitos and Thymus look at each other with new horror, Kleitos dropping the pails where he stands and scurrying back round the corner of the Queen's granary to press himself against the building, heaving. Thymus is right beside him.

"Holy mother god, Thymus, it is a riot! They will swarm down the Bridge Road next and take the ship! We must return to tell Ramicus! We must pull her out into the harbor!"

"Easy, Kleitos. They are busy looting the city. It could be hours before they think of the storehouses. We must tend to the dogs or else face the assassin's wrath ourselves. And I would personally rather face a hundred of those cowards up the road than one Rush the Assassin."

"To hell with the dogs. Let us release them. We cannot return here to feed them once the looters come down to the docks to plunder, at any rate. We must return to the ship and tell the captain to pull out into the harbor or lose the ship altogether."

At this Thymus lets go a hoot of relief and gives his friend a poke in the chest. "That is it, Kleitos! How simple! Leave them hungry. Let those thieves open the door looking for something to steal, eh? Let them release the dogs!"

"Yes!" Kleitos grabs his mate, embraces him, sighs a sigh of exhaustion and gratitude, and follows him back to the ship to tell Ramicus, and the captain, of the impending danger. In half an hour the Queen's vessel is safely off shore, settled in the harbor, with Ameg's skiff tied to the stern. By early afternoon the city is sacked and the looters are making their way down the Bridge Road toward the storehouses on the harbor.

It is late afternoon on the same day when Cara, exhausted to the point of near delirium, rounds the mountain on ass-back along the well worn cart road, and sees the settlement of the Priests of the Dead.

At first her heart jumps in her chest with relief and gratitude. Here she can rest. Surely this group of religious will see her plight and give her something to eat and drink, allow her to leave the asses in a pen with theirs and offer her a comfortable place to sleep for a few hours. She is as yet unaware that the place is a storehouse for the bones of the families of Knossos, or that the priesthood is little more than a collection of family rejects, dim-wits and drunkards, spastics and cripples, whose parents or siblings relegated them to a life of isolation to defer the public shame of their existence. The sect itself is controlled by a small group of junior priests from each of the four Houses, so that the families' religious leanings are represented. There are three from the House of the Moon, two from the House of the Sun, one each from the houses of the Bull and the Sky. These are rotated in and out of the City of the dead bi-yearly, so that at some point in his career, every priest has spent his required time there.

Down the mountainside she can see the sea gleaming in the late afternoon haze. Unaccustomed to life in a port town, she is not alarmed to see that the harbor is very nearly abandoned, that the huge shipping vessels that normally clog the port are missing. Cara pats the side of the ass she rides, even gives it a scratch at the withers.

"There now, look. We are only a few miles from the city. And here is a place where we can rest. The priests will see we have met with misfortune and comfort us. We are safe now."

She has come to call the smaller ass Mary, the larger Portia. She can no longer remember what these names mean to her, but finds the habit gives her some relief from her loneliness. As she continues toward the eastern side of the settlement, she approaches a small pasture of sheep and goats.

"Here are friends for you to graze with, Portia. And you, Mary, a place to lie down in safety."

It is not until she reaches the barns that the hair on her arms lifts as if with a chill. The utter silence of the place is disturbing to her. No voices break the stillness, not even the lowing of oxen, nor the bleating of goats, though some meander about the yard freely, picking on bits of vegetation and scraps behind the ramshackled sheds that house the animals. There is not even the trill of a bird, nor the buzzing of honey bees in the vegetable gardens on the opposite side of the road.

Still she continues, kicking Portia around the empty barns toward the center of the compound, expecting at least to find a priest or two moving about among the huts.

But when she turns the corner into the yard what she finds turns her blood cold. Her head reels, unable to make sense at first of the sight, and then she draws breath enough to power all of the unvoiced horror and emotion, the anger and the fear, that she has denied a voice since the second quake turned the world upside down.

And Cara screams.

By late afternoon the hell hounds of Rush the Assassin are following their master's stale scent up the Burial Mound Road toward the City of the Dead.

The dogs, brothers in a litter of wolf-mastiff crosses bred for war on the plain of Urartu near Mount Ararat, have never known freedom. They were purchased by the assassin when they were whelped, and have known only one alpha, Rush. Now they follow his scent up Mount Ida, along the Burial Mound Road, muzzles down, at a lope.

Earlier that morning a pack of looters from the east end of the city descended on the docks to raid the storehouses. They came with stolen carts, wielding kitchen knives and clubs, intent on pillaging the grain houses and killing anyone who tried to stop them. But the docks were already deserted, and their way clear. By mid-afternoon most of the buildings were burning, the raiders, many of them drunk on palace wine or mead that they had confiscated earlier, having set fire to what was left after they took all they could carry.

From the Queen's ship the dock, and the city itself, looked as if Knossos had been at war. Dark smoke billowed from the windows and rooftops of buildings, and the streets were strewn with wreckage. Loosed livestock roamed among the debris, pecking and foraging. Thymus and Kleitos had told Ramicus that they fed the dogs and left them in the storehouse. What more could they do?

"Well they will have to fend for themselves now," said Ramicus, watching the world go mad from the prow of the Queen's ship. "As will we until and unless the assassin returns."

In the din, the two looters who came upon the storehouse where the beasts were trapped could not hear the animals barking wildly within. When they released the bolt, the door crashed open, knocking the doorman to the ground, and to safety. The second man lost his face when the first dog out, assuming the din around him was battle and the man an enemy and an obstacle between he and his master, dispatched him. Then the two hounds picked up the assassin's scent, and followed it up the Bridge Road toward the City of the Dead, where his path would split from the common road and follow a more direct climb over the mountain toward Cyrus.

But the dogs never made it past the City of the Dead.

They never made it past Cara's scream.

For the dogs were trained to protect their master, and all of his possessions. Left in the yard of his compound in Knossos when he was away, they had one occupation and one only, to guard the compound and all that was in it, including Josepha and the boys, with their lives. Though neither Ameg's wife nor his sons could control the beasts, nevertheless they were kept safe day and night by their virtue of being his, and more than one foolish burglar lost his life testing the theory.

Now the dogs, which are fast approaching the City of the Dead from the north, are within earshot of Cara's vivid soprano scream. Excited by the sound, they charge on, for their master has, on more than one occasion, brought them with him here and kenneled them in a work shed while he carried out business. They take his route through the place, traversing the cemetery itself, which is first to greet patrons on the road from Knossos, and gallop over mounds and between tombs to the colony of huts where the priests live and work. Rounding a burning hut they charge toward Cara, who is yet astride the ass but fast being separated from it by a handful of drunken plunderers. The smaller ass is being pulled away by two men. It too is screaming in fear and rage for it will not be taken from the larger ass. Strewn about the yard are the bodies of several priests who fled from their huts when they were torched by the raiders, and were then cut down or clubbed to death in the yard. One has been set on fire and is even now whirling and shrieking, a flaming ghost trying in vain to put himself out in the dirt.

Cara is clinging to Portia's neck as the men attempt to yank her off the animal. One has her by her hair, another has pulled her skirt from her and left her naked from her waist. The men are drunk and frenzied, intent on rape, and do not see the dogs rounding the burning hut at a gallop.

The dogs are trained to protect Rush's things, and his scent has led them here. A woman is being attacked and screaming. And the woman smells of Rush.

The dogs can yet trace the scent of their master amongst the many smells that assault their senses on this battlefield. It is what they are trained to do.

The war dogs of Rush the Assassin attack the attackers.

Not far from the melee, Rush, Nikolaos and Rah are making their approach to the City of the Dead from the south west. They cannot hear the battle, for the breeze carries Cara's aria of screams north and east, toward Knossos, and the dogs work in silence. The sun is setting over the Aegean in a clouded sky. Steam from Thera has turned the belly of the clouds orange and magenta, a sight that stops Rush in his tracks.

"What is it?" asks Nikolaos, coming up behind him on the right.

"It is the end, Captain," answers the assassin. After a moment, he turns to Rah, who has come to stand in his lengthening shadow. He takes the boy by both arms and draws him close. Rah looks up at him, startled, his strange, prismatic eyes reflecting the reds and yellows in the sky. He stiffens in the assassin's grip.

"There may be trouble ahead, little cat, and I cannot fight thus." Rush takes the golden chain that links them, lifts it. Rah looks down at his leash, looks back up into the assassin's face.

"I must release you," continues Rush. He takes the boy's chin. "I have killed ten men thus far to have you, and I shall kill as many more before we reach the harbor. I have stolen you, when I was paid to assassinate you. I have lived," he shakes the chain," in chains since I first laid eyes on you."

"Rush," begins Nikolaos, setting a hand on the big man's arm.

"Be quiet, Captain, or lose your tongue," says Rush, still holding Rah's face in his hand. "I will not leave Crete without you, Rah, do you understand?"

Rah does his best to shake his head, affirmative, in the vise of the man's grip.

"I will not leave without you."

Rah is beginning to tremble.

Rush releases his face, takes the chain, unfastens it from the boy's belt, still holding the boy by his arm. He unsnaps the chain from his own belt and hands the length of it to Nikolaos, who quickly shucks his rucksack off his shoulder and stuffs it into the bag.

Suddenly Rah twists his arm out of Rush's grip and points past him, down the incline toward the south wall that hides the burning pit of the City of the Dead.

"Sing," says Rah.

Rush looks at Nikolaos, puzzled. It is the first word Rah has spoken since they left Cyrus.

"Sing, Rah?" says Nikolaos gently, recalling the night the boy told him of the woman's voice he could not hear himself. "Do you hear singing?"

"She sing!" Rah is becoming excited. He hops a few steps further down the path toward the wall of the cemetery colony. He makes a pleading gesture toward Nikolaos, even tugs his arm. "She sing, Nikolaos, she sing lullaby! This same lullaby!"

Nikolaos looks at Rush. "He heard a woman sing a lullaby the night before we left, from his window at the palace. He says this is the same lullaby."

"Cara sings," says Rush, looking from Rah to the Captain.

"Cara sing!" says Rah, pointing down the path.

"Come, little cat," says Rush, taking off at a loping trot down the path toward a sound he cannot hear.

"Your wife?" shouts Nikolaos, now running to keep up with the assassin. Rah has already passed them both and has darted out of sight through the thickening trees.

"She is not my wife!" Rush shouts back, now running at top speed to keep up with Rah. Nikolaos is soon left behind.

Ten minutes after she enters the City of the Dead Cara is crawling out from under a corpse. The man was attempting to yank her off Portia by an arm when the two monstrous black wolves rounded a burning hut and attacked. The first beast to reach the conflict leapt into the air and took her attacker's throat in its jaws and the man, still clutching her arm, fell beneath it. Cara was dragged from Portia just as the ass bolted. She landed atop the man who had intended to mount her and was soaked in the blood pumping from his pounding heart through the gruesome spigot that had been his throat. The second hound had the man who had ripped off her skirt and was shaking him by the face like a doll. It took him some time to die while the animal dragged him about the courtyard, its fangs hooked in his eye sockets, shaking him and growling playfully as if engaged in a friendly tug-of-war. Cara's first instinct was to disguise her scent from the dogs with the corpse of the first man. She pulled his still-warm body atop her own as best she could, struck in her own peculiar way with the irony of the outcome of his decision to rape her.

Now Cara is pushing the man's cooling corpse off her half-naked body and looking about for signs of the beasts that saved her. But the animals are gone. The two asses are standing together not twenty meters from where she lies, grazing in a patch of vegetation. The rest of her attackers are nowhere to be seen, no doubt having fled into the countryside pursued by the wolves.

Cara finds her skirt, filthy with dirt and blood, still in the frozen hand of the faceless, and forever nameless, man who tore it from her. She makes a weak attempt at modesty, discovers there is not enough left of the rags to cover her, and looks about for a substitute. The stink of the battlefield is almost overwhelming. The priest who has cooked in his own robe smokes like a dampened torch in the center of the courtyard. Even without a smoking priest, the place has the smell of death about it, as the bodies of the families of Knossos lie in various states of decay and dismemberment not far from the huts, in the burning pit on the southern edge of the colony. She is downwind of the pit.

Cara feels her head begin to reel and a sense of lightness come over her. I am going to faint, she thinks, and if I faint I cannot run nor defend myself and I will die. Nevertheless she finds herself falling as if in slow motion to her knees when a wave of nausea burrows like a mole up from her gut. Retching bile onto her hands, which are splayed before her in the muddy grass, she determines to stop the world from spinning. I will find a note. I will find a center note.

Cara quiets her mind, forces herself to concentrate on the tip of her left index finger where the nail has been ripped off in the struggle and is now bleeding and turning a blade of muddy grass pink. Center note. Left index finger. She makes a little hum, chokes, spits the remaining bile from her mouth, tries again.

She hits the first note of the lullaby she sang to the owl at her window two nights earlier.

And defeats the death that is all around her with her voice.

Rah is first to reach her. Despite two days of grueling travel, the voice of the lady who sang the lullaby has brought his injured brain back to his human mind and charged his athletic limbs with stamina. He rounds the smoking huts on the north side of the courtyard and comes to a slippery halt in the damp grass when he sees the woman who came to Cyrus with his master, naked from the waist, on her knees and singing to her hands. Rah stops in his tracks, balancing on his toes to break his entrance, and to keep from startling this mare and risk losing her.

But the ethereal presence of the Grain God is impossible to ignore. The motion of his golden invasion into the hell that surrounds her lifts Cara's attention from her fingers, with which she has been playing out the notes she sings with fastidious attention. She looks up, and sees in the dimming light the vision of an angel, flickering like the diaphanous wing of a dragonfly in the haze of the smoking huts.

A pale blonde halo of hair, limbs as fine and balanced and pleasing as those of a prized colt, and the bewitchingly beautiful face of a cat, all planes and cheekbones and tip-tilted blue-green eyes.

She knows this vision, has seen him dance, land like the feather of a dove on the floor of the arena at the palace of Cyrus.

And where Rah is, Ameg cannot be far behind.

"Lady sing," says Rah carefully, stepping toward Cara as if approaching a spooked horse. He seems oblivious to the horror that surrounds him and focuses only on Cara, moving cautiously and silently forward, until he is only a meter or so away. Somehow he has brought himself to the ground, to her level, in his approach, and now reaches tentatively for her, tilting his head softly down and to the left to imply meekness, but still fixing her with those impossibly blue eyes.

"Rah," chokes Cara, reaching for him, forgetting her nakedness, forgetting her filth. She finds his fine shoulders with her bleeding fingers, gulping and choking on the strange dance of laughter and sobs her voice has invented.

"Cara safe now," says Rah, a gentle curve in his lips. "Wolf here."

And so he is. In the near darkness of the smoky sunset, his dark is darker. She lifts her eyes to see the massive black shape of the assassin, weapons glinting from his ankles and his sides. Her heart gives her chest a mule kick. He is worse than anything she has seen thus far. Then she realizes that this is Ameg. And her heart gives a few more mulish kicks, for a different reason.

"What has happened to you, Cara?" says the man behind the mask with Ameg's voice. Rah is still on his knees, allowing her to hold him. He is like a pretty male doll. She cannot let go. Not yet. For now, Ameg, you must share him with me.

Another voice, another man coming round the smoking hut and calling. "Rah!" It is the Captain of the Palace Guard of Cyrus, the handsome one, Nikolaos. Why is he here? Why is he here with Ameg and with Rah?

Ameg has turned to see the two asses yet grazing in a patch of vegetation near the smoking hut. "Where is the cart, Cara? Where is Marta?" He looks down at her, waiting for her answer.

She pulls in a breath through her sobs. "The quake," she says. "I couldn't-" Now she is safe. But Marta is still gone. "I couldn't save her," she looks up into the single eye that is exposed through the mask. It is impossible to read his reaction.

Nikolaos has come round his left. He has been walking about the courtyard as if looking for something. Now he hands her a priest's white robe. He has stripped one of the dead to offer her a covering. When she fails to take it from him he opens it and puts it over her shoulders. At the same time Rah rises, helping her to her feet.

"Marta gone," says Rah. He looks at Ameg. The single exposed eye has slid to meet his, and suddenly there is readable emotion in it. The black wrapped monster lifts a hand to Rah's face, strokes his cheek with the flat of one thumb.

"Marta is gone," he repeats in a hush tone.

"But," says Rah, "still have Cara. Still have sing." He flicks his brilliant eyes up at his master, then looks down shyly, as if he has said too much.

Cara has slipped her arms into the robe at the gentle direction of Nikolaos. He has even found me a belt, she thinks, taking it from him and tying it around her waist to keep the robe closed.

The sudden boom of great hounds baying breaks the stillness. Cara shrieks and stumbles back into Nikolaos, who instantly pushes her behind himself and draws his sword.

The two black wolf dogs have returned. They break the tree line to the west and hurl themselves across the courtyard at Ameg.

The assassin steps forward, takes the brunt of their momentum against his chest as they leap and wriggle in the air, lapping at his face and whining with delight.

"Ta-hah!" says Rah, pointing at the wild greeting at the same time that Nikolaos grabs his arm and pulls him away from the animals, then tosses him behind himself with Cara. But this upsets the beasts and they instantly turn to him, snarling and ready to leap at his throat.

"Hup, Hup!" barks Rush, and the dogs obediently drop to their bellies, eyes yet riveted on Nikolaos and growling lowly.

"They know the boy is mine, Captain, and will not tolerate his abuse," says Rush softly.

"They are yours? These wolves?" cries Nikolaos, a look of utter bewilderment on his face.

"They seem to know the woman is mine also, Captain, which makes you doubly a thief in their eyes. Put down your sword, it will do you little good against them. They are war dogs. They have been trained to outsmart a swordsman."

"By you," says Nikolaos. "You really did command an army, didn't you, Rush? Who are you?"

Rush looks at him, his one uncovered eye smiling. "I have commanded many armies, Captain," is all the answer that Nikolaos will get. "Now drop your sword in an attitude of surrender. I will not let them harm you."

Nikolaos swallows, looks back over his shoulder at Cara and Rah, considering. Cara is gazing from the dogs to Rush and back at the dogs with a look of dreamy wonder on her face. Rah is giggling his dusky giggle.

Nikolaos purses his lips. "Very well, Rush." He slowly lays his sword at his feet, keeping his eyes on the dogs as he does so.

Rush steps past the beasts and takes the Captain's sword by the handle. Then he puts his hand on the Captain's shoulder.

"Leave it!" he barks. The dogs sit up, panting canine smiles and dripping saliva from mouths made of gleaming white, dagger-sharp hills. "Come," says Rush, and the two animals trot up to Nikolaos, who is gritting his teeth with the fear he refuses to acknowledge. "Let them know your scent, Captain, and that you are mine now, and they will defend you with their lives, as they did Cara."

"How did you know-?" blurts Cara from behind Nikolaos.

"Look around you, girl, does a man kill thus? Someone has let them loose from the storehouse at the harbor where they were being kept for me. Looters, come down to the harbor from a city without a government, no doubt. They followed my scent here, found you under attack. Took the matter unto themselves."

"But how could they know I was-" this gives her a minute of pause, "your property, Ameg?"

"They make it their business to know what is mine and defend it," responds Rush matter-of-factly.

"I came round the huts from the east." Cara is looking up at Rush in awe. "I thought I would be safe here. I didn't see. What was happening. Until it was too late. They were like animals, they were pulling me off Portia. One tore off my skirt. And suddenly the dogs, they came... like lions... from the south, out of the cemetery. They attacked the men. I thought they were wolves. I pulled-" she points to the man lying not far from them, the man with no throat, "his body on top of mine. It was all I had to hide behind." She swallows, looks down at the dogs, who are smiling widely at her, tongues lolling, as if proud to have their exploits recounted to their alpha. "They must have chased the rest of the raiders into the woods." She looks up at Rush.

"They will have caught them and dispatched them," responds Rush, releasing Nikolaos' shoulder and turning to the animals. "Assu suwanna," Good dog, is all the reward the hell hounds get, but it is enough to send them into paroxysms of canine delight.

"We cannot enter the city at night. The ship will be pulled out into the harbor. We must remain here until morning."

"Here, Rush, in the City of the Dead? Here in this burned out hell?" responds Nikolaos, turning to put his arm around Cara protectively. Rah has dropped to his knees, open mouthed and panting in response to the greeting he is now getting from the dogs. They lap his face, snuffle him under the skirt and arms, wagging and wiggling.

"This is war, Captain. This is anarchy. This is not the Palace of Cyrus. Nor even the training fields in Mycenae. Civilization in Knossos has disbanded. And we bring with us the reason."

At that, Nikolaos looks at Rush with new horror.

"Are you telling me they will blame Rah for this?" his voice has fallen to a near whisper.

Rah is oblivious to his words. He whimpers and pants in happy unison with the dogs at the assassin's feet. But Cara has understood his meaning. Her eyes grow large and owlish. She has had enough of anarchy.

She steps back, out of the protective circle of Nikolaos' free arm.

"They will kill us all," she murmurs. "If it is their Grain God they blame, then to save themselves from the wrath of the gods, they will kill their Grain God, and us with him."

"Men without government are less than animals," says Rush evenly. "They have no logic, only fear and greed. They will look at events and find a scapegoat. Thera and Rah have always been married. While Thera steamed, the fields of Knossos flourished, and the Grain God was celebrated. Then he vanished, and the coast has been battered by sea storms and word of quakes has reached the province. The monarchy has fled. Now the cause of their cataclysm has returned. They will not allow him to board a ship and flee as did their Queen. As did the priest who made him. They will do what they believe that priest should have done, had Rush the Assassin not intervened. They will sacrifice the slave god of Rah, who has so displeased the gods, and hope for a reprieve. The servants of the priest will have talked, and all over the city men will know that it was Rush, who is also Ameg, who stopped the priest from killing the boy. When they see the Grain God return to Knossos, in my possession, they will not allow either of us to flee the island they believe that we have doomed. "

After a moment of silence, Nikolaos takes a breath, looks down at Rah still playing with the war dogs, and sighs.

"You might have told me this when I insisted you take me with you, Rush," he says.

"Would you have done any differently, Captain?"

"I cannot say. Perhaps I would have remained with my Queen, as I should have."

"You have a habit of lying to yourself, Captain Nikolaos," says Rush, turning to find a suitable place to bed down for the night.

An hour later the company is settled in a ring around a small campfire in the cemetery. Everyone has had some dried provisions from Nikolaos' store, and a bath in the priest's cistern. Their clothing has been washed and left out to dry overnight on the low limbs of trees. Rush is flanked by his war dogs, Rah is happily curled up on the opposite side of one, using its haunch for a pillow, Nikolaos is leaning his back against a tree, set to sleep upright. Cara is wrapped in her priest's white robe, which has become a comfort to her. Her face is hidden under the hood. Across the campfire she watches Rush though the brief opening. His assassin's camouflage is hanging on a tree limb over his head. He lies on his back, naked, and seems oblivious of her feminine presence.

She wants nothing more than to crawl over to him on her hands and knees, past Nikolaos, past the dogs, and curl herself against his chest to trace paths with her fingers through the curling hair that forms a black star over his heart. I could ask you a thousand questions and never be satisfied, though you answer every one. You are a devil. You are a monster. You are my lover, and my master. She forces herself to look past him, at Rah, also naked, lying on his belly in the grass with his face against the dog's haunch. My rival. No. Nothing could rival that. That is an angel. Fallen from heaven to turn the world on its end. And this is no place for angels, she thinks. If I had to choose between Rush and Rah, which would I chose? But what a silly thought. These two are locked forever together, like it or not. He will never let you go, Rah, and you are like light, impossible to hold. It is nothing to do with me.

Presently she whispers to Nikolaos, who is staring up at the stars, "Why do we not approach the city by night? Is it not safer to travel in darkness?"

Nikolaos turns, surprised she is addressing him. "I suppose his ship is out in the harbor, to avoid the looters boarding and taking her. Perhaps he has no means with which to identify himself to the captain from the pier at night," he answers, then adds softly, "You are not his wife."

"No. He took Marta and me from a brothel in Malia."

"You are a-?" but the chivalrous Captain cannot finish.

"No. I was kidnapped from Pheistos. I was to be sold a virgin." At this she gives a rye chuckle. "No. No one was ever to get their money's worth from me, either way."

The Captain looks at her strangely. "You are an unusual woman."

"How so, Captain?" says Cara.

"I suppose because-" Now he has put himself in a quandary. It seems he cannot finish a sentence without being unkind.

"Because most females overrate their value?" she answers for him.

"Well-"

"I may yet be one of them," she murmurs, looking over at Rush through the opening of her hood in such a way that the Captain cannot follow the direction of her glance. From here, with this hood on, I can look you up and down and back again without being observed. I can make lips of my eyes and devour you with them. I can taste again and again all that sinew and strength. From under this priest's cowl, I can imagine playing that instrument of yours. My fingers, in my imagination, can stroke you like the great beast you are, and I can envision pleasuring you. From here under this hood, my eyes can rape the rapist. And I can believe that I can tame the master. Here, behind this hood of invisibility, my hungry eyes can consume you. Perhaps I am meant to be a priest, and hide in mystery behind a white hood. But no, a woman cannot be a priest. What can a woman be that I desire to be? They were right to sell me for a whore, if only you were in the market for one, my darling.

"What are you dreaming, Cara?" says Nikolaos softly after a time.

"He will sell me for a soldier's wife," she answers.

"Rush? He took you to sell you?" The Captain looks over at Rush with disgust. "Bastard."

"No, no. He took us to complete his disguise in Cyrus, I think. Rich merchant, wife and child. He tries to be a monster, but look at him. Everything he does, he does for love, no? Why are we here? To save Rah. No, he took Marta to save her from the whoremaster. Then he needed me to be her mother."

"He is quite good at being a monster, Cara," answers Nikolaos.

For that, he gets the black opening of her priest's hood to peer into as she turns her head to him.

"I will bet you your sword you would be dead by now if it was not for him, Captain Nikolaos. Am I wrong?"

Once again, Nikolaos blinks at her in surprise.

"You are an unusual woman, Cara," he answers. "What would you do with my sword?"

She blows a bit of air through her lips. "Fall on it and cut my own head off, no doubt," she answers. "Good night, Captain." Then she rolls over on her side and gives him her back.

It is not long after midnight when the dead awaken Rah.

He is sleeping soundly, and has rolled off the dog's haunch and facing Cara, for the little group has bedded down in a circle. A glow brings him out of his dream of the last dance of the Story of the Grain God, when he meets his death in the teeth of the wolf, and rises from his own corpse, the true Rah. He opens his eyes and sees that he is in a cemetery, and at first he thinks he is once again in the hands of Turios and Aktor, until he realizes he is free to move his limbs. Then he looks about to see if he is still dreaming, for a glowing mist is hovers over the ground like fog and the bodies of his companions are muted by it.

But there are priests moving all about the camp, priests in the white robes of the Priests of the Dead, their faces hidden by their cowls. They move about as if searching for something. They peer at the sleeping Captain. They shuffle about. One lifts Cara's hood, another stares down at Rush, who lies on his back under the black flag of his assassin's tunic, which billows in a thin breeze.

Rah rises to his feet. He walks up to the priest who is staring down at Rush. He puts his hand on the man's arm. It is solid. This is not a dream. But the man only shuffles off in the direction of the burned out huts. As if responding to some internal signal, the others lift their heads and follow him. Rah takes a few steps in the same direction, then stops. He turns his head. Cara is whimpering in her sleep. She tosses her head, throws an arm out at an invisible adversary.

Rah forgets the ghostly priests and goes to the woman.

Cara is flailing her free arm at the man who is trying to pull her off Portia. But this time the man has the head of a wolf. I will put him to sleep with a lullaby, she thinks to herself, and she begins to sing. Now the man has caught her wrist and is stroking her forearm ever so gently. His fingers tickle like feathers along the back of her arm, raising goose bumps on her skin. A shudder of pleasure ripples down her arm and into her throat and makes her giggle but how can she? He is a monster! With the head of a wolf! But no, he smells of myrrh and cherry blossom and his skin (for he has bent to hold her) is warm silk. Rah.

"Cara safe," whispers Rah in his guttural, thick-tongued voice. He has taken her up in his arms and is rocking her, his mouth against her hair. "Cara have bad dream."

He gives her a brotherly kiss on her scalp and rocks her back and forth, cradling her in his arms.

Cara's head is swimming. He smells delicious. Her mouth is open against his shoulder and without thinking she pokes her tongue out to taste his skin. It is fresh butter, salty sweet. Her arms circle the boy's body, independent of her will. His torso is narrow, athletic, the body of a leopard. She draws him close. She longs to run her teeth along his jaw, lick at the fine stubble there, taste his mouth. She forbids herself. But she cannot stop herself from trailing kisses up that lovely golden throat and follow the muscles along his neck to nibble on his ear.

Rah giggles, pulls his head lightly away. Moonlight is making a silvery gold halo of his curls. She reaches up, must touch that leonine mane, and gets a shock when she discovers its softness.

"Oh, Rah," she murmurs, twisting her fingers in his hair and pulling him down on top of her.

"Wolf is be angry, Cara," purrs Rah against her mouth, attempting to lift himself free and untangle from her embrace. But she is not letting him go. She slips one hand down to find his maleness, she draws his head back by the hair with the other, she shifts her weight, he is so light! then slips out from under him, straddles him, and slides herself onto his sex.

Rush is awake at dawn. The little Grain God is the first thing he thinks of. He rises, looks about, finds the boy is no longer pillowed on the dog's haunch, and feels fury build in his brain as he grabs his assassin's garb from the tree above his head and peers about for Rah's pale curls.

He would not be surprised to find him riding Cara, now that there is a female in the group. But the woman is turned over on her side, facing away from him. She is a few yards from Nikolaos, who sleeps against his tree, his sword lying in his lap. Rush moves silently across the little camp space. He does not wish to wake Nikolaos. But his theory about what might have caused Rah to rise early plays with his patience. He will talk to the girl.

He kneels beside her, pulls her hood from her head, and slaps a broad palm over her mouth. She comes abruptly awake, huge brown eyes flying open at him. They do not soften when she sees what has awakened her.

"Where is the boy, Cara," hisses the assassin. She shakes her head beneath his palm, her eyes darting about the campsite. He moves his hand slightly so that she can speak behind it, but not so far that he cannot silence her in an instant if he needs to.

"He is not here?" she whispers. Good. She will keep that voice of hers down.

"He came to you last night?" With the assassin's hood over his head Rush has only one eye available for her to search. She blinks into it, swallowing nervously.

"He-" she swallows again uneasily.

"I have no time for nonsense, woman. Did he lie with you? I care not if he did. He is missing. I need a trail."

"He came to me, Ameg. I was half asleep, I don't know why, the trauma of the last few-"

"Spare me. Where did he go when he left you?"

"I thought he fell asleep here in my-" another swallow. "I did not see him leave me."

"Do not wake the Captain. Be still till I return, you understand?" says the assassin. "You tread a thin rope, woman. You are become more nuisance than value to me."

"Yes sir," murmurs Cara, miserably.

Rush rises to his feet in the dark. His dogs have come to his side. "No," he tells them, pointing to the place he had been sleeping. "Stay. Watch." The animals trot back to their sleeping spot dutifully.

"Rush," whispers Cara. It is the first time she has called him by the assassin's name. "I-"

"Spare me, woman," hisses the assassin, looking about in the dark, and then moving off toward the burned out huts to find the boy.

Just shy of dawn, Brother Crispo, nephew of Ananou and next in line to head the House of the Sun, awakens in the City of the Dead when a goat nibbles at his ear, mistaking it for a bit of hay. Brother Crispo has been hiding in the chicken shed since dusk, since the massacre. He had been gathering the evening eggs when he heard the shouts of the raiders and the cries for mercy from the priests, coming from the colony of huts in the center of the compound. Brother Crispo had seen this coming and he was no hero. He closed the shed door, burrowed under a pile of hay left in a corner for replacing the bedding in the laying boxes, and prayed.

He locked himself in with a goat.

Now, just shy of dawn, Brother Crispo swipes at his ear, slapping the goat in his muzzle and throwing off the hay he has used both as a covering and a bed. A hen that has been setting on the hay clucks indignantly and hops off his chest. The goat bleats, as if to ask, what now Brother Crispo? Forever since his arrival at the compound five months ago, he has been the source of information for every dim-wit relegated here by family, and every unfortunate junior priest doing time in the City of the Dead as a part of their religious purification.

Brother Crispo sighs, blows a bit of hay from his lips. He takes a few more breaths and then heaves himself onto his feet. He is an exceedingly corpulent man, round as a pomegranate, with a generally pleasant demeanor and a face so wide and chubby that his eyes fairly disappear when he laughs. He scratches at his shaved head, wiping off a few more stems of hay, and looks to the goat.

"Well Ephram, this is a fine mess. Mess enough for a goat to love. But I can stand this coop, and your stench, not a moment longer. It is time to go out and see what is left of our world."

And with that he waddles to the shed door, having to crouch for the shed is built for chickens and not for grown men, nor hardly for men of his breadth. With one more, heavy sigh, he braces himself for the worst, and opens the aperture.

And is greeted by the most breathtaking sunrise he has ever witnessed.

"White chicken," smiles Rah, looking up from where he squats on his haunches just a few feet from the doorway of the chicken coop. And sure enough, Lydia is scratching about in the hard soil not three feet from him, as if there were anything there of interest other than the boy.

It takes Crispo a moment to catch his breath. In the little yard outside the shed, which faces east, the Grain God of Knossos, the missing Rah, squats with one arm extended toward Lydia the white hen. Above his golden curls a red dawn peeks, chasing the night across the heavens and back into the west.

"Rah hungry," says the Grain God, lifting himself easily from his squat and stepping toward Brother Crispo. "You cook egg for Rah?" He points to Lydia. "This hen? She lay, no? Rah can eat."

Brother Crispo gives himself a moment to compose a response as he takes in the scene.

"This is Lydia," he says softly, suddenly overcome with concern that he might spook the boy and lose him with a careless gesture. "She is a good layer." He takes a step toward the boy. "And I am Brother Crispo." He lifts a hand. "I'm glad to meet you, Rah."

Rah makes no effort to take his hand. "Can cook egg for Rah, Crispo?

Rah hungry."

The corpulent priest looks over the boy's lean frame and frowns. Why does the House of the Moon starve their slave gods so? He puts his hands on his ample hips and shakes his head sadly.

"Well, we shall see, Rah, what is left of the world. If I can find the means, we shall cook you an egg. Come," he lifts an arm, hoping the boy will allow him to guide him back into the chicken shed where he can show him Lydia's laying box. But Rah looks at him suspiciously and moves back out of his reach.

"No, you get."

Ah, thinks Brother Crispo, you are not going to let a grown man lure you into a shed. Smart boy.

"Very well, Rah," says Brother Crispo agreeably. "I will collect some of Lydia's eggs, and then we will see if we can find a pot and boil them for you."

Rush is approaching the courtyard of burned out huts from the east when he spots Rah and Brother Crispo rounding the barns on the southwest end of the colony. He is already annoyed that Rah has disobeyed him and wandered, doubly annoyed that the boy has copulated with a woman he had every reason to believe was his wife, or at least his property. Now he sees the boy gamely entertaining the attentions of the fat, fool priest, Crispo, who has headed the City of the Dead these past five months. Even more annoying is the fact that Crispo, nephew of Ananou, has somehow escaped yesterday's massacre.

"Oh dear," says Crispo, when he sees the assassin standing in the center of the still smoking ruins of the colony. "Oh dear, oh dear. If it isn't the devil himself, the very devil. What on earth is he doing here?"

He will not wait long to find out. Rah has dropped like a rag to a full bow at his side, his face hidden as his curls fall over his knees into the dirt, and Rush is striding toward them with enough impulsion to knock down a line of house guards, were there any here to protect him.

"Oh, dear," whispers Brother Crispo. "That is a very unhappy assassin. What have I done to displease him?"

"Crispo!" booms Rush into his face when he reaches him, loudly enough to wake the dead priests whose bodies are strewn about the courtyard. "What are you doing alive, and in possession of my little Grain God, eh? Your head needs loosening."

"Is it my fault I have avoided death, sir? You see what has befallen us!" responds Brother Crispo, more out of sheer terror than argument. He lifts his arms to gesture at the wreckage all about them.

"Captains go down with their vessels, Crispo, or hang when they reach port," responds the assassin, shoving the man a few paces back and reaching down to grab a fist full of Rah's curls. With it he yanks the boy onto his toes. "You wander from me again, little cat and I will make a maiden of you," he grumbles into the boy's face.

"I was gathering eggs when they came," offers Brother Crispo, cringing as Rush gives Rah a shake in mid air.

"A chicken in a chicken coop," answers Rush, still holding Rah so that his toes skim the ground. "Why did you leave camp, boy?" He takes the boy's face in his free hand. "Answer me!"

"Hungr-" grunts Rah, unable to finish the word with the assassin's grip dislocating his jaw.

"He was hungry," offers Brother Crispo. "Look at the poor little thing, he is skin and bone. Don't you feed him?"

Rush shoots the priest a vicious look, then looks Rah over as if examining a calf he means to slaughter. The boy has lost weight since they left Cyrus. After three grueling days of travel he more nearly resembles himself in his coma than at his athletic apex. He has eaten little more than dried fruits and nuts, and these from the Captain's personal provisions and only because Nikolaos was there to coax him. A hot ball of guilt pulses in Rush's throat. He sets the boy down on his feet, still holding him by the scruff, and looks back at the priest.

"Have you something for him to eat?" he says, awkwardly. "He is very particular-"

"We were just going to find a pot to boil these," says Brother Crispo, pulling two eggs out of the pockets of his robe with a satisfied smile.

CHAPTER 47

In the city of Knossos, anarchy has reigned for a single day.

But the falcon cannot hunt without the falconer, and Knossos is a tame city that knows only the rule of bureaucrats, not soldiers, businessmen, not generals.

The rabble has had their time, their moment to take what they have envied from the houses and businesses of the rich who have deserted them. But as morning breaks over the still lovely skyline of the greatest city in the Aegean, the people look for hope. This is a people who have been governed by queens and high priests for two hundred years. Their Queen is gone. As are their two most powerful religious, Mochlos and Ananou. But there are two high priests left to look to for governance. There is Enenoch, High Priest of the House of the Sky, and Tyrus, High Priest of the Bull God.

These two have always been heads of lesser houses of worship, given less importance and so, less financial strength in the scheme of things. But today they are the highest-ranking officials left in the city. And the people want guidance.

Perhaps because of their smaller stature as religious powers, Enenoch and Tyrus have always been allies. Today, Enenoch has come to visit the house of the Bull God, with a contingent of guards to keep him safe in the streets, to discuss their future.

"It has settled down, Enenoch, as I knew it must. These people are a peace loving, greedy lot. Take away their government, they will steal. But in the end they will look for leaders to return the peace."

"There is no army, no insurgence," agrees Enenoch. "Just a bit of rabble from the east end. They plundered the palace, what was left in it, and the Houses of the Moon and Sun. When they came to my gates my men took down a few with arrows from the roof and the rest fled. Most have gone back to their homes with their spoils. Fools. It will all mean nothing if the gods release the fires of Tartarus on us from Thera."

Enenoch is picking at his fingers as he speaks. He is a nervous man, tall and lank, shaven bald, as are all of the high priests of Knossos but for Tyrus, whose crowning glory is his luxurious mane of black hair, which he allows to flow to his shoulders to give him the appearance of a Minotaur. "A priest of the Bull God does not shave his head, nor his member," Tyrus has been known to say in defense of his peculiar style. "The hair is a feature of strength and manhood." But in reality, he simply has a love of hair, his own especially.

"Had I but a ship in harbor," murmurs Tyrus for the umpteenth time. "I would be in Egypt, or Hatti, where I have family."

"You would be all the rage in Hatti, Tyrus," responds Enenoch, finding the image humorous. For Hatti is a land of hair, the warriors there believing their strength to be in it and wearing it long, like women.

"But my two vessels are far out to sea, trading with China. And you, Enenoch, have no vessels at all."

"What does a priest need with trade, Tyrus? The people provide my house with all I require to discharge my duties as a religious."

"Oh, pah, Enenoch. You simply can't afford one. What with Mochlos and his Grain God hogging the people's charity and the Queen's favor. The clever bastard."

The two men stand on Tyrus' northern balcony, which overlooks the back of the palace and beyond it, the sea. The church of the Bull God is located just south of the palace, as is fitting. Each house has been built in the appropriate quadrant of the city. The House of the Sun is in the east, for the Sun God rises from that horizon each morning. The House of the Moon is nearest the harbor, for the Moon dominates the Sea. The House of the Sky God is built on the southwest edge of town, nearest to Mount Ida. And the church of the Bull God is tucked into the hills on a rise just south of the palace, for the Bull God lives in the earth.

"If only we could get our hands on the little Grain God, Tyrus, we could pacify these fools. They believe it is his disappearance that has caused their woes. If he were to show up in our possession ..." Enenoch does not finish his thought. He is drumming his fingers on the balcony wall and tapping his foot as if an internal rhythm is ever playing in his brain.

"Well, it would buy us some time, I suppose," responds Tyrus. "But in the end it will all be the same. I fear what the sailors tell us is true, Enenoch. The only safety is distance. The steam from the nipple of Thera blows west. East is safest. What we need is a ship."

"What we need is a miracle," answers Enenoch, tapping a nervous finger against the mud brick wall.

By late morning the corpulent Brother Crispo has been introduced to the rest of the company and has provided his new friends with a generous and much appreciated meal. In the colony of huts in the center of the compound there is little left of value. Most of them are burned down and what little food and housewares the priests possessed have been taken by the raiders. But Crispo is not a man to leave his comfort in the hands of others. Behind the courtyard, in the cemetery, he had commandeered a tomb not a week after he was assigned to spend six months in the City of the Dead. Cool and dry, with a short stair facing south and a door on either end, it was a perfect place to hide a kitchen. Crispo, being of superior rank in the colony, had the remains of the dead removed and relegated to the fire pit, to be cleaned and laid to rest with distant relatives. Then he borrowed some brick from several other graves and converted a corner of his new kitchen into an oven. He used the bottom half of a palace amphora, which one of the families of the dead had left filled with grain as an offering for their deceased, to make himself a stove, and dug a pit on the opposite side of the tomb for cool storage. This accomplished, he set to work doing what he loved bests—cooking---and quickly earned the affection of his peers and a reputation as the best superior the colony had ever known.

Once he is satisfied that his hidden kitchen has not been raided, and that he still has the means to do so, he sets to making a decent meal for Rah, and for the other travelers in the assassin's company. Crispo returns to the barnyard, taking Cara along with Rush's permission, and together they gather enough eggs and goat's milk to provide for a party of five hungry guests. For Brother Crispo is not one to mourn. He is a man who believes in sunshine and celebration. And so with what seems little effort, he is soon entertaining his visitors not twenty meters from where they spent the night, outside his kitchen tomb in the pleasant mid-morning cemetery breeze.

"You may be worth your weight," grunts Rush, who lies on his side enjoying a home-cooked breakfast for the first time since he left his own house in Knossos three weeks earlier. He has pulled off his hood, and leans on an elbow in the grass, his eyes on Rah, who is wolfing honey-soaked grain cakes across from him.

"There, you see?" quips the priest, handing Cara another plate of freshly baked cakes from the door of the tomb, to pass around the group. "And you were angry I was not to be counted among the dead, sir. A chicken's place is in the coop!" And the group laughs, knowing from earlier conversation how it was that Brother Crispo escaped death.

"And had you heard my scream, would you have come to save me, Brother Crispo?" smiles Cara at the big man, knowing full well that he must have heard it.

"Dear girl, what could I have done for you, but harmonize?" responds

Crispo, earning another round of laughter from his guests.

"My little slave god needs his priests," muses Rush, after the chuckling has died down. He is still watching Rah eating voraciously. His comment brings the Captain's attention from the plate of grain cakes Cara is offering him.

"You are planning something, Rush," he says, narrowing his eyes at the assassin.

"I am always planning something, Captain," responds Rush humorlessly. Cara has come to sit on her heels in front of him with the plate of fresh cakes before her, waiting for him to accept another helping. Her priest's cowl is back, her hair cascades over her shoulders, and the V of the robe has fallen open to her waist. "For instance," he continues, his eyes wander down Cara's throat to the swell of her breasts and back, "your wedding."

This nearly causes Cara to tumble over onto him in shock. Her eyes flash open, and stare into his a moment too long for her own good before she recovers and drops them respectfully to the ground.

Crispo has returned to his kitchen and can be heard bumbling around and humming to himself from within. Rah has become distracted by something in the tree line west of the cemetery. But Nikolaos has understood the assassin's meaning. He peers at him, then allows his eyes to wander over Cara, who remains crouched before Rush as if in a bow.

"A gift, Rush? What have I done to deserve such consideration," he says acerbically.

"You could use a distraction, Captain," answers Rush, waving Cara and the plate of cakes away.

"I cannot afford a wife, sir, I have yet to make my way in the world," responds Nicolaos when Cara is out of earshot, having returned to the kitchen tomb to help Brother Crispo. Turning to see what has caught Rah's attention he adds, "and it will take more than a wife, no matter how appealing she may be, to distract me from my promise to myself and to my Queen to preserve the safety of the Grain God."

"Perhaps, but when we reach my ship I become captain and commander, and as captain, I intend to make a husband of you, pup. And to pull that burr from my buttocks at the same time," he nods in the direction of the kitchen.

Rah has jumped to his feet as he speaks. Now Rush casually walks over to him, his war dogs flanking him, all three peering east, ears lifted. Nikolaos comes to his feet as well to stand at the assassin's side.

"More raiders, Captain," smiles Rush. "Returning to pick over what may be left from yesterday's slaughter. Perhaps my dogs have left me something to play with after all." He takes Rah by the arm and pushes him toward the kitchen tomb stairs. "Watch," he says to the dogs, giving Rah a little shake, then nods to the boy and directs him down into the kitchen. The dogs obediently follow him down the stairs.

"You too, Captain," says Rush, motioning for Nikolaos to join the others. "Close the door behind you, and do not give away your position."

Nikolaos stares at the assassin, hesitating. "There could be dozens of them. I cannot leave you here to defend us all, sir. I am no coward."

"No, but I have come to like you, pup, and do not wish to see you cut down in battle behind my back while I am yet engaged. Put yourself out of harm's way," says Rush, nodding to the kitchen door and speaking with more gentle humor than Nikolaos imagined he was capable of.

Nikolaos turns dutifully to the stairs, descends them, hesitates, then closes the tomb door and returns to the surface.

"I will not disobey an order, sir, but respectfully ask once more for permission to remain at your side," he says to Rush.

Smiling, Rush takes his shoulder and gives it a painful squeeze. "Granted, Captain. Now take my left flank, around to the north. We will let them pass through, then come up behind them. It matters not their number. They will search the raided huts, and finding nothing of value will go to the barnyard to steal livestock. We will pick off stragglers coming through the cemetery, decreasing their number and determining who is in charge, if anyone. We will corral the remainder in the barnyard when they are distracted by their work. Stay always on my left flank. Understood?"

"Understood, sir," responds Nikolaos, and then adds without thinking, "You speak as if we are an army, Rush. But we are only two."

"I am an army unto myself, Captain," responds the assassin, "and together we make an alliance."

As it happens, the men coming to raid the City of the Dead are not remnants of yesterday's massacre, but renegade palace guards from Knossos who have formed their own band. They are easy enough to identify, for they still wear their palace uniforms, in whole or part. Just as Rush predicted, they cut through the cemetery, passing Crispo's hidden kitchen (the clever priest had doused the oven fire by then) within a few hundred feet, and moving in a disjointed group toward the colony of huts.

Hesitating only a moment when he sees the uniform of a palace guard, Nikolaos takes two heads himself when a pair of stragglers, lagging behind the others, notices the breakfast debris outside the kitchen tomb and stop to investigate. He has counted a dozen men by then, and hurries to catch up with the remainder. But by the time he has reached the burned out huts, he has passed five fresh corpses, men Rush has taken down like a sly wolf, picking them off from behind, the first four in pairs of two, without drawing the notice of the leaders. All but the last has been dispatched in the peculiar style that Nikolaos will come to know as the assassin's trademark, a dagger through the space under the jawbone, into the back of his victim's throat and up into the bottom of his brain. The last man has had his head bashed in with a rock.

Leaving the cemetery, Nikolaos spots Rush signaling to him from the tree line north of the courtyard. When he sees he has caught the Captain's eye, Rush makes two deliberate gestures, the first, a splayed hand: "five are left." The second, a point toward himself and then a circling motion: "Stay on my left flank." Nikolaos obeys, circling the huts to the south as he approaches the barnyard behind Rush.

He is determined not to let the assassin out of his sight, but loses Rush almost immediately when two men exit the ox barn with a cow and he must drop behind a shed for cover. In the next instant he hears shouting of men mingled with the lowing of the frightened cow and the clash of battle. It is time to join, making it two against five. He jumps from his hiding place and rushes toward the skirmish.

And sees that three more renegade palace guards are running toward the barnyard from the cemetery.

"Damn!" Nikolaos turns to confront them.

The first plows into him with his sword forward but close to his body as the second and third circle, containing him on the right and left. He lifts his sword and smashes the man's weapon down and away. In less than an instant he has been pressed into a defensive position. His first thought is that the Palace Guard of Knossos has been better trained than that of Cyrus. These men know how to carry and spar. It is three against one and he must continuously turn in a circle to maintain sight of all three of his opponents. He cannot keep this up for long and with Rush engaging five men on his own, he cannot hope for help from the assassin.

Nikolaos jumps back and parries as the first man to engage him lunges again. I must think like Rush, he says to himself, and then the man to his left draws a blade of blood on his upper arm and the hot, driving anger that is never far from him leaps from his breast into his brain and chases fear off like a deer.

Nikolaos spins, his sword not held to spar but to dismember. He takes the man behind him by surprise and cuts open his face.

The man lets out a high-pitched scream and drops his sword. He lifts his hands to his wound, and blood gushes through his fingers and runs down his arms.

Nikolaos' sword continues on its arc and slices across the next man's breast. The blade cuts clean through to the man's ribs and splits his free arm open from elbow to wrist, cutting his right hand in half.

The third man has backed off. He takes a moment to consider his friends, then turns and dashes back toward the cemetery and the road to Knossos.

Nikolaos looks to the assassin, ready to come to his aid. But there is no need. Rush is watching him from the center of a pile of dying palace guards, his feet apart and his broad shoulders eclipsing the cow shed. He has taken down four men and seems to have saved a fifth, a man nearly his height but half his girth, for Nikolaos to watch die. He has twisted the man's right arm behind his back and the man is on his toes moaning in pain, though it is obvious by the odd angle of his arm that his shoulder is already dislocated.

Rush slaps his free hand onto his captive's forehead and pulls his face back. He gives Nikolaos a moment to comprehend, then brings his teeth down on the man's throat.

You are insane, thinks Nikolaos as Rush releases his opponent and the man crumples to the ground at his feet. But the man's throat is not opened, nor is the assassin's beard dripping with his blood. Still, the man is down and finished.

As if dreaming, Nikolaos walks toward Rush.

He looks about at the assassin's work. Most of the men are still alive, moaning or weeping like boys. One man has lost his hand at the wrist. The hand still clings to his sword. Another man has had his face sliced at the scalp and holds the skin that has been ripped down over his eyes as if it might somehow reattach itself.

The man at the assassin's feet is wheezing for air through his crushed windpipe.

"I lost my dagger in that one," Rush nods at a man lying in a patch of cow manure behind him. He turns to recover it from the man's chest.

"You cut down five swordsmen with nothing but hand held blades," murmurs Nikolaos. "And threw one at an opponent, leaving you with none, when you still had one man to face?"

Rush looks at him with exaggerated patience.

"You did well, pup," he says, placing his foot on the chest of the man with the dagger in his heart and giving the golden handle a firm yank to dislodge it. "You are learning."

Nikolaos is looking down at the last man Rush dispatched.

"I don't understand," he says, as Rush bends to wipe the blade of his dagger in the grass and then return it to the holster strapped to his ankle.

"Look here." Rush steps in front of him, and instantly has him by the side of his neck in one hand. Nikolaos flinches involuntarily. Rush holds his gaze, strokes his throat with his thumb along the thorax, gently, like a lover. Then he presses. Nicholoas chokes and grabs at the assassin's hand.

"The windpipe is made of cartilage. Crush it, it cannot recover. Your man is down." One hand still cupping the side of Nicholoas' neck, he looks down and kicks the dying man in the throat for good measure. Then he returns his gaze to Nikolaos with a wicked smile before he releases him.

"How will we get to your ship without a contingent of guards, Rush?" says Nikolaos as they head back to the cemetery kitchen.

"Robes, Captain. Crispo has one, as does Cara. And I keep one in my rucksack. We need two more. Let us look about the courtyard for a few. The dead no longer need them."

After stripping two of the less bloodied corpses of their vestures the two return to the tomb kitchen, where Crispo and Cara have been busy packing what is left of the priest's supplies into baskets saved from the offerings of families of the dead.

"Good," says Rush of their work, "it will complete our disguise. A few priests, having survived a raid, coming into town with what is left of their possessions."

"I must take Lydia also," says Crispo, hands on hips. "And a white nanny. The boy needs the eggs and milk and I doubt you thought of it when you loaded your ship, sir." He has learned that he can berate the assassin for neglecting Rah's divine needs and yet live, and he is fast becoming a habitual abuser of the privilege.

"Very well, Crispo, go and collect them. No, you stay with me now, boy," says Rush, taking Rah by the arm when the boy moves to follow the priest back to the barnyard. "Take the woman with you."

By noon the little company, dressed in the robes of the Priests of the Dead, are heading down the mountain toward the harbor of Knossos. Crispo and Cara, each holding an opposite handle, carry a basket of housewares and provisions, and a trussed hen, between them. Rah and the Captain carry the second basket, with the nanny tied to Rah's belt by his golden chain. Rush leads, his two war dogs tracking him on either side of the road, deep in the brush and invisible. Their journey takes several hours but meets with no misfortune. As they descend the mountain they are relieved to see that the city is calm. Although there is no travel up and down the Bridge Road, nevertheless the streets appear to have normal activity. The harbor is all but deserted, and only the Queen's ship lists in the moderate waves half a kilometer out from the shore.

"What is it, Rush?" says Nikolaos when the big man stops in the road ahead of him.

"It is not my ship," he answers. "That is the Queen's vessel. And yet look there, a skiff is tied at her stern."

"But the Queen has deserted her city, you said so yourself. Else the dogs would have never been released from the storehouse. Else the palace guards would not be raiding the City of the Dead."

"Just so," says Rush, peering out over the harbor. "Ah," and he turns to clap Nikolaos on the shoulder and bring him close, pointing. "Look at her flags, Captain. See the black one, beneath the Queen's trident?"

"The Tears of the Bull," murmurs Nikolaos with some resentment, touching his own cheek unconsciously.

But Rush only offers him an unlikely laugh. "You may well thank me for that mark someday, Captain," he says mysteriously and then continues down the road toward the harbor.

CHAPTER 48

In Knossos, Tyrus, High Priest of the Bull God, has been taking advantage of misfortune. His men have moved him into the palace, where he has a greater look of authority, and what is left of the Palace Guard has been taken into his service. Now he looks out to sea from the Queen's own chamber window. He looks out over the harbor at the ship she left behind, and he considers its meaning.

Several days ago the ship moved from the dock out into the bay. One or two palace guards were sent down to the wharf this morning to see if there was any movement aboard the vessel. They came back with the most interesting news Tyrus has heard since he learned that the Queen was deserting her people. He learned that beneath the Queens flag flies the flag of the Aegean Assassin.

Tyrus has always believed in looking for the advantages in life. It is how he became High Priest of the Bull God in the first place. He has used this method of approach throughout his life, ever since the first real opportunity to do so exposed itself.

It has served him well.

For when Tyrus was only a boy of fifteen he was taken in battle on the plains of Troy. He was taken by the Greeks. Not a pleasant proposition for a fifteen year old Hittite boy who passed easily for eighteen.

Tyrus was large for his age, of course, and this contributed to his look of maturity. But he also had a beard, a good beard, by the time he was fifteen. It was what got him into the army in the first place. His father had died in battle, a terrible disadvantage to a boy of fifteen. And his mother was simply no match for him. Another disadvantage. When she begged him to stay home and work in the local pottery to help feed the family, he threw her into the cow shed and bolted the door. Then he went back into the house, picked up his infant sister, and a torch from the kitchen fire, and brought them both outside, positioning himself so that his mother could watch him through the little window above the shed door.

"Give me your permission, woman, or I will set her aflame and you can watch her cook!" he said, holding the torch dangerously close to the babe's swaddling.

It was an easy enough choice for the mother. She had two more sons, one older, one younger, than Tyrus. She gave the boy permission and swore to his commander that he was seventeen. She never saw him again.

Tyrus should have been put to death in the province where he was captured. Greeks rarely spared Hittites or made slaves of them. They were simply too dangerous and bull headed and it never ended well. But Tyrus was a clever boy. He convinced the Greeks to let him fight their best dagger man in a game of sport. If the Greek won, Tyrus would at least lose his life in battle, and the Greeks would have had a good fight to bet on and a bit of fun to break up the monotony of daily life in the field. If he won, he would be brought back to the coast when the Greek army returned home in the fall, and would be put up for auction. The Greek commander could hardly lose in either case. Tyrus would either die in the contest, or be sold to a merchant on the coast, no doubt for a handsome sum, and taken across the sea. His own commander in Mycenae would never be the wiser. He agreed to the challenge.

The man they put up against Tyrus was a swordsman who had special training in knife fighting and at first it seemed an unfair match and not much sport. Tyrus' opponent had years more experience than he, was taller and broader, and had the advantage of the knife. All but two of the Greeks bet on him, expecting the fight to be over before it began. The two Greeks who bet on Tyrus had both had some hand-to-hand combat with Hittites at one time or another in their careers. They sat together quietly beside the bet holder and waited to clean up.

It was the first true test of Tyrus' theory that there is advantage in every disadvantage.

Tyrus came out into the center of the fighting pen, an area about twenty meters wide, around which soldiers watched the game leaning against a ring of carts. He made a few attempts to lunge at his knife wielding opponent, jumping nimbly out of the way when the man's dagger came within striking distance, then took a more passive roll and simply danced around on his toes avoiding the knifeman's slicing swings. In truth, he was deliberately setting the man up to give away his fighting technique. And after several turns around the circle, he had a pretty good grasp of it.

Tyrus allowed the man to advance, drawing him always around the outside of the circle so as not to be cornered, and encouraging him to begin repeating the same swings, the same three steps thus, two that, until the soldiers watching the contest were beginning to bore and become irate, until they were jeering their own man and urging him to rush to finish the fight. He knew that his opponent's movements were engrained, habitual, because of his training, and that he was liable to display the gist of his technique even in this short space of time. Thus, Tyrus anticipated that he could turn the man's advantage, that is, training and experience, into his disadvantage, and his own disadvantage, being his inexperience and lack of a weapon, into his advantage.

Tyrus waited a bit longer, leading the man around the circle, dodging and testing his skill with erratic moves. Before he made his decision to strike he had learned that the man had a weak left side, the side on which he held his knife, perhaps due to poor vision in that eye. As a matter of fact, the man had only partial vision on the left side, the result of a blow to the head in battle two months earlier and a thing he had not admitted to his commander, who would have sent him to the rear.

Tyrus let the knifeman continue chasing him around the ring, over-confident in his armed advantage. Soon Tyrus would make an unexpected move that would cause his opponent a split-second of hesitation. And that was all any warrior needed.

Round and round the two opponents went with Tyrus leaping back away from the knife blade, first to the left, then to the right, the knifeman moving rhythmically and redundantly forward. It seemed that he had been dancing backwards for a good ten minutes when without warning the doorway of advantage that Tyrus was looking for presented itself. One of the bystanders, leaning forward and goading his man to strike and have it over, tripped over his own boot heel and took a short step into the ring just in front of the knifeman. It was a minor thing and could have come to nothing. But it was enough of a break for Tyrus.

Without warning he too tripped, but purposefully and to the man's left, falling back onto his buttocks and sweeping his legs round in front of himself as the knifeman continued to advance one instant too many. Tyrus swept the man's legs out from under him.

The rest was easy, for the Hittites were the finest wrestlers in the Aegean and Tyrus was the best in his province and could put a boy twice his size in a hold faster than a man can truss a goat. Once down, the knife man was a fish pulled up on shore. Out of his element of advantage, he was easily put on his face. Then Tyrus twisted his knife hand back and under until he heard the pop of a shoulder coming out of its socket. He relieved the man of his knife and opened his throat with it.

After that, the Greeks held Tyrus is awe. They kept him with them for two years, allowing him to train their recruits in the art of hand to hand. Of course, Tyrus kept his best Hittite secrets to himself, knowing full well that to do anything less was treasonous to his own countrymen. But he used his position of servitude to his advantage, making sure to impress his masters with his willing service and unerring respect. He earned his freedom when he was but seventeen, was offered a commission in the Greek army, and declined, though the alternative was a lifetime of slavery. He would not fight against his own.

"You must sell me into slavery, sir. I will sabotage an entire regiment if you give me the opportunity," he openly told his master. "I am always a Hittite."

He was taken to the coast and sold to a Minoan slave merchant, none other than Kephas, who was so impressed with his strength and endurance as a rower that he kept him aboard his ship for three years.

In the three years he had rowed on the galley of Kephas' ship, he had never made the slightest move to escape from his master. He had no reason to. He did not wish to return to his homeland, where he would be obligated to work to support his mother and younger siblings. He disliked the colonies along the coast of Canaan, mostly due to his inherent hatred of small town living. Egypt was enticing, but the politics made it difficult for a clever slave to make something of his disadvantages. And Tyrus was determined to do just that.

Then, on the morning of Tyrus' twentieth birthday, Kephas' ship anchored in the harbor of Knossos.

And Tyrus of Troy fell in love with a city.

From the ship, the skyline of Knossos was like nothing he had ever seen. It glimmered in the sunlight like a pearl necklace, lying along the beach in the sand. One could see the coral roof of the palace from here, cresting the white villas that rose all along the shoreline. There was the bridge leading into the city, an immense mural painted on its face in startling colors.

Tyrus never wanted anything more in his life, and he determined at that very instant that he would make Knossos his home. He learned everything he could about the Minoans from his shipmates that day as they waited in the harbor for Kephas to return from his business in the city.

"Who are these people?" he asked the boatswain. "What do they worship? Who governs them? What entertains them?" And once he had learned what he needed to know, he set about to convince Kephas to sell him to the Queen.

That night, in the hold of the ship, he killed another man. He did it using the horn of a bull, a trinket that Kephas had kept in his own personal items, a thing dipped in gold that had been given the merchant by an Egyptian priest in exchange for a beautiful Nubian boy who had been captured on the coast of Africa. Tyrus had known about the horn for two years but had never touched it. He knew that it had symbolic meaning to Kephas and that he would never part with it, and somehow this stayed in his mind. Perhaps it was his belief that such sentimentality was a weakness in his master, a disadvantage. And wherever there was disadvantage, there was advantage. One day the horn would be his ally.

He made no effort to disguise his work, though he could easily have done so. It was very clear who the murderer was. He left the horn lodged in the man's ear, then cut a coin sized hole in the back of his own scalp with a healthy lock of his hair attached. He tied the grizzly thing to the horn. When the body was found, Kephas ordered Tyrus to pull his Hittite braid up and reveal his scalp. There was the matching wound.

"What have you done, Tyrus? I have treated you like a son," said Kephas then, heartbroken, for Tyrus was like a son to him, or at least a damned good slave until now, and he had considered giving him his freedom when he was twenty five and offering him a position of rank on his ship. "And this is how you repay me?"

"I have killed, sir, and I will kill again and again. Like a snake in the grass, I will pick off your best, until one day, when we are out to sea, and I see my advantage, I will kill you, Master, and take your ship, for you have taught me everything I need to know to become a successful merchant," said Tyrus, remembering now his mother's sobs for mercy as he held the torch to his baby sister's swaddling cloth what seemed a lifetime ago. If it comes to this, if I can have this city, he thought, then it has all been worth it, and I have turned my disadvantage into a life of luxury amongst a soft and silly people.

"Why do you tell me this? When you know I must hang you for it," said Kephas, looking down with dismay at the golden bull's horn, which he could not bring himself to dislodge from his second mate's head.

"I have worked for you like a bull at the plow, for three years pulling your oars from morning 'til night," responded Tyrus. "You say you have loved me like a son. Now decide. Will you put me to death because I would rather die than remain on this ship? Or can you see an opportunity for profit when it presents itself? Look here at this island people. They worship the sun and the moon and the sky. They set up queens to govern. They jump bulls for entertainment and make gods of slaves. Sell me to the Queen and I will make us both rich. Tell her I am come from Egypt where I have fought and killed a hundred bulls to entertain the Pharoah. Give me nothing but this golden horn with which to fight. Tell them it is imbued with the spirit of the Bull God. They have no priest to honor him. Let her put me in a ring with a bull. How can you lose? Either I kill the beast and become a god myself, the Priest of the Bull God, or I die. You lose nothing."

"What have these peace-loving people done to me to deserve you, Tyrus? You are a strong rower, it is true. But you are also a murdering Hittite. It would be like letting loose a weasel into a hen house."

"Not so, Master. I will give them what they need. I will give them a new church, and a male deity with which to strengthen their people."

Now Tyrus put a hand on his master's shoulder, a dangerous thing for any slave, even one already looking down the throat of death, to do. He spoke as if to an equal. "This man was a thief and well you know it, Master. He had been stealing from you for years. This horn," and Tyrus leaned down to pluck the thing from the dead man's ear, "was given to you in payment for a slave you loved enough to sell into a better life. Now give it to me, and let me use it for the same purpose."

"No man can kill a Cretan bull with a golden horn, Tyrus, not even a stone-headed murdering Hittite like yourself."

"Then I die trying." was all that Tyrus answered. "Not hanged, but gored to death, for killing a man on your ship."

Kephas knew he had been beaten. He could not kill Tyrus, least of all for disposing of a sneak whom he had never been able to pin to his acts of thievery. Besides, he was too fond of him. But he had no choice now. If he did not hang him, or sell him, he would lose the respect of his crew, and that was as good as suicide for a merchant captain.

"Very well, Tyrus. May the bull be palsied. I will approach the Queen with your story. But I cannot guarantee she will use you for the purpose you propose."

But Queen Nanaea was in love with the idea as soon as she heard it. A man who could kill a bull with a golden horn? A bull's horn? And if he could pull it off, a new priest? A new church? More revenue for the palace. It was genius, and just what she needed at this point in her life as a Queen, a Queen without daughters. A diversion. A spectacle for the people!

And so Tyrus was sold to the Queen for an enormous sum, and kept with the bulls for three days while the palace prepared for the fight. The city was astir with the story and buzzing with anticipation of the contest. A man who could kill a bull with a golden horn! Who says he is the agent of the Bull God himself! Come to establish a proper church here in Knossos! Well this is what we have needed all along! A House for the Bull God!

On the night before the contest, Tyrus did a simple thing. He cheated. He eavesdropped on the bull keepers and learned which bull they planned to match against him the following day. Then he waited until the palace was asleep and went down to the bull pen. He fed the animal the stem of a certain yew tree, a plant used medicinally on board merchant ships but known to be highly poisonous to oxen. In the morning the animal was walking in circles in his pen, sweating and digging the ground. By early afternoon, an hour before the contest, he was dead.

It did not take a statesman to convince Knossos that the Bull God had sided with the man from Egypt. That the city was in dire need of his services.

And thus the House of the Bull God was established.

To his credit, Tyrus returned the golden bull horn to Kephas, who kept it until the day he died, much as he did his memory of Rah.

By late afternoon the man Nikolaos failed to kill in the barnyard battle that morning has made his way back to the city. He has learned that the Priest of the Bull God, that Hittite bastard, Tyrus, has taken up residence in the abandoned palace. He has learned this from several guards who returned to the employment of the palace themselves when they discovered that the two high priests who had not abandoned them were taking up residence there, and had brought their households with them. Tyrus, whom by now everyone knew was a Hittite by birth, had taken the Queen's wing, Enenoch the King's. The main and second floors had been plundered by thugs from the east end that morning, but the maze of storage rooms and tunnels beneath the palace were untouched. The plebian fools did not even know of their existence. Tyrus, though not especially beloved of the people, was the best game in town, and so a good number of palace guards had returned to service with him. The man who Nikolaos failed to kill soon joined them. He had had enough of being a renegade palace guard.

It was not long before his story of the skirmish with the assassin, and a man dressed in the uniform of a Cyrian guard, reached Tyrus. And it was not long before Tyrus, who had always been careful to keep an ear to the street, put together the pieces of the puzzle of the Queen's ship and the assassin's flag.

"Here is our miracle, Enenoch," says Tyrus, standing at the northwest window of the second floor of the Queen's suite and looking out over the harbor and the last vessel left in the bay. "The assassin has returned with the Grain God, and the Queen has left him a ship in the harbor with which he might flee this doomed city and return to his home in Anatolia."

"How can you be so sure the boy is with him, Tyrus?" responds Enenoch nervously. "The man said he had a Cyrian palace guard with him. There was no sighting of the boy."

"Enenoch, what was he doing in Cyrus? Is it not obvious that he had reason to believe the boy was there, in the possession of the Queen? Thus the palace guardsman?"

"Why would Nanaea leave him a ship?" counters Enenoch, ever searching for the mold in the bread.

"Because the assassin and Ameg are one and the same. Clearly they had a relationship, one perhaps we will never fully understand."

"Ameg was a pansy," responds Enenoch, looking down at his fingers irritably. "I have never believed this talk that Ameg is the Terror of the Aegean."

"You will, my friend," answers Tyrus pleasantly, slapping him on the back and nearly toppling him over the window ledge. "For you are soon to meet him."

"And how do you propose to divert them to the palace?"

Tyrus smiles with self-confident satisfaction. "A rumor should do it."

CHAPTER 49

By the time Rush and his company have reached the paved road leading into the city, a mob has formed on the dock.

It was not a difficult rumor for Tyrus to start. The people of Knossos already knew that Ameg had returned on a skiff a fortnight earlier, revealed himself as none other than Rush the Assassin, and after leaving the House of the Moon orders to board his own vessel when it returned for him, took off like a wolf in the night to recover the Grain God of Knossos for his own purposes. They knew, too, that it was the assassin who was responsible for Mochos' failure to sacrifice the boy properly to the god Rah at the end of summer. Now a servant of the House of the Sky, who claimed to have overheard a conversation between two guards at the palace, swore that Ameg was on his way into the city with the missing Grain God and that he planned to board the Queens ship and take him away with him to Anatolia. As she told it, a contingent of palace guards had spotted him pillaging the City of the Dead and attempted to arrest him. They had been sent out that morning by Tyrus, who hoped to recover the stolen Grain God and return him to Knossos so that he could be sacrifice, thus saving the city from disaster.

Now Rush and his company, having made it safely down to the wharf, are confronted with a crowd of angry men and women who have prepared for them. They have gathered a pile of stones, and one, who seems to have taken the role of their leader, steps forward as the five travelers approach them.

"Ameg, we want the slave god, Rah, and we will have him. Hand him over and we will let you board the ship the Queen has left for you. Your own family and household, as well as that of the House of the Moon, have departed for Anatolia. The Queen's ship waits for you in the harbor. Go, join your family. But the Grain God is the property of the people of

Knossos. You have caused all of our misfortune by preventing his sacrifice on the Mountain to the god he represents, as is proper. Give us the boy, and you are free to go. But deny us, and you die." With this he hefts the first rock toward Rush. It lands with a thump in the sand at the assassins feet, rather ineffectually. But it is only a gesture, a means of instigating the crowd to follow suit. The mob behind the man are all lifting their stones and readying, on a sign from him, to begin throwing them.

Rush instinctively holds his arms out on either side, forming a barricade with his body in an attempt to keep the others from being struck by a premature stone.

"Cover the boy," he says to Nikolaos over his shoulder so that only he can hear. "Keep him behind you. I will get the others safely aboard ship. Then we will have to negotiate with this mob."

Nicholoas steps in front of Rah and reaches for his sword under his priest's robe.

"No," says Rush. "Your sword will do no good now Captain, and will only provoke them. Be still."

Nikolaos reluctantly returns his hand to his side.

"Show us the Grain God, Ameg." says the man who is in control of the mob.

"Here he is," responds Rush, reaching back to pull Rah's cowl from his head. There is an instant groan from the crowd, like the sound of a lost animal that has been reunited with its master. Rah's platinum gold head is a dizzyingly beautiful thing in the late afternoon light. His pretty eyes sparkle, green and gold, reflecting the shimmering waves that lap the nearby beach.

"This is what you wish to put to death?" says Rush. His tone is casual, but beneath his hood the muscles against his jaw clench with anger.

"He must die," says the leader of the mob, more subdued, almost apologetically. "We have angered the god by our failure to return him to him. He gave us rich crops and wealthy seas all summer long. But now the coast is plagued by storms, and the volcano threatens. We must take him to Mount Ida and let the priest sacrifice him, as is just. Or else we all die."

"Ah," says Rush to Nikolaos, whose feet are planted in an aggressive stance behind him. "Now you have it. It is the two remaining priests who have instigated this crowd. Tyrus," he snarls to himself. "I will have your balls for breakfast before this is over."

"Very well, sir, you speak with authority," he says to the mob leader, and now it is all Nikolaos can do to keep himself from laughing. How do you say such a thing to so small a man, and sound convincing? You are many things, Rush.

The man relaxes and the crowd lowers their stones, although they do not drop them. Rush takes a casual step forward, pulling back the cowl from his priest's robe. The crowd moves in a cohesive group a few steps backward. For Rush is wearing his assassin's mask, and there is not enough light in the Aegean to soften the picture of the assassin beneath the priest.

"You may escort us to the priest, Tyrus, and thus put the slave god, Rah in the proper hands. But you must allow me to accompany him for I believe that without me your island would already be under the sea. It is I who control the Aegean and always have. And it is I who control the Grain God. Why do you think the volcano has remained appeased? It is because I have rescued Rah from Cyrus, where he was to be put to death, so envious are the people there of Knossos' prosperity. I took Rah, and Cyrus is no more. It has been swallowed by the earth, by the Bull God. Now you wish to take him from me and put him to death. Do so, and the same will become of you. I mean only to remove him from this land to spare you."

The mob leader has been growing agitated. He looks back and forth from the assassin to the mob behind him, knowing full well that the animal he is in control of at the moment could turn on him at any moment. And this man has been a senator in the court of Knossos. He can speak, and will take the mob if he is allowed to speak for long.

"You may accompany the boy," he says suddenly, hoping for a quick ending to the confrontation. He looks back at the crowd for their approval. Several of the men in front nod.

But Rush is not finished. He takes another step forward, toward the beach, toward the crowd. The mob lifts their stones, defensively now.

Rush turns his shoulder to them and in one quick movement opens his sash and allows his robe to drop to the sand. The crowd makes a startled hiss, for the man is a nightmare. Wrapped like a black mummy, his weaponry glints in the sun. But the most disturbing thing is that he seems to have grown to twice his size by removing the robe. Nevertheless, he pays them no heed, but lifts his arms up and spread-eagled, signaling the ship. The crowd turns to discover that there is movement aboard. In a moment, the skiff has been launched and begins to head to shore.

"HUP!" barks Rush, and the two wolf dogs trot up to his sides from behind a building on the wharf. Now the crowd is roused and fearful.

"What the hell are you doing!" hisses Nikolaos at the assassin.

"Making a point, Captain," says Rush. Then he lifts his voice for the crowd. The leader has retreated into the group and is indistinguishable from them. It seems Rush has defeated his authority.

"I have with me a priest," he gestures to Crispo, who quickly removes his cowl to expose his bald head, "and a woman." He gestures to Cara, who does the same. "Surely you will allow me to put them safely aboard ship."

"Put those wolves aboard as well, sir," says the leader from within crowd.

"I cannot. For they will not leave the Grain God, nor allow for his abuse. You will have to separate them from him yourself, sir, if you choose. Or else allow them to accompany us into the city, and let your priest figure out what to do with them."

"Tyrus will know," says someone from within the crowd, and there is a murmur of consent.

"And who is this man beside you who guards Rah?" says another, pointing boldly at Nikolaos.

"He is the Captain of the Palace Guard of Cyrus, who deserted his own Queen to serve the Rah. He has proven in battle that he will lay down his life to protect the boy, and you will have as good a chance of separating the two as you do those two war dogs."

With that, Rush is allowed to put Cara and Crispo on the skiff when it arrives.

"Tell the captain of the ship what has happened," he tells Crispo as he takes Cara's arm and guides her onto the boat after the priest. "Tell him to give me until noon tomorrow. If I am not here then, leave without me."

"No!" cries Cara, struggling to rip her arm out of his impossible grip. "You bastard! Then I stay also!"

"Woman," Rush lowers his voice, taking her by her shoulders, and giving them a painful squeeze, "do as you are told. I will be back with the boy, or there will be no one left alive in Knossos."

Looking into his face with the single-minded focus of a bird of prey, she whispers back, "Gods damn you, Rush, but I swear by them. If you do not return, if you and he do not both of you return, there will be no one alive on the ship either."

This earns her a chuckle and a rough pat on the head. "Only because you have capsized her, Cara, and by mistake," he says, shoving her onto the skiff with enough force to send her to the floor on her bottom. Then he tosses the little nanny goat on top of her.

"I think she did not mean her betrothed," says Nikolaos, shaking his head as they begin climbing the Bridge Road toward the palace, surrounded by the crowd.

"No. She means the boy. And you may as well begin your marriage by knowing she coupled with him last night right under your upright-seated nose, Captain," answers Rush cheerfully.

"You are wicked," says Nikolaos, opening his eyes in shock at him.

"No, Captain, I am your ally. She will give you fierce sons," Rush winks his uncovered eye.

In front of the palace, Rush stops and turns to the crowd, which has long since fallen behind his bold stride. All along the way they have been dropping their stones in the street. They are now without weapons, and subdued.

"You will return to your homes now and leave the politicking to the politicians. Else the assassin will visit you in your sleep. Remember, you must always sleep, and now the assassin knows you," he turns with deliberate slowness to the man who led the crowd at the beach, "and where you sleep," he adds, his voice plummeting into a dark, Hittite growl. The man steps back, as if it were not too late to disguise himself in the crowd.

Then Rush turns to the two men guarding the palace doors. He snaps his finger and the war dogs step forward, smiling dripping jaws at the two men. The men stand stupidly, their hands on the hilts of their swords, looking down at the beasts. They are the same two guards that Ameg confronted several weeks earlier at the doors of the palace.

"These dogs go where I go" says Rush in Ameg's mild and lilting voice, mimicking himself. "And only attack on a single word from me, a word, if spoken by me even in error, that will raise their hackles and put whomever I address inches from a bloody death." It is the precise warning he gave them the first time, but now he gives the admonition with a spine tingling edge. He is dressed as Rush the Assassin, but speaks with the soft voice and high toned Greek accent of Ameg. With another wink from his exposed eye, and leaning into the man on the right, he suddenly adds in a vicious, hell-deep baritone, long with Hittite vowels, "I think it time you learned it."

The two men jump away from the huge double doors, fairly falling off the palace steps as they do so. Rush barks, "Guard!" at the dogs, and they turn to sit where the two men stood moments before. Then the assassin swings open the heavy double doors with a single heave.

"Bar them!" he orders to the guard standing just inside when he and Nikolaos and Rah are within. And the man jumps to attention and throws the massive bolt. Several more guards have come running forward from the interior of the palace.

"Now bring me that cheating whore, Tyrus, and that pathetic housefly, Enenoch so that we may do business!" He grabs the closest man, one with a captain's emblem on his hat. "You have left the wolf in, Larabus" he smiles through his mask into the man's face, close enough to bite off his nose. "What were you thinking, eh?" He releases him with a shove, and the man hurries away toward the Queen's courtyard.

"Take the robe off, Captain, we are no priests," he says to Nikolaos, who gratefully drops his to the floor and then turns to Rah to remove his disguise as well.

"No," says Rush, "Leave it. Pull the hood back up."

Nikolaos obeys.

In a few moments, the sound of fast moving feet slapping the tile hall announces Tyrus' entrance. Behind him, Enenoch fairly runs to keep stride with the younger man. The captain of the guard brings up the rear.

"Tyrus!" booms Rush in a voice that shakes what is left of the palace wall art, finery that was hung too high for the pillagers to steal. "You want what is mine? Come and get him! And bring your best men with you! I will kill every last man in this palace, and then I will skin you and make a new suit for myself from the strips of your hide!"

"Good gods," mumbles Nikolaos, pulling Rah back and drawing his sword.

But the burly, Hittite-born Tyrus only smiles his broadest smile and even dares open his arms to Rush.

"You may accuse me of many things, sir, and I would agree. But you cannot call me a fool!"

"I am a bull who will have his chance with you, Tyrus of Troy," spits Rush, unappeased. "I will not eat the yew. You will face me."

"Perhaps, Master, but not today. Today I am your ally!" spouts the confident Tyrus, still offering the assassin his breast like a long lost relative.

Rush rewards his impertinence by stepping forward and slamming a forward strike into it, sending Tyrus back across the polished tile floor into Enenoch and his captain. All three fall like stooges to the ground.

But even this does not change the High Priest of the Bull God's course. He rights himself, using the others to climb to his feet first, and brushes himself off casually.

"Ah, a proper Hittite warrior welcome if ever there was one," he smiles, rubbing his bruised and probably cracked sternum as he offers Rush a low bow.

"Now, sir, let us talk plainly. I am a citizen of Knossos by choice, not by chance, and have loved this city from the first day I lay eyes upon her from the harbor. But I am also a young man who does not wish to die in the arms of his lover, but go on and find another. And I know as well as you do, sir, that this city is even now taking her last few breaths."

Here Tyrus takes a dramatic risk by turning his shoulder to Rush in order to finish his speech whilst pacing back and forth in front of him.

"You have a ship, and you are headed west to Anatolia," he says, stroking his luxurious beard. "You have a Grain God whom the people believe is the cause of the disaster. You cannot safely leave now that the climate is stirring. You will be stoned to death. And even you, Rush, Master Assassin, can lose your life to a crowd of rock-wielding fools. But I," and here Tyrus allows himself the luxury of stroking back a lock of his shoulder-length hair, "can guarantee your safety."

He looks at Rush, smiling broadly, arms once again extended from his side as if offering a king a gift.

Enenoch, standing several feet behind the captain of the palace guard now, takes a hard swallow and another few steps back. He has begun muttering a prayer to the Sky God under his breath.

Rush has pulled his hood from his head as Tyrus speaks. Even under his beard it is clear that his jaw is clenching. Now he narrows his eyes at Tyrus. His lids at half-mast, the obsidian irises glitter like the blades of his weapons.

"I think I shall make a woman of you before you finish this speech Tyrus," he growls through his teeth. "Which ball do you like to die choking on, right or left?"

But Tyrus is unfazed. Excitedly, he turns conspiratorially to the assassin.

"Rush!" he whispers. "I know I am no match for you, who is? Nor can I better sway a crowd than can Ameg, a man who has been a bureaucrat, or lead as can Antaris, a general. But I tell you, you need a priest now, to convince these fools that their salvation lies in that which benefits you! I am that priest! They believe, because a priest told them, that the boy must be sacrificed to his God on the Mountain. So now I do as you do in war! I take their thrust, and use it to my advantage! I do not convince them that the boy must live! It is too late for that! I agree with them that he must die! Yes! Absolutely he must be sacrificed to Rah! But it is not Mount Ida where he must be sacrificed! No! The gods have spoken plainly! Whose belly is rumbling? Thera's! You see where I am heading? He must be thrown into the very maw of the volcano on Thera!"

Tyrus takes a moment to let his plan sink in. Once again, he has lifted his arms to Rush, who ignores them, but regards him with a pitch to his brow.

"Brilliant," murmurs Nikolaos, looking from Rah to Rush. "We take the priests, we escape Crete, and the boy lives."

"And you will take your chances with me once I have you on board, Tyrus?" is all Rush says in answer.

Tyrus shrugs. "One thing at a time. We are not so different in one thing, Rush. I believe you are, like me, a man who makes advantage out of disadvantage. I believe you will come to find me of value to you."

"You are an overconfident ass, Tyrus,"

"Perhaps," shrugs Tyrus again. "I think not. I think I am just confident enough to get us out of this mess."

In the blink of his eye his throat is in the assassin's grip.

"Do not use the word 'us' when addressing me again. You are a traitor and a whore, and I sleep with neither," snarls the assassin.

This time, Tyrus appears cowed. He pulls at the assassin's fingers, to no avail.

"I did what I needed to do to survive, sir," he rasps. "But I never divulged a single secret of Hittite warfare. Not one."

"You trained the enemy. Even if badly. Better you should have died with honor," answers Rush.

"What good is honor, once a man is dead?" wheezes Tyrus.

"Oh for the gods' sakes, Tyrus, will you never know when to shut up?" squeals Enenoch. "He will close your throat for good, you arrogant fool!"

This draws Rush's attention. He releases Tyrus and regards the High Priest of the Sky, who brings his own hand to his throat fearfully. "I have nothing but the utmost respect for you, Ameg ... er ... Rush," he stutters. "I am at your humble service," he adds, dropping to the floor in a handmaid's bow.

Rush regards him with little interest. Then he returns his attention back to Tyrus.

"My servants will make you comfortable for the night," says the Bull priest, rubbing his neck. "I will address the people in the morning. You will be on your ship before noon. You have my word."

"No tricks, Tyrus."

"You are my passage, sir, out of this doomed place. As I have said, I may well be a whore. I am not a fool."

From out of nowhere, Rush backhands the burly man, sending him to the floor alongside Enenoch.

"A fool," says Rush then, "Would try to steal the Grain God. A fool would take his chances with the volcano, hope for the best. Hoping to make himself a king once the crisis is passed. Using the boy like a toy for his own gain. Setting himself up a priest-king and the boy his slave-god."

"Not I, sir," says Tyrus, who has climbed to his knees but no further.

"Get up, Bull priest, before I kick your balls into your throat that you may choke on your own arrogance." Rush turns to Nikolaos.

"Take off his robe, Captain."

Nikolaos has been watching this exchange with a mixture of pride and shame. Is he now the underling of an assassin and a madman? Or a general and statesman? He only knows for sure that he is on the stronger side of this argument so long as he stands beside Rush. Careful not to direct the assassin's temper at himself, he does as he is told. He takes Rah's robed arm and draws him forward, so that the boy stands between himself and the assassin. Rah has been silent throughout this confrontation, indeed, since his return to Knossos, and Nikolaos is wondering if they have lost him once again to the animal that ever threatens to possess him. He unties the belt that keeps the robe closed, then pulls the boy's hood back, taking the entire garment with it and dropping it to the floor behind him.

It is as if the palace entryway had been darkened beneath a clouded sky and suddenly the sun has crested the mountains and filled the air with southern light. The atmosphere has brightened, the light now warming and eerily hazed.

"Oh," says Tyrus involuntarily. He is still on his knees and must look up into Rah's feline face from the floor.

Rush looks at Nikolaos over Rah's head, a muscle in his cheek twitching with angry energy.

"He is . . ." begins Tyrus, pushing himself to his feet.

"Exquisite," murmurs Enenoch, also rising.

Tyrus has stepped up to the boy and is peering into his face. "What eyes he has!" He looks at Enenoch. "Do you recall...? I have seen him dance, of course..." he lifts a hand to touch a lock of Rah's hair and Rah flinches, taking a nervous step back into Nikolaos.

Nikolaos puts his hand on the boy's shoulder and looks to Rush.

"It's alright, little cat," says the big man. "Let the priests see for themselves."

Tyrus' fingers stretch to capture a lock of Rah's curls. He seems to have lost all sense of the assassin's presence.

"It is like silk," he murmurs to himself. He lifts the lock, then allows it to spill through his fingers like gossamer in the hazy light.

"Now you see what I have sacrificed my own safety to protect. Beware, Tyrus, this is not a trifle."

"Perhaps he really is the Rah," says Enenoch, unable to keep himself from moving forward to stand beside Tyrus and peer into Rah's eyes. "They are like the sky over the Aegean. Like the sky. Perhaps he really is the cause of all of this."

"Perhaps," says Rush. "But no one is throwing him into a volcano, nor cutting out his heart on a mountain to appease the gods. The gods can come and deal with me themselves, for he is mine now. He is mine and I will take him with me to Anatolia, along with his priest, Mochlos. I will offer him, a new God, to a people who meander between idols and phantoms left over from the days before we conquered them. And when the ash has settled and the crops have recovered here on Crete, I will return with him and his priest and re-establish law and order."

"Yes, he will need priests, this god," says Tyrus hopefully, combing his fingers through a thatch of Rah's curls. "But not just the Priest of the Moon. This is a god for the earth. For the crops, the grain. He will need a priest of the earth. He will need the House of the Bull."

Rah has begun to make an uneasy burring noise, but Tyrus seems oblivious of it.

"Look at this mane. Is he not a little lion?" says the priest, stroking Rah behind one ear. "What is more of the earth than the lion. King of the plains of Africa. And I have seen him leap!" he continues, making little circles against Rah's scalp with his fingers. "Like a great cat, he leaps and spins-"

The burring has lowered to a satisfied grunt. Rah's lids flutter sleepily, his fan-like lashes setting puffs of air against the Tyrus' wrist. "A young lion," muses Tyrus, involuntarily continuing to massage little circles behind

Rah's ear. Rah has closed his eyes. The single grunt has begun a series of them, a human purr.

"No," says Enenoch, leaning over Tyrus' shoulder. "You are blind, Tyrus." He pokes Rah's chest and the boy's lids flutter open to narrow at the Priest of the Sky, then flutter closed again. He tips his head, leaning against the hypnotic stroke of Tyrus' fingers.

"Those eyes!" continues Enenoch, unfazed. "Sea-sky eyes. And the sun in his hair, above. I too have seen him leap and spin. Weightless, he is. Like a cloud. Like a bird. He is the offspring of the Sky! Why had I never seen it?"

"This is like Ananou," murmurs Nikolaos to Rush over Rah's head. "He said Rah was the Sunrise, and fell at his feet. I did not believe him sincere then, but-"

"He will have all four houses," says Rush, watching Tyrus and Enenoch with a curl on his lips. "Sun, Moon, Sky, Earth. I will reestablish all four when I return to Crete." He snatches Tyrus' wrist and draws his hand away from Rah, who seems to be falling asleep on his feet.

"You planned it, all along!" says Tyrus, his attention suddenly returned to Rush.

"The thought occurred," smiles Rush. He draws Rah out of the priest's reach with a little shake, and Rah rouses and looks up at him, a cat-like sourness crossing his brow.

Rush narrows his eyes at him, gives him another, warning shake.

"Nikolaos, you must return to the harbor and board the ship," he says, still looking down at Rah, who squints up at him disagreeably. "You must speak with the captain. We need to know if there is room aboard for the Houses of the Sky and the Bull God."

"Why me, sir?" blurts Nikolaos irritably. "Why not let me stay here to guard the boy?"

Rush shoots the Captain a ferocious look. "Because you are not enough an army to guard the boy, Captain."

Now it is Nikolaos who is giving him a sour look.

"You will provide a guard to take the Captain back to the harbor and await his return," says Rush, addressing Tyrus. "I will not sink the vessel attempting to carry more than it can bear."

"Fair enough," says Tyrus, pleased at this outcome. He hoped only for his own life. Now it seems the assassin intends to save his entire household, intact, and Enenoch's as well.

"My little cat and I need rest," says Rush then. "Prepare your address to the people, Tyrus. Spread the rumor that you will make a speech at sunrise in the street outside the palace. I will take the King's wing tonight. Send us something to eat." He lifts his brow. "You know how to feed him?"

"This one needs much from Rah. Grain, fruit-" begins Tyrus.

"And white fish, and milk and cheese from the white goat-" adds Enenoch, nodding.

"Yes, yes. Well, send it up. And meat for me. Rarely cooked. And good wine from the cellar."

"You may depend upon it sir. The House of the Bull has an excellent kitchen."

"Yes, I can see that," says Rush, frowning. For Tyrus is not the fit rower he was when first he arrived in Knossos.

"Larabus!" Tyrus turns to the palace captain, snapping his fingers importantly. "Take a score of guards. Get down to the harbor with the Captain before we lose the light."

"Sir." The man responds with a short bow, then marches off to fetch some sober men.

CHAPTER 50

At twilight, Nikolaos returns from the ship with the guarantee of the captain that there is sufficient room on board, and stores, to carry twenty more men. There are ten junior priests in the House of the Bull God, eight in the House of the Sky. A perfect equation. And a good omen. While the priests prepare their households for the journey, Rush instructs Nikolaos to guard Rah while he goes out for an hour.

"Where are you going, sir, in this hostile environment? If you are seen in the street without the priest's guard on you, you will be stoned."

Nikolaos is finishing his own meal, seated on a chair by the window of the King's chamber. Rah is lying on his belly on a pallet in the steward's chamber just next door, snoring into a feather pillow. He ate well and fell into a deep sleep within minutes of being put to bed.

Rush has returned from the baths and is pulling on his assassin's garb.

"Never ask me where I am going, Captain. I do not even allow my wife such a luxury."

"Your pardon, sir," responds Nikolaos cagily. "But I fear for your safety."

Rush looks up from his ankle, where he has been strapping the holster of his gold handled dagger.

"Another luxury I do not allow my wife."

Nikolaos frowns, but is yet undaunted. He casually sops up the last bit of gravy on his plate with a round of bread, then looks back toward the steward's room where Rah sleeps.

"I think it not my safety you concern yourself with, Captain. And that is wise. It is the boy, eh? Not so much afraid for the wolf who hunts at night, but for the lamb who sleeps while the wolf is hunting. You fear my return more than my departure, do you not?"

"You are not a champion of self control, sir," responds Nikolaos, putting his plate to the floor and rising.

Rush has finished strapping on his weaponry and lifts his head. He nods toward the King's huge bed, which he will occupy when he returns.

"You wish to sleep with me tonight, Captain? You do not like the room at the end of the hall? Too far from Rah? Perhaps I take my frustration out on you instead, eh? This palace has no women in it, save the old dame who tends the laundry. And you are prettier than she."

"You threaten vainly, sir," says Nikolaos, unmoved. "Your guise is wasted on me. It is only the Rah that tempts you to your own sex."

Rush has pulled his hood over his head. Now he approaches the window where Nikolaos stands with his arms crossed over his chest. He is face to face with the younger man when he turns to whisper in his face, "Go to bed, Captain. It could be hours before I return, and tomorrow is a big day."

Nikolaos peers into his one uncovered eye. He frowns, flicks his eyes back toward the steward's chamber, considering.

"I will sleep here with you then," he says boldly.

Even through the mask it is clear that this amuses Rush. He shakes his head with a chuckle, then turns to slip through the window. "Brave to the point of comedy," he comments before dropping out of sight.

At the east end of town, two streets over from the House of the Sun, the man who led the mob is readying for bed.

He is a man of moderate height and medium age, a man who worked as a laundry steward in the palace until the Queen departed, taking his livelihood with her. Then, suddenly, he found himself both unemployed and unwed, for his wife left him within the week for the lover she had been keeping, a cook who worked for the House of the Sky. She herself worked in the palace kitchens, and when the House of the Sky moved with Enenoch into the palace, she openly took up with the cook and moved there with him.

The man, whose name is Peleos, has never considered himself much of a leader, although he held a rank above several others in the laundry and was therefore used to giving orders. His wife had given him no children. He was her second husband and she had had three by her first, but those children were half grown when he married her and they never paid him much heed. Therefore when he was chosen to speak for the mob, chosen by straws of all things, he considered it a good omen, and was grateful for the chance to make a name for himself. He, Peleos, first laundry steward to the king, to speak for the people! To address the assassin! Perhaps his luck was changing. Perhaps Tyrus would take note of his ability to handle this mob, and hire him back at the palace! Perhaps this was the thing that would convince his wife that he was not the spineless creature she claimed he was.

Then she might return to him.

So Peleos is in good humor when he finishes dousing the house lamps, sets the bolt to the door, and heads down the narrow hall to the stair at the rear of the house leading to the upper floor. Nothing has been heard from the palace, save that the Cyrian Captain was escorted back to the harbor by a handful of guards, allowed to board the assassin's vessel, then escorted back to the palace. Apparently Tyrus was getting along reasonably well with Ameg. No doubt they would be taking the boy to Mount Ida tomorrow to finish what Mochlos should have done weeks ago.

Therefore it is something of a shock to Peleos when he rounds the doorway of his bedroom with the last lit lamp in his hands, and finds the assassin in his bed.

"I have learned much about you Peleos, from the kitchen help at the palace," says the assassin from his bizarre recline, hands locked behind his head, on Peleos' wife's side of the bed. "First laundry steward to the King. Quite a challenge for the Terror of the Aegean." He brings one hand out from its hiding place behind his hideous hood, regards the tip of his left index finger, picks at the nail, brings the other hand round and with a panther-like quickness releases the gold handled dagger from its holster at his ankle and flips it once in the air, catching it by the handle casually. He begins trimming the nail with its tip. "You lost your wife to your spinelessness," he continues, looking up from his work and gesturing with the blade in the direction of the palace. "She lies with the sauce man in the kitchen barracks even as we speak. A sauce man! Her children think you an ass, though their father was nothing more than a cart maker who drank himself to death. Beat her religiously whether she needed it or not." He looks at Peleos with his exposed eye. It is a handsome eye, thick with black lashes and tipped slightly down, as if some perpetual sadness resides within.

"Sir, I-" begins Peleos. And the assassin waits, politely, the tip of his dagger poised in mid air.

"No," says the assassin. "I thought not. Not even now, Peleos, when death has come to make a husband of you," he pats the empty side of the bed, Peleos' side, "you have nothing much to say."

"I-"

The assassin has tipped his head, almost comically, waiting for the finish of the thought. But none comes. "You have no use for that tongue, Peleos," he says, shaking the dagger at the man like a remonstrating finger. "But I do."

Peleos has begun to make a clumsy attempt to back out of the bedroom door and flee. He gets no further than the hall before the assassin has leapt from the bed and pinned him by his throat against the hall wall.

"You are nothing to me, laundry man. Just something that has been carrying around a tongue, until I found a use for it." With that, the hand on

Peleos' throat releases and a blow that could stun a bull smashes into his jaw. Peleos' mandible cracks in half with a strange popping sound that echoes in his head for several seconds. Stunned but conscious, he gives the assassin little resistance as his mouth is pried open and his tongue severed at the half.

An hour into his nap, Rah is awakened by footsteps outside in the King's hall. Still on his belly with his face in a pillow, his eyes fly open. He stiffens, straining to hear the muffled struggle, then the grunt, that follows. Presently the handsome vee of Nikolaos' silhouette appears in his doorway, backlit by the light from the hall torches.

Rah lifts himself from the pallet, makes his customary cat-like leap onto his feet, stands with head tilted as if still listening for sound in the hall. He regards Nikolaos with innocent torch-lit gold eyes.

"I won't have anyone sneaking around up here while you sleep, Rah," says the Captain in explanation. He looks down the hall, obviously at the man he has just dispatched with some indiscretion. "The assa- ... the wolf... is gone and I am left here alone to keep you safe." He gestures to his left. "He had no reason to be up here."

Rah takes a step toward Nikolaos, as if to see beyond him into the hall.

"No. Stay here. Keep your door barred. Here," he steps back and closes the door, then says loudly from the hall, "Bar it. Let me test it."

Rah does as he is told. He hears the Captain try the door, then sigh heavily before moving off to dispose of the unfortunate servant who thought to douse the lamps in the King's hall as he always did before bed.

Rah stands facing the barred door. There is no source of light in the room, save the glow of a full moon from the small window above the bed. Still, his sharp eyes make out the priest's robe lying on the floor to the right of the door, where he had dropped it earlier. He tips his head at it, then picks it up and opens it by the arms. He spreads it wide, then whips it over his shoulders. It trails heavily to the ground.

Rah frowns. He drags the robe to the bed, steps up onto the mattress and peers out of the casement into the moonlit dark. The steward's window faces a small courtyard. He has been in the palace at night before, though never in the King's wing. He and his troupe had entered the palace from the rear to reach the gymnasium, and when it was time to perform, climbed an incline to a passageway that led into the Great Hall. But he has also been to the Queen's wing, though much against his will and more than once too intoxicated to have his bearings. Rah strains to remember how he was brought there from the palace entrance. Each time he was taken to the Queen he was taken down a hall along the right side of the Great Hall, but then turned left, traversing a corridor behind the hall, behind the place where the King and Queen and their court viewed the dances, to the

Queen's suite on the eastern side of the palace. This time, as he was brought to the King's wing, he again passed the Great Hall on his left. But then turned right. So he is on the west side of the palace.

Rah tips himself out of the casement and twists to look into the sky above. Moonlight pours over his shoulder. The moon is behind him, in the east. So he must follow the moonlight. Then he will find an aperture with which to climb back into the palace and reach the Great Hall without alerting the Fox.

The clouded, eerily lit sky mesmerizes him for a moment. Visions splash through his head. A moonlit ride on horseback in the company of his barbarian master, a quiet evening on the prow of Kephas' ship, waves lapping the hull. The night of the Dying of the God ceremony, the night he became Rah. His dance with the bare-breasted maiden and his coupling with his concubines all night and into the morning. Suddenly he is in the Great Hall of Knossos, in the center of the arena, surrounded by torchlight and the awed faces of his audience. It is the last scene of the Tears of the Moon Goddess dance. The wolf, made of two dancers dressed in black and carrying the wolf skin over their heads, the upper half of the lead dancer's body encased in a hideous, snarling mask, follows him from the shadows as he leaps and whirls, pretending to be unawares of its presence. His face is painted white and ringed with feathers, and he wears the fine silken wings that Aros fashioned for him. Unhampered by the light fabric, he executes a line of jumps and spins that draws a collective sigh from the audience. His wings are real, they lift in the currents of air that his movement creates. He is the Dove boy, beloved of the Moon. But the Moon walks the far side of the earth tonight. She fails to light his way, and so the wolf may slink in the darkened corners of the arena, stalking him.

Suddenly the wolf leaps from the shadows and faces him. He scampers back, wings lifted up and away, too late. The beast takes his torso in its jaws, tear his wings from his back, intent on devouring him. Even so, even on his back and in the mouth of the wolf he is still dancing. He writhes and bucks under the horrid jaws of the double bodied beast. The crowd is hysterical.

Rah leans out the window, looking for a place to scale the wall. Only vines. But he is light and needs little purchase. He can easily manage his way to the roof, then over and into an aperture nearer the Great Hall.

Rah hops off the bed, lifting the heavy robe up behind him with both arms wide. But the material is like a shroud. It refuses to take air, but hangs in a sullen drape from his hands. Frustrated, Rah bunches the garment into a ball and throws it on the floor.

"Pah! No good! This is no wings. Rah need wings!" He looks about the dark room for something else to use in his reenactment. But there is only a heavy linen sheet on the bed and a thick green drape hanging from a series of hooks over the window and pulled with a sash to the side.

Rah looks back down at the robe. He picks it up by one sleeve, stands on the body of the garment and gives the sleeve a yank. The thing comes easily apart, the threads rotted by much laundering and time. Rah holds the sleeve up in front of him, then pulls it onto one arm. He has pulled it on backwards, wrist first.

"Need Aros now." He pulls the wrist of the sleeve up over his shoulder, holding it by the wide end against his golden collar. The garment is made for a much bigger man and the bottom of the sleeve now falls to his hip. He swings his arm forward and back. The worn fabric moves freely, becomes airborne, unhampered by the body of the robe.

"Hah! This can be wing! This how Aros do." He ties the wrist end of the sleeve to his collar, then, using his teeth and one hand, ties a bit of the shoulder end to his golden bracelet. He moves to a mirror across from the bed. Swings the wing. Content, he turns back to the torn robe and stands on the body of it, yanking the second sleeve away. He pulls the second sleeve, backward, onto his opposite arm, then secures it to his collar and bracelet as he did the first.

"Paint face," says Rah, looking about the room for something suitable. To his delight, he finds a jar of talc, used for cleaning up liquid spills, on the steward's dresser. He picks up the jar, sniffs, sneezes, and sets to work whitening his face.

Rush enters the palace from an eastern window on the second floor, in the Queen' wing. He has one visit to make before he returns to the King's chamber for a well deserved rest.

There is no need of the assassin's hood now, and he quite deliberately and playfully pulls it from his head and tucks it into his belt. He is smiling. It is not often that fate provides him with this much entertainment in one evening.

Rush finds his way down the hall to Nanaea's private chamber, knowing that the arrogant Tyrus will have taken her quarters. There are no guards, and it is almost too easy for him to enter the Queen's suite, then move on a panther's silent feet past the ladies' rooms, now occupied by junior priests, enter the royal bedroom and settle on the priest's chest before the man has a chance to take a breath and cry out.

Rush drops his weight on Tyrus, straddles his middle, and waits as the priest bucks like a panicked bull under his seat. But the man is already losing air, for Rush has clapped a hand over his nose and mouth and pinched them shut. He waits, secure in the knowledge that panic will subside as the priest's crafty brain realizes that although he is a powerfully built man himself, he is no match for the assassin, and must find a more sophisticated method of escaping death.

Tyrus quiets quickly, as expected. Though suffocating, he looks up into the assassin's face with determined calm.

"You can survive, traitor, if you are clever enough. Are you clever enough?" smiles the assassin.

Tyrus nods, then blinks with some confusion. There is a lump in the assassin's cheek, as if he is carrying something in his mouth. Now he removes his hand from Tyrus face and the priest takes a grateful breath.

"I pray I am, Master," Tyrus whispers carefully.

"Hah, a priest that prays. There is a new idea," says Rush humorlessly.

"I pray that I can be of more service to you alive than dead, Master, and I pray you have already decided on that service, and decided that I may live, for if not, I am already dead," responds Tyrus.

"So true, Tyrus the Traitor. Now give me a kiss," says the assassin leaning down into the priest's face, his dark brow lowered over pitch eyes at half mast. "And I will forgive you."

Tyrus swallows, staring with concern at the bulge in the assassin's cheek. He takes a deep breath. "Yes, Master. As you wish."

In an instant the assassin's mouth is on his, his iron fingers catching the man on either side of his neck, causing him to open his jaw to gasp for air. Something meaty and warm, like chewed grizzle, has been deposited into his mouth and pushed by the assassin's tongue into his throat. Terrified that it is lodged there, Tyrus makes a frantic attempt to turn on his side and cough.

But Rush claps a bear sized palm over his mouth and holds his head to the pillow a few seconds longer, allowing panic to burn through the man's body like fire. He feels hot urine soak through the priest's sleeping gown and dampen his own legging. Only then does he release the priest and lets him choke out Peleos' tongue.

"What is it?" gasps the priest, looking at the pinkish wad he has just coughed onto his mattress.

"It is your other tongue, Tyrus. The one you put in the mouth of the mob that detained me here. You see I bring it back to you, for it is your servant." Rush has sat back onto Tyrus' thighs, removing himself from the moisture that has collected on the front of the priest's sleeping gown. Now he casually removes the two crescent blades from their holsters under his arms and holds them apart, much as Tyrus held his arms out to the assassin earlier in the foyer of the palace.

"Will you kill me then?" murmurs Tyrus, looking from one blade to the other.

"Embrace me now, villain, as you wished to embrace me this evening!" snarls Rush in Hittite.

"No sir," answers Tyrus, "I will not. Nor ever again be so bold. You come to convince me I am a fool. You have done so, Master. Would that I had never fallen in love with this city, and never left Kephas' employ. Would that I were even now rowing in perpetual hell aboard a merchant vessel, slave to Greece. Would that I had never been a Hittite boy of fifteen summers who failed to die in battle, and then took advantage wherever he could find it."

"You break my heart, Tyrus," responds Rush, yet he lowers his blades.

"Can you never forgive me for it, Master? For choosing to live when life was yet available to me? And I only a boy of fifteen?" says Tyrus again, hopeful that he may have stumbled upon a soft spot in the assassin's black heart.

Rush frowns. He takes a deep breath, and his massive chest strains at the fabric of his tunic. He looks down at it, as if considering.

"Skin would make a better suit," he says suddenly. "More give. I have thought about it often. A suit of human skin. What do you think, Tyrus of Troy, hm? Have I not a fine idea?"

Tyrus' eyes have widened with horror, for the assassin's penchant for skinning a man alive is well known.

"You have two tongues now, Tyrus. Can you not give me an answer with either?" Rush lifts one brow, waiting.

"Human is too thin I think," answers Tyrus hoarsely. "Better to use goat, or sheep."

"Mmm," nods Rush, slipping his blades back into their holsters and lifting himself off the priest at last. "Perhaps. But it might do to try human some time. A trial run." He looks back at Tyrus as he moves toward the chamber doorway.

"Yes sir, I take your meaning," answers Tyrus from the bed. "I will be ever aware of your plan to try out such a suit, and do whatever it takes to postpone that fitting."

This elicits a broad smile from the assassin.

"Even a fool can learn from his mistakes, Tyrus," says Rush, nodding. "I do not wish to waste such a crafty brain as yours to make a suit, but I will if ever you give me another reason to consider it."

Sensibly, Tyrus says nothing, but remains where he is, though soaking in his own urine, until the assassin has been gone for some time.

In the Great Hall of Knossos, the torches have been lit. A crowd of several thousand are packed into the hall, yet there is silence. It is the silence of anticipation. The King and Queen of Knossos watch from the dais at the far end of the arena. Rah stands in the center of the arena floor, a waif in white wings and bare feet, gold glinting at his neck, waist, wrists and ankles. His head is down, his mop of silvery golden curls curtain his talc-white face. For he is thinking hard, pushing his injured mind back in time to remember. And backward is ever a direction it refuses to go.

In fact Rah stands in moonlight, the torches only lit in his mind. There is no crowd, nor do Aros and Pyrus and Dimius watch with proud hearts from the performer's entrance, which is like a tunnel at the back of the arena that leads down an incline to the bull pens. Nor does the wolf, made of two dancers dressed in black, the leader encased in a snarling mask, now slink about the darkened corners of the dance floor as Rah prepares himself for the final act.

Rah returns to the routine in his mind, taking fast little panting breaths in preparation, fast little breaths that lift and fill his breast, where a sliver of moonlight, entering through the clearstory windows above, has painted a perfect white diamond on his heart.

Rush is returning to the King's wing, using the hall behind the south end of the arena, when movement to his right, through the Queen's entry to the dais, catches his attention.

He is still filled with the fuel of death and dominance when a spinning white light in the center of the arena sends the double blade of lust and anger through his loins. The force of his own emotion is like a kick in the chest by a wild ass. He takes a single step backward, then lowers his muzzle and advances.

Rah moves forward, head down, arms back and body arched, spiraling outward from the center of the arena floor. Behind him slinks the double-bodied wolf, tacking from side to side but ever behind his motion, crouched and waiting for a moment in which to spring and take him down.

Rah lifts his head, to the right, the left. Where is the moon tonight? He searches the sky, so convincingly that the eyes of the audience follow his gaze up to the ceiling of the hall. But she is not out tonight, any fool can tell that by the way the boy circles and spins, searching the domed ceiling of the Great Hall, and failing to see the wolf crouching just a few yards away in the dark. He turns and turns, eyes up, the innocence of a lost child in his whitened and feather-ringed face. The timpani and lyre accompany his movement, following him into a series of brilliant leaps and breathtaking spins, lifting him to impossible heights as he flees across the arena floor, now pursued with hungry excitement by the double-bodied wolf and the hideous mask head.

Rah takes flight on the wings of doves, airborne though no horse gallops beneath him to carry him over a fence. Airborne of pure energy. For what is stronger or faster than light?

And suddenly, a mis-step. Deliberate, just there, ten meters out from the dais, where the wolf must take him in full view of the Queen and her court. He stumbles, even this with immeasurable grace, and the invisible double-bodied wolf catches him in its horrifying jaws. He writhes and bucks under the teeth of the beast. The audience is a beast itself, a beast that must be held back by Ramicus and his men.

Rah stills under the jaws of the wolf.

The applause is wild. The stomping of feet deafening.

When the crowd has quieted, the torches are relit and Rah raises himself to his feet and drops into his signature bow in a lozenge of moonlight that has found him, at last, ten meters out from the dais.

Head bowed, curls falling over his talc-whitened face, Rah is unaware that a living wolf watches from the platform. He maintains his bow, spent and panting, his torso glistening with sweat.

"Spit at me now, little cat," whispers the assassin through his teeth from the very edge of the dais.

Rah raises his head, still crouched but eyes big with confusion. His world is gone. There is no King and Queen, no audience, there is no torchlight, only he, bowing low on the arena floor before the grizzly vision of Ameg, dressed but for his hood in the garb of the assassin.

Rah rises softly to his feet, gazes into the eyes of the true wolf, his chest heaving from exertion and now shock. Disoriented, he gives the assassin a bewildered look and tucks his chin.

"No spit at master," he offers contritely.

But Rush will not be placated so easily. He wanted to see the boy turn his head, in position, to the right while still at the bottom of his bow. He wanted to catch the very corner of that beautiful face, tilting at him, one silvery brow flattened hard against the brush of lynx-long lashes. He wanted to be the recipient of all of that ineffectual kittenish fury, that delicious look of absolute hatred he received at the end of this very dance what seems a century ago.

I want an excuse, little cat.

Rush pounces off the dais and lands halfway between Rah and the platform. The boy starts, eyes dart up, flashing. But he manages to maintain his posture, as if knowing that giving flight will only stimulate the wolf's lust to chase.

Rush takes one step toward him, then another. Rah drops his eyes again, still heaving from his performance but now trembling as well.

Rush stops where he is. He allows himself a long and lingering look at the moonlit spectacle that is Rah in self-made costume, drenched in sweat, heaving and trembling like a winded deer. The boy has tied the disembodied sleeves of a priest's robes to his golden collar and bracelets. They hang like dead chickens from his sides. Even more preposterous, he has found some powder, probably cleaning talc, with which to smear his cheeks, exaggerating those already impossibly blue eyes.

The combination of loveliness and absurdity is dizzying, even for a wolf.

I could eat you like a rabbit, raw and still warm, thinks the assassin, taking a step closer. Now he is only an arm's length away.

Rah lifts his head. "No spit at master," he says again. "Rah is wrong to spit-"

"Don't you apologize now, you little devil," whispers the assassin, breathing through his teeth. "There is no apology for what you've done to me."

In an instant he has slammed the boy onto his back and pinned his braceleted wrists over his curls, clamping them together in one hand. The wind knocked from his lungs, and his brain reeling from the force of that tackle, Rah can only twist his face as far as possible from the assassin's. But he is trapped in a cage of black, muslin-wrapped fury. His vigor already depleted from his performance, he is a moth under the assassin's colossal strength. His back stings from the force of the tackle. Infantile tears leak from his eyes as Rush brings his face low and grumbles into it, "Why do you fear me, you little bastard, eh? Do you not see what you have done to me? To the Terror of the Aegean? I am your whore."

Rah makes a sudden attempt to yank his wrists from the assassin's grip but his effort is futile. He strains to take a decent breath, but the assassin only shifts his weight, pressing down even harder against his ribs.

"I am in love with you, Rah," Rush murmurs into the boy's face, pulling his head back by the scruff with his free hand. "Had I not been in love with you I would have put your pretty head in a sack the first time I caught you, and brought it back to Cyrus as I was paid to do."

Rah has squeezed his eyes shut, twisted his face away and gritted his teeth.

"Had I not been in love with you," continues the assassin, running his teeth casually along Rah's windpipe now, "I would have cut out that wounded little tongue of yours the day you spat at me. I would have smashed those pearl teeth from your mouth the day you bit me."

He shifts his weight again, giving the boy a chance to take another breath, no more.

Then he lowers his mass back down, pressing Rah's lungs to the sand flooring of the arena. "Not so good, being the devil's lover is it? Not much fun. Better to be gored by a bull, I suspect. Better to be taken up to the mountain and slaughtered by the priests."

He lifts his weight one more time, allowing the boy a few more breaths. Rah takes several hungry gulps of air, mouth open. Then he squeezes his eyes and mouth shut against the onslaught of the assassin's lips as they explore his lashes, his nose and mouth. The man's organ nudges him, even lifts his skirt, pressing against his own sex. Winded and weak, Rah is nevertheless unable to suppress a feeble growl.

Rush chuckles. The chuckle is long and deep. And angry. There is far more anger in that sound, meant to express happiness, than is in Rah's little burr.

"You think I want to be a slave's slave?" sneers Rush, pulling Rah's head back again and nipping at his mouth until he must open it. When he does, Rush fills it with his tongue. It is like a weapon, that tongue, a thing made for devouring prey, or gagging an opponent.

"I am not made for love, little cat," murmurs Rush, releasing the boy's mouth and staring into his face with the intensity of a wolf that is about to take a rabbit after a winter's long hunger.

Rah's burr has become a sing song warble. He makes another futile attempt to twist out of Rush's grip. His brow has flattened, his ears pulled back. His lips pull into a silent snarl, exposing his teeth.

Rush is smiling.

"Still you fight, little golden one." He licks at the boy's lashes again, then runs his teeth over the fine blonde stubble at his jaw. "Wild little beauty." Suddenly he lifts himself onto one elbow, giving Rah's head a little shake.

"Spit at me, dancer," He says again. "Spit at me now."

Rah focuses his brilliant eyes on the assassin's face, brow wrinkling. "No spit at master," he says through clenched teeth.

Rush gives his head another shake. "Spit at me!" Without warning he brings his hand up under the boy's skirt and takes him there, his fingers firm, possessive, and insulting.

Rah's jaws clench. Fury alights in his gold-green eyes. He gives a snarling grunt and spits into the assassin's face.

The assassin releases his scruff, wipes the spittle out of his lashes, licks it from his fingers.

Rah gives one final, unexpected twist. With all he has left, he slips from the assassin's grip and manages to sink his incisors into Rush's left shoulder.

Rush grunts in pain and surprise, then gives his shoulder a powerful flex, dislodging the boy's teeth.

"Now I break you, boy," he sneers and brings his hand up, slapping Rah hard across his jaw, then taking him by his hip and flipping him onto his belly.

But something is wrong. The boy is convulsing beneath him.

Rush pushes himself off the boy's chest and turns him back to face him. Rah's eyes have rolled back in his head. His muscles jerk in a single spasm so fierce it nearly bucks Rush off his torso. Then the ugly epileptic fit tears him out of the assassin's arms, out of the assassin's world, and out of danger.

"My god, what has happened to him?"

It is Nikolaos, who, moments later, stands on the dais behind Rush in the weak moonlight. Rush pays him no heed, but maintains his hold on Rah's spasming body, determined to keep the boy's jaw closed and his head still until the fit passes.

Nikolaos springs off the dais to kneel at his side.

"I made him bar the door to his room," he explains, confused and guilt ridden. "It was still barred when I went to check on him. He must have slipped out of the window." He looks over the boy's weakening convulsions. "What the hell has he done to himself? What is all this?" He has taken up the tip of one of the wings. "A sleeve," he answers himself. He looks into the boy's chalk smudged face, puzzled and disoriented by the assassin's stony silence.

Rah's fit has begun to lose momentum. As it does, the assassin sits back on his haunches in the sand, releasing him. When the boy is quiet, he remains still, his big hands hanging loosely at his sides. Nikolaos looks from Rah to Rush, then back to Rah. The boy is sleeping peacefully now, a fallen angel with chicken wings and talc-smudged cheeks.

Rush is looking down at Rah like a man who has just taken a lance through his heart. Nikolaos takes hold of his shoulder and shakes it. Rush gives him no response.

Both men stare down at the boy for what seems an eternity. The lozenge of moonlight that lit Rah's final bow has moved out into the center of the arena, leaving the three players in the dark.

Still, Rah does not awaken from his slumber.

Rush reaches down to brush a curl from the boy's forehead. He takes a moment longer, then he scoops Rah up into his arms and rises slowly to his feet. Nikolaos follows him onto his own.

"She said that if I put this light out, then I must learn to live in darkness," says the assassin, looking down into Rah's sleeping, talc-smeared face.

"Who has said this, Rush?" asks Nikolaos softly.

"His mother," responds Rush, a single tear glistening on the lashes of one eye. "Already," he continues, "I find the dark unbearable."

CHAPTER 51

Throughout the night the assassin maintains a vigil at Rah's bedside, but the boy made of motion remains motionless, and darkness reigns.

"It is the coma," says Nikolaos. "He was never fully awakened from it. It has come back for him. It has nothing to do with you."

Rush has spared Nikolaos the details of the previous evening. Nevertheless, it is obvious to him that Nikolaos has imagined what has happened, most of all, by his failure to ask for further explanation. It is a kindness Rush cannot fully comprehend. But kindness now, especially from Nikolaos, is unbearable.

"You know what I am, and what I have done, and yet you forgive me. Is this the noble man's method of torturing a criminal, Captain?" he asks.

"It is because I know what you are, Rush, that I cannot hold you responsible. Is a wolf a thief because it takes the lamb?"

"If I am a wolf and this a lamb, why is my belly not full, Captain Nikolaos? Why am I yet unsatisfied? And would have been, even more so, had his illness not prevented me from fulfilling my hunger?"

"You know the answer to that, I suspect. It is as I said in the wine cellar. Rah without purity is no longer Rah. Rah tamed ... is no longer Rah."

"Nor is Rah without motion Rah," answers Rush heavily.

"Just so."

At daybreak Rush informs Tyrus of the boy's coma. "So now you will tell the people you have drugged him to ready him for his death on the volcano. Have the priests lay him in a stretcher. They will form a procession to the harbor. Then I will signal the ship and we will leave this island and sail immediately to Anatolia. I would not have him die before my wife, and all those who have known and loved him, see him again, though they must see him thus."

To his credit, Tyrus meets the occasion with his usual optimism. "This is nothing, only a design of the brain, a kind of self-protected sleep. He has been under great stress. Kidnapped. Recovered from certain death by you, Rush, more than once. And by your Captain, here. He will recover. He has given us a perfect ruse with which to convince the people of our sincerity!"

His speech to the people that morning is moving, and when he turns to gesture to the procession of priests, bearing Rah on a stretcher of lamb's skin and olive wood, Rush offers him a nod of approval. The people follow behind with bowed heads, some weeping, and upon their arrival at the harbor, line the beach with lilies upon which the priests may tread as they load the stretcher onto the skiff.

Nikolaos and Rush, along with the assassin's two war dogs, accompany Rah and two priests on the skiff's first trip back to the ship. It will take another hour and three more trips for the remaining priests to be taken on board.

The Queen's ship is equipped with both sail and rowers. The hold is deep enough at the center to house the gift of twenty horses and the area in which they are kept is open above, with a canvas awning for bad weather. Having learned from Nikolaos that the horses Rah played with in the King's field are stabled in the hold, Rush lifts Rah from the stretcher when the skiff reaches the ship, intent on bringing him there. He picks him up as a man would his own sleeping child, then turns him gently onto his shoulder, resting the boy's hip against his neck securely, before climbing the rope ladder. Nikolaos, as always, follows close behind. It is Ramicus who gives them both, and the two priests, a steady hand to help them over the bulwark.

On deck, Rush turns to Nikolaos.

"I would give a king's ransom to feel this cat's teeth and claws in my back now," he says matter-of-factly.

"Yes and then you would give another to have him off your shoulder." Nicholaos nods generously, putting a hand on Rush's free arm.

"Let us put him in the stables," Rush says heavily, recalling the boy's antics on the dapple colt so long ago in the King's pasture, "for he so loved the horses." He turns from Nikolaos to find Cara and Crispo standing before him, both still wearing the robes they boarded the ship in on the previous afternoon.

Cara is looking down at Rah's pale face and weeping, and Crispo holds her against his rotund girth in an effort to comfort them both. When she looks up into the assassin's face, it is with silent accusation.

"He is not dead, but only sleeping, Cara," says Nikolaos then, taking her from Crispo. Cara gratefully leans against him, laying her head against his chest.

"We saw the procession on the beach," she says, gulping back a sob. "We thought-"

"You think I would let them kill him?" growls Rush then, irritably. "No, but you are right to blame me, for I brought on the seizure he does not awaken from."

"A seizure?" says Crispo, and then, "Yes! They said he took to fits! Proof of a soul's marriage to the godhead. So this is Providence, you see? His coma signals the end. The god will have him back, whether you like it or not, and if you do not give him back, then the god will take him! And all of us with him."

"What are you saying, Crispo," says Nikolaos. "That the mountain will explode because we do not sacrifice Rah?"

"Then prepare to die, priest," mutters Rush, "for I take him with me to Anatolia, and heaven nor hell will stop me." With this, he looks down at the unconscious Rah, who seems to rest quite peacefully in his arms, a comic angel, his face is still smudged with talc, though Nikolaos has thought to detach the disembodied sleeves from his collar and bracelets and has wrapped his body in a fresh linen.

"Wake, little cat, and I will give you the world in which to jump and play," says the assassin with reddened eyes.

"And then chase you to the ends of it," remarks Nikolaos, giving Rush a gentle smile when the assassin looks up at him with a flash of fury in his depthless black eyes.

"I fear he may not, sir," injects Crispo. "The god will have him, one way or another. Either by sacrifice, or by a calamity of nature."

"Nonsense, Sun Priest," it is Tyrus, who has just joined them on the deck, Enenoch in tow. "Where is your daybreak? Must the Priest of the Bull God instruct a Priest of the Sun to remember his master's habits? Daybreak always comes, no matter how dark the night. This light will shine again. He sleeps, because the end is near, and will awake when it is over. Now we must flee this place! Home to Anatolia! East of east! Autumn's western headwind will hold the death cloud back. I have spent enough time at sea to know this. But further east still, at the compound of the assassin, we will be safe."

"And you think destruction will not follow us wherever we may go, so long as we defy the god?" squeaks Enenoch, wringing his hands, yet looking down at the face of the Grain God with a peculiar longing.

"I am destruction," says Rush. "Let destruction follow me, for I deserve her. Still, I will not give him up to the god, nor leave him here to perish, even to save myself. Ramicus! Give the captain my orders to set sail, full speed. If what you say is true, Crispo, there may be only hours left to spare."

For two full turns of the sun the Queen's ship sails on western headwinds, making good time. The Grain God sleeps in a bed of straw in a corner of the stable block in the center of the hold, and nearby the dappled colt blows and chews, now and then lifting its head over the crib to nuzzle the boy's cheek, as if encouraging him to awaken.

The sea is calm, the air unusually warm for mid-autumn, the sky clear as glass.

The boy sleeps, and now and then he dreams.

He dreams of a voice, and of a dove. He dreams of a dapple colt, and a wolf made like a man, a great black wolf with pitiless eyes and a heart like a volcano, who leaps up from the sea to snarl and snap at his wings and bring him down into its jaws to devour. A wolf who is in love with him, whose hunger is so great that all the world must perish from the heat of it. In his dream, he is soaring on silver wings, high above the Aegean, unchained and free of the jaws of the wolf. But the world is not. And from the clouds, from the bed of his mother the moon, he looks down to see that the wolf would have him even if it must destroy the world to do so. And so the wolf opens its jaws. And out from its jaws springs a column of fire, a column of fire so fierce it can be seen in Egypt, heard in the northlands where the boy was born, and felt a thousand leagues away.

And the column is the tongue of the wolf, reaching up for him, intent on burning his wings so that he might drop into its fearsome maw. But the boy flies on, ever upward and away from the mouth of the wolf, whose mouth is a volcano, whose heart is a fire.

At an hour past mid-day, Thera erupts, and the world is forever changed. And yet changes can bring us back again to the beginning. Choked under a death cloud of burning ash and dust, and a darkness that will last for three days and cool the world for three years, the kingdom of Minoa is snuffed out. The voices of the Queens and Kings, of their lively courts, and of the people, the crowds that went mad to watch Rah dance, are forever muted. A year later, vegetation will burst through the ash and flourish, using even the charred cinders of the people of Minoa for fertilizer. A year after that, a certain wolf, lean with war and fierce with unfulfilled desires, will return to dominate the island, using it as a military stronghold. A sentimental wolf, he will return with four high priests and their priesthoods, with two queens and their households, and for a brief and unrecorded time in history will rebuild Crete under his own rule.

But for now, there is Thera to deal with.

When the volcano erupts, the Queen's ship is two hundred miles east of Eden, east of Knossos, and east of the epicenter of destruction. But she is not out of danger. The massive plate shifts beneath the sea lift the

Aegean back like a bed linen, changing the seascape for hundreds of miles, even thousands. In Egypt the Red Sea will part, allowing Josepha's people to cross into Jordan. In Anatolia, just north of the Island of Rhodes, an eight hundred foot high wall of water will crash onto the shoreline collapsing the floodplains of Ararat, destroying all in its path. But at the compound of the assassin, further east yet, the wave will fail to rise above the cliffs upon which the settlement is built.

The ship itself will drop like a hat in the wind, two hundred feet below sea level and will be drawn back toward the death cloud and toward Knossos as the waters yawn north to Troy. But the ship is sturdy, the hull flat and designed by the finest maritime engineers that the world will ever know. She stays upright and survives the fall. When the sea levels, she gains as many leagues as she has lost and flies toward Anatolia, as if on angels' wings.

On the morning of the third day at sea, in the main hold of the Queen's ship, Rah passes into a dreamless sleep. Still bedded down in a crib beside the dapple colt, on the orders of the assassin, he is under constant watch. This morning it is Crispo's turn to take his vigil. But as usual, there are others gathered round to keep the watchman company. Rah is, by some odd coincidence, surrounded by his priests. Tyrus and Enenoch have come to sit beside him, as well as Cara, still dressed in the robe of the Priest of the Dead, and representing perhaps the House of the Moon, being woman.

"He is an angel at rest," comments Enenoch.

"In flight as well," responds Cara, who has crawled into the crib so that she might offer Rah her lap upon which to rest his platinum head. Now she strokes a puff of pale curls back from his brow and begins to hum a simple tune.

"The Queen of Cyrus called him Kitten. Is he not a kitten?" she interrupts her melody to murmur, her large eyes shimmering with unwept tears.

"Just so, a young lion," answers Tyrus cheerfully. "You will see how he grows into one! Now he is but a kitten, a cub. But in a year or so, this Rah will seem as nothing compared to that!"

Tyrus has joined Cara at Rah's head. Now he leans casually over the crib, scratching the boy behind an ear as he did in the palace entry, and no one takes much notice when the boy, in his sleep, makes a little row of grunts and turns slightly toward the priest's fingers.

Cara has returned to her melody. It is a lullaby, and begins with center note. Yesterday Rush heard her humming it on board and forbid her to make the sound in his presence.

She hums the tune, reflexively focusing on her left index finger, where the nail was ripped off in a forgotten struggle only a few days ago. For the moment, the group is silent but for her tune.

"You are a most optimistic man, sir," says Crispo to Tyrus. "If he goes much longer without food and water, he will surely perish."

"He will awake when he is thirsty enough, Crispo," answers Tyrus, his fingers making circular strokes against Rah's scalp and eliciting a strange new noise from the sleeping Grain God.

"What is that? Is he choking?" Enenoch puts his hand to his own throat, looking at the others with alarm.

Cara halts her lullaby once more, bending to put her ear closer to Rah's breast. Then she giggles. She looks up at Tyrus and gives him a smile.

"He is purring, Tyrus. You have made him purr!" She gestures with her index finger for Crispo to come and lean over the boy's chest to listen.

The Sun Priest bends over Rah, putting an ear to his clavicle. Then his face opens into a great, round grin and he straightens.

"Just like a little cat!" he nods to the others, who have gathered closer to the sleeping Rah to hear for themselves.

"Yes," comes the hiss of the assassin behind them. He has approached on a wolf's silent feet, and without exception, the priests flinch. "My little cat," murmurs Rush, shoving them aside.

All three give the assassin a wide berth as Rush moves to the side of the crib. Only Cara stays where she sits, cross-legged in the straw, refusing to release the burden of Rah's head from her lap.

"I will not have Josepha see you without your pearl," says Rush gruffly to the sleeping boy, then pulls the earring from his own right ear, brushing aside a thatch of Rah's curls to find the piercing hole in his left.

"Closed," he mutters. "No matter, I will open you," and with that he takes the boy's lobe between his fingers and pushes the wire through.

"Gah," says Rah irritably as a drop of scarlet blood welling from the reopened wound spills onto Cara's white lap. Brush-thick blonde lashes flutter, and a pair of impossibly blue-green eyes open and lift to the assassin's.

Rush blinks down at the boy, clearing his vision.

And, as if knocked from a horse, is stopped cold.

...to be continued.

ABOUT THE AUTHOR

Susan Shepherd has authored four novels and two memoirs. She is a retired law enforcement officer who spent most of her career interviewing criminals and writing reports for the Court. She lives on the North Fork of Long Island, New York with her husband, three horses and four cats.

And coming soon, Book Four of the Saga Of The Rah series: Returning Rah